Lisa Jewell is in her thirties an
where she lives with her husba
worked as a secretary before redundancy, a bet an
her away from all that. She is the author of four huge bestsellers:
*Ralph's Party*, *Thirtynothing*, *One-Hit Wonder*, *Friend of the Family* and most recently *Vince & Joy*.

# LISA JEWELL

*Perfect Partners*

# RALPH'S PARTY

# THIRTYNOTHING

PENGUIN BOOKS

PENGUIN BOOKS

Published by the Penguin Group
Penguin Books Ltd, 80 Strand, London WC2R 0RL, England
Penguin Group (USA) Inc., 375 Hudson Street, New York, New York 10014, USA
Penguin Group (Canada), 90 Eglinton Avenue East, Suite 700, Toronto, Ontario, Canada M4P 2Y3
(a division of Pearson Penguin Canada Inc.)
Penguin Ireland, 25 St Stephen's Green, Dublin 2, Ireland (a division of Penguin Books Ltd)
Penguin Group (Australia), 250 Camberwell Road,
Camberwell, Victoria 3124, Australia (a division of Pearson Australia Group Pty Ltd)
Penguin Books India Pvt Ltd, 11 Community Centre,
Panchsheel Park, New Delhi – 110 017, India
Penguin Group (NZ), cnr Airborne and Rosedale Roads, Albany,
Auckland 1310, New Zealand (a division of Pearson New Zealand Ltd)
Penguin Books (South Africa) (Pty) Ltd, 24 Sturdee Avenue,
Rosebank, Johannesburg 2196, South Africa

Penguin Books Ltd, Registered Offices: 80 Strand, London WC2R 0RL, England

www.penguin.com

*Ralph's Party* first published by Penguin Books 1999
*Thirtynothing* first published by Penguin Books 2000
This combined edition published 2005
1



Printed in England by Clays Ltd, St Ives plc



ISBN-13: 978-0-141-02735-7
ISBN-10: 0-141-02735-5

# RALPH'S PARTY

For Jascha and Yasmin

# ACKNOWLEDGEMENTS

Thank you, Katy, Sarah and Nic, for reading as I wrote, chapter by chapter, month by month, and being unfailingly positive, constructive and enthusiastic. And thank you, Yasmin, for putting me up to this in the first place and continuing to encourage and inspire me throughout. I truly couldn't have done this without you. And lastly, thank you, Jascha, for not knowing anything about contemporary women's fiction but for being a great boyfriend and taking a risk anyway. Thanks for paying the bills, paying for dinner, buying me a computer and keeping a roof over my head. What a man!

. . . IT IS ALWAYS LIKE THAT AT PARTIES, WE NEVER SEE THE PEOPLE, WE NEVER SAY THE THINGS WE SHOULD LIKE TO SAY, BUT IT IS THE SAME EVERYWHERE IN THIS LIFE . . .

– *A la recherche du temps perdu,* Proust

# PROLOGUE

Smith put the phone down and glanced around the living room. A few people had already been round that night, and the flat was still relatively tidy after an earlier blitzing.

He picked up empty mugs and glasses and carried them through to the kitchen. It was strange and vaguely unsettling to think that these objects still carried the lip marks, the fingerprints, the traces of saliva and microscopic organisms left there by the strangers who had been into his home that evening, strangers he had shown his bathroom, who had seen his grubby dressing-gown hanging behind his bedroom door, strangers who had sat on his sofa in unfamiliar clothes with unfamiliar mannerisms and names and lives, strangers who had been given the opportunity to peer into other strangers' private lives.

Ralph and he had reached decisions quickly and cruelly. It would be obvious in a moment that someone was unsuitable, but they all got the tour: 'And this is the kitchen – you'll be pleased to hear we've got a dishwasher *and* a washer-dryer!'; the talk: 'Smith's up with the lark during the week but we both like a lie-in at the weekends'; the interview: 'What do you do for a living?'; and the conclusion: 'Well, there's still a few more people to see the flat – give us your phone number and we'll let you know.' Always the full fifteen minutes, so that the unwanted stranger would leave feeling like he'd been in the running, like he'd been given serious consideration.

Jason had sounded hopeful on the phone but turned out to be looking for a ready-made social life. 'I just want to live somewhere that's got a bit of life – d'you know what I mean?' he'd said, his eyes wide and over-keen.

'Erm, maybe you could explain?' Ralph had asked, thinking of the nights that he and Smith spent hopping mindlessly through forty-seven cable channels without talking and going to bed, stoned, at midnight.

Jason sat forward on the sofa and cupped his kneecaps with his hands. 'Like, for example, where I live at the moment, all that happens is I get home from work every night and nobody wants to do anything. It pisses me off, d'you know what I mean?'

Ralph and Smith had nodded sympathetically and felt old.

Monica had been a born-again Christian – would it bother them if she spoke in tongues occasionally? – and Rukhsana appeared to be on the run from an abusive arranged marriage. Her hands shook throughout the meeting, her dark eyes unable to rest on one object or hold a gaze. She explained that she and her husband were having a 'trial separation'. Ralph and Smith decided that a permanent separation from Rukhsana's sad but unpalatable situation would be best for them.

Simon had been sweet but at least twenty stone, his frame throwing the rest of the flat temporarily out of proportion, the sofa making a painful noise it had never made before as he gingerly lowered his bulk on to it.

Rachel had the sort of skin condition that made them want to hoover the flat the minute she'd left, and John smelt of Pedigree Chum. They'd just about given up hope.

'Who was that on the phone?' Ralph switched on the television and spread-eagled himself on to the sofa, the remote control poised for action in his hand.

'Someone about the flat,' Smith replied from the kitchen, 'a girl – she's on her way over now. She sounded nice.' He kicked the door of the dishwasher closed. 'Her name's Jem.'

Jem took the first turning off Battersea Rise, which brought her into Almanac Road, a small sweep of three-storey Edwardian houses, long and thin with basements – unusual for this part of South London.

As she walked down the road, peering nosily into uncurtained basement flats, she began to feel strangely like she had been here before. There was something familiar about the proportions, the width of the pavement, the colour of the bricks and the spacing between the weedy saplings that lined the road.

Jem stopped outside number thirty-one, and the feeling of familiarity increased further. She suddenly felt safe, like a child coming home after a tiring day out, to a warm house and Saturday-afternoon television.

Jem glanced down into the basement flat and saw a young man, his back to the window, talking to someone out of view. It was then that she knew she had been here before. Maybe not this exact place, but somewhere very similar. In her dreams, since she was a teenager – a basement flat in a tall house in a terrace; a view through the window, at night, the room lit up; a man on a sofa smoking a cigarette, whose face she couldn't see. Her destiny. Was this him?

Jem rang the doorbell.

# CHAPTER ONE

The girl standing in the doorway was tiny, about five foot two, black curly hair held on top of her head with pins and clips in some complicated but very feminine style that looked as if it should have sported ivy wreaths. She was post-coitally pretty, with cherry-red cheeks and a bitter-sweet mouth, the bottom lip drawn back very slightly under the top, and her eyes were bright and mustardy, framed by mascaraed lashes and faint but lively eyebrows. She should have been wearing wood-nymph muslins and lacy leather sandals but instead had on an equally beguiling soft flannel suit with fur at the collar and cuffs and a short skirt that would have looked obvious on a taller woman. The tip of her nose was winsomely pink.

Smith let Jem walk in front of him down the hall, watching her as she turned her head this way and that, examining the pictures on the walls, peering through half-open doors and patting table-tops as she went. She was definitely cute. She turned to Smith.

'This is lovely, really, really lovely.' She smiled widely and suddenly turned to face the wall, grabbing the top of the radiator with both hands and letting out a sigh of relief. 'Sorry,' she laughed, 'my hands are freezing, like blocks of ice – feel.' She made her small white hands into fists and placed one on each of Smith's cheeks. 'It's so cold out there!' Smith started and felt suddenly shy.

'Shall we go to the kitchen? I'd love a cup of tea.'

'It's just through the living room,' offered Smith, attempting to overtake her.

'Oh, yes. I know where the kitchen is. I saw it through the window. Outside.' She laughed again. 'Sorry, I'm really nosy. And I've seen so many horrible flats tonight I don't think I could have faced coming in here if it hadn't looked nice.'

They walked into the kitchen.

'My flatmate's around somewhere,' said Smith, filling the kettle. 'He's probably in his room. He's called Ralph. I'll take you to meet him when the tea's done.'

Jem was examining a rack of herbs and spices. The plastic lids of the jars were covered in a layer of greasy dust; all of them were full. 'Do you and Ralph ever cook?' she asked.

Smith laughed. 'Erm, I think this speaks for itself.' He opened the door of the fridge to reveal shelves laden with colourful packets proclaiming 'Thai-style Green Curry', 'Creole Chicken with Cajun Rice', 'Chicken Tikka Masala', and floppy see-through bags containing fresh pasta sauces and soups.

'Oh, God – typical boys! That's such an expensive way to eat!' exclaimed Jem. 'Cooking's brilliant, you know – I'll teach you. And Ralph, if you like.' She used the name Ralph comfortably, as if she knew him. 'I'm very good. I think. Well, so I've been told. I can cook a Thai curry. These ready-made things are dreadful for you – it's all the salt they put in them to make them taste of something.' She closed the fridge and wandered back into the living room.

'Do you want to ask me some questions?' she called,

picking up a paperback from a shelf and examining the back cover.

'Milk and sugar?' Smith called back.

'Have you got any honey?'

Smith futilely opened and closed a few cupboards. 'No,' he shouted. 'Got some golden syrup, though.'

'This is a gorgeous room, you know. No offence or anything, but it doesn't look like two boys live here.'

'Thank you.' Smith was embarrassed, and slightly shocked at being referred to as a boy in his thirtieth year.

Jem quickly took note of the objects strewn around the top of the dark wooden coffee table inlaid with ornate brass work. She approved of a good messy coffee table – they held so many interesting clues to the day-to-day content and clutter of people's lives. Smith and Ralph's coffee table held a selection of remote controls, a satellite TV guide, an ashtray full of stubs, two packets of red Marlboro, a business card, a box of matches and a home-delivery pizza menu. Somewhere underneath it all she could make out a proper coffee-table art book, a set of car keys and, barely visible but unmistakable, a small piece of green cardboard torn from a packet of Rizlas. Jem smiled quietly at her discovery.

'Let's go and say hello to Ralph,' Smith was lingering in the doorway, his face cocooned in wreaths of steam from his tea, 'and then I'll show you around.'

Ralph barely noticed Jem the first time he saw her. He was arguing with his girlfriend Claudia, sitting at his desk, the phone cradled under his chin as he carelessly pulled elastic bands into tight ligatures around his wrists in an apparently subconscious attempt to cut off his blood supply and end the painful predictability of it all.

As Smith entered he grimaced and took the phone from under his chin, holding it a foot or two from his ear so that Smith could hear the tinny drone of the unhappy woman. He hit the speakerphone button:

'*I just feel like I'm the one doing all the work here, Ralph, d'you know what I'm talking about? No, of course you don't. Who am I kidding? You can't see anything beyond the remote control – as long as you've got a piece of technical equipment in your hand that will prevent you from doing something else, something that might, just might involve you getting up off your arse and doing something . . .*'

'Ralph,' whispered Smith, 'this is Jem.'

Jem twinkled at Ralph from the doorway.

Ralph saw a small, smiley girl, tendrils of hair framing her face.

'*Are you listening to me, Ralph, or have you put me on that fucking speakerphone?*'

Ralph smiled apologetically at Jem and mouthed a 'Nice to meet you' as he hit the speakerphone button again and began murmuring inaudibly into the phone.

Smith and Jem left the room, closing the door quietly behind them.

'Claudia can be very . . . demanding. They could go on like that for hours. Poor bastard.' Smith smiled smugly and took a slurp of tea.

'You don't have a girlfriend, then, Smith?'

'Very perceptive,' he replied ungraciously. 'No, I don't.'

Not for the first time since Jem's arrival, he found himself feeling uncomfortable. He wanted to be friendly and welcoming, to create a good impression, but try as he might, he just couldn't, and was coming across instead as frosty and impolite. He put his hand out to grasp the antique door-handle in front of him and pushed the door open.

'This would be your room.' He reached to the left for the light switch. 'It's quite small, as you can see, but it's got everything.'

The room was tiny and L-shaped. The walls were clad in caramel-coloured wood-panelling, and the room was lit centrally by a ceiling lamp housed in a brass and glass star-shaped shade. A single bed stood at the far end, covered with a vivacious Indian throw and several large cushions with tassels and fringes. A 1920s wardrobe with mirrored front panels stood in front of it, and at the other end of the room was a single sash window hung with densely patterned heavy curtains and a small chest of black-lacquerwork drawers.

Jem turned and grasped hold of Smith's hands. 'I absolutely love it. I love it. I knew I would. Please can I live here? Please!' Her face was glowing and childlike, her hands felt small and warmed by her mug of tea.

'Let me show you the rest of the flat first and then we can have a chat.' Smith could still feel where Jem's hands had covered his. 'I need to talk to Ralph as well – lots of other people have been to see the room. I'll need to consult him.' He could feel himself blushing and turned his back on Jem.

'OK,' she said lightly. She wasn't worried. She already knew that the room was hers.

## CHAPTER TWO

Siobhan knew she should feel happy. I mean – ALR, All London Radio. That was something else, it really was.

When Karl had first told her, earlier on that evening, she had felt ecstatic – all his dreams come true. He was on the phone to his Irish mother and Russian father in Sligo now, telling them the news. She looked at him over the top of her book; his soft, handsome face was alive with an energy she hadn't seen for years as he explained to his no doubt bursting-at-the-seams-with-pride mother that her one and only son, her precious, sweet Karl, had just been handed a peaktime slot on London's biggest radio station.

She couldn't quite imagine it: 'Good evening, London, and welcome to the Karl Kasparov Show.' Her Karl, not some faceless, naff DJ, but her Karl, having thousands of listeners, his own jingles, doing interviews. His name would be there in the radio listings: '3.30–6.30 p.m. – Karl Kasparov.' *Drive Time*, that's what they called it, Karl's slot. Karl was going to have a *Drive Time* radio show.

Siobhan imagined a classic 'Hot in the City' scenario, a traffic jam on a steaming summer's day, bumper-to-bumper gridlocked traffic and the sound of Karl's voice purring from car radios, 'It's hot out there – so keep cool by staying tuned to *Drive Time* ALR' before seguing into 'Up on the Roof'.

A barely perceptible whimper jolted Siobhan from her train of thought. It was a quarter to eleven – they'd forgotten about Rosanne in all the excitement. She was now sitting stoically by the living-room door, aware that tonight was not a normal night and trying, without irritating, to convey the message that she still had a bladder and it was getting late.

'Oh, baby, did we forget about you?' The sympathetic tone of Siobhan's voice elicited a tentative wag from Rosanne's tail, which increased with velocity and force as Siobhan headed towards the hook in the hall that bore her lead.

'Karl, I'm taking Rosanne out for a pee. Come on, baby! Come on, we're going out!'

Siobhan struggled into her winter coat, so much tighter around her upper arms and chest than it had been last year, and Rosanne panted delightedly at the door waiting for her mistress to join her.

Siobhan was glad to be out in the cold night air. The central heating, the excitement and the champagne had fuzzed up her mind. It was a beautiful October night and the tall, elderly houses of Almanac Road looked elegant beneath a jet-black sky brightly illuminated by a huge full moon.

Rosanne seemed to sense the fullness of the moon above, uncertainly sniffing the air around her, her black coat looking extra glossy beneath the bright white light. They walked to the end of the road, Siobhan thinking hard about her feelings. She'd got so used to she and Karl bumbling along in their unimpressive lifestyle. It had never mattered to her before that she hadn't really worked since losing her job as a technician at a fashion college in Surrey – she'd made ends meet with the odd wedding-dress commission and handmade cushions for an interior-design shop on Wandsworth Bridge Road. And Karl's weekend deejaying at local pubs and functions, plus what he earned at the Sol y Sombra teaching Ceroc had been plenty to meet their paltry mortgage repayments and modest-lifestyle expenses.

Karl and Siobhan – a strictly small-time couple. That's how Siobhan had always seen them, and she knew plenty of people who were jealous of their way of life, and their relationship. She couldn't have wanted for any more really – they had a lovely flat which they'd been lucky enough to buy for next to nothing before Battersea had up and come, a beautiful dog, friends they'd known since university, a relationship full of laughter and ease that was, their friends informed them, the strongest they knew, an example to everyone else, a yardstick. Neither of them was going to suffer from executive burn-out. The idea that all this might change, would change, filled Siobhan with dread.

Suddenly it would matter that she was getting fat, Karl would notice that her life was going nowhere. He would get back from his *Drive Time* slot, hyped and driven, full of fame and crappy Top Ten pop songs and find Siobhan's bulk sprawled all over the sofa, glued to *Coronation Street*, her belly swollen from the enormous meal she'd eaten while he was out because she didn't like to eat in front of Karl any more, and what would he think?

Would he still drive the little black 1966 Embassy he'd shipped back from India the year after university? Would he still wear his old American Classics chinos with the split on the knee and the scuffed old Bass Weejun loafers he'd had since before she even knew him? Would he still put on his funny Tibetan socks with the leather soles when he got in and make them both a cup of tea and watch documentaries on the sofa with Rosanne on his lap?

Would he still love her?

It was cold now – winter had stopped knocking tentatively at the door, had forced its way in and made itself at home. Siobhan looked up in time to see a wispy violet cloud pass over the moon and then disappear back into the blackness.

'Come on, baby, let's go back.'

They moved briskly up Almanac Road towards the light and warmth of number thirty-one. As Siobhan felt in her coat pocket for her front-door keys she heard voices and looked down to see a pretty dark-haired girl leaving the basement flat below theirs. There'd been visitors in and out of that flat all night. She wondered what was going on.

She unclipped Rosanne's lead in the hall and the dog dashed into the living room and straight on to Karl's lap. Karl hugged her and let her lick his face and Siobhan watched the scene from the hall while she tugged at her too-tight coat sleeves. She smiled deeply and warmly to herself and allowed the scene to etch itself firmly on the slate of her mind, allowed the joy of her current life to overcome her, because, she knew for sure, it was all about to change.

# CHAPTER THREE

Ralph and Smith had been best friends for fifteen years. They had been enemies for four years before that, since day one at grammar school, Smith offended by Ralph's creative aura and vaguely effeminate manner and Ralph threatened by Smith's easily gained popularity and effortless academic success. They kept different circles of friends and, on the rare occasion that their paths crossed, they sniffed and snarled at each other like unfriendly dogs passing in the park, their friends keeping them at bay like impatient owners tugging on leads.

It took a girl to bring them together. She was a foreign-exchange student from Baltimore called Shirelle and she was staying with Smith and his family for two months. She arrived in London in May wearing flared jeans with turn-ups and a hairy turquoise woollen jumper with a cowl neck. Her hair was long and plain, like her face.

She spotted Ralph getting off the bus on her first morning at Croydon Grammar. His trousers were tighter than school rules allowed, his dark-blue blazer was held together at the back with a safety-pin and his hair was dirtily tousled, sticking up in meringue-like peaks sculpted with soap. He had a smudge of something black and sooty under each eye. Smith thought he looked like a right tosser. Shirelle fell in love.

Over the course of that term Shirelle became Skunk.

She shaved her hair and dyed it black with a peroxide streak running through the middle. She spent her allowance in Carnaby Street on fishnets and studded belts and leather skirts. She smoked and drank snakebites and followed Ralph around like a lovesick Rottweiler. She asked him over to the Smith residence with the invitation 'Fuck me,' an offer that, although it scared him half witless, Ralph as a hormonal young man of sixteen felt he could not refuse.

Smith as a hormonal young man of sixteen was both fascinated and repulsed by these sessions and the fact that they were happening, audibly, under his own suburban roof. Any previously held notion of Ralph's dubious sexuality was well and truly rubbished by the noises that emanated from the Smiths' spare room. As time went by, his curiosity got the better of him and one afternoon, feigning interest in the phone book in the hall, he watched Ralph saunter down the stairs, tucking his T-shirt into his combat trousers in an awe-inspiringly macho way, smelling of something unfamiliar and exciting.

'So, what's going down, then, Ralphie-boy?' Smith enquired, in what he hoped sounded like a casually offhand, sneeringly condescending manner. 'How's it going with the skunk-woman?'

Ralph glanced ceilingwards. 'Fancy a walk?' he'd said, shoving his hands deep into his pockets.

And that was that. Shirelle went home at the end of term, despite her threats to stay and bear Ralph's children, bring them up in the squat they would share with the Sex Pistols and Siouxsie Sioux, take heroin and die of an overdose, and Ralph and Smith became friends.

Theirs had developed into a friendship based around the ability to comfortably spend hours in each other's company without the need to speak or move. Now, as it had been at school, they each maintained different circles of friends and took part in different activities outside the flat, but their time together there was a precious opportunity mutually to make no effort whatsoever, a form of behaviour that they found unacceptable to themselves and their friends in any other circumstance.

Obviously they weren't always silent. Sometimes they would discuss which channel to watch, occasionally they even bickered about it and conducted small tussles over the remote control when one felt the other lacked the judgement required for captaincy of such an important tool. And sometimes they would talk about women.

Women were a pain in the arse, they were balls and chains, never pleased, always aggrieved. Smith and Ralph thought of themselves as nice blokes. They weren't bastards, they didn't have affairs or lie to women, or stand them up, or hit them, or expect them to perform menial tasks. They didn't ignore their women when they were with their mates or go out with the lads and refuse to see them; they didn't stick pictures of Melinda Messenger over their beds. They were *nice blokes*. Phoned when they said they'd phone, gave their girlfriends lifts, paid for things, didn't demand sex, even handed out the odd compliment. Ralph and Smith tried to treat women as equals, they really did, but women just kept proving to them that they weren't worthy of it – they were a strange, alien breed with a list of unreasonable expectations as long as the M1 and a feast of paranoias and insecurities that Smith and Ralph were expected to deal with, daily. And then of course there were the women who weren't like that. They were the ones you fell in love with almost immediately, told all your mates about, made fantastical plans for the future with and then felt surprised when three weeks later they dumped you in a pool of your own foolishness and went off with someone who *would* have affairs, lie to them, stand them up, hit them and expect them to perform menial tasks.

Ralph, blessed with an insatiable libido, couldn't do without the sex and still threw himself regularly into the fray, emerging every now and then broken and crippled, hobbling and limping, his over-enthusiastic genitalia still pointing proudly like a bayonet towards the next battle. But Smith had given up fighting this frightening nineties version of the battle of the sexes years ago and retired, bruised but intact, to his corner.

Smith was saving himself anyway, so he said. Saving himself for a woman about whom he knew nearly nothing, a woman with whom he'd never progressed beyond the occasional awkward exchange of smiles, waves and nods, a woman who, in his opinion, encapsulated in one blissful arrangement of cells, organs, pigment and genes, the absolute epitome of female loveliness. For five years he'd imagined a day when their paths would cross. He'd bestow upon her a charming smile of teeth and self-confidence, engage her briefly in witty conversation, extend an invitation to dinner at the wonderful restaurant that had just opened up in St James, smile again at her acceptance, drape his overcoat over his shoulder and walk away with a well-paced swagger.

Instead, he'd spent five years grimacing gruesomely at her like a socially and intellectually inept toad, sometimes raising a limp, sweaty hand to wave at her if he chanced upon her from a distance and occasionally adding yet more to his plight by tripping over obstacles, dropping fragile objects, missing steps and failing to find his door keys whenever he was within her sights. He was in love with a vision of blonde, honeyed gorgeousness, a tall, slender, toned slip of perfection that no other girl he'd encountered before or since had come close to matching in any way. He was in love with a girl called Cheri, a girl who lived two floors above in the flat at the top of the house, a girl who shared his address. Until he made her his, no other girl would do.

Smith's love for Cheri remained undiminished by her haughty arrogance, her sneering indifference to his attempts at friendliness. It remained unsullied by the frequency of middle-aged men visiting her flat, their Porsches and BMWs double-parked on Almanac Road, by the thought of wives left at home while their husbands wooed his beloved with gifts of jewellery and perfume and dinner at all the best restaurants in London. Smith failed to see beyond her beauty; all he knew was her cool exterior, the layers of self-protective skin she wore to hide the nothingness inside.

While Smith waited on a fantasy that he was emotionally incapable of engineering into reality, Ralph filled his life with a succession of vacuous blondes with accommodating beds, and the two of them killed time . . . until what? Until they were too old to do anything about it? Until all the opportunities in life had gone, like unclaimed raffle prizes, to other people?

Smith knew that they needed a change. Things had been the same for too long. They were grinding each other down. He'd put an ad in *Loot*, one in the *Standard* and a card in the newsagent's window. And along had come Jem.

As far as Ralph was concerned, things hadn't changed too much in the week since Jem had moved in. She was out most nights, and when she was around she was barely noticeable. There were a few strange things in the bathroom, like cotton-wool balls and jumbo boxes of Tampax, and the fridge had suddenly become home to fresh vegetables, chicken breasts and skimmed milk. But apart from surface changes, it was still, to all intents and purposes, the same flat.

Except it felt different. The dynamics had changed. Ralph no longer felt comfortable walking around in nothing but his boxers; he became self-conscious about his toilet habits, which had always been protracted and unpleasant-smelling but which Smith had learned to live with a long time ago. And, more unexpectedly, Ralph was curious, very curious. Here was a stranger, in his home, a stranger about whom he knew no more than a first name, a strange woman at that, with all the exotic and delightful paraphernalia that surrounded women – knickers, bras, make-up, heels, roll-on deodorants in pink bottles, hairbrushes entangled with long, clean-smelling hairs, Pearl Drops, lacy things, silky things, fluffy things. He'd spent many hours extracting varying degrees of enjoyment from the women in his life, but he'd never, in all his thirty-odd years, lived with one before.

And now there was one in his flat. His curiosity was aflame and, really, he had only peeped into Jem's bedroom. He hadn't searched through her things or opened drawers or anything, just walked around a bit and looked at stuff. He was sure there wasn't anything wrong with that. If there'd been anything she hadn't wanted anyone to see she'd have put it away somewhere, out of sight. And besides, she'd left the door open. Ralph didn't like to think of himself as a snoop and was feeling slightly guilty now about his little investigation, especially in the light of what he'd seen.

Ralph had intended to spend this week at the studio. He hadn't been for over three months now. He'd made that brochure-design job for the travel company last more than a fortnight when he could have finished it in a week and had spent the last ten days or so cocooned in his room working his way through all thirty-three levels of some computer game or other. He'd reached the end this morning and, after the rapturous programme of congratulations and flattery from the computer had died down, he'd sat back in his chair and realized with some sadness that he now, officially, had nothing to do.

He'd persuaded himself that at eleven-forty it was way too late to make it to the studio but that he would definitely go tomorrow. He'd thought about the possibility of calling Claudia at work and decided against it – he always called her at the wrong time: 'Not now, Ralph, I'm in the middle of something'; 'Not now, Ralph – I'm on my way out'; 'Not now, Ralph – I've only just got in.' He imagined Claudia, in one of her silly shiny suits, busily walking in and out of the office all day, endlessly, like a film on a loop. It made him smile to himself.

The usual cloud of boredom descended upon him, and he decided to go for a short walk. As he strolled down Northcote Road, past market stalls of jewel-coloured autumn flowers and cheap plastic toys and joss sticks and African beads he began to think about Jem. He really hadn't wanted another flatmate – he liked his lifestyle with Smith, an easy life, watching telly, getting stoned – but it was Smith's flat and so he'd gone along with it, and anyway, Jem seemed quite nice and he trusted Smith's judgement.

The first week had been a bit awkward. Smith and he weren't very good at making an effort with strangers, and he'd felt guilty ordering that home-delivery Indian without asking Jem if she wanted any and then embarrassed when he'd heard her slipping into the bathroom moments after he'd made that festering rodent-corpse smell in there. She'd offered to cook for them tonight, and although he appreciated the gesture he found himself rather selfishly resenting this disruption of his normal routine. Monday night was his staying-in night and he liked it to be as socially undemanding as possible; when Smith was out he quite often switched on the answerphone and ruthlessly screened his calls. But it was nice of Jem to offer and he would try to rise to the occasion.

To give his walk a purpose he went into his local overpriced 'corner shop', one of those ubiquitous upmarket chains which sell bags of imported tortilla chips for extortionate amounts of money but never stock anything you really want to eat, which sell only one kind of washing powder but at least twenty-two brands of Mexican chilli sauce. Ralph didn't know why he frequented these places – they were so obviously designed to line the pockets of some youthful laughing-all-the-way-to-the-bank ex-City-boy types ('Ere, Paul, let's buy some retail space and flog the yuppies a load of wine and tortilla chips for three times the recommended retail price') and they annoyed him intensely. He bought himself a packet of Marlboro, although he had two packs at the flat, and walked back to Almanac Road.

Lunchtime television consisted of a selection of cookery programmes and Australian soaps, and Ralph found himself mindlessly absorbed in some frenetic shopping-channel programme, watching a camp guy with a tape measure around his neck feverishly extolling the myriad virtues of a horrible acrylic tunic with beading around the neck: 'Not just one, not two, but three, *three* different types of beading. You've got the bugle beading here, the button beading around the appliqué and, look – this *beautiful* tear-drop beading on both sides!'

Ralph wondered what planet these presenters came from and what drugs the channel fed them to make them sound so sincerely and genuinely excited about the naff and uninspiring products they were being asked to pay homage to.

He switched off the television and felt silence engulf the room. He felt empty and useless. He had nothing to do. He picked up a mug of lukewarm tea he'd made earlier and a packet of Tuc biscuits and walked aimlessly into the hall. It was then that he found himself, almost subconsciously, pushing open the door to Jem's little room.

It was strange to see the spare room full of someone's things. He'd only ever seen it empty before. It already had an unfamiliar smell. Jem's belongings lay semi-unpacked in boxes around the edges of the room – empty boxes had been flattened and folded and left near the door. The bed was unmade and there was a blue cotton dressing-gown draped across it with a white Chinese dragon embroidered on the back.

Ralph stepped further into the room to examine a pile of CDs balanced on the table next to Jem's bed. He was impressed with her taste in music, like his, still stuck somewhere in 1979: the Jam, Madness, the Cure, Generation X, the Ramones – he might ask if he could borrow them. Next to the CDs was a framed photograph of Jem in a thick winter coat, her nose reddened by the cold, crouching to hug a handsome golden retriever. Ralph looked closely at the photograph, realizing that he couldn't really remember what Jem looked like – he hadn't paid her much attention – and that she was extremely pretty. Not particularly his type, though. He always went for blondes, blondes with long legs and designer clothes and attitude problems, blondes with names like Georgia, Natasha and, of course, Claudia, blondes who worked in PR or for art galleries or fashion houses, blondes who wished he was wealthier, trendier, tidier, smarter, earlier, later, cooler – someone else.

In contrast, Jem was tiny and quirkily pretty. She had good taste in music and she kept a picture of her dog by her bed. She was also nice and polite and gave the impression that she'd be a pleasure to be with. Not Ralph's type at all.

He bit into a biscuit and a large chunk fell to the floor. As he stooped to pick it up he noticed a pile of books under the table, worn and battered looking, with various years inscribed down their spines in gold blocking, or handwritten in pen and marker. They were diaries – and, by the look of them, not impersonal desk diaries but proper, from-the-heart, highly personal girls' diaries. They stretched from 1986 to 1995. He wondered what had happened to 1996, the current diary, and then he saw it just peeping out from under Jem's dressing-gown.

It was open but obscured by the gown; he could see the date – it was last Thursday's – and snatches of handwriting, small and curly like Jem herself: '. . . beautiful flat . . . might be shy – I'm sure they're not . . . this be my destiny – I'm so excited . . . Smith could be him but seems a bit . . . Ralph . . .' Ralph stopped abruptly. What the hell did he think he was doing, snooping around in this poor girl's room looking at her fucking diary, of all things? This really was very, very sad indeed. He almost left at that point, but his interest had been stimulated to boiling-point.

His heart was racing as he pulled the dressing-gown out of the way and his jaw dropped as he read the entry in full. It seemed Jem thought she was here because of some dream or other, she was following her destiny, she was excited because she thought that either Smith or himself would be the man of her dreams – literally. Ralph was inclined to think that Jem was some sort of fruitcake, but as he read on he found himself warming to her dream, her destiny. Not only was he in the running, he had the advantage. Look, she'd written it: 'Smith seems a bit uptight, and he's not really my type to be honest. Ralph seems more likely – very lean and sexy and sort of dangerous looking' – Ralph's stomach tingled pleasantly as he absorbed the compliment – 'he seems like he'd be more fun to be with. The problem is, he's got a girlfriend.'

This was all true, thought Ralph – apart from the bit about Claudia being a problem. He *was* more fun to be with than Smith these days. That hadn't always been the way, but over the last few years, since his obsession with Cheri had taken over his life, Smith had lost some of his old sparkle and self-confidence.

There was no entry after that. Ralph put down the book and took a deep breath, resisting the urge to turn back the page, to read more. He placed the diary on the bed at the same angle he'd found it, painstakingly rearranging the blue gown over it and hoping she hadn't left a hair draped across it, to trap sad, snooping diary-readers.

He sat on her crumpled bed now, so unlike Claudia's, which took ten minutes to make, with new bedsheets every day and complicated throw and cushion arrangements that had to be just so, otherwise she'd complain. One of Jem's bras was folded into the sheets. It was black and plain and old looking. He picked it up and examined the label – little Jem was not so little: 34D. Where the hell had she been hiding those? Claudia had breasts that complemented her willowy stick-insect frame, small and pointy and incapable of forming a cleavage even when pushed firmly together from both sides. Ralph realized that he missed breasts, he missed that projection of soft voluminous womanliness that moved when it was touched and was always warm and welcoming. Other bits of women's bodies sometimes felt like they might bite or strangle or constrict, but never the breasts – they were friendly and relaxed.

Ralph was disturbed to find himself running the strap of Jem's bra across his top lip and smelling the thin strip of worn black elastic. He removed it quickly and placed it on his lap, turning his hand into a fist, which he inserted into the cup. It fitted easily, leaving plenty of room for a second fist. My God, he thought, Jem is what Claudia would describe as a 'clever dresser'. Whenever Ralph disagreed with Claudia's assessment of another woman as fat she would explain that he had been fooled by clever dressing – underneath that strategically placed scarf or sweater the woman was really a vast rolling mound of fat, he just couldn't see it because he was a man and oblivious to the tricks that women played. Maybe she was right, he thought now, admiring the capacity of Jem's bra. He certainly hadn't noticed those before.

He placed the bra back into its crevice in the bedsheets. He was beginning to feel a bit seedy and uncomfortable with himself and was relieved to note that he didn't have an erection.

Ralph was tempted to stay in Jem's room; he was enjoying its snugness and femininity. He wanted to see what she kept in the drawers, take the top off her deodorant and smell the ball, read all her diaries and find out what she was doing on specific days years ago, he wanted to climb into her bedclothes, under her duvet and between her sheets, his head on her aquamarine-cased pillows, to smell her and feel the echo of her warmth.

Instead, he stood up slowly and ruffled the duvet back into shape, checked there were no traces of his visit, left the door ajar as he'd found it and stepped back into the hall. Tonight could be quite interesting.

As he sat back down at his desk, trying to think of something constructive to do which didn't involve leaving the flat, using the phone or expending too much energy, his thoughts kept returning to the tantalizing snippets he'd read in Jem's diary, and he felt an overwhelming wave of intrigue and curiosity. What was all this about dreams and destiny? What else had she written about them? And more to the point, what else had she written about *him*? He couldn't quite explain it, but for some reason Ralph suddenly had the feeling that life was about to become very complicated.

## CHAPTER FOUR

It seemed to Siobhan that her body was just one big hair-sprouting machine. She'd expected to wrinkle as she aged, she'd expected her hair to lose its pigment, her skin to lose its tautness, but she hadn't been expecting the slow but insistent arrival of so much bloody body hair.

Starting from the bottom up, she had developed little lawns of mousy hair on the fleshy bits on her big toes. Then of course there were the legs, but she'd always had hair there – that was socially acceptable. Even supermodels had hairy legs, and there were aisles full of products in Boots that you could buy without shame or embarrassment.

It was what happened at the top of her legs that bothered Siobhan the most, the dense jungle of coarse hair that seemed more and more intent as the years went by to find its way out of her underwear and join the party taking place on her thighs and creep up her stomach in a thin arrow pointing to her belly button. The line looked particularly unpleasant in the winter, standing out starkly against the now-spongey white expanse of her stomach.

But it didn't stop there. She had noticed lately, among the pale soft down that slept between her breasts, a few renegade hairs growing longer, darker and thicker than the rest. Why? And nipple hair, spidery legs forcing their way through the otherwise unblemished surface of her breasts to spoil the aesthetics and make her feel ugly. Hair on her upper lip, too, that made her self-conscious when people stood too close to her, and even the odd whisker growing quietly but determinedly from cheeks and chin.

The soul-destroying, time-consuming rituals to rid herself of so much unwanted hair were almost daily now. Bleach for her moustache, a razor for her legs and under her arms, rancid-smelling cream for her pubic hair, and tweezers for her toes, nipples, chin and eyebrows. Did men have even the vaguest idea how much work went into women keeping themselves smooth and childlike, into removing anything from their bodies that might even begin to be described as masculine? Would men themselves be prepared to do it if fashion and society had decreed that they, too, should be alabaster-smooth?

And how come in other countries it was acceptable? How come a million Italian women could walk shamelessly and proudly along beaches every year, a veritable bearskin of black hair cascading from their bikinis and lush pelts of foliage dangling from their armpits? How come in France they had a special and affectionate word to describe the female moustache, yet an English woman would be embarrassed to walk down the street with more than a quarter-millimetre of stubble on her legs in case she were branded a dyke?

How high would it be, if she were to pile up the last ten years' worth of hateful hair? It was all so thankless. Like housework. From the very second it was done it was getting worse again, closer to needing to be done again. Hair was so insidiously persistent and never ending – it just grew and grew and grew, relentlessly. It never went on holiday or had a day off and it didn't care how fond you were of a particular part of your anatomy, it just decided to grow there anyway, like weeds on a smooth stone wall.

Siobhan had once tried to cultivate an interest in gardening, thinking herself the type, but it had quickly become clear to her that it was just like housework and unwanted hair – frustrating and for ever. Hair, weeds and dust – Siobhan hated them.

She was doing something that she seemed to spend more and more of her time doing lately – hating her body. Not only was she getting hairier by the day but she was also getting fatter, and it was now no longer a case of having put on a few pounds and her clothes being a bit tight – she had reached a size that meant people who didn't know her might refer to her as the 'fat woman'. Most of her clothes now hung redundant in her wardrobe, while she lived in the same pair of leggings and a small selection of shapeless tunic tops and jumpers. If she bought anything new it would mean having to go to shops she'd never been to before and buying clothes in sizes that screamed to the world 'I am fat.'

Karl never said anything about it – and it remained unspoken. He still touched her and stroked her and hugged her, still held her hand in public and told her he loved her. He'd never really been a compliment man anyway. Siobhan wondered what he really thought. She certainly didn't undress in front of him now or walk around the flat naked, and their habit of taking baths together had petered out unnoticed and, again, unremarked upon. She could always ask him straight out like other women would, 'Karl, do you think I've got fat?', but she knew that he wouldn't lie like other men would, he was the most honest man she'd ever known, and he would say, 'Yes, Shuv, you have,' and then where would the conversation go? What would happen next? It might emerge that he found her repulsive, that he hated her for letting herself go, for not loving him enough any more to care what she looked like.

The truth was that Karl didn't find her repulsive. He actually quite liked the shape of Siobhan's body now. She'd always been a bit out of proportion, with skinny legs, a too-wide back and a flat bottom, and now she was more balanced, her breasts looking less incongruous, her bottom more rounded and feminine. She felt nice, especially in the dark, firm and ripe and plump, her arms solid and corpulent, her thighs smooth and soft. It was almost as if the extra layers of fat had given her body a new lease of life, put the bounce back into her thirty-six-year-old skin – she felt like a chubby young schoolgirl, and Karl had never slept with a chubby young schoolgirl, even when he was a chubby young schoolboy.

Siobhan still had the most beautiful hair he'd ever seen, thick swags of summer corn down to her waist, always shiny and clean and smelling of good things. So much of the early romance and attraction in their relationship had revolved around her magnificent hair. He would see it everywhere he went around campus, either swinging freely to her waist, catching the light even on a cloudy day, or tantalizingly folded and pinned up like lustrous puckered gold. That hair tormented his soul for six months. His heart would miss a beat and then pump uncontrollably whenever he saw it; it was like a deafening siren signifying the faint possibility that he might have to walk past Siobhan and display his blush, his desire, his embarrassment. He fantasized about removing those tortoiseshell combs and clips, seeing her hair spread thickly like freshly churned butter over his pillowcase, or spilling over the back of the passenger seat of his 2CV. He wanted to wash it for her, comb and look after it for her, almost like it was a pet, an animate part of her – something living and breathing that encapsulated everything he wanted in a woman and everything that was wonderful about Siobhan.

Siobhan had been unaware of any of this. As far as she was concerned, Karl was the good-looking Student Union guy, the one with the Russian name and the Irish accent, the one she saw pinning posters up on noticeboards, the one who seemed to know everyone on campus, the one with the 2CV and the rockabilly quiff, and the one who had been quite conspicuously going out with Angel, a bleached-blonde, gamine-cropped, baby-faced wet dream of a girl from the first year, since for ever. Siobhan found him charming and attractive, loved his Irish accent, his sunny disposition, his well-formed bottom but, as far as she was concerned, there was a certain level of inevitability when a couple were as attractive and popular as Angel and Karl, and it was hard to imagine them enjoying anything less than a flawless, companionable and highly sexually charged relationship. She imagined the two of them sometimes, legs entwined on sun-drenched pure-white sheets, biting and digging their fingernails into each other, or laughing together in a pub with friends, their chemistry overwhelming and infectious. She smiled at him from time to time, and he smiled back, but that was as far as she imagined it would ever go.

Siobhan's hopes and her heart were hydraulically lifted one day by a conversation with a friend who was on the Student Union with Karl.

'She's a little cow,' he said, unprompted, of Angel.

Zing! Hope Alert!

'Really? I always presumed she'd be nice, you know, going out with Karl and everything. They seem like a perfect couple.'

'The man has the patience of a saint. I don't know how he puts up with her, I really don't. They row non-stop, and she gives him such a hard time. Karl's a great bloke, he could do much better than her, and between you and me, I don't think it's going to last much longer anyway. I reckon she's seeing someone else – but I didn't tell you that.' He tapped the side of his nose and winked at her.

Siobhan didn't need to hear anything else. The passing smiles turned into passing chats, which evolved into long, animated lunches in the park when Angel was in lectures. And, when Karl told her one night after they'd officially been going out together for six weeks that their mutual friend had been so sick of Angel and so tired of hearing Karl going on and on about Siobhan that he'd taken it upon himself to set the wheels of romance in forward motion, it had filled Siobhan with such a deep glow of warmth that she hadn't needed to wear her coat home.

Her hair had lived up to his expectations, and even up until a few months ago when they stopped sharing baths, he had shampooed it for her occasionally, gently and meticulously, marvelling at its quality and length and the fact that it was in his hands and he was allowed to touch it whenever he wanted.

Some men were breast men, some were leg men and some were bottom men. Karl was a hair man. It was hair that turned his head and made mincemeat of his senses.

Cheri had lovely hair too – not impressive, imposing hair like Siobhan's, but it was silky and long and a pretty shade of vanilla. He'd noticed her hair before he'd noticed her, last summer; it shone with streaks of sunshine-bleached blonde. It hadn't been too long before he'd also noticed her long brown legs dangling from tiny summer dresses and short cotton skirts, her elegant shoulders, tanned and angular, and her finely featured face with those wonderful cheekbones and perfect teeth.

He admired Cheri's hair now, in an aesthetic, casual sort of way, over the top of his *Evening Standard*, as he sat behind a large window in a Covent Garden dance studio and watched her in a crop top and Lycra knickers high-kicking her way through the last five minutes of her Acid Jazz class.

While Siobhan sat naked on the side of the bath ruefully grabbing handfuls of wretched, hateful flesh, three miles across town Karl stood up, folded his paper, greeted Cheri with a kiss and a stroke of her firm, neat buttocks and took her out for lunch to her favourite Modern European restaurant.

# CHAPTER FIVE

It was just starting to get dark as Jem walked from her office in Leicester Square to Gerrard Street to buy ingredients for the moving-in meal she had promised to cook for Smith and Ralph. She'd been living with them for just over a week now and she still knew absolutely nothing about them. She'd been out a lot and spent the rest of the time in her room, giving them their space, but now it was time to make friends.

On the day she'd moved in they had chivalrously although unenthusiastically helped her transport her boxed and bagged belongings from her dirty, French-mustard-coloured Austin Allegro to her room, the three of them processing quietly and industriously up and down the concrete steps like some sort of modern day chain-gang. They had then left her to her own devices for the remainder of the evening while she unpacked in the now somewhat cramped confines of her tiny room, popping their heads around the door every now and then, proffering tea and coffee and asking her politely how it was going.

Funny, this modern day thing of sharing homes with strangers, Jem had thought. Strangers had always lived together, of course – domestic staff and their employers, lodgers and their landlords – but not like today. Today people were expected to share an equal footing in their homes with strangers; there was no hierarchy. You watched the same television in the same living room, you used the same toilet and bath, shared the fridge, cooked on the same cooker and had some sort of obligation to treat this new person in your home as a friend, not an employee, not a lodger. Jem had moved around a lot from flatshare to flatshare and always found the first few nights strange and lonely. She had felt Smith and Ralph's awkwardness as they tried to go about their normal business but she knew that they didn't feel as relaxed as they would usually as they watched the Australian Grand Prix or Topless Darts. Even though she wasn't in the room with them, the fact that there was a third person in their home had thrown the dynamics of their nightly routines slightly out of kilter.

She thought about them now as she crossed over Lisle Street and remembered with a thrill that one of these two awkward but seemingly likeable men might be her destiny. It sounded daft, she was well aware of that, but fate had always made itself very plain to Jem and she had learned to trust in it unquestioningly. The only cloudy issue that fate had left her to deal with this time (and it was a very cloudy issue indeed) was which of the two men it was. Since it wasn't about to hit her between the eyes, she'd spent the last week looking for signs.

She couldn't go on looks, although they were both good-looking men, in very different ways. Smith had the public-school, floppy-haired, well-structured sort of look that she would have swooned over when she was eighteen. He was tall and nicely but unathletically built, with soft brown eyes, handfuls of thick minky hair and a fine nose with the most perfect nostrils. But he was a bit 'grown up' for her tastes, a bit too mannered, a bit restrained, too much the gentleman. She got the impression he'd be taken aback if she ordered a pint in the pub and that his idea of romance would involve long-stemmed roses and surprise trips to the theatre – yuck. She liked her men quite rough and ready, men who didn't treat women like 'ladies'.

Jem sorted through a box of shiny red and green chillies, long, thin and beautifully misshapen, feeling for firmness, while she contemplated her destiny. She placed the chosen ones into a clear plastic bag torn with some effort from one of those useless bag-dispensing contraptions and moved her pale hands to a box of baby aubergines, small and apply-green with waxy skin.

Jem found this sort of shopping therapeutic. A packet of M&S picked, peeled, topped and tailed, polished and prepacked vegetables just couldn't compare. How much nicer to wade with your hands through boxes of colourful and excitingly exotic produce, fresh from Thailand, China, India that morning, the scent of distant sunshine still clinging to their skins.

Ralph was probably more what she would have called 'her type'. He had the lean, slightly undernourished look that she liked, emphasized by his shorn hair and too-large clothes. His face was sharp but the angles were well-defined and his round blue eyes were set inscrutably deep into his face, giving him a streetwise but somehow sweet look. And he had one of those wonderful lazy, lop-sided smiles that started on one side of his face before the other side caught up. Sexy. He had the traces of a South London accent, which she loved, and he would *def*initely not expect her to drink dry white wine when they went to the pub or be impressed by expensive meals for two in trendy restaurants.

She reached the butcher's counter.

'Hello, Jem!' The butcher smiled widely as she approached. He was wrapping a large slab of pork belly for the elderly Chinese customer in front of her. 'What'll it be today?' he asked in a soft Mancunian accent. She'd always wanted to ask him how he'd ended up being the only English person working in a Chinatown supermarket.

'Hello, Pete.'

She surveyed the trays of ducks' feet and pigs' ears, the yards of shiny lilac intestines, the hunks of glistening white fat and rows of pink trotters.

'I'll have a pound of chicken breast, please, with the skins off.'

'What are you cooking tonight, then?' he asked. He always wanted to know what she was cooking.

'Oh, just a Thai Green Curry.'

'Making your own paste, are you?'

'Of course,' she smiled. 'Don't I always?'

'Thin slices?'

'Yes, please.'

'Who's the lucky dinner-guest tonight then?' he asked, deftly slicing through the pink meat with a lethal-looking knife.

'New flatmates – I'm trying to make a good impression.'

Jem took the chicken and put it in her basket. Who knows where the chickens from which these breasts had been wrenched came from? There was no handy label explaining their origin, no soft white-paper duvet for the breasts to rest on as they travelled from supermarket shelf to the purchaser's fridge. They were anonymous, and Jem felt that bit more adventurous for choosing them from among the gory remnants which other supermarkets would never put on view.

The shop was crowded, full of Chinese locals buying food for supper, of souschefs from Chinatown restaurants picking up an extra sack of rice or two for the evening rush, of tourists just looking, and amateurs. Amateurs were people who liked the atmosphere but didn't know what to buy, and their baskets invariably held a couple of packets of twenty-five-pence instant noodles, a jar of oyster sauce and a can of something preposterous like Squid in Malaysian Curry Sauce that Jem knew would end up in the bin because it stood to reason that squid in a can would be disgusting. Jem always felt a rather nasty sense of superiority as her basket went through the check-out in front of an amateur, feeling proud of her bunches of fragrant fresh coriander, packets of glossy green lime leaves, cans of creamy coconut milk, spindly sprays of lemongrass and hairy bunches of rose-pink shallots.

She looped her carrier bags over her wrists and headed for Shaftesbury Avenue. The sky was darkening to a deep plummy shade of black and the streets of Soho were assuming the night-time air of temptation and provocation that always excited her. She glimpsed the animated faces of couples over pints in pub windows, absorbed and stimulated even on a Monday night by the conversation and facial expressions of their obviously new-found love, and she felt lonely for a moment, until she remembered where she was going and the romantic potential that lay ahead.

Smith couldn't tell whether Jem was a wine girl or a beer girl so he picked up both. Maybe she didn't drink at all – he grabbed a bottle of Perrier. He was in the vintner's around the corner from his office in Liverpool

Street. 'Vintner's.' The City was just as pretentious as the West End in some ways, with its fake antiquity and overblown traditions. What was wrong with calling it an off-licence, for Christ's sake?

He took his purchases to the recently distressed mahogany counter and a traditional shopkeeper wearing a deep-green cotton apron and steel-framed glasses zapped them through the till with an olde-worlde barcode gun. Smith realized he was in a bad mood. He almost threw his card at the unfortunate vintner and bristled with unnecessary impatience as he rolled the bottles in tissue paper and put them into a bag. The copper bell on a spring which rang as he closed the door behind him irritated him.

He walked across Finsbury Circus noticing how cold it was and thinking how it had seemed like only days ago that he had sat here basking in his shirtsleeves watching old farts playing bowls in his lunch hour. He was always much happier in the summer.

He wished that Jem wasn't cooking tonight. He really wasn't in the mood to be pleasant and interested and conversational, he just wanted to sit in front of the television and have a big fat spliff and a lager and not talk to anyone. He was aware that this was exactly why he had decided that a flatmate would be a good idea in the first place, but just not tonight, that's all. Tomorrow night would be fine. The presentation would be finished by then, James would be off his back and he would probably have bought a bottle of champagne and a bunch of flowers to celebrate, and Jem would have been impressed by how friendly he was, how amusing and how sincere in his appreciation of the great effort she had made to cook them this meal. Just not tonight.

Smith arranged his briefcase and bag in one hand to grab the escalator rail with his other as he descended into Liverpool Street station. He took large confident strides and fumed as someone in front of him, a tourist who obviously had absolutely no understanding of escalator etiquette on the Underground, came to a halt.

'Excuse me, please,' he muttered huffily. The tourist turned and shuffled into the space to the right good-naturedly, apologizing with a smile. Smith felt guilty for a second, thinking of the times he had been a tourist himself.

He sweated on the Circle line, feeling irritated by every other person in the carriage with him – they were too smelly, too noisy, too close, too tall, too fat, holding too much newspaper or just offensively unattractive. Smith had fantasies about embedding pickaxes into their skulls.

He wondered what he and Ralph and Jem were going to talk about that evening over supper. As he thought about it, it occurred to him how little he knew about Jem. He'd avoided talking to her whenever possible and didn't even know how old she was, where abouts in London she worked, whether or not she had a boyfriend – for some reason he found himself hoping that she didn't – all he knew was that she had a name nearly as silly as his, she liked honey in her tea, she drove a horrible Austin Allegro and she was really quite attractive. Not a Cheri, of course, not a magnificent specimen of well-toned, shiny, angelic goldenness like Cheri. But she was approachably pretty, small and sexy and sort of fluffy, like a proper girl. She had a sweet, unthreatening voice and she never wore trousers –

Smith respected that in a woman. But for some reason, he had no idea why, she made him feel uncomfortable.

The doors of the Tube train opened at Sloane Square and Smith tumbled out of the carriage gratefully, glad to breathe in the fresh, crisp night air. When he'd first bought the flat in Battersea, eight years ago, Smith had got a real kick out of alighting at Sloane Square. After all, the plebs waiting for friends and dates outside the station weren't to know that he didn't live in SW3, as he breezed past them swinging his briefcase confidently down the King's Road. He couldn't give a toss now what anyone thought. He was way past that sort of immature posing and knew that nobody waiting outside the station even noticed him, let alone gave a shit about where he lived.

The flower stand outside the station caught his attention – it looked brave and colourful against the now almost leafless, grey October backdrop of Sloane Square and he decided that he would buy some flowers for Jem after all. She was paying for dinner and he didn't suppose she had much money. He selected three fat posies of peonies, bright and unpretentious – he didn't want it to look like a come-on.

The act of buying the flowers seemed to trigger a calming chemical in his brain and he felt his mood improve as he boarded the bus, flashed his pass at the driver and took his usual seat at the back.

As the bus passed over Battersea Bridge and filled with the glow of the pomegranate sunset filtering through the birthday-cake lights of Albert Bridge, Smith felt a small rush of euphoria. He allowed himself a little smile, and began to look forward to the novelty of a home-cooked meal and a conversation with a pretty girl.

# CHAPTER SIX

As usual, Siobhan had eaten by the time Karl got home after his Ceroc class. Siobhan had gone with him when he first started teaching. She would don one of her old fifties dresses bought from Kensington Market and fill it out with frothy petticoats, slide on some ruby-red lipstick and black eyeliner, put her hair up in a pony-tail, and the two of them would get into the black Embassy and drive down to the Sol y Sombra feeling like Natalie Wood and James Dean. But when they got Rosanne she felt guilty about leaving her on her own five nights a week and had gradually stopped going. And these days she wouldn't be able to fit into any of her old dresses anyway.

Now she would watch Karl as he slicked Black and White gel through his black curls and slid into his peg trousers and genuine Hawaiian shirt, looking, apart from a little less hair along his hair-line, exactly as he'd looked fifteen years ago. He was a brilliant dancer and an even better teacher; some of his ex-pupils had gone on to teach their own classes. He was always much in demand at weddings and parties because he made women look and feel as if they could dance.

'Has someone else moved in downstairs?' he asked, unlacing his worn but shiny brogues. 'There was a girl in the kitchen just now when I walked past, cooking.'

'Was she small and dark?'

'Yes.'

'I've seen her coming in and out all week. She must be a new flatmate or something.'

Karl wandered into the kitchen and put his arms around Siobhan's substantial waist and his chin on her shoulder. She reached back to ruffle his hair and realized, too late, that it was Ceroc night.

'Eugh, I've got Black and White all over my hands. Yuck!' She made a dash for the tap. Karl slapped her bottom gently.

As he left the room, the smile disappeared from his face. He sat down on the sofa and put his head in his hands. He could hear Siobhan next door, singing softly as she washed her hands. Her voice was gentle and melodic. She sounded like a little girl, an innocent little girl. He wanted to cry. He wished he was on his own so that he could sob and sob until his heart broke. He had been robbed, robbed of his baby. It had been taken away from him without his permission, without his knowledge.

Just one floor away, in the flat upstairs, his baby had been growing and breathing and sleeping in Cheri's womb, a mass of cells the size of a fingernail, with eyes and feet and thumbs, carrying in it the strands of his DNA, of his black curly hair and his bad temper in the mornings and his funny big toes, and she'd killed it without even thinking to mention it to him.

The fact that she'd ended their affair today, casually, over pan-fried scallops with lime juice and fresh coriander, meant nothing. *Cheri* meant nothing to him, except hair and sex and a dancing partner. But she'd killed his baby and she really didn't seem to care. He'd looked at her cold and untroubled face – she'd seemed more concerned with the texture of her scallops than the murder she'd committed – and he'd hated her, really, really hated her.

'One in three pregnancies ends in miscarriage, you know, it's not such a big deal. It could have just died anyway and you'd never have known, neither of us would ever have known,' she'd explained wearily, as if she had to explain away an abortion to some distraught, cheated-out-of-fatherhood ex-lover every lunchtime. 'And what would you have said to Siobhan anyway? "Oh, darling, you know that girl who lives upstairs, that one you don't like, well, I've been fucking her and guess what? Marvellous news, she's pregnant." Yes, I'm sure dear, fat, barren Shuv would have been *very* pleased for you.' She'd arched her perfect eyebrows impatiently and turned to inform a passing waiter that her scallops were too tough, and would he mind bringing her a linguine with chilli and clams?

Karl had no idea what he would have said to Siobhan had circumstances been otherwise; practicalities were not prevalent in his helter-skelter thought processes – all he could think about was the fact that his chance had gone. His baby had been in a womb. Suppose he and Siobhan had been so desperate for a child that they'd gone to a surrogate mother – it would still have been his sperm, another woman's egg, another woman's womb – what was the difference? He had about as much feeling for Cheri as a plastic syringe would have.

As he sat listening to Siobhan preparing his dinner in the next room, remembering the pain on her face when she'd been told at the age of twenty-one that she was infertile, that she'd never be able to have a baby, he vowed he'd have his revenge. He wasn't sure how he'd do it, but when the opportunity arose, he would make Cheri feel bad, as bad as he felt now.

Smith hadn't known whether to laugh or cry all day. He'd had two hours' sleep, eight cans of lager and two tequilas the night before and now it was Tuesday and he only had another couple of hours to complete the presentation that his financial PR company was putting together for one of the largest banks in the country. The office was in a state of complete panic and James was being more painful than Smith could have ever thought possible. He was usually an unruffled, dignified sort of a chap, who prided himself on his elegance, but when the heat was on, the loose brush of silvery hair that usually covered his balding skull stood upright, his silk tie refused to sit in a neat vertical line and small wet patches appeared under the arms of his Jermyn Street shirt.

His face was florid now, and he was shouting at Diana to 'Open some fucking windows in here! It smells like a Bedouin fucking-tent.' Diana, who hated working and was waiting for her pink-faced jellybaby of a boyfriend to propose and allow her to live the life of leisure she felt she deserved, had reached breaking-point half an hour ago and was about to cry.

Smith moved back to his desk and looked at his screen. He'd written one line of the proposal so far, 'Quirk & Quirk is one of the City's longest established PR houses with a reputation for . . .', and it sat on the screen now, reminding him vindictively of his hungover state, mocking him for being so irresponsible, daring him, challenging him to write another line without thinking about last night.

Smith felt his bowels begin to move. He picked up a copy of *PR Week*, and checking that James wasn't watching his every move, as he tended to do when he was in a panic, he walked towards the toilets.

Sitting in the shiny white cubicle staring blankly at the magazine on his lap, his reflections on the previous evening persisted. What a night, what a completely unexpected night. And what a mess. He put his face into his hands and smoothed back his thick hair with his palms, enjoying the feeling of the skin on his face stretching taut.

What was he supposed to do now? It was all going to be so horribly embarrassing. Smith just wasn't used to women coming on to him. In the days before Cheri, before he'd given up on women, it had always been up to him, he'd always made the running. Jem had really taken him by surprise last night, and he'd been too drunk to think about what he was doing. He felt guilty now, almost like he'd been unfaithful to Cheri. He'd saved himself for five years, five whole years, and now he'd blown it – just like that. It was all very flattering, the first time in years his ego had received a massage. And it had been enjoyable, *extremely* enjoyable. But he really shouldn't let it go any further. He hoped to God that Jem regretted it as much as he did. Maybe she would prefer to forget about it too. And if not? He'd have to tell her, tonight, tell her it was all a dreadful mistake. Then what? Shit. The atmosphere would be terrible. She'd move out and he'd have to find another flatmate. What was he supposed to say to her? What the hell were they going to do? And why the fuck hadn't he thought about this at the time?

He stared dismally at his reflection in the mirror

above the sink. He looked appalling. He felt appalling. He had to write that proposal. He felt like storming into James's office, slamming his fists on the desk and saying, 'I'm sorry, James, but I have a life, and I don't give a shit about Quirk & Quirk's long-established reputation. Write it yourself, you manic old bastard – I'm going home.' But he wouldn't, of course. He took a deep breath and walked back into the claustrophobic mayhem of the office. James was frantically pressing buttons on the fax machine.

'Diana, Diana, what the hell is the matter with this stupid machine?' he was muttering, his upright hair making him look like some kind of ageing budgerigar.

'Have you pressed Send, Mr Quirk?' she asked with weary impatience.

'Of course, I pressed Send. Look, can someone else please do this, I really don't have the time.'

Diana made a face at James's retreating back and headed towards the fax machine. She noticed that Smith was back.

'Someone called for you while you were out, a girl. There's a message on your desk.' She raised her eyebrows.

Smith peeled the yellow note from his computer screen. '*Gem called – thanks for last night and fancy going for a drink tonight? Please call back.*' His heart lurched in his chest, and he felt a hot flush rise up from his neck.

Oh, shit. Now what?

## CHAPTER SEVEN

'Morning, Stella.' Jem was exhausted and hungover and could feel the bags beneath her eyes pulling at her eyelids.

'Morning, Jem, you look well today. Is that a new lipstick you're wearing? It suits you.'

'Thanks, Stella.'

Ridiculous. Jem knew she looked like shit. Jem and Stella had been working together at the theatrical agency for over three years now, and every single morning without fail Stella would furnish Jem with a compliment and every single morning it would be one that she had never heard before. Taking account of holidays, Jem had calculated that five compliments a week equalled two hundred and forty compliments a year and a grand total of seven hundred and twenty compliments in all, all of them different.

'How did it go last night?' Stella enquired, in her usual ingratiating manner. She was hovering over Jem's desk with that desperate look on her face, like she'd been waiting since six o'clock that morning for Jem to get into work so she could ask her just that question.

Stella was thirty-three years old, six foot two, and still a virgin. She had hair the colour of yellowing newspaper, the remains of a perm at the ends, which never seemed to grow or change. She wore the same pale-blue eyeliner every day, which only succeeded in making her round eyes look even more damp and watery than they were. As far as Jem could tell she had no life whatsoever, and chewed gratefully on whatever scraps of Jem's not particularly exciting life she chose to throw her. 'How did your sister's eye test go?' she'd ask concernedly. 'How's your friend Lily getting on with her new boyfriend?' (She'd never met Lily.) 'What colour wallpaper did your mother choose in the end?' (She didn't know Jem's mother.) 'Oh, the duck-egg . . . lovely.'

Jem wished she could say she was fond of Stella, that she had a soft spot for her, that she'd miss her if she wasn't around, but it wasn't true. She was a huge galumphing giant of a pain in the arse, and on a morning like this morning, with a thumping dehydrated headache and a lot on her mind, she found it took all the patience and civility she could muster to form even the curtest of replies.

'Oh, fine, fine. It went fine, thank you.' Jem smiled tightly and tried to look busy.

'Good,' trilled Stella, thrilled that Jem had had a Monday night good enough to be described as fine. 'Still enjoying the new flat?'

'Oh, yes, lovely – super. Very much, thank you.' Jem was running out of fake enthusiasm.

Stella's phone rang at that moment and Jem breathed a sigh of relief. She felt a small blush of coy embarrassment and excitement spread across her face and towards her chest as snapshot images of last night's events flashed unbidden through her mind. Smith had bought her peonies – he'd actually bought her peonies, her favourite flowers in the whole world. The minute he walked in and shyly handed them to her muttering, 'Just to say thanks for the meal,' she'd known without the slightest doubt that it was *him*. She'd stood in the kitchen and looked at the two men last night, and it was blindingly obvious in an instant. On one side was Smith looking handsomely careworn in a nice grey suit and a pale lilac shirt and tie, and on the other was Ralph wearing a foul baggy grey jumper that he appeared to wear every day and a most unbecoming pair of vaguely obscene-looking longjohns.

'D'you need any help?' Smith had asked, as Ralph wandered back into the living room and back on to the sofa to watch *EastEnders*. Smith – two; Ralph – nil.

Finally they sat down to eat. The entire flat was infused with the aroma of coconut, garlic and coriander and the almost heavenly scent of Thai fragrant rice. Ralph and Smith were in raptures.

'This is the most delicious thing I have ever eaten in my whole life!' declared Ralph.

'Better than anything I've had in a restaurant,' agreed Smith.

It had taken a few of cans of lager to lubricate the evening, after the seam of compliments on the quality of the food had run dry, and Jem had found herself doing most of the work to start with, asking the two men about themselves.

Smith worked in the City, she discovered, for a PR company dealing largely with financial institutions. He'd worked as a City dealer before that but had been in danger of burning himself out so had taken a fairly substantial cut in salary to change career. But, reading between the lines, he was still earning somewhere in the region of four times Jem's modest salary. He'd lived in Almanac Road for eight years – he'd saved vast amounts of money working in the City during the boom and living with his parents in Croydon after he left university and paid cash for the flat when Battersea was still relatively good value. Ralph had moved in shortly afterwards.

To her surprise she'd learned that Ralph was an artist. She had a clichéd idea of what an artist looked like and it wasn't Ralph. She'd been wondering what he did for a living and had noticed that he never seemed to leave the house. He hadn't painted for a few months, he'd been doing sporadic freelance graphic design on his Apple Mac, but it seemed that his income was chicken-feed, just enough to cover living expenses, beer, cigarettes and drugs and the odd cab home. He seemed uncomfortable talking about his lack of direction and stalled career. He'd been the star of his year at the Royal College of Art, and his degree show had been met with much over-excitement from critics and buyers. He showed Jem a small book of press cuttings from the time, moody black-and-white photographs of 'the artist' accompanying glowing articles full of phrases like 'formidable talent', 'genius', 'exciting new star of his generation'. He'd had a few successful exhibitions, sold some paintings for what had felt at the time like extraordinary amounts of money and then everything had gone quiet. New 'exciting stars of their generation' had displaced him and for the last few years he'd been relegated to exhibiting his work in City wine bars and hotel foyers.

'I'd love to see some of your work,' Jem had said. 'Have you got any of it here?'

'Yeah, Ralph, I'd love to see some of your work too,' said Smith, turning to Jem. 'I've lived with this bloke for eight years and I've never seen anything he's done at the studio. Not a Polaroid, nothing. Show her your degree-show book, Ralphie.'

Ralph grunted but loped off to find it.

He'd returned with a large hardback book which fell open easily to a double-page spread headed 'Ralph McLeary' and a picture entitled 'Dangerous Sands Shifting 1985.' Jem didn't understand or care much for modern art but the picture made an instantaneous impact, and she turned the page with interest, to 'Noxious Gases and Ultraviolet 1985' and a smaller picture entitled 'Violent Electrical Storms 1985'.

The paintings were abstract but rich in colour and although seemingly flat and one-dimensional, Jem felt surges of energy bursting from them.

'Ralph, these are great, really . . .' She searched for a word that wouldn't sound ignorant, '. . . dramatic, energetic, scary almost. And I don't usually like modern stuff. These are brilliant!'

'Thanks.' Ralph had looked pleased despite himself and closed the book. 'Anyway, you've had to ask enough questions tonight. Tell us about yourself.'

Jem always hated talking about herself, but she told them in as few words as possible about Smallhead Management, the theatrical agency where she'd worked for three years, how she'd recently been promoted from secretary to Junior Talent Manager and was learning the ropes from Jarvis Smallhead (they'd laughed at his name), the outrageously camp agency boss who had high hopes for her. She recounted the almost never-ending series of mini-dramas and crises she had to deal with every day involving a bizarre collection of aged luvvies and prima donnas. She told them about the painful Stella and her obsession with Jem's life, about her eccentric mother and her long-suffering father and her idyllic childhood growing up in a cottage in Devon. She explained that her name was short for Jemima and that before she moved into Almanac Road she'd been living with her sister Lulu in a vast, partially furnished flat off Queenstown Road. Lulu was moving her boyfriend in, and his three children from a previous marriage, and although she'd been welcome to stay, Jem had decided to move on.

They'd carried on chatting as Smith and Jem cleared the table (Smith – three; Ralph – nil), and the more Jem watched Smith the more she felt sure. He was definitely the quieter of the two, the more restrained. He sat straighter at the table, his table manners were more precise, his laugh more controlled than Ralph's, and there was something vulnerable about him that appealed to her, a certain sadness, a loneliness. Ralph was good fun and probably more similar to Jem in a lot of ways, but although Smith seemed more uptight, she felt a closeness to him.

Once she'd decided she knew it wouldn't take much to set the ball rolling, to lead Smith gently by the hand into a relationship. She just hadn't expected the ball to start rolling quite so soon, or quite so fast.

Ralph had got up from the table at about eleven, kissed Jem unsteadily on the hand, thanked her profusely for the meal, proclaimed it a milestone in his gastronomic life and gone to bed, leaving Jem and Smith alone.

Jem hadn't wasted any time. 'Do you believe in fate?' she'd asked, rolling a spliff on the pine surface of the kitchen table.

'What do you mean?'

'You know, everything happening for a reason, events

and moments being preordained. Like me being here tonight. If I'd seen a double room I liked last week I wouldn't have come to see your room. I would be sitting in someone else's kitchen now, talking to someone completely different, and I wouldn't even know you and your lovely flat existed.' She paused briefly. 'Except, that's not quite true.' She stopped to search for a Tube ticket in her handbag to use for a roach. She wondered how much she could say to Smith.

Smith wondered what on earth she was going on about and wished he could focus on her a bit more clearly.

'This is going to sound weird – do you promise you won't think I'm a nutcase?' she asked, tearing off a small piece of cardboard.

Smith reached for a bottle of tequila. 'Promise,' he said.

'Well, ever since I was a teenager, I've had a recurring dream.'

'Ye-es,' Smith slid the shot glass in front of her. God, she really was cute.

'Just a really nice image of a tall house on a curved road with a basement and little trees outside. I'm walking down the road and I look into one of the flats and there's a man sitting on the sofa with his back to the window. He's smoking and talking to someone I can't see and he's smiling and happy and relaxed and I really, really want to go in. The flat looks warm and welcoming and I just have this very strong feeling I'm supposed to be living there – it doesn't feel right that I don't, that I have to walk past and never get to know the man inside, never be part of his life. And that's it, that's the dream. And then, that night I came to see the flat, I just knew it was the same flat – I felt it. It was so familiar, so safe, just the way it felt in the dream. And I looked down, just like in the dream, and I saw a man sitting on the sofa and talking to someone out of view.' She paused. 'Do you think I'm mad? Are you going to kick me out?' Jem laughed nervously.

Smith fought the smile that was twitching at the corners of his mouth. He didn't know where this weird conversation was going, but for some reason, he felt compelled to keep it going. He arranged his features into an expression of serious consideration. 'No, I don't think you're mad at all. I think that's really rather amazing.'

'But that's not all. I hope you don't think this is really heavy or anything . . . Oh, I don't know whether to say this or not . . .'

Smith looked at her intently and rested his head on his hands. 'Please – go on. This is fascinating – I promise you.'

'Well, it's not just the flat. It's the man. I know in my dream that I'm supposed to be with the man on the sofa – he's my destiny. Do you realize what I'm saying?'

Smith had no idea what she was saying, but she was getting cuter and more attainable by the minute. All of a sudden he could imagine taking her face in his hands and kissing her sweet little red mouth, and then he thought about Cheri, imagined her upstairs now, while they spoke, elegantly tucked up between her ivory silk sheets (he'd never actually seen them, of course, but they had to be, didn't they?), her lithe, supple body encased in a tiny slip of satin and lace, her perfect head ever so slightly denting her pillow while she slept. He imagined her lace-clad chest rising gently up and down as she breathed, pictured her turning in her sleep, stretching and writhing slightly, the slippery sheet sliding off her body for a second and revealing one long, brown perfectly formed leg. She would sigh as she turned, a long, deep, sensual sigh, and then drift back into sleep . . .

'You do think I'm mad, don't you? Shit. I knew it. I knew I shouldn't have said anything.' Jem was staring at the floor and wringing her hands.

'What? No! No. God, I'm sorry – I was just thinking, that's all.' Smith smiled modestly and sincerely at her. He still wanted to kiss her, and all of a sudden it didn't seem like too much of a challenge. He lifted his shot glass and nodded towards hers.

'Cheers, then,' he said, watching her as they downed the repulsive liquid and grimaced.

'Yeek,' scowled Jem.

'Bleugh,' shuddered Smith.

They fell silent for a moment, looking into their glasses and glancing at each other every now and then, both waiting for something to happen.

'Smith,' said Jem eventually, 'I hope you don't think I'm being unbelievably forward, but – I've just had this overwhelming compulsion to hug you. What do you think?' She grinned nervously and put out her arms.

It had been a monumental hug, a coming-home hug. Jem had almost felt the energy flowing between them as she pushed her head into his chest and breathed him in deeply, his smell enveloping her in the same feeling of rightness and safety and destiny as her dream, but better, because this was real.

Smith had gripped her tightly, unexpectedly enjoying the sensation of shared physicality; it had been so long, so bloody long since he'd had any kind of decent human contact. He'd forgotten what it felt like to put your arms around another human being, without embarrassment, and share their warmth and their body. He'd always thought this moment would've happened to him and Cheri, but this was good, this was nice. Jem was nice.

They had stood like that for what felt like hours, their arms around each other, Jem's head in Smith's chest, Smith's chin on her head, breathing deeply, sighing, allowing unspoken feelings to flow through them, a silent communication between two people looking for entirely different things and finding them in exactly the same place.

# CHAPTER EIGHT

Ralph could not believe it. He really could not believe it. It was beyond the pale, it defied belief, it was rude and . . . and . . . and . . . unbelievable. He could not believe it. The girl had only been here two minutes and already Smith was . . . was . . . fucking her. He was fucking her. He was fucking well fucking her. Unbelievable!

He could not understand how it had happened. One minute they'd all been sitting together having a nice chat and a laugh and breaking the ice very nicely, thank you, and they were all friends, all equals and then Ralph had taken himself off to bed and then – then what? What the hell had old Smithie said or done to that girl to get her into the sack so fucking quickly? Maybe she was some kind of nymphomaniac who moved from flat to flat shagging her flatmates – saved getting cabs home, he supposed. Jesus.

Ralph had lain in bed all morning with an achingly full bladder, waiting for the other two to leave the flat so that he wouldn't have to bump into either one of them on his way to the bathroom. Smith was gone by eight o'clock and then Jem had got up and left at nine. He was standing over the bowl now, watching the colourless jet of piss escaping gratefully into the water below, and breathing a pleasurable sigh of relief.

Jem just didn't seem the type. A nice girl, a decent girl. He'd found her completely charming over dinner the previous night and had been thinking how refreshing it was to meet a girl who was intelligent and funny and pretty, and drank lager from the can, and loved curry as much as he did, and who was a good talker as well as a good listener. He'd been delighted and flattered by her reaction when he'd shown her some of his paintings. He'd been overwhelmed by her culinary ability and her highly impressive capacity for searingly hot food. He'd been entranced by her stories about her family and the strange characters she worked with at the theatrical agency. He'd found her Italianate hand gestures and scrunchy facial expressions beguiling and endearing. She wasn't like any of the girls he normally met. She was special.

So what was a lovely girl like Jem doing, leaping willy-nilly into bed with a prat like Smith? Ralph was intrigued. He was confused. And he was also a little jealous.

He headed for the kitchen and a pint glass of tap water, gulping greedily. It was a filthy day, just visible outside the kitchen window; the sky was uniform paper-flat white, and a fine drizzle was slowly moistening the bricks and concrete of South London, turning the crunchy leaves strewn messily around the streets into mulch. The combination of bad weather and bad hangover was rapidly making the journey through London to his draught-ridden, rat-infested studio in Cable Street seem unlikely.

Maybe all that stuff in her diary was rubbish and she'd wanted Smith from the first moment she saw him. Maybe something had happened between them that night when she'd come to see the flat and Ralph had been in his room. Maybe the air had been thick with the scent of unbridled lust since Jem had moved in and Ralph just hadn't noticed, like some sad insensitive bastard. Maybe (Ralph hated to think it) maybe the dinner was only really intended for Smith, and they'd both been waiting all night for him to go to bed, giving each other looks across the table every time he'd opened his mouth to say something else, thinking 'Fuck off, Ralph, Fuck off, Ralph.' Ralph felt stupid.

For five years he'd had to listen to Smith droning on and on about that God-awful woman upstairs, that snotty, stuck-up bitch with the attitude problem from hell, who didn't have even the slightest awareness of Smith's existence. And now, the first time an eligible woman set foot in their flat and showed a little interest, he'd bedded her. Just like that. That really was the epitome of laziness.

The post landed on the doormat and Ralph padded down the hall. A cheque from the travel company – £540. Just enough to clear some of his overdraft so that he could start building it up again. Ralph could not remember the last time his account had been in credit. He put the cheque on the hall table – he'd make a trip to the bank later in the day. He noticed that the door to Jem's room was ajar again. He remembered the tantalizing passage he'd read in her diary yesterday and, his resolve and sense of honour weakened yet more by curiosity, he pushed open the door and scanned the room for the book. Maybe there would be a clue in there, something to explain the extraordinary goings-on of last night.

The room was still in disarray. Jem's bed had been slept in, so she'd obviously managed to find her way out of Smith's bed at some point, the curtains were drawn and the weak light outside struggled through the thick fabric, casting a pink glow over the room. Ralph reached for the light switch and the little glass star lit up. The diary sat with its predecessors under the table by the bed.

Ralph was caught off guard by his reflection in the wardrobe mirror – so, this is what he looked like, snooping in someone else's bedroom. He was wearing a pair of old grey longjohns and a baggy grey V-neck jumper, displaying a spray of dark chest hair and a silver chain he'd bought in Bangkok. His hair was short but dishevelled, receding into two gentle dips of baldness, which seemed to retreat at exactly the same rate of acceleration as the hairs on his chest, back and shoulders advanced. His blue eyes were looking a little dull this morning, as they always did when he'd been drinking. But, on the whole, not at all bad for a totally unfit, twenty-Marlboro-a-day, very nearly thirty-one-year-old man.

Ralph wasn't a vain man, just one who appreciated how lucky he was not to have to worry about being unattractive – life was difficult enough without being ugly as well. His image looked after itself; he didn't need to cultivate it. He never put on weight, and the muscles he'd developed during a summer spent labouring on a building site when he was twenty-two had somehow lasted him almost a decade. Losing his hair suited him, and hair care was just a matter of going to the same barber's he'd been frequenting since art school and asking for a number two. And girls always seemed to buy him clothes. Especially these PR fashion types who got discounts all over the place and half-price designer samples. The jumper he was wearing had been bought for him by Oriel, a beautiful but tedious girl with an obsession with handbags and a small dog called

Valentino. He'd seen the same jumper in a shop a few weeks after they split up and had been shocked to see it sporting a price tag of £225. That hadn't stopped him wearing it at least five times a week without washing it; it was now peppered with small burns caused by hot rocks falling from spliffs, and smelt at close range like an ashtray full of curry which had been stuffed up someone's armpit for an hour during a heatwave.

Ralph turned away from the mirror. He wasn't used to studying himself – it wasn't unpleasant, just vaguely unsettling. He pushed open the dark wooden doors of the wardrobe.

The floor was lined with shoes, lots and lots of shoes, little tiny shoes. Some were flat and some had heels, but they all looked as if they had been worn; unlike the impulse buys that constituted the extravagant shoe collections of other girls, these were old friends.

Her clothes formed an eclectic kaleidoscope of rich browns and reds and greens, and floral prints on chiffon, velvet, suede and silk. They emitted a sweet odour, perfumed with subtle undertones of pubs, cooking oil, wood smoke and spicy food; an aromatic diary of her social life. Ralph pulled out a particularly pretty dress, ankle-length diaphanous georgette printed with small red roses, with thin straps and a stream of impossibly small buttons down the back. He could picture Jem in it, her black curls studded with flowers, her abundant bosom pushing upwards, running barefoot through the grounds of some imaginary grand house, a pink-cheeked Renaissance babe.

No no no no no *no* NO! Ralph stopped himself abruptly. He hadn't come in here to sniff Jem's clothes and form elaborate Mills and Boon-style fantasies about her. He hadn't come in here to get a crush on her. Jem was not, was most definitely not, *not*, NOT, Ralph's type. No. Blonde, tall, whippet-chested, cool, arrogant, wine-drinking, label-wearing, *Elle*-reading, ball-attending – that was Ralph's type.

Time to get down to business; time to find out what was going on here. Yesterday he'd been in the running, had been, in fact, ahead of the game; yesterday he'd been 'lean' and 'sexy' and 'more fun to be with'. Yesterday he had been the object of Jem's strange and mysterious dreams. Yesterday he'd been Jem's 'type'. One day later and he was a spare part.

All of a sudden he could see the future mapped out before him, and it wasn't pretty. Jem and Smith were going to become inseparable; he would have to spend hours listening to them having sex, sitting on his own in the armchair while they snuggled together on the sofa. They would decide to get married, and Smith would approach Ralph nervously after the engagement party to broach the subject of him moving out. He'd end up in a cardboard box (no one else would be as understanding about Ralph's sporadic rent-payment style), and he'd have one Tennents Super too many and be set on fire by hooligans while he lay unconscious in a doorway.

Why the hell had she gone for Smith? What had he, Ralph, done to put her off? Maybe it was all those smelly shits he'd done; she always seemed to walk into the toilet moments after he'd exited. Or it could be because he hadn't fussed around her, offering to help when she was cooking, like Smith had. She must have got a fair idea last night of how much money Smith earned – that was always attractive in a man. And Smith had bought her flowers as well, the smarmy bastard – that had to be it. Girls liked flowers. God, if only he'd thought of that. Why Smith? Why not him? Why not him when she'd fancied him more to start with? What was wrong with him? Smith already had a flat and a great job and loads of money, he didn't need a girlfriend, too. And besides, he was in love with someone else. Ralph felt suddenly nauseous with rancid jealousy, rising to the surface of his soul like lumps of wet toilet paper in a blocked toilet bowl.

His pulse racing, his resolve and sense of honour now absent, Ralph sat down on Jem's bed and pulled the diary from the top of the pile. He began to read from the beginning, from January 1996, when Jem had been somewhere else, non-existent, someone he was yet to meet. If Smith was going to go out with her and sleep with her, then *he* was going to get to know her.

Lunchtime came and went, and elsewhere people with jobs went out, shopped in Boots, ate sandwiches, bought the *Evening Standard*, walked around town in suits and shoes and coats. Ralph read.

By mid afternoon the people with jobs were on the phone, in meetings, making cups of coffee, flirting at the photocopier, immersed in the safety of office life. Ralph read on.

As the light died at five o'clock and the people with jobs rushed to meet deadlines, tidy their desks, switch off their computers and frank the mail, Ralph still read.

At six o'clock, or thereabouts, he closed the book, put it back under the table, ruffled the duvet, turned out the light and left the room. He sat at his desk, tapped a Marlboro out of its packet, lit it, smoked it and waited for Jem and Smith to get home.

# CHAPTER NINE

'What's she doing here?' Siobhan asked, in a tone which she hoped sounded casual and light-hearted and didn't betray what she felt inside – insecure, jealous, nervous. She was just so bloody pretty and sort of fit looking, glowing with health and vitality; all the stuff that had waved goodbye to Siobhan years before. And she had such lovely hair.

It was Karl's leaving party at the Sol y Sombra, just a few drinks with his students, some of whom he'd been teaching for five years, to wish him luck in his glittering new career.

'She's one of my students, didn't I tell you?' Karl was drinking from a bottle of lager.

Definitely not. 'I don't think so. You might have, I don't remember.'

Cheri didn't really strike Siobhan as the Ceroc type, she seemed more aerobic, more of a sweating-at-the-gym sort of girl.

'She's very, very good actually. She was my partner for a while, after you stopped coming.'

'Oh, really.' A filthy flash of unaccustomed jealousy pierced her stomach. Brightly, brightly, keep smiling, Siobhan; don't let him know you're jealous.

'You really don't like her, do you?' Karl asked unexpectedly.

'Well, I mean, I don't know her. She just doesn't seem

like a particularly nice girl, that's all. Not really my type. She doesn't pass the Pub Test.' Karl knew about Siobhan's Pub Test; it was her way of ascertaining whether or not a girl was her type. She imagined being in a pub with the girl in question. If she could envisage sharing a couple of pints, a bag of crisps and some easy chat with her, she passed; if not, she was happily consigned to the not-my-sort-of girl pile.

'Yeah, I don't like her either.'

Brilliant! 'Oh really, I thought you thought she was all right.'

'No, you were right, Shuv. She's a selfish cow. I didn't even invite her tonight, one of the other girls did.'

'So what don't you like about her?' Siobhan's curiosity was aflame. She wasn't used to Karl forming such forthright opinions about people, doing vindictive things like deliberately not inviting people to parties, calling people 'selfish cows'.

'I don't know. I just agree with you, that's all. There's something about her I don't like. I can't put my finger on it.' In fact, Karl was furious. He'd told the little bitch not to come tonight and she'd promised she wouldn't.

'Why would I want to come to some sad little drinks with all those sad little Ceroc people? Don't worry. Bring your fat girlfriend – she'll be safe, I promise you.'

And now here she was, dressed up to the nines in some skin-tight black cotton dress with a low-cut back, drinking lager from a glass and flirting with poor Joe Thomas, the permanently sweaty looking bank clerk with the Buddy Holly glasses and too much Brylcream, who looked as if he was about to die of entirely unconcealed excitement.

Karl couldn't remember who'd started this whole mess

any more. Obviously he'd noticed Cheri – any man would notice Cheri. But then, life was full of women to be noticed; if you started doomed affairs with all of them you'd never get anywhere. Picking up women wasn't Karl's style. It must have been Cheri.

He'd bumped into her one day at the front door, struggling for her key. He'd just got back from a dance class, so he had on all his fifties gear, and she'd asked him if he'd been to a fancy-dress party. When he'd explained about Ceroc, she told him that she was a dancer, that she'd trained as a ballerina until she was twenty, that she loved rock 'n' roll, her father had taught her to jive as a child. So Karl had invited her along to the Sol y Sombra, and she'd come. In retrospect, knowing what sort of a girl she was, she'd probably been flirting like mad with him then, sending out frantic sexual signals that he – honestly – had been completely oblivious to.

It wasn't until the first time he danced with her that he felt anything beyond a purely aesthetic appreciation of her. She was quite simply the best dancing partner he'd ever had. Her classical training added beauty and grace to the most basic Ceroc moves and she felt like a hollow doll, light and effortless, feathery and feminine. Ceroc was a man-led dance, and she followed his moves almost telepathically, injecting just the right amount of energy and enthusiasm into her dancing, smiling all the time.

Karl had been blown away. So blown away, in fact, that he hadn't mentioned it to Siobhan when he got home that night – not because of guilt, but because he knew he would blush vivid red and Siobhan would ask him why, and then he'd blush even more vivid red, and it just wasn't worth sowing seeds of doubt in her mind over nothing. So he hadn't said anything. He hadn't hidden it either, but Siobhan was obviously never looking out of the window when he and Cheri got back from class together, and since there was no chance of Siobhan and Cheri forming any sort of neighbourly friendship, she had never known.

Which of course made it easier for Karl neatly to compartmentalize his life when the dancing partnership turned into something a little more carnal. Karl had been shocked rigid when Cheri had first kissed him. It was definitely a scenario that had been swirling pleasantly through his mind for a few weeks, but then, life is full of enjoyable imaginary scenarios, and it would be impossible to enact all of them.

'Let me buy you a beer,' she'd said one night. And then, when the beer was gone and it was time for them to go, 'I really fancy another drink. Let me buy you a tequila.' And then, when those were gone, 'Let's have another, go on.' She'd had to persuade him, jolly him along, but he'd agreed in the end. After a third tequila they were laughing and relaxed, and Cheri had swivelled around towards him on her barstool, smooth brown legs conspicuously crossed, eyelids lowered, her body closing the gap between them and, before any embarrassment had a chance to creep in, she'd locked her eyes on his and kissed him. Gently at first, hoping that she wouldn't have to do all the work, that he'd respond to the sensual brush of her lips and kiss her back. She'd looked at him again. 'I love dancers,' she'd said, her eyes moving from his lips back to his eyes and to his lips again. She'd grazed his lips, a little harder this time. 'I especially love Irish dancers,' she'd drawled, 'with soft lips.' He'd kissed her then, and Cheri felt a rush of triumph.

Their kisses had become longer and harder, and his tongue probed deeply into her mouth. He'd brought his chest up close to hers, gripped her back and emitted a small, slightly animal grunt. 'Let's go to the office,' he'd groaned, searching his pockets for the key, and they'd stumbled into the small, stifling room, pungent with the smell of stale cigarette smoke and warm plastic at the end of a long, hot summer's day.

Cheri had let her dress drop to the floor, a practised procedure, and smiled at the look on Karl's face as he saw her for the first time, unwrapped, pert, smooth and naked. He'd been awkward, fumbling with his clothes, clearing a space, never taking his eyes from her body. 'God you're beautiful,' he'd said, rolling a condom on to his erect penis. It was all over in five minutes, hard, fast and uncomfortable. Karl was sweating profusely, his trousers still around his ankles, his quiff drooping and falling into his eyes. 'Oh, Jeez,' he kept saying as he came, 'Oh, Jeez.' And then he'd pulled up his trousers. 'Shit, it's hot in here,' he'd said, and handed her her dress from where it lay on the floor. 'I'm going to wash my hands.'

That should have been it really. They should have left it there. But, it seemed, as far as Cheri was concerned, it wasn't over. It wasn't over because, although she'd seduced him and aroused him and led him astray, he wasn't grateful. And she wanted him to be grateful.

But he wasn't. He never asked for more than Cheri offered him and took even that with an affronting lack of graciousness. She'd almost had to drag him up to her flat one weekend when he'd told her that Siobhan was away. She'd cleaned the flat from top to bottom, cooked a romantic meal, and Frank Sinatra, his favourite, wafted alluringly from room to room. There were clean sheets, new underwear, flowers. But it hadn't made any difference. It was longer and more comfortable and less sweaty, but it was still entirely perfunctory, and Karl had wolfed down his dinner afterwards and gone back to his flat to watch telly on his own.

For his part, Karl wasn't sure why it had dragged on for so long. In a strange way which he couldn't quite explain, he was scared of Cheri. Her emptiness and coldness frightened him, and he couldn't help feeling that if he tried to extricate himself, he might pay dearly for it – Rosanne in a pot of boiling water sort of thing. She'd been so determined to have him, so determined to make him want her that he hadn't dared go against her wishes. And if he was honest with himself, there'd been something strangely aphrodisiac about that intensity, about his fear – pathetically, it had turned him on.

He had truly believed that he would never, ever, in a month of forevers be unfaithful to Siobhan; it was more than unthinkable, it was ridiculous. And he certainly would never have thought it possible that he'd end up having a torrid affair with a bimbo – which is all Cheri was, a blonde bimbo with legs up to here and lovely tits, who could dance like an angel.

He knew he was nothing special to Cheri, but then he didn't suppose that anyone would be anything special to Cheri. It was, had been, purely and simply, fucking as an extension of dancing, a natural conclusion in a way to a traditionally sexual art form. They danced so well together that it stood to reason they would fuck well together.

It had been much easier than Karl could have imagined, lying to Siobhan, facing her fresh from the Sol y

Sombra, coital sweat still drying on the back of his neck, the tang of rubber still perceptible in his boxer shorts. Funny how he didn't blush now, now that he actually had something to feel guilty about. He'd spent his entire life blushing at inopportune moments, his face reddening for no reason whatsoever, and now, he could walk into his flat, face his faithful and trusting girlfriend of fifteen years, his dick smeared with the vaginal secretions of the blonde bimbo from upstairs, and remain perfectly alabaster white. Ironic.

It hadn't occurred to him that girls like Cheri got pregnant. She was just so utterly soulless, so cold, so vacant and devoid of emotion, so different to how he expected a real woman to be that he hadn't thought for a moment that she even possessed a womb. Cheri was a dancer, a looker, not a mother. The thought of a baby suckling at those perfect rose-coloured nipples was ludicrous, the idea of Cheri pushing a pram, of Cheri changing a nappy, was laughable.

Siobhan was what Karl imagined a mother to be like. Siobhan was real, she was alive, she had a heart so big she could have mothered the entire country and still had room for the rest of the world. Karl had never been loved by anyone the way he'd been loved by Siobhan, such clean, easy, honest love, not the possessive, clingy insecure love so many people mistook for the real thing. She had never tried to change him, to alter him in any way. She loved him just the way he was, and Karl didn't think you could ask for much more than that. Except, for some reason, passionate sex with unsuitable, unpleasant women.

Karl was feeling incredibly uncomfortable now, with Cheri and Siobhan in the same room. And Cheri had a look about her, like she was here for a reason, had a hidden agenda. She turned away from Joe Thomas for a moment and caught Karl's eye – she smiled widely at him and, to Joe's obvious disappointment, started to make her way over towards Karl and Siobhan.

'Hi!' she beamed, 'Hi! It's Siobhan, isn't it? I haven't seen you around for ages. Haven't you been getting out much lately?' she held out her tanned hand for Siobhan to shake. Karl felt sick as the two women's flesh touched. 'I'm going to miss your boyfriend so much.'

'Oh, really?' Siobhan replied amiably.

'Yes, Tuesday nights will never be the same again,' she said, looking at Karl.

Karl found himself almost glued to the spot, his bottle of lager frozen half-way between his mouth and the table, watching the scene unfold before his eyes.

'You must be so proud. When do you go on the air, Karl?'

He collected himself, conscious of a small stream of sweat wriggling down his temples. 'Erm, Monday week, isn't it, Shuv?' he said, handing the conversation back to the women.

'Yes, that's right. He's at the station all next week, though, to learn the ropes, you know, learning how to put those jingle cartridges in the jingle machine, all that technical stuff,' Siobhan replied with a little laugh.

'Well, Karl, good luck and everything. I'd have to have stopped coming to the lessons anyway soon. Look' – she held out her left hand, palm down – 'I'm getting married.'

'Oh, what a beautiful ring.' Siobhan held Cheri's fingertips gently in hers while she examined it, turning it to catch the light.

'Yes, it belonged to my fiancé's mother. She was one of the most beautiful women you've ever seen.'

'Your fiancé – is that the tall guy with the blond hair?' Siobhan asked.

'Oh, no, that's Martin. Oh, God, I wouldn't marry him. No, it's Giles. I've known him since I was nineteen. He's very wealthy, very important in the City. He's got a house in Wiltshire and one in Australia and a flat in Docklands.'

'Where will you live? Are you going to move out of Almanac Road?'

'No, I think I'll keep it as a *pied-à-terre.*' She sounded uncomfortable using the expression. 'You've got to have a bit of space, haven't you?' She tossed her hair over her shoulder and laughed. 'Anyway, you two, I hope you don't mind but I'm leaving now. I've got a big day tomorrow looking at dresses, and I've got to find a venue for the reception.'

Karl and Siobhan both murmured their lack of disappointment.

'Karl, my coat's in the office. Would you mind opening it up for me?' Cheri placed her hand on his bare arm and he jumped slightly, the first time he'd moved since Cheri had approached them.

'Erm, why don't I just give you the key?' he said, fumbling in his pockets.

'Oh, you know how awkward that lock is – I can never get the hang of it. Do you mind?' She was wearing a sickly smile, one of her eyebrows raised slightly higher than the other.

Karl gripped Siobhan's hand. 'I won't be a second. Will you be all right?'

'Yeah, sure,' she replied weakly, wondering why she

was feeling so uncomfortable about Cheri and Karl going to the office together.

He returned a few minutes later, looking red faced and flustered. 'Do you mind if we go?'

Siobhan was secretly relieved. 'No, of course not. What's the matter?'

'Nothing. I've just had enough, that's all,' he said distractedly, surreptitiously trying to wipe away the now solid stream of sweat rolling down the sides of his face.

He was so angry he could hardly breathe. That little bitch, casually moving from man to man, taking things as she went, holidays in Antigua, engagement rings, flats, babies, honesty, decency. What was she going to do to this poor Giles character?

Everyone seemed to let her get away with it, just carried on giving her things and giving her things and never expecting anything in return. Well, he was different. He expected things. He wasn't going to let her walk away just like that, into some cosy life with a rich man who'd give her anything she wanted for the rest of her life. Especially when she'd come here tonight to show him she was in control, to flaunt herself at him, to prove to him that she could fuck him, finish with him, abort his baby and still get a decent man to marry her.

That was why he'd done that to her in the office just now, forced his hand down the front of her dress, squeezed those perfect breasts hard with his sweaty fingers until she'd yelped with pain and then kissed her hard, ignoring the clash of his teeth against hers, sucking hard on her tongue and grabbing her crotch with the other hand, kneading the hot flesh inside her knickers while she struggled against him. He'd thrown her coat at her then and held the door open. He wasn't scared of her any more.

'Go home, you slut,' he'd said. 'If you ever come anywhere near Siobhan again . . .' He was shaking, and the anger inside him filled out the whole of his six-foot frame.

She was a whore, a slut – it didn't matter whose engagement ring she was wearing – and he wanted her to feel it, wanted her to leave the Sol y Sombra cheap and dirty, not the righteous, virtuous wife-to-be she'd convinced herself she was tonight. She'd looked frightened when she left, clutching her coat, her lipstick smudged around her mouth, her dress dishevelled. He'd ruined it for her, her little wedding fantasy. Good.

'Shuv,' he said later on when they'd got home and he'd regained his composure, 'let's have a baby.' He hadn't planned to say it, it just came out. But the moment he said it he realized it was right. It was what he wanted, more than anything.

'Oh, Karl, you know . . .' Siobhan began sadly.

'Yes, yes, I know. It's going to be difficult, it's going to be hard. Especially for you. But let's try. Properly. We'll be able to afford it now – you know, different treatments and stuff. Shuv, please. I really want us to have a baby.'

He was on his knees now, holding Siobhan's hand. 'Please . . .' He laid his head on her lap.

Siobhan was still feeling unsettled by the incident in the club, and this was the last thing she'd expected. She thought they'd written it off years ago, after the doctor had told her that the infection in her ovaries had made her infertile. That's why they'd got Rosanne. She hadn't thought the subject would arise again; it had been philosophically dealt with and it was closed.

'But what if it doesn't work, you know? It could take years and years, and I'm thirty-six now. Maybe I'm too old – they don't like dealing with older mothers, more risks, it would take up all our time. I've seen the documentaries – it might tear us apart, and you and I are more important to me than a baby. I couldn't bear it, all the disappointments and the waiting . . .'

'Please, Shuv, please.'

Siobhan looked down at the mop of black glossy curls on her lap, the solid neck and the curve of his wide shoulders, the bright design of his Hawaiian shirt. His legs were bent up under him, his whole being prostrate and vulnerable. God, she loved him. All she wanted in the whole world was for Karl to be happy. That was all she'd ever wanted, from the day she'd met him.

'OK – we'll see.'

Karl grasped her tightly and buried his head further into her warm flesh. 'Thank you, thank you, thank you,' she heard him breathe. 'Thank you.'

She stroked his hair, ignoring the slick gel, and felt quietly scared.

# CHAPTER TEN

Ralph should have gone out, he realized that now. He shouldn't have sat in on his own all night. Claudia had invited him out to some press party for the launch of a new perfume her agency was handling. It would have been a nightmare, but there would have been free food and booze and lots of PR babes to admire and he could have just got totally pissed and spent the night at Claudia's and let the two of them have the flat to themselves. But instead he'd decided to be selfish and interfering and hang around to see what happened next with the red-hot lovers. He'd been expecting to hear the key in the lock all night and was positioned ready for the entrance of either one of them, feet up on the coffee table, spliff on the go, lager in one hand, remote control in the other.

At about nine o'clock he'd got bored of maintaining this pose even though it was a fairly natural one, and had decided that a reading-the-paper-in-the-kitchen pose would be more suitable. By ten o'clock he'd read the obituaries and the gardening column, had tried and failed to get even one word on the cryptic crossword and had thoroughly depressed himself by reading the executive job pages. Was he ever, ever, going to be in a position to earn £120,000 p.a. *plus* car *plus* healthcare *plus* bonus? No, he wasn't, and the thought made him miserable.

By half-past ten he had concluded resentfully that Smith and Jem must be together somewhere and he'd made toast and experimented with a lying-on-the sofa-making-a-phone-call-and-eating-toast pose but couldn't think of anyone he wanted to speak to.

By the time Jem and Smith finally got home he was back in his original sofa, spliff, beer and telly pose. They were glowing horribly and the noise of their playful chatter in the hall had preceded them upsettingly.

They stood in the doorway, all teeth and smiles and breathless hilarity.

'All right, mate. Had a heavy night?' Smith enquired sarcastically. Sarcasm was not something Ralph was in the mood for.

'Yeah, well, I was going to go to one of Claudia's poncey press things but I couldn't face it. I didn't fancy another heavy night after last night, so I thought I'd have a quiet one. Where've you two been, then?' He was trying to be pleasant. He really didn't want to know where they'd been, he didn't give a shit where they'd been.

'Just for a drink with a couple of Jem's friends and out for a meal.' Smith placed his hand on Jem's shoulder as he spoke; Ralph felt dejected.

'You missed a great programme on Discovery,' he countered, 'about killer sharks. They cut this one shark open on the beach and found the partially consumed remains of four men inside it, including their oxygen tanks.'

'Aw, fuck, what a way to go,' Smith said. Ralph could tell that he was feigning interest; he was looking at Jem and playing with her hair.

'Does anyone need to use the bathroom? I'm going to get ready for bed,' she said, taking Smith's hand from her hair and holding it at her side. Ralph watched her gently.

I know about you, he wanted to say. I've been inside your head all day long and I know everything. I know every thought you've had for the last ten months, every place you've been, every meal you've eaten, I know more than Smith. I know you haven't had a single date all year, that you've been starved of sex but resisted the temptation to go to bed with your friend Paul.

I know you eat curry at least twice a week.

I know that you're not as confident as you make out and that you hate yourself sometimes. I know you worry what people think of you, that you're sensitive, that you can be paranoid sometimes, that when you're being chirpy you think you're getting on people's nerves.

I know that you haven't spoken to your mother for two years and how unhappy that makes you.

I know you get terrible PMT. I know your periods are as regular as clockwork (thirty-one-day cycle, first thing in the morning) and that you worry obsessively about your bowel movements and that's why you eat two pounds of All-Bran every morning.

I know you had chronic piles in June.

I know you think you're two-faced because you think dreadful things about people you're nice to in the flesh.

I know you chose Smith because he bought you your favourite flowers. I know about your dream and I can see why you thought that Smith was the one. I should have made more of an effort, I should have put some decent clothes on and offered to help, I shouldn't have been so offhand and I shouldn't have gone to bed. And I know you're wrong, Jem – it's not Smith, that was just a coincidence: buying flowers is a cheerful thing to do.

It was me sitting on the sofa when you looked through the window and it's me you should be with.

But how could he say it, when it would mean admitting that he was a sneak of the lowest sort, the kind of person who reads other people's diaries? He looked at Jem now and realized that she was a different person to the stranger he heard leave the house that morning. He'd been inside her head all day, inside her thoughts. He knew more about her than Smith did, Smith who'd spent the evening with her and met her friends and had sex with her last night. He knew her secrets and insecurities. He desperately wanted to be close to her.

'Na, na, go ahead. I'm going to be up for a while,' he replied.

'You go first,' Smith said, pulling Jem back towards him with both arms around her waist.

'OK. Night night, Ralph, see you tomorrow.'

'Don't I get a kiss?' he said, getting up from the sofa. He suddenly wanted to touch her, too.

'Why not?' Jem smiled. 'Night night, Ralph,' she said again and gave him a peck on the cheek.

'Sleep tight, Jemima.'

'So, what do you think, then?' Smith whispered excitedly, as the door closed behind her.

'About what?' muttered Ralph. He really didn't want to discuss Smith's revolting good luck with him.

'Jem, of course. What do you think of Jem? Of me and Jem? Oh, come on – you must have worked out what's going on.'

'Oh, right, very nice. Yes, very nice.' Then, seeing from the look on Smith's face that something further was required, 'Lovely hair, very pretty, very nice. I'm very pleased for you, Smithie, really I am.'

Glancing at Smith, he could sense that this line of new-girlfriend flattery still wasn't sufficient.

'I'm not talking about what she looks like, I'm not asking you to fancy the girl, I just want to know what you think of her – of us.'

'Look, what the fuck do you want me to say? The girl's only been here five minutes. She's very nice – I like her. I just hope you know what you're doing, you know, after the last few girls. You've got a bit of a track record for rushing things . . . remember Greta? You asked her to marry you after two weeks and then couldn't understand it when she ran a million miles in the opposite direction. And then that fuck-awful Dawn girl, the one you told you loved on the first night you met her and then she turned up the next day with all her stuff, expecting to move in. And *I* had to get rid of her for you. And that Polish girl you took home to meet your parents after less than a week, who made off with their Camcorder and your dad's laptop to support her boyfriend's crack addiction. And . . .'

'OK, OK,' Smith conceded, 'I know what you're saying, but this is different. Jem's different. I feel different. That's what's so great. I'm not going to fall in love with her, it's all under control! I was going to tell her tonight, tell her that I didn't want to take this any further, tell her about Cheri and everything. And then I thought, why? Why the hell shouldn't I have a bit of fun for a change, a bit of sex? I forgot how much I enjoyed it and I think I deserve it, don't you? Jem's a really lovely girl, I really like her. But for once, I've got the upper hand, I'm in control. I'm older and wiser and I won't make the same mistakes again. It's just a bit of fun. Really,' he stressed, noticing the look of scepticism on Ralph's face.

'So you haven't told her about Cheri – about your deeply unhealthy five-year obsession with an unattainable woman.'

'Of course I haven't! You've got to be kidding, haven't you? I'm not going to mess it up before it's even started. She thinks I'm great, she thinks I'm the man of her dreams – really! She told me last night. She thinks – now get this – she thinks that this flat has appeared in her dreams and that I'm her destiny. Isn't that hysterical! Anyway, Cheri's a different thing entirely. Cheri's a dream-woman. I've waited long enough. It's time to get on with my life. And maybe if she sees me getting on with my life, you know, without her, with a pretty girlfriend who worships the ground I walk on, she'll see me in a different light, come round a bit. It might make me more attractive to her.' Smith's face brightened at the thought.

'But you will tell Jem – at some point – won't you? I think she has a right to know what sort of a prat you really are.'

'Yeah, yeah, and I suppose you've told Claudia all about your colourful past, have you?' said Smith, knowing full well that Ralph hadn't.

'Yeah, but that's different, I don't love Claudia. She doesn't need to know.'

'Whoa! Who said anything about love?' Smith laughed, 'I think you're rushing things a bit here! That's what's so fantastic – I actually think, for the first time in my life, that I've met a woman who's more into me than I'm into her. D'you have any idea how great that feels? And she lives here, which means I don't have to worry about all that phone-call and date hell – I've got her on tap. This, Ralph my old mate, is what I would call a result!'

Ralph swallowed the bile-like sensation of distaste that rose in his gut as he listened to Smith. He pulled a cigarette from the packet in front of him and tried to bring the conversation to a halt. 'Well, can you keep it down tonight, please? I've got to get up early tomorrow morning and I don't want to have to put up with you two caterwauling all night.'

'Why not? I've had to put up with Claudia the Queen of Grief for the last six months. And I can assure you that Jem is as quiet as a kitten compared to that bloody banshee. You know, Ralphie, there are decent women out there. You don't have to go out with a nightmare like Claudia.'

'Look, I don't want to piss on your only-just-ignited fireworks here, but all girls seem great when you first start going out with them. Claudia seemed great: "Hey, I don't want commitment, I don't want to be tied down, I just want to have fun, I just want you to have fun, of course I don't mind if you go out with your ex-girlfriend tonight, of course I don't mind if you cancel dinner, I'm a grown-up woman, I'm cool." And now look at her. Just watch it, Smith – women, they're all the same, and don't you forget it.'

They heard the light in the bathroom being switched off, and the door being shut. Smith got to his feet and stretched.

'Yeah, yeah. Just you wait. Once you get to know Jem, you'll know what I mean – she's just not like that. You'll love her too.'

'Nah, Smithie – not my type,' Ralph said, forcing a grin. 'And anyway, I thought we weren't allowed to talk about love.'

As the door shut behind him, and Ralph found himself

as he had been all night – alone – he felt a great sense of loss. Things were never going to be the same again. For years life had unfolded nicely, predictably, easily. Now everything was in jeopardy – his home life, his relationship with Smith, his finances, his security, his routines and habits. And, he realized suddenly, more than anything, his heart.

# CHAPTER ELEVEN

'Look, I like the music, I'm not saying that I don't like it. I think it's great music, classic stuff. But I'm fifty-three, I'm a balding fifty-three-year-old executive with three kids, a house in the country, a Land Rover and acid indigestion, I'm supposed to like it. Hmm, hmm . . . d'you see what I'm getting at?'

Jeff, programming director at ALR and Karl's new boss, looked at him across his huge status-symbol desk with his hands held palms up and his face wearing an expression that said 'There's a queue of people outside my door waiting to talk to me about budgets and scheduling and I'd really rather just bawl you out and get you out of my office, but because you're a new boy I'm going to have to be pleasant about this.'

'Hmm, hmm . . . d'you see what I'm saying, Karl? Hmm, hmm.'

Karl wished he'd stop doing that 'hmm, hmm' thing.

'Kids just don't want to listen to Al Green or Jerry Lee Lewis – I do, oh yeah, yeah, I do – but they don't. D'you understand? Hmm, hmm . . .'

Karl was beginning to feel like the only guest at a party who hadn't been told that it wasn't fancy dress. He'd been brought in to ALR to play a wide range of music, from Top Ten to Tom Jones. That was what had appealed to Jeff when he'd been a guest at a wedding Karl was Deejaying at and that was why he'd got the job, over the heads of all those other DJs struggling for years in hospital radio and small-time local radio stations in Nuneaton and Truro. He was knowledgeable, not just poppy and happy and chirpy. They'd wanted someone their listeners could respect, someone with impeccable taste in music. They'd wanted him to build some sort of reputation – if it's on the Karl Kasparov show then it must be good.

*Drive Time* was captive-audience time, listeners trapped in cars. People did other things during the breakfast show, they brushed their teeth, they fed the kids, they made love. Daytime radio was for working to, background noise; as long as the DJ churned out a lot of pop and fun nobody was going to turn the dial.

*Drive Time* was different, a time for unwinding at the end of a hard day, a time to be selective and demanding and to turn that dial if the DJ was getting on your nerves or the music was repetitive.

Karl, with his deep, lilting Irish accent, his unabrasive sense of humour and his intelligent taste in music was exactly what they were looking for.

And now, after less than two months, they were telling him that they were wrong, that they were losing listeners. The critics loved him, but his audience was 'turning the dial' in its thousands.

'Phone-ins, celebrities, characters, comedy, chat, that's what you need, Karl, and more Top Ten, hmm, hmm.' He picked up his phone and dialled. 'Rick, you got a second, mate? I'm here with Karl, you know, discussing the show, hmm, hmm. We need your expertise here mate, some Rick-style advice. Could you come and see us? Yeah, yeah now, that's right, great, OK great . . .'

'Rick – you know Rick, don't you – he's the producer,

you know, on Jules's show? Yeah, right, anyway, he's got some great ideas, he's a great bloke full of energy, and funny? – God, he's funny – I want you to spend some time with Rick, you know, talk talk talk. I'm talking about your free time here, Karl, I'm talking about . . .'

He stopped and began to search in the top drawer of his vast cyclamen melamine-topped desk with one hand outstretched as if ready to pull Karl back by the lapels were he to attempt to escape. His other hand surfaced with a large bunch of keys. He looked at Karl triumphantly.

'I'm talking about Glencoe. I've got a place up there, an old Presbyterian chapel, converted, miles away from anywhere, it's ab-so-*lute*-ly be-*yew*-tiful, right on the banks of the loch. At this time of year the sun sets right over it – it's stunning, Karl, really, really stunning – makes you feel kind of small and pointless, that sort of landscape. Puts everything into perspective . . .' He fell into a thoughtful silence and then suddenly slammed his hands down hard on the desk. Karl jumped slightly in his seat. 'And I want *you*,' he pointed at Karl, 'and my mate Rick to get yourselves up there this weekend, with your partners of course, and really have a mess-around, you know, hmm, hmm, get pissed, get off your faces if you want, you know, really unwind and relax, get to know each other and start throwing some ideas about – anything that makes you laugh, anything that makes your girls laugh. You got kids, Karl?'

Karl shook his head numbly.

'Good. Anyway, I'll get Sue to give you directions and stuff and money for booze and anything else you want . . . yeah, that's a good idea . . . yeah, take some drugs with you, I want you to come back with some really zany ideas, something for the kids, hmm, hmm. And take some watchables up – you know, Jack Dee, Lee Evans – I'll get Sue to sort that out for you. Don't worry about it, I'll get Sue to sort everything . . . ah, Rick.' Jeff stood up. 'Rick, my favourite producer. Karl, mate, this is Rick de Largy.'

Karl turned around in his chair.

'Good to meet you – I love your show.' The man standing in the doorway smiled and held out his hand. He was ridiculously good looking, not in a flash way but quietly and horribly handsome. Karl could suddenly imagine how women felt in the presence of greater beauty. With all this talk of 'zany' and 'kids' and 'chat' Karl had imagined that this Rick character would be naff and toothy and unpleasantly sweatered, with too much hair and a fake tan. Even his name had sounded tasteless and gaudy. But the man standing in front of him was elegantly dressed in a white cotton shirt, well-cut jeans and what looked like handmade shoes, his gentle-featured face framed by understated wire-framed glasses and his hair a soft champagne blond, short at the back and sides and thick and effortlessly unkempt on the top. He looked about the same age as Karl but much healthier. His skin actually glowed – Karl had thought that only women's skin glowed.

'You two,' said Jeff leaning forward into his desk, 'are going to be great, great friends – just you wait.' He beamed like a proud father. 'Now, what about a bit of lunch then, boys, hmm, hmm?' He laughed and shook both men's hands. 'Let's go and talk about how Rick here is going to make you the funniest man on *Drive Time*.'

Funny? *Funny?* Karl felt his heart drop. He'd never

felt less funny in his life. His home life was falling apart. Things just hadn't been the same since that night at the Sol y Sombra and afterwards, when Karl had begged Siobhan to have a baby. The atmosphere of warmth and love in their little flat had died and Karl didn't know why. It should have grown from that night – Cheri was out of his life, he and Siobhan were making plans for the future, he was just about to embark on a fantastic new career, everything should seem new and fresh.

He'd lain in bed on the night of his leaving party and watched Siobhan sitting on the edge of the bed swiftly removing garments, pulling her top over her head, her hair spilling over her smooth white back, and he'd felt a strong rush of love and arousal, not just a need to ejaculate but a need to probe every area of her body, to explore her like he used to when they were younger. He stroked her hair and wound it around his hand into a thick coil that gleamed in the muted lamplight and brushed it against his face – it felt like satin and the lustrous silkiness aroused him further. He placed his arm around her waist, feeling it melt into the pliant rolls of flesh, and reached his hand upwards until it found her breast. He'd groaned then and buried his face into her back and breathed in the scent of her skin deeply, gently massaging her breast, feeling her nipple suddenly bloom under his fingertips, a small warm bullet of flesh.

For years their sexual routine had been fun and frolicsome, rollicking romps, good clean fun. Tonight he wanted more. Every bone and muscle in his body had quivered with desire as he gently pulled Siobhan around and lay on top of her. He pulled her hair from around her shoulders and arranged it carefully into an abundant fan over the pillow – she looked like a Titian archangel. He kissed her hair, her forehead, her plump white cheeks, her eyelids, her ear lobes, her neck – oh God, he wanted to feel every part of her with his lips, his tongue, his fingers. He groaned again and slid his face between her breasts, the tip of his nose feeling the moist pool of sweat that lay between them, damp and hot and pungent. He licked at it, enjoying the taste of the sweat on his tongue while his hands pushed her breasts gently together – 'oh God oh God' – he could come now, he really could. His erection was bursting, ripe and angry and pressed hard into Siobhan's groin – he rubbed it up and down against the coarse hair, the abrasion spreading feelings of desire from the shaft of his penis to the tips of his fingers. He felt Siobhan wriggling slightly under him and stroked her face, wanting the love he was feeling for her to spill from his fingertips into her head, so that she'd know without him breaking the spellbinding silence that was fuelling his desire.

'Karl . . . Karl . . . please, please.' Siobhan's voice had sounded like a distant echo, her hands gently pressed down on his shoulders. His tongue continued to forage, his hands grasped her flesh harder and harder . . .

'Karl, stop it, please . . . I . . . I . . . don't want to.' Karl took Siobhan's nipple into his mouth and sucked hard on it, running his tongue around the hard warm flesh . . .

'Karl, STOP IT, STOP IT, STOP IT! Get off me!' She pushed hard down on to his shoulders and tried to roll him away.

'WHAT?' screamed Karl. 'What the fuck is wrong?' He was on his side of the bed now, his hair wild and on end. He turned to look at Siobhan, who had pulled the duvet up over her body and still lay in the same position. She was crying, silently, huge effortless tears flowing down the sides of her face and on to the pillowcase, a completely blank expression on her reddening face.

'I don't want to, Karl, I just don't want to . . .'

'You don't want to what? What don't you want to do, Siobhan? Tell me, for fuck's sake.'

'I . . . I . . . I don't know.' She wiped away the teeming tears with the back of her hand to make room for the endless flow.

'You don't want me to make love to you – is that it? You don't want me to love you, to love your body – what, Siobhan? What?' Karl demanded.

Siobhan sniffed but the tears kept coming. 'I don't know Karl. I don't know . . . I'm so sorry, I just can't. I'm sorry . . .'

'Well if it's all the same with you, I'm going to have a wank,' he snapped, striding through the bedroom towards the bathroom and slamming the door behind him.

Siobhan had watched his angry naked body, still in good shape, defined back muscles, firm round buttocks, his scrotum just visible as the light from the hallway silhouetted him briefly. It was a body she was so familiar with, had loved for so many years, enjoyed for so many years, and as she watched it walk out of the room, away from her, she cried and cried and cried.

She didn't know what the matter was, or how good her intuition was. But it was something to do with the party at the Sol y Sombra, something to do with that girl, the blonde from upstairs, the one who was getting married. She made Siobhan feel ugly, she made her feel insecure, and for some reason she made Siobhan feel sad and scared, as if something until now immutable had changed for ever.

She wanted to tell Karl, but she couldn't. How could she explain that she'd rejected him because she thought he wished he was doing those things to Cheri? That she'd lain there while he caressed her and licked her and loved her, and all she could think was that he was fantasizing about that girl, fantasizing that Siobhan's fat unkempt flesh was Cheri's taut brown flesh, that her densely haired, pungent genitals were Cheri's neat soft mound, that the woman underneath him was young and firm and beautiful?

She'd seen the way he looked at Cheri, how he'd blushed, the way he used to blush on campus all those years ago. And what had happened in the office, why had he looked so flustered when he got back? There was no doubt in Siobhan's mind that Karl fancied Cheri, that he wanted her. It all tied in with the glamour of his new job. How could a top DJ possibly be satisfied with a fat, lazy, hairy woman? He wanted more now, even the way they had sex wasn't good enough for him now – he wanted steamy Hollywood sex, passion and heavy breathing and grasping flesh, not the usual routine of fun and laughter.

He was probably thinking about Cheri now as he sat on the toilet and vented his frustration, probably enjoying it more than he would writhing around on top of Siobhan's vast, wobbling body pretending she was someone else.

He obviously didn't see her as a woman any more. It all made sense. That was why he suddenly wanted her to have a baby after all these years, so she would become a mother, a vessel, not his lover. Young fresh girls were for fucking; fat ugly women were for staying at home and having babies and getting even fatter. Their breasts were for suckling, for hard greedy babies' mouths to drain of their suppleness and femininity and leave dry and pendulous and ugly, hanging like strips of biltong. And while she nursed his child he would be fucking one of those awestruck girls who congregated outside the ALR building, wanting a piece of DJ.

The door opened quietly and Karl tiptoed in. 'Shuv, I've brought you someone.'

A weight fell on to the bed and a wet tongue stroked Siobhan's cheek. The aroma of dog wafted in the air. Siobhan hugged Rosanne to her and cried until the tears stopped coming. Karl put a hand on her shoulder.

'Shuv, I'm sorry, I didn't mean to storm out like that. I didn't mean to shout. I was just so . . . so . . . I just wanted to make love to you so badly tonight.' He stroked her hair. 'Please, Shuv, talk to me, tell me what's on your mind.'

Siobhan just shook her head sadly, put the dog at the foot of the bed and turned on her side away from Karl.

'I love you,' he whispered in her ear, 'I need you.'

He turned over then, the other way, and a heavy wall of silence divided the room, a dense knot of unresolved unhappiness and uncommunicated thoughts hung in the air.

They hadn't made love since. They hadn't really talked either. They'd gone about their lives in an apparently normal fashion. Siobhan had given him a hero's welcome when he returned after the transmission of his first show, and he'd given her flowers. They'd been out to buy a new sofa together and bid an emotional farewell to the old one when they left it at the tip. But things just weren't the same, there was a distance between them that would have taken a million yards of rope to bridge, an intolerable distance that they were both too afraid to cross, because below was infinite darkness, impossible depth.

The baby had been forgotten about; it hadn't been mentioned since that night.

Things were not good and now they were getting worse.

No, Karl had never felt less funny in his life.

# CHAPTER TWELVE

Jem had always found that men seemed to fall in love very quickly. The full-blown declaration of love usually came within the first week, sometimes sooner. When she was younger she'd been so shocked by these revelations that she would clumsily repeat this much-abused statement in reply, not knowing how else to bring the embarrassing moment to a close. And then, of course, after it had been said once it had to be repeated like a mantra every time it was offered to her like a desperate gift from the love-afflicted soul. She soon learned when the 'I Love You' moment was imminent and discovered that when it was countered by a firm but affectionate 'Don't be silly, of course you don't', it rendered the afflicted one even more desperately in love and devoted.

Which is why, even though she'd been going out with Smith for nearly two months now, she wasn't in the least worried that he still hadn't said it, that he still hadn't told her he loved her. He didn't have to. Jem knew he loved her, without a word leaving his lips. As far as she was concerned it was yet another sign that Smith was the One. It was all so easy, so effortless. Smith was so undemanding, he didn't put any pressure on her.

Jem found it refreshing that he didn't plague her with romantic gestures and overblown declarations and gifts and pukey tokens and acts of love. He didn't go on about how beautiful she was, or how she was the most amazing woman he'd ever met, or how she was *so* sexy and *so* wonderful and *so* special. She'd had enough of all that to last her a lifetime and she knew that such devotion usually came with a price tag attached – the jealousy and possessiveness of an insecure man.

Jem was aware that other women might find her attitude hard to understand. She realized that many women spent the majority of their lives dreaming of a man who would finally notice the dazzling flecks of amber in their eyes, the fine golden hair on the back of their necks, the porcelain smoothness of their skin, a man who would stroke, caress and soothe, utter words of adoration and talk endlessly of the years to come and the joys of commitment, a man who would place them carefully and reverently upon a diamond-encrusted pedestal, throw rose petals at their feet and hand-feed them morsels of their favourite food, all the while unable to unglue their eyes from them for fear of missing just one second of their incomparable beauty.

Not Jem. All that stuff turned her stomach and made her want to vomit.

She'd loved it the first time it had happened, of course she had, especially coming as it had at the tail-end of a hideously awkward adolescence just as she'd finally convinced herself that she was to remain unloved and unpenetrated for ever.

His name was Nick and he was a comfortable-looking bloke with a strong jaw and the sweetest smile imaginable. He'd just come through an equally awkward adolescence and at the ripe old age of nineteen was just about to resign himself to a lifetime of virginity when Jem came along.

It was a classic summer romance, full of picnics and trips to the cinema, drunken nights in beer gardens and hours of fumbling in the front seat of his mother's car, where Jem had found herself, after years of trying to keep other boys' hands out of her knickers, frankly, quite desperate to get hers into his.

They finally dispensed with their long-standing virginities that summer, the day after Jem's eighteenth birthday and, in comparison to stories Jem had heard subsequently from her female friends, it was a truly magical event that had lived up to both their expectations. They were madly, madly in love with each other.

So everything was perfect and Jem was happy.

Until one night, a few weeks later. She'd been well into her third pint and enjoying a raucous conversation with a raucous friend at a raucous girls' night out – when in walked Nick. He'd ambled self-consciously into the bar, scanning the room for his precious Jem, his face opening up like a blossoming flower when he spotted her, his pace quickening as he approached, his arms outstretched to pull her into a desperate embrace.

'I was missing you,' he said, 'my mates were boring me. I just wanted to be with you,' and he'd gripped her to him, burying his face in her hair and Jem had *tried* to smile, *tried* to reciprocate the depth of feeling, the strength of passion, but failed miserably, feeling instead completely suffocated, trapped and compromised. Nick felt like someone different after that night. They were no longer equals. The scales had been tipped. And try as she might, Jem just couldn't revive the warm, solid, easy love she'd felt for him before.

At the end of that summer, she went to university in

London and he went to university in Newcastle, and although things were OK at first, their weekend meetings gradually became more and more stressful. Nick would spend hours interrogating Jem about her newfound male friends in London, about her every movement and action, and quiz her about every boy she'd kissed before they met. Then he started to cry with alarming frequency, huge, wailing, snotty, unstoppable tears. 'I only went to Newcastle to prove to myself that I could live without you – and I can't! I can't live without you, Jem!' When he'd started talking about transferring to a London university, Jem decided it was time. Enough was enough.

It was one of the hardest things she'd ever done and he reacted badly when she phoned him, blowing his grant on a flight from Newcastle to London because the train would have taken too long, and searching London's student community, house to house, for her. He'd finally found her, trying to hide from him in Lincoln's Inn Fields. They spent three traumatic hours going over and over the details of their relationship, Nick begging and pleading for another chance, until the sun started to sink and the vagrants began to set up their makeshift homes, and Nick finally gave up and went home.

Jason hadn't believed Jem loved him, either and demanded her attention, her love and her reassurance constantly, for ten months, disappearing into huge black sulks for days on end when he felt that she had wronged him in some way. Danny had insisted that she stop seeing her friends – he couldn't understand why she should possibly need friends, now that they'd found each other. Clem wanted to marry her after six weeks and then fell into a deep depression when she said no, claiming that he no longer wanted to see her because 'it just hurt too fucking much.'

And then, finally, there was Freddie, a fantastically charismatic, hysterically funny and deeply sexy saxophonist, who Jem had been all set to fall miserably in love with. He was totally removed from all the 'nice' boys she'd loved before and she was more than ready to experience the other side of the coin, to hand him her heart on a plate. But he beat her to it. Within weeks he'd had his long tousled locks cut short, swapped his jeans and waistcoat for a pair of chinos and a check shirt and was talking seriously about selling his sax and getting a job in sales so that they could get a mortgage and maybe think about starting a family.

Jem had been amazed. Wasn't that the way girls were supposed to behave? Wasn't it women who wanted commitment, security, babies, and men who just wanted to get drunk with their mates, have fun and play the field for as long as possible? Not in her experience. As far as Jem could tell, men were the ones with a strong need for commitment and security. How else could you explain the fact that at least nine times out of ten it was the man who proposed marriage? They can't *all* have been arm-wrestled into it.

Another thing Jem had learned about men was that they were threatened by a woman who *didn't* crave commitment and security, who wasn't straining at the leash to walk up the aisle, who didn't stop and drool at the windows of every jewellery shop she passed or turn to melted butter at the sight of every passing pink-cheeked cherub in a pushchair. As much as men might moan and whinge about these traditionally female traits, at least they knew what they were dealing with – 'the nag', 'the ball and chain', 'her indoors'. It had all been tried and tested by their father and their father's father and his father before them; women like that were a known quantity. It gave joyous meaning to nights at the pub or out with the lads – you deserved it after all you'd had to put up with from the demanding old harridan all week. It was part of life's rich tapestry and eventually, a couple of years down the line, the man would pretend to be strong-armed up the aisle, just to keep the tradition going, even though it was really what he wanted, too.

But these days – well. These days all the rules were broken and for some reason a lads night out isn't quite so enjoyable when you're worrying about what your free-spirited girlfriend is up to with her mates, and it takes the edge off rolling home pissed at one in the morning when she rolls in at two in the morning, completely slaughtered and having had a much better night than you. Where's the fun in being a bloke if you can't dangle the carrot of commitment in front of your girlfriend for years on end? And if she doesn't want commitment, the ring, the babies, then what the hell does she want? So Jem had found that most men, when confronted with a girl who just wanted to have fun, became confused and for some reason took over the role of the traditional woman, going to extraordinary lengths to try to tie their girlfriend down, break her spirit and control her.

But not Smith. Smith was perfect. He was happy for Jem to do her own thing, in her own way. He was generous and kind and easygoing and so affectionate. Jem had never known such an affectionate man. He never left her alone, was always dropping kisses on the top of her head, squeezing her hands, stroking her neck and grasping her to him in rib-crunching bear-hugs. Jem knew why. He'd confided to her on their first date that he'd been celibate for five years. Five years! He hadn't had any physical contact with a woman for five years. It was another sign. It had to be more than a coincidence, his celibacy. He must have been waiting for her, waiting for Jem. And she was more than happy for him to make up for lost time with her.

He smelt nice, he looked nice, he dressed beautifully and he felt gorgeous. He didn't hassle her with his emotions and insecurities, he gave her space, he gave her time. She really liked all his friends. He really liked all her friends. And the fact that he was rich enough to pay for meals out and cabs home without Jem feeling guilty was just the cherry on top of it all.

OK, so it wasn't love's young dream. OK, so they'd bypassed all the usual courting rituals – the long, animated talks over late-night drinks, the endless hours spent in bed inspecting each other's moles and scars and belly buttons, the hour-long phonecalls you never wanted to end and pizzas in the park on freezing winter afternoons. And maybe they didn't really have all that much in common – she'd been right about the dry white wine and the fancy restaurants. But they were so easy in each other's company. Even now, at this early stage in their relationship, they were able to sit comfortably in silence, in public. It didn't matter when they ran out of things to say. There was no embarrassment. And Smith wasn't the most adventurous and spontaneous of people. But that didn't matter to Jem. She'd had her share of romance, and she didn't want any more.

She really didn't mind that Smith had forgotten both their one-month anniversary and their two-month anniversary. She found it refreshing. And she didn't mind that he never paid her compliments or noticed when she changed her hair or wore a new dress. She certainly didn't mind his lack of discomfort about her nights *à deux* with her close friend Paul or his complete lack of jealousy about her ex-boyfriends and old loves. She was happy that he spent so much time at work and didn't put any part of his life on hold to make room for her. She didn't want any of that. She didn't want the attention, the demands, the neediness. She'd been under the magnifying glass, the spotlight of insecure love for long enough. And now, she just wanted Smith.

## CHAPTER THIRTEEN

Ralph had given up reading Jem's diary over the last two months. Well, the current diary, anyway. It was just full of Smith this, Smith that and Smith the bloody other. It was like Ralph had ceased to exist the moment Jem had slept with Smith. He had been hoping for some doubts to creep into her entries, some reference to the fact that Smith wasn't quite right for her, wasn't good enough, that she'd made her decision too soon. But it hadn't come. She was utterly blind to it, she was 'in love' with Smith and her diary was a constant, gurgling, gushing, vomit-inducing account of how perfect he was and how wonderful they were and how great the sex was.

But Ralph hadn't given up the long periods of time spent just sitting in her room. He liked it in there. It smelt good and he felt safe and warm with all Jem's feminine artefacts, it was second-best to her actually being there herself. He felt close to her when he was in her room.

He was sitting on her bed now, thumbing through her old *A–Z*, taking note of all the little roads that had been circled and wondering what they'd been circled for. Parties? Job interviews? Flatshares?

It was two o'clock in the afternoon. Claudia was away. All his mates were staying in with their girlfriends. A Friday night in. Ralph had felt unloved and depressed so he'd headed straight for Jem's room.

He put the *A–Z* back in her top drawer and his eye fell again upon the pile of old diaries under her table. He'd managed to resist the temptation of looking at them so far – it made him feel more disciplined, less unethical, marginally better about himself and his underhand behaviour. He looked at them and looked away again. No – he mustn't. He looked again. Fuck it, he thought, and reached for the bottom diary, an old accounting book covered in UCL stickers and smiley faces. Written on the cover was '1986'. He pulled back the front cover, the old, brittle paper crackling slightly as he turned over the first page. He started reading.

Six hours later, he stopped. A whole day had gone by and Ralph had learned an awful lot more about Jem. He'd learned about her adolescence, how much she'd hated her frizzy hair and her anaemic complexion and the fact that she was so short; how while other girls were losing their virginity and getting pregnant and coming into school with florid lovebites adorning their necks, Jem was busy crossing streets to avoid having to walk past anyone remotely resembling a teenage boy. She'd been painfully shy and painfully unconfident, crying into her pillow every night because she was so ugly and no man would ever want her. She'd been fifteen before she'd had her first kiss and then it had been so unpleasant and shared with such an ugly specimen of male youth that she'd rubbed at her mouth with the back of her hand for a good ten minutes after it was over, shuddering at the memory.

She'd then gone out, briefly, with a succession of ugly youths, desperately trying to cling on to her honour and her virginity, before Justin Jones had asked her out. Justin Jones had, apparently, been the school heart-throb, a dark-haired dish with the pick of the school's girls at his feet.

'Why me?' she'd asked, referring obliquely to the contrast between herself and the more overtly attractive female students who would queue up daily just to stand in Justin's wake. 'I dunno,' he'd said, half-smiling, 'it's not the way you look, it's just something about you. I just really fancy you.' Justin Jones had unwittingly instilled in Jem with that one, long-ago, offhand comment a confidence that any amount of fawning compliments from lovesick suitors could not have achieved. He had paid her *personality* a compliment. He'd flattered her *spirit*, and Jem knew she didn't have to be anyone else but herself. She was an attractive person and anyone who couldn't see that was not worth knowing.

Since then, it seemed, Jem had had a whole string of relationships with nice blokes who'd made complete pains of themselves, smothering her with love and making unreasonable demands of her. Until Smith.

At last Ralph was beginning to understand what Jem saw in Smith, why she was so in love with him. Smith didn't call on her emotionally, he didn't restrict her or control her.

How ironic that she should have fallen in love with him because he didn't give a shit about her. How ironic that she thought he was so different from the other boys when, in reality, he was exactly the same, and the only reason he wasn't showering her with gifts and adoration and proposals of marriage was because he was in love with another woman. How ironic . . .

Ralph took a beer out of the fridge and flopped on to the sofa, searching through the rubble on the coffee table for the remote control. He'd just missed *The*

*Simpsons* and now *Real TV* was on Sky, a series of totally unamusing real-life videos of people nearly drowning under white-water rafts and being rescued from burning buildings.

Smith was out tonight, at a press do. It was possible that he and Jem might be alone tonight. Maybe, instead of shuffling around trying to find reasons not to talk to her like he usually did, he should use it as an opportunity to get her to open up. Find out even more about her. He already knew more about her than he'd known about even his longest-standing girlfriends. He knew all her insecurities, her romantic history and her needs and desires. Now he wanted to get to know her better than anyone had ever known her before.

He heard female voices outside and shifted round on the sofa to peep through the open curtains. It was Jem, laden down with shopping as ever – he'd never met a girl who spent so much time in supermarkets – and she was talking to that blonde tart from upstairs. He strained his ears trying to catch what they were saying, but it was muffled. He smiled at the irony of Smith's girlfriend so easily and quickly engaging herself in a situation which Smith himself had been dreaming of, ineffectually, for the last five years. He stood up to check his reflection in the mirror, ruffled his shorn hair and sat down again.

Eventually he heard the front door open, and seconds later Jem burst into the room – Jem always burst into rooms, such was the force of her enthusiasm – all parcelled up in a big black coat and a deep-purple furry stole.

'I've just had a really nice chat with that girl from upstairs. She's very friendly, isn't she?'

Ralph had always found Cheri to be absolutely the opposite, but maybe Jem was a better judge of character than he was.

'She's a dancer, you know. She trained to be a ballerina until she grew too tall. It explains why she's so elegant, she holds herself very well.'

Ralph just thought she was a stuck-up bitch with too much attitude even for him.

'What are you doing tonight, Ralph?'

He shrugged and scratched his head, 'Um, fuck all actually. Pretty sad for a Friday night.'

'Excellent. Look, I've been blown out by my friends so I thought I'd just cook a curry, drink a load of lager, have a bit to smoke and then go to bed early. D'you fancy joining me? Well, apart from the going to bed early bit, of course.' She giggled adorably.

Ralph couldn't think of anything else he'd rather do tonight, he tried to hide his excitement: 'That sounds absolutely perfect – I'd love to. I can't promise to be much help in the kitchen, but I'll skin up.'

'Done.'

It was all Ralph could do to stop himself punching the air as Jem left the room.

'Right, I've decided,' Jem was back, barefoot in thick black stockings and a short dark-green jersey dress with capped sleeves and a flirty skirt, 'Have you ever seen that programme *Can't Cook Won't Cook*?'

Ralph looked blank.

'Oh, come on, you must have, you're at home all day. It's for people like you' – she pointed at him – 'people who write off cooking without even trying it. This chef guy gets two pathetic people to cook a dish by watching what he does – well, anyway, it's crap but that's not the point. I think every bachelor should know how to cook at least one dish, and since you like curry so much I thought I'd teach you. Come on, get up.' She held out her hand for him and he smiled and followed her into the kitchen, enjoying the feeling of her tiny little hand on his.

'I thought we said that I'd skin up and you'd cook.'

'Yes, well, I've changed my mind. OK, as you know, there are many, many different kinds of curry. Tonight I'm making a chicken jal frezi – actually, you can make a spliff while I'm doing the talk bit – yes, tonight I'm making a chicken jal frezi, it's very, very easy. You can pretty much do it to your own taste – I like mine quite green and stinking hot! So, I've got the chicken breasts, we can chop those later, and a really big bunch of coriander, lots of these monster-hot little green chillies – the big ones are crap, don't bother with them. Keeping up so far?'

'Oh, yes, so far so simple.' Ralph was sitting at the table crumbling grass into a translucent paper balanced on an upside-down box of Shreddies. He was entranced: why had none of his girlfriends ever taught him to cook before?

'You can get ready-made pastes but it's better to make your own – you can put what you want in really. OK, I'm going to put in loads of this coriander, some fresh fenugreek leaves and some ground fenugreek – smell that' – she held the plastic packet under Ralph's nose – 'that's what your armpits smell of the day after a curry . . .'

Soon enough Ralph was chopping up pieces of chicken and slicing onions and mincing garlic. He must have eaten a million curries in his life but he'd never heard of half the things that went into one. Ghee? Cumin? Curry leaves? He was amazed to find that he was thoroughly enjoying himself, even suggesting additions and asking for more jobs to do, and he was feeling wonderfully relaxed with Jem, for the first time since he'd found out about her and Smith. They were chatting and laughing together like old friends, singing along to the Pogues and dancing around the kitchen.

They laid the table together, and Ralph was ecstatic to be served with a plate of curry and rice that he'd helped to cook. And even more ecstatic when he tasted it – it was delicious.

'Ralph,' Jem began as they ate, 'can I ask you a question?'

Oh, Lord, one of life's most worrying openers.

'How do you feel about me and Smith – be honest?'

Oh, gawd. What was he supposed to say? '*I* want you *I* want you *I* want you, that's how I feel about you and Smith.' That would have been honest. Smith doesn't know you like I know you; you don't know Smith like I know Smith; it's all wrong and I'm as jealous as hell.

'I'm very happy for you both,' he said. How about that for honesty.

'So you don't feel excluded or, or left out or anything? It's just that you and Smith have lived alone together for so long, maybe you feel I'm crowding you, pushing you out?'

'Ooh, no, not at all, it's nice having you around.' Well, that was true at least.

'You would tell me if it was a problem, wouldn't you? I'd hate you to feel uncomfortable in your own home.'

'I promise you, it's not a problem, it's been so long since Smith was even interested in a woman, it's a relief in a way.' Pinocchio, eat your heart out. 'I'm glad to see him happy. I've never seen him this happy before, you're very good for him.' But you'd be even better for me.

'Oh, good, that's a weight off my mind. So why aren't you seeing Claudia tonight?'

Claudia, Claudia? That was a conversational quantum leap. Ralph had to think hard to remember exactly who Claudia was, let alone why he wasn't seeing her.

'Oh, yes, yeah, she's gone to Paris for the weekend, something to do with work – fashion shows or something.'

'Ooh, very glamorous. I've not met Claudia yet, what's she like?'

'What, honestly?'

'Yes, we're being honest, aren't we?' She tore off a piece of kitchen roll and blew her nose, which was running from the heat of the curry.

'Well, she's very attractive, very tall and slim. And she can be quite sweet sometimes. But mainly she's a real pain. Everything I do is wrong. If I phone her it's inconvenient, if I don't I'm a bastard. If I invite her out with my mates she complains that she doesn't like them, if I go out without her she complains that I'm leaving her out. She tells me I'm scruffy and should make more of an effort, and then when I buy something new she says, "Oh, you can afford to buy new clothes but you can't afford to take me out for dinner." I can't do anything right.'

'Do you love her?'

'No.'

'Do you like her?'

'Sometimes.'

'So why are you going out with her?'

'For the sex, I suppose.'

'Well, that's honest, I guess. Wouldn't you like to be with someone you were in love with?'

Ralph reached for the kitchen roll – the heat was getting to him too. 'I have to admit, just lately I've wanted something more. I've been too scared for a long time, you know – the emotional investment, the insecurity, the vulnerability.'

'You've been hurt in the past?'

'Well, not hurt as such, just too involved, drained almost – it took over my life and I haven't wanted to risk getting entangled like that again. But now, I don't know, I think I might be ready for something real – the love thang.' He laughed nervously. He couldn't believe he was talking like this, he hadn't talked to anyone about real feelings for so long.

'Just haven't met the right girl yet?'

Oh, Jem, if only you knew.

'Yeah, something like that.' Time to redirect the conversation: 'So, you and Smith – is it a love thang?'

Jem smiled. 'Oh, yes, definitely. Very, very much so. Smith is everything I ever wanted, he really is. He's perfect.'

No, Jem, he's not. He's a prat and he doesn't deserve you.

'Yeah, he's a great bloke.' Ralph wanted to say something bad about Smith, put him down, but that was really small-minded and mean. He wanted to tell Jem about Smith's disastrous romantic history, that would take the shine off her rose-tinted glasses. He wanted to tell her that Smith thought her ideas about dreams and destiny were ludicrous but a good way to get into her knickers. He wanted to tell her that Smith would drop her like a hot potato if Cheri was so much as to glance in his direction. There was so much he wanted to say but he couldn't possibly say any of it. Jem saved him from his thoughts.

'How come you don't paint any more?'

Well, they really were getting to the nitty-gritty tonight.

'Phew – that's a big question. I wouldn't say that I don't paint any more, more that I don't paint at the moment. I've tried, but the inspiration just isn't there. Maybe I've got too complacent. I was very unhappy when I was younger, very introspective – it was easy to paint then.'

'You've cut yourself off, haven't you? Cut yourself off from feeling things. I bet if you were to meet someone and fall in love it would all come back, all those emotions would be unlocked and you'd be straight down to the studio. It wouldn't feel like a chore, like an effort. Yes, that's Dr Jem's remedy. Get yourself a decent woman and fall in love.'

Irony was just so painful sometimes.

Ralph's eyes were starting to stream now, the chilli heat was on slow-release and his mouth was burning, his lips were swollen, his nose was running and his mind was in overdrive, full of things he wanted to say but couldn't.

'Not finding this too hot, are you, Ralph? All that talk about how you've never had a curry that defeated you?' Jem teased.

'Absolutely not.' Another lie, but there was no way he was going to admit that to this girl! 'Just how I like it. You look like you're suffering yourself, Miss I'm-So-Hard.'

'Humph – no way! This is mild compared to my usual curries, I was being kind for your sake.'

'Oh, I see, you think you're a bit of a chilli queen, do you?'

'I don't think it, I *know* it. I've never met anyone who can eat food as hot as I can.'

'Well, I think you've just met your match.' Ralph was well and truly fired up with competitive enthusiasm now. He leapt up from the table and took a handful of raw chillies from the bag on the counter.

'OK, one chilli each, whole, no nibbling. Let's separate the men from the mice.'

'No problem. Go on, let me have it.'

Oh, the pain, the sweet searing pain as the astringent oils from the chillies slowly released themselves over their tongues, first a crack as the shiny green skin broke under teeth, then a hint of flavour followed by an exhilarating burst of fire ineffectually doused by a sudden flow of saliva.

'You can't swallow it, you've got to chew the whole thing and display it on your tongue,' said Ralph.

Fingers of fire licked at the back of their throats, their brains sending frantic signals to all areas of the body. Jem and Ralph chewed feverishly, rapidly inhaling and exhaling through puckered lips like antenatal mothers and waving their hands in front of their mouths in a futile attempt to calm the flames.

'Oh, fuck – fuck fuck fuck – it's burning a hole through my tongue!'

'It's burning a hole into the back of my throat!'

Heart racing, sweat flowing, Ralph beat his fists off the tabletop, his eyes bulging slightly out of his head and tears rolling down his cheeks.

'OK, OK, time to show, time to show – I've got to swallow this thing before it kills me,' Jem shouted, her cheeks pinker than ever. 'Tongue out, please.'

Ralph and Jem stuck out their tongues, displaying small beds of green mush, and swallowed.

'Water, water!!!' yelled Ralph.

'No, water makes it worse. Lager!'

They gulped greedily but the liquid made no difference.

'Oh, God, I think I'm going to die! Rice, eat some plain rice!'

They both made a dash to the cooker and picked up handfuls of rice with their fingers, stuffing it into their mouths.

'Ice! Is there any ice in the freezer?!' cried Jem.

Ralph pulled open the door to the freezer and frantically searched through its contents. 'Got some, got some!' He turned the ice tray upside-down and bashed it hard against the work surface, ice cubes flying out in all directions, on to the floor and into the sink. They each picked one up and stuffed them into their mouths, sucking hard to extract every last drop of icy coolness.

'Oh, Jesus,' cried Ralph, 'Jesus Christ!' The flames were finally beginning to subside but his whole body was still in a state of sublime shock, endorphins flowing through him like some sort of wonderful drug.

'My God!' Jem was sliding the ice cube around her swollen lips. 'That was unbelievable! That was like sex!'

Their heads were spinning and their pulses racing. Both of them were laughing uncontrollably at nothing.

'That was *better* than sex,' replied Ralph.

Slowly they sat down again at the table.

'So, who won?' asked Jem.

'I think we can call that a draw!'

'Oh, no, I don't think so. Someone's got to win. Best of three!'

By the time Smith got home the flat was filled with an air of barely contained hysteria. He followed the sound of insane laughter into the kitchen and found Ralph and Jem with their heads in the freezer.

'What the hell are you two doing?' he asked, putting his briefcase down on the table amid the sea of empty lager cans, dirty plates and melting ice cubes.

They spun around guiltily, mouths full of ice, cheeks aflame, eyes streaming.

'Chilli Challenge,' replied Ralph through his ice cube, desperately fanning his mouth, 'five each – raw ones – it's a draw.'

'What! You're both fucking mad,' said Smith, shaking his head slowly. He caught Jem's eye. 'Look at you, you look like a lunatic. You look deranged!'

Ralph didn't think Jem looked deranged, he thought she looked absolutely stunning. Her hair was down now, long black curls framing her brilliant red face, glowing with heat and exhilaration as she hugged Smith. She was hugging Smith. It hurt Ralph to see how quickly she was drawn away from the special cocoon of madness they had woven for themselves tonight and into the arms of Smith, like she was a child he'd been baby-sitting all night whose beloved parent had returned. It had been him and Jem, close and totally together, and then Smith had walked in and crushed the atmosphere like a beetle under the weight of his stupid fucking briefcase. There'd been one brief beautiful moment when Smith had walked into the kitchen and he'd felt like Smith was the odd one out, the spare part, and Jem was his.

But now the night was over, painfully over. Jem was clearing away the debris on the kitchen table, Smith was unknotting his tie and talking about his night with a load of Swiss bankers. It was over.

Ralph was anchored to the spot by the weight of his sadness. 'Um, I reckon I'll push off to bed then,' he murmured quietly. 'Thanks for a lovely evening, Jem. Thanks for the Chilli Challenge and the curry and everything – it's been brilliant.'

He leaned down to kiss her on the cheek, just as she turned her face towards him, and caught her fully on the lips. The unexpected sensation sent shock waves through his system, a current of excitement from his lips, down via his heart to a loop-the-loop through his stomach, and ended in a hot glow of pleasure in his groin. It was more powerful than the chillies!

''Night, then.' His body was suddenly contorted by the conflicting desires to stay and ravish Jem and to leave the room as fast as his legs could carry him. He stumbled into the bathroom and sat down hard on the covered toilet. He was shaking.

He loved her. He was totally and utterly, stupidly and wonderfully in love with her. Shit.

# CHAPTER FOURTEEN

'Och aye, this is the life, is it noo?'

'Och, and so it is, Siobhan, it's a bonny wee country and that's to be sure.'

Rosanne sat in the back seat of the Embassy, her snout stuck through the small aperture in the window, her eyes slanted closed against the bitter December wind that was blowing through her long black ears.

'Considering you're the Gaelic one, you do a crap Scottish accent, Mr Kasparov.'

'Well,' retorted Karl, 'have you ever heard Sean Connery trying to do an Irish accent? Bloody dreadful!'

Siobhan and Karl had left urban Scotland behind them now, and the landscape was slowly building up momentum, growing from tentative undulations in the south to the full-blown tidal-wave formations they were driving through now, along unending, empty roads, a wonder of nature, a spectacle of breathtaking beauty around every corner. For the last forty-five minutes, since they'd hit the Highlands, their conversation had consisted of nothing else but 'ooh's and 'aah's as the sharp Scottish light picked out shimmering threads of silvery water cascading down sheer black hills, or a tiny enchanted island artistically placed in the middle of a loch. The voluptuous landscape that loomed all around them was soft and womanly, carpeted in what looked from a distance like bright-green velvet, and the late-afternoon sky touched the land below with gentle wreaths of pale-blue mist.

Neither of them had been to Scotland before, and they felt like over-excited children now, dying to see what lay around the next corner yet wanting to linger every time they encountered a view which they knew would stay in their dreams.

'I hate to say it, but this knocks spots off Ireland. I've never seen anything like it,' said Karl.

Siobhan was studying the atlas on her lap. 'One more loch and we're there,' she said, brushing her windswept hair out of her face.

'That's a shame, I could keep driving for ever.' This was definitely the easiest they'd been with each other for weeks. They'd obviously needed this, a break from London, some distance from their problems. Karl wished it was just going to be the two of them for the weekend, but he liked this Rick de Largy character. He was a nice bloke, maybe it wouldn't be so bad.

It was four o'clock now and the low northern sun was already starting to set.

'Should be just in time to see the sunset over the loch. Jeff said it's breathtaking.' Karl couldn't wipe the smile off his face. He took his left hand from the steering wheel and placed it around Siobhan's shoulders, giving her a little squeeze. 'Are you nervous?' he asked.

'No, well, not really. A tiny bit maybe.'

'Yeah, me too. It's going to be fine though, you'll see. And if you don't want to join in you can just say you're not feeling well and sit and watch the view.'

Siobhan forced a laugh. Karl registered its false sound with pain. He couldn't remember the last time he'd heard a genuine, raucous Siobhan belly-laugh. He loved that laugh; it was a laugh which resonated throughout restaurants, which made people on buses turn and look, which would have got her kicked out of public libraries. Now it was paper-thin, so brittle it sounded as if it could turn to tears, just like that.

They drove on for a while, deep in singular thought, while the sky hung above them like a kaleidoscopic mosquito net, changing colour every second.

'Glencoe two miles: we're nearly there. Are you ready to party, girl, hmm hmm? Ready to take some class A narcotics and just be wild and crazy, hmm hmm!!'

They were looking out for a tiny turning off the main road. The trees were painted white apparently; that was the only way of identifying it.

'There – there!' Siobhan pointed to the left.

They pulled off and followed a short dirt-track to a fork. A peeling green wooden sign to the right said 'St Colombas.'

'That's the place.'

The little black car bumped up the track for a while in darkness, but within a couple of minutes Siobhan and Karl were transported to Fairyland; the sides of the tiny lane were lined with bright pink and red Chinese lanterns, hooked on to the branches of diminutive cherry trees, prettily delineating the meandering route through the dark towards the chapel.

'My God, this is beautiful,' whispered Siobhan.

More was waiting for them at the head of the lane: the last dramatic red moments of the sunset reflected in the loch, the clapboard chapel lit up with fairy lights, a set of winding wooden steps from the graveyard down to the banks of the loch hung with more Chinese lanterns, shining the same warm crimson as the sinking sun, a picturesque wooden boat tied to an ancient wooden jetty bobbing blissfully in the still, icy water. An owl called from one of the towering chestnut trees around the chapel clearing, and windchimes hanging from the windowframes tinkled gently in a small gust of refreshingly clean air.

'I want to be buried here,' said Karl, his jaw hanging.

Even Rosanne was extra quiet, seemingly as enchanted as her masters by the unbelievable beauty of the place.

'I thought it was going to be really flash but it's not, it's just beautiful. I reckon Jeff must have been a real old hippie when he did this place up.'

They slowly unbuckled their seat-belts and collected their bags from the boot. There was already another car in front of the chapel.

'OK. Ready, Shuv?' Karl held his hand out for Siobhan.

'As I'll ever be.'

Karl rang the large copper bell hanging outside the vast wooden doors. Within seconds the door was answered.

'Karl, mate, good to see you. What a place!' Rick was barefoot, in jeans and a big jumper, and holding a glass of wine.

'Yeah, isn't it! I've never seen anything like it.' The two men shook hands.

'Rick, this is Siobhan, my girlfriend.'

'Lovely to meet you, Siobhan – Karl never stops talking about you.'

Siobhan attempted to smile, but she could barely breathe. This man was absolutely gorgeous! He was beautiful. She almost felt weak at the knees. Why did men never tell you things like that; they never said 'Oh, by the way, so and so's really good looking.' She wished Karl had warned her.

'Pleased to meet you, too.' Siobhan had suddenly remembered how to behave in a social situation. She smiled her most gorgeous smile and shook his hand firmly and confidently. She was *not* going to be a fat aunt in front of this angelic man, in this magical place. 'Isn't this the most beautiful place you've ever seen?' She was thin, thin and beautiful and desirable. She shook her hair round so that it framed her face.

'Stunning. I can't believe old Jeff would be capable of doing something so nicely. I thought it was going to be all shagpile and satellite dishes and log-effect gas fires. Anyway, come in the two of you – it's freezing out there. We've put the central heating on and Tamsin's just lighting a fire.'

They followed him into the chapel – the damp stone hallway was full of wellingtons and waterproofs and piles of wood – and then through the main hall and into the body of the building. They both gasped. The room was at least thirty foot high, raftered, galleried and cavernous. It was floored with antique boards and old rugs and lit up by an eclectic mix of dozens of Art Deco lamps and Victorian chandeliers. There were three enormous cream sofas at the far end, dressed in Chinese tapestries and an old oak banqueting table at the near end, covered in candelabras and vases of flowers.

'Wow!'

The girl kneeling in front of the monstrously large sandstone fireplace around which the sofas huddled got to her feet and rubbed at the knees of her jeans.

She was small, petite even, with soft, sandy-coloured

curly hair tied back in a pony-tail and a light smattering of freckles over her nose and forehead. She wasn't wearing any make-up, and she was, Siobhan was pleased to notice, ordinary – pretty, but ordinary.

'Siobhan, Karl – this is Tamsin.' Karl and Tamsin looked at each other quizzically as their hands touched and a strange atmosphere suddenly descended upon the group.

'Shit – Tamsin – what a coincidence!' Karl was saying.

'Oh – yeah – hi.' Tamsin was looking slightly uncomfortable, stepping from foot to foot.

Siobhan looked at Karl in confusion. Rick looked at Tamsin in confusion.

'You two know each other?' asked Rick.

'Erm, Tamsin used to be a student of mine – Ceroc – last summer . . .'

'Aaaah,' said Siobhan.

'Oh, right,' smiled Rick. 'Cool! What an amazing coincidence. I didn't know you'd been a dance teacher.'

'Well . . . you know . . . mortgage to pay.'

'Yeah, yeah.'

The atmosphere was inexplicably and negatively charged and, instinctively, Rick changed the subject. 'Well,' he said, clapping his hands together in an attempt to quell the unsettled mood, 'let's show you your room.'

Karl and Siobhan exchanged glances and followed Rick up the stairs and on to the gallery.

'What's going on, Karl?' whispered Siobhan, as they unpacked in their over-the-top Rococo bedroom, walled with swathes of dusty satin Jacquard and batches of browning Victorian and Edwardian photographs in chipped wooden frames.

'That's that girl,' whispered Karl. 'Remember? That one I told you about. The nympho, steam-train chick – it's her. The one who had that *ménage à trois* with those two French guys.'

'What?' Siobhan put her hands to her mouth to muffle her delighted shriek. 'God, no wonder she looked so awkward. D'you think she was going out with Rick then?'

'God knows. Probably,' said Karl, painstakingly arranging his trousers over a large wooden hanger. 'They live together.'

Siobhan suddenly felt that everything was going to be all right. The house was beautiful, Rick was gorgeous, and his girlfriend was ordinary – an ordinary girl with an extraordinary secret that she bet Rick didn't know about: it was Tamsin's place to feel uncomfortable this weekend, not hers. She smiled as her hopes for the weekend elevated towards the woodworm-ridden rafters like big pink helium balloons. She was going to enjoy herself. This was going to be fun.

She flopped backwards on to the huge four-poster, her hair flying out around her head. 'Isn't this brilliant! I feel like a princess, the one in the Princess and the Pea!' She began to bounce around on the vast bed. She was suddenly feeling unbelievably overexcited.

'Careful, Shuv, that's a really old bed. You might break it.'

Siobhan stopped bouncing and looked at Karl with disbelief. 'Oh, charming! You wouldn't say that if I was some slender young size-eight thing.'

'I'd say it if you were Will o' the Wisp, Shuv. Don't be so sensitive, for God's sake. It's probably an antique, and it wasn't made for bouncing up and down on, that's all I'm saying.' Karl zipped up his holdall and shoved it into the back of the towering tallboy.

A few of Siobhan's pink helium balloons had burst, leaving her feeling resentful and annoyed. 'He's very good looking isn't he, Rick? You didn't tell me he was so handsome.' Siobhan felt the insecure need to wind Karl up, get a reaction.

'Yeah, he is, isn't he? Especially for a radio producer!'

Typical – no reaction whatsoever. Siobhan had never tried to make Karl jealous before. She'd never felt the need to test his love, to push him to see how far he could go, how much he could take. But after the way things had been between them for the last two months, since that night at the Sol y Sombra, Siobhan didn't trust him any more.

Well, sod it. She certainly wasn't going to let Karl's attitude stop her from having fun for the first time in, oh, as long as she could remember. She was going to flirt with Rick, she was going to get roaring drunk, take any drugs that were offered to her and she was going to shine, even if it was only for a day and a half.

She decided to get changed, she suddenly felt uncomfortable in her old leggings and Aran cardigan. And she was going to put on make-up and do her hair. Just because Karl hated her fat, it didn't mean that other men would.

She pulled her neglected make-up bag from her case and sat at the dressing-table under the huge stained-glass window. Two small pink glass lamps illuminated the area, casting a soft flattering glow. As Siobhan delicately puffed at her face with a big soft brush and carefully applied a thin line of black liquid-liner to her eyelids she felt prettier than she'd felt in months. This was a magical house: it wasn't 1996 any more, it could be any time, past or future, but it was a time when your dress size was irrelevant, a time when you could be beautiful just because of where you were, because of the particular light of a pretty pink lamp. Fairy lights; magic lamps.

Karl watched her from the bed. 'I guess we should try not to bring up the subject again,' he said.

'What?' murmured Siobhan, disturbed from her reverie.

'Tamsin. We shouldn't say anything else about Tamsin and the dance class.'

'Oh, no, you're right. I don't want to talk about London and everything anyway, I just want to get lost under the spell of this place.' She was twisting her mane into an intricate knot of golden strands and stabbing it aggressively from behind with pins from a cardboard holder.

'Do you want a hand, Shuv?' asked Karl eagerly. Siobhan always asked him to put pins in her hair in the old days, when she used to wear it up regularly. He'd loved doing it, it was such a feminine act, and he'd thought himself privileged to be allowed to play such a vital role in Siobhan's grooming.

'No, I'm all right, thanks, nearly finished. You can go down if you like, I'm going to get changed now.'

'I don't mind waiting for you.'

'No, really, you go down. It'll spare you the unpleasantness of watching me get undressed.' Siobhan hadn't meant to say that, it had just come spilling out; an unbridled, feral thought had just escaped from her mouth. It was something she'd thought a million times over the last few weeks, few months in reality, and had never, ever intended to say, and now it was out, free, independent of her. She waited the split second for a reaction with her breath held.

'Shuv, what the fuck are you going on about?' Karl was incredulous. 'You think I don't like seeing you naked – Jeez, you're so wrong – I love you naked.'

Oh, nice try, Karl, thought Siobhan, you expect me to believe that? 'Karl, go downstairs. We'll talk about this another time.'

'No! I'm staying here and we're going to talk about this now. Is this what everything's been about, all this, all this . . . sadness, this sadness between us?'

'Karl, go downstairs. Go downstairs now or I'll scream. I do not want to talk about this. I do not want to listen to your bullshit. Get out!'

Bald-faced lies. Bullshit. Bullshit, Karl Kasparov. If you liked me this size, why would you be getting sweaty and flustered by that girl from upstairs, why would you think I'd break the bed, why would you want me to get pregnant? Liar.

Karl slowly left the room, and Rosanne followed him, unsettled by the unfamiliar atmosphere, and scared by the anger on Siobhan's usually placid face.

Siobhan felt no regret; she'd show *him* tonight. She'd be the old Siobhan, happy, poised, funny and attractive, except it wouldn't be for Karl's benefit – he wasn't worthy of such a performance – this would be for Rick.

She slipped on her black tunic, the one she'd made for herself, with the indiscreet split down the front that revealed a good few inches of cleavage – this was the first time she'd had the nerve to wear it – and matching trousers, and slid her feet into strappy sandals.

She opened the door out on to the gallery and looked

down into the room below. Karl and Rick and Tamsin were all sitting on the sofas, drinking wine and talking quietly and politely. As the door closed behind her the trio turned around and looked upwards. Siobhan saw Rick gulp.

'Siobhan' – Rick stood up – 'just in time. I was just about to break open the champagne.'

Siobhan moved as elegantly as she could down the stairs, her heels making a feminine click against the wood as she walked. She felt like a contestant in a beauty pageant.

'I feel a bit underdressed now,' said Tamsin light-heartedly, gesturing at her jeans and fleecy top. 'You look fantastic.'

Rick handed Siobhan a champagne flute. 'Here's to a wild and wacky weekend!'

'Here's to Jeff!'

'Here's to Scotland!'

The four almost-strangers clinked their glasses together. Siobhan met Rick's glass with a smile that emanated almost entirely from beneath her eyelashes.

'And here's to new friends,' she beamed.

# CHAPTER FIFTEEN

The first bottle of champagne lasted half an hour, the second twenty minutes, and the third was gone almost before it was opened. Siobhan was feeling flushed and was waving goodbye to the last vestiges of her inhibitions. She, Karl and Rick were talking animatedly and frankly about work, and Tamsin was in the kitchen heating through a fortune's worth of party food from M & S. Siobhan would usually have volunteered immediately to help in the kitchen, and it had crossed her mind, but she didn't want to, not this time. She wanted to stay out here with the men and elegantly cross and uncross her legs and join in the conversation. She was preoccupied with her posture, keeping her back straight and her chest out and her stomach in, occasionally smoothing her hair back with her hand or fiddling with her rings, watching Rick's body language and responses, gauging his interest in her and then turning to Karl, wondering if he'd noticed yet.

Tamsin appeared, laden with plates of chicken wings and pizza squares and trout goujons. She put them down on the table unnecessarily hard, hoping to attract attention to herself and her efforts, but none of them even looked around from their conversation.

'If anyone's interested,' she began, then decided to take the unattractive sarcasm from her voice, 'there's some food here – it'll soak up the champagne.'

'Excellent,' someone murmured, but still no one moved, still they sat there and laughed and joked and revolved around Siobhan like balls on a weather-vane.

Rick poured the dregs of the champagne into Siobhan's glass.

'Oh,' said Tamsin, clutching her empty glass, 'was that the last of the champagne?'

'Sorry, darling,' said Rick, 'it was only a drop. There's some wine in the kitchen, do you want me to get you some?'

'No, it's all right,' said Tamsin, unashamedly playing the martyr. 'I'll get it. The food's getting cold, by the way,' she added as nicely as she could.

'Oh, go ahead – I won't be eating anything,' said Siobhan. No way. There was only one thing more unattractive than a fat woman and that was a fat woman eating. Things were going really well with Rick, she was feeling wonderfully in control, she'd forgotten just how easy it was to turn a man to mush. She didn't want to blow it now by stuffing her face with chicken and pizza.

'Are you sure you wouldn't like me to bring you back a little something?' asked Rick, getting to his feet.

'Oh, no, really, we had a big lunch on the way down. Maybe I'll have something later.'

As Tamsin and Rick made their way over to the table, Karl approached Siobhan shyly.

'Are you all right?' he asked tenderly, leaning into her shoulder to whisper in her ear, brushing her neck with the tip of his nose.

'Never better,' she replied stiffly, trying to ignore the bolt of sadness and bitter-sweet love that coursed through her at his touch and the feeling that she wanted to comfort Karl, to reassure him.

'You look a lot happier,' he whispered.

'Well, I'm having a great time. Rick's fantastic.'

'Yes, he's great, isn't he? I told you you'd like him.'

Siobhan gritted her teeth in irritation. 'I'm going to get some more wine,' she said, getting to her feet, suddenly aware that she was drunk, as she felt her legs wobble slightly underneath her. She quickly gauged the distance from her seat to the kitchen door and the number of obstacles she would encounter on the way. The last thing she'd want to do now was trip over something or start weaving across the room like a dodgy shopping-trolley.

Unfortunately, she was already too drunk to start trying to regulate her drinking. But then, so was everyone else. The little bag of white powder made an entrance at about eleven o'clock and Siobhan was the first to accept the rolled-up fiver and square mirror from Rick. She turned away slightly in case she messed it up and dabbed lightly at her nose, dislodging a couple of small crumbs before passing the mirror on to Karl.

'I guess this is when we're supposed to start being wild and wacky,' she said.

'Ah, well remembered,' said Rick. 'I brought a tape recorder.' He walked to the hallway and returned with a tiny, state-of-the-art machine. 'It occurred to me that we'd come up with all these brilliantly witty ideas and we'd be so pissed that none of us would remember them. This thing's brilliant, it tapes for six hours and the sound quality is breathtaking.' He placed it on the mantelpiece. 'Are we feeling funny yet?'

A general cheer went up and he switched on the machine.

Jeff was right about Rick. He was very funny and his humour infected the other three. They sat for three hours and talked complete nonsense, inventing quiz games and characters and role-playing, Siobhan and Tamsin pretending to be listeners phoning in. It was actually working. Jeff obviously knew what he was doing – there was no way they'd have managed to come up with so many good ideas sitting in a boardroom in the ALR building. The coke had given them all the confidence to contribute ideas they might have felt foolish about in other circumstances, and the alcohol had also lowered their inhibitions and freed up their imaginations.

Siobhan was having the best time ever. Rick thought she was marvellous, and her confidence was sky-high: she knew she was being funny, funnier than Tamsin, and she was thrilled to find that she hadn't lost the ability to flirt, to twist men around her little finger. Rick was hers, and she sat close to him on the sofa, her arm draped carelessly behind his back, not touching, but possessing him none the less. She'd forgotten how good it felt to be the centre of attention.

Finally the hilarity began to die down. It was early morning, the coke was wearing off and the conversation began to pall. Siobhan got up and stretched.

'Do you think we've got enough stuff?' she asked Rick.

'We've got enough stuff to last us the next five years,' he replied happily.

'Well, I need some fresh air,' she said.

'That's an excellent idea,' Rick said, standing up quickly. 'Let me get my coat – I'll come with you. Are you coming?' He turned to Karl and Tamsin, as an afterthought.

Siobhan went up to her room to fetch her sheepskin jacket. She checked her reflection quickly in the mirror and tidied up her hair, smoothed her eyebrows and applied a little more lipstick. Adrenalin was coursing through her. What was going to happen? Would Rick try it on? How would she react? She thought of Karl and then quickly put him to the back of her mind. She'd go with the flow, see what happened – the worst thing that could happen was a kiss; it was too cold outside for anything else.

The night air hit them like a cold shower as they closed the chapel door. A wind had picked up now, a gentle low wind that whipped around their legs like a cold, ghostly cat. They wandered in silence towards the banks of the loch and sat down on the wooden steps leading to the jetty, listening to the windchimes and hugging their clothes to them to keep warm.

'Blissful, isn't it?' murmured Rick.

'Heavenly,' agreed Siobhan, her elbows on her knees, her face in her hands, watching the loch rippling in the pink glow of the Chinese lanterns.

'You could fall in love here.'

Siobhan bristled slightly. 'Yes,' she said, 'I suppose you could.'

They fell silent again.

Rick cleared his throat. 'You're a wonderful girl, Siobhan, really you are. I've never met anyone like you before. Karl's a very lucky man.'

'I don't think he sees it like that,' she said with a nervous laugh.

'Oh, no,' said Rick, 'he thinks you're marvellous. He

talks about you a lot – he made you sound amazing and he wasn't exaggerating.'

'Oh,' said Siobhan, 'well . . .' She was embarrassed.

'No, really, I think you're gorgeous . . .' he stopped, 'Do you mind me talking like this?'

'Oh, no, please carry on. I'm not going to look a gift compliment in the mouth.' She couldn't look at Rick, he'd see her vulnerability.

'I just think you're . . . you're . . . stunning. You're so funny and, and warm and clever and beautiful. God, I shouldn't say this, Siobhan, but if I was single and you were single . . .'

She turned to face him.

'Go on,' she said.

'Well, you know, if I was single and you . . . you were single, I'd just love to kiss you now.'

Siobhan's whole body was tingling with excitement and nerves. A flush was rising from her lap to her face.

'Do you think that would be wrong?' he asked, his body turned completely towards hers, his eyes searching her face for approval.

'Well, we could always try it and see if it *felt* wrong and then we could stop it if it did.'

'But what about Karl?' Rick pushed some stray hairs behind her ear.

'What about Tamsin?' she replied, every hair on her body to attention as a result of his touch.

'Well, to tell you the truth, we haven't been getting along so well lately. Tamsin . . . Tamsin's not a very stable girl, she's not a very happy girl. I sometimes think I may have bitten off a little more than I can chew with her. She's hard work . . .' He was stroking her cheek now, with the backs of his fingers. 'God, you've got wonderful skin,' he whispered, 'it feels like satin.'

Siobhan's groin felt like it had been plugged into the mains. She groaned softly.

Rick brought his face towards hers. 'Just like a child's skin.' He rubbed his nose gently along her forehead, teasing her with his lips. He held her neck with his hand and massaged her jawbone with his thumb. Finally his lips met hers and Siobhan succumbed, turning around to meet his body and his lips, goosebumps and tingles and deep hot flashes of sexual excitement and lust suffusing her body. She hadn't felt like this for years. She opened her mouth to allow Rick's tongue to caress hers. His lips were soft and warm, and his breath tasted of red wine and fresh air. Oh, God, French kissing was good. Why did people stop doing it after they got to know each other? Why was such an intimate and erotic act reserved mainly for strangers? She wound her tongue around his and up around his teeth, pressing her body against him as he leant her back against the steps and started to move his hands inside her coat and over the silky fabric of her tunic. She pulled his shirt out of his jeans and caressed the skin on his back, appreciating the solid feel of the muscle underneath and the tension, knowing it was his desire for her that was making him feel so good.

She was lost in their kiss, entirely oblivious to the windchimes and the owls, and to Karl, a few hundred feet away from her, inside the chapel. Rick moved his hands under her top and towards her bra. He let out a stifled moan as his hands found her breasts. Siobhan could feel his frustration at the fabric that encased them and sloped her shoulders slightly to enable him to slip the straps off and pull it down. Rick moaned again as his hands felt the bare flesh flow from her bra, she felt his excitement and she could understand it, two huge breasts in his hands: if she were a man she would be excited. He kneaded them gently, still kissing her, his tongue growing wilder and wilder in her mouth, her lips feeling wonderfully raw and sore. She wanted him to kiss her until they bled.

Suddenly he tore his lips away from hers and buried his head inside her coat, under her tunic, between her breasts. He was sighing and groaning and licking her breasts and sucking her nipples. 'Oh, God, Siobhan,' he kept saying. 'Oh, God, Siobhan.'

Siobhan bent slightly to watch him – she'd been staring at the stars, lost in desire and lust – and as her gaze fell upon the top of his head, his sandy blond hair glowing peach in the lamplight, the spell broke. What the hell was she doing? Why was she letting this man suck her nipples, this man with blond hair? For fifteen years she'd looked down on Karl's black mop, my God – Karl! – what was she doing?

Suddenly she was sober and she was cold, physically cold. Rick's hands were sliding down her body, towards the elasticated waist of her trousers, his fingers pulling at it, feeling their way down to the top of her knickers, but she was fully conscious now, wide awake, aware of her surroundings and her circumstances. She was with another man, on the banks of a loch on a sharp December night, her hair was unravelling, her back was aching, she was cold. She felt the last glimmer of passion desert her and anxiety begin to set in. Her body tensed and she pulled back slightly, wanting Rick to calm down too, wanting him to stop but not wanting to tell him to. She looked down at him again; he was completely consumed, carried away, he wasn't aware of Siobhan's change of mood. This was all wrong, all wrong, it was just supposed to be a kiss – she could've covered up a kiss, walked back into the chapel still feeling confident and in control. This was getting out of control, how could she hide this from Karl? This was all wrong! Oh, shit! What had she done?!

She sat up, and Rick moved his head from between her breasts and tried to find her mouth again. 'Oh, Siobhan, I want you,' he picked up her hand and put it to his groin. 'Feel how much I want you.'

That was it.

'Rick!' she said firmly, 'we've got to stop.'

'Oh, no, Siobhan, we've got to carry on. I want to be inside you, you feel so good, you smell so good,' he rubbed her hand up and down the solid shaft inside his jeans.

She pulled her hand away, pulled up her bra and her tunic, closed her coat. 'No, Rick, we've got to stop. Karl and Tamsin are in there. What if they come out and find us?'

'We can hide somewhere – let's go into the woods.' His hand still rested on her knickers.

She pulled his hand away gently. 'No, that's enough. I want to, I really do want to, but I can't, we can't. It's not right.' She tried to smooth down her hair.

Rick's face wore the expression of a thwarted schoolboy who'd kicked his football into a forbidden garden. Siobhan took his hands in hers. 'I'm sorry,' she said gently, 'if circumstances had been different, if we weren't here, if I didn't have Karl and you didn't have Tamsin . . . but, thank you.'

'What for?' asked Rick incredulously.

'Thank you for wanting me, for making me feel sexy and beautiful.'

'Why would you need me to make you feel sexy and beautiful? You *are* sexy and beautiful!' he said, kissing her hands.

'I don't feel it, Rick, but you made me feel it. I didn't used to be this fat, you know, I used to be slim. I'm not used to it.'

'You're not fat!'

'Oh, Rick, don't be such a typical man. Of course I'm fat.'

'OK, so you're not Kate Moss, but you've got a lovely body, really you have. It's . . . it's soft and warm and it smells good and it feels good and, OK, it might not look great in a mini skirt, but it looks great to me, like a real woman's. The first girl I had sex with was round and sexy. She was called Drew, and she was so pretty and full of life and love, and I've never really stopped loving her, you know. People are just prejudiced, Siobhan, because maybe they've never had a chance to really appreciate someone who doesn't conform to the ideal. Well, as far as I'm concerned, they don't know what they're missing. I mean, look at Tamsin, she's tiny and she looks great in Lycra and all that, but sex is just, you know – it's just not all that exciting, she's very unconfident, restrained. I'd rather have a big woman who loved it than a skinny woman who wasn't too bothered. And besides, you're firm, you're not all flabby. I think that's perfect.' He kissed her cheek. 'I think you're perfect.'

Siobhan smiled a small smile and squeezed Rick's hands.

'Thank you,' she said again, fighting back a little tear, 'thank you, you're a very, very nice person.'

'So, is that it then?' He smiled. 'I have a feeling I've just been therapy for you.'

Siobhan felt bad. 'Oh, no, I mean . . . well . . . I'd love to get to know you better . . . but, well . . . you know . . .'

'Yes, I think I do. You really love Karl, don't you?'

She nodded.

'So why all this? What was this all about?' he asked tenderly.

'Oh, God. I'm not sure any more. I thought he was interested in someone else. Well, I still do actually. I think. I don't know. I just thought he was changing, going off me, didn't fancy me any more. I've been feeling so insecure, incredibly insecure . . .'

'Have you spoken to Karl about it?' Rick pulled her jacket closer around her as a gust of wind hit them from the surface of the water.

'No, I just can't. I've got some kind of block, I don't know where to start. I've always been so confident and I don't know if Karl could cope with me being like this, knowing the truth about how I feel.'

'Look, Siobhan. I don't know Karl very well, but from what I've seen and the way he looks at you and talks about you, he could cope. What he *won't* be able to cope with is you not telling him. I wish things could be different, I really do. I wish I could have taken you into the woods and made love to you all night and then taken you home with me and made love to you some more, but things aren't like that, so I think you should use what's just happened here as a chance for a new start with Karl. Talk to him, tell him how you feel before it's too late.' He looked into her eyes seriously. 'Really, I mean it. Don't put it off – do it now, tonight, while you're feeling like this, now! Come on, let's go inside.'

They stood up and tidied themselves and slowly walked back towards the chapel.

'Thanks,' said Tamsin awkwardly to Karl's back as he poked at the fire. He turned around. 'Thanks for not saying anything earlier on, you know, about last summer. I was . . . it was . . . a strange time . . .' She brought a bitten fingernail to her mouth and began to chew.

'Hey. Forget about it. It's none of my business.'

They sat in silence for a second.

'I wonder where they've gone,' said Tamsin, as pleasantly as she could.

'Oh, they're probably looking at the view or something,' said Karl, sitting back on the sofa.

'Aren't you worried?' she asked impatiently.

'No – why should I be? Rick's with her, he'll look after her.'

'That's not what I meant. For Christ's sake, haven't you noticed what's been going on tonight?'

Karl looked blank.

'Your girlfriend. Flirting with my boyfriend. Blatantly. Don't tell me you haven't noticed anything.'

'Oh, that's nothing to worry about. Siobhan always used to be a terrible flirt, it doesn't mean anything. I'm just glad to see her enjoying herself for once.'

All the resentment Tamsin had been swallowing that night was starting to erupt. 'God, you really are stupid, aren't you! That wasn't just flirting, that was a fucking mating ritual going on in front of your very eyes. They're probably out there fucking each other's brains out right now!'

Karl laughed. 'I think you're being a bit paranoid, if

you don't mind me saying so. I think you've probably had a bit too much coke and booze.'

'Look, why don't we go out and see for ourselves!' she shouted, jumping to her feet.

'Sit down, for Christ's sake. You're being ridiculous. Just because you don't trust your boyfriend . . .'

'This has got nothing to do with not trusting my boyfriend! It's your fucking girlfriend I don't trust. She's like a bloody black widow, all over him all night, spinning a web around him, like a great fat predator!'

'God, you're mad!' said Karl calmly. 'Siobhan is the sweetest, nicest, warmest person I've ever known and you're just jealous. And you should learn to trust your boyfriend.'

Karl's easygoing attitude and condescending manner were pushing Tamsin over the edge. 'That's it! I'm telling her! When she gets back, I'm telling her. About you. I know about you.' There was a wild glint in her eyes as she stabbed the air above her with a finger to accentuate her point. 'You tell me I should trust my boyfriend! You fucking hypocrite! Why should I trust anyone when there are men like you around? Adulterous, slimy, two-faced, dick-led creeps who'll fuck anything with a decent pair of legs!'

Karl should have known this was coming.

'Oh, yes – you think no one knew about you and Cheri in the office at the dance club? Did you think we were all stupid?! Cheri told me all about it. All the sordid details. She told me about the abortion, too – your baby that she had to get rid of. What makes you think Siobhan's any different to Cheri? What makes you think I should believe that Rick's any different to you?! It's what makes the world go round, you smug arsehole – sex,

sex, sex! Siobhan wants it, you want it, Rick wants it, we all want it, and you can't trust anyone. So don't sit there telling me I'm paranoid, thinking that you're any different to anyone else, 'cos you're not. Wake up and smell the coffee, dick-for-brains: your girlfriend wants to have sex with my boyfriend and they're probably doing it right now!' Tamsin was crying, angry tears. 'And if they're not doing it they're sure as hell thinking about doing it!'

Karl adjusted himself in his seat and eyed Tamsin thoughtfully. He was still utterly collected.

'I have to say that I am not at all comfortable with the concept of blackmail,' he began, 'so let's just call this a deal, OK? But, if you even so much as think about mentioning my affair with Cheri to Siobhan, there are some things I could tell Rick over lunch one day that I feel sure you'd rather he didn't know about.'

'Huh!' said Tamsin, wiping at her tears, 'you don't really know anything. You can't prove anything.'

'OK, OK. Look, I'm not stupid either, y'know. Everyone knew what you were up to. Those two French guys couldn't keep their mouths shut about your little rosbif-sandwich interlude. There's no point going into this any more than necessary. As I say, this is a deal. I think we should just drop the subject now. If you're really that worried, then why don't you go and have a look outside, but I can assure you, it'll only make you feel worse about yourself. Trusting people has nothing to do with other people, it's in here' – he pointed at his head – 'and you can call it complacency, or smugness, but I call it dignity and happiness. I call it the only way to get through life and stay sane.'

Tamsin couldn't think of anything to say to that.

'Well, it doesn't look like we're going to be able to make any more small talk tonight, so I may as well go to bed,' said Karl. 'I'm very sorry things got a bit unpleasant there – I guess it's been a long day and a long night. Do you think we could make a fresh start in the morning?'

Tamsin shrugged and stared at the floor.

Karl put out his hand to shake hers. She gave him hers, limply.

'Whatever will be will be, Tamsin. Sleep tight.'

He tapped up the stairs, followed by Rosanne, who'd been sleeping in front of the fire, and Tamsin curled up on the sofa with the intention of crying and worrying and revelling in anxiety. Instead the huge amounts of alcohol in her system sent her into a deep and instantaneous sleep.

She didn't hear Rick and Siobhan tip-toe back in, and she didn't even wake up when Rick picked her up like a baby and carried her up the stairs to their room.

The lights went off around the house, toilet chains flushed, floorboards creaked, and suddenly it was silent.

Silent except for the windchimes, the owls and the gentle hum of the tape recorder still going round and round on the mantelpiece, where they had left it recording . . .

# CHAPTER SIXTEEN

Ralph woke up with a start. He'd been dreaming, deep disturbing dreams he wasn't used to having. He tried to remember them, but the details had fled his memory already. Something was strange, something was different. The alarm? Yes, the radio, music blaring out from the other side of the room where he'd left it . . . Why? . . . What? He'd set the alarm, last night. What time was it? 7.30 a.m. – fucking hell. He pulled the thin pillow from under his head and put it over his face, trying to block out the music and the light strobing through the minuscule gap between the curtains. As consciousness returned to him, slowly and painfully, he became aware of the lyrics to the song playing on the radio: 'I feel so dirty when they start talking cute . . . I wanna tell her that I love her but the point's probably moot . . . I wish that I had Jessie's girl . . .'

Jesus Christ! Ralph took the pillow from his head and sat up slowly. It was seven-thirty in the morning and he could relate to Rick Springfield – this was a very strange start to the day.

Ralph pulled himself from under the warmth of his duvet towards the radio, trying to find the Off button on this alien piece of equipment. Eventually he unplugged it in desperation and sat back on his heels as silence returned to the bedroom.

Someone out there was trying to get at him; it was

the first time in months that Ralph had set his alarm and it woke him up with fucking 'Jessie's Girl'. Unbelievable!

He was utterly disoriented. What the hell was going on? The studio – of course! He was going to go to the studio today. Why? Because he was an artist? Sort of. Because he wanted to? Not really. Because . . . because Jem had told him to . . . that's right. Because Jem had told him to. Well, not told him to exactly, but encouraged him to, advised him to, *wanted* him to.

He'd promised her he would, just to make her happy. You're right, he'd said. Tomorrow – I'll go tomorrow, bright and early. Don't do this for me, she'd said, do it for yourself, promise me. I promise you, he'd said.

So here he was, seven-thirty on a Friday morning, shell-shocked, exhausted, cold and confused. He certainly did not feel like he was doing this for himself – this was for Jem, plain and simple, to make her proud of him, milk her interest in him. He would be her little project if that's what she wanted: he didn't mind playing the tortured artist for her if it meant that he occupied her thoughts for a while and displaced Smith. Smith was a banker, more or less, a boring old bloody banker, nothing there to capture Jem's imagination.

He walked over to the windows and threw open the curtains, ready to face the day now he remembered why he was doing this. What a beautiful day! That helped. He'd borrow Smith's bike and cycle there, get some oxygen into his lungs, as his mother used to say.

He pulled on some boxer shorts from a pile on the floor and made his way into the hall, quite perky now, humming to himself, '"I wish that I had Jessie's gi-i-irl, I want Jessie's gi-i-irl . . ."'

'Didn't know you were a Rick Springfield fan.'

'What?' Ralph jumped. It was Jem, coming out of Smith's bedroom wearing one of his T-shirts that barely concealed her . . . her knickers? Her hair was unruly, her face sweetly sleepy and swollen; she looked like a baby mouse. She yawned.

'So,' she said, 'what do you think of seven-thirty in the morning, then? Horrible, isn't it?!'

Not so horrible after all – not when you got to see Jem, braless and fantastically dishevelled, in a T-shirt with the tantalizing promise of maybe, if she was to bend over just the weeniest bit, glimpsing the last centimetre or two of her bottom, or maybe . . . maybe . . . if she was just to stretch a little bit and the front of her T-shirt was to . . . augh, God. He pulled his gaze away from her legs.

'Grim!' he agreed.

'I got up especially early to give you some moral support. I hope you appreciate it!'

'Oh, God, you didn't have to. That's very sweet of you.' She'd got up early, just for him! Left Smith alone in bed, for him. Yes! 'D'you want to use the bathroom first?'

'No, you go first. I'm going to make you some breakfast, set you up for the day! I wouldn't mind a quick wee, though.'

'Oh, sure, of course.'

He moved out of the way to let her get to the bathroom, her body just barely brushing up against his as she passed, just enough to induce an unexpected erection inside his baggy shorts, which forced its way jauntily through the gap at the front and emerged squinting into the brand-new day, like an overzealous mole. Shit. He pushed it back inside, buttoned the fly quickly with fumbling fingers and crossed his hands in front of his crotch. Jem had left the door slightly ajar and he could hear her peeing, that strange gushing, jerky sound of girl's pee hitting water, and then the sound of toilet paper being unravelled from the wooden holder and folded and wiped across her. And then she was out again, grinning widely at him.

'I didn't flush it – hope you don't mind. See you in the kitchen!'

She skipped off down the hall. Ralph watched her as she went, her T-shirt rising just not quite high enough with every bouncy step she took. He exhaled deeply the breath he'd been holding since their bodies had touched and walked into the bathroom. He stared down into the toilet bowl at Jem's pee and the raft of pink paper floating on top of it, sinking slightly as it became waterlogged, and aimed his semi-hard penis at the yellow water, feeling strangely gratified by the sight of their fluids mingling before his eyes. Yes, he liked the idea of their bodily effluents becoming as one . . . and he absolutely adored the idea of Jem now, in the kitchen, tinily T-shirted and cooking his breakfast . . . mmmmm! He smiled smugly to himself. Things were looking up.

It had been two weeks now since their first night together, their chilli night, and Ralph had been working incredibly hard to sustain the bond they'd formed. He realized now that this was more than a crush, more than jealousy or lust. He was most definitely in love and he had no intention whatsoever of ignoring it, of putting his feelings to one side. He'd never been in love before and he was not going to let this opportunity slip through his fingers. He was going to take it slowly and cautiously.

He had suddenly started taking an interest in Smith's social and professional affairs, subtly discovering when he was going to be out and making sure he, Ralph, was in, that he had some time alone with Jem. He'd bought a couple of new tops and had finally washed his jeans, a job he'd been putting off for six months. He also bought flowers regularly now, from Northcote Road – peonies, of course – and made sure that he timed it so that he was artistically and sensitively arranging them in a vase when Jem got in from work. He'd even cooked for her a couple of times. And they'd developed a banter about hot food. 'Oh, you must go to such and such a restaurant in Earlsfield/Bayswater/Brick Lane. Best vindaloo I've ever had – really, really hot'; or 'Guess what? They've started selling Thai Bird chillies in Asda.' Ralph had even found some chilli seeds for sale in Northcote Road, and Jem and he had planted them, taking it in turns to water them and discussing their progress together, anxiously, like fretful parents.

This was a particularly successful development as it not only brought Jem closer to him, but also alienated Smith, who suffered from a tendency to order lamb pasanda and things with almonds and cream in. It was a tiny but effective little spanner in the works of Smith and Jem's cloying complicity. Ralph shared something with Jem that was somehow outside the realm of a non-romantic relationship – their own complicity. And now there was the tortured artist thing.

They'd been watering the chilli seeds in the airing cupboard the night before, and Jem had brought the subject up.

'Had any more thoughts about painting, Ralph?'

'Painting what?' he'd replied absent-mindedly, thinking maybe she was suggesting a new lick of paint in the living room.

'You know. Painting. You – studio – artist,' she'd said, with her palms outstretched, emphasizing his obtuseness.

'No. Was I supposed to?'

'No. You weren't *supposed* to, I just thought you might have, that's all.'

'Why's that?'

'I don't know. You just seem different lately, somehow. More . . . more . . . purposeful. More alive. I had actually been wondering if you might have met someone!' she added playfully, nudging him in the ribs.

'No, I haven't "met" someone,' he retorted, nudging her back and laughing. 'I've got a girlfriend, remember.'

'Oh, yes – the lovely Claudia.'

'And what have you got against Claudia all of a sudden?' Ralph was surprised and faintly pleased by the mild sarcasm in her voice.

'Nothing' – Jem took a deep breath – 'except she doesn't make you happy and I think you could do better for yourself.' She patted ineffectually at the moist soil in the small plastic pots, for something to do to cover her embarrassment.

'Oh, bless you, Jemima. I didn't think you cared.' Ralph was coming across as light-hearted, but inside his chest his heart was racing like a Formula One car. Finally, finally, she was cracking – she cared, she cared!! 'So, who do you think would be better for me then?' he asked cocking one eyebrow slightly in an attempt to look coy.

'Oh, I don't know. Someone who makes you feel good about yourself, someone who appreciates what a lovely bloke you are and doesn't just complain the whole time, someone who would inspire you to do what you're best at and not just treat you like a . . . like a . . . like an airhead gigolo!' She was practically kneading the already smooth soil now, her face reddening slightly.

Ralph laughed, hard and loud.

'"An airhead gigolo!!" God that's funny. I've never thought about it like that before, but I think you're right! I think that's exactly how she sees me. A gigolo!'

'No, really, Ralph, I'm being serious. There's a desperate shortage of nice blokes around in this world and you're wasting yourself on Claudia. Believe me, there's thousands of girls out there, nice girls, who would just love to go out with a guy like you. And if you had a nice girlfriend you'd spend less time bloody worrying about what you were going to do wrong next, and being inadequate and not good enough for some souped-up Sloane, and more time doing what you're good at. Painting. Really. I mean it,' she finished, closing the door of the airing cupboard and heading for the kitchen. Ralph followed closely behind, not wanting to miss a syllable. 'Girls like that make me so angry – they give other girls a bad reputation. Dump her and start painting, Ralph. Please.'

Oh, blimey. This was getting a bit heavy now. 'Can I just try the painting bit first and then see if I still need to dump Claudia afterwards?'

She punched him playfully. 'God – can't live without the sex, can you!'

'I'm not going to deny it, I'm a voracious animal,' he smiled, leaning backwards against the work surface.

'Well, I wouldn't want you to do all this just because I say so,' Jem said, replacing the water-spray under the sink, 'but if you thought you were up to it you should definitely give it a bash, just one day at a time – see how you feel. That's always the way in life: the longer you leave things, the harder they are to do . . .' She trailed off. 'Do it, Ralph, go tomorrow. Get up early, get to your studio and see what happens. Maybe you won't paint anything, maybe you'll just come straight back again, but at least you'll have got out of this cycle of just staying at home all day doing nothing – eh?' She was standing in front of him, looking up at him through her eyelashes, a stern but amiable expression on her face which stopped Ralph from feeling that he was being pressurized and more like he was being cared for, warm and nice inside. It had been a long time since he'd felt that way.

'OK,' he said, feigning defeat under duress, 'OK. Just one thing, though – what exactly do you mean by "early"?'

'Oooh, no point being half-hearted about this. Seven o'clock?'

'No way! Eight,' he countered.

'All right. Seven-thirty and no arguing!'

'OK, but that stinks, it really does. Even you don't have to wake up that early.'

Jem smiled. 'You'll feel good about it, I promise. You'll feel happier with yourself.'

And then that all too familiar moment arrived – the depressing sound of Smith's key in the lock, the twinge of pain in Ralph's heart as Jem's face lit up like the woman's in the Terry's All Gold advert, and she was gone, gone from him, and into Smith's arms.

But she was his again now, for a few delicious moments, before Smith got up; she was in the kitchen cooking him breakfast – she'd never cooked Smith breakfast – and she was wearing that teeny-weeny, itsy-bitsy T-shirt. He rushed his shower, not wanting to miss a moment, dressed quickly but thoughtfully in his cleanest clothes, splashed on a bit of designer aftershave (a present from an ex), fluffed up his hair and made his entrance.

Jem was coaxing the last few baked beans from the bottom of the can. 'I always feel mean if I leave a few stray ones,' she said, 'like they'll feel rejected or something.' She flicked on the gas ring and gave the beans a quick stir. 'Could you handle laying the table?' she asked. 'I'm just getting to the brain-to-hand co-ordination bit.'

She had put an apron on over the T-shirt, tied in a bow at the back, forcing the precarious garment a little higher up her legs but still . . . still just not quite high enough. Maybe if she had to reach for something from one of the cupboards higher up, like . . . the ketchup!

'Jem, would you mind passing me the ketchup? It's in that cupboard just over your head.'

He watched with bated breath; Smith's T-shirt had been clinging stubbornly to the back of Jem's thighs all morning like a prudish nanny, but now it was time. There was no way its resolute spirit could survive the impact of reaching for the ketchup.

Jem raised herself on to tiptoes, her back started to stretch, her arm left its side to begin the journey to the cupboard, the T-shirt moved a millimetre, two millimetres, three millimetres, and there it was! Almost. Oh, God, just another millimetre . . . Ralph was frozen to the spot with painful anticipation . . . Just another millimetre . . . Shit! Shit!! Jem's free hand suddenly grabbed the hem of the hateful T-shirt and pulled it down staunchly over her thighs as she completed the stretch and grabbed the bottle. Ralph couldn't believe it.

'There you go.' She handed him the bottle, seemingly unaware of his intense disappointment and frustration.

Let's face it, he thought, I was not meant to see her bottom, it's not going to happen, forget about it. But, dear God, he wanted to see her bottom. If it was anything like her silken thighs he absolutely had to see it.

'Sorry, Jem. Mustard?' He gestured at the same cupboard with his eyes.

She tutted good-naturedly and reached for the cupboard again. The mustard was further back in the cupboard and she had to stretch that little bit more, using her spare hand to steady herself on the work surface. Ralph stopped and stared again: one millimetre . . . two millimetres . . . three, four, five – Jesus! There it was! Six, seven . . . his mouth was dry, his eyes bulging . . . oh, sweet Jesus . . . the most beautiful, edible, luscious little bundle of bottom, pale and smooth and . . . bottomy . . . and, oh God, want to bite it want to bite it . . .

'I hope you're not looking at my bottom, Ralph McLeary!' laughed Jem, turning around.

Ralph spluttered. 'What? Me?'

'Yes, you. Here's your mustard.'

Ralph reached out for it with trembling hands, trying to look unfazed and innocent, turning too soon and missing the jar entirely. It dropped to the floor and, quite contradictory to Ralph's expectation of what would happen if you dropped a jar of mustard on to a linoleum-covered floor, it smashed into several pieces, depositing a splat of dirty yellow paste all over Jem's bare feet.

'Oh, God, Jem, I'm so sorry.' He rushed for the kitchen roll and pulled far too much off, bundling up the mass of paper and soaking it under the tap. 'I'll wipe it off for you. I'm so sorry.'

He got down on his knees at Jem's feet and began to dab at the mustard. 'There,' he said, 'it's coming off.'

'Of course it's coming off,' said Jem. 'It's mustard, not creosote!'

Ralph held her ankle tenderly as he wiped her tiny white feet. 'There,' he said, letting his hand slide a little further up her calf, his whole body stiff with the excitement of being so close to the hem of her T-shirt, his face inches from her naked groin, his hands encasing her legs and her feet, the mustard suddenly an erotic lubricant; he would quite happily have licked it off her.

'There. Almost done.'

He tore a single sheet off the roll and dried her feet with it, delicately, moving the paper in between her toes with his finger, his other hand still moving slowly further up her leg, almost behind her knee now. He was disappointed to realize that the job was finished; all the mustard was gone. He patted her leg and got slowly off his haunches, leaning his body in a little bit as he rose, keeping his nose close to her body, breathing her in deeply. Suddenly his eye was caught by a couple of small yellow specks on her legs.

'Oh,' he said, breathlessly, 'there's a bit more.'

He put his finger back in the paper and brushed at the splashes, wobbling slightly on his tired knees and grabbing the top of her leg quickly to keep himself steady. Warm, soft, lovely, lovely legs. She didn't flinch at all, just stood still, looking down at him with a small smile on her face.

'You're very thorough,' she said.

'All gone,' he said nervously, slowly, very slowly getting to his feet, his nose almost brushing against the protrusion of her breasts through the T-shirt. He was standing perilously close to her, towering over her, his heart beating so hard he could hear it in his ears.

She didn't move. 'Thank you,' she said.

He didn't move. 'My pleasure,' he said.

'No mustard for your sausages, then,' she said.

'I guess not,' he said.

Neither of them made any attempt to return to their respective chores. They stood where they were, for what seemed like eternity but was probably only a few seconds.

'Ralph?'

'Jem.'

'Remember what I was saying yesterday – you know, about thinking that you deserved someone better, how I think you're quite special?'

Ralph hardly dared breathe. He felt like he was being kept upright only by the magnetic force that Jem was radiating, like if she was to walk away he would just collapse in a heap on the floor. 'Yes?' he replied expectantly. Oh, God. What was she going to say?!

'Well, I just wanted to say . . . oh, shit!' Her face became panicked and she turned around abruptly, 'Shit – the bacon!' She pulled the pan off the heat and opened the window over the sink.

The kitchen was thick with grey, caustic smoke, the bacon annihilated, shards of brittle black charcoal sitting shame-facedly in the pan.

'Oh, bollocks!' she exclaimed, laughing. 'No bacon either, I guess.'

'Never mind,' said Ralph, 'the beans are my favourite bit anyway. Don't worry about it. Carry on. What you were saying, you know, just now . . .'

'Oh, yes,' said Jem, 'That. I was just going to say . . .'

A deafening wail obliterated her sentence, a high-pitched shriek emanating from somewhere in the flat.

'What the hell is that?' shouted Ralph over the din.

Smith was standing in the doorway in a green towelling dressing-gown, looking dazed, his hair all over the place. 'What's going on?' he mumbled with annoyance. 'Why's the smoke alarm going off?'

'Oh, God. I burnt the bacon,' said Jem. 'Quick, Smith, blow on it – blow on the alarm!'

The three of them congregated in the hall. Smith stood on a stool and blew on the alarm, fanning away the small amount of smoke with his sleeve.

'What were you making bacon for anyway?' he asked, bristling with irritation.

'For Ralph. For his breakfast,' she added unnecessarily.

Smith continued blowing and fanning until, eventually, the unbearable siren died down.

'Jesus,' he said, getting off the stool and smoothing down his hair.

'Sorry, boyfriend!' said Jem, holding out her hand to him. 'At least we know it works, though.'

'Hmmmm,' replied Smith, gruffly. 'Well, I suppose it was time to wake up anyway. Is there any breakfast for me?' he asked.

She smiled at him radiantly. 'Of course there is. Coming right up!'

Smith went for a shower then, and Ralph and Jem returned to the kitchen, Jem cracking eggs into a clean pan and turning the heat down under the now almost solidified beans.

'Jem,' said Ralph, putting out knives and forks, 'what you were saying . . .?'

'I'll tell you later,' she said, and carried on with the breakfast.

Later. Later? It was another one, two, three, four, five, six, seven, eight, nine, ten, TEN! hours until later. How could he possibly wait ten hours to hear what Jem had to say? That was impossible.

'Can you not just give me a little clue?' he said, wincing.

'Oh, God, Ralph! It's no big deal. I'll tell you later, OK?'

'OK,' he said, taking a seat at the table and watching her deftly co-ordinating the final stages of the greasily aromatic breakfast.

Smith came into the kitchen and breakfast was served.

'There you go – a proper working man's breakfast for proper working men,' said Jem, placing plates covered with eggs and sausages and beans and mushrooms and huge slabs of hand-sliced toast dripping with butter in front of them. 'Get stuck into that!'

'You are an angel, you're a saint, you're totally and utterly perfect! Thank you!' Under the circumstances Ralph felt able to blast Jem with superlatives and adoration without arousing discomfort or suspicion (the way to a man's heart and all that) and Jem took it as it sounded rather than as it was meant, smiling happily at her satisfied customer.

His overpowering need for satiation, stimulated by the morning's string of oddly sensuous encounters, was projected on to his food, and he ate like an animal, wolfing down the huge plate of food in moments. He wanted to go now anyway. Smith and Jem were playing footsie under the table and smiling at each other over their breakfast plates. He took his plate to the dishwasher, packed a small rucksack with a radio, some mini Mars Bars and a spare jumper, grabbed Smith's bike and helmet and set off down the road. Smith and Jem waved him off sweetly from the top of the basement steps, arms around each other, looking almost like proud parents. The notion made him feel queasy, quashing the whole air of ripe desire and eroticism that had inflamed his morning.

## CHAPTER SEVENTEEN

Ralph cycled quickly, taking the scenic route along the river, over Battersea Bridge, past the desirable residences of Cheyne Walk, down Grosvenor Road towards Millbank.

'"Where can I find a woman like that – like Jessie's girl . . ."' He sang loudly to himself as he pedalled, not caring who heard. He was bursting at the seams with pent-up everything – lust, jealousy, love, hurt, excitement, disappointment. This was unbearable, totally unbearable. How could he go on like this, living under the same roof with the two of them, Jem not minding if he saw her bottom, telling him he was 'special' and then playing footsie with Smith as if he didn't exist? Was she doing it on purpose? Maybe she was a nymphomaniac after all. No. No. That wasn't right. There was more to it than that, much more. There was something between them, something . . . spiritual. Oh, what rubbish. Spiritual! No, they got on, it was as simple as that. They got on very, very well together, they had a 'special' relationship. If he didn't fancy her so much he could very well have been friends with her – that would have been novel, a female friend. But that was impossible now, especially after this morning, especially after the pee in the toilet and the T-shirt and the mustard and everything.

What was it she wanted to say to him? He couldn't

get it off his mind. Oh, well – he only had one whole enormous, never-ending day to wait to find out.

He turned right and left at Parliament Square and followed the river on to Victoria Embankment, still cycling suicidally fast, ignoring the burning in his leg muscles and the possibility of errant pedestrians walking into his path.

It was a glorious day, cold in the nicest possible way, the sky an unfeasible blue, the Houses of Parliament gleaming like freshly washed bedsheets.

Fucking Smith. Fucking bloody Smith. Smith had always had the better luck. From early on. Smith had the smart house in Shirley, the nice liberal parents, the coolest friends, the best-looking girls after him, the flash car on his eighteenth birthday, the holidays, the job, the money, the flat, the career. Ralph had just tagged along to start with, feeling out of his depth and insecure.

His parents were old, much older than anyone else's parents, and timid of nature. He couldn't have invited anyone back to their house in Sutton – his mother would have laid a table of Viscount biscuits and cardboardy jam tarts and wanted to chat with his 'young friends' about school and the weather. His father would have taken refuge in the garden, pottering around in his twill cap with his rake and his hoe or whatever, looking like an elderly groundskeeper in a stately home. The television would be switched off – it was rude to have it turned on in company – and the small beige living room would have resonated with the sound of the old wooden clock on the wall ticking away the interminable seconds.

He'd had to work hard to find his feet in Smith's world. The first time he'd been round to see Shirelle, he'd been almost morally shocked by the attitude of Smith's parents, who swore frequently and shouted loudly over the din of every television in the house, and let Smith's friends come and go without the slightest interest in who they were or how their schoolwork was going or whether they were about to have sex with a foreign-exchange student in the spare room.

He hadn't lingered at first, servicing Shirelle as speedily as possible with one eye on the door, not quite able to comprehend the fact that Smith's parents didn't actually care, and leaving rapidly, dressing on the way out, not looking to the left or the right for fear of making eye contact with one of the many people who appeared to be constantly milling around the large, comfortable house.

And then of course he'd gone for that walk with Smith and found that he was not a bad bloke and was obviously disproportionately impressed by Ralph's supposed sexual prowess, and Smith had welcomed him into his life.

He'd been uncomfortable for a while, worried that he was the subject of some enormous joke, but he soon learned to relax and enjoy the advantages of having wealthy, happy friends. The jealousy he'd always felt towards Smith began to wane, and as the years went by and their friendship developed into one of brothers, the initial discrepancies between them faded and they became equals. Ralph was cool now, too, he could hold his own – he was the star of the Royal College, he had press coverage, beautiful blondes, a wide circle of friends and invitations to smart parties.

But now all those old feelings were rising to the surface again, the feelings of inadequacy, of being the country mouse, the poor relation, the social misfit, the butt of someone's joke. Because Smith had the one thing in the world that Ralph hadn't even realized until now he'd wanted – a real relationship with a real woman who really loved him.

Fucking Smith. Fucking bloody Smith. Not. Fucking. Fair.

He hurtled up Thames Street towards a bank of impatient cars queued four-wide at the traffic lights. He rode on, faster and faster, up Lower Thames Street and towards Tower Hill. The burn in his legs had stopped ages ago, he was an automaton, the bike was cycling itself. He heard a car horn for the millionth time that morning. 'Ah, fuck you!' he shouted out, sticking his finger in the air.

He took his hands from the handlebar, got to his feet and closed his eyes against the wind that whipped across his face like a leather glove. He took in a huge deep breath, bigger almost than his lungs, and opened his mouth wide enough to feel the rush of air against his tonsils.

He was about to yell but the sound was lost in the blaring screech of yet another car horn, of rubber against Tarmac, of metal grinding metal as Ralph's bike hit the bonnet of a shiny red Mercedes 350SL convertible, his dream car, and his body flew up into the London skyline, across a parked car, over a parking meter, finally landing with a menacing thud of flesh and bone against the wall of an office building on Minories.

His body was soon surrounded by a concerned group of strangers oohing and aahing and asking if anyone was a doctor, and shouldn't they call an ambulance, and putting their ears to his mouth to see if he was breathing.

'Shhhhh!' said a small fat man who, for some unofficial

and peculiar reason had taken control of the situation, 'shhhhhh, everyone, he's trying to speak.'

He put his gelatinous face an inch from Ralph's mouth, his cheeks turning red with the effort of leaning over. He sat back, exhaled and scanned the faces of the attentive crowd gathered around him.

'He's saying that he wishes he had Jessie's girl,' he announced with confusion, 'over and over – "Jessie's girl."'

'"I want Jessie's girl . . ."'

'Why the hell does he keep singing that?' whispered Smith.

Jem shrugged and squeezed Ralph's hand again. 'Oh, God, look at him!' she wailed. 'It's all my fault! He would still have been in bed at that time of the morning if it hadn't been for me.' She put her head down on the side of Ralph's bed and began to sob.

'Oh, Jem, don't cry. Don't blame yourself.' Smith stroked her small, quivering head. 'It's *not* your fault. Remember what the driver of the car said. He was cycling unbelievably fast, with his eyes closed – it wasn't just bad luck . . .' He trailed off as the image of his poor mangled bike flashed through his head again. He'd only had it for two months and now it was a write-off, dead, deceased. Thanks a lot, Ralph.

The doctor had informed them that Ralph had a fractured wrist, severe bruising to the left side of his body, a broken rib and mild concussion. He would come around soon, he told them, any time now. He was very lucky apparently; the wall had, perversely, broken his fall. If he'd hit the pavement first he could have injured his back or broken a leg.

They were sitting with Ralph, in the quiet of the ward, either side of his bed, Jem holding his hands, Smith holding his own crossed in his lap, waiting for Ralph to do something, anything at all rather than lie there looking so pale and still and bruised, singing that bloody song over and over again.

'Let me get you a cup of tea,' sighed Smith, getting to his feet and stretching, looking quickly at his watch. He had so much work to do.

Jem turned back to observe Ralph. He looked so sweet, his face scuffed and tinged with purple, his big round eyes so distressingly closed, his left arm in plaster, a bandage around his chest holding his broken bones together. He looked like a child, a vulnerable, lovable, sweet, broken child, and it was all her fault. It didn't matter what Smith said, what anyone said, it was she who'd steered Ralph down that particular path of fate, whether he'd also been to blame or not. If it hadn't been for her he'd still have been in bed at that hideous moment when his bike hit the bonnet of that car; she'd determined his destiny that Friday morning, she and no one else.

'"Jessie's girl – I want Jessie's girl,"' Ralph was humming again in that strange, rasping voice.

'This is Jem, Ralph – can you hear me?'

'Where can I find a woman like that . . . ?'

'Oh, Ralph, this is Jem. Please, Ralph, open your eyes, look at me.'

Ralph just lay there.

'Ralph – Ralph – it's me!'

Ralph awoke. 'Jem . . .' Ralph's voice sounded weak, tired.

'Shhhhh . . . shhhhh,' said Jem, putting her hand to his cheek, 'don't try to speak.'

'Jem.' He smiled at her and closed his eyes again, nuzzling his cheek against her hand. 'Jem.'

Smith returned at that moment, grasping two polystyrene cups of tea.

'Smith, Smith, he's awake! He talked to me!'

Smith put the cups down on the bedside table and reinstated himself quickly on his chair. 'Ralph – Ralphie – can you hear me?'

Ralph nodded and opened his eyes slowly. He smiled at Smith. 'What the fuck's going on?' he croaked.

'You tell me,' laughed Smith, grinning widely at Ralph and taking his hand, 'you lunatic bloody kamikaze cyclist! What the hell were you playing at?'

'I – I don't remember,' he replied, speaking very slowly. 'Oh, yes, I do! I was singing. Singing. I was singing. I was on your bike. Yeah – that's right.'

'I'll get the nurse,' whispered Smith to Jem, 'they probably need to know.'

'Jem,' said Ralph, after Smith had gone, 'so nice to see you – you look . . . lovely.'

'Oh, Ralph, thank you, but I think your judgement's probably a little impaired at the moment.'

'Has Smith gone home?'

'No, he's gone to get a nurse. You've been unconscious for hours.'

She watched as he drifted into a happy slumber. She felt overwhelmed with tenderness and affection. All of a sudden she wanted to hold Ralph, to protect him, to look after him, to love him? . . . It had been such a strange morning. The whole episode with the mustard had unsettled her. There was something nice about it; she'd enjoyed the feeling of his hands on her legs, his finger between her toes . . . and there'd been that moment, before the bacon burnt, when the world had stopped for a second, literally stopped, and he'd stood over her, close to her and her heart had beaten so hard it had felt like her eardrums were going to explode and now . . . now . . . for some reason she was feeling very confused.

She looked at Ralph, his cheek still resting against her hand, his body still and shattered, his mind elsewhere. He looked so gentle, so in need of love and care.

Her heart tied itself up in a knot.

# CHAPTER EIGHTEEN

It had been a very happy fortnight for Siobhan and Karl, the happiest for months and months. Siobhan had taken Rick's advice that night at the chapel and talked to Karl about everything, absolutely everything. And Karl, in his usual strong and compassionate way, had listened and understood – even the bit about Rick.

'You kissed him,' he'd stated matter-of-factly, sitting bare-chested under the counterpane on the huge four-poster bed, Rosanne curled up at his side with her head on his lap.

'Uh-hum,' Siobhan had nodded, looking glumly at the floor, long strands of scruffy golden hair falling from the pins that had held it in place all night, her eyes streaked with black mascara and smudged eyeliner, her dainty heels clogged with mud from the banks of the loch.

Karl had felt a small jolt of surprise. That mad Tamsin girl had been right – sort of. They'd kissed. Rick had kissed Siobhan. Siobhan had kissed Rick. He found himself feeling a little sick.

'Jeez. What . . . what . . . er, how . . . how long . . . how long did you kiss for, exactly?' he said slowly, rubbing his chin, feeling awkward about this unexpected scenario but also that he needed to handle it like a grown-up.

'Ten minutes, twenty minutes, I don't know. I thought

of you,' she added, wanting to turn the conversation back to what was important – them. 'I thought of you and I stopped . . .'

'Why? Was it . . . was it . . . because you were drunk, high – what?' Karl was talking calmly, rationally, genuinely trying to understand what had happened that night but still shaken by the image in his mind of Siobhan, his Siobhan, in the arms of another man, kissing him, her tongue in his mouth . . .

'Partly – well, no, not really at all. I was . . . I was thinking about it even before we started drinking, the minute I saw him, in fact,' she gulped, feeling maybe she'd admitted too much but then realizing that this was just the beginning of what needed to be said.

'Well, yes. He's a great-looking guy, I suppose . . .'

'Oh, Karl, stop it! Stop being so bloody reasonable. Do you think that's all there was to it? You think I just liked the look of him and suddenly, after fifteen years with you I just thought, Oh, what the fuck, I'll have him? Yes, he's good looking, of course he's good looking, but . . . but that's not it.'

'Well, then, tell me, Siobhan. Please tell me. Why?'

'To show you that I'm still attractive, that other men, good-looking men, would find me attractive. I wanted to make you jealous, Karl. I know how immature that must sound, how . . . how stupid. I wanted you to stop me, before, when we were flirting, I wanted you to get angry, to be possessive, to think, That's my girlfriend and if I'm not careful she's going to have sex with someone else – but you didn't. You were so typically Karl – so unfazed, cool, oblivious – so fucking smug! It didn't occur to you did it, Karl, it didn't cross your mind that someone else might want me? You just think I'm some great ugly inkblot, some fat bird that no other man would look twice at . . .' She broke down in angry tears.

'Oh, God, Siobhan, this is what we were talking about before, before we went downstairs tonight. Shit. I wanted to talk to you then but you were so angry, so defensive, you wouldn't talk about it.' Karl could feel tears welling up behind his eyes now. 'Come over here, Shuv.' He patted the empty bed beside him. 'Please. I want to be close to you.'

She got up from the dressing table and walked slowly to the bed, sitting gingerly on the edge, wanting to be close also, but still full of so much uncommunicated anger and resentment that she was unable to yield herself to him entirely.

'Shuv,' he began, 'I'm not going to lie to you. You have put on quite a lot of weight. I've not mentioned it because it just didn't seem important. Really,' he added, registering the raised eyebrows and scepticism on Siobhan's face. He took her hand. 'You are the most beautiful woman in the world. And I'm not going to say "to me" because that's not true. You're beautiful to me, but I can also see that you're beautiful to other people as well. I've seen the looks men give you when we walk down the street. You're overweight, yes, but that doesn't matter. I mean look at you – you're magnificent, Siobhan – your hair, those blue eyes, the way you carry yourself, the way you are with people, your laugh. And when you're naked you look voluptuous, feminine, round . . .'

Siobhan was smiling now through her tears, a soft spot in the pit of her belly aching with pleasure.

'I don't want you any less, Siobhan, if anything I want you more. That night, that night when all this started, after the drinks at the Sol y Sombra, I wanted you more then than I can ever remember, more than when we first met.'

Oh, yes – that night. Siobhan had to tackle this now, while she was feeling able to talk honestly. She took a breath.

'Karl – about that night. I want to explain.'

He held her hand encouragingly.

She continued. 'It was that girl, that Cheri girl – you know, the one who lives upstairs. Well. When I saw her there at your drinks party and she looked so young and slim and beautiful and you were obviously so . . . so in awe of her, I just felt really inadequate and ugly, and later, when you were, you know, trying to make love to me, I just kept thinking that you wanted me to be her, that you were imagining I was her, that I was young and slender and smooth and . . . and . . . and that's why I pushed you off me – I just couldn't bear it. I felt so hideous – like a freak, like a whore or something, like a great fat whore. I thought that that was why you were being so passionate, because you were turned on thinking about her, not me, and – oh, God – does this all sound really pathetic?'

Karl felt sick. What had he done? He was to blame. Why had he ever gone within a mile of that horrible, horrible bitch? He had the most wonderful girlfriend imaginable, a girlfriend who loved him and trusted him and cared for him. And his selfish, pathetic actions had forced her into the arms of another man. In a way he deserved this. He'd been plagued with guilt for months now, for what he'd done to Siobhan. It was time he paid the price for his treachery, his deceit.

'No . . . no,' he sighed, pulling her to him. 'It doesn't

sound pathetic, not at all pathetic. I'm the pathetic one, Siobhan, not you.'

'What do you mean?' asked Siobhan.

'Nothing. Nothing. Just that you've always been the strongest one. Always. I've leant on you through the years, relied on you. It was you who made all the best decisions in our relationship. If it wasn't for you we'd still be living in that grotty bedsit in Brighton, I'd still be trying to be a rock star, playing to a bunch of pissed eighteen-year-old students in a stinking union bar knee-deep in snakebite and vomit, convincing myself I was enjoying it, that I was living some sort of worthwhile life. You made me grow up. I'm a better person because of you, Siobhan. And I promise you, really, really promise you, Siobhan, that when we got home that night, when we were in bed, it was you I wanted, it was you I saw when I closed my eyes, that I felt under my fingertips, with my mouth, with my tongue. Only you. That girl, that Cheri girl, she's very pretty, y'know, obviously but – oh God, Siobhan, it's you I want, you I've always wanted, eight stone or eighteen stone . . . Well – maybe not eighteen stone!' He laughed and Siobhan hit him playfully and let him hold her in his arms and love her and comfort her.

Well, that wasn't so much of a lie, about Cheri, Karl thought guiltily. Just selective truth, protective lying, protecting them, their love, their future. But, God, he felt awful, he felt so, so awful. He stroked her hair.

'Jeez, Shuv, your hair's full of stuff – bits of twig and grass and God knows what. Are you sure you were just kissing out there?'

'Well, it was lying-down kissing, wasn't it?' she giggled nervously. 'Karl, do you forgive me? You know, don't you, it was nothing? It was me being childish and I used poor Rick to get at you . . .'

'Oh, I shouldn't imagine he minded too much. What man would, you devilishly beautiful woman, you!'

They'd hugged tightly and properly then and talked into the night, talked about the last twelve months, about Siobhan's unhappiness, and they'd made plans to make sure that Siobhan would be happy in the future, to make sure that never again would they allow their relationship to become stifled, silent and thick with unspoken thoughts. And then they'd made love, for the first time in nearly two months, and as Karl slid down between her breasts, Siobhan looked down at his mop of black curls and lay back and smiled.

They'd heard the rumble of Rick's Peugeot early the following morning – he and Tamsin had obviously thought better of hanging around to see what happened next – and spent a blissful day and night on their own in the enchanted chapel, talking, walking, eating and making love.

The first thing she'd done when they got back to London on Monday was to phone her gynaecologist to arrange an appointment to talk to someone about their options for infertility treatments. During their late-night conversation in the chapel, it had transpired that Siobhan had been in denial about her inability to conceive for years; it had been a long-held dream, an assumption about the path her life was going to take, and when she'd been told it was denied her, she'd brushed the dream under the carpet like a shrivelled-up dead spider, bought Rosanne and decided to get on with her life, refusing to consider the option of fighting for what she'd always believed would be her natural right. Not, she understood now, the action of a decisive, pragmatic woman, but the action of a woman in shock, a woman who didn't know what else to do. They would make the most wonderful parents, they realized that night. So many awful parents in this world, so many who didn't deserve children, who didn't want them, who hurt, stifled, spoiled and damaged their offspring. As they talked and basked in the warmth of their revived closeness they knew that they deserved children, they were ready for them, and they wanted them more than anything.

The next thing Siobhan did, anticipating the advice she was bound to be given prior to any treatment being offered to her, was to enrol with her local Weight Watchers group. Funny, now she knew that Karl loved her any way she came it was so much easier to make the decision to do something about her weight. For herself, not just for Karl; for their future, for their baby. And, more practically, in the short term, so that she could resurrect some of her lovely old clothes from early retirement and throw away her horrible leggings. It was boredom that had led her to overeat, the hours and hours spent at home on her own, with a fridge full of unhealthy food, eating meals alone, huge plates the size of a funeral pyre, without the constraints of the embarrassment of someone watching her.

She and Karl had decided that she needed more to do, she needed to be busy, too busy to eat, so she'd put an ad in a bridal magazine advertising her dressmaking services. The ad had only been in for a week and she already had three commissions. The phone rang every day with enquiries from prospective brides, and she was turning the spare bedroom into a proper bridal room.

They'd discovered the hard way that the ease that had always been the bedrock of their relationship had also been its undoing. They'd never discussed things in any great depth because they hadn't needed to. Siobhan had always decided when to move on, and Karl, compliant and utterly full of faith in her foresight and wisdom, had followed blindly. He'd been too blind to see when the time had come for him to take the lead and take Siobhan firmly by the hand and into the future, their future.

It had been hard for Karl to come to terms with what had happened between and Rick and Siobhan that night on the banks of the loch. He'd had to control a lot of rather unpleasant feelings of jealousy and he really didn't like the emotion at all – it was alien to him, against his nature. But he'd managed, somehow, and now he was feeling strangely touched by the revelations that night at the chapel, touched that, for once, Siobhan had needed him. He was being called on to be a man, called up for service almost, except his country didn't need him, his lover did, and he felt proud and strong and ready to do whatever was necessary.

He felt very grown-up, and it was a great feeling. He wanted to spend some money on the flat, get rid of all the studenty artefacts and shabby bits of old furniture they'd brought with them from Brighton, take the posters off the walls, buy some light shades for the bare bulbs, buy a really nice duvet cover, maybe take out the horrible orange plastic bathroom suite and put in something expensive and Italian.

He couldn't be a rockabilly for the rest of his life; he was thirty-five years old: if he had children, their schoolfriends would tease them for having a father who looked like Bill Haley. It would be painful, but he was going to do it – go to the barber's and ask them to remove his beloved quiff and sideburns. On the bright side, it wouldn't take him so long to get ready for work in the mornings, and he could stop using that Black and White gel that Siobhan hated. Maybe build some cabinets for his oversized record collection too; the yards and yards of neatly stacked rows of records currently dominated their living room, like some dubious modern-art exhibit at the Tate Gallery. They were a trophy, a testament to his life to date. It was time to hide them, maybe even sell some. Time to move on.

They'd been so happy for so long that Karl and Siobhan had forgotten to press Play after depressing the Pause button of their lives – they'd been stuck in the freeze-frame for years, transfixed by its perfection, by the smiles on the faces of the people in it. It had taken that night in Scotland to remind them that there were new scenes to come, new developments to be worked through and that the important thing, the most important thing in the world, was to keep the film moving, whether the film had a happy ending or not.

Karl's work was going better, too. He'd been called to Jeff's office on his return to work on the Monday afternoon, and he was smiling. He'd just received the latest ratings and figures were up for Karl's show – only a fraction, but enough to suggest to Jeff that it would be best to leave things be for a few weeks, give things a chance to settle down, see how the figures went. 'Keep hold of the tape from Glencoe, though,' he'd said, 'Rick tells me you came up with some blinding stuff – keep it, just in case.'

But Karl felt confident that they wouldn't need the

tape. The following week's figures had shown a further increase and he felt sure that the trend would continue. He didn't mind playing the odd bit of Top Ten bilge to keep the younger listeners on board if it meant that he could educate them by playing pop classics in between.

Karl had decided from the outset to be honest with Rick about the events at Glencoe. He liked him, he respected him and he wanted their relationship to work.

'Rick,' he'd said in the station canteen after his show on Monday, 'I know what happened. I know what happened with you and Siobhan on Saturday night.'

Rick had visibly receded in his seat then and stared down at his suddenly unappetizing plate of broccoli and cheddar bake. 'Oh,' he'd managed to reply in a voice a few octaves higher than his normal bass.

'Look, I'm not the jealous type, Rick. I was a bit shocked, it has to be said. But I hear that you were very kind to Siobhan, offered her some very wise advice and, well, we needed it, to be frank with you. I just want you to know that I don't feel bad about what happened, you know, that night . . .' This wasn't true. It wasn't true at all. Karl still felt sick about what had happened, but he knew that if he allowed his jealousy to get a foothold the whole situation would turn in on itself and become negative. He had to keep things positive, it was the only way.

Rick finally exhaled and began to regain his bulk. 'You know, she's a great girl, Karl, really, really . . .' he said nervously.

'Yeah, I know. I know.' Karl didn't want to hear this; he had no interest in Rick's opinion of his girlfriend. He took a breath to control himself. 'Look, all I'm saying is, basically, no hard feelings, eh? I respect you and I don't want this to come between us, especially when it's turned out to be such a . . . such a positive thing ultimately – for both of us, for me and Siobhan. We needed a kick up the arse – you know, we'd got stale, stuck, complacent, so anyway,' he smiled then, and stuck his hand out to Rick, who took it uncertainly but gratefully and shook it hard, 'forget about it – eh?'

'Yeah,' said Rick, still feeling a little embarrassed by Karl's candidness and his part in the situation.

'So, how are things with you and Tamsin? She was a bit upset that night?' said Karl, thickly buttering an insipid bread roll, wondering how much he could say to Rick about his patently unstable girlfriend.

'Um.' Rick gulped. 'Gone . . . she's gone.' He spoke quickly, in that strange, high-pitched voice.

'Oh, Jeez, mate, I'm sorry. What happened?'

'Well, I told her – what happened.'

'You told her! Why?'

'Well, she guessed really. I woke up the next morning and she was just sitting at the foot of the bed, staring at me.' He shuddered. 'It was scary actually. And she was holding my clothes, from the night before, and they were sort of . . . dirty. You know, grass stains and stuff.' He averted his gaze from Karl's at that moment. He breathed in deeply and let it go slowly and audibly through puckered lips. 'She just went fucking ape, completely mad, you know? Telling me I was a cock-sucking bastard motherfucker son of a syphilitic bitch – that sort of thing. I'm surprised you two didn't hear, she was screaming so loud.'

'Jeez,' said Karl.

'You know, I've been with Tamsin for six months, but I don't think I know even half of what makes her tick.

There's a lot of stuff going on under the surface with her, d'you know what I mean? She's got a lot of secrets, that girl, a hell of a lot of secrets.'

'Hmmmm,' said Karl. That was undoubtedly true.

'I guess it's just as well I found out sooner rather than later, eh?' he added with a small, nervous laugh.

'How are you feeling about it?' asked Karl.

'Worried, more than anything. I don't know how she's going to cope.'

'Look, if she needs help, she'll contact you. She'll probably change her mind and try and come back. She's a grown woman, she can look after herself. It's the people who seem weak who are always surprisingly strong, and the ones who seem strong who are unexpectedly weak. She'll be just fine.'

'Yeah, I hope so, I do hope so. Oh, by the way' – Rick dipped into his leather briefcase – 'I . . . er . . . I brought this.' He handed Karl the small silver tape recorder from the night in Glencoe. 'I haven't listened to it yet, and it doesn't seem like you're going to need it now, but you may as well have it.' And then he'd passed the little machine to Karl who nodded his thanks and put it in his back pocket.

Karl got up to leave and they shook hands. The cleaning-up operation was over for the time being; everything that had to be said had been said. Karl was glad he'd done it, glad he'd been so controlled, so mature. But he still couldn't rid himself of the feeling that he'd like to take Rick outside and break his jaw.

It had been a most, most excellent two weeks for Karl and Siobhan and now it was almost Christmas and Karl had left the ALR building in Olympia and was driving up Kensington High Street. It was dark, the streets glowing phosphorously orange, and the pavements on both sides were thick with shoppers and slush from the snow that had fallen briefly that lunchtime and melted quickly in the brilliant white sunshine that had followed. A Salvation Army band played carols outside Barkers and the pleasant noise of shiny brass and scrubbed voices added to Karl's already great sense of well-being. He miraculously found a parking space in Derry Street and quickly pushed his way as charmingly as possible through the dense hordes of shoppers towards the warm welcoming doors of the department store, fully appreciating the gorgeous gust of artificially warm air that hit him as he entered. He walked briskly through the perfumery department, avoiding the plastic-faced assistants wielding large bottles of headache-inducing fragrances and headed through to the quiet inner sanctum of the jewellery department. This was no good, he thought, eyeing up the display cases of oversized pieces of gold and amber and cubic zirconium, they were all costume pieces, gaudy and garish.

'Excuse me, please,' he said to a friendly looking young man behind a counter, 'excuse me. Can you tell me where I'll find the real jewellery?'

He pointed Karl in the right direction. Oh, yes, he thought, this is more like it, this is the stuff.

'Can I help you, sir?'

'Yes, please,' replied Karl eagerly. 'Yes. Can you show me a selection of rings, please, in the region of . . .' – he quickly calculated how much he could afford – 'in the region of £1,000 to £1,500. No, sorry, actually can you make that £2,000?' He smiled widely. It was going to be worth it.

'Certainly, sir. And what sort of ring were you looking for?'

Karl would have thought that was obvious – there was only one kind of ring, wasn't there?

'Oh, engagement rings, please.'

Yes! He was going to marry her. He was going to marry his beautiful, beautiful Siobhan. He was so excited he could barely breathe. Why had he never thought of this before! He stared down at the glistening tray in front of him, rows and rows of shiny, perfect troths, tiny sparkling symbols of love. Oh, which one? Which one would end up on Siobhan's delightful finger for the rest of her life? Because it would be for the rest of her life; for the first time ever, the concept of being with Siobhan for the rest of his life seemed unbearably romantic, not just some inevitable destiny, some unspoken certainty, but the most wonderfully, fantastically romantic notion imaginable. Just think, the two of them for ever, children, grandchildren, a nice house in . . . in . . . Chelsea maybe, glittering careers, and the two of them, always the two of them – Karl and Siobhan Kasparov, that fabulously grown-up, happy couple, still so in love after fifty, a hundred, three hundred years together . . . aaaaaaahhh. Makes your heart melt, dunnit . . . ?

He had to think about what Siobhan would like, not what he liked. He'd have chosen some great hunk of rock; Siobhan would prefer something more subtle, daintier, maybe something with a coloured gem in it, blue maybe to match her eyes, or yellow to match her hair. The salesman patiently showed him every tray in the department, calculating his commission with each ring Karl looked at, encouraging him and sharing his enthusiasm. Finally Karl saw it – the right ring, the one that had

'Siobhan' written all over it: an intricate cluster of tiny pearls, diamonds and sapphires mounted on a white-gold band, feminine and unusual, with a vaguely Celtic feel to it, and entirely unpretentious – just like Siobhan.

The excited salesman placed the ring in a beautiful red-leather box and Karl left the store £2,200 poorer and in a rush to get home. They'd invited their friends Tom and Debbie over for dinner that night, nothing fancy, just some pasta, maybe watch a video after. Now he was hoping they wouldn't want to stay for the 'maybe-watch-a-video-after' bit and would leave as early as possible, giving him time to propose before they were both too tired to celebrate.

He could barely contain himself as he flitted around Siobhan in the kitchen that night, watching, or rather hindering her while she prepared the evening meal, chopping up huge flat mushrooms and strips of streaky bacon for a carbonara sauce (made with virtually fat free crème fraîche, she hastened to inform him).

'Tom and Debbie are running a bit late,' she told him. 'They called just before you got back.'

'Oh, God. How late?' he asked impatiently.

'I don't know, only about half an hour or so, I suppose.'

'Oh, God.'

'What's the matter with you? Since when were you a stickler for time-keeping in other people?' asked Siobhan, laughing at Karl's curious vexation.

'Oh, nothing – I just want this evening to be over, that's all. I want to be alone with you and I can't wait because I'm an impatient fecking bastard, that's all,' he said, grabbing her from behind and planting a vampire kiss on the back of her neck.

'Control yourself, Karl Kasparov!' giggled Siobhan. 'Another half-hour won't kill you!'

'It might well do, it might well do . . .'

Karl was bursting at the seams. It had been Jeff, Jeff of all people, who'd put the idea into his head. He hadn't done or said anything in particular, it was just the way he referred to his wife all the time – Jackie this and Jackie that. And his kids, he talked about them constantly, called them 'the kids' even though they were probably in their twenties by now. 'Jackie and the kids.' 'Siobhan and the kids.' It seemed that Jeff and Jackie had a great marriage; it had lasted more than thirty years already and they were still very much part of each other's lives, firmly interwoven like threads in a piece of fine silk, not a rag-bag fraying old patch of canvas like a lot of marriages seemed to be. There was a wonderful, dignified finality to their marriage, an immutable permanence. They hadn't reached a dead end and stopped, they'd gone on and on, growing and changing, up the same path, towards the same horizon, hand in hand. It was corny but it was also exactly what Karl wanted. He wanted a great marriage.

Tom and Debbie finally arrived and the four of them enjoyed a relaxed evening together. Before too long it was eleven o'clock, too late to watch a video and, as far as Karl was concerned, time for them to go, time for the big moment. He'd contained his excitement long enough, imagined the look on Siobhan's face, the plans they would make about venues and guests and which church and what vows and talking into the night and going to bed to make love and celebrate their future together. The past was important, of course it was, but nothing was more important than the future now.

Eventually Tom began to yawn and look like he was going to leave.

'Do you want me to call you a cab?' asked Karl.

They saw them to the door as the cab waited outside, its engine breaking the silence of the still December night. Siobhan yawned, too, as the front door closed behind their guests. 'I'm going to brush my teeth,' she said.

'No! Wait!' said Karl, his smile so lively that it pulled his face in a hundred different directions at once. 'Just wait there. Don't move.' He motioned to her with his hands.

'What are you up to?' asked Siobhan, Karl's ludicrous smile infecting her.

He returned from the hall with his hands behind his back. 'Siobhan,' he began, 'this is the most important thing I've ever done. It's also the best thing I've ever done and I only pray that you agree with me!' He laughed nervously and Siobhan stared back at him with curiosity, amusement and apprehension.

'Siobhan McNamara, the most beautiful woman in the world' – he pulled the red box from behind his back and clumsily forced it open – 'Siobhan McNamara, will you marry me?'

He stood, for what felt like an eternity, holding the little box aloft, searching Siobhan's face for a reaction.

'Oh, my God, Karl, you daft bugger! You madman! What the hell have you done?' She picked the box cautiously from the palm of his hand.

His face dropped and a look of panic spread across it.

'Yes, please!' She threw her arms around his neck. 'Yes, please!'

# CHAPTER NINETEEN

Smith had gone away for an entire weekend. Some idea of James's apparently, an office 'team-building' exercise, completely bizarre given that the members of the small office were so vividly disparate it was obvious no amount of 'building' would ever make a team of them. But James had been sweet-talked by a charming, long-legged rep from a management consultancy and persuaded that after a weekend of 'motivational, incentivizational, inspirational deconstruction and reconstruction' not only would his odd little company somehow be transformed into a model of modern working practices but that he would also live longer, attract women and suddenly experience a regrowth of his long-absent hair.

So Smith had grumpily packed a small bag on Friday morning, and he, Diana, James, three ageing account executives, two dumpy secretaries and a bad-tempered receptionist had squeezed themselves into a rented Renault Espace and trundled up the A1 to a hotel in Hertfordshire. Jem had been heartily amused though, of course, very sympathetic and embraced him tightly as he left the flat, looking stony-faced and muttering, 'Only get one fucking weekend a week and I've got to spend it with a bunch of psychos.'

Jem had arranged to meet up with some friends at the Falcon on St John's Hill that night for someone's birthday and had gone home after work to change.

Ralph was in. He hadn't been out since he'd got back from hospital two weeks ago. He was still a bit sore, especially around the ribs, and it hurt like buggery when he laughed, but his doctor was pleased with his progress – he was young and strong and healing well.

Jem joined him on the sofa with a can of lager. Ralph had looked at her, a strange smile hovering about his lips. 'What is it?' asked Jem.

Ralph kept smiling. 'Guess what?'

'What?'

'I've done it!'

'Done what?'

'I've been a good boy,' he beamed. 'I'm sorting my life out.'

'Oh, yeah? Meaning what?'

'Meaning I've finished with Claudia,' he said smugly.

'What!' she shrieked. 'What do you mean, you've "finished with Claudia"?'

'Well, what do you think I mean? I've finished with Claudia, simple as that.'

'Good God. I don't believe it! Let's get this straight. You saw Claudia – Claudia with the legs, Claudia with the face of an angel, Claudia who lets you have sex with her – you saw her, and you said, "I'm sorry, it's over, I don't think we should see each other any more," just like that?!'

'That's right,' he replied, his arms folded across his chest, grinning indulgently.

'Not "It's over but can we still have the odd shag for old time's sake?"'

He shook his head.

'Not "It's over but do you mind if I sleep with your best friend?"'

He shook his head again.

She'd thrown her arms around him then and hugged him quickly.

'Bloody hell, Ralph. I'm so proud of you! How did she take it?'

'Oh, typically Claudia. "You would do this just before my sister's wedding, wouldn't you, you're so selfish, who am I going to go with now, all my sisters will have their boyfriends and husbands there and I'll be the sad old spinster – God I hate you!"' He finished his impersonation with a camp flounce. 'And then she cried. Wasn't expecting that, I have to say, old Clauds, crying. She tried to play it down, y'know, but I think she was really upset.'

'So what next?' Jem asked. 'How are you going to control your sexual urges? What are you going to do on Friday nights? Who's going to be your next girlfriend?'

'What makes you think there has to be a next girlfriend? No, I think I'm going to steer clear for a while, "find some time for myself."' He said this in a cheesy American-therapist voice. 'I haven't been single since I was, since I was . . . ever. I've never, ever been single – I think it'll do me some good. And I reckon I can live without sex for a while, a little while anyway. I've got my sources if I get desperate, I've got my Little Black Psion Organizer!'

'Well,' said Jem, moving to get up, 'it's a start, it's a very good start. Well done. Now we've just got to find you someone to fall in love with . . .'

A strange mood fell across them both briefly at that moment, and for a second they sat, suspended. Ralph noted the fleeting tension with some satisfaction. He had realized that Jem thought he was a little sad, going out with a girl he didn't care about purely for the sex, and so he was putting a new plan into operation: Operation Mature and Available. His decision to chuck Claudia hadn't been entirely rational and prescient. It had been hard for him lately, spending time with Claudia, wishing she were more like Jem, everything she did and said irritating him with its cloying girlishness and irrational female 'logic'.

But mainly he'd finished the relationship because Jem wanted him to, because Jem would think more of him if he did and because, more than anything right now, he wanted Jem's respect. He'd done a lot of thinking since the accident and understood that there was no point in mooning around after Jem, trying to impress her with his choice of flowers or the latest vindaloo. Jem was twenty-seven years old, the age when a woman, consciously or not, starts to look for different qualities in a man, an age when charisma alone is not quite enough to clinch the deal, when a healthy bank balance, a solid future and a practical nature become just as attractive as a trendy haircut, a wacky sense of humour and the romantic allure of a failed artist.

That was another reason she'd chosen Smith, and he didn't blame her really, he'd always been quite taken with the thought of being supported by a rich woman and could see no reason why Jem should be beyond the allure of a man in a position to keep up the mortgage payments and pay for Baby Gap clothes in the event of a maternity break, a man you could seriously envisage making a good impression at a Parent–Teacher meeting, a man who would have no qualms about assembling a set of bookshelves, a man with AA membership. So, there was no point in getting all bitter and resentful about Smith and his seemingly obscene good luck. He just needed to rise to the level of the competition. Surely a girl would rather a fabulously successful artist type than a fabulously successful banker type.

He'd been in touch with his 'mentor', Philippe, who had unexpectedly been pleasantly surprised to hear from him after so many months. They'd discussed the future, the market, the prevailing stars, his past work, his state of mind, and Ralph had left feeling nicely needed and worth while and itching to get the cast off his wrist so he could start painting again. He'd made another, less eventful trip to his studio and pottered around for a while, clearing out the cobwebs and rat droppings, throwing out dead-bristled brushes and dried-up tubes of paint, familiarizing himself with the draughty old shit-hole.

Less is more, he'd decided, and he'd backed off from Jem in the two weeks since his accident, spending more time with his friends, even when he knew that Jem was going to be on her own in the flat, deliberately forgetting about the chilli plants in the airing cupboard, dispensing with the constant flower-buying and compliments. And the more he backed off, he'd been gratified to note, the more she came to him. Part of that was to do with guilt, he realized that. She still blamed herself for the bike accident and fussed around him like a delightful little hen, making sure he was comfortable, fetching him things from the kitchen, cooking for him. But she was missing the rapport they'd developed, it was obvious – she'd talk to him about the chilli plants, give him progress reports, like a sad mother to an absent father who needed reminding about the welfare of his children. She took up his flower-buying role and brought home unusual chillies she'd discovered in food halls and Asian supermarkets.

Once Ralph had established that Jem cared, truly cared, it was time to put step two of Operation Mature and Available into practice: finish with Claudia. And now this remarkable opportunity had arisen, Smith, away, for a whole weekend, two whole days. He didn't know what was going to happen but he knew something would. Definitely. He could feel it in his water.

Jem could feel something in her water, too. Ever since the day of the accident she hadn't experienced a moment's peace. She had spent the last fortnight battling with feelings she'd never encountered before. Jem had always been so solidly sensible in love, a serial monogamist, as they called them these days, two years here, a year there, all nice blokes and clean breaks.

Despite the fact that for one reason or another Jem usually ended up breaking men's hearts, it wasn't because she was cruel or unkind or had anything against men. She didn't *want* to hurt them, she just had to sometimes. She'd never been unfaithful and, as far as she knew, no one had ever been unfaithful to her. She'd never had a 'bad' relationship, just relationships that didn't work out because men wanted more than she could give. She wasn't one of those girls who was constantly attracted to the wrong sort of man, who suffered from unrequited love, who couldn't commit or who 'loved too much'. She'd never had a passionate love affair with someone, been consumed with desire. She'd never experienced irresistible lust. She'd loved, or at least been fond of everyone she'd ever been out with, and they'd loved her back. All her relationships had been strong learning experiences, passing the time until the right man came along. And now, when finally she thought the right man *had* come along, and she was happy and could see a long-term future ahead of her with Smith, she was suddenly feeling horribly attracted to someone else. To Ralph. It was utterly ridiculous. This wasn't how she operated.

Jem wasn't stupid, she could read people like books, had always been able to, and it was quite obvious that Ralph was attracted to her, too. It was touching, the way he'd been so pleased when she'd congratulated him on his choice of flowers that he'd gone out and bought them every week, and the way he was always making nice comments about her clothes, and that he was happy just to hang around the flat with her when Smith was out and chat about things which were 'their' things now, like chillies and music and recipes. She'd ignored the signs at first, put it down to vanity on her half. Why would Ralph, with his penchant for willowy, upper-class blondes, be interested in her? She was imagining it, paying herself compliments. But then there'd been that peculiar morning, the morning of the accident, and she'd found herself behaving quite outrageously by her standards. She knew he'd been titillated by the shortness of her T-shirt and she'd been conscious of the fact that she wasn't wearing any knickers; she had known, deep down, that he'd deliberately asked her to reach for items from the top cupboard so that he could look at her bottom. She'd been wickedly happy to oblige, titillated by his titillation.

She hadn't been fully aware of any of this at the time, of course. People never really are. Jem believed that very few people were as calculating as other people assumed them to be when they did something wrong.

Things *did* just happen, and it was only afterwards that you could look back and see the points at which you allowed yourself to lose control, to make the wrong decision, to behave badly. Ralph's interest in her made her feel good, and she couldn't ignore it. She'd been ashamed of herself when she'd experienced a flutter of excitement at the prospect of spending a weekend alone with him. But nothing, absolutely nothing, of any description, shape, size or form was going to happen this weekend, or ever for that matter. *Nothing. No way. Never.*

His announcement tonight about Claudia had unleashed a whole new set of unwelcome emotions. He was free, he was available. Jem had no idea why this was important, but the moment he'd told her her stomach had done a backward flip and triple pike. She was pleased because over the two and a half months she'd been living at Almanac Road she'd become very fond of Ralph and wanted him to be happy, not henpecked by a dissatisfied, uptight, walking nightmare; she was pleased that he at last appeared to be taking his life in hand. But there was also a part of her that was pleased just because he was single, because he was no longer with someone else. And then she'd made that remark about finding him someone to fall in love with, and a strange feeling had overcome her, for a second she'd felt awkward and uncomfortable. Stupid, really. After all, she wasn't in love with him, she was just day-dreaming; she was in love with Smith and that was that. She was flattered by Ralph, fond of him, cared about him. But she was *not* in love with him. And he was not in love with her.

'What are you doing tonight?' she asked him abruptly, to diffuse the peculiar mood that had descended on her.

'Your first night of freedom,' she added, finally getting to her feet.

'Not a lot,' he replied. 'I was going to stay in and do a bit of sketching, now that my wrist's stopped hurting so much.'

Jem looked down at his bandaged wrist and started laughing.

'What's so funny?!' asked Ralph, laughing too.

'I just thought of something.'

'What?' said Ralph, smiling widely.

'I just thought, you sure chose a bad time to finish with Claudia! No sex and now no wanking! You're going to get pretty frustrated!'

Ralph looked down at his impotent right hand as well, and a look of dismay came over his face. 'Shit,' he muttered, 'I hadn't thought of that. Supposed to be good for you, though, isn't it?' he added, brightening. 'A bit of abstinence, holding on to your seed. Good for the mind and soul. Still . . . shit . . .'

Jem continued to laugh at the look on Ralph's face. 'Looks like it's the old hoover attachment for you, then,' she cackled, slapping her thighs with her hands.

Ralph winced.

'Come out with us tonight, Ralph, we're only going up the Falcon. Come on, it'll take your mind off your predicament!'

'Who's "we"?'

'Oh, just some friends. It's Becky's birthday, it'll probably be quite a big group.'

Ralph quickly weighed up the pros and cons: night in alone *v.* night out with Jem. 'OK. When do we have to be there?'

*

Ralph rolled a spliff for the walk, using some grass he'd just acquired from a friend of a friend.

'I don't know what this is like,' he said, pinching it out of the bag between his fingertips, 'but it was fucking expensive and it smells amazing.'

'Looks like skunk,' said Jem. 'Go easy on it.'

'Nah,' said Ralph, smiling wickedly and piling it on to the Rizlas with the abandon of a man who has a brand-new bag of weed.

They took the spliff and a can of lager, wrapped themselves up in as many clothes as possible and began the freezing walk down St John's Road, smoking as they walked. Half-way down they both suddenly realized that they were completely stoned.

'Shit,' said Jem, 'I'm wasted.'

'Me, too,' agreed Ralph. 'That's completely taken me out.'

'I told you to go easy on it!'

St John's Road was empty and gaudy, brash chain stores twinkling with fairy lights and sale banners, the occasional group of revellers passing them drunkenly in swaying bands. It was the last weekend before Christmas.

They walked up to the traffic lights giggling at their predicament, quickly finishing the lager, finding a bin for the empty can. St John's Hill was busier, chilly commuters still pouring out of Clapham Junction station clutching Blockbuster Video cases and hoping they weren't too late to make it to Marks and Spencers. They crossed the road and pushed open the door to the Falcon and were greeted by a blast of warmth and Oasis and loud male talk, accented by the occasional shard of female laughter. The huge U-shaped pub, replete with traditional Victorian fixtures and fittings, was packed, and they had to push their way to the bar.

'I'll get these,' said Jem. 'What do you want?'

She stood on the foot rail to gain a few inches and leant into the bar, years of experience teaching her that this was her only chance of being served at a busy bar lined with tall men, smiling at the barmaid, who was serving someone else – barmaids always served girls first.

'Two pints of Löwenbräu, please,' she shouted, when it was her turn.

They took their drinks and Ralph followed Jem while she manoeuvred her small frame through clusters of office workers in suits and skirts, circles of friends in jumpers and jeans, scanning the room for a familiar face.

Eventually, the glimmer of recognition, the raised hand, the introductions, the sea of strange faces and barrage of instantly forgotten names, the echoing question, 'Where's Smith?', the quizzical looks, the friendly handshakes, the gradual separation of the group back into the individual conversations which had been momentarily halted by their arrival.

'Jem tells me you're an artist.'

Oh, God. Ralph turned to face the architect of this dreadful opener, a lanky young man with an agreeably lop-sided face wearing a *Reservoir Dogs* T-shirt and drinking a pint of cloudy bitter that looked like it contained frog spawn.

'Um, well, sort of . . . lapsed, you could say, but trying.' He managed a snigger and looked down into his glass before taking a large gulp.

'Actually, I'm a sort of artist, too – sort of,' replied

Reservoir Dogs, unfazed by Ralph's lack of interest. 'I'm a graphic designer; Jem tells me you do a bit of that, on the old Mac.' He was grinning and wriggling with excitement as he spoke, and Ralph knew what was coming: 'You know, I think Macs are finally coming into their own . . .'

And he was off. Ralph died inside. He loved computers but he hated talking about them. And he was stoned. So stoned. It was all he could do to keep up with what Reservoir Dogs was saying, let alone think of one single response that wouldn't make him sound like he'd just landed in a time machine from the year 3000 BC. It was loud; the music was so loud, he kept asking Reservoir Dogs to repeat himself and then wondering why he'd bothered. He'd lost the ability to make eye contact. He glanced across at Jem every now and then, and she would glance back from the conversation she was conducting with an unattractive girl with a squandered bosom, and he could tell that she was having a hard time too. He smiled, he chuckled, if the intonation of Reservoir Dogs's voice suggested that that was appropriate, he nodded agreement, he shook his head with disapproval, he said 'Yeah, I know' a lot. But he didn't have the first idea what the man was talking about and he didn't care. He had to get away, this was a nightmare. He finished his pint; he'd only had it for ten minutes.

'Can I get you a drink?' he asked, affecting an angled glass with his empty hand in case his voice got lost in the atmosphere.

'Yeah – thanks. I'll have a pint of Parson's Codpiece please.'

Ralph made his way gratefully to the bar. This was such a bad idea. Why had he loaded that spliff? He was a paranoid, twitching, nervous wreck. The vibrant pub was electric with colours and movement and noise. He felt like he was walking on a moving carousel and everyone, but everyone was looking at him. He wanted to go home.

'How you doing?'

He turned around. Oh, thank God. It was Jem. 'I'm completely fucked, I can't cope. Who *is* that bloke? He's so weird.'

'What – Gordy?! He's not weird, he's lovely – that's just you being stoned.'

'How are you doing?'

'Oh, I'm fucked too. I've been trying to talk to Becky but I've got no idea what she's talking about, and I can't take my eyes off her tits.'

'I don't blame you – better than looking at her face!'

Jem hit him with mock indignation and then laughed.

'Listen, Jem, d'you mind if I go after these drinks? This really is not a good night for me to meet a bunch of new people.'

'This is not even a good night to be with a group of really close friends. I'll come with you.'

They took their drinks back to the crowd. Gordy slapped Ralph on the back: 'Thanks mate, nice one.' They had strange disjointed conversations with people with overexpressive faces and booming voices, concentrating hard to keep up, losing the thread, worried that they had HOPELESSLY STONED written all over their blank, uncomprehending faces. They finished their beers, made their excuses, pushed their way back through the crowd, '*Mega Mega White Thing*,' clouds of smoke, faces, backs, voices, shouting 'Excuse me, please, excuse me,' '*Lager Lager Lager,*' until they reached the doors, opened them and, as the last few bars of Underworld died away, emerged into the cool, beautiful, empty silence.

'Aaaaaaaaah!' they both exhaled in unison.

'Nightmare,' said Ralph.

'Shit,' said Jem, adjusting her furry wrap and putting on her gloves. 'OK, I need to be somewhere very quiet and very mellow where I don't have to talk to anyone I don't know . . .'

'Shall we go home?' asked Ralph, blowing coils of steamy breath into his hands.

'No, come on, let's turn this to our advantage. Let's go into town and have a really weird time. Let's pretend to be German tourists and go to all those places we don't normally touch with a bargepole. Come on. Look! There's a number 19: it's an omen, quick!' She grabbed his hand and they ran towards the bus stop on Falcon Road. They leapt on to the platform just as it began to pull away.

# CHAPTER TWENTY

They started in Piccadilly Circus, and for the first time in their lives they sat with the tourists under Eros. A duo of African drummers provided a suitably irregular soundtrack as they sat and watched the lights of Piccadilly from, they both agreed, a far superior vantage point to the more well-trodden areas. They wandered in zombie-like awe around the Trocadero, blinking at the harsh illumination, gawping at the peculiar array of shops. They took a ride on the Emaginator and screamed themselves hoarse as they careered down bottomless pits and around blind corners at a million miles an hour. They walked up Gerrard Street, a street that Jem walked down every day of her life, which in her current state of mind took on the air of a film set filled with a cast of weird and wonderful extras. London was alive; it smelt of Christmas. Everywhere they went they were filled with wonder. What a fascinating city, what an interesting shop, look at that person, look at that restaurant, those noodles look good. The world was full of colour and activity and sound and music and the most remarkable people.

They went into the Chinese supermarket and wandered up and down the aisles for ages, oohing and aahing over packets of all sorts of God Knows What. Jem's friendly Mancunian butcher was there.

'Hello, Jem,' he said.

‘Oh, hello, Pete!’ she replied. ‘Don’t you ever get a day off?’

‘Nah, I love it, don’t I? Can’t get enough of touching raw meat and playing with offal.’

He was just finishing up, they were about to close, and he only lived just up the road. He invited them back to his flat for a beer and a smoke. This evening was becoming more and more bizarre.

He lived in a flat over the Hong Kong bank. It belonged to his boss, the manager of the supermarket and, by the sound of it, most of Chinatown. Pete would not be drawn on the subject of Triads, but Jem and Ralph had reached their own conclusions. It wasn’t the smartest of flats, the stairway overwhelmed by camel high-gloss paint and tan shaggy carpets with shiny track-marks, the furniture in the high-ceilinged living room obviously expensive but sparse and tasteless.

They followed Pete down a cavernous hallway, papered with beige bamboo-design paper and lit by grimy faux-candle wall-lights. He pushed open a white plywood door at the end.

‘This is my boudoir,’ he announced proudly.

Ralph and Jem laughed out loud. The room was huge, three large sash windows framing the bright lights of Gerrard Street outside, the changing colours bouncing off the mirrored walls and ceiling. But it was the bed that had really made them laugh. It was at least eight foot square and topped by an enormous arched bedhead which looked like the console on the *Starship Enterprise*, with flashing white lights and an abundance of knobs and switches.

‘Shit,’ said Ralph, ‘have you got a licence for that thing?’

'Wild, isn't it?' laughed Pete. 'D'you fancy a ride?'

Ralph and Jem looked at each other. It had suddenly occurred to them that they were in a strange butcher's flat late on a Friday night and he was getting undressed and inviting them on to his potentially perverted bed.

Pete sensed their unease. 'It's not mine, you know,' he smiled, 'it's my boss's. This is his Shag Palace, like – it's where he brings his birds. Come on. I'm totally sound. I promise ya. It's just a laugh.'

He leapt on to the bed and it wobbled like a fat girl's stomach.

'It's a water-bed!' Jem shrieked with delight. 'I've always wanted to go on a water-bed!'

'Well, now's your chance – get your shoes off.'

She threw her shoes aside, joined him on the bed and began to bounce around a little. 'Come on, Ralph,' she called, 'this is fun! Get on.'

Ralph still wasn't sure. He was feeling less stoned than earlier but he was still nervous, a bit edgy. Maybe there was a gang of twisted psychotic fetishists hiding in the mirrored wardrobes that lined the walls. Maybe this Pete guy regularly brought gullible strangers back to his sick flat so that he and his mates could have a bit of fun. Maybe they were Triads. Maybe it was part of the deal for living in his boss's flat. He scanned the room for video cameras, shackles, handcuffs, lengths of rope, torture implements. All he could see was a thousand reflections of the strange tableau of him and Jem and the butcher and a kaleidoscope of coloured lights. He was totally weirded out.

'Um, nah. I'm all right, thanks,' he muttered, shoving his hands into his coat pockets and stepping nervously from one foot to the other.

'Suit yourself,' said the butcher.

'What do all these buttons do?' asked Jem.

He smiled and hit a knob. The bed started to vibrate. He hit another one. The bed undulated like a belly dancer. He flicked a switch and the lights started to flash and the bed began to play music. A tray popped out of the flush console bearing a gold pot of cigarettes, an inbuilt lighter and an ashtray. Another panel opened to reveal a shelf of miniature gin bottles and two tumblers.

'This is the best one, though,' said Pete, fiddling with a joystick.

With a gentle hydraulic hum, the bed lifted itself a few inches off the ground and slowly turned on its axis through 180 degrees until it faced the other way.

'Wow!' laughed Jem.

'Isn't it great!' agreed Pete 'And this is *my* secret compartment.' Another panel lifted to reveal a small wooden box. He brought it out, opened it and gave it to Jem. It was a stash box full of Rizlas and cardboard and a large lump of black. 'Help yourself. I'm going to have a quick wash and a shave – I'm going out later. Make yourselves at home on the bed and I'll be back in a mo.'

He closed the door behind him and Jem peered around the bedhead at Ralph, who was still standing on the same spot.

'You all right?' she asked.

'No, actually I'm totally freaked. What are we doing here? This is really dangerous, you know – he could be anyone. There could be anyone here.' He moved across the room and began to open and close the mirrored doors.

'What on earth are you doing, Ralph?' asked Jem, getting off the bed and walking towards him.

'I'm just checking, that's all,' he replied, a little embarrassed by his own paranoid behaviour.

Jem crossed her arms and looked at him, smiling fondly.

'What?' he demanded gruffly. 'What are you smiling at?'

'You.'

'Why?'

'Because you're sweet.'

'Oh, stop it.' But a small smile had started twitching at the edge of his lips.

'Come here,' she held out her arms, still smiling.

Ralph's stomach flipped. She wanted to give him a hug! He moved shyly towards her, his smile now almost fully formed. She was tiny in her bare feet. Her hair was falling down. Radiohead played 'Creep' quietly in the background. The lights on the bedhead flickered in rhythm. The room was dark but alive with light and colour. It seemed to spin around them. He would never forget this moment.

He wrapped his arms around Jem's neck. He wanted to say something but he didn't want to talk. She wrapped her arms around his waist. They squeezed each other tightly. She stood on her tiptoes and buried her head in his chest. It was the best hug of Ralph's life. The moment was magical, enchanted. She smelt like happiness. She felt like happiness. If only, if only she was free, free to lift her head up and offer him her ripe, red sweet mouth . . .

'Ralph . . .'

'Um?'

'D'you remember that morning, the morning of the accident?'

'Uh-hum.'

'When we were in the kitchen and I was going to tell you something?'

They separated and held each other's hands.

'Yes.' Finally. He had known it would only be a matter of time before she remembered that unfinished business.

'Well, I just wanted to say . . .'

'Yes.'

'I just wanted to say that I think you're very special . . .'

*So fucking special.*

'. . . and that I'm very, very glad to know you and that . . . that . . . well, whoever you finally fall in love with is going to be a very lucky girl. I really enjoy being with you and I feel very close to you – very close. I hope you feel the same way.'

Ralph smiled and squeezed Jem's hands. 'Oh, God, oh, yes, I really do. Really, really. I . . . I . . . I . . .' Was it the moment? Was this the time to come clean, to tell Jem that he was hopelessly in love with her? 'I . . . I . . .'

'What?' urged Jem. 'Spit it out!'

He exhaled. 'Nothing – nothing. I'm very glad to know you, too, that's all. I think you're extremely special, too. Smith's a very lucky bloke.' He laughed nervously. No, it wasn't the right moment. Not yet.

Jem kissed him on the cheek and leapt on to the bed again. 'Come on!' she grinned, 'chill out. This is one of life's great surreal experiences – don't miss out on it!'

He smiled, finally relenting to the spirit of the night, unlaced his shoes and joined her on the bed.

'It's your fault if we get gang-raped and hacked to

pieces by twenty-two Triads with machetes and stainless-steel dildos, though.'

Jem made them a spliff and they sat on the gently bobbing bed watching Chinatown from the window, feeling like they were on the deck of a huge white yacht moored in the middle of Soho. Pete came back into the room with a handful of lagers and they passed him the spliff.

'What a place to live,' said Jem, cracking open her can. 'Something to tell your grandchildren about.'

'Too right,' he said, inhaling. 'But it's got its drawbacks. I have to be out of here in seconds if the man wants to bring a whore back. And then I have to change the sheets afterwards. And if I want to chuck in the job – bang goes the flat. But you're right, it's a real experience.' He wandered towards one of the wardrobes, rustled around for a few moments and came back clutching hangers.

They watched him slip into a pair of flat-fronted purple jacquard trousers, a silk lilac-patterned shirt with a monstrous collar and enormous flapping double cuffs, a fat orange satin tie and a black frock-coat with preposterous lapels.

'So,' he said, giving them a twirl, 'whaddaya think? Cool or what?'

'Incredible,' said Jem, stunned by the transformation. He looked amazing. He looked like a pop star. 'You look amazing,' she said, 'you look like a pop star.'

'Thank you,' he said, smiling happily. Jem had obviously said the right thing. 'This is all vintage stuff, you know – collectors' items. I get it all from a stall at Greenwich market,' he said, clipping on enormous diamond-studded cuff-links. 'Here, do you two fancy coming out for a boogie? I'm going to Nemesis, it's just around the corner,' he added, noting the blank expressions on their faces. 'It's a really nice place, not pretentious or anything.'

Ralph and Jem looked at each other. They both knew that the other didn't really fancy it and shook their heads.

'Nah, thanks, Pete. Not really dressed for it, are we?' Jem said, looking at Ralph.

'Thanks anyway, mate,' said Ralph, who had finally satisfied himself that Pete wasn't about to make them the grizzly victims of a butchering that would have hardened Soho detectives turning green and throwing up into their hands. Psychopathic murderers just *didn't* wear silk lilac shirts and diamond cuff-links.

Pete stood at the mirror, adjusted his sideburns, tweaked his hair and straightened his cuffs. He offered them his flat for the night as he wouldn't be back till mid-morning. When they declined, he insisted they take a spliff for the road and a couple more beers.

'Any time,' he said, 'any time you're round here, just come and see me at the supermarket or this place, and we can go out for a drink next time.'

'Do you always let strangers into your flat?' asked Ralph.

Pete snorted. 'Of course, mate. There's no adventure in life if you don't trust people, is there? No experiences. I work hard, I play hard, and if I die tomorrow, at least it would be better than ending up like me dad. Hates change, complains if they alter the layout in Tesco's or if *Countdown* starts five minutes late. Doesn't trust anyone, thinks everyone's out to get him. He's never been to London, let alone out the country. How I see it is like this: Some people have like, a travel-bug thing, don't they? Want to go to Thailand and Africa and have adventures and wear shit clothes and carry all their stuff around in a fucking great bag on their back.' He shook his head and grimaced. 'Not me. I can have all the adventures I want right here. You've just got to have the right attitude. Look where we are – the greatest city in the world . . . all the people in the world are right here. Poor people living in dog-shit and second-hand clothes, rich people driving cars that cost as much as houses, artists, bankers, models, drug dealers, the ugliest people in the world, the most beautiful people in the world, Cambodians, Swedes, Nicaraguans, Israelis, Ghanaians, Portuguese. Go to Stamford Hill and look at the Hassidic Jews there, that's an adventure. Rich Americans in St John's Wood, or South Kensington. Japanese in Finchley Central. Arabs on the Edgware Road. Irish in Kilburn. Greek Cypriots in Finsbury Park. Turks in Turnpike Lane. Portuguese in Westbourne Park. And then here, Chinatown, noisier, ruder, more bad-tempered bunch of people I've never met before. But I love it. I'm open to anything that comes along in this city.

'Ninety-nine per cent of the people in this city wander around in a little bubble. Like you, Jem. I see you at least twice a week and we have a little chat, and I can tell you're a really nice girl and that you've got a bit of spirit, like, a bit of adventure, but you were still too scared to take it any further, weren't you? We'd reached our little London point of contact, you were comfortable with that and if it hadn't been for tonight we would have gone on like that for eternity.

'Nah – life's too short to live in Beckenham and lock

your door every night when you get off the six-fifteen, not to let strangers into your flat. See you two, tonight, I bet you never thought you'd end up on an eight-foot water-bed watching some butcher getting tarted up for the night. I bet you're glad you did though, arntcha?' He laughed.

'Ever seen that film *After Hours* about that straight guy who follows Rosanna Arquette into downtown New York and ends up stranded in the middle of the night with no money and meets all these weirdos and freaks? Now, some people might have watched that film and thought, Oh, God, what a nightmare, I hope nothing like that ever happens to me. Not me. That's what I want my life to be like, every day – *After Hours*. I always think of it like this: You're walking down the street and you pass a phone booth. The phone's ringing. Now, there are two kinds of people, people who think, Don't want to get involved, and walk on by, and people who are curious, nosy, and want to answer it. Chances are it's a wrong number. But there's always a chance you could be getting involved in some mysterious rendezvous, a lover's tryst, anything. A phone ringing on the street – it could be anything. It could be the start of a film, like, or a book' – he paused for effect – 'I love it!' He looked at his watch and slapped his thighs. 'Anyway, enough of me philosophizing, I've got some partying to do.'

They followed him down the dreary stairwell and back into the bright, multicoloured mayhem of Chinatown.

'If I don't see you before, Happy Christmas and all that – have a good one,' said Pete, shivering a little in the icy midnight air.

He gave Jem a kiss on the cheek. He leant into Ralph's ear as they shook hands.

'Lucky man, Ralph,' he whispered, 'very lucky man.'

Ralph almost corrected him, almost said, 'Oh no, she's not my girlfriend,' but stopped himself. He wanted Pete to think he was a lucky man; he wanted Pete to think he had something special.

And then he went. Jem and Ralph stood where they were, not quite sure what to do next that wouldn't feel like an anticlimax after their rather peculiar experience and Pete's closing inspirational philosophy.

'Gosh,' said Jem.

'Indeed,' said Ralph.

'Food, then?' said Jem.

'Guess so,' said Ralph.

Jem's face suddenly lit up with a wicked smile. 'Come on,' she grabbed his hand, 'can we just do something before we eat – there's something I've always wanted to do.'

Ralph shrugged, smiled and followed her.

# CHAPTER TWENTY-ONE

A fat Mexican in a sombrero played panpipes by the pagoda phone boxes, watched and appreciated by no one. Restaurants closed down for the night, scrawny men in grubby overalls wheeled large bins of leftovers into the street. Two drunk transvestites in feather boas and Baby Jane make-up passed them noisily and disappeared into a bar above the Chinese barbers' with red velvet curtains at the window and fairy lights around the door. A couple stood outside the Dive Bar lost in a neverending kiss.

They crossed Shaftesbury Avenue, weaving through the perpetual traffic jam and crowds of coated, scarved and hatted people.

'Where're we going?' asked Ralph.

'Just you wait!' smirked Jem.

They turned left from Greek Street into Old Compton Street, Ralph peering as inconspicuously as possible into the steamed windows of chrome-and-glass gay bars, into a world he had no place in, an exclusive world. Funny, he thought, how the word 'exclusive' had come to mean chic, fashionable, private, select, when what it really meant was that you weren't allowed in, you were excluded. It was quite a horrible word really.

Right and left into Brewer Street.

'Here,' said Jem, stopping outside a darkened shop with beaded curtains at the doorway and an amateur window display filled with sun-bleached packaging and nasty nylon underwear. A sign in the window proclaimed WE SELL POPPERS. A grotesque mannequin with chipped skin like a horrific burns victim sported a leather basque and brandished a whip in arthritic fingers. Unfeasible dildos stood side by side on a shelf, like suspects in a police line-up.

'Here?' asked Ralph, his voice betraying a little middle-class disapproval. 'What for?'

'Just for the hell of it, of course, I've never been in a sex shop before.' She was excited, a bit nervous. 'Come on,' she urged.

They entered the shop together, trying to look blasé, as if they often browsed around Soho sex shops on a Friday night. An Amazonian woman with backcombed black nylon hair down to her thighs, wearing more black eyeliner than the average woman would apply in a lifetime and a tight leather dress that must have required the removal of at least a couple of ribs glanced up at them with a look of practised disinterest and then continued to read the vintage comic she had spread open on the counter in front of her. Her skin was a dead, matt white which appeared to have been sprayed on with an aerosol can. She looked like she might have fangs.

A large black guy in a T-shirt and jeans stood silently by the door, his hands clasped in front of him, his legs a couple of feet apart. Security. At the far end of the shop an unlikely couple browsed through a rail of French-maid outfits and Miss Whiplash leather ensembles. She was tall, young, perfectly blonde, expensively dressed; she would have looked fantastic on a large black horse in a pair of jodhpurs and a hairnet.

He was small, old, powerfully bald, expensively dressed; he would have looked intimidating at the head of a huge corporate boardroom table. Maybe not such an unlikely couple. They'd done this before. There was no humour between them as they quietly discussed the preposterous pieces of shoddy nylon and PVC which hung like oversized dolls' clothes from cheap plastic hangers – this was a business transaction. What were they? Boss and secretary, client and high-class whore, husband and second wife? Maybe she was his daughter's best friend at boarding school? Another couple stood and examined the video racks. He was fat and unkempt. So was she. Again no humour. They might have been browsing through the reference section of the local library.

The shop was silent, there was no music, no television, just the reverent, businesslike hum of muted embarrassment. This was not what Jem had expected.

She wandered towards the video display and the fat couple moved a little to the left to give her some space. She picked up a box. A shocked-looking peroxide blonde with a mouth like a vagina squeezed her dome-like breasts together while a faceless, torsoless, armless man pinned beneath her penetrated her anally and another man who appeared to have only a two-foot penis and a fabulous head of hair impaled her from the front. No wonder she looked shocked. Jem put the box down. She surveyed the display of extraordinary leather and chrome bondage accessories that hung from the ceiling like carcasses in a butcher's window. Masks, hoods, cuffs, straps, whips and chains, implements for hanging someone from the ceiling, tying them to the bed, gagging them, constraining them, contorting them, whipping them. An all-in-one, head-to-toe PVC bodysuit with a barely sufficient mouth-slit straddled the wall. It looked uncomfortable, sweaty.

Jem walked towards Ralph, who was flicking through a magazine filled with badly photographed images of men and women looking uncomfortable and sweaty in similar erotic garb.

'I'm going to buy a vibrator,' she whispered to him, cupping his ear with her hand.

'What?!' he exclaimed, almost silently.

The vibrators were located in the glass-fronted cabinet which served as a counter to the vampire woman with the comic. Jem felt a little uncomfortable as she eyed the selection, trying to look expert, trying not to look self-conscious under the stagnant aura of the bizarre shop assistant. She wasn't sure what she was looking for. Did she want a sixteen-inch shiny black one or a discreet, cream, handbag-sized model? She beckoned to Ralph, who put back his copy of *House of Correction* monthly and crouched down next to her in front of the cabinet.

'What d'you think?' she whispered.

Ralph shrugged. He felt like the unwilling boyfriend in a clothes shop on a Saturday afternoon. This was girl's stuff – how was he supposed to know? He was feeling awkward. He'd been inside a sex shop before, of course he had. With his mates, when he was younger, for a laugh, to buy poppers, leer over dirty magazines. But this was different, very different. Now his head was full of images – Jem on her unmade bed, lying on her Chinese-dragon dressing-gown, her knickers around her ankles, her skirt hitched up, knees apart, applying her new vibrator to herself. Oh, God, it was fantastic. But he didn't want to think those things about her; as erotic and exciting as the image was, he didn't want it in his head. He wanted the hug in Pete's bedroom in his head. He wanted the subtly erotic image of Jem's bare toes smeared with mustard in his head, the barely there glimpse of her soft white bottom. He wanted her face, open, smiling, bright and joyful. He wanted to imagine them together, in the future, in love, laughing, making love, taking their dog for a walk.

He looked down at her smiling face, the tip of her nose pink and pinched, her eyes looking brightly and fondly at him, and the unwanted image disappeared. This was Jem, gorgeous, lovely, wonderful, angelic Jem. He didn't want to be like Smith. He didn't want to be a fusty old stick-in-the-mud. She was asking him to be open-minded, to go with the flow. He smiled and turned to eye the display.

'I mean, I don't suppose it really matters how big it is, as long as it vibrates – unless you want to stick it inside you, of course,' he offered helpfully.

'That's true,' whispered Jem thoughtfully. 'I don't think I want a black one, or one with veins. They're a bit vulgar, aren't they?'

'Yeah,' agreed Ralph. 'I think you should just go for a cheapo one. There's no point in spending a lot of money.'

'Hmm. What about attachments?' she asked, gesturing to the pop-up tongues, cactus-like probosces, alien plastic fingers and fierce nodulated rubber balls.

'Nah,' said Ralph, warming to the subject now that he was no longer embarrassed, 'just gimmicks, waste of money. That's a good one,' he said, pointing to an innocuous slim cream model with no veins, helmet, tongue, balls or inadequate pulsing movement, 'and it's only £7.99. I'd go for that one.'

'OK,' said Jem, getting to her feet, wishing suddenly that they were available in boxes on shelves, like in a supermarket, so she wouldn't have to ask the frightening androidal creature above her to get her one. She took a deep breath and forced herself to be brave. This was like having a smear test. Unpleasant for the recipient but all in a day's work for the administerer. Old Morticia must have seen all sorts – a nice middle-class girl buying an inoffensive vibrator on a Friday night would be nothing to her. The girl looked like she'd had a frontal lobotomy anyway.

'Can I have one of those, please?' she asked, as confidently as she could in such a low voice.

Morticia leant down to see where Jem was pointing, unlocked a cabinet behind her, took out a box, opened it, showed the contents to Jem, waited for her to nod approval, put it back in the box, put the box in a white plastic bag, took the ten-pound note from Jem's hand, handed her two pounds and a penny and a receipt and carried on reading her comic. The whole transaction took place in deathly silence.

'Thank you very much,' said Jem, reeling as she heard her nice home counties voice and good manners resonate inappropriately around the hushed shop.

The black security guard remained waxwork-still as they passed him at the door. Ralph held back the clacking beads for Jem and they stepped out into the street, relieved that it hadn't suddenly turned into a strange, uninhabited ghost town, that there were still normal-looking people milling around the streets, queuing for night-clubs, waiting on corners for non-existent cabs to take them home.

They walked back towards Lisle Street and enjoyed

an MSG-rich meal of crispy beef and chilli, chicken in chilli-and-black-bean sauce and Kung Po chilli pork in a near-empty restaurant, under the watchful gaze of a bored young waitress who had appeared thoroughly confused by their request for their food to be 'extra spicy' and was now observing them curiously for signs of spontaneous combustion or insanity while they chatted about Pete and the sex shop and their strange evening.

'What Pete said just now, before we left – it really made me think you know,' Jem said, pouring the remains of a Tsingtao lager into her glass, 'about adventure, and trusting people and everything. He's right, you know. I like to think of myself as a bit of a "free spirit"' – she fashioned the quote marks out of the air with her fingers – 'I like to think I'm up for anything, open to adventure. But Pete was right. Everyone in this city is scared, aren't they? There are lots of weirdos out there, but I don't suppose many of them are likely to kill you or kidnap you, are they?

'It's like, d'you ever walk past people in a train station, say, or walking down the street, a group of friends meeting up, talking about their other friends – "Oh, how's so and so?" – talking about their lives, and you can tell they're quite close, known each other for a while, shared experiences? D'you ever get a twinge like maybe you're missing out on something? Like, how come their paths crossed and ours didn't, maybe they're great people but I'll never get to know them? I'm just a stranger on the street to them, I've got my own friends, my own shared experiences with other people who *they'll* never know. And it just seems sort of sad. D'you know what I mean? So many people in this world and the law of averages says that you can only ever get to know such a tiny percentage of them. And fear means that you'll get to know even less. Why are we so scared of each other? Someone at work invites you over for dinner and you're filled with horror, you bump into an old friend on the train, they suggest going out for a drink, you swap numbers and then pray they won't call you, you've got your nice safe circle of friends, your Tuesday friend, your Thursday friend, your weekend friends, you've got your night in on a Monday, your gym night on a Wednesday, and all of a sudden you haven't got any room left for anyone new. Is that what God intended? Is that right? Surely we're all living point nought nought nought nought one per cent of our potential lives. I'm only twenty-seven – what am I going to be like when I'm fifty? Don't you think it's sad?'

'I think you're being a little rose-tinted about the whole issue, to be honest, Jem. Friends are an investment, they're not always easy. It's not always fun and laughter and super shared experiences. Friends have needs, problems, demands, insecurities, expectations, and in order to be a good friend you have to at least try to satisfy all of those things as well as enjoying the good times. I just don't think it's possible to offer that sort of relationship to everyone you pass on the street. I think we're forced to be selective, to take just a couple of chocolates out of the box and leave a few strawberry creams and hazelnut whirls for someone else.'

'Ah,' said Jem, enjoying Ralph's analogy, 'but who gets the montelimar?'

Ralph smiled. 'I think the montelimars end up working in Soho sex shops and going home to an empty flat covered in bat droppings.' He picked up the bill that the eagle-eyed waitress had prematurely planted on their table.

'Yeah, I suppose I'm being a little idealistic. Friends can be a pain. They can be demanding and hard work. But maybe that's because they're the wrong friends. I read a quote once, can't remember who by, but they said that your friends aren't necessarily the people you like the best, they're just the people who got there first. You spend your whole life searching for the right partner but maybe you settle for your friends too soon and then just make do for the rest of your life, never knowing what you're missing out on. Oh, I don't know,' she sighed, resting her head on her hands and smiling at Ralph across the table, 'maybe I'm talking complete crap. I just feel . . . Pete's just made me feel like I'm missing out, like I'm not living properly. I'm grieving for all the strangers I've never known!' She turned the bill around on its saucer to have a look at the total.

'Pete's one in a million,' said Ralph, 'it just isn't possible for everyone to be like that. We really would be in trouble if they were – human nature couldn't support that level of openness, there's too many of us, we're not equipped for it. We've evolved like this for a reason: survival, the most basic of all human instincts, adapted to living in a city with eight million other people. It makes sense.' Ralph peeled a ten-pound note from his wallet.

'I guess I've just always been the sort of person that can't bear to feel they're missing out on anything. If I've got a choice of two parties to go to I'm always convinced I've chosen the naff one and the one I missed is going to be the party that people will be talking about for years to come. Grass is always greener sort of thing . . .'

She stopped abruptly and they looked at each other. There was a moment's silence. Jem stopped fiddling with her napkin.

'Does that apply to your relationships, too?' asked Ralph, semi-flirtatiously, semi-seriously.

'Not usually,' Jem said, looking down at her hands and examining them nervously.

'Not usually?' Ralph stared at the top of her head. 'So, sometimes?'

The atmosphere was suddenly deliciously awkward.

'Yes, sometimes,' Jem lifted her head slightly and smiled behind her hand.

Ralph could feel that they were clinging on to the precipice by their fingernails – one more millimetre and they'd be there, falling. He couldn't blow it now, couldn't say the wrong thing. He took a deep breath and waited to see if she'd say anything more. She didn't. They stared at each other, breathlessly, across the table. She opened her mouth, lowered her eyes. Ralph's heart stopped beating. Still she didn't say anything. His turn.

'When?' he asked gently. Jump, Jem, he thought, I'll catch you. It'll be fine. Just jump, please, let go . . .

Jem pleated her napkin into a fan. 'Oh, just sometimes – not usually.'

'So, you have felt that the grass was greener while you were in a relationship? Was it? Greener?'

The waitress removed their bill and two ten-pound notes without either one of them noticing.

Jem shrugged and carried on pleating. 'I don't know.'

'You never found out?' Ralph was fishing.

Jem stopped pleating and looked up at him.

'No,' she said, 'I haven't found out. Shall we go?' She got up abruptly from her seat, which lost its footing and fell backwards. She flustered and tried to pick it up but got her bag tangled on the table leg. Ralph helped her untangle herself and straighten the chair. They stood inches from each other. Jem awkwardly adjusted the strap of her bag on her shoulder. She looked up at Ralph. He was gazing at her with an intensity that made her glance away immediately.

'Excuse me,' she said, making a pointless effort to get past him.

Ralph took her shoulders and looked into her eyes. 'You haven't yet – that's what you said. Do you think you might find out? Ever? In the future? Maybe?'

Please say yes, Jem, please, for the love of God, say yes.

'No,' she lowered her eyes, 'I don't think so. It doesn't work like that does it?'

'You mean Smith?' said Ralph.

'No, I don't mean Smith. We're not talking about Smith, are we? We're talking hypothetically here.'

'Oh, right – I see,' Ralph felt himself shrinking. 'Cross wires!' He attempted a small laugh. Fucking Smith. 'Guess we'd better go. Let's see if we can find a cab.'

Neither of them had allowed the atmosphere to linger. The conversation, as blatant, as explicit as it had seemed at the time, seemed more and more ambiguous as it receded into memory.

They took a deft U-turn in the conversation as they sat in the back of the heated cab and watched early-hours London flash by in a multicoloured series of twinkling vignettes. By the time they got home they were friends again. But it was a rather poor patch-up job, a temporary fix, because they both knew deep inside that they hadn't imagined the conversation – there were no cross wires.

*

Ralph lay in bed that night, flat on his back, his duvet up to his chin, his hands clasped together underneath on his chest, staring at the ceiling. He was tired but he didn't want to close his eyes. If he did his head would fill with images, images that hurt too much now. Images of a parallel universe in which he had brought home the peonies, had made more of an effort, hadn't gone to bed first on that fateful evening, had taken more care over his career, his destiny, a parallel universe in which Jem had made the right decision, had chosen him. Tonight had been one of the best nights of his life. He'd never had such fun with a girl before, never had such adventures. The whole night had been like a film – magical, surreal, wonderful. And he was more in love with Jem than ever before.

A tear formed, he blinked and it ran down the side of his nose. She'd said no, it wasn't going to happen. He'd never felt so sad in his life.

## CHAPTER TWENTY-TWO

'Morning, Jem,' chirruped Stella.

'Morning, Stella,' Jem replied.

'New jacket?'

'No – very old jacket, actually.' Maybe Stella was finally beginning to exhaust her repertoire of compliments.

'It's lovely – it suits you. How was your weekend? How's your poor flatmate?'

'Oh, he's much better now. The bruising's gone down, his wrist's starting to heal – the doctors reckon there won't be any lasting damage.'

'Oh, good, good. That's marvellous news. My auntie Kate broke her wrist – it never healed, gave her pain for the rest of her life, she was never able to use it again, but then, she was eighty-two, I suppose, and old bones are so weak. Like my mother's hip – she broke one hip and had to have it replaced, waited three years for that operation, dreadful NHS, and then her knee went and she had to wait another two years to have that replaced, she walked like a duck after that, waddle, waddle, waddle, and . . .'

Jem's thoughts began to wander, as they did on the rare occasions that Stella talked about her own life. They wandered back to her weekend, such a strange, but wonderful weekend. It had been magic, their night in Soho. And then there'd been that big, plump moment of awkwardness in the Chinese restaurant, when they'd nearly . . . oh, God. They'd been so close to going to a place that Jem didn't want to visit. Ever.

Jem's feelings were all over the place and she suddenly found herself subconsciously making mental pro and con lists:

Smith: sweet, generous, handsome, peonies, her friends liked him, she liked his friends, good job, lots of money, nice flat, reliable, affectionate, easy to be with, man in her dream?

Ralph: sweet, generous, handsome, sexy, stacks in common, great sense of humour, easy to talk to, always in a good mood, creative, passionate, vulnerable, potential for *After Hours* living, man in her dream?

Smith: a bit restrained, tendency to moodiness, not very adventurous in bed, predictable, likes kormas, thinks girls should drink dry white wine, not creative, introverted, settled, no potential for *After Hours* living.

Ralph: unstable career (but he *was* trying), bad taste in women (but he *had* finished with Claudia), oversexed (no, she crossed that one off her mental list) . . . she racked her mind for more cons . . . longjohns (no, he didn't wear those any more) . . .

Jem shuddered slightly, trying to shake the thoughts out of her head. Stella had finished her catalogue of OAP joint-replacement stories and Jarvis, her boss, had arrived in a flurry of paper and camp complaining. 'Oh, Jemmy, darling, please, please can I relieve myself on your desk – I'm desperate,' he whined, dropping a thick folder in front of her. 'It's that repugnant Scots witch, she's in full broomstick mode – wants me to negotiate another 5 per cent for her from Carlton for that dreadful quiz show. I ask you! She's lucky anyone will hire her at all – face like a rhino's arsehole with piles. Could you, would you, Jemmy darling? I've got the hangover from Gomorrah and my back feels like Roy Castle's been tap-dancing on it all night in stilettos – thank you, thank you.' He blew her a kiss, disappeared into his office and fell asleep face down on his sofa.

Jem and Stella looked at each other and exchanged a small smile. Jem sighed and pulled open the folder. What a start to the week. She hated having to negotiate rates, especially with the people at Sin 'n' Win, who were notoriously tight with their budget. The phone saved her from having to contemplate this unpleasant job.

'Good morning, Smallhead Management,' she trilled in her silly phone-answering voice.

'Morning, Smallhead Management,' said a strange nasal voice, 'I've got quite a small head and it's a bit out of control at the moment and I was wondering if you could manage it for me. And, do you do big ears and fat ankles by any chance?'

Jem smiled and turned away from the office towards her desk.

'Ha ha ha, McLeary – funny boy, very, very funny.'

'Too quick for me, Ms Catterick, and how are you today?' He sounded terribly bouncy but just a little nervous, a slight breathlessness catching in the back of his throat.

'Not bad, not at all bad. How are you, and to what do I owe this delightful honour?' Her heart was pounding. This was Ralph, for God's sake, dear old Ralph. Why on earth was she feeling so . . . so . . . giddy?

'Oh, knackered, bored, miserable without you.' He produced a peculiar strangulated laugh that said he shouldn't have said that – that was the sort of thing you said to your girlfriend, not your flatmate, not your best mate's girlfriend.

'Not going to the studio today?' Jem replied, deliberately ignoring his last comment.

'Yeah, yeah,' he said, 'I'm here already. I've been here since nine o'clock. My fingers feel really supple today, I think I might be able to use them – give it a bash anyway.'

'That's the spirit.'

They were silent for a second, awkward, almost.

'And I just wanted to say, thank you – for the weekend – I really enjoyed myself.' Ralph cracked the silence.

'Yeah – it was good, wasn't it? I enjoyed myself too.'

'And I wondered if maybe . . .'

'Uh-huh . . .'

'. . . Well, there's this restaurant in Bayswater . . . and I know Smith's working late tonight . . . does the best jal frezi in town . . . and maybe . . . well, you're probably going out or maybe you fancy a night in, but if you fancied it we could meet up later . . . er . . .'

'Uh-huh . . .'

'It was just a thought. Nothing fancy, you know, just a curry . . . and . . . um . . .'

'OK.'

'Yeah?'

'Yeah, OK. What time?'

'Straight from work? Six-thirty maybe. I could meet you outside the Tube. Bayswater, not Queensway.'

'OK.'

'OK, then. Excellent. Well . . . have a good day and I'll, er, see you later, then.'

'Yeah, see you later. Work hard.'

'I will. You too. Bye, then.'

'Bye, then.'

'Bye.'

'Bye.'

Jem put the phone down. She needed to take a few deep breaths to bring her heartbeat back to normal human resting levels. Bloody hell. If she wasn't quite mistaken, Ralph had just asked her out on a date – and she'd accepted. This was it. The beginning of the end.

She ignored Stella's curious gaze and began fumbling through the folder on her desk.

Shit. What had she done? And why was she so bloody excited?

## CHAPTER TWENTY-THREE

The tape recorder made a hissing noise, then a whirr, then a click. The room fell silent. Siobhan jumped slightly. She lifted her hand heavily to tuck her hair behind her ear. She put her head in her hands. She stood up. She paced the room. She sat down again. The clock said eight-thirty. She stood up. She squeezed at her temples and stared at the floor. A car pulled up outside. She went to the window and threw open the curtains. It wasn't him. She looked in the mirror, adjusted her hair and wiped away the deathly streaks of mascara that had formed under her eyes from the tears she'd cried. When she was hurt. Just before she got angry. A long time before she'd started hating him.

She searched through the debris on the floor for her hairbrush, pushing pieces of broken vinyl out of the way, lifting cushions off the floor and putting them back, peering under the up-ended Christmas tree and shattered picture frames. She found it in the hallway, where she'd thrown the contents of their 'bits and pieces' tray – the carpet glittered with multicoloured foreign coins and hairpins, plectrums and keys. She untangled her hair from its velvet elasticated band and began to comb it vigorously, till it gleamed and every strand was in place. She tied it back again, making sure there were no ridges or tangles in it, and smoothed it down with her hands. She felt calmer now.

Another car pulled up outside. It wasn't him. She paced the room again. Fucking bastard. Fucking smug Irish piece of shit. Cunt. Cunt cunt cunt cunt cunt. She was ready for him now. She stood at the window, waiting. She saw the dark-haired man and the girl from downstairs leave the basement flat clutching cans of lager and laughing. Out for a normal Friday night – lucky them.

Come home, you bastard, come home, you bastard.

She tapped her fingernails on the windowsill. Come home.

Finally, the familiar rumble of the old Embassy. She watched him slowing down, looking for a parking space, not finding one – good – reversing back down the road with his chin on his shoulder and his arm over the passenger seat, into the space in one smooth movement – he'd always been a very good parker – reaching into the back seat to pull out his briefcase and a carrier bag from the off-licence, locking the door, striding up Almanac Road. Look at him, she thought, just look at him. Who the fuck does he think he is? Prick. Oh, yes, skipping up the stairs now with a bounce in his step. Cunt. She remained where she stood by the window and waited for the sound of his key in the door.

'Hi.' Bastard.

Silence for a second and then his voice from the hallway.

'Shit. What's happened here? Shuv, where are you? Are you all right? What's this stuff doing all over the floor? Shuv? Shuv? Shit!' He walked into the living room and a tiny pink-glass bauble crunched under his foot. He took a step sideways and looked around the room in horror. 'Jesus Christ, Shuv, what's happened?' He walked precariously towards her. 'Are you all right?' He reached out a hand to touch her arm. She jerked it away from her.

'Get your filthy hands off me. Don't you dare touch me!'

He backed off. 'Oh, Jesus, what's happened? Who did this? Has someone hurt you?'

Siobhan laughed bitterly. 'You could say that.'

'Who? Tell me.' He attempted to touch her again.

'It's you, you revolting piece of shit. Get off me!'

'Me?' asked Karl incredulously. 'How?'

'Yes – you! You'd love it if it was someone else, wouldn't you? Then you could get all angry and phone the police and roam the streets seeking revenge. But there's no one else to blame. I trashed the house and it's your fault, you fucking bastard.' She pushed him out of the way and stormed into the bedroom.

'What are you talking about? Shuv – please – talk to me.' He followed her through the hall and into the bedroom. 'What've I done wrong?'

Siobhan turned to face him. Her face was red with anger. She slowly lifted her head up to the ceiling and pointed above her with a finger. She put her other hand on her hip and stared at him.

'What!?' asked Karl in exasperation. What the hell was going on? This was insanity. All day long he'd been looking forward to coming home. It had been a hectic, problem-ridden day of hassle upon hassle, but at the end of the tunnel were Siobhan and Rosanne and the flat and a blissful weekend of relaxation and warmth and television and the pub. Not this. What was this?

'That!' she hissed, still pointing upwards, 'that's what

you've done wrong. That trashy little tart up there. In the office at the dance club, apparently . . .'

Karl's jaw dropped and his heart began to hammer against his ribcage. This could not be happening. Not now. His mind hurtled through a million possible responses in a couple of seconds. Denial? Admittance? Tears? How the hell did she know? Had he left something lying around the flat? No. It must have been that venomous little bitch. She must have told her. Why? Why now after so long?

'Are you going to say something or are you just going to stand there looking like a retard? You know what I'm talking about, don't you? You're not going to deny it, are you? I'd hate you even more than I already do if you did.' She folded her arms and regarded him with icy disdain.

Karl felt his stomach constrict and the contents swill around nauseatingly. He sat down heavily on the bed and exhaled a deep, painful breath. He had to find out how she knew.

'Shuv, oh, God, I . . . er . . . who told you?' He looked at her desperately.

'You did. You told me, you stupid fucking careless bastard. Here,' she said, turning to walk out of the room, 'wait here.'

Karl heard the sound of glass and vinyl crunching underfoot as Siobhan walked through the living room. He felt, like people he'd heard on talk shows and films say a thousand times before, as if his world was falling apart. He knew, without a shadow of a doubt, that this was the worst thing that had ever happened to him.

Siobhan returned a second later holding something small and silver in her hand: Rick's state-of-the-art tape recorder. Karl mentally rewound and fast-forwarded through his memories until he found what he was looking for. That night at the chapel, when Siobhan and Rick had gone outside, he and Tamsin. He heard Rick's voice in his head, word for word: 'This thing's brilliant, it tapes for six hours.' Siobhan rewound the tape a little and pressed Play – it was Tamsin's voice, shrill with bitterness and alcohol: '*you think no one knew about you and Cheri in the office at the dance club? Did you think we were all stupid?! Cheri told me all about it. All the sordid details. She told me about the abortion, too – your baby that she had to get rid of . . .*' He screwed his eyes closed. How stupid. Oh, God, how painfully stupid.

'OK, so now you know,' said Siobhan, waving the gadget at him. 'You fucking bastard.' She threw it on to the bed beside him. 'I want you to go, Karl. I want you to pack a bag, right now, this instant, and leave. I'm going to my mother's tomorrow. You can come and move back in then. I can't live under this roof any more, I can't share a roof with that whore. I don't want to talk about this and I don't ever, ever want to set eyes on you again.' She choked on her tears as she left the room, slamming the door behind her.

Karl sat numbly on the edge of the bed for a minute. This could not possibly be happening. His stomach churned and his head ached with tears that he was too shocked to set loose. This could not be happening. But it *was* happening. This was real. This was horribly, horribly real. He had to stop it!

He leapt to his feet and strode into the living room. Siobhan was sitting on the sofa, their new sofa, staring into space, Rosanne lying uncertainly across her lap, her eyes darting awkwardly around the room. Karl got down on to his knees and began to collect small shards of coloured glass and black vinyl.

'Leave it, Karl!'

'It's dangerous,' he whispered. 'Rosanne might hurt her paws.'

'I'll do it,' Siobhan snapped, 'after you've gone. Talking of which – can you please leave.' She wouldn't look at him.

'Siobhan – please – can't we talk about this . . . ?'

'Why on earth would I want to talk about this?! Listen to your excuses. Hear all the sordid details. It's pathetic. You're pathetic! Nothing means anything any more. Just go!'

'Oh, God, Siobhan! No! Please! Please don't do this! I love you. I need you. I . . .'

'Oh, stop it, for God's sake, stop it – you sound pathetic! Look, Karl, I mean it. I want you to go. I don't want to talk about it!'

Karl's face crumpled and he began to cry.

'Shuv – no!' He dragged himself on his knees to her feet and wrapped his arms around her legs, his whole body quaking with silent sobs. 'No . . . no! I won't go . . . it was nothing, it was a mistake, it was crap, rubbish, I was stupid, I was weak. It was . . . all a huge mistake. I'm so sorry, so sorry . . .'

The sight of Karl prostrate at her feet, crying, opened Siobhan up. It broke through the cold hard shell she'd been determined to wear, and she started to cry too. 'I trusted you. I always trusted you. I asked you about her, remember, in Scotland? And you made me feel like a silly little girl. How could you?! I was honest with you, about Rick. Why couldn't you be honest with me too? That's what really hurts. The lies. The dirty, ugly, stinking lies. You made a mistake. I made a mistake. Why couldn't you admit it? And why, Karl – why did you do it? Because I was fat, that's why! "Oh, no, Shuv, you're beautiful, I love you whatever size you are." Bollocks! You lied to me! You must have thought I was so fucking stupid. I hate you, Karl, I hate you so much!' Tears flowed down her face and her shoulders heaved up and down. Karl gripped her legs even tighter and cried even harder.

'I'm so sorry. I'm so sorry! Oh, God – what have I done?'

'Ruined everything, that's what you've done, you stupid cunt.' The unfamiliar word felt like poison spilling from her lips. 'Ruined absolutely everything.'

For a few moments they sat stock-still, Karl still wrapped around Siobhan's legs, crying so deeply and painfully that neither of them could talk. Rosanne looked from one of them to the other, her dark eyes full of concern and confusion. She whimpered quietly and snuffled at the top of Karl's head. Karl raised his head and looked up at her. He kissed the top of her head. He caught Siobhan's eye, the first eye contact they'd had since he'd got home. He knew what to do. His face brightened slightly. He took Siobhan's hand.

'It doesn't have to be ruined, Shuv. We can work on it. We're strong enough. We can get through this. Other couples couldn't. We're not like other couples. We're special, we can get through this. I'll do anything it takes – anything. I'll move out for a while if that's what you want. But please, let's fight for it. We can't give up on this because of something so . . . so . . . stupid. If we gave up it would be the most tragic thing imaginable, we'd regret it for ever – please.' He squeezed her hand tightly and looked up at her pleadingly. 'Imagine it, Shuv. Us, not being together. Me, on my own here. You, somewhere else. Not together. Imagine what it would really be like. Imagine it. We can't do it, we can't let that happen to us – can we?'

Siobhan looked down at him in her lap. She couldn't imagine it. It filled her with dread and pain. But she couldn't imagine making it work again either. She didn't trust him any more. He'd had sex with their neighbour, impregnated her, he'd lied to her, he wasn't the man she'd thought he was, the honest George Washington, incapable of telling a lie. How many other lies had there been? She would become an insecure wreck, worrying constantly when he was out of her sight, like one of those women she'd always pitied. She'd go through his jacket pockets, interrogate him about his activities, sniff the air for perfume when he came in from work, steam open suspicious-looking mail, eavesdrop on his telephone conversations, look for his love, his attention, all the time. She didn't want to become like that. She couldn't live with someone she didn't trust. She'd rather be alone for the rest of her life. She looked away from Karl's intense gaze and withdrew her hand from his. Every muscle in his body was taut with anticipation. She shook her head sadly.

'No,' she said quietly, 'it's too late. It's over.'

Karl wailed. 'No! Please, God, no! Don't say that. It's not over, it'll never be over. We're soul mates. We have to be together, Siobhan, we just have to!'

She pushed him gently off her lap and stood up heavily.

'I don't trust you any more, Karl. I can't live with someone I don't trust. Now, please, I beg of you, pack a bag and go. If you really care about me you'll go. Please!'

Very slowly, Karl got to his feet. 'Tomorrow,' he sighed, 'I'll go tomorrow.' Siobhan shook her head again. He walked numbly to the bedroom while Siobhan waited in the living room, listening to the desolate sounds of cupboard doors opening and shutting, drawers being slid back and forth, the zipper being pulled open around the circumference of Karl's suitcase, and then pulled shut again. The saddest sounds she'd ever heard in her life. Her tears ran silently.

Karl stood slackly in the doorway, weighed down by his suitcase and his misery. Siobhan wanted to ask him where he was going but didn't let herself. That would be too caring, too personal, too . . . ordinary. She saw him for a second, as he'd looked skipping up the front steps just half an hour before, light-footed, ready for the weekend. In another world they'd be eating now, watching a video, drinking a bottle of wine, curled up together on the sofa, bathed in garish, twinkling reflections from the fairy lights on the Christmas tree they'd put up the weekend before. They'd discuss his show like they did every evening and Siobhan would tell him how the wedding plans were progressing. One of them would take Rosanne out for a walk and then they'd go to bed together, cuddle up in each other's arms for a while to get warm and fall asleep.

But this was a different world, a world in which she'd been bored in the afternoon and had found that little tape recorder of Rick's. She'd switched it on and enjoyed listening to it, laughing out loud to herself. Because she was cooking she hadn't switched it off at the end, she left it playing. And then everything had gone psychedelic. She'd thought it was a joke at first, Tamsin and Karl messing around together, so she'd rewound it and played it again. And then she was sick, physically sick, shivering and gasping and heaving over the toilet bowl. She'd splashed her face with cold water and the shock woke up the anger in her and she'd gone insane for quarter of an hour, destroying their home. This was the world she was in now. This was reality, Karl standing in the doorway with a suitcase about to leave home. The tears kept coming.

'I'll phone you later,' he said quietly.

'No,' she said. 'No. Don't phone me.'

'I'll phone you later,' he repeated. Rosanne jumped off the sofa and walked up to Karl. He crouched to hug her, muttering tear-stained farewells into her soft ears, and then he stood up, looked at Siobhan and walked out of the front door. The slam echoed around the barren flat.

Siobhan walked slowly to the window and watched him unlock the boot of the little black car, swing the suitcase in and then manoeuvre himself into the front seat before starting the engine and driving away.

As his car passed the window he slowed down and looked up at the flat. Their eyes met for less than a second and a look of unbearable intense pain passed between them. The Embassy made a small, bloodcurdling screech before disappearing from view and out of Almanac Road.

## CHAPTER TWENTY-FOUR

Ralph checked the clock on the bare white walls of his studio for the hundredth time that hour. It was 5.18. Time to go, nearly. Well, if he took his time, dawdled a bit, he could probably leave now. It wouldn't matter if he got to Bayswater a bit early; it was a nice evening, he could wait outside the station. And that way, if Jem got there early, too, they'd have longer together.

He switched off the little radio, put it in his rucksack, picked up his jumper and coat from the chair by the blow-heater where he'd been warming them up, threw them on hastily, turned off the light and locked the doors behind him.

The concrete corridor was cold and filled with the clackety-clack of interlock machines from the dress-maker's studio next to his and muted drum 'n' bass coming from her CD player. He took the steps two at a time out into the dark courtyard, past Murray, the permanently stoned security guard, and into the bleak, traffic-infested thoroughfare of Cable Street.

Another wasted day. Another totally wasted day. He hadn't even picked up a brush. He'd spent the first hour pacing the studio, getting up the nerve to go to the payphone down the corridor and phone Jem. And then, when he'd finally done it, he'd spent the rest of the day pacing the studio in anticipation, watching the minutes die slowly on the studio clock, his stomach clenched tight in a knot of excitement, fear and dread. Shit. He didn't know what the hell to do, how to handle it. His loyalties were split asunder.

Smith, you arsehole, you stupid, stupid fucker. Why did you have to tell me? And that was the irony of the whole situation. Smith had told Ralph because Ralph was Smith's best friend – who else was he going to tell? And since Jem had moved in, that was something that Ralph had almost forgotten. For the last three months he hadn't seen Smith as his mate any more, his best buddy. He was his rival, his opponent. He was the person who was getting in the way of his dreams and his destiny, the person who stood between him and happiness. Ralph had forgotten, forgotten that, first and foremost, before Jem, before nearly everything else, Smith was his best friend. He'd felt bad about it – but not as bad as he'd felt about Smith's pathetic little outburst of childish excitement when he had got back from his team-building weekend the night before.

Smith had been edgy from the moment he'd got back to the flat on Sunday night, overanimated, overblown, loud and irritating, going on and on about his weekend. Jem had gone to have a bath. Smith had waited until he heard the bathroom door bang shut and then leant towards Ralph conspiratorially.

'It's happened!' he'd said, his face almost splitting at the seams with delight and excitement.

'What's happened?'

'Finally, finally!' continued Smith, oblivious to Ralph's lack of comprehension, 'I knew it. Didn't I tell you? Didn't I tell you!' He punched Ralph playfully on the thigh and grinned at him like the Cheshire Cat.

'Spit it out, Smith, for Christ's sake. What the hell are you going on about?'

'Cheri, of course! Cheri!' He was rocking back and forth. '*Ma Cheri amour*! Ha!'

'What? What are you talking about?'

'Well, Ralph, my friend. My patience has paid off. It is, as they say, in the bag. Tonight I bumped into the glorious Ms Dixon outside Sloane Square Tube station. Uh-huh! We shared the bus stop for a while and we just chatted . . . like you do.' He raised his eyebrows mock-nonchalantly and then broke back into a ludicrous smile. 'Can you believe it? Me and Cheri. Just chatting! I didn't stutter, stammer, grimace, drop anything, break anything, sweat or trip over. We . . . just . . . chatted. Ha! And she is *only* about three hundred and eighty-five times more beautiful when you're talking to her than when you just glimpse her in passing. God! It was amazing. Anyway, we waited ages for a bus, just chatting, as I said, and then I suggested we go for a quick drink at Oriel to warm up and then maybe get a cab a bit later. Cool, or what?! So we did. I asked her what she wanted and she ordered a bottle of wine. A whole bottle! So I knew she wasn't just being polite – she'd have ordered a tomato juice or something then, wouldn't she? And she is just unbelievably nice, you know – really, she is. I know you think she's a snooty cow but she isn't at all. Oh, Jesus, Ralph. She is beautiful. She is *so* beautiful. I have never seen skin like that in my life. And her hands are perfection and her hair is like . . . like . . .'

Ralph had been momentarily speechless. He'd breathed in deeply as he felt his heart fill with a mixture of joy and horror. Smith still loved Cheri! In spite of Jem, in spite of everything. This was wonderful news.

But it was terrible news, too. Poor Jem. She didn't deserve this. As much as he wanted Smith and Jem to split up, as much he wanted her for himself, he couldn't bear the thought of her being treated so badly by anyone.

'Oh, my God, Smith. I thought this was all over. I thought you were over this. What the fuck are you playing at?' He'd eyed Smith with horror and disgust.

'I thought I was, too. I thought it was over. But then I saw her tonight and . . . and, well, God. She's just so beautiful. And I can talk to her, Ralph. I can really talk to her . . .'

'But what about Jem? You can talk to Jem, too. I've never met a woman as easy to talk to as Jem . . .'

'Oh, yeah. I know that. But Jem's Jem and Cheri is something completely different . . .'

'What, Smith? What *is* Cheri? What the fuck is going on here?'

'OK. OK. Keep your undies on. Look. I don't know. I don't know, all right!' Smith had put his head in his hands. 'Christ – talk about pissing on a bloke's fireworks. Jeez . . .'

'Look, Smith. I am not here to piss on your fireworks. I'm here to point out to you that you have a girlfriend. Remember? Jem? Sweet, trusting, loyal, faithful, loving Jem? Christ . . .' He looked away, revolted. 'So,' he sighed resignedly, 'what happened next?'

Smith brightened a little and sat up straighter. 'Well, so, we were in Oriel, chatting, drinking wine, just getting on, really. And she was telling me all about herself, about how she used to have loads of lovers, but now she's got rid of them all because – and get this – she's looking for Mr Right! Is that amazing, or what! She's basically cleared the decks for the right man. It's got to be, hasn't it? It's got to be me! I've waited five years, I've wanted that woman for *five years*, I've dreamed about her, I've thought about her, I've even . . . Shit, I've even imagined her when I've been in bed with Jem . . .'

Ralph wrinkled his face in distaste. 'You really are a cunt, aren't you?'

'Jem was just all a big part of the way things panned out. Jem took my mind off Cheri for long enough for my obsession to shrink to a manageable size, so that when Cheri was ready for me, I wouldn't blow it. D'you see? It's all timing. It's destiny.'

'I thought you didn't believe in all that.'

'I don't . . . I didn't. I do now. I didn't believe in Jem's destiny, but I believe in my own. This is it, Ralph. This is it!'

'This is *what*?! Will you please tell me what the fuck is going on? You have a drink with the girl from upstairs, she tells you she's not going out with anyone at the moment and you're already making plans for the future. I mean – *what*?' He shrugged and held up his hands in frustration. 'You're just going to dump Jem, are you? Just throw her away like a used tissue?'

'Fuck, Ralph – I can't believe you're reacting like this! I thought you'd be pleased, excited for me. You know how long I've been in love with that woman, you know the hell I've been through. Christ, before Jem came along I hadn't had sex for five years. Five years! Do you have any idea what that feels like? Jem's been great for me, really great. She's brought me out of myself, reminded me about shared physicality, about sharing everything. And, no, I'm not going to dump her. Not yet, anyway. It's still early days for me and Cheri. I've got to earn her trust. Just because *I* know we're meant for each other, it doesn't mean that she'll know. No, I've got to take it slowly . . .'

'. . . and meanwhile, you'll just tag good ol' Jem along for the ride, will you? Smith, I'm horrified. I am horrified and I am disgusted by you. In fact, I am so disgusted by you that I can no longer talk to you.' Ralph stood up and looked down at his friend. 'Jem is just about the best person I have ever known – no, actually, she *is* the best person I have ever known, and I refuse to sit here and allow you to treat her like this. I'm going to tell her, and I'm going to tell her now!'

Smith leapt to his feet. 'Don't you fucking dare! Don't you fucking *dare*! One word, just one word leaves your lips and you're homeless, mate' – his face was millimetres from Ralph's – 'and I mean that. *One word*, and you're out of here. You're my mate, Ralph,' he said, running his fingers through his hair, 'and I hope you'll always be my mate. But mates stick together, don't they? They don't take sides with girls. You've known me for fifteen years. You've known Jem for fifteen minutes. It's your choice. OK? But don't think I wouldn't do it. Because I would.'

He'd picked up the remote control, then, stretched his legs out on to the coffee table and switched on the telly.

Ralph had looked at him there on the sofa in his rumpled suit and tie, his blandly handsome face bare of feeling, and wondered for one stupefied moment how a girl as perceptive, wise and reasonable as Jem had ever thought that an emotional cabbage like Smith could be the right man for her, the man she'd been dreaming about since she was sixteen.

Ralph quietly and sadly left the room, and headed straight for his bedroom.

He hadn't got a wink of sleep that night. His emotions were all over the place. Excitement, because he knew something that would put a speedy end to Jem's silly infatuation with Smith. Frustration, because to tell her would be apocalyptic. Feelings of hypocrisy, because he was no angel himself. He felt sorry for Smith because he was an arsehole, and he felt sorry for Jem because Smith was making a fool of her. In a way, this was all his dreams come true, confirmation of everything he'd always thought – that Smith was not worthy of Jem and her unconditional love. Confirmation that Smith didn't deserve a girl like Jem.

He tossed and turned and turned and tossed, his emotions going around in his head like marbles in a tumble-drier, and then he'd got up early, before Jem and Smith, and made his heavy-hearted way to the studio. He still hadn't decided what he wanted to say when he'd phoned Jem, he just knew that he had to talk to her. They'd had such a wonderful weekend together and, despite the scene the night before with Smith, he didn't want to break the spell.

And now he was standing on the dreary platform of Limehouse DLR station, waiting impatiently for a rare sighting of a train, his mind still in total and utter pandemonium, wondering what the hell to do. Should he? Shouldn't he? The complete devastation if he did. Smith would know it was him who'd told Jem and would throw him out of the flat. But then, he'd had a free ride for long enough now. Smith was going to settle down with someone at some point, whether it was Cheri, Jem or anyone else, and he'd be out on his ear then anyway.

Maybe it was about time he learned to stand on his own two feet, stopped using Smith as a security blanket.

But he'd have lost a friend, his best friend. Did that matter any more? He was vaguely surprised to feel a twinge of pain in his heart when he contemplated it. But it was nothing like the enormous spear of agony that pierced right through the fibre of his being when he imagined losing Jem; that really would be the greatest loss imaginable. Maybe Jem would hate him for telling her, for dismantling her happiness and taking apart her dreams. Maybe she'd take out her anger at Smith on him, direct her hurt and her disappointment at him. That would be the worst-case scenario – then he'd have lost everything.

He realized that the safest possible alternative was to say nothing. Smith was a slimebag, he'd proved it now, and the best decision all round would be to say nothing, bide his time, capitalize on his wonderful relationship with Jem and then be there for her, help her to pick up the pieces when it all came tumbling down, as it was bound to, at some point in the future.

But that was the problem – the vagueness of that concept: 'some point in the future'. What sort of way was that to live a life, waiting for your best friend to break your true love's heart before you could claim your destiny, before you could be happy? And, in any case, maybe all this bullshit about Cheri would come to nothing and Smith would keep Jem hanging on in second place for the rest of their lives. Maybe he'd fuck up in ten years' time when he and Jem had four children and a house in the country and invited Ralph over for dinner once or twice a year because they felt sorry for him. No. He couldn't let that happen. He didn't want to be staring wistfully and meaningfully at Jem over the dinner table when he was forty, still resenting Smith.

A train finally slunk apologetically into view, and Ralph boarded it, too grateful for the warmth to feel angry about the wait.

And then there was the matter of personal morals. In some people's books, and maybe in Jem's, reading someone else's diaries would be perceived as being on a heinous par with infidelity. Did he really have any right to moralize about Smith's actions? Did he have any right to unload Smith's secret on to Jem without coming clean about his own sneaky, dishonest behaviour? Not really. But how could he do that? How could he tell Jem in one short sitting that (a) her boyfriend had been fantasizing about an unattainable woman he'd been in love with for five years while he was in bed with her, (b) her flatmate had been reading her diaries and snooping in her room for the best part of three months and (c) aforementioned flatmate was hopelessly, passionately and devotedly in love with her and wanted to spend the rest of his living days with her. And how're you finding your jal frezi, by the way? Shit.

As he made his way towards the Circle line, he was no closer to deciding what to do. Every option seemed to offer nothing but down-sides – not an up-side or a fringe benefit in sight. Where was the option that resulted in Jem realizing she was madly in love with Ralph, leaving Smith without telling him why and everyone living happily ever after? Non-existent, that was where.

He'd have to play it by ear. See how he felt when he was sitting there in the restaurant, with Jem. Maybe she had her suspicions, you never know. Then he would only be confirming what she already knew, not maliciously sabotaging Smith's life. Yes, that's what he'd do. Plan nothing, decide nothing, Play It By Ear . . .

The Tube finally arrived at Bayswater station and he tumbled off and up the stairs towards the bright lights and open-all-hours bazaar atmosphere of Queensway above. Jem wasn't there yet. He glanced around him for a clock – it was six twenty-three. He stood at the lip of the station, his hands deep in his pockets, his nose starting to run slightly in the cold night air, brusquely dismissing thoughts from his head as they entered, chanting mantra-like to himself, *Play It By Ear, Play It By Ear*.

An old woman in the opposite corner to him was muttering obscenities to herself and slowly hitching up yards and yards of filthy grey skirt. He looked away, embarrassed, but then couldn't resist a quick look back. She was showing him her prune-like, hairless fanny and smiling at him through blackened, wizened teeth. 'That's what you want, innit darlin'?' she was chuntering. Ralph looked away again. How disgusting . . .

Queensway never slept, but that was because no one English lived there – it was all company lets and pay-by-the-week hotels, Australians and Arabs and Africans, big-screen sports pubs, all-night coffee shops, noisy restaurants, and the sound of loud foreign chatter everywhere you went. It always felt vaguely like being on holiday when you were in Queensway. Not the place for cocoa and slippers and *Coronation Street* with your shepherd's pie.

Ralph glanced at the clock again, careful not to attract the attention of the repugnant female flasher still standing across from him and now, he suspected, urinating down the wall. It was six twenty-nine.

*Play It By Ear. Play It By Ear.*

'Who's your mate?'

Ralph spun around as he heard a soft female voice centimetres from his ear. It was Jem.

'Oh, shit. Thank God. It's you. I thought it was my knickerless friend over there.'

'Lovely, isn't she! Has she shown you her fanny yet?'

They began to walk.

'So, how was your day?' Jem asked.

'Oh, crap. Didn't get a thing done . . .'

'Oh, that's a shame. Why not?'

'Just had a lot on my mind, I guess.'

'Like what?'

'Oh, nothing much. You know, just stuff . . .'

'Anything you want to talk about?'

'Nah – not really – maybe. I may bend your ear yet.' Yes. That was good, Ralph thought. Lay the foundations for possibly discussing it later. 'How was your day?' He looked down and smiled at her. He loved that he had to look down to smile at her. It was so . . . so . . . beguiling . . .

'Dreadful, absolutely dreadful. The Monday from Hell. But far too boring to talk about. So, tell me about this jal frezi.'

They chatted as they walked, about curry, about this and that, about nothing. Ralph began to feel himself simmering to the surface like boiling milk, but he couldn't turn the heat down. He didn't want to make small talk. He didn't want to pretend that they were just friends. He didn't want to just go and have a curry with Jem and come home and watch Jem disappear into Smith's slimy, second-rate arms. He wanted . . . he wanted . . . *Play It By Ear*, he reminded himself, *Play*

*It By Ear*. But it was no good. He was playing it by ear and his ear was telling him to do it, to take a risk with everything in his life, gamble the lot. Yes, please, Mr Croupier, I'll put it all on red, the limousines, the yacht and the house in Colorado . . .

He took a deep breath and then exhaled. They'd reached the restaurant. The abrupt change in atmosphere brought his temperature back down to a simmer for a few moments.

'Wow!' exclaimed Jem, 'what a place!'

Dozens of unsmiling waiters in skinny black trousers ran nimbly through a vast sea of tables, holding aloft huge silver platters filled with red, green, brown and creamy pink curries, and cushiony white naan breads like miniature moonscapes. Hundreds of loudly conversing diners sat framed by colonial murals in mint green and ice blue, between towering wrought-iron palm trees and under six-foot ceiling fans spinning desperately to keep the intense heat down.

A frenetic waiter showed them to their table, threw a pair of menus at them and disappeared without a smile.

'It's not the friendliest place in the world,' whispered Ralph, 'but just take a look at the prices.'

They discussed the menu, decided on their order, and within less than a second of them closing their menus the same wiry waiter was back, gruffly taking their order and disappearing quickly again. Their Cobra beers arrived in thirty seconds.

'Fast turnover,' Ralph laughed, suddenly realizing that he'd chosen a bad venue for a heart-to-heart – if you took longer than fifteen minutes in this place they sent waiting customers to hover over your table.

'Well,' said Jem, smiling up at Ralph over the top of her beer glass, 'this is very nice, isn't it?'

Ralph was slightly taken aback. He'd forgotten that this was very nice. He'd just been thinking of it as purgatory.

'Yes,' he said happily, 'I suppose it is – very nice indeed.'

'Um' – Jem looked away from Ralph and then back towards him – 'what's it . . . what's it in honour of?'

'What d'you mean?'

'It's just that – I hope you won't take this the wrong way – I kind of had the feeling, when you phoned this morning, to ask me about tonight, that you were . . . asking me out?'

'Really! What made you think that?' Ralph choked on his Cobra.

'Oh, I don't know. You just sounded sort of nervous and the conversation was a bit stilted. It just . . . reminded me of being asked out on a date. That's all,' she finished, waiting for a response.

The small talk was over.

'So' – Ralph rubbed his chin – 'let's get this straight. I phoned you, entirely innocently – bored, nothing better to do than phone boring old Jemima Catterick – invited you out for a curry, purely, of course, so I wouldn't have to sit here on my own, and you thought I was asking you out on a date. The cheek of it!'

'Oh, stop it!' laughed Jem.

'And then,' Ralph was getting into his stride now, 'and then, having quite unbelievably mistakenly thought that I'd asked you out on a date, which is, of course, rid*i*culous, instead of saying "But, oh, Master Ralph Sir, I couldn't possibly, my heart belongs to another, you are a scoundrel and a cad," proceeded to accept what you had so brazenly misinterpreted as an invitation of an *amorous* nature and are here now, sitting at this table with me, *unescorted*!! What am I to make of this?'

'Oh, Ralph, you old git!' Jem was blushing furiously.

'I'm sorry,' Ralph laughed. 'Your face. It's a picture. You look so sweet.' He looked down at his large, long-fingered hands, now covering Jem's tiny white ones, and felt a glow in his stomach. They looked so right together, those hands. He wanted to see them together for the rest of his life. He caressed the side of Jem's hand with his thumb. She made no attempt to move it. 'Such tiny hands,' he murmured. He squeezed them and looked at Jem, giving her a slightly cheesy smile because it was all he could manage, and then down at their hands again. 'You were right.' He glanced at her shyly through his eyelashes. 'I *was* asking you out on a date earlier. It's true.' He smiled again and gave her a 'Caught me' look with raised eyebrows. 'I . . . we had such a great time at the weekend – it was . . . it was one of the best weekends of my life – honestly. And I wanted to see you again – away from the flat and from Smith and everything. I just . . . I just love being with you, Jem, I really do, and . . .' He gulped and looked quickly up at Jem, who was watching him with an expression of anticipation and warmth. He sat up straight and looked her in the eye. 'I hope you don't mind,' he finished, looking away again.

'Of course I don't mind,' replied Jem. 'I've told you before, I love being with you, too. I know I've only known you for three months, but I already think of you as one of my best friends.'

'Oh, God, Jem, that's sweet. But it's not what I'm

talking about. I'm talking about love. Real love. Not palsy-palsy love, not matey love. I *really*, *really* love being with you. I . . .' He faltered for a moment and felt a tingly sweat begin to break out on his brow as the floodgates opened. 'Oh, God, Jem. I love you. I've never said that to anyone before. But I mean it. I'm mad about you. I think you're the most wonderful person I've ever met. I think about you all the time and I can't pretend I don't feel this way any more. I'm jealous as hell of Smith for having you. I never really thought about love before, about the right woman, about settling down with one person. And then you moved in and at first . . . at first I didn't realize how special you were – you were just a flatmate I didn't really want. And then I got to know you, got used to having you around, and gradually started liking you more and more. And then one night I knew – the night we had the chilli challenge. I suddenly knew, without a doubt, that I was in love with you. Jem, we were destined to be together. We're right for each other. We fit. We would be the most special couple in the world, you know – magic, it's magic when we're together, haven't you noticed? I can't just be friends with you any more, Jem, d'you understand? I don't want you to like me as a friend. I want you to feel the same way about me as I do about you, and there are times . . . sometimes, when I think you already do.' He breathed out, a long, cool wonderful breath, full of relief and elation. He felt about ten stone lighter, the weight of the feelings and emotions he'd been hauling around with him for the last two months finally lifted from his soul.

'I also know that you've heard all this before. I know about Nick, and Jason, and the other ones. I know you've had enough declarations of love to last you a lifetime . . .'

'What!' Jem's eyes were saucers.

'. . . but I promise you, I'm not like that. I wouldn't want to change you, to control you. I want you exactly as you are now. So, if I don't hassle you and I don't bombard you with flowers and poems and love letters, it's not because I don't love you, it's because I do. D'you see?'

'What!? Rewind! How the hell do you know about Nick and . . . and Jason, and everyone?'

Ralph looked across at Jem's furious face and exhaled heavily. Oh what the hell, he thought. Nothing to lose now. May as well go for broke. He took a deep breath.

'Oh, God. Jem. Please don't overreact to this, please try to understand. This is going to sound dreadful, but . . . but . . . I read your diaries. I'm so sorry. I've been reading your diaries since the day you moved in. I mean, not just reading your diaries, it was more than that. I've spent hours sitting in your room, just breathing you in, just being among your things. I know everything about you. I know how ugly you felt when you were growing up, I know about all those lovesick boys, all those clingy, demanding men who tried to change you, tried to control you. I know everything about you and I think it's only fair that you know everything about me. I know it was wrong – I've never done it before, I promise you. I was just sort of . . . drawn to them . . . drawn to you. I know that sounds like bullshit, but it's true. And it made me feel so close to you. I wanted so much to feel close to you. I'm not good with intimacy, Jem. It was the only way I knew. I'm very, very, very sorry. Really I am. I'm so sorry, Jem.' He smiled nervously, his gorgeous, lop-sided, lazy smile, from left to right. 'Please, Jem – say something.' He held his breath and awaited her response.

Jem's face was puce. 'I can't believe it! I can't believe you read my diaries! That's . . . horrible! Christ, Ralph. I thought you were my friend! Well, look. You can forget about that, you can forget *all* about that. Friends don't destroy their friend's sense of privacy, friends don't snoop around their friend's personal things. It makes me feel sick just thinking about it . . .'

'Please . . . Jem . . . please try to understand . . .'

'No, Ralph. I don't understand. And from this day on, from this *moment* on, you and I are flatmates – nothing more, nothing less – no more curries, no more chat, no more anything. Just keep away from me and everything will be just fine. Let's just forget any of this ever happened – OK?!'

'No! Jem! Please! I don't want to forget this ever happened. I'm glad this happened. I *wanted* this to happen. Please – let's talk about this.'

'Ralph, didn't you hear what I said? No more. It's over. I want to go home. Let's get the bill.'

She leant down to pick up her handbag then, rustling around in it for her purse, her chest rising and falling violently with the effort of not crying. Her world was spinning around her head like a broken helicopter. She had never felt so confused in her entire life. She was angry, so angry, about Ralph reading her diary, snooping in her room. But she was feeling more than that. She could live with the idea of Ralph reading her diaries. She wasn't a secretive person, she had nothing to hide. It was a terrible thing for him to have done, but she could handle it. What she couldn't handle was the avalanche of feelings triggered by Ralph's declaration of love, his declaration of what, if she was honest with herself, she'd known all along. Ralph was in love with her! He'd laid his hand on the table, he'd let the cat out of the bag, and there were beans all over the bloody place. This was no longer a game. The situation was no longer under control. And she wished she could have laughed lightly, patted Ralph's hands and told him sweetly that she loved him too, but not in that way, that her heart and her destiny belonged to Smith, that she wanted nothing more from him than friendship. But she couldn't. Because it wasn't true.

Damn and blast and fuck it. She loved him. She loved Ralph. She loved the way he held his pint and his fag in the same hand. She loved that he watched *The Waltons* in bed every Sunday morning. She loved the way he always stopped to pet dogs he passed on the street. She loved the way he shouted at people on the telly he disagreed with. She loved his hands and his long bony feet. She loved his lazy smile and the way he started wheezing when he was hysterical with laughter. She loved the fact that she could say absolutely anything to him and he'd make a conversation out of it, no matter how silly or banal. She loved his fascination with the detail of life, how he always noticed a good sunset or an unusual cloud formation, a hidden gargoyle on the side of a building or a ladder in someone's tights. She loved the gap at the back of his mouth where he'd lost a tooth in a football match and she loved the little scar that ran into his hairline where he'd head-butted an amp by mistake at a Clash gig in 1979.

She loved him and now he loved her. They could be together, they could just hold hands, disappear into the sunset together and live happily ever after. They could love each other.

She looked up at him quickly. He was facing away from her, forlornly trying to attract the attention of a waiter She looked at the sweet V-shape of hair at the nape of his neck that she'd always wanted to touch, the defeated slump of his shoulders. He was adorable. Even as the adrenaline of anger flooded her body, even as she put a dam over her feelings towards him, she yearned to turn around and take him in her arms and kiss the living daylights out of him. She loved him. She wanted him. She'd never even kissed him . . .

But she couldn't love him. She just couldn't. *What about Smith?* The floodgates snapped closed.

Ralph turned around and met her gaze.

'Jem . . .' he beseeched.

'No!' she snapped.

'Please . . .'

'No!'

They left the restaurant in a heavy cloud of silence, hailed a cab and went home, the atmosphere between them setting like cement as they drove.

# CHAPTER TWENTY-FIVE

Karl drove straight round to Tom and Debbie's that night, after Siobhan had kicked him out, and phoned her, repeatedly, every ten minutes, listening with disbelief to the sound of his own voice on the answerphone, informing him that he wasn't there, but that he could leave a message. Of course he wasn't fucking there!

The following day he tried her at her mother's, every half-hour, until Mrs McNamara had finally snapped and told him she'd call the police if he tried again; Siobhan did not want to talk to him. He couldn't really remember much about it all now, it was a big, black, drunken blur. He'd got himself to work somehow on Monday afternoon.

And that was when it happened – when everything changed.

He hadn't planned it at all. The last thing he'd been thinking about in the previous seventy-two or so hours was work, his show. But he was a DJ. He couldn't phone in sick. So he'd driven in, in a daze, his automatic pilot changing gears for him and looking out for traffic lights.

'You all right, mate?' his producer John had asked, as he stumbled blindly into the studio.

'Yeah, yeah.' Everything was different. His studio felt different. John seemed like a stranger. They went through the playlist. Funny, he thought, he was the DJ, he was the man who played the records, the man who played the songs with the lyrics that cut right through the heartstrings of the broken-hearted throughout London. How many times, he wondered, had he put on 'The Sun Ain't Gonna Shine Any More', and how many times had some poor, devastated, lonely fucker in an empty flat switched on his radio and heard it and felt the pain of loss even more greatly than before. He'd done that to people, without even realizing it. And now it was his turn. But he could control it, he could change the playlist. He could play the Spice Girls and 'I Will Survive' and 'Aga-fucking-doo' and keep it all at bay, all the pain. He could play God.

But he didn't want to. He would stick with the playlist and deal with the consequences. Who wanted to be God anyway?

He'd glanced through the list, viewing it for landmines, but he knew the emotions wouldn't hit him until he was listening to the song, till the lyrics were real in his ears.

'Are you sure you're OK?' asked John, again.

'Yeah, yeah.'

Why wasn't he feeling anything? He *wasn't* feeling anything. Just numbness and weirdness and emptiness. He didn't want to cry. He didn't want to run. He didn't want to be here. Things were just happening to him, words were coming from his mouth, his hands were moving, holding his cup of coffee, his legs crossed and uncrossed themselves, his eyes read and translated words for him, but he had nothing to do with any of it, it was all just happening. He wondered if his face might actually smile, if his throat might just laugh out loud. Probably.

'Mr Pitiful', Otis Redding: that was first up. He

remembered that song. It was on a tape he'd made for Siobhan when they'd only just met. You know, how you used to, when you were too young to know who you really were so you'd make tapes for each other, a way of saying, 'This is me, this is who I am, this is what I like, and because I like you so much, I want you to like it, too,' before you had a job or a car or a flat or a history or a proper personality that could say all that for you. So he'd made her endless tapes, spent hours painstakingly picking through his record collection for just the right track, hours recording them on to C90 tapes he bulk-bought from Woolies. And then he'd handed them to her proudly, wanting her so much to love them, to love his music as much as he loved it. And she had. And that had made him love her even more than he already did . . .

The news was read, the weather forecast and the traffic reported. Karl's mind went blank. What was he supposed to say? What did he usually say? He had no recollection. He couldn't even remember what day it was, what month. The clock ticked down the seconds. Five . . . four . . . three . . . two . . . one. Karl's mouth was bone dry. His voice had vanished. His whole spiritual being had disappeared from sight. Karl had ceased to exist . . . His jingle ran, and then there was a minuscule moment of silence, magnified ten-thousand-fold by the number of people who heard it. John stared at him, bulgy-eyed, the studio assistant reached for the mike, ready to step in, and then, finally Karl opened his mouth.

'Good evening, London, you're tuned in to ALR, London's finest, and I'm Karl Kasparov. It's 3.30 p.m. and it's *Drivetime* here in the country's capital. Just three shopping days left till Christmas, so I've been told, and here's one of my favourite songs, for all you useless guys, just like me, who haven't bought a single gift. It's called . . . "Mr Pitiful".'

He slipped the cans from his ears and stared in wonderment around him. He hadn't given a single thought to what he was going to say when he went on the air, and then he'd managed that – it was second nature. John gave him the thumbs up, relieved. Karl was a pro. It was going to be all right.

And it was all right. For the next fifteen minutes or so, at least, he was quite amazingly good. He breezed through the link-ups; sailed through REM and the Manic Street Preachers; 'Oliver's Army' was a piece of piss; 'Respect' by Aretha, no problem; 'Wonderwall' didn't even come close to cracking his professional veneer. He had some on-air banter with John, drank his coffee, smiled and even laughed a little. He was just doing his show. He began to feel almost normal again.

And then . . . he wasn't expecting it, it wasn't one of his favourite songs, it didn't really remind him of Siobhan, or even of his youth: 'The Bitterest Pill', the Jam.

Something about the song tore right through his emotions. He loved the Jam. Siobhan had loved the Jam, too. And it was so true – this was the bitterest pill he'd ever had to swallow, the end of everything, the beginning of nothing. And it was all his fault. His mind filled involuntarily with images of Siobhan, smiling, laughing. His senses filled up with the smell of her and the sound of her.

And then he started crying. Slowly at first, tears just trickling down the side of his nose. He turned away from

John and the rest of the team, wiped them away, took deep breaths. There were forty-five seconds left of the song. His breath came faster and faster, the tears thicker and thicker; thirteen seconds to go.

His body started to heave, and he suddenly realized that there was no way he was going to be able to stop the flow. John was talking to someone on the phone, the assistant had gone to the toilet, no one had noticed. Three seconds . . . two . . . one. He should have lined up another song, segued straight into something else, given himself a chance to recover. But he didn't, it hadn't occurred to him. The airwaves were silent, except for the sound of his laboured breathing as he tried to regain control of himself. It was like an awkward silence at a dinner party except a thousand times worse. John put down the phone and stared at him in horror. The silence continued. Karl kept crying.

And then, at last, he spoke. He knew he shouldn't. He knew that eventually John would have played a jingle, a trailer, something. This wasn't what radio was about. Radio was about professionalism, seamlessness, technology, music. It wasn't about his heartache or his misery. It wasn't about him.

'I . . . I'm sorry,' he began, his voice quavering dangerously, his vowels thick and doughy with mucus, 'I'm . . . I'm . . .'

Everything in the studio stopped; John was rooted to the spot, his jaw hanging open, his hand glued to his cheek. There was no bustle, none of the usual activity, just an unhappy man talking quietly into a microphone like it was his best mate down the pub, while tears poured down his cheeks.

'I've had a bad weekend . . . my girlfriend left me.'

John winced and covered his face with his hands. 'Oh, my God,' he muttered, 'he's doing a Blackburn, he's doing a fucking Tony Blackburn.'

'Siobhan, my girlfriend. Fifteen years. And . . . it's all over . . . and . . . oh, God, I'm sorry. I thought I'd be able to do this but . . . but, it's so hard. God, it's *so hard*. It's only just hit me, y'know. She's gone. Siobhan's gone!' He let loose a gigantic sob. 'Oh, God! If you knew what Siobhan was like. She was . . . she was like an angel. Just like an angel. I wanted her so badly, I've never wanted anything in my life like I wanted Siobhan and then I got her – I don't know how, I didn't deserve her, y'know. She was too good for me, *way* too good for me – a different class. She was so beautiful. And, God, you should've seen her hair, it was like pure gold, y'know? She could've had anyone and she chose me. And I don't know what I'd've done without her all these years, without her smile and her laugh and her goodness and her wisdom. God, she was wise. And her love. She loved me so much – d'you understand? D'you know what it's like to be loved that much by someone so beautiful and so . . . so good. And I . . . I . . .' His voice began to crack up again. 'I never took it for granted. Really. I never did. I always thanked God for that woman, always appreciated her.

'But . . . but, but . . . listen! Now just you listen to me, all you men out there. And women. This is important! This is just so bloody important, you must pay attention. If you've got a man, or a woman, and you love them and they love you, don't mess around, don't cheat on them. Please. Just don't do it. I did it. I took the trust of the most incredible, beautiful woman in the world and I made a mockery of it. And for what? For nothing! For disposable sex with a disposable woman who meant less than nothing to me. Can you believe it! Can you believe anyone would do something that stupid?! It was a pathetic little ego-boost. I can see that now. I always thought Siobhan was too good for me, too beautiful, too special. I tried to pretend it didn't bother me, but I always felt smaller than her, and then this other girl came along and made me feel like the Man, y'know? I was cleverer than her, nicer than her, better than her, or so I thought. And she wanted me. And my sad little male ego just took what was on offer, just grabbed it without a thought, for anything or anyone, not even myself probably. Oh, God! I didn't even enjoy it that much, y'know! But at least I felt special – *I* was the special one. It made me appreciate Siobhan even more, when the affair ended. It made me realize things about love and relationships that I hadn't thought about before. About continuity, about growing old with someone. How that can be as romantic as falling in love. I wanted to marry Siobhan, then, be with her for ever and ever and ever. But it was too late. She found out about the affair, she found out exactly what I was like. That I was pathetic and selfish and weak. And she deserved someone better than me. So she left. And now I'm alone. And it's over. I'm going to go back to our flat tonight, where we used to live together, and she won't be there. It'll be empty. And . . . and . . . and I didn't know it was possible to feel this unhappy and this sad and this bad. I loved her so much, and I broke her trust, and now I'm swallowing my bitter, bitter pill, and I deserve it. So – so just don't do it, OK? Just don't. Because if you're with someone you love, who loves you back, then you're the luckiest person in the world. *Ignore* that sexy bloke in the marketing department or that horny girl who lives upstairs, or whatever. Because it is not worth it. D'you hear? It . . . is . . . not . . . worth . . . it.' Karl took a deep breath and sat up straight. The tears had stopped. 'Well,' he began, looking cautiously around him at the open-mouthed assistants and secretaries and producers who were now standing five-deep in the booth, gathered together from all corners of the ALR building, staring at him, some glossy-eyed, some embarrassed, some horrified. One young girl wiped a tear away from her eye and looked away from him. There was absolute silence. 'I . . . erm . . . I'm sorry. I – er – sorry. Sorry.' He laughed a tight little laugh and looked around again at his waxwork audience. Jeff stood at the front now, his arms crossed, eyeing Karl with a look that was impossible to define. 'I've got a feeling this might be my last show on ALR – I'll put another song on. And, I'm sorry . . .'

He slid up the volume, pushed the cans away from his ears and rubbed his face hard with the palms of his hands. Shit. What the fuck had he done? He'd just lost control. All he'd been aware of was the mesmeric, soothing sound of his own voice in his earphones, nothing else – not the listeners at home, not the procession of shell-shocked people gathering in his studio, certainly not the fact that he was waving goodbye to his career. He'd been talking to himself, sorting out his own head, over the airways, to thousands upon thousands of strangers. He felt better for it. It was better than the dreadful, numb nothingness he had been hauling around with him all weekend. At least things felt real again now . . . painfully, horribly real.

'Karl.' He felt a warm hand on his shoulder and turned

around. It was John. 'Shit, Karl. That was something else. You OK?'

'Oh, Jeez. John. Shit . . .'

'Jules is out there. She'll take over for you. Come on, let me get you out of here.'

'Shit. Am I going to get the sack? Is that it? Is this over too?' He got heavily to his feet and pulled at the hem of his denim jacket, awkwardly.

'Nah, nah, nah. Come on, Karl. Let's go. Jules is here.' He put his arm gently around his shoulders and guided him through the swing doors and out into the corridor.

It was like a film: people just stopped and stared at him, shamelessly, craning their necks over partition walls and around doors; a hush fell wherever he went. He felt he should have a blanket thrown over his head and be bundled into a waiting van. They passed the reception desk.

'Karl – Karl!' June had one hand over the mouthpiece and was calling his name across the foyer and beckoning him with her eyes.

Oh, God. What did she want? Karl just wanted to keep walking, until he was out of the building and on the pavement and in his car.

'Karl, stop!' June was wobbling across the marble floor on her stiletto-heeled ankle-boots. 'Stop, it's Jeff – on the phone.'

Karl looked helplessly at John. This was it. He was going to get the sack. He took the phone from June.

'*Karl – mate – get back here this instant.*'

Karl's heart sunk deep into his stomach.

'*The fucking phones are going fucking ape, Karl – hmm, hmm – they want you back on the air. Get up here right now.*'

And then Jeff dropped the phone half-way through his last sentence like he always did, like only powerful people ever do.

'It's true,' cooed June, aflutter with unexpected Monday-afternoon excitement, 'the phones haven't stopped ringing for the last ten minutes – and they all want you. What *have* you been up to, Karl?' she asked with a middle-aged, happily married, flirtatious smile.

Karl turned to John again. John shrugged and smiled and led him back up the corridors, into the lift and back to the studio. It was mayhem. Three extra secretaries had been brought in to help man the phones. The atmosphere was electric. A small ripple of applause broke out as Karl walked slowly back into the room.

'Karl – mate.' Jeff strode towards him, smiling widely, and slung his arm across his shoulders, giving them a bone-crunching squeeze. 'They fucking loved it! You're a star, mate! We've taken two hundred calls in ten minutes! Get back on the air – give 'em what they want – tell 'em what you're feeling.' He guided him back towards his seat.

Jules smiled, slipped off her headphones, stood up and kissed Karl on the cheek, handing him the cans.

Karl sat down and looked around him at the sea of warm, sympathetic faces.

'I don't know if I can,' he muttered.

'What?' said Jeff. 'Of course you can, 'course you can. Just carry on – just as you were.'

'But . . . I've said it now, said everything I wanted to say.'

'Well, just say it again! They want it, mate. You can say anything you like. Just keep talking. We'll put some calls through to you; there're some fucked-up people out there who can really relate to you – they want to talk to you. You can do it, Karl – hmm, hmm. Jules will stay here if you need back-up. Go on, just be yourself, no rules at all . . .' He squeezed his shoulders again and began to back out of the room, 'No rules . . .'

Karl was terrified. He wanted to go home. All this . . . expectation. All these people, staring at him. Fucked-up weirdies waiting to talk to him on the phone. Jeff winked at him. Jules patted his arm. John brought him another cup of coffee. The clock said he had forty-nine seconds. Shit. He felt so alone . . .

The clock ticked away the last three seconds. Karl took a deep breath, and held it. He cleared his throat. 'Well,' he began, 'I've er . . . I've been asked to come back. Ha!' He laughed nervously. 'It seems that you all like me better miserable than happy! Um, I'm going to try, to keep things going and we can all, maybe, just be miserable together. I'm not quite sure how this is going to work . . . but . . . I think I'll play another song now. This one's for Siobhan. For us. It makes me think of university, before I knew her, when I just used to watch her, y'know, and dream about her. When she was just a fantasy, something out of my reach. It's one of the most perfect pop songs of the last ten years. It's the La's. "There She Goes" . . .'

Thumbs up all around the room. Karl breathed a sigh of relief. He grabbed the playlist and began to scribble all over it, striking through it with his pen and rewriting it. This show was going to be for Siobhan. There were no rules, that was what Jeff had said. No rules. So he'd do the whole show for Siobhan, for them, play all their songs, all their favourite songs. Wallow in it. And if people wanted to listen to him wallowing, then they were most welcome to. He didn't mind in the slightest.

So for two hours, he talked about Siobhan, he played hauntingly sad and heartbreakingly happy music. He took phonecalls from listeners who'd made the same mistake as him, some of them in tears, from listeners who just wanted to wish him all the best. He played requests for them, *their* songs.

It was two solid hours of pure emotion, of honesty and humanity. The phone rang constantly, there were tears and torment and anger, sadness, misery and regret. All the sad, lonely people in London came out from under their emotional duvets and felt part of the world again. It was unbelievably naff. It was horribly corny. It was Oprah on a bad day. But, it seemed, it was what people wanted. And it was what Karl needed.

There were people queuing on the pavement, clutching bunches of flowers and autograph books when Karl left the building that night. They'd been waiting for him. It was bizarre, it was madness. 'Thank you,' they kept saying. 'Chin up.' Pretty girls in clumpy boots gave him their phone numbers, pale men with dark eyes shook him by the hand. The atmosphere was peculiar. Karl shuffled through, said 'thank you' a lot, took the phone numbers, accepted the flowers, signed the autograph books and finally made it to his car, slamming the door behind him.

'Jeez,' he muttered to himself, 'what the fuck's going on?'

Little did he know that this was just the start of the madness. For the next few days, he was London's best-loved celebrity. They did a piece about him on *Newsroom South East*, his picture was on page three of the *Evening Standard*, accompanying an article about infidelity in the capital, every day there were increasingly more people standing around outside the ALR building, waiting to speak to him, to thank him.

But as far as Karl was concerned it was all completely ridiculous. It didn't make any difference to him; Siobhan didn't call.

He stayed with Tom and Debbie that night, and the next, and the next. He couldn't face going back to the flat. Siobhan knew where he was staying; he'd left a message with her mother, dictating the number twice, to make sure she wrote it down properly. She never called. She must have read the newspapers, listened to the radio, seen the news, but it didn't seem to have touched her at all. Not that that was why he'd taken on this role as the capital's favourite agony uncle, but you'd think, wouldn't you, that if the rest of the metropolis was awash with sympathy for him, that she would have felt it too? She really didn't want to know.

So, for three days he went to work, went home, got drunk, talked to Tom and Debbie about Siobhan, talked about life, talked about finding himself single, childless and alone in his mid-thirties when he'd always assumed he'd be just like everyone else, and wondering what the hell had gone wrong.

After the third day, he began to get angry. For fuck's sake – she'd gone off with Rick, hadn't she? She'd betrayed his trust too. After all, what's the difference between lying down and letting someone kiss you for half an hour, and lying down and letting someone shag you for five minutes? Which is the more intimate really? And supposing he *had* told her about Cheri, before she found out, would she have forgiven him? Would she have said, 'Karl, you've done a dreadful thing but, because you've told me all about it, and I didn't have to find out for myself, I forgive you and I know I can learn to trust you again'? Of course not. She'd have felt just the same, just as awful, just as unforgiving. She'd still've moved out.

Finally, after the show on Thursday night, Christmas Eve, he plucked up the courage to go home, back to Almanac Road.

He sat in the back of the cab, staring out of the window at the miserable, wet, dark night, his head pounding with frustration, anger, misery, loss and rage, and a blinding, all-consuming, heart-palpitating terror.

His key sounded strange in the lock. Like a distant echo of something from his past, a shadow of a memory from a forgotten dream. He'd never noticed the sound of his key in the lock before, never been aware of the sharp metallic click and the smooth hydraulic movement. It was so familiar yet so new.

It was cold in the flat. The central heating had been off for five days. Siobhan had always had it on full blast, claiming she felt the cold more than most, something to do with her circulation. He'd always wished it was cooler, complained, tried to open windows when she wasn't looking or slip the thermostat down a bit. It was cold now and he wished it was so hot that the paint on the walls would melt . . .

She'd cleared away all the mess. There were three huge black bin-bags in the kitchen, full of his broken records, and the Christmas tree stood naked and pitiful on the fire escape by the kitchen door, what was left of its decorations piled into a carrier bag and left by the fireplace. She'd taken all the nice bits and pieces that had made it their home, the vases, the clocks, the dhurrie rug. It was spotlessly clean. Everything was in its place. It smelled of furniture polish and Windolene. It was horrible.

He'd wanted to turn around and leave the moment he'd walked in. Rosanne's scruffy wickerwork basket, outside the bedroom door, was gone and her lead no longer hung from the hook in the hallway. It was silent, cold, dead and empty.

Karl sat heavily on the sofa, their sofa. Where she had sat six nights ago and told him it was over, where he had clung on to her legs and begged her to let him stay. He put his head in his hands and let the silence and the chilling emptiness of the flat engulf him. It occurred to him, for the first time since she'd gone, that she wasn't coming back. They hadn't had a tiff; they weren't having a breather from each other; it was over. She wasn't coming home.

For the very first time in his whole life, Karl was alone.

# CHAPTER TWENTY-SIX

Cheri had seen him come home on Christmas Eve, two months ago now. It was the first time he'd been back since that radio show. She'd stood in her pure-white fluffy bathrobe and watched him from the window; he looked grey and dull and monotone, not like the Technicolored Karl she remembered. She'd watched him put his key in the lock and had almost been able to see the pain flicker across his face as he slowly pushed open the door . . .

She could imagine what he was feeling. Of course she could, the whole country knew what he was feeling, for God's sake. He was a celebrity – which was just so bloody typical. When she'd met him he'd been nothing but a lowly dance-teacher. Then she'd dumped him, and now, because of their affair, because of *her*, he was famous, splashed all over the papers, his face popping up with grating regularity on the pages of gossip magazines and on TV chat shows. He'd even – and it made Cheri's blood boil just thinking about it – been interviewed by Richard and Judy. Richard and Judy! First London and now the whole bloody country was enraptured, smitten, head-over-heels in love with Karl bloody Kasparov. Poor Karl Kasparov.

Poor Karl, my arse, Cheri had thought. Poor Karl, who'd taken her with such ferocity and regularity on that chair at the Sol y Sombra. Poor Karl who'd caressed and licked every inch, every corner, every soft, supple, delightful nook and cranny of her firm, ripe body, groaning and grunting like an animal with undisguised desire. Poor Karl, who lied to, cheated, deceived and betrayed the woman he'd publicly professed to loving so much. Cheri really didn't feel much sympathy.

OK, so she'd made the running. He'd been harder than most. In fact, he'd been her greatest conquest. She'd wanted him because she thought he was unattainable, because every Saturday morning she'd look out of her window and see Karl, Siobhan and their sweet little dog walk back from the shops, laden with bags, and they'd be laughing and chatting about wonderfully domestic issues and mutual friends and their plans for the day, and he would casually place a hand on Siobhan's shoulder and look at her as if she was the only woman in the world, as if she wasn't fat, as if it didn't matter. Karl patently had no idea what he was missing. He was a handsome man. The hair and the sideburns were a bit silly and some of his shirts were a little loud but she could see that he was fit; he had a good solid neck, wide shoulders, a great bum, accentuated by his tighter than currently fashionable trousers and wonderful thick black hair, shiny with gel. And she just loved Irish accents, had never been able to resist them. He could do better than that, she'd decided. He just needed something, or someone, to make him realize. She was doing him a favour.

It had been hard at first, getting his attention. 'Come on,' she'd wanted to shout at him, 'come over here, take a look at a real woman, look at what you're missing – you can have me, I'm yours. I promise you, you'll never look back, never be happy with a fat woman again.' But to no avail. He looked at her, he smiled, he said 'Morning' when they passed in the entrance or on the street, but he didn't 'notice' her. And the more he didn't notice, the more she wanted him. It became almost an obsession, deciding what to wear in the mornings, listening out for the slam of his front door, ensuring that their paths crossed at least once a day. She'd followed him once, wondering where he went every evening at six o'clock in his Hawaiian shirts and peg trousers, and had discovered that he taught a dance class. At last, a connection, a way in. She could jive, her father had taught her when she was a little girl. She'd waited until the class finished and then followed him home again, colliding with him at the front door and engineering a conversation towards an invitation to join his next class.

Even then it had been hard. She'd turned up every Tuesday and summoned every ounce of her passion to inject into the childish steps of the dance, ensuring that she always partnered Karl, that every move she made shouted '*sex*', lassoing him with her eyes, hooking him with a grind of her hips, and smiling, always smiling. But still, nothing. He would compliment her on her dancing, express his gratitude that at last he had a partner who had a true appreciation of Ceroc, buy her a beer, walk her home afterwards. But nothing. Siobhan this, Siobhan that, he talked about her all the time and eventually she understood that if she wanted Karl she would have to take him. So she did. But she'd soon tired of him.

And now he was famous – rich and famous. And where was her credit, her glory? Where would Karl be now if it hadn't been for Cheri? Just another low-profile, anonymous DJ on local radio, that's where.

It wasn't fair. All her life Cheri had dreamt of fame, had dreamt of being a prima ballerina, until she'd suddenly shot up to five foot ten and realized that she wasn't going to be the next Margot Fonteyn, she wasn't going to be showered with roses and pursued by millionaires. And as far as she was concerned, her unwanted growth-spurt was the only reason why Darcey 'bitch-face' Bussell had ever made it; it should have been her.

It wasn't right that Karl was famous and she wasn't, that she received no recognition, stuck in the chorus line of undistinguished musicals in London's less dazzling theatres while Karl was partying it up with celebrities all over town. She was twenty-six, talented and beautiful, but she wouldn't be for ever – it would be too late one day; she'd be old and ugly and her chance would have gone.

The more Cheri thought about Karl and his sudden fall into the lap of celebrity, the more she wanted to take up her role. She was, after all, the woman referred to constantly in interviews with Karl, in newspaper articles, she *was* that 'disposable woman'. In a way, she was famous already – famous for being a marriage-wrecking bitch from hell.

And, then, one day the previous week, she'd had a sudden revelation. She'd been watching something on the telly, about a woman who regretted her part in breaking up some relationship or other, so had plotted and planned and brought them back together, and then everyone thought she was wonderful. She could do that! Of course she could. And then *she* would be famous. And famous for being good, not for being a bitch, famous for bringing Karl and Siobhan back together. She'd be a heroine, everyone would love her. She could already imagine the stories in the newspapers: '*34–24–34 beauty Cheri said she could bear the guilt no longer. "I never meant to hurt anyone," she said today from her Battersea penthouse, "I was just lonely. All I want now is for Karl and Siobhan to be happy."*' Cheri knew how the media worked – a griefstricken DJ publicly emptying his soul over the airwaves was great, great press; the unnamed ex-lover suddenly emerging from the woodwork to mend his heart was pure media nectar.

Cheri felt a small shiver of excitement fizz down her spine – this might just work! All she had to do was work out the logistics. Where was Siobhan? How could she contact her? How would she convince her that she had her best interests at heart? It would mean playing the 'nice girl', she realized that, but she reckoned she could pull it off.

Cheri let the curtain drop and curled herself up on the sofa with a mug of fragrant peppermint tea and a bottle of pale-oyster nail polish. She had some thinking to do.

Siobhan had been a wreck when she and Karl had first split up, as the full realization of what had happened began to sink in. It was over, she and Karl were over, and for the first week she'd done nothing but pull Rosanne to her and cry into her fur. Karl had kept phoning and kept phoning and she'd resolutely refused to take his calls even though a soft, aching part of her heart was desperate to talk to him, to hear his gentle voice and make him feel better. She'd heard his radio show and listened to every single song he'd played for her, sat and hugged her knees in her old bedroom while Karl shared their most intimate memories with half of London. She'd talked to his voice on the radio, hoping that he'd answer back, and when he hadn't she'd cried and cried.

Her mother had tried to reason with her, tried to persuade her to take Karl's calls. It was a mistake, darling, she'd said to her, that boy really loves you, you know that, why can't you give him a second chance? Siobhan knew that part of her mother's wish for a reconciliation was an instinctive maternal fear that her daughter would be left on the shelf, that she was thirty-six years old and Karl might be her last chance, but she also knew that her mother was talking sense. After the horror of discovering Karl's secret had faded away and she was left, alone, in her draughty old bedroom in her mother's house in Potters Bar, it did occur to Siobhan that Karl should be forgiven, that she could, probably, learn to trust him again, that he did love her as much as she deserved to be loved and that the two of them could repair the damage and still make a beautiful life for themselves in the flat in Battersea. But something stopped her thought processes from advancing beyond these vague notions, something stopped her from taking his phonecalls or picking up the phone or packing her bags and driving back to the flat and saying 'Darling, I'm home.'

She was haunted, haunted by images of Karl, naked and sweating, pumping up and down and in and out of Cheri. Every time she closed her eyes, she imagined it, Karl's rump clenching and unclenching, quivering and wobbling, ramming and pounding, driving himself in and out of Cheri, deeper and harder and faster. It made her feel sick. It disgusted her. And try as she might, she couldn't exorcise the image. It was with her every moment of the day, inexorably linked with her thoughts of Karl, tainting every attempt she made to be reasonable about the whole sorry situation. It was like someone had spilt a bottle of ink over all the wonderful memories she had of Karl and their life together.

So she didn't call and she didn't go back and she stayed in her room in Potters Bar growing more and more unhappy, waiting, she supposed when she thought about it later, like a princess at the top of the tower, for Karl to come and rescue her. But he didn't. He talked about her to half the entire population of London, about them and their relationship, he tried to talk to her on the telephone. But he didn't come for her.

Then, one Sunday evening, at the end of January, she picked up the phone in her mother's hallway and she called Rick. It was a most unexpected thing to have done. She hadn't really thought about it, hadn't given herself a chance to feel nervous about what she was doing, she'd just picked up the phone and dialled. She supposed, in retrospect, that she'd needed a lift, an ego boost. Her confidence levels had never been so low, and the only thing that lifted her spirits was the memory of that night in Scotland and the way Rick had looked at her, touched her, made her feel.

She and Rick chatted for half an hour, about how cold it was, about how dreary Potters Bar was, about Christmas and New Year, family and friends, Fulham and food. It was an ordinary conversation, it was full of small talk and inconsequentialities, but it was warm and bound together with unspoken words of friendship and caring, and after Siobhan had put the phone down she'd felt better than she'd felt for weeks.

They'd chatted a few more times after that and then, one day in mid-February, Rick had suggested she get out of Potters Bar for a night, come for a night out in Fulham; he'd take her to the Blue Elephant because she'd mentioned that it was her favourite restaurant, and she could stay at his, in the spare room, of course.

It hadn't sounded like a date when he'd suggested it, just an invitation from a friend, worried that another friend was about to die of boredom. He'd come in for a cup of tea and utterly charmed Siobhan's mother. 'What a delightful, delightful young man,' she'd said, with a slightly girlish tone to her voice, 'and so handsome. And fancy driving all the way from Fulham to Potters Bar to pick you up. Not many men would do that, you know.'

Rick had raved about how much weight Siobhan had lost – which she had; she couldn't eat when she was unhappy and had gone down to a healthy size fourteen. 'Not that you weren't gorgeous before, of course!' he'd smiled. They hadn't talked much in the car on the way into London, just listened to music and grinned at each other a lot. 'It's so good to see you,' Rick kept saying, '*so* good.'

And Siobhan had smiled and told him how good it was to see him, too. Which it was. Absolutely wonderful, in fact. He'd put his hand over hers and squeezed it, beaming at her and then beaming to himself.

In retrospect, Siobhan could see that it was really quite strange. After all, they didn't really know each other, had only actually met once before, but there had just been so much *warmth* between them, they were like old friends. It had felt so comfortable sitting there in the passenger seat of Rick's new BMW, not talking, just listening to music and smiling at each other. It was as if they'd known then that they had all the time in the world, that this was just the beginning.

Rick had parked outside his house and then they'd walked, arms around each other and terribly slowly, like new lovers do, down Fulham Broadway, towards the Blue Elephant. It's easy to gauge the newness of a relationship by how slowly a couple walk together. Siobhan and Karl had reached the medium canter of the established couple years earlier, their motivation for walking becoming a desire to get from A to B rather than a chance to spend time together.

But even though any passing stranger might have assumed that they were brand-new lovers in the first blissful throes of romance, as far as Siobhan was concerned, they *weren't* on a date. They just weren't. She was still raw and in pain, and the idea of a date, of getting involved in another relationship was quite out of the question. She was enjoying Rick's company more than she could possibly have imagined, but she was still in love with Karl.

Which is why, after the tiny little Thai waitress had taken their order and removed their menus, the first question Siobhan had asked Rick was, 'So, how's Karl?'

Rick had shrugged, wryly. 'You tell me.'

'What – haven't you spoken to him?'

Rick shook his head.

'Really?'

'Of course not. He blames me, doesn't he?'

'What for?' Siobhan was confused.

'For you finding out about his affair. Because it was me who gave him *that* tape recorder.'

'What?! God, that's so pathetic! So unfair. You didn't make him take it home with him, you didn't make me press the Play button and you *certainly* didn't shove his dick into that slag!' Siobhan looked around her as she realized that she'd started shouting. 'Sorry,' she said. And then she'd started crying. 'I'm sorry. It's just . . . it just hurts so much.'

Rick had passed her a tissue, made a joke, made her smile through her tears. He'd ordered champagne and they'd talked all night, about Karl, about Tamsin, about love, about life, about everything. It was the first chance she'd had to really talk about her feelings, to put into words the disgust that she felt about what Karl had done with Cheri. None of her female friends were single and they were all Karl's friends, too. She hadn't wanted to put them in an awkward position. But it was different with Rick. *He* was different.

'OK,' Rick had said as they left the restaurant three hours and two bottles of champagne later, 'enough talk-therapy – you need some fun. You need to drink a lot more champagne and get horribly drunk.'

'Oh, Rick, I don't know,' Siobhan had laughed. 'Look what happened last time you and I drank too much champagne together.'

They'd both giggled, but then Rick had turned and held Siobhan's hands in his and looked into her eyes. 'Siobhan,' he'd said, 'you know how I feel about you. And I have to say that nothing's changed. I still think you're the most amazing woman. You're . . . you're . . . well, you know. But right now you don't need that of me. You need a friend. And I really, really want to be your friend. Hey!' he smiled, 'I'll be your girlfriend, if you like! I can do that!'

'What?' Siobhan had laughed.

'Yeah! Come on. Let's go back to mine, have a couple of Sea Breezes and get tarted up, and then we'll go to a club and see who can pull the ugliest person, and then we can come home, put on our dressing-gowns and moan about men over a cup of decaff! It'll be excellent!'

So they had. Rick had put on a Boyzone CD, they'd drunk more than a couple of lurid-pink Sea Breezes and danced around his flat together while they got ready, Rick camping it up ridiculously: 'What do you think – does this make my bum look fat? Beige chinos or the khaki chinos – or do they clash with my hair?'

They'd caught a cab to a dive of a club off the New King's Road, full of foreign-language students, Australians and South Africans, and Rick had ordered them white-wine spritzers at the bar. 'Mmmmmm,' he'd said, 'I've never had one of these before, they're quite nice, aren't they!'

They'd danced for ages, to Oasis and Counting Crows and REM, chatting and laughing and eyeing up everyone on the dance floor. 'See that guy over there,' Rick had said, 'he's looking at you.'

'Which one?'

'That tall one, with the white T-shirt on – brown hair – over there.' He'd indicated with his eyebrows.

'No, he's not – don't be stupid.'

'Yes he is! Look – he can't take his eyes off you. D'you want me to go and say something to him?'

'No!' Siobhan had grabbed his arm. 'No! Don't you dare! Please – don't!'

But it was too late. Rick was already winding his way across the dance floor. Siobhan had turned away in horror and stood rooted to the spot, hoping that the flashing plastic tiles would open up and swallow her until, a few minutes later, she'd felt Rick's hand on her shoulder.

'His name's Mike, he's American, he's an engineering

student, he's nineteen and he thinks you're gorgeous.'

'Oh, don't be ridiculous.'

'I'm not! Look! He's waving at you.'

And sure as could be – he was. Siobhan had waved back, a feeble little gesture and turned away again.

'Aren't you going to talk to him?'

'No way!'

'Oh, go on!'

'No. Really. I couldn't. I just couldn't. I don't even fancy him.'

'What! How can you not fancy him? Look at him. He's handsome, he's clever and he's only nineteen!'

'Exactly! What the hell am I going to have in common with someone who's probably never seen a black-and-white television, who's never owned a vinyl record and who thinks that all-night TV is a God-given right?'

They'd both dissolved into hysterical laughter then, and Rick hadn't pushed it. 'Fair enough,' he'd said, 'fair enough!'

By the time she and Rick got back to his flat, at three o'clock in the morning, they'd drunk another five spritzers, chatted to dozens of people, all young enough to conceivably be their children, had two phone numbers a piece, Rick had been thrown out of the ladies' toilets twice and Siobhan was laughing so hard she could barely breathe.

'Oh, Rick,' she'd giggled, 'you really are the best friend a girl could possibly ask for!' Siobhan hadn't had so much fun since Brighton, before she'd met Karl. She'd never been a single girl around town. She and Karl had moved to London together and made all their friends together, and because she'd never worked in an office she'd never really had 'girlfriends' as such, just couple friends. And even though tonight had just been a joke, a piss take, it had given her an idea of what she might have been missing out on for the last fifteen years. Fun. Spontaneity. Childishness. Silliness. It had been brilliant.

'Feeling a bit happier now?' he'd asked, handing her her coffee and joining her, dressing-gowned, on the sofa.

'Well, let's see. I've been taken out to dinner to my favourite restaurant, I've drunk champagne, vodka and white wine spritzers, I've been lusted over by a nineteen-year-old American, a twenty-year-old South African and a twenty-two-year-old Estonian, I've danced myself silly for three hours, I've walked home in the rain singing motown and now I'm wrapped up in an airing-cupboard-warm dressing-gown on a squidgy sofa in a beautiful flat, drinking real Colombian coffee. Yes, I'd say I'm feeling a bit happier now.'

'Glad to be of service,' he'd said.

They'd fallen silent for a moment then and stared awkwardly into their coffee cups feeling that something more should be said, that this was a special moment. Siobhan had been the first to look up and had been suddenly startled by the blue of Rick's eyes, by the softness of his skin, the sincerity of his expression, the kindness of his mouth and the warmth of his smile.

'Oh, Rick,' she'd said, 'who are you? You always seem to be in the right place at the right time, saying the right things. You always make me feel so much better, so much like I want to feel.' She'd looked deep into his eyes. 'Are you an angel?'

He'd smiled and put down his cup, taking Siobhan's hands in his. 'No,' he'd said, 'no, I'm not an angel.' And then they'd instinctively moved towards each other, across the ivory damask skin of the sofa, and grabbed hold of each other in a deep, warm embrace.

She'd clasped him to her and rested her head against his, breathing him in, breathing through the layers, the slightly herbal aroma of his hair gel, the fruity tang of his shampoo, the oily pungency of his warm scalp and, underneath it all, the base notes that words couldn't describe – the smell of him. It seeped through her nostrils, down the back of her throat and rushed into her heart. She caught her breath and held him tighter.

Siobhan really hadn't expected to fall in love with Rick. She'd thought she was still getting over Karl. And maybe she was. But she was unable to control the feelings that swept through her like a magical hurricane whenever she was with him. He made her feel as special as Karl had always told her she was, he made her feel beautiful and secure and brand-spanking-new, like she'd just been taken out of the box.

She truly felt that Rick was an angel. They were two angels together and she had never felt so serenely, perfectly happy in her whole life as she had in the last month, since she'd been going out with Rick. This was as good as it got, as it could ever possibly get.

And one day soon, she didn't know when, she was going to have to tell Karl all about it . . .

# CHAPTER TWENTY-SEVEN

*The Evening Standard 27 February 1997*

## A Star is Reborn

In today's faddish, fickle world, in which fashion, fame, opinion and favour are fleeting and so dependent on the vagaries of the media and its self-appointed pundits (and I include myself in this possibly quite disagreeable fraternity), it is gratifying to discover that from time to time a talent can emerge that is so unquestionable, so prodigious, so undeniably brilliant, that it can survive a backlash from even the most vicious hack's keyboard. I stand humbled.

The name on the invitation sounded familiar. Ralph McLeary. Those of you with elephantine memories may well recall the artist – I certainly didn't. The accompanying press release filled in the gaps for me. Ralph McLeary was a Royal College luminary back in 1986, whom I, in this very column, once described in a glowing, almost embarrassingly gushing manner as 'a young man with an incestuous relationship with his medium, a young man who has created, at the tender age of twenty-one years, works in oil on canvas of such magnitude and importance, of such precocious maturity that I am obliged to employ the word "genius" to describe him.' I was not alone at the time. The press was united in a froth-mouthed frenzy. It all came flooding back to me.

However, I have no recollection of his works, not one brushstroke or colour or shape; the detail has been cleared from my ageing and ragged memory to make room for the proliferation of fresh young painters paraded before my jaded eyes in the intervening years, whose works I am contractually bound to find words, daily, to describe.

I am, I fear, a fickle old man, my head so easily turned by a pretty canvas and the indulgent pleasure of my own words on paper. But, like the abandoned wife who makes a dramatic re-entrance – years after she has been traded in for a younger model, whose charms soon fade – thinner, happier, more confident, and glowing with inner beauty, Ralph McLeary has re-emerged to put us all to shame. His show, currently on display at the Notting Hill gallery of his one-time mentor Philippe Dauvignon, is a reminder that art is not, and nor should it ever be, prey to the same fads and foibles as the eminently more disposable, high-turnover worlds of fashion, film or popular music, and that a true genius can quite happily survive and, in McLeary's case, positively flourish without the ego-driven attentions of some fossilized Fleet Street flunkey.

These are McLeary's first works in over five years and I find my fingertips nervously twitching above my keyboard with the effort of not gushing forth, once again, in the manner of a lascivious old man. I will restrain myself.

McLeary's work has matured in a most satisfactory manner, his earlier anarchic stabs, jabs and thrusts at the canvas being replaced by a soft, almost romantic realism in a series of portraits of heart-breaking beauty and haunting eloquence. Maybe the previous McLeary incarnation was suffering from a delayed and troubled adolescence, but the McLeary of today is all grown up with a freshly pressed shirt, a decent haircut and is, no doubt, nice to his parents. And all the better for it. In these days of toilet bowls, chocolate bars and maimed animals masquerading as art, it makes an old man very happy to view a collection of paintings that speak so traditionally and with such beauty of the simple concepts of love and happiness and light and dark. I will not say another word . . .

Ralph's back was a mess, his shoulders ached, his hands felt arthritic. His nose was streaming, his throat was raw, his sinuses felt like they had fishing hooks stuffed into them. His clothes hung off his rake-like, emaciated body like enormous flaps of skin, dark circles surrounded the grey pits of his eyes, he hadn't had a haircut in nearly two months and his hair was matted into small grimy peaks of grease and paint and dust.

He looked appalling, he felt appalling, but he didn't care. He was a man possessed. He hadn't had a decent night's sleep since Christmas, he hadn't been out for a meal, touched a drink, seen his friends, watched telly, been to the shops, had sex, had a bath, read a paper, sat on a sofa. Nothing. All he'd done, for nine weeks, was paint and smoke. Paint and smoke. Paint and smoke.

He'd survived on Ginster's pasties, plasticy sandwiches and microwaved burgers from the Esso station around the corner on Cable Street. His social life consisted of sharing the occasional spliff in the wheelie-bin area with Murray the security guard.

Bed was a large, smelly piece of foam, covered over with an old dust-sheet, and his pillow a couple of T-shirts folded into each other. Entertainment was his paint-splattered old tranny and sex was the odd half-hearted wank.

Everything else was painting and cigarettes.

It had been a small life, an uncomfortable life. It was cold and dark and lonely and unhealthy. He lay on his mattress at night, listening to the wind whistling through the cracks in the window-panes, the scurrying of rats outside his door, the never-ending drone of four lanes of traffic speeding by on Cable Street. He awoke each morning at five, he washed in the toilets down the corridor, he painted, he popped out to the Esso station, he ate something, he painted, he painted and he painted, he went to bed at midnight, one in the morning, two in the morning, and then he woke up and did the same thing all over again.

He was prolific. Pro-lif-ic. After so many barren, stagnant years, he was unstoppable. He'd phoned Philippe, who'd been to visit him after the first two weeks, seen what he'd already produced and immediately written him out a Coutts account cheque for five hundred pounds, which Ralph had banked and spent on canvases and paints.

Day by day the walls of his studio were lined with more and more paintings – twenty-one paintings to be precise, small and large, portraits and still lifes. Twenty-one paintings in sixty-four days. Quite an achievement. Philippe said he'd never known anything like it.

What Ralph didn't explain to Philippe, because it sounded so naff, was that his inspiration through it all had, strangely enough, been a DJ, a DJ called Karl Kasparov.

Ralph had tuned into ALR one afternoon, by mistake. He didn't usually enjoy commercial radio, all those adverts and brain-dead DJs. But something about the desolate tone of the Irish DJ's voice had appealed to him and then he'd understood what he was talking about – lost love – and he'd been almost moved to tears by the empathy he felt with him. He sounded like such a nice bloke and his honesty was breathtaking. And then he'd seen a picture of him on the front of some trashy magazine in the petrol station and had put two and two together and realized who he was. He was the guy from the upstairs flat at Almanac Road, the one with the quiff and the spaniel and the fat girlfriend, the guy he'd said hello to in passing dozens of times, but had never really spoken to . . .

He'd started listening to his show every day, like the rest of London, just to make sure Karl was all right, to find out how he was feeling, poor bastard. And he'd found that Karl's misery had fuelled his own, motivated him, inspired him. Cut off from humanity, from reality, and from the source of his own unhappiness, Ralph had needed Karl to remind him why he was there in the first place. Three-thirty p.m. had been the high spot of his day, his chance to feel something again, to feel human. He had a lot to thank Karl Kasparov for. He'd never really met him, but he felt like an old mate now, a really good mate. Once this is over, he'd promised himself, I'm going to buy that bloke a drink; actually, I'm going to buy that bloke a lot of drinks.

*

Ralph sat back now, a cigarette burning between his fingers, his stiff, sore back against the wall, his knees brought into his chest. He sucked hard on his Marlboro and blew out a thick cloud of soft, white smoke. He had finished. He couldn't paint another stroke even if he wanted to. His collection was complete and he was satisfied. He looked around his studio and breathed a sigh of relief. And then he felt a small stab of sadness.

God, he missed Jem. He missed Jem so much. He couldn't wait to go home.

He'd managed two days of attempting normality at Almanac Road after their disastrous curry in Bayswater, two days of hiding out in his bedroom, trying to avoid Jem, trying to avoid Smith, controlling his urge just to leap on her, shake her by the shoulders and tell her all about Cheri, to tell her that Smith was a tosser, before he realized that he had to go. Jem barely acknowledged him, the atmosphere was foul. He couldn't live like that. So he'd packed a small bag and gone to the studio, started painting and not stopped since. He spent Christmas Day painting, New Year's Eve painting. He'd phoned Smith to say he didn't know when he'd be back, he'd phoned his parents to wish them a Merry Christmas and a Happy New Year and, apart from Philippe, he hadn't contacted anyone else for more than two months.

But now it was over and time to start living again. Besides, he had a party to organize. Thursday night was the press launch but Friday was his night. Invite whoever you want, Philippe had said, your mum and dad, your friends, your flatmates, your Uncle Fred. Get some caterers in, a sound system, have a party, you deserve it – and for God's sake, get a haircut, you look appalling.

He had a plan. He'd go back to Almanac Road now. He'd have a bath, he'd get one of those £3.99 spit-roast chickens from Cullens and have it with mashed potato and gravy and eat it with *cutlery*! The thought excited him. He'd dig out his address book, he'd whack out some sort of groovy party invite on his Mac, print off a few dozen, go down to the Post Office, buy some stamps and send them out to all his friends. He'd put one in Jem's room and one in Smith's room.

And then he'd go upstairs. On the way to the first-floor flat he'd stop and put an invitation through Karl Kasparov's letter-box. It was the least he could do for him after everything he'd, albeit unwittingly, done for him.

Then he would wander up the stairs to the first floor and he'd knock on the door and ask that Cheri girl if he could come in for a moment. He'd accept her offer of a cup of tea and then he'd ask her a favour. She'd be confused at first but then he'd explain, in graphic detail, why he wanted her to do this for him and, hopefully, she'd smile and say 'Sure', and she'd be glad to help. He'd finish his tea, thank her from the bottom of his heart, shake her hand, maybe even kiss her cheek and go back downstairs.

And then he'd walk into his bedroom, take off his shoes, strip to his boxers, peel back his soft, heavy duvet and slip into bed. Aaaah! And then he'd sleep, all night and most of the next day, and he wouldn't wake up until the sun had already started to sink in the sky, until the sky was the colour of blueberries and plums and the football scores were tap-tapping their way through to *Grandstand*. And then . . . and then what?

And then he'd smile from ear to ear because he'd be half-way to happiness, half-way to where he wanted to be, half-way to Jem.

## CHAPTER TWENTY-EIGHT

His coat was hanging in the hallway, his clumpy boots stood side by side by the doormat, laces loose and undone, toes slightly turned in, just like his feet. Jem's heart missed a micro-beat. She hung her coat over his and wandered into the living room, looking for more signs of his return.

The ashtray on the coffee table overflowed with Marlboro butts and the remote control sat where he had always left it, on the arm of the sofa. In the kitchen a plate smeared with congealed gravy and shreds of crispy chicken skin sat at an angle in the sink, half-heartedly rinsed. A packet of Smash sat on the counter, by the kettle, surrounded by hard, floury nuggets. The door of the dishwasher was open, again like he had always left it, and a tea-bag sat in a pool of its own tan emissions on top of the bin.

So, thought Jem, the Phantom Diary-Reader is back.

The bathroom was humid and slick with condensation – large wet footprints steamed on the bathmat still on the floor, his old green toothbrush with the long-flattened bristles lay on the side of the sink. Small globs of toothpaste clung to the white enamel.

Jem allowed herself a smile and walked quickly across the hall to Ralph's bedroom, her heart racing with anticipation. She knocked tentatively at the door and pushed it slowly open when there was no reply. Her spirits dropped as she encountered an empty room. He was out. He was out, but he was definitely back! Ralph was back!

She'd really, really, *really* missed Ralph. She'd missed everything about him, his sleeping presence behind the closed door of his bedroom while she got ready for work in the mornings, his half-drunk mugs of old, cold, milky tea lying around the flat in the most unexpected places – she'd found one in the bathroom cabinet once – his bare-footed padding around the flat, the packets of Marlboro stored all over the place like a squirrel's nuts, but most of all she just missed him being there.

She'd tried her hardest to put all that love stuff to the back of her mind. It was just silly. She didn't love Ralph – how could she love him? She didn't really know him, she'd never kissed him, never slept with him – she was just fond of him. And he was just being silly, too, as silly as all those other boys, all those other 'I Love You's. She was sure he'd realized how silly he'd been over the past couple of months, probably had a new posh, skinny girlfriend by now. And she'd got over her anger about the diary-reading business. It was good that Ralph had gone away, away from Almanac Road. It had given her time to put her mind into order and make sense of that night in Bayswater. If he'd stayed around she'd have been confused and bewildered, constantly comparing Ralph and Smith, wondering what to do. She'd have worried about the falling-off of her feelings towards Smith, the growing intensity of her love for Ralph. She might even have started to believe that Ralph was right, that they were supposed to be together and Smith wasn't her destiny.

Which, given the way things had been going between

them for the last two months, was not quite such an outlandish theory.

Things weren't going well. Things were, in fact, quite hideous. Smith had changed so much lately, since his weekend away in St Albans. At first she thought maybe he was sulking, maybe he was jealous about her and Ralph having such a great weekend together, going out for *that* curry together, maybe he *was* just like all the other boys after all. But after a while she'd realized that he wasn't jealous, he wasn't sulking, but that he quite simply wasn't interested in her any more. And she didn't have the first idea what to do about it. He was no longer affectionate, no longer funny, he didn't make an effort, hadn't been out with her and her friends for two months, hadn't held her hand, taken her out for dinner, phoned her at work, nothing. Jem was well aware that she didn't have very high expectations as far as men were concerned, she didn't demand much in the way of attention or romance, but this was ridiculous! She'd tried to talk to him about it, tried to voice her concerns without coming across as insecure or paranoid, which she most definitely *wasn't*, but each time he'd reassure her that really, he was fine, of course he was, he was just a bit tired, a bit stressed, a bit overworked, a bit preoccupied. And he'd apologize and stroke her hair absent-mindedly and that was that. She didn't like to go on about it because she knew from her own experience how trying that was, the incessant questioning: 'Are you all right? . . . Are you *sure* you're all right? . . . Why are you so quiet? . . . What's the matter? . . . Is it me? . . .' etc etc. She'd hated it and she refused to inflict it on somebody else. Even if they quite patently *weren't* all right.

At first she'd been worried by Smith's change in

attitude, alarmed, had spent hours agonizing over what might be the problem. Boredom? Depression? Someone else? And then a couple of days ago she'd stopped thinking and stopped worrying and all of a sudden she'd stopped caring. And that was more worrying than anything. If she truly loved Smith, surely she'd still care? No matter how awful he was, how cold, how distant? But she didn't.

Somewhere along the line, she realized with horror, they'd turned into one of those hideous middle-aged couples you see staring into space together in restaurants and pubs, seething with uncommunicated resentment and loathing, staying together for years on end, compromised to the nth degree, because neither one of them ever had the guts just to get up and walk out, one of those couples who just *don't care about each other any more*.

Jem had tried to be positive about it; she knew that the early pheromone-induced passionate phase of a relationship was not a long-lived state of affairs and the fact that she and Smith had been living together from day one had probably hastened the whole process towards its inevitable conclusion a little, but still, it had only been five months. Surely they were allowed a little more love-hued bliss than that? But it appeared not.

And now, Ralph was back. Ralph who *did* care about her. Lovely, lovely, lovely Ralph. Dearest, darling, gorgeous Ralph. It was the happiest she'd felt in weeks.

She wandered into her bedroom and kicked off her shoes.

There was a small red envelope sitting on her bed, addressed to Miss Jemima Caterick, in Ralph's untidy handwriting. She leapt upon it and ripped it open. Inside was a brightly coloured invitation on shiny colour-printer paper.

*Ralph is about to be stinking rich.*
*So come and celebrate at*

RALPH'S PARTY

*Get drunk, dance, flirt, do whatever you want – I'm paying.*
*You can even have a look at my paintings if you like.*
*Galerie Dauvignon, 132 Ledbury Road, London W11,*
*Friday 6 March 8.30 onwards.*
RSVP

Jem's spirits lifted substantially. A party! How thrilling! She could wear that lovely rose-printed dress with the skinny straps and all those little buttons down the back that she'd never had a chance to wear before. She'd be able to see Ralph's paintings, as well, these amazing paintings that the press were raving about. There'd be dancing, she hadn't danced for ages – Smith didn't like dancing, of course, boring old git. But she'd dance anyway. With Ralph. She'd dance with Ralph. Sod Smith. Sod him.

She penned a reply and propped it up against Ralph's door.

'Ten pound forty, mate.'

The cab driver held out his hand and peered up at Karl through the open window. Karl slowly ransacked the pockets of his jacket, his coat, his jeans, swaying ever so slightly in the cold, damp night air. He eventually located his wallet, licked the tips of his fingers with a delicate pink tongue, and awkwardly pulled out a twenty-pound note.

'Keep the change,' he slurred, turning heavily on his heel and weaving towards the front steps of number thirty-one. The cab driver eyed the twenty, eyed Karl, shook his head and drove away.

Karl lumbered precariously up the stone steps, left foot, right foot, left foot, right foot, leaning in towards the door to maintain balance, scraping his front-door key around the lock in clockwise and anti-clockwise circles before it finally, more through luck than judgement, slid into the hole. The door opened heavily under his weight and took him somewhat by surprise. He closed the door gently behind him and surprised himself again when a loud slam echoed around the hall. He winced and put his fingers to his lips. Shhhhhhh! He giggled and fell back against the door.

A small pile of letters sat on the shelf in the hall. He picked them up between unwieldy fingers and his face puckered into an absurd mask of concentration as he screwed his eyes open and closed in an attempt to focus his two perfect fields of vision into one perfect field of vision and read the envelopes.

'Miss Shee Dickshon – ha! – shlag.' He tossed the top one away from him, towards the stairway leading to the first-floor flat. 'Miss Esh McNamara – huh! She's no' here, nah – she's fucking *gone*!' he shouted at the envelope. He fished in his inside pocket for a pen, removed the lid with his teeth and began to scrawl all over the front of the envelope: '*She's not fucking here – she's at her fucking mother's – 78 Towbridge Road, Potters Bar, Herts – send her my fucking love.*'

'Siobhan-fucking-McNamara, Mish McNamara, Mish Dickshon, Mish Dickshon, Siobhan.' Cheri's letters flew from his hands all over the carpet and up the stairs. He turned towards his front door in disgust and negotiated the lock, falling on to the floor of the hall, front first. Picking himself up, he noticed a red envelope on his doormat, handwritten, with no stamp.

He tore the envelope open, wobbling gently from side to side and stifling a dainty hiccup. He moved the letter within away from him and towards him until it made itself readable, squinting like an old man reading the *Times*. There was some handwriting scrawled on the back.

'*... listened to your shows ... made me cry ... live downstairs ... know lots of beautiful single women ... thought you could do with a good party ... next Friday ... just a thought ... bring a guest ... champagne all night ... just turn up ...*'

Karl smiled crookedly.

Free champagne, huh? He'd be there. What a nishe bloke, he thought to himself. What a nishe, nishe, nishe, nishe bloke. He smiled again, left his overcoat where it fell on the floor, stumbled into his bedroom and collapsed on top of his unmade bed and into a deep and instantaneous sleep.

Cheri watched Karl from her window, sliding into the front seat of his funny old black car and driving away down Almanac Road. She waited until he was out of view and then strode quickly and lightly to her front door and down the communal stairs, her cashmere-socked feet barely making a sound as she tiptoed across the floorboards.

She stopped outside Karl's door and quickly peered through the hall window, checking that he hadn't unexpectedly returned, before reaching into the back pocket of her jeans and taking out a screwdriver, a nail file and her expired American Express card.

Cheri's plan was starting to gather momentum. She'd had a most unexpected visitor the day before, one of the guys from the basement flat – not the good-looking one she'd had that drink with at Oriel just before Christmas, but the scruffy one – Ralph. He'd asked her for a favour. It was all a bit weird really, and her first instinct had been to say no, but then Ralph had told her who else was going to be there and she'd thought about the journalist at the *Daily Mail* she'd phoned the day before, the one who said they'd be interested in her story, and she'd decided that it might be to her advantage to help out. And besides, he'd been really quite sweet, that Ralph bloke, and such a nice smile.

So she'd said yes and now all she had to do was get into Karl's flat somehow to find what she needed. She knew it was possible. One of her old boyfriends had managed to get her door open a couple of years ago when she'd locked herself out. All the doors in the house were the same, the original ones that had been put in during conversion, so the locks were probably the same, too.

After a good fifteen minutes of manipulation and stress and desperate attempts not to damage the paintwork and gouge large chunks of wood out of the doorjamb, the door suddenly and happily creaked open. Cheri smiled with satisfaction, put her tools back in her jeans pocket and wandered into the flat. She wrinkled her nose a little with distaste. It was a mess: the curtains were drawn, there were piles of old Sunday papers all over the floor, mugs and plates everywhere, takeaway containers balanced precariously on top of the television, and the whole flat was imbued with an overwhelming odour of musty bedsheets and old shoes.

She surveyed the room and wondered where to begin. She didn't even really know what she was looking for. An address book would be a start, she thought, so she headed towards a table that looked like it might, at one point, have been a desk. Her heart was racing under her sweatshirt, reverberating against her ribcage. Her hands were shaking and her breath was short and sharp. She was enjoying this! She began leafing through piles of paper on the table and then trying the drawers. Nothing.

She wandered into the kitchen and then backed out again when she saw the state of it. Why didn't the stupid bastard get a cleaning lady for Christ's sake? He could afford it. To think that she could have . . . yuck . . . with someone so unclean, with such low standards. She shuddered a bit and put the thought to the back of her mind.

Gingerly, she pushed open the bedroom door and took a deep breath against the assault of the smell of his unwashed bedclothes and un-hung-up clothes strewn about the room. She switched on the light and balked at the sight of a pair of unappetizing-looking boxer shorts resting at her feet. She sneered and stepped daintily over them, towards the dressing-table at the far side of the room. Bingo! There it was – exactly what she was looking for. A letter, addressed to Siobhan but covered now in a barely legible scrawl. *78 Towbridge Road, Potters Bar, Herts.* She memorized the address, repeating it to herself several times before placing the letter back on the dressing-table, switching off the bedroom light and softly retracing her steps back to her flat upstairs.

It was all systems go!

Ralph? Ralph? Ralph?

Who the fuck was Ralph?

Siobhan had gone to school with a boy called Ralph – Ralph Millard, a pretty, fey boy with a reputation for being 'posh', but he wasn't even in her year. Her doctor was called Ralph, or was it Rupert? Rodney? No – she didn't know any Ralphs.

So who the hell had sent her this invitation?

She picked it up again and looked at it, turning it over to see if any give-away clues had suddenly appeared on the back. No. Nothing.

It had arrived a week ago, in a parcel of forwarded mail from her mother, in a red, handwritten envelope. It was addressed correctly, to Siobhan McNamara, but without a postcode. The postmark said it had been posted in W1 – could have been anyone. She certainly did not recognize the handwriting and, although it had been marked RSVP, there was no address or telephone number enclosed to which to do so. It was a total mystery. And Siobhan did love a mystery.

She'd deliberately passed by Ledbury Road earlier on that week and satisfied herself that Galerie Dauvignon did actually exist and was actually showing a collection of paintings, but she'd suddenly been too shy to go in and, besides, she was quite enjoying the suspense and didn't want to spoil whatever surprise it was that was awaiting her on Friday night. Maybe it *was* Ralph Millard. He might well have been the type to end up an artist. Maybe he'd always had a secret crush on her and had kept her mother's address all these years, waiting till he'd made a success of his life before getting in touch again, to show off. Or maybe he'd been bearing some sort of grudge for twenty years and now it was pay-back time? No, Siobhan had never said more than two words to the boy.

It was all a wonderful, great, gooey mystery and, as the days had gone by since she'd first opened the invitation, she'd become really quite excited at the prospect, planning her outfit and booking an appointment at the hairdresser's. Whatever it was, *who*ever it was, she was ready for it. The worst thing that could happen would be that it was all a mistake – so what? At least she'd have a chance to get dressed up and show off her new figure and her trendy new haircut. If it was an awful party, all she had to do was leave, hail a cab and go back to Rick's. Back home. She'd only been living at Rick's for a couple of weeks and hadn't quite got into the habit of calling it home yet.

Rick hadn't decided yet whether or not he was coming, although he was every bit as intrigued and excited as Siobhan by the mystery of it. Siobhan knew he was just trying to be cool, trying to play the easygoing boyfriend, giving his new girlfriend some 'space', showing that he was happy to let her go out on her own to a strange party on a Friday night, just like Karl had been in the early days of their romance. 'Oh, no,' Rick had said, so sweetly, 'you don't want me hanging around, cramping your style, you go on your own.' Bless him. Such a sweetheart. Siobhan secretly hoped he wouldn't come. She was still enjoying the euphoria of new-found freedom, the reincarnation of her old independent spirit, which had been buried away for years inside layers of routine, boredom and fat. She wanted to enjoy her adventure tonight alone.

She wandered into the bathroom, the expensive designer bathroom in Rick's flat with the stainless-steel shower compartment and the curved mirrors, the expensive designer bathroom that was polished every two days by the Hungarian cleaning lady who came in every day to clean all the rooms in Rick's expensive designer flat.

She'd lost even more weight after she moved into Rick's flat; it just wasn't the sort of flat that a fat girl could feel comfortable in, it was a thin girl's flat. Something about the sparse fixtures and fittings, the long, flowing swags of curtains, the elegant vases of slender flowers, the glass and chrome objects on skinny, barely-there shelves, the tall, thin Georgian windows, high ceilings and shutters, the soft, elegant minimalism of the place, had just sort of *sucked* the fat off her. She hadn't had to try. And of course, it was a well-known fact that falling in love was one of the most effective diets known to woman.

Once the excess weight had gone she'd been filled with confidence to try different things. So she'd gone to the hairdresser's and winced while they snipped painfully through her pony-tail, screwing her eyes shut as she heard the severed hair fall quietly to the floor, like a whisper. They'd cut her hair to just below her shoulders, into big chunky layers, a 'Rachel' she supposed it was called, although she hated to admit it. They'd put some blonder streaks at the front and blow-dried it upside-down. She'd shaken her shorn hair and thrown back her head, and there in the mirror in front of her was a young woman! A young, modern woman of the nineties. Karl would have been horrified. He'd loved her hair almost as much as he loved her, Siobhan had sometimes thought, and he hated change.

From the hairdresser's, Siobhan had gone straight to Covent Garden, to Oasis and Warehouse and French Connection, and bought herself a rather extravagant amount of clothes – fashionable clothes to go with her fashionable hair! And not a pair of leggings among them.

Rick had loved her new look, commenting in a very unboyfriendlike way on how her old hair had dragged her down, as beautiful as it was, and how much better the new cut framed her face and accentuated her fine, Irish features, the blonde streaks bringing out the dazzling blue of her eyes.

She was shampooing her new hair now, marvelling still at how much less hassle it was and wondering why she'd saddled herself with such a ridiculous amount of hair for so many bloody years. She was free – free of her hair and free of her fat and free of the past.

She rinsed it through, stepped out of the shower and into a soft, cream towel, shaking her head to loosen the droplets of water from her ears, while she dried her neck and shoulders. She picked up the glass of wine she'd left sitting by the sink, now sparkling with beads of jewel-like condensation, and took a large gulp. She rolled the glass between the palms of her hands, turned to look at her reflection in the mirror behind her and smiled a little smile of excitement.

## CHAPTER TWENTY-NINE

'Oh, ma' God – look at you! You are elegance personified – no?!' Philippe slapped Ralph on the shoulder and looked around the room for a reaction from the caterers who were wheeling in trolleys of food and champagne from a van parked outside. Philippe always did everything for effect.

Ralph pulled at his tie and shifted nervously from foot to foot. He'd felt self-conscious all the way to the gallery. It was the first time he'd worn a suit and tie since his aunt's funeral the previous year. It was a nice suit, though. Dolce & Gabbana. Ha! If Claudia could see him now! It was grey (this season's black, apparently) with nice neat little pockets. They'd talked him into a rather radical stripy shirt with a cutaway collar. 'Natural clothes-horse,' the small, painfully fashionable Spanish assistant had told him admiringly as he held ties up to his chest. 'Yes – 'ave you ever thought about modelling?' the tall, painfully fashionable French assistant had agreed. 'You 'ave the 'eight, the post-yure, you know? Ees so nice, for me, when you wear these clothes, ees so nice!' They'd stood and beamed at him.

Ralph had been flattered but embarrassed. But he'd liked the suit and the groovy shirt and he particularly liked the natty thin black tie they'd chosen for him – more Madness than Kid Creole, and not too trendy. He'd walked out into Bond Street, six hundred pounds poorer, but feeling ten inches taller. He'd faced the trauma of designer-clothes shopping and he'd triumphed. Male model indeed!

It was important that the suit was right. Very important. He wanted everything to be right tonight. This was more important than the opening night, more important than any of those overblown old farts and pretentious tossers who'd come to criticize his work for the papers. He'd been up to James Street to have his hair cut that morning and had finally relented to one of those proper old-fashioned wet shaves with steaming towels that his barber had been offering him for years. New shoes. New whistle. Soft chin. Best socks. It was party night.

'So, Ralph, for what honour do we owe these new clothes, this 'andsomeness, this' – Philippe sniffed the air to either side of Ralph's collar – 'this sexy perfume.' He raised his eyebrows and patted Ralph's cheeks gently with both hands.

'You'll see, Phil, you'll understand,' he replied, a little stiffly. He wasn't in the mood for piss-take. He was far too nervous.

'Is a woman, no?' Philippe's brown eyes sparkled with mischief.

'No – is not a woman – it's just a suit, that's all.' He bristled slightly. His heart was racing. He slipped a finger under the collar of his shirt. 'God, it's fucking sweltering in here, Phil – is the aircon switched on?'

Philippe nodded. 'Full power. Here, come see the beautiful flowers – they just arrived. Peonies, just like you asked. Come – see.' He guided Ralph across the gallery, over flawless bleached-blond maplewood flooring, to the office at the back.

Ralph's head moved to the left and right as he walked,

looking at his paintings, trying to see them through Jem's eyes. What would she think? Would she freak? Would she laugh? Would she love them? Oh, God, he hoped she'd love them. They were all for her, after all. He'd hung them with Jem in mind, placed them on the walls in the exact order he wanted her to see them in, imagined her in her black coat, furry stole and gloves, imagined her swivelling her head this way and that, stepping closer to look at the captions, turning and smiling at him every now and then.

The small office at the back was awash with peonies – Ralph had ordered two hundred and fifty pounds' worth – and the fresh floral aroma permeated his nerves and dissolved his tension a little. He ran his fingers absent-mindedly over the soft, silken tips of the multi-coloured petals and slowed his breathing.

'Any chance of a glass of wine, Phil?' he asked, adjusting his tie.

Philippe raised his eyebrows. 'Wine? Ralph. What is going on? Yesterday, and the day before, and the day before this, it was jeans and lager – now, today, is suits and wine. Is me – yes? I am rubbing off on you – you are becoming a Frenchman – no?!' He giggled and pulled a bottle of wine from the fridge behind him and took two glasses from the cabinet.

Ralph picked up his wine, lit one of Philippe's cigarettes and walked back into the gallery. He reached beneath the reception desk and changed the CD on the music system located there. Radiohead. There. That's better.

And then he paced for a while, enjoying the muted thud of his leather soles against the springy floorboards, following the lines between the boards, balancing on one foot, seeing if he could splay his feet, heel to heel, into a one-hundred-and-eighty-degrees angle, without falling over. He could.

He put his hands in his pockets and pulled them out, admiring the expensive sweep of his trousers and the perfection of the creases that ran from hip to ankle. He buttoned his jacket, felt even hotter and unbuttoned it. He flapped the sides of the jacket back and forth to ventilate his armpits. Shit, it was hot.

He stood at the front door, his cigarette and wine in one hand, his other in his pocket, leaning against the door-frame. He probably looked like a pretentious twat, hanging out in a trendy Notting Hill gallery in his Dolce & Gabbana suit, drinking wine and smoking French cigarettes. He didn't care. He was nervous.

He watched people walking past. Most of them didn't look in. Art. Not Really My Cup Of Tea. Don't Care For It Much. He didn't blame them really. It was a funny old thing, art, when you thought about it. His paintings. They were for him. Bits of him. His fantasies and dreams. No wonder most people wouldn't want it in their homes. The sort of people who did want it, the sort of people who were prepared to pay £2,500 for one of his paintings, didn't really have proper homes, they had houses, or offices, or 'spaces'. He tried to imagine one of his paintings on the living-room wall at his mother's, next to the clock with the swinging pendulum. He smiled.

A glance at the clock on the wall behind him told him it was only 7.30 p.m. Another hour to go. Again he paced the room. He drank morc wine. He smoked a dozen cigarettes. 'You want we call this exhibition "Study in Nicotine"?' Philippe had complained.

The caterers worked around him, placing artfully designed platters of canapés on to white-clothed tables. Miniature Thai crabcakes festooned with sprigs of fresh coriander, dwarf sticks of satay with tiny little bowls of gloopy peanut sauce, diminutive pink bundles of prawn wrapped around baby butts of sugarcane, the smallest samosas Ralph had ever seen in his life, saucers of sweet chilli sauce, hot chilli sauce, chopped green chillis, minced red chillis and chilli pickle. Ralph had taken a lot of care over the food order.

Two large black bins behind another table were full to brimming with ice and champagne and a young girl in a black skirt and smart white blouse was busy putting shiny glass flutes in rows on the table in front of her.

Philippe was fussing with the peonies, arranging them around the room in huge extravagant bouquets, humming quietly to himself as he went. He was the girliest heterosexual Ralph knew.

Ralph felt his stomach contract and his bowels move. He tried to ignore it, but as his excitement mounted it got more and more unbearable. He rubbed his stomach through the cotton of his stripy shirt and clenched his buttocks tightly. The hair on his arms stood on end. He paced the room some more. He squeezed his buttocks some more. He smoked another cigarette. He stood at the door again and watched the traffic and the W11 trendies and the foreign couples walking into expensive restaurants. He took off the Everything but the Girl CD Philippe had chosen and put Radiohead back on. He put 'Creep' on repeat play. 'You want your guests to die of depression?' muttered Philippe. His stomach kept churning. His bowels kept moving. He could feel sweat patches under his arms. It was 8.28 p.m. Where the bloody hell was she? Christ – if she didn't come – no, she'd come, she would . . .

His bowels were going crazy now, every cigarette he smoked loosening them even more. She wasn't here yet – she should have been here by now – he wanted to wait for her, be at the door when she arrived, but he *had* to go to the toilet. He dashed through the office and into the cubicle by the back door. He sighed with relief as his nerve-racked insides fell into the toilet bowl. He pulled up his lovely new trousers, tucked in his shirt, straightened his tie and mopped under his arms with some balled-up toilet-paper. He looked at his reflection in the mirror. He looked frightening – pale and clammy with an expression of pure terror in his eyes. And he was so thin. Shit. He'd wanted to look so together, so successful. He looked like a drug addict in an expensive suit. He dried his hands and walked into the office, taking deep breaths and pinching at his cheeks to restore some colour.

There was so much to think about, so much to worry about. What had started off as a nice idea, a little party with all his friends to celebrate his success and the end of his self-imposed exile, had turned into a potential soap opera peopled with strange, complex characters and woven through with convoluted story-lines. It could all go horribly wrong. He hoped it wouldn't end in farce.

Oh, where was she?

She said she'd be here before everyone else – she said she'd be here at quarter past, and it was now 8.45 p.m. He walked back across the gallery towards the door just as she arrived, gliding into the room in an electric puff of perfume and glamour. Her silken hair was piled tousily on top of her head and her burnished skin gleamed like copper under the merest hint of make-up.

'Oh, God, Ralph, I'm so sorry I'm late, I couldn't get a cab and . . .'

'Don't worry, it's fine, they're not here yet anyway. Here, let me take your coat.' He slipped it awkwardly from her shoulders, revealing long, bare brown arms and an ankle-length sliver of sheer, black, body-clinging lace.

Ralph's mouth sprang open like a cash register. 'Jesus Christ – you look absolutely – Christ – you look fantastic!'

Cheri smiled, trying not to look as if she was too used to such compliments.

'And I can't thank you enough for this, really I can't. Thank you so much for coming and thank you for looking so . . . fucking gorgeous. You're absolutely perfect . . . umwah, umwah.' He grinned and kissed her theatrically on each cheek. Suddenly his muscles relaxed, his heart rate slowed down and a smile returned to his face.

'This is going to be great,' he said, clasping Cheri's arms and smiling widely into her eyes. 'It's going to be great!'

# CHAPTER THIRTY

Smith hadn't so much as given Jem a second glance, let alone commented on her appearance when she'd emerged from her bedroom, looking, quite frankly, stunning, in her rose-printed dress, with her hair pinned up all over her head with tiny little satin rosebuds, and wearing a pair of extremely sexy strappy sandals that fastened all the way up her finely-turned ankles with suede laces.

'Have you finished in the bathroom yet?' he'd asked with a hint of impatience in his voice that was wholly misplaced as it was *his* fault that they were running late in the first place, and Jem had only been in there for fifteen minutes, not really a terribly long time for a girl to make herself look so utterly ravishing.

He'd refused to wear the white shirt that Jem had suggested he put on, and was now grumpily undoing the shirt he'd chosen because he'd discovered a stain on the sleeve that was, to judge by the tone of his voice, also Jem's fault (although she'd never laid a finger on the shirt in her life) and moaning under his breath about what a bloody hassle the whole evening was turning out to be and he hadn't even left the house yet.

The cab finally arrived twenty minutes after the third time the increasingly unconvincing man at the cab office had informed them that it was 'just around the corner'.

By the time the cab had fought its way through an

unexplained, slow and extremely long traffic jam on Holland Road and pulled up outside the gallery, it was 9.30 p.m. and Smith and Jem had lost all interest in talking to each other.

They paid the driver, who may well have been in a good mood when he'd arrived at Almanac Road to pick them up but had obviously been infected by the general atmosphere of hostility and resentment that had suffused his cab for the last thirty minutes and was now as grumpy as both of them, if not more so.

Jem adjusted her furry wrap and waited on the pavement for Smith to get his change.

'I'm not staying late,' he muttered, tucking his wallet into his back pocket and joining Jem on the pavement. 'Ralph's friends are a bunch of nobs.'

Jem raised her eyebrows behind Smith's back in a very married way and they walked towards the door, at precisely the same moment that Karl sauntered towards the gallery.

'Oh, all right, mate! Didn't recognize you for a moment there, out of context sort of thing!' Karl grasped Smith's hand.

'Yeah, nice to see you.' Smith shook hard, a look of confusion spreading over his face at the sight of his upstairs neighbour. 'What are you doing here, then?'

'Your mate, Ralph, he sent me an invite. Said he'd been listening to me on the radio and felt sorry for me. Hah! Half of London feels sorry for me y'know – it's a strange predicament. But then again, I do get invited to an awful lot of parties these days.' He winked and nudged Smith in the ribs and Smith and Jem both saw that he was drunk.

Realizing that Smith's general mood was unlikely to

bring forth an unprompted introduction to the large Irishman, Jem stuck out one small hand and pointed it towards Karl. 'Hi, I'm Jem. I live downstairs with Smith and Ralph. Nice to meet you.'

'Ah, yes – you're the flatmate. Is that right?'

Jem smirked. 'Yeah, sort of.'

'Nice to meet you, too. I'm Karl.' Karl smiled a warm drunken smile and squeezed Jem's little hand, a bit too hard. 'You're a lovely looking girl, if you don't mind me saying.'

Jem didn't mind him saying, in the least. It was the only compliment she was likely to get tonight and she embraced it warmly.

'Not at all,' she smiled, looking towards Smith to make sure he'd registered the comment and was feeling suitably inadequate for not having matched it earlier. He was already half-way through the door.

The party appeared to be in full swing. Smith, Jem and Karl wove their way through the room, looking, respectively, for the toilet, Ralph and the champagne. Bloody hell, thought Jem, as they squeezed past bare backs, designer labels, skinny blondes, male models and fashion victims, Ralph really has got some glamorous friends. She felt very short. The air was thick with Issey Miyake, pretentious talk, dense clouds of cigarette smoke blown from bored round mouths and the high-pitched whine of plummy girls moaning about other plummy girls. They were greeted with disinterest as they moved through the room, or the occasional slow and deliberate eyeing up and down, followed by a look of vague disappointment when no labels of note or drop-dead good looks were spotted among their number.

Jem started to feel her spirits droop. Smith was right. Ralph's friends really *were* a bunch of nobs. She could actually feel Smith's bad mood increase as he followed behind her.

She scoured the room desperately for Ralph now. She was scared that he'd have suddenly turned into a pretentious artist-type and that he'd ignore her when he saw her and pretend not to recognize her in front of all his supercool friends: 'Excuse me, do I know you?' She shuddered. She had to see him, to reassure herself that he was still lovable, gorgeous Ralph, despite the throngs of two-dimensional magazine-cut-out people he'd surrounded himself with. She kept walking.

Karl was glad he'd had a few drinks before he came out. He looked around him at the plastic people and suddenly felt very alone and very old. He was glad he'd bumped into these two at the door, at least he hadn't had to walk in on his own. Karl hated this 'being single' business. He absolutely hated it. All his friends kept telling him he'd get used to it, come to enjoy it, in fact. He'd soon realize the benefits, they insisted. Instead, Karl came to hate it, more and more, every day. Not a day went by that he didn't miss Siobhan and their cosy lifestyle and their nights on the sofa. Life was so simple, then, he hadn't had to make an effort, hadn't had to go to parties full of strangers and make conversation with people he didn't like. Life with Siobhan had been pure, domestic bliss.

He was still sure she'd come back. She couldn't stay in her dreary little bedroom in Potters Bar for the rest of her life. She'd forgive him soon enough, she just needed time and space. It was his birthday next week. He was sure she'd phone him then – it was the perfect opportunity to start afresh, to forgive and forget.

In the mean time he had a party to get through. He reckoned he'd put away a few glasses of champagne, down some of those delicious-looking morsels of food he'd spotted over the other side of the room, make a wee bit of polite conversation with his lovely neighbours and then slip off and back to the rather good bottle of single malt he had waiting for him back at the flat. He started fulfilling his evening's resolutions by grabbing a glass of champagne off a passing tray and knocking it back in one, wiping at his mouth with the back of his hand and stifling a little burp.

Smith had spotted Ralph's head at the far side of the room. 'There he is,' he muttered with relief. His little band of followers shadowed him as he headed Ralphwards.

Ralph was wearing an incredibly smart grey suit and had finally had his hair cut. He was, thought Jem, looking absolutely delicious. He had his body turned away from them and was chatting to yet another tall, skinny blonde in a black lace dress whose face they couldn't see. The conversation seemed quite animated and their heads were pressed close together, their body language insinuating that they were making more than polite chit-chat. Jem felt a little nausea rise in her gut and swallowed it quickly. Ralph could talk to whoever he liked; it had nothing to do with her.

Ralph spotted them approaching and broke away from his intimate chat. When he saw Jem his face broke open into an enormous smile and he opened up his arms to embrace her. Jem breathed an enormous sigh of relief – he was being Ralphy – and let him absorb her in a bear-hug.

'Jemima Catterick, you look breathtakingly beautiful,' he whispered in her ear and brushed her cheek with a tiny kiss that sent shivers down her spine. She blushed and felt her heart pump under her breast.

'So do you,' she giggled.

The tall, golden woman had turned around now and Ralph broke away from their embrace to put an arm around her bare shoulders. Jem felt jealous again.

'Um, I think you all know Cheri, don't you?'

Cheri beamed at the trio.

'Cheri, this is Karl . . . you know each other, don't you? . . . Smith, my flatmate – I believe you've met . . . And this is Jem – Smith's girlfriend – I think you've met her, too, haven't you? Well, isn't this a nice, neighbourly little gathering! Sorry about all these pretentious bloody Notting Hill trendies . . . didn't invite them . . . someone else's friends. My real friends are probably still in the pub . . .'

Ralph continued talking, but no one was listening.

Smith was swaying on the spot, his hand still where he'd left it, in Cheri's, when they'd been introduced. He'd gone a rather bilious shade of puce and looked like he was about to faint. He was grimacing and was obviously trying to form a word in the back of his throat, his dry mouth forming and unforming circles, like a tongue-tied trout. He wished he'd worn that white shirt.

'Didn't know you knew Ralph?' he finally managed, in a rather unattractive squawk.

'Well,' said Cheri, trying delicately to extricate her hand from Smith's, 'he's a new friend' – she imbued the word 'new' with half a ton of innuendo and put her arm around Ralph's waist, proprietorily – 'and he's just such a little sweetie.' She puckered up her voluptuous lips and kissed him softly on the cheek.

Jem stood rooted to the ground, feeling even smaller, and foolish and over-flowery. She felt unexpected and entirely uncalled-for tears well up from her chest and breathed deeply, clinging on to Smith for dear life, while he stuttered manically about how much he liked Cheri's dress and how stunning she looked and what a pretty hair-do that was.

In the general atmosphere of hatred, jealousy, lust, embarrassment and shock, no one had noticed Karl, whose face was slowly turning from a pale lobster-pink to a bright, lurid crimson and whose large frame was filled with so much anger and rage he looked like he might explode like a microwaved sausage at any moment.

'What the FUCK is going on?' he began, slowly and deliberately, looking directly at Cheri. 'Is this some sort of FUCKING joke?' This was said almost silently except for the final 'fucking' which was bellowed so loudly that they all jumped from their skins and clutched their throats.

The group turned towards Karl. Cheri put out one nervous hand towards his arm. 'Calm down, Karl. It's not what you think. I promise you, you'll understand . . .'

Karl jerked his arm away from her touch. 'You FUCKING SLAG. Don't you fucking touch me. JESUS! I feel sick. Isn't it enough that you destroyed my life?' He leaned in towards Cheri, who cowered into Ralph's shoulder, and began spitting into her face. 'Now you're going to destroy this fella's life too . . .' He pointed viciously towards Ralph.

'Now, mate, come on . . .' Ralph tried to intervene with

an outstretched arm. Karl swiped it away like it was an annoying fly. He was approaching boiling-point.

'No, mate, *you* come on. I don't know what the fuck's going on here, but I don't like it. Not one bit. Is this all a joke, huh? Is that it? Why did you really invite me here tonight? Did this BITCH put you up to it?' he snarled.

'Karl, please! I promise you, it's not a joke. You'll see,' Cheri beseeched, theatrically, 'it's just not like that at all, it's because I care . . .'

'WHAT!' Karl began to laugh, a deep, ominous, unpleasant laugh that made all three of them flinch. 'You! Care! You're incapable of caring about anyone or anything but yourself. You are the most selfish, self-centred, manipulative and evil woman it has ever been my misfortune to meet. You've already ruined my life once and I'm not going to stick around here while you and your "friends" entertain yourselves at my expense.' He slammed his empty glass down on a shelf. 'Thanks for the invite – *mate*,' he spat at Ralph.

'Please, Karl, don't leave – you can't leave now!' Cheri was desperately holding on to him. If he left now, then all her work would have been for nothing and she'd be stuck at a party she didn't really want to be at, with a bunch of people she didn't even know, and she'd never be famous.

But Karl extricated himself from her grip, turned on his heel and began to stride through the room, knocking dahlings and It girls out of the way with his large elbows as he moved. The twittering and chattering had died down during the confrontation and everyone now fell silent, apart from one hooter-nosed idiot on the far side, who was so taken with the sound of his own voice that nothing, it appeared, could stop him talking.

Karl had almost reached the door when someone grabbed him from behind and spun him around. It was Smith, who had watched the whole sorry scene unfold in utter horror and had chased Karl uncertainly across the floor of the gallery, through the gap in the crowd that Karl had left behind him, and to the door.

'Now listen here . . .' he began.

Jem watched from the other side of the room and winced, thinking for the first time how silly Smith really was. 'Now listen here' – it was the sort of thing that only a really silly man would ever say. It would be entirely his fault if Karl were to wallop him one.

'. . . now listen here. I don't know exactly what your problem is, but you are *way* out of order and I suggest you go back immediately and apologize to Cheri. That is no way to talk to a lady.'

Karl stared at Smith. He suddenly looked a lot taller than six foot and certainly a lot taller than Smith. His lip curled up in a Rottweiler-like sneer.

'That BITCH over there is no lady. And what – the fuck – has it got to do – with you?' he asked, poking Smith in the shoulder in what looked like an extremely irritating manner. 'Oh – don't tell me – she's got you in her nasty little grip as well, has she?' Karl laughed and pushed Smith gently away from him. 'Well, good luck to you, mate, you'll need it.' Karl turned away and towards the door.

Smith bridled a bit, looking as if he was seriously contemplating grabbing Karl's arm again and taking this argument outside, but was saved by the timely entrance of another guest, a pretty blonde woman in a black coat and heels.

'Oh, my God! Siobhan!'

'Karl!'

'Christ! What . . . what the . . . what're you doing here?'

'What are *you* doing here?'

'I don't know. Who invited you?'

'I don't know. Wasn't it you?'

'No.'

'I've got no idea.'

'Christ, Shuv, you look amazing. What happened to your hair?'

'I had it cut. Look, what the hell's going on? Whose party is this?'

Karl pointed at Ralph, who was watching with an open jaw at the far end of the room. Cheri had repositioned herself discreetly behind a pillar.

'His?' said Siobhan, her face contorted with confusion. 'But . . . why? Who is he?'

'He's Ralph.'

'Oh, yes. Ralph. Of course. The invite. But who is Ralph?'

'*That's* Ralph. He lives downstairs, Almanac Road. Remember?'

Siobhan struggled to recall. 'Oh, yes, but – why? I don't understand, Karl. What the fuck *is* this?'

Karl shrugged. 'I have no idea.' His frame relaxed, his face softened and he smiled. 'Jeez – who cares? Shuv, it's so good to see you. It is *so* good to see you . . .'

He petted her hands and grinned manically down at her.

Smith was still standing behind him, his fists clenched, his hackles still at attention. He turned to face the rest of the room, which had already grown bored of the drama and resumed halted conversations as if nothing had ever happened. What did you have to do to entertain these people? He looked down at his fists and unfurled them slowly, rubbing at the indents his fingernails had left in the palms of his hands. He straightened his tie, ran his fingers through his hair and began walking slowly back across the room, embarrassed that his attempt at a fight, his only ever attempt at a fight, had been stalled like that in front of a room full of Ralph's twattish friends.

He headed straight towards Cheri, who had now emerged from behind the pillar, and put an arm protectively around her shoulder, rubbing gently at the bare skin under his hand. His heart raced. She felt exactly as he'd expected her to feel – like silk spun from the thread of the silkiest silkworm that ever lived.

'Are you all right?' he asked in his best sensitive and caring voice.

Cheri nodded glumly. 'Yes,' she said, 'but I suppose after everything I've done, I deserved it.' She looked away poignantly.

'What! Don't be ridiculous. He was drunk. He had no idea what he was talking about.' Smith was quite beside himself with indignation.

'No, Smith – really. He was absolutely right about me. It's all true.'

'No!' Smith made them all jump with the ferocity of his dissension. 'He's mad. Really, Cheri. Don't you pay any attention to him.'

Cheri sighed and Smith continued to rub the small patch of lustrous skin that lay just beneath his thumb. It was the best piece of skin he'd ever touched; he could quite happily rub it all night.

'Look, Smith,' Cheri continued, 'I told you all this –

don't you remember? – at Oriel? All about my past, my problems with men.'

Jem stiffened and gripped her glass in her fist as if she was armwrestling it. Smith finally stopped rubbing Cheri's shoulder and let his hand drop to his side, aware of Jem's existence seemingly for the first time that day. Ralph flinched and looked away. It was starting. He hooked his hand through Jem's arm and deftly began to wheel her away from Cheri and Smith.

'Jem, let me give you a personalized tour of my exhibition – a true honour for you.' He smiled cheesily and dragged her away, just as she was beginning to open her mouth to say something. Jem didn't resist. Oriel? What? Smith didn't know Cheri. What the hell was happening? Why was he being so protective of her? What did he know about her? All that thumb-rubbing and concern and all those compliments about her dress and her hair. And, anyway, wasn't Ralph supposed to be with Cheri?

'Ralph,' she asked in a small, confused voice, 'what the fuck is going on here?'

Ralph was beginning to feel a little guilty now, but not in a bad way – a bit like a vet giving an injured animal a painful injection. This was for Jem's good; she might not like it at the moment, but she'd appreciate it in the long run. He put his hands on her shoulders and steered her towards the front of the gallery.

'I dunno,' he laughed, 'it's just one of those nights, I guess.'

Jem's head was in too much turmoil to demand a more articulate response and she let him move her around like a mannequin. What was all that business with the couple from upstairs – that Irish DJ guy and his ex-girlfriend? They were standing together now at the door, Siobhan giving Karl a little twirl to show off her new figure, Karl grinning from ear to ear, looking like he'd never been happier in his life. And what did he have to do with that Cheri girl? And how did Ralph know Cheri? And Smith? And . . . and . . . and . . . oh, God. Jem felt quite giddy. Up until this evening Jem had thought that Cheri was just the girl who lived on the first floor, the one she'd had that chat with ages ago, the one who used to be a dancer, the one who was getting married. Yes, that's right, she was getting married wasn't she? And now she was Ralph's date, Karl's enemy and Smith's . . . Smith's what? And she certainly didn't seem to be getting married any more. She glanced across the room and saw that Smith had placed his hand back on Cheri's shoulder and was whispering into her ear, his groin twisted pointedly towards her thigh, his eyes glued to her face. Cheri was smiling and laughing and looking very coy.

'Jem? Jem, are you all right?' Ralph was leaning into her face and staring into her eyes, looking concerned.

'Yeah . . . sure . . . I'm fine.' She tore her gaze from the unpleasant and unsettling little scenario; she couldn't deal with all this right now. Besides, she had Ralph to herself for a few moments and he was about to show her his paintings, which, in all the drama, she hadn't even glanced at yet. She took a deep breath.

Ralph was still staring into her eyes. He opened his mouth as if he was about to say something, closed it and opened it again. 'I know I've already said this, Jem – but I'm going to say it again anyway. You look drop-dead gorgeous. You really do. That dress is . . . stunning. And I love, absolutely *love*, all these little roses in your hair.' He touched one gently with a fingertip. 'You are, without a doubt, the most beautiful woman in this room. I'm so glad we're friends again – so glad.' He picked up her hand and gently kissed the back of it.

'Oh, Ralph, so am I. I really missed you, you know.' Jem blushed and giggled and kissed the back of his hand too, feeling immediately that this was an embarrassing thing to have done, clearing her throat and turning away to hide her blush. 'So, er, are you going to show me these famous paintings of yours, then?'

Damn Ralph, she thought, always sending me into these paroxysms of confusion.

Ralph flushed slightly, pleased as punch with the little damp patch on the back of his hand that Jem had left there with her lovely soft lips.

'OK.' He placed one hand gently on her waist and pointed her towards the first painting. 'This one's called "Pink Lipstick and Peonies".'

Jem gasped and put her hand over her mouth. 'Ralph – that's – is that? It's me, isn't it?' She spun around towards him with wide eyes.

It was a small portrait, rich in colour and detail, a close-up of Jem's face wearing a huge, open smile that showed all her teeth, her head surrounded by a bed of pink, purple and mauve flowers in full bloom.

Ralph nodded and steered her towards the next painting.

It was Jem again, head and shoulders this time, in a field of shiny red and green chillies. The next one was of Jem, and the next, and the next. There were still lifes, too, of flowers and spices and chillies. Jem suddenly felt embarrassed and self-conscious.

'Ralph . . .' she began.

'Shhhhh' – Ralph put a finger to her lips – 'just look – just enjoy.' And there she was, just as he'd envisaged, twisting her head this way and that, peering at the captions, turning towards him every now and then with a quizzical look on her face that said 'You're mad,' but that was also full of affection, wonder, excitement and, he was absolutely sure of it, love.

## CHAPTER THIRTY-ONE

'So, is there any particular reason why you didn't tell Jem about our little drink at Oriel at Christmas?'

Smith looked momentarily nonplussed and scratched his chin. 'Oh, but I did. I guess she just forgot,' he sniggered, and pushed his hands deeper into his pockets.

'Hmmm.' Cheri let it pass. 'She's a lovely girl, isn't she? I bumped into her once, outside the house and we had a little chat. I thought she was gorgeous.'

'Yeah. Yeah. I suppose so.'

'It's funny, because we spent all that time talking at Oriel and you didn't mention her once . . .'

'Well . . .'

'Quite gave me the impression you were single, actually.'

'Yeah, well . . .'

'Which is a shame, because I sort of hoped that you would be.' She circled the rim of her glass with one long, brown finger. 'We got on very well that night, didn't we?'

Smith's eyebrows shot up to his forehead and he stood up straight. 'Oh, God – I mean, Jem and me – it's nothing serious, really.'

'That's not what she told me.'

'Huh?'

'That time I chatted to her outside the house. That's not what she told me. She told me all about her dreams and how you and she were – how did she put it? – destined, that's right, *destined* to be together.'

'Well, Jem's very sweet but she can be a bit –' He pulled an extraordinary face involving crossed eyes, a protruding tongue and an index finger circling around his temple, then snorted and shoved his hands back into his trouser pockets.

'Really! Hmmm, I have to say she seemed very sane to me. But she's absolutely mad about you, she really is.'

Smith smiled smugly and shrugged. 'I know,' he said.

'But I thought you said it wasn't very serious . . .'

'Well' – he scratched the back of his neck – 'it's not – for me. D'you know what I mean? I think' – he looked around him and lowered his voice an octave – 'I think it's a bit of a case of unrequited love, to be honest. I mean, I'm very fond of Jem – don't get me wrong – really very, very fond of her. She's a lovely girl, as you so rightly said, but . . . she's not "the One". You know what I mean, don't you, about "the One"?' He raised his eyebrows conspiratorially and moved his body an inch or two closer to hers.

'Oh yes,' she replied, 'Mr Right. That sort of thing.' She flashed him a dazzling smile. What a slimy bastard, she thought to herself, gritting her teeth. Ralph had been so right about him. She'd had her misgivings about this whole scenario – she was only here for Karl and Siobhan, after all. And now they were happily ensconced together at the other side of the room, looking terribly pleased with themselves – it looked like her plan had been a resounding success – and she could just call it a night, go home. But she was in full flow and after just five minutes with this scumbag she was keen to do whatever it took to get him out of Jem's life. She watched Jem and Ralph move across the room, his large hands on her small shoulders, guiding her gently around the pictures he'd spent nine weeks locked in a damp, cold studio painting for her, pictures of *her*. She'd noticed the little *frisson* of discomfort that had flickered across Jem's face when she'd walked in and seen her and Ralph together, looking like a couple. Cheri knew that look better than most. She'd been jealous. She felt more than friendship towards Ralph, it was obvious. They looked right together. Ralph had been right, she could see that now. This awful Smith character was just an obstacle.

She looked across the room again at Siobhan and Karl, deep in conversation and laughing together, and smiled to herself. She was having so much fun being a good person! Now, if she could just get Smith out of the way tonight and clear the path for Jem and Ralph, then she really *would* be a fairy godmother! Cheri smiled again as a lovely feeling swam through her stomach, a big, fat, happy fish of goodness. She turned back to Smith and stunned him with another of her prize smiles.

By eleven-thirty, most of the fake guests had left – they had to get up early the following morning to catch flights to New York and Tokyo and Sydney, for shows and shoots and castings – and Ralph's real friends had arrived, fresh from the pub around the corner, loud and drunk and ready to party. The evening, it seemed, was only just beginning.

Someone put Abba on the CD system and within the first three bars of 'Waterloo' pretty much everyone was dancing, clutching champagne bottles in their hands and swigging from them as they moved to the music, singing along to the lyrics at the tops of their voices. Smith had Cheri by the waist and was spinning her around the room, rather heavy-handedly.

Siobhan and Karl were sitting quietly in a corner absorbed in conversation.

And Jem was in the toilet, crying her eyes out.

She hadn't spoken to Smith all night. Not one word since they'd got there. First of all he'd been so deeply involved in conversation with that Cheri girl that she hadn't liked to interrupt, and then he'd whisked Cheri off on to the dance floor and they hadn't stopped dancing since. And Smith didn't even *like* dancing. She brought her tissue to her face as fresh tears began to cascade down her pink cheeks. She was embarrassed and she was humiliated. She wasn't used to being treated like this. Ralph had tried to console her, tried to put her mind at rest, convince her that there was nothing to worry about, but for God's sake, Smith was all over that girl.

And then there was Ralph. It looked like all that love stuff was going to come to the surface again any minute. Jesus – a whole room full of peonies and paintings of her and all their favourite food and compliments and hand-kissing and tingles up and down her spine and the way . . . the way he'd put out his finger to touch one of her little satin roses . . . it was all so intimate, so exciting, so gorgeous and so fucking wrong. It was all so fucking wrong. Smith was her boyfriend – although you wouldn't think it judging by his behaviour tonight – and Ralph was her friend, and now her feelings were every bit as confused as they'd been before Ralph had gone away. No, they were more confused, much more confused . . .

Jem marched out of the cubicle, splashed her face

with water from the sink, mopped it off with a paper towel, adjusted her dress, poked at her hair and squared her shoulders. She needed reassurance. She needed to know that Smith loved her. For the first time ever, she needed to hear him say it. She was going to walk out there and grab him away from that horrible girl and make him tell her then and there, so she could hear it, so she could get her mind straight and stop all this Ralph nonsense once and for all.

She gave herself one last stern look in the mirror, turned on her heel and strode out into the gallery.

Siobhan had been trying to tell Karl, all night, about her and Rick. She'd taken a dozen deep breaths at appropriate moments, steeled her nerves, and then lost it. How could she? He looked so happy, his face was aglow with joy. He was so thrilled to see her and was trying so hard to make a good impression, to say all the right things. He'd asked her how things were going at her mother's; that would have been the perfect opportunity to have said something, but she just couldn't. He'd be so hurt, so angry. She'd said something inconsequential in reply and changed the subject. She'd suggested that they get up and dance, to avoid conversation, but he'd said no – I just want to sit here and talk; I've missed you so much; I want to talk all night. So they sat and talked and now they were talking about Karl's radio show, the infamous one, and Siobhan knew that any moment now the conversation was going to get serious – very serious indeed.

Smith was absolutely plastered. Completely, totally and utterly hammered. It was only because Cheri was such a good dancer and was so strong that he hadn't fallen over yet. His thick hair was matted to his forehead with sweat, his shirt was damp and crumpled, and he had a ridiculous expression on his face which he probably thought was a suave smile but which looked more like the village idiot's on a bad day. He was hopelessly out of rhythm and kept singing the wrong lyrics to the songs, without noticing.

Cheri had had enough of dancing with this cretin – he was making her look bad – and she encouraged him off the dance floor with the suggestion of getting a drink. He followed her like a pissed puppy.

'Cheri,' he slurred, leaning awkwardly against the wall, clasping a glass of champagne, quite obviously trying to look cool and failing miserably, yet again, 'you and me. We should get together, y'know – some time.' He raised his eyebrows lazily, in a 'How about it?' sort of way.

'Oh, yeah?' Cheri replied wearily. She was tired of this now.

'Yeah,' leered Smith. 'You and me – we're good together, aren't we – we've got something – special. Can't you feel it?'

'Yeah, I suppose so.'

'That night at Oriel, that was great, wasn't it?'

'Uh-huh.'

'And tonight. Shit – it's been brilliant. We've talked all night and danced and everything . . .'

Cheri was looking frantically around the room, for Ralph or Jem or anyone to come and rescue her. She was bored stiff.

'. . . and I really think that you and I – well, I think it's destiny . . . d'you agree?'

Cheri wasn't even listening any more. 'Yeah,' she murmured. 'Yeah, sure.'

Smith had failed to notice that Cheri was stifling a yawn and looking at her watch. He'd decided that enough was enough. He'd waited long enough and now, this instant, this very moment, was the right moment. This was it!

He slammed his drink down on the bar, threw himself to his knees and grasped Cheri's hands in his. 'Oh, God, Cheri! I love you. I've always loved you!' His voice rang out around the room; he didn't care who heard! Ralph looked away from the conversation he was having with his mate John's girlfriend and watched with horror. He closed his eyes and covered his face with his hands. Smith was up to his old tricks. 'I've loved you for five years and . . . I want us to be together for ever.' Smith slavered wet kisses on to the backs of Cheri's hands. Ralph's eye was caught by someone emerging from the toilet at the back of the room. It was Jem, looking red-eyed and walking forcefully towards Smith and Cheri with a determined look on her face. He saw her jaw drop when she noticed Smith's lips on Cheri's hands and he watched her stop in her tracks when she heard Smith, at the top of his voice, with all the abandon of a man in love who has had too much to drink and is no longer in control of his senses, shout out for the world to hear, 'Cheri, I love you. Will you marry me?'

For the second time that night, the room fell silent. Cheri looked horrified, Ralph gasped, and Jem screamed. Smith turned around, almost falling from his knees in the process, saw Jem and began one of his trout impersonations, turned back to Cheri, saw the look of disgust on her face and dropped his head into his chest.

Jem picked up her coat from a chair, threw on her furry wrap, grabbed her handbag and ran from the gallery, out on to the dark, wet street, her sobs swallowed up by the sound of passing traffic as the door opened and closed. Ralph threw Smith a look of pure contempt, picked up his coat and ran out after her.

Cheri looked down at Smith's slumped figure at her feet. She tugged at his hands and pulled him into a standing position. 'Pathetic,' she sneered at him. 'Absolutely pathetic.'

Siobhan and Karl had missed all this drama. They were already in the street, having some of their own. Karl was pacing up and down the pavement, gesticulating wildly with his hands. Siobhan stood with her head downcast and murmured gently under her breath. They stopped their conversation momentarily as first Jem and then Ralph emerged from the gallery and began running down Ledbury Road, Ralph shouting 'Wait, Jem, please,' after her receding figure. They looked at each other, shrugged and continued. What they were talking about was too important to allow even the most dramatic of goings-on to disturb them.

'So – if you're not living at your mother's – where exactly are you living?' Karl turned away from Siobhan, not wanting to watch the discomfort on her face. 'With your *new boyfriend*?' He spat this out. He felt sick, violently sick.

Siobhan nodded glumly.

'Oh! And where exactly does this *new boyfriend* live? Somewhere nice?'

This was horrible, truly horrible. They'd been getting

on so well, and then Siobhan had dropped the mother of all bombshells. She was seeing someone. 'Is it someone special?' Karl had asked. 'Yes,' she'd nodded. 'Is it – serious?' She'd nodded again. 'Jesus – how long?' Karl was becoming increasingly distressed. Siobhan had shrugged. 'A few weeks.' Karl's face crumpled and his lip began to quiver. 'But . . . but . . . we've only been split up a few weeks.' Siobhan had started crying then and had buried her head in Karl's chest. They'd hugged and Karl had moved their trauma out on to the pavement to avoid becoming a topic of conversation amongst the party-goers.

'Well?' he demanded, a sob catching at the back of his throat. 'Do you and your *new boyfriend* live somewhere nice – Siobhan – tell me, tell me all about it . . .'

'Oh, please, Karl, don't . . .'

'No. Siobhan, I want to know everything. Tell me everything. What's his name? What does he look like? What does he do for a living? Is he handsome? Huh? Is he? Is he good in bed?'

'Oh, Karl . . .'

'Well – is he? Jesus. Siobhan. What's going on here?' Karl ran his fingers through his hair and drooped backwards into a shop doorway, draping his coat over his knees and rubbing his face with his hands. 'I thought we were having some time apart. Why couldn't you wait, Siobhan? Shit – how did you manage to get over me so quickly? Over *us*?'

'I don't know, Karl, I don't know. It didn't feel quick, it felt like an eternity, sitting in that bedroom, alone, missing you, missing the flat, missing everything. It felt like for ever, just waiting, hoping that you'd come and get me.'

'I called you! I called you every day, every hour of every day. You wouldn't take my calls.'

'Oh, God, Karl, it's easy to call. I wanted you to take action. *Do* something. I wanted to hear the sound of your car engine turning over in the driveway, wanted to hear the car door slam and your footsteps in the gravel. I wanted to hear the doorbell and I wanted my mother to call up the stairs to tell me that you were there, that you'd come for me. Every night I waited – and you never came . . .'

'But your mother said she'd call the police if I even *phoned* again. How could I, Shuv? How could I just turn up? I didn't know what to expect.'

'Oh, please! Don't tell me you were so scared of my mother, my tiny little sixty-nine-year-old mother, that you couldn't fight for what you really wanted. I always had to do *everything*, Karl – everything. Don't you see? That was the whole problem. You just always wanted everything to stay exactly as it was – me, the flat, life, everything. If I hadn't dragged you up to London all those years ago, we'd still be living in that shithole in Brighton. If I hadn't phoned Jeff after that wedding you'd never have gone for that interview. If I hadn't sat up half the night with you, persuading you, you'd have turned down the job. I even had to be unfaithful to you to get you to notice that I was unhappy, that there was something seriously wrong with our relationship. I had to kick you out when I found out about you and Cheri and I was *damned* if I was going to be the one to make the running again, Karl, to reconcile our relationship – it was your turn! It was your *fucking turn*! I waited for you, Karl, and you didn't come. You didn't write. You didn't give me one decent reason why we should try to save our relationship. You just sat around, drinking whiskey and feeling sorry for yourself, crying down the airwaves to a million total fucking strangers, making everyone feel sorry for *you*! Well, what about me! Who felt sorry for *me*! No one. No, Karl, you had your chance. You had a thousand chances and you blew all of them. I have to take control of my life again, Karl. Be me again. And there's no room for you any more. I love you. I will always love you. You've been my best friend for half my life. But you're a dead weight, Karl, and I've cut myself free. Just like I cut my hair, see' – she pulled the shorn locks to her chin and waved them at Karl – 'and don't you think it suits me better?' She turned away then and began to cry.

Karl felt like someone had slapped him in the face with a side of salmon. Tears stung his face. What could he say? What could he do? She was right. Shit! He wanted to kick himself. He wished that he could be split in two so that he could chase himself down the street, into an alley and kick twenty-six different types of shit out of himself.

'Shuv . . .' He reached out to touch one quivering shoulder with his hand. She spun around.

'Oh, Karl – I'm so sorry. I'm so sorry that you thought there was still hope. I heard you on the radio and you sounded so defeated, so much like you knew what I already knew – that it was over, finished. If only I'd known. We could have talked before. We *should* have talked before.'

'It's too late now, huh? Too late for all those could'ves and should'ves.' He exhaled noisily and began to cry again. 'Oh, Shuv, what the fuck am I going to do without you? What am I going to do, Shuv? Eh?'

He turned towards her and the two of them held each other in a sad, wet, desperate embrace, sobbing loudly into each other's ears.

So loudly in fact that, at first, they failed to hear the engine of the car that pulled up on the road next to them and the gentle whine of an electric window being lowered, and then the soft, shocked tone of Rick's confused voice calling out, 'Siobhan?'

# CHAPTER THIRTY-TWO

Ralph finally caught up with Jem at the junction with Lonsdale Road. She was striding purposefully but awkwardly in her skinny heels. 'Jem – please – stop!' He followed quickly behind her, accelerating a little to overtake her. 'Please – stop!' He grabbed her wrists and pulled her to a halt. 'Stop!'

'What?' Jem barked, struggling to free herself from his grip. 'Leave me alone!'

She began to thrash out violently at Ralph, futilely flailing her arms around. 'Jem, I'm sorry,' Ralph said, bringing her arms into his chest and putting his around her, restraining her in a tight embrace. 'I'm so sorry.' She relented to his mollification and collapsed silently into his arms. 'I'm so sorry. Oh, Jem.' He rested his cheek on the top of her head, feeling the little indentations in his skin made by the satin roses and smelling the floral freshness of her shiny hair. 'My poor, poor Jem.' Her small body heaved under his arms for a moment and he hugged her tighter.

Jem sniffed and wiped her fingers across her nose. 'Ralph,' she said, 'I didn't just imagine that, did I? That was my boyfriend in there, proposing to that girl? Was it a joke, Ralph? Tell me it was a joke. What the fuck is going on? Huh? What is that girl doing here? How do you know her? How does Smith know her? Don't give me any bullshit, just tell me the truth. Is this all some sort of sick joke? Huh? Huh!'

Ralph exhaled. He knew he had to explain. He had to explain everything and not leave out one single detail, including his own sneaky part in the whole hideous scenario. He led Jem to a bench and they sat down.

'Well,' he began, 'this all started five years ago, when Cheri first moved in upstairs . . .'

And he told her, all about Smith's pathetic obsession, about his self-imposed celibacy while he waited for Cheri to notice him, about the night he'd bumped into Cheri on his way back from St Alban's and they'd gone for that drink in Oriel, about how Ralph had wanted to tell Jem *then* but Smith had threatened him with homelessness. He told her how Smith had laughed at her dreams and destinies and how he thought she was a bit mad but that having a girlfriend would make him more attractive to Cheri. He even told her how Smith had fantasized about Cheri when he was making love to Jem . . .

'Oh, my God! Oh, God, I feel sick! I can't believe you didn't tell me all this, Ralph,' Jem sobbed, 'that night, in Bayswater. You just let me . . . oh, God, I feel so humiliated – I've never been so humiliated in all my life!'

'Think how it would have sounded, Jem! You wouldn't have believed me! I'd just told you I was in love with you, it would have sounded so convenient, so . . . untrue! I had to prove it to you, that Smith was a slimebag. You had to see it with your own eyes. That's . . . that's,' Ralph lowered his eyes, 'that's why I invited Cheri tonight. I've never been friendly with the girl, never even really liked her very much. But I just had to let you know what was going on – I couldn't let him treat you like that any more. And I knew that was the only way you'd really believe what was going on.'

'So, you deliberately ruined my evening, did you? You deliberately humiliated, hurt and destroyed me in front of dozens of people! You deliberately made a complete and total arsehole of me, and . . .'

'No! No! Not of you – of Smith. I made an arsehole of Smith. And I have to say, he surpassed himself. Even I had no idea that he was that ridiculous, Jem, I promise you. I thought he'd flirt with her, at worst, but *that* – that was quite remarkable. And I'm sorry that I ruined your evening, but I thought it was a small price to pay for the potential ruination of the rest of your life, which, as you well know, I happen to care a great deal about, so, please, Jem, don't take this anger out on me – take it out on Smith. He's the one who deserves it, not me. I know I've managed to develop something of a reputation with you for being devious and underhand but please, please, please believe me – I *had* to do this. I couldn't watch him making a fool of you for one second longer. Smith's an arsehole. He's my best friend, but he's an arsehole. I know it and now you know it. Please don't be angry with me, Jem – please!'

Jem caved in visibly and began to wail. 'Oh, Ralph, I hate him! I never ever want to see him again.'

'No, Jem. Don't let him get away with it. Give him hell. If I were you I'd want to go in there and kick him right in the bollocks, kick them so hard that he could cough them up and use them for tonsils. He's made a fool of you, Jem – he's treated you with a complete lack of respect. And you, more than anyone I know, more than anyone I've ever known, deserve to be treated with respect.' He stroked a crooked finger against the wetness of her hot, red cheeks. 'You're so special, Jem. You are so fucking special.'

Jem looked up at Ralph through her tears and into his eyes and suddenly she saw it. Destiny. The man in her dreams. She had never seen love like that in anyone's eyes, ever before. Ralph really, really loved her. And it *wasn't* like all the other I Love Yous. He didn't want anything from her, he wasn't besotted, he wasn't obsessed, he wasn't looking for her to fill any holes in his life, he didn't want to change her, control her or adore her – he just loved her. Plain and simple. He loved her. She reached out one small, cold hand and placed it on his cheek.

'Thank you, Ralph. Thank you for caring so much. Thank you for the paintings and the food and the peonies. Thank you for being there for me and for what you did tonight. I'm sorry I got angry with you, I'm sorry I'm so stubborn. It's just . . . it's just . . .'

'Yes – I know – you like to be in control. I know that. I know *you*. That's why I knew I had to do what I did tonight.'

'You really care, don't you?'

Ralph nodded and took Jem's hand from his cheek and put it to his lips. 'You know I do, Jem. And you know I love you . . .'

'Oh, Ralph!'

'. . . and you know that that was part of why I did what I did tonight – because it would give me a chance, a chance to be with you, because as long as you were in love with Smith, that wasn't going to happen . . .'

'Oh, Ralph!'

'. . . and I have so much respect for you for not wanting to hurt Smith. You're a better person than I am – he's my best mate and I don't have that level of loyalty to him. But now, now you know, now you know what he's really like, and you're free, Jem! Free! I'm not expecting you to tell me you love me, I'm not expecting anything from you at all. I know that reading your diaries was a bad thing to do and I don't expect you to forgive me, but now we can be friends, and then, if nothing else ever happens, at least I'll know it's because you don't love me and not because of some misguided sense of love and loyalty you have for a pathetic little man who doesn't deserve to even breathe the same air as you. D'you understand?'

Jem smiled, enigmatically. Ralph continued. 'So, if we both live to be a hundred and you never fall in love with me, then that's cool, because at least *you could if you wanted* and . . .'

Jem put a hand on each of Ralph's cheeks and kept smiling at him.

'. . . I mean, especially so soon after all this stuff with Smith, you're probably feeling a bit *vulnerable* right now and so I wouldn't expect, you know, *anything*, you know, like that . . .'

Jem watched while Ralph talked, a look of tenderness and love spreading, like the rising sun, over her face. She leaned her body in a little nearer to his.

'. . . so, as long as we can still be friends, you know, go out for meals, go to the pub sometimes, I don't need you to fall in love with me, well, you know, not yet anyway, not immediately . . .'

Jem brought Ralph's face close in to hers and put one finger over his lips.

'It's all right, Ralph,' she whispered, grinning from ear to ear. 'It's all right. I love you.'

'What?' Ralph stopped his blabbering and screwed up his face.

'I love you!'

'But . . . but . . . but . . . really? Really and truly! You love me?'

Jem nodded.

Ralph's insides stood up and performed a standing ovation, his heart let off a volley of fireworks, his stomach fluttered with the wings of a million doves and a shower of ticker-tape spiralled joyfully through his mind. Jem loved him! She loved him! He leapt up from the bench and ran around it in circles, punching the air and whooping with joy. 'She loves me! She loves me!'

'Oh Jem,' he beamed, sitting down next to her and gripping her hands in his, 'you have just made me so happy. You'll never know how happy I feel right now. I love you! And you love me! We love each other, Jem, we love each other.' He pulled her to him and almost crushed her in the best hug in the history of the world and then, suddenly, just when Jem thought he was going to kiss her, he stood up, grabbed her by the hand and began to run with her towards the party.

'Come on,' he laughed, 'we've got some unfinished business to attend to, haven't we? We've got to go back to the party and retrieve your dignity! Let's go!' he said, 'let's go and crucify Smith!'

But their mission was unexpectedly delayed by the sight, as they approached the gallery, of Karl, red in the face, showing all his teeth and smashing his fist into the terrified face of a pretty blond man who lay stretched precariously across the bonnet of a showroom-new silver

BMW while Siobhan stood and screamed, tugging ineffectually at the back of Karl's shirt.

'You FUCKING BASTARD!' Jem and Ralph winced at the sound of cartilage cracking under knuckle and the sight of a small plume of blood erupting like red ink from the flattened nose. 'You FUCKING BASTARD!!'

'Karl, get *off*! Get off him! Please! Leave him alone!' Siobhan tugged again at the hem of his shirt, but it was useless to try to pull him off Rick: Karl was strong at the best of times; in his current rage he was superhuman.

'You FUCKING BASTARD!' Jem and Ralph flinched as another blow cracked off the unfortunate Rick's cheekbone and yet another burrowed deep between his ribs with a sickeningly brittle popping sound.

'*Help me! Help me!*' Rick's voice sounded tiny beneath Karl's armpit. '*Will someone please help me!*'

'Ralph?' Jem nudged Ralph.

'What?'

'Can't you do something?'

'Oh, right – yeah.' He wandered uncertainly towards Siobhan.

'What's going on?' he asked.

'Oh, please,' sobbed Siobhan, 'please do something. He's going to kill him!'

Oh, God. This really wasn't Ralph's scene at all. But he took a deep breath and launched himself at Karl's waist, linked his hands around him and tried to peel him off Rick like a mussel from a shipwreck. Without turning, Karl swung a seemingly double-jointed arm at him and clouted him around the ear, but Ralph clung on, using his foot against the side of the car for leverage. Karl turned to see what exactly this annoying little parasite was playing at, realized it was Ralph and immediately let Rick drop, like an out-of-favour toy, on to the bonnet of the car, with a resounding thud.

'It's you!' he boomed, 'it's you, you fucking bastard. This is all YOUR FAULT!'

Ralph's expression changed from one of a hapless have-a-go hero to one of terrified incomprehension within a millisecond.

'What?'

'You FUCKING BASTARD!'

Oh, God – hadn't Ralph heard that somewhere before?

'Why are you doing this to me, eh? What have I ever done to YOU? Why are you trying to RUIN MY LIFE?'

Ralph shrugged and began to back away from Karl, surreptitiously. And then, unfortunately, he smiled.

'What THE FUCK are you laughing at, you FUCKING BASTARD!! You think this is FUNNY! You invite me to your party, to humiliate me and break my heart and you think that's FUNNY!'

'Look, mate, I'm sorry, I really am, but I promise you, I'm not laughing at you and I'm not trying to ruin your life and I have no idea what the hell is going on here . . .'

'Oh! You don't know,' Karl laughed, ominously. 'So, you *didn't* invite that slag Cheri, in there then, eh?'

Ralph nodded tautly. 'Yeah – I did.'

'Right. So I suppose you *didn't* invite me then, huh?'

Ralph gulped and nodded again. 'Yeah, sure, I invited you.'

'And of course, you *couldn't possibly* have invited my girlfriend Siobhan then, could you?'

Ralph shook his head violently. 'No – no! I didn't. I didn't invite her. I don't even *know* her – I promise!'

Karl grabbed Ralph by the neck of his lovely new Dolce & Gabbana shirt and brought his face inches from his own. Jem gasped and gripped hold of Ralph's arm.

'So, who did? EH? Who invited her? It's your party, isn't it, you're the FUCKING HOST! So! Who else could it have been? I want to KILL YOU, you bastard, this has been the worst night of my life and I want to kill you!'

Siobhan gently touched Karl's elbow.

'Karl, please, it's not his fault. It's not anyone's fault. Please leave him alone.'

'No, Shuv – you keep out of this! This BASTARD'S playing games with me and he's not going to get away with it.'

'I really don't think he invited me, Karl. Please, leave him alone. Please don't fight any more.'

'But, Shuv, I thought this was what you wanted! I thought you wanted me to be like this, to take action, defend your honour, fight for what I want . . .'

Siobhan looked him deep in the eyes and held his now limp hands. 'Karl – it's too late. It's me you should be shouting at. I should have told you about Rick. I should have been more honest with you. I should have told you everything. It's too late for fighting, Karl. It's too late.'

'But . . . but . . .' he looked helplessly from a breathless Ralph to a beseeching Siobhan. He didn't know what to do any more. He didn't know what to think. He didn't know who he was or why he was or where he was. He lifted his hands to his eyes and began to cry.

'Oh, God,' he mumbled through spitty breath, rubbing his eyes hard with the heels of his hands. 'Oh, God.'

Siobhan put an arm around him and led him away from the small group of onlookers. She turned to give Rick a reassuring wink as she went, which he returned with a small, pained grimace through the encrusting blood surrounding his nose and mouth. He knew what

Siobhan had to do. He understood. He straightened himself painfully, dabbing gently at his nose and mouth.

'Any chance I could come in and use some ice, mate?' he asked Ralph quietly, after they'd gone.

'Oh – sure – yes – of course.' Ralph came to his senses – he'd been in some sort of fear-paralysis ever since Karl had first called him a FUCKING BASTARD – and gave Rick a shoulder to lean on as they walked slowly back into the party.

'Oh, thank God, you're back.' Cheri approached Jem and Ralph anxiously as they returned. 'You've got to get rid of Smith – he's doing my brain in.' She indicated Smith, at the far end of the room, stumbling towards the toilet, unaware of Jem's return. 'He won't leave me alone,' she whispered.

He'd spent the hour since Jem had fled desperately trying to convince Cheri that he wasn't drunk, that he wasn't pathetic, that he wasn't a sad, ridiculous bastard, and that his proposal of marriage was not only sincerely and passionately intended but was also a fabulously good idea and that Cheri would regret it for the rest of her life if she turned him down.

Cheri looked at Jem with pity and compassion and put a hand on her arm. 'Are you all right?' she mouthed. Jem nodded and smiled at Ralph, and then back at Cheri. 'I'm fine now, thank you. Angry, embarrassed and humiliated, but fine! Unlike this poor bugger.' She moved out of the way to reveal poor Rick, slouched against Ralph's shoulder, his face quickly swelling up into tight shiny bumps of purple and grey.

Cheri eyed Rick's bloody, broken face with concern, and then a flicker of recognition passed across her face.

'Rick?' she questioned, taking his hand and helping Jem and Ralph to lead him to the large black bin full of semi-melted ice behind the bar.

Rick's face crumpled with the strain of remembering.

'Cheri,' she said, placing her hand on her chest, 'remember? I'm – I was – a friend of Tamsin's. We all went out one night, last summer, to that restaurant on Fulham Broadway and your car got clamped, remember?'

'Oh, yeah. Of course. Cheri. I remember you, yeah. What are you doing here?' He winced as Jem and Ralph gently lowered him into a chair.

'Oh, God,' Cheri laughed, 'don't ask!'

Ralph and Jem looked at each other. This evening was in danger of collapsing under the weight of too much drama and coincidence.

Cheri wrapped some ice in a linen napkin and rested it against Rick's face. 'Are you O K?' she asked. 'Are you sure you don't need to go to a hospital, or something?'

Rick shook his head and smiled bravely. 'Nah, it's just superficial. Really. I'll be fine.'

Cheri smiled kindly and continued her administering. She was enjoying playing the role of a benevolent Florence Nightingale-type. There was a time when she'd have been ill at the thought of touching someone else's wounds, someone else's blood, when it would have been a huge inconvenience. Now it was a pleasure. Maybe she should have been a nurse? She smiled again.

The party had started to thin out a little now. Ralph's friends had begun asking for minicab numbers and people milled drunkenly about on the pavement outside the gallery, waiting for black cabs.

Abba were still playing on the CD a little forlornly now, as only one drunken, maudlin-looking fellow with lipstick kisses all over his face was dancing to it, holding an empty bottle of champagne to his chest and humming along sadly to 'Dancing Queen'.

Philippe was wandering disconsolately around the room with a bin liner, collecting cigarette butts and licking the tip of his finger occasionally to moisten the small, barely visible burns left all over his lovely maplewood flooring, and tutting softly to himself.

A few couples lined the room, still absorbed in conversation and unaware that the party was closing down around them, and a group of Ralph's friends surrounded him, thanking him noisily for a great night, congratulating him on his exhibition and his good fortune and making the scrag ends of conversation that only get used at the close of a party – invites to other parties, promises to phone, last-minute exchanges of news and gossip – trying to cram into two minutes all the chat and talk that hadn't been shared earlier in the evening because you were talking to someone else. Or, in the case of this particular night, because you were showing your muse your paintings, watching your best friend propose to a woman he shouldn't have, convincing your true love to fall in love with you and breaking up a fight between an extremely angry jilted lover and his girlfriend's new boyfriend.

Siobhan and Karl had still not returned from their cooling-down walk, Cheri continued to tend poor Rick's wounds, Jem stood with Ralph while he saw off his friends, and Smith . . . where was Smith? Smith was nowhere to be seen.

No one had seen him, in fact, since about half an hour

ago, when Jem and Ralph had first returned from their drama on the street.

'I think I saw him heading towards the toilet,' Cheri offered helpfully, patting daintily at Rick's wounds with a napkin-wrapped fingertip.

Ralph and Jem looked at each other mischievously. It usually meant only one thing when someone disappeared into a toilet for that long at a party. They walked softly across the wooden floor towards the toilet door, and Ralph tried the handle. It was unlocked, and he pushed the door open slowly, while Jem held on to his arm and peered over his shoulder.

Jem and Ralph had seen all sorts of sorry sights in their life before, all manner of pathetic, drunken individuals in undignified positions and situations, but nothing they'd ever seen before could have prepared them sufficiently for the sight that confronted them when they opened the door to the toilet in Philippe's gallery.

A huge cloud of steam fled the room as the door opened, revealing Smith, completely unconscious, slouched on the toilet seat, his trousers unfurled around his ankles, his penis flopping sadly and shrunkenly to one side amid his shirt tails, while his head rested in the sink, surrounded by a halo of putrid-smelling yellow and green vomit, matched by the Pollockesque lumps splattered all over his face and embedded in his wet hair. The hot tap ran violently down the side of the sink, missing the vomit entirely and kicking up billowing fugs of steam into the room. Nestling in the bottom of the toilet bowl, plainly visible thanks to the perky angle of Smith's naked bottom, sat an enormous and rank-smelling turd. It was quite the most undignified vision that either Jem or Ralph had ever encountered.

'Oh, dear,' said Jem, putting her hand over her mouth and turning away.

'Oh, dear,' repeated Ralph, stifling a laugh. 'Stupid bastard.'

'What shall we do? Poor Smith.'

'Huh!' exclaimed Ralph. 'Poor Smith, my arse!'

'What's going on?' Cheri had heard the commotion from the other side of the room and was standing behind them, unaware that she was about to witness a scene that would put her off her food for at least a week. She peered curiously over Ralph's shoulder and squeaked a little when she saw what was in the toilet, turning away in horror.

'Smith!' shouted Ralph, kicking at his shins. 'Oi, wake up – wake up! Your fiancée's here! Ha! Wake up!'

Smith slowly opened one eye and made a strange groaning noise under his breath, which sounded like 'Leave me alone', but no one could be sure.

'Cheri's here, mate – your fiancée! Wake up.'

'Ugh,' said Smith, opening his other eye and lifting his head an inch or two from the gory sink. 'Cheri?'

'Yes. Cheri.' Ralph smirked to himself.

'Oh, Ralph,' cried Jem, 'leave him alone. That's enough!'

Ralph knew Jem was right. He was enjoying himself, but it was cruel and mean and wholly unchristian. 'OK,' he said, 'you're right.' He leaned in towards Smith and shouted in his ear: 'I'll just leave you to make sweet talk with Cheri here, shall I then?' and he and Jem left him there, gradually gaining consciousness and, with it, the dreadful realization that there was vomit in his hair, shit in the toilet, his penis and naked arse were on full view and that his beloved Cheri was standing over him, eyeing him with an almost tangible expression of pity, disgust and horror.

'Ugh, God,' he mumbled, as he let his head fall back into the sink and kicked the door shut with one outstretched, half-naked leg, 'ugh, God.'

Siobhan and Karl had returned from their walk and found the gallery almost empty, except for poor Rick still sitting where Cheri had left him on the chair by the bar, his face now so swollen and purple that it was almost unrecognizable. Karl shuffled uncomfortably in the background, while Siobhan gently lifted Rick to his feet.

'It's all right, mate,' Rick said, as he and Siobhan shambled past Karl, towards the front door. 'I deserved that.'

Karl followed them out on to the street and watched Siobhan place Rick tenderly into the passenger seat, buckling him in and lightly brushing away a tendril of hair from the blood that was coagulating around his eye.

She walked over to the driver's seat, opened the door, sat down, adjusted the chair, put the key in the ignition and stared up at Karl as the electronic window wound itself down. She put a hand on top of Karl's hand, resting inside the window.

''Bye, Karl,' she said. 'I'm glad I saw you tonight. I'm glad this happened. Well,' she indicated Rick, 'maybe not *everything*. But, whoever it was who invited me, and I'm pretty sure I know who it was' – she indicated Cheri standing in the window of the gallery, watching them sadly – 'I'm glad they did it.'

Karl couldn't deny it. It had been the most painful,

awful night of his life. It had been worse than the night Siobhan kicked him out. But it was good that it had happened. It had to happen. They'd had a much needed talk while they wandered together around the twinkling old lamp-shops and cosy, over-priced antique shops of Ledbury Road. They'd talked about everything, but mainly the future, and Karl realized now, without a doubt, that he had no place in hers . . .

'We're better off apart,' she'd said, smiling brightly at him. 'You've got to let go, Karl. The sooner the better. Start looking at the world with different eyes – you'll be surprised what you see – it's quite amazing! Think of the last fifteen years as a myopic haze and the last few months apart as brand-new glasses. I've been wearing mine. And you haven't. Now you've got to put yours on. Really, Karl! Put them on and see how bright life can be, how new and fresh and colourful.'

Karl wasn't too sure about this strange analogy. It sounded unlikely. And, whatever Siobhan might think, he was glad he'd had the opportunity to kick the shit out of Rick. He'd enjoyed it – right or wrong, he'd enjoyed it. He gripped Siobhan's hand hard and smiled at her through gritted teeth as the window began to close. 'Maybe we could go for a drink, one night.' He squeezed the invitation through the final inch of open window and drew his hand away from the car.

Siobhan nodded, put the car into drive, smiled one last smile at Karl and pulled away.

Karl stood on the pavement, swaying slightly in the wake of the car and the brisk winter wind that was picking up around Ledbury Road. He put his hands into his coat pockets, watching until the car had disappeared from view, and then he turned around and began to walk back into the gallery. He wiped a small tear away from the side of his nose, took a deep breath and put a spring in his step.

It was time to go home. Time to start afresh. Time to see things differently.

It was time . . .

It was a strange quintet who shared a black cab back to Almanac Road that night. Karl sat quietly on one side, staring intently from the window, nursing his scuffed knuckles absent-mindedly with the thumb of his other hand, wishing that the cab would hurry up and get him home and trying not to look at Cheri, who was sitting primly on one of the fold-out seats, desperately trying to keep her distance from the foul-smelling Smith, who'd attempted to wash every trace of sick and bile from his person but still carried with him a strong and heavy aroma of vomit. He had his head out of the window, like a dog, the bitter wind gusting through his hair and making his eyes water, but at least it meant he didn't have to watch Cheri eyeing him with contempt and reminding him that never, in the whole history of mankind, had one man managed to blow it so spectacularly and so completely. It also meant that he didn't have to look at Jem, snuggled up under Ralph's arm and watching him with a small sad look of pity and regret, designed to make him feel even worse than he already did about the awful unfolding of events that had occurred tonight, at Ralph's party.

Nobody spoke as the cab trundled dejectedly across Battersea Bridge. The sky was jet black overhead and illuminated brightly by a fat, white full moon. A party boat lit with fairy lights and loud with chatter and music passed beneath the bridge as they crossed. A skinny girl in a tight Lycra dress waved a bottle of champagne at them from the deck. Smith waved back half-heartedly.

The cab pulled up quietly outside number thirty-one and its passengers spilt heavily and gratefully on to the pavement, all glad that the cab ride from hell was finally over.

Cheri made her way briskly to the front door, keen as ever to avoid Karl, especially given the disastrous outcome of her attempt to bring him and Siobhan back together by sending her that invite. He caught up with her on the front step and waited awkwardly behind her while she unlocked the door.

'Well,' he began, unexpectedly, 'that was some night, wasn't it?'

Cheri spun around at the sound of his voice. 'Yeah,' she laughed nervously, 'unbelievable.'

'Um,' he scratched at the back of his neck, 'I don't know who, er, invited Siobhan tonight. I suspect it was you' – he put a quieting hand out as Cheri began to explain – 'it's fine, Cheri. It really is. I'm glad, you . . . someone . . . invited her, and I'm glad I saw her tonight and I'm glad I hit Rick. So . . . just don't worry. OK? It's all all right and I'm sorry, as well, about earlier, shouting at you like that. It was unfair. I was drunk. Sorry.' He smiled at her, a warm, sincere smile full of hope for the future and death to the past. Then he slipped his key into his lock and disappeared quietly into his flat, leaving Cheri standing at the bottom of the stairs, her coat clutched in her hands, a look of surprise, gratitude and pleasure slowly pinkening her face.

She turned and walked up the stairs, towards the top floor, smiling to herself, and wondered, yet again, at the joys of goodness . . .

Smith vanished quickly into the basement flat. He wanted to go to bed, more than anything in the whole world. His head ached, his throat was sore and his heart felt like it was slowly bleeding to death. He let the door slam behind him, not caring that Jem and Ralph were on their way, not wanting to look at them for one more single, solitary second. Everything was a mess now. Ralph was a bastard, Jem hated him, Cheri despised him. He had no friend, no girlfriend and no fantasies left. It was all over. Everything. But he was too tired to start trying to wonder about the future now, about his living arrangements, about Cheri, about everything. He'd deal with all that tomorrow. He'd buy flowers for Cheri tomorrow, to apologize, and he'd give Ralph and Jem their marching orders, kick them out. Tomorrow.

Right now, he was going to bed . . .

Jem and Ralph stood at the top of the basement steps and watched the full moon for a while.

'It was a full moon the night I first came to see the flat, you know?' said Jem, her arm tucked firmly around Ralph's waist.

'Oh, yeah?' he murmured happily, dropping a kiss on to the top of Jem's bedraggled head. 'Weird stuff always happens on full-moon nights, doesn't it? People behave strangely, act differently.'

'They certainly do!'

They fell quiet for a moment, contemplating the unbelievable sequence of events that had occurred that night.

'D'you remember,' asked Jem, suddenly, 'd'you remember when I first came to see the flat? You were on the phone, to Claudia, you didn't even look at me!'

'Ah, but what I bet you don't know is that seconds before you arrived, I'd been sitting on the sofa – there' – he indicated the sofa through the window – 'sitting there, waiting for this mysterious girl called Jem to arrive and . . . *smoking a cigarette.* So, you see, it was me all along. The man on the sofa, the man of your dreams! Maybe you'd have realized sooner if fucking Claudia hadn't phoned at that precise moment . . .'

'And if you'd bought peonies! And hadn't worn those disgusting longjohns! And . . .'

'OK!' laughed Ralph, squeezing Jem to him, 'you're right! Destiny moves in mysterious ways, doesn't it?'

'You know Smith will probably make us move out, don't you?'

'Yeah. Well. We'll deal with that when it happens. I know a lovely little place on Cable Street!'

They started to walk down the steps and then Ralph stopped abruptly and turned to face Jem. 'Wait!' he exclaimed, beaming. 'Wait! I've had an idea. Just stand there and don't move until I tell you! OK?' He leapt down the steps two at a time and disappeared through the front door, letting it close behind him.

Jem stood on the steps, uncertainly, shivering a bit in the cold wind and wondering what the hell Ralph was playing at.

A moment later, she noticed a light shining from the living-room window and turned to look down.

A man was sitting on the sofa. A long plume of pink-tinged smoke hovered above his head. He had a slender neck and an oval skull covered in short black hair that ended in a sweet triangle of stubble at the nape of his neck. Jem shuddered. It was her dream. Exactly! And then she smiled, a huge, belly-achey, involuntary smile. The man on the sofa turned slightly in his seat. He looked at Jem and shared her smile.

And then Jem lifted the hem of her rose-printed dress with one small fist and ran down the steps, her heels echoing on the concrete, pushed open the front door, and the living-room door, grabbed hold of her destiny, threw him down on the sofa and kissed the living daylights out of him.

# THIRTYNOTHING

for Oliver Cannon Jewell
*nephew extraordinaire*

www.lisa-jewell.co.uk

# ACKNOWLEDGEMENTS

Thank you once again to my loyal and lovely readers, Nic, Katy, Sarah and Yasmin. Don't worry – I won't ask you to do it again. Thank you to my agent, Judith, for killing off my excess characters so humanely (so long, Rudy, Rebecca and Tony) and making this almost readable. Thank you, too, to Louise 'Editor of the Year' Moore, for not making me kill off anyone else and making this almost publishable.

Thanks also to all those people I was too shell-shocked to thank last time: Harrie, Sarah and all the fantastic editing types, Peter and his incomparable sales team, Nicky and Katrin, the sanest and calmest PRs I've ever met, John and his hugely imaginative marketeers, to the two Sophies and to Ami for yet another stunning cover.

Thank you to every bookseller who piled the last one high and prominently – I'm eternally grateful. To the panel of the *Late Review* who were so nice about my book on 6 May '99 – I love all of you. To all the readers who have sent me such great e-mails and letters – send me more. And to all the readers who didn't write to me – thanks for buying the book, anyway.

Thank you to Lee for all his advice about A&R and to Seb for never ceasing to inspire me with the vagaries of his love life. And finally, but never leastly, to my top-of-the-range man Jascha, without whose hardworking presence I would spend all day on the Net and this book would never have been written – thank you for being so proud and so supportive. Without you, the days would seem empty and long and I would talk to myself a lot.

# CHAPTER ONE

Dig woke with a start.

The first thing he was conscious of was the taste in his mouth, a rancid coating of . . . what was it? Onions? Garlic? Some kind of battery-acid-type thing going on in there as well. He slowly brought a hand from beneath his duvet and cupped it around his mouth. He let out a small puff of coagulated breath and sniffed it back in. Jesus. Grim beyond belief. He clamped his mouth shut again.

The second thing he was conscious of was his head, which appeared to have had a large shipment of ball-bearings dumped in it overnight, while his blood felt as if it had been transfused with silica and come to a grinding, desiccated halt somewhere around his temples.

The third thing was his stomach, a solid, churning area of gas and corrosive fluids, swishing and swirling around together like a kind of miniature primordial soup. He felt a bubbling tube of gas begin to wriggle through his stomach, around his intestine and down towards his bowel. He could tell it was going to be bad when it departed his body in a hot and silent *phut*, and before long his airless room was ripe with the stench of yeast and garlic.

'Oh, Jesus. What the fuck is that smell?'

Which is when Dig became aware of the fourth thing.

The girl in his bed.

He turned his head slowly, and there she was. A girl. A girl with messy blonde hair and black stuff smudged under her eyes and bare bony shoulders and a tattoo of a sea horse on her left arm and one hand covering her mouth and nose while her face wrinkled up in distaste.

'Jesus!' The girl turned over on to her side with a disgusted flounce. She had some sort of accent, and another tattoo on her back, of a butterfly. It was very nicely done. Dig slowly manoeuvred himself up on his elbow and surveyed the girl as if she were some kind of strange sea creature which had been washed up on his bed by the tide. She looked young. Surprise surprise. About twenty, probably. And thin. Very thin indeed. Another surprise. He wondered what she was called.

'Do you have any Nurofen?' Her voice was muffled through her hand but was now recognizably Irish. Northern Irish, to be precise.

'Uh-huh.' Dig's hand found the little tablets on his bedside table, and the glass of water he'd put there last night, a sign that at some point between getting home and going to bed he'd obviously been mentally and physically functioning to some extent. Which also indicated to him that relations had more than likely been had with this small, bony girl in his bed.

He turned to look down at the floor by his bed. Yep. There it was. A shimmery sliver of pearly latex with a neat little knot at the top. Well, that was something, at least.

The level of traffic noise wafting through the half-opened window from Camden Road outside led Dig to believe that it was probably some considerable time after the six in the morning his head was telling him it was.

He turned painfully to look at his radio alarm: 11.48 a.m. It was also hot, stiflingly hot. Strange for the middle of November.

He passed the glass and pills to the bony girl.

'Thanks.' She gulped them down in one. 'What time is it?'

'Ten to twelve.'

'What! Fuck, you're joking!' She sprang out of bed, like a little pink whippet and began jumping into her clothes: a tiny black vest top, no bra, hard little nipples poking through, G-string, no buttocks, combat trousers, pierced belly button, trainers. 'Fuck fuck fuck.' She heaved the curtains apart, sending Dig recoiling across the bed with one elbow over his face. She surveyed the street below.

'Where the fuck am I? Is this Tooting Broadway?'

'What? No – no – Kentish Town – Camden Road.'

'Oh no! Oh fucking no. I have to be in Clapham in ten minutes. Jesus! Can I get a bus from here? Where's the Tube? D'you have a car?'

'No. Five minutes that way. Yes, but it's in for repairs.'

'Oh, Christ – I'll have to get a cab. I only have a fiver. D'you have any cash?'

Dig peeled the last crumpled tenner from his wallet and handed it to her.

She kissed it. 'I'll pay you back.'

'Where are you going?'

'Work.'

'On a Saturday?'

'Yeah – I'm a waitress – shit – it's going to be murderously busy today – look at that sunshine – but it's only a temporary thing, y'know, part time.'

'You're a student?' Something had come back to him from the night before.

'Yeah, that's right.' She was scraping her hair back into some kind of knot. The sun was playing on her and she looked quite pretty. She seemed strong and bright.

'Where d'you study?' Dig was suddenly feeling vaguely sociable, as if he might quite like to see her again.

'God, you can't remember a thing we talked about last night, can you?' She smiled. She pulled a pair of yellow sunglasses from her rucksack and sat them on top of her head. 'Well' – she looked pleased with herself, a little embarrassed – 'I'm at sixth-form college right now, but my tutors reckon I'll get a place at Oxford next year – *if* I get my grades.'

Grades? *Grades?* Jesus! 'What – er, what grades?' Dig rubbed at the stubble on his chin.

'A Levels, of course.'

'So – you're – how old?'

'Seventeen.'

Oh dear God!

She was standing at the door now, her rucksack on her back, looking all of a sudden like a child, like a small girl wearing big girl's clothes. She seemed to transmogrify before his eyes, her hips disappearing, her breasts deflating, her waist expanding, her hair morphing as he watched from stylish topknot to perky pigtails. Oh Jesus Christ! Seventeen!

'Hey, look,' she was saying, waving his ten-pound note at him, 'I'll find a way of getting this back to you – I promise. I have your number, I'll ring you.'

I'll ring you. *I'll ring you!* There was a child standing in his bedroom doorway, with a pierced belly button, waving his money at him and telling him she'd ring him. Jesus, what was the world coming to?

'Oh, and by the way – Happy Birthday.' She smiled at him, a nice, warm, intelligent smile, and then she was gone.

Happy Birthday. Oh yes, Happy Birthday indeed. Thirty years old. He was thirty years old. A thirty-year-old pervert. A dirty thirty old man. A heinous, raincoat-wearing, boiled-sweet-carrying, dribbling, drooling old man.

He'd slept with a seventeen-year-old.

OK, so it was the stuff of dreams, the stuff men of his age made lascivious, lustful jokes about over pints in pubs. But to have really done it, to be confronted with the reality of a seventeen-year-old in his bed. His little sister was eighteen and if he'd found out that she'd . . . with a man of thirty . . . he'd have . . . Well, anyway, it just didn't feel right. Dig suddenly felt a little too old to be chasing after much younger women.

The previous evening was starting to come back to him in dribs and drabs. Tequila slammers at Nadine's. Opening presents. Pints at the Lady Somerset with the rest of the crowd. All piling into a cab at midnight. Some club somewhere in town. (A club? They never went to clubs any more.) More tequila. And then dancing – dancing for hours . . . God, he'd probably looked a right arse. And that girl, that child . . . Katie! That was it, that was her name – Katie – except she'd pronounced it 'Kayday'. Dancing with her and telling her, over and over again, 'It's my birthday! It's my birthday!' And then – a curry? Shit, it must have been nearly morning by then . . . where the hell had they managed to find a curry at that time of night?

And that girl, Katie, had been there. And . . . yes, that's right, Nadine had started on Maxwell in the restaurant and she'd tipped her raitha into his korma for some reason or, more probably, for no reason whatsoever. Poor Maxwell. It looked like his days were numbered. And then? Well, they must have got a cab or something. He couldn't remember anything after that.

Dig wrapped himself up in his dressing-gown and made his way to his gleaming little Ikea kitchen, where he got himself some coffee. He switched on his ionizer, lit a cigarette and let his hangover wash over him for a while, as he trawled his memory for more detail, but nothing came to him, just blurred images and fuzzy fag-ends of conversation.

The coffee and cigarette, combined with the unimaginable gunk that had already been in his mouth when he woke up, had pushed his breath to crisis point. He absolutely *had* to brush his teeth.

He stared at his reflection in the mirror as he brushed. There's the crunch, he thought, there it is. A couple of years ago I could have had a heavy night and woken up the next morning looking like something that vaguely resembled a human being, instead of this monstrous, clammy-complexioned, open-pored, dark-shadowed, grey-skinned sack of old bones that's staring back at me from my bathroom mirror. But now I'm thirty, and although I still have youth ahead of me, I have left the greatest part of it behind me, and my body is no longer on my side, will no longer collude in my systematic abuse of it. My body is asking for a break, and my punishment for not giving it a break is to make me look this hideous in the mornings.

Still, he thought, he didn't have much to complain

about as he entered his fourth decade. He had a great social life and friends he'd known for years. He was liked and respected by nearly everyone he came into contact with. He could pull pretty girls; he owned his own flat – OK, so it was small and noisy and it was up three flights of stairs, but it was his; he had the job of his dreams working as an A&R manager for a small record label in Camden – all right, so it was poor pay for long hours and very little success, but he loved it. Unlike most men he knew of his age, he still had all his hair and a pretty firm stomach. His family lived just round the corner so he got to see his precious mum at least once or twice a week. And now he was thirty.

Thirty wasn't so bad.

Yeah. Thirty was fine.

Actually, it wasn't that different to twenty-nine.

## CHAPTER TWO

Nadine rolled sideways towards Maxwell and let his big, bear-like arms wrap her up in a sleepy embrace. His neck smelled sweetly musty, and traces of last night's aftershave lingered on his skin. She could feel the hairs on his chest rubbing against her breasts and his resting heartbeat echoing through her ribcage.

The sun was streaming through the yellow and red sari silk draped over her bedroom windows and the calming sounds of outside activity floated over her bed like a summer breeze: a dog barking, a child discussing his plans for the day with his mother, car engines starting, front doors opening and closing.

'Cup of tea?'

'Ooh, yes please.'

Maxwell pulled his huge frame from the bed, squeezed himself into Nadine's much-too-small red-silk robe and gently padded off towards the kitchen. Nadine stretched herself out in the newly spacious bed and smiled as she heard Maxwell performing his usual clattering pillage of the kitchen drawers and cupboards, unable even after three months to lay his hands on teaspoons, mugs and teabags without first exploring every possible location.

She clicked on the radio and listened to the homely babble of Radio Five Live presenters for a while, and suddenly realized that despite the traces of a headache lingering around her temples, a vaguely nauseous sensation emanating from her stomach and the slightly embarrassing memory of yet another scene with Maxwell in the restaurant last night, she was feeling quite inexplicably, deliriously happy. It was a Saturday morning, the sun was shining, there was a man in the kitchen making her tea, and she had no plans whatsoever for the rest of the day. Maxwell wasn't usually here at the weekend. She'd only seen him last night because it was Dig's birthday and Dig liked Maxwell and had insisted that she invite him. She wasn't used to waking up with a man on a Saturday morning. It was nice. They could do couply things: they could go for a walk, or go out for lunch somewhere and read the papers. Or they could just stay in bed all day, watch the telly, eat bacon sandwiches, chat and have sex.

This, she decided, was one of those moments, one of those utterly perfect moments in life, which you absolutely had to draw into your lungs and hold there and absorb every drop of, because that was what life was all about. If you expected eternal happiness, then you missed the essence of life that was contained in moments like this.

'There you go,' said Maxwell, gently placing steaming mugs of tea on the bedside table – mugs, Nadine noticed, that she never used, her emergency mugs, ugly ones her mother had given her, decorated with insipid roses fading defeatedly after ten years of washing-up and kept at the back of the cupboard, mugs that only someone with no sense of design or aesthetics would have pulled from her cupboard when presented with a selection of at least twenty more attractive mugs. She felt a sudden burst of irritation and her little happiness bubble exploded over her head. Why couldn't he be perfect? Was that too much to ask?

'For God's sake, Maxwell,' she bristled, waspishly, 'why do you always have to choose the ugliest mugs in the kitchen?'

'Eh?' Maxwell looked stumped, and Nadine felt flooded with disdain, at the precise moment she should have felt guilt.

'Haven't you noticed,' she continued, 'that when *I* make the tea I always use those Deco mugs or the Simpsons mugs or the South Park mugs. You know – the nice mugs? Haven't you noticed that I never, ever use these mugs?' She pointed at them in disgust.

Maxwell shrugged and shook his head. 'What's wrong with them?' he asked sadly.

'Huh! Exactly! That's exactly it! If you don't know what's wrong with these mugs then there is no point in having this conversation.' Nadine knew she was being unreasonable but she couldn't help it.

'Do you want me to change them?' he offered.

Nadine jumped out of the bed in exasperation and gesticulated angrily. 'No, Maxwell. I don't want you to change them, I just want you *not* to have chosen them in the first place. I want you to be as unspeakably *repulsed* by these mugs as I am. I want you to look at these mugs and feel a deep sense of pity for the men and women of . . . of' – she picked up a mug and read the inscription on the bottom – 'of Lichfield Pottery, Staffs, who were actually paid to paint these disgusting flowers on to the sides of these disgusting objects and who probably think they're highly talented artists. That's what I want, Maxwell.'

Maxwell's kind face crumpled up with the strain of

comprehension, and Nadine could see that he was trying, he really was trying to understand what she was saying to him and this annoyed her even more. She was being a complete bitch and a real man would have told her to shut the fuck up. But he wasn't a real man, and he had actually picked up one of the mugs and was now turning it around and around in his hand, gazing at it from every possible angle, his face a picture of studious contemplation.

'Mmmm,' he said, 'I suppose it is a bit *plain*. A bit old-fashioned . . .'

'Oh, put it down, for Christ's sake!' she fumed. 'Put the fucking mug down.'

The badly chosen mugs, taken in isolation, were not, evidently, a big deal, but set in the context of their three-month-old relationship they were yet another sign that Maxwell was the Wrong Boyfriend. She'd been trying to convince herself for three months that it could work, that despite the differences between them, despite his penchant for brightly coloured designer menswear, his infatuation with Celine Dion, his unflappable demeanour and his unfeasibly good manners, despite his home being ten miles away from hers, just outside Dagenham in Essex, and despite the fact that he was a courier and she was a photographer who earned five times as much as him, she could make it work. Because Maxwell was as nice a bloke as you could ever hope to meet and Nadine felt that she deserved a nice bloke. But nice blokes aren't necessarily perfect blokes and Nadine was sorry for her pettiness and intolerance, but she couldn't, just couldn't, abide the differences between herself and Maxwell for another moment.

'Nadine,' Maxwell was saying, softly, 'I'm not really

sure . . . could you explain to me why you're getting so wound up about a pair of mugs?'

Nadine appreciated that this was a fair question. 'Oh God, Maxwell. It's not just the mugs. It's not the mugs. It's everything. It's us. It's me . . . this just isn't working . . .' Nadine listened to the words echoing in her head and thought how hollow they sounded. She wondered how many times in her life she'd used the same words before. 'It's me,' she always said, 'it's not you, it's me.'

And it was true. It *was* always her. She hadn't been dumped since she was twenty-one. It had been fine when she was younger, going out with unsuitable men, because all her friends were going out with unsuitable men, too. They'd all get together and compare horror stories, revel in the imperfections of each other's ill-advised relationships, bond over mutual disdain for the inferior sex. That's what you do when you're in your twenties. But then, gradually, one by one, all her friends had found decent men, good men, and splintered off. And now, in her thirtieth year, Nadine found herself hanging around, like the Queen of Spades in a game of Old Maid. The game was over, the rest of the pack was in pairs, but she was still playing. And until a few weeks ago, she'd still been enjoying it.

But then she'd turned thirty and had begun to evaluate her situation, and all of a sudden the life of a serial monogamist didn't seem like so much fun and there wasn't the time to waste any more. Her youth was running out, her choices were diminishing, and it had hit Nadine then, the real reason why she went out with so many losers: she only went out with men who didn't threaten her friendship with Dig. The moment a boyfriend started to make claims on her time or her emotions, it was over. The moment a boyfriend began to show any signs of resentment about the amount of time she spent with Dig, it was over. There existed between Dig and Nadine this sort of unwritten law that said that they weren't allowed to spend quality time with anyone but each other. Weekdays were for boyfriends and girlfriends; weekends were for Dig and Nadine.

Dig was Nadine's best friend, her favourite person in the entire world, and as long as they were friends she didn't actually *need* to be in love with anyone else. It would just complicate everything if either of them ever fell in love with another person.

The only problem was that they just didn't fancy each other; each one epitomized the antithesis of the other's 'type'. Dig liked tiny, girl-child-type women (which Nadine most certainly *wasn't*) who made him feel manly, and Nadine liked enormous hairy men (which Dig most certainly *wasn't*) who made her feel delicate. If they'd fancied each other, they would have been married by now. Probably.

Nadine looked at Maxwell, staring warmly but blankly at her, and she suddenly realized that he was going to be the last Wrong Boyfriend. Definitely. Without a doubt. No more Wrong Boyfriends. Only Right Boyfriends from here on in. She would have one last crack at trying to find a suitable man, and if that failed, she'd marry Dig, skinny legs and all.

She took a deep breath. 'Maxwell,' she said, sitting down beside him on the bed and gently removing the mug of tea from between his enormous fingers. 'I think we should talk.'

*

Well, thought Nadine, as she closed the front door quietly behind Maxwell's slightly stooped figure, at least he didn't cry. That was the worst thing, the most horrible thing imaginable, to see a grown man cry, especially a man as big as Maxwell. He'd taken it quite well really, almost as if he'd never before considered the concept of being dumped and was going to go home and give it some thought, as if she'd given him some unfathomable lateral-thinking test to consider. Poor Maxwell, she thought. But he'd be fine. He'd be just fine – he was good-looking and funny and caring and generous – he'd find someone else in days. A nice Essex girl who would look up to him and respect him and love every inch of his hairy, chunky body, a kind girl who would appreciate him and make him happy, happier than Nadine had ever made him.

He'd be just fine. Unlike her.

Nadine glanced around her now empty flat, at the dents in her gaudy Bollywood duvet cover left by two bodies, and the hated pair of mugs still sitting accusingly on the bedside table. She absorbed the change in the atmosphere, the stillness of the air, the sudden silence from outside her bedroom window – and then she remembered how she'd felt twenty minutes ago, the thought of the day ahead which had pleased her so greatly and the pure moment of unblemished happiness she'd experienced and embraced.

It occurred to Nadine that maybe those moments weren't meant to be fleeting, that maybe they were like seeds, and you were supposed to plant them and water them, and that if you tended them well, eventually you would grow a Tree of Happiness.

And if that was the case, she wondered, how come every time she was lucky enough to find a Happiness

Seed she mashed it up, spat on it, stamped on it and then threw it out of the window? Why did she have to spoil absolutely everything?

Nadine felt her stomach begin to rumble with fake, post-late-night-curry hunger. She contemplated rustling up a quick bacon sarnie but then decided she had to get out of the flat, go for a walk, see someone, talk to someone.

She picked up the phone and called Dig.

## CHAPTER THREE

'So,' said Dig, regarding Nadine disbelievingly over a large plate of greasy meat and chips, 'let me get this straight. You dumped Maxwell because he chose the wrong mugs?'

'Well, yes. Among other things. I mean – we both know he wasn't right for me, don't we?'

'I really liked him . . . well, compared to some of the other men you've been out with this decade.'

'Yes. Of course. So did I. Who wouldn't? But he was so annoying, you know? The way he dressed, and the way he was always going on about his mum, and Celine Dion, and the fact that he was allergic to *garlic* of all things – I mean, how can you go through life being allergic to *garlic*? – and he was so pathetic, sometimes, so . . . so . . . so . . .'

'Nice?'

'Very nice. But just so . . .'

'Kind, pleasant, generous?'

'Yes. But, so . . . so . . .'

'In love with you?'

'Look' – Nadine pointed a speared chip at Dig – 'he held his knife and fork like he was going to knit a sweater with them, OK? That's just one of those things I, personally, can't live with.'

'Oh my God, Deen! You complete fucking *snob*!'

'Well, it's the truth. I can't help the way I am, can I?

It just used to make my blood boil. And he couldn't spell either, and there is nothing worse than a man who can't spell – it takes all the romance out of cards and love letters and things.'

'You are unreal, Nadine Kite,' said Dig, slowly shaking his head from side to side in wonderment, 'you really are. What planet are you from?'

Nadine looked at him sniffily, sensing that her defence was shaky, to say the least. 'OK,' she conceded, 'I admit it. I am a snob, and I am a fussy cow and I do demand a lot of men but, the bottom line is this: Maxwell wasn't right for me and I didn't want to go out with him any more and I've found a whole load of excuses not to love him back. But, I know, *I know* that when I meet someone who *is* right for me, then I won't care whether or not they can spell, or how they hold their cutlery.'

Dig snorted sceptically.

'Yeah, right. Take the piss. But I know it. OK?'

Dig cut a swathe through the juices on his plate with a chunk of toast and smiled wryly at Nadine. 'Deen,' he said, popping the toast into his mouth, 'you know I love you dearly, you know you're my best girl and I would do anything for you. But you are a nightmare. You are a complete and utter nightmare . . . If you were a bloke, you would be a bastard.'

Nadine dropped her jaw in mock indignation.

' . . . And one day you are going to get your comeuppance. You are going to meet this so-called "perfect guy" and you are going to put up with his appalling table manners and his shocking shirts and he is going to turn around and shit all over you. He is going to turn around to you one day and say, "Nadine, you're a great girl, but I just can't stand those purple trousers you wore last Thursday and the way your ears wiggle when you laugh and, quite frankly, your ginger pubes make me want to puke. So, no hard feelings, eh?" And Deen – and I say this with all the affection and love in the world – I for one cannot wait for that day to come.'

Nadine took a sharp intake of breath and clutched at her neck. 'You bastard!'

'Since you were twenty-two years old, since the day you left university and realized that you were never going to see Phil again, you have been out with every bloke who was stupid enough to ask you. As if three years with that weirdo wasn't enough. You have never once stopped and asked yourself if you actually *wanted* to go out with them, whether they were suitable, whether you fancied them, or if it stood a chance in hell of working out. You just use men to flatter your ego. You spend a couple of weeks doing everything within your power to ensure that they fall in love with you, and then the minute they do, you spend another two months building up a big enough list of faults and grievances to justify dumping the poor bastard.'

'*I do not!*'

'Yes, you do. Every bloke who asks. Doesn't matter if they're thin, fat, young, old, rich, poor or ugly. All they have to do is ask. Is it any wonder that it always ends in disaster? Is it any wonder that you spend half your life dumping them? Is it any wonder that you haven't met the right guy yet?'

'I do not go out with every guy who asks me.'

'OK then. Name me one guy you've turned down – one guy.'

Nadine thought for a moment and then smiled wickedly. 'Well. Let me think. Oh yes, that's right. There was one bloke – you!' She smiled smugly. 'Got you! I turned *you* down.'

Dig shook his head. 'No no no. That doesn't count. We were kids then. I'm talking about *after* university, after the thing with Phil.'

Nadine went silent for a while as she flicked rapidly through her memory files, her face wrinkled in concentration. 'Well,' she said eventually, 'it's not as if I get asked out every day or anything. You have to take these opportunities when they're offered.'

'Oh, come on! You haven't been single for more than a week in the last ten years and you haven't been out with anyone for longer than a few months. Work it out for yourself.'

'Oh yes,' leered Nadine, triumphantly, 'oh yes, of course! I forgot I was talking to the world's leading relationship expert. I forgot you were the man who had his heart broken when he was eighteen and hasn't let one single woman near it since. I forgot I was talking to the man who hasn't known the surname of the last six girls he's slept with, who thinks commitment is staying the night, who thinks a date is a chewy version of a prune and who *woke up in bed this morning with a seventeen-year-old girl*!'

An old man who had been working his way slowly and disagreeably through a plate of overcooked roast beef and congealed gravy since they arrived threw Dig a look of profound admiration, and a young couple in the corner looked up from their newspapers with raised eyebrows, turning subtly for a glimpse of this apparent paedophile. Dig blushed.

'Yeah, right,' he whispered, 'but at least I don't lead them on, at least they know what they're getting into. I never give them any false hope. And besides, girls that young, they don't actually *want* anything serious, anyway. Not like you lot.'

'You lot, who lot?'

'You,' he said, pointing at her, 'you thirty-something women.'

Nadine raised her eyebrows ceilingwards. 'Oh,' she growled, 'don't start all that business again. I'm far too hungover for that argument. And anyway, I'm not thirty-something, I'm thirty-nothing.'

'What's the difference?'

'Well, thirty is more like a full stop on your twenties, really. I don't think you're actually *in your thirties* until you're thirty-one. Anyway, all I'm saying is, you're in no position to preach to me about how I should be conducting my love life. You're the nicest bloke I know and one day you're going to make somebody a wonderful husband. But right now you should carry a health warning.'

'OK, OK,' sighed Dig, smiling, 'so we're both as bad as each other. You dump perfectly decent men because they choose the wrong mugs, and I'm the Jerry Lee Lewis of Kentish Town . . . Let's face it – we're both crap.'

'Oh God, Dig. Look at us. We're both thirty now – we're *too old* to be crap, we're not supposed to be crap any more. We're supposed to be getting it together. My mum had two kids by the time she was my age and, as far as I can tell, I still *am* a kid. Where's my biological clock, Dig? Where is it? Why haven't I got one? Maybe if I had one then I'd be a bit more selective about who I went out with because I'd be subconsciously looking for a good gene pool, you know, a hunter/gatherer type, a sperm donor rather than a temporary ego boost.'

'And I'd be looking for a good, heavy-hipped, child-bearing woman instead of chasing after ectomorphic breastless androgynes with body piercings.'

'What have we been doing for the last ten years, Dig? I mean, I'm under no illusions about everlasting love, but we haven't even come close. We haven't had one long-term relationship between the two of us. Other people spend their twenties learning lessons about love and relationships, and you and I have just been going round and round in circles, learning nothing. We're pathetic. Maybe that's what we should be doing, Dig. Maybe we should at least *pretend* that we're looking for a partner to have children with, even if we're not – that way we might choose a little more wisely.'

'But I don't like heavy-hipped women.'

'Oh, Dig. Don't be ridiculous. Women don't have to have heavy hips to bear children. Look at Pamela Anderson – she's had two and she doesn't look like she could give birth to a clothes-peg. No, it's more a frame of mind, an attitude. I think we should give it a bash, you know. I mean, look around this place. Look at her.' She pointed towards a pretty girl in her late twenties sitting alone with a bacon sandwich. 'She's nice-looking, she's got lovely hair, she's slim and she's most probably single. I bet if you asked her out, she'd say yes.'

'Yeah, but why? Why is she single? If she's so great then why isn't she sharing her bacon sandwich with someone?'

'God, I don't know. Maybe she's just split up with someone, maybe she's just dumped her boyfriend because he put too much sugar in his tea. Maybe she's as bad as us.'

Another girl walked into the café then, and the bacon-sandwich girl's face lit up. The two women greeted each other warmly with a kiss on the lips, and Nadine saw their feet entwine underneath the table.

' . . . Or maybe she's a lesbian. But that's not the point. The point is, we're thirty years old, we're healthy, we've got flats, cars, jobs and security, we're both unbelievably nice people and we're going to wake up one morning and find ourselves all alone. All our friends will have big messy houses full of teenagers and grandchildren and noise and activity, they'll be arranging weddings and going to graduation ceremonies and discussing their children's achievements and sending them off to see the world, and we'll be alone, you in your anally tidy flat, me with fifty years' worth of glossy magazines arranged in piles, with nothing but memories of how it was to be young. That's not right. I don't want that. And the only way we're going to be able to avoid that is by doing something about it *now*.'

Dig had been nodding throughout this and now stuck one hand out towards Nadine. 'I agree,' he said, 'and I think we should make a pact here and now. I'll start looking for a more mature woman and you start looking for a bloke who measures up to your standards.'

'And the first person to start seeing a decent man or woman gets . . . gets . . .' Nadine quickly calculated the chances of Dig recognizing a 'real' woman if she slapped him around the chops with her handbag, smiled and stuck out her hand, 'a hundred quid.'

Dig's eyebrow shot up into his hairline but he grabbed Nadine's hand and shook it hard. 'Yeah,' he said, 'OK. A hundred quid for the first person to start dating a decent person.'

'So that means a woman over the age of twenty-six,

for you and a man who I actually *like*, for me. OK?'

'OK!'

They shook hands hard and smiled at each other across the table, each one as certain as the other that this was one bet that would never be called in.

## starfish and kites

Dig thought Nadine was a bit of a drip when he was allocated the seat next to hers on his first day at the Holy Trinity Convent School for Boys and Girls in Kentish Town.

She had unruly red hair and squidgy white hands with dimples where she should have had knuckles. She was very small and very round, and her grey school skirt stood out starchily from her legs in an angular 'A' shape, ending somewhere near her ankles, which were densely clad in thick-ribbed tights.

Nadine thought Dig was a bit of a nerd when he awkwardly approached the desk next to hers. He was very skinny and very pale, with an overdeveloped head of thick black hair that looked, to her, like a bad wig. His uniform wasn't crisp and brand-new like hers, it looked sad and threadbare and out of sorts. She guessed that he was wearing his big brother's cast-offs and then thought that he probably came from one of those huge Irish Catholic families that her mother had told her all about. He only had one eyebrow and he looked to Nadine like one of the children in *Planet of the Apes*.

Not surprisingly, none of the other children rushed over to get to know Dig and Nadine when the bell for their first break rang at 10.30 a.m., and consequently they had to make do with each other for company while they sat in the playground.

'Dig,' stated Nadine, swinging her plump little legs back and forth, 'that's a really stupid name. Why are you called Dig?'

'It is not a stupid name. It's short for Digby.'

'Well, that's a stupid name, too.'

'No it's not – it's French.'

'Yes it is. "Dig". It's not a name. It's a *verb*.'

'What about you? You can talk. Nadine *Kite*. That's not a name, that's a thing that you fly in the sky.'

'Yes. I *do* know what a kite is, thank you very much.'

'Oh yes – I bet you've never flown one, though, have you? I have. My dad bought it for me. We take it out on Primrose Hill.'

Nadine fell silent for a second and took an extra big slurp of her Banana Nesquik before shrugging. 'Who cares?' she said. 'Kites are for kids. Anyway,' she continued, changing the subject, 'how come you've only got one eyebrow?'

'It's not *one* eyebrow – it's two eyebrows that meet up in the middle, that's all.'

'Looks stupid.'

'Oh,' said Dig, 'thanks a lot.'

'Don't mention it.'

They both stopped talking and began sucking aggressively on their cartons of drink. Dig turned to Nadine and pointed at her hands. 'How come you've got no knuckles, then? How come they're *inside out*?'

'What do you mean?'

'Look,' he said, taking one of her little hands in his own and rubbing his thumb over the dimples in her joints, 'the skin there goes *in*, instead of *out*. They're not normal.'

'Yes they are!' She spread them out like starfish and gazed at them.

'No, they're not. Look at my hands.' He splayed his long white hand open, placed it over her starfish hand and pointed out his sharp knuckles. 'That's what knuckles are supposed to look like.'

'Hmph,' said Nadine.

There was a short silence.

'You can come with us – if you like,' said Dig.

'Where?'

'Kite-flying. Me and my dad.'

'Oh,' said Nadine. 'OK, then.'

They both sat then and stared at their touching hands, and let the warmth seep between their fingers while their cartons of drink sat on either side of them warming up in the September sun and the playground echoed around them with the sounds of a thousand other children.

Nadine looked up at him then, into his kind, brown eyes, and decided at that moment that whatever happened in her life, she was going to marry Digby Ryan.

# CHAPTER FOUR

By the time Dig and Nadine had finished breakfast it was early afternoon, and a fairly strong wind had picked up around Primrose Hill, tugging clouds across the sun and throwing dead leaves into the air.

'Fuck it,' said Dig, kicking up a drift of leaves with his trainered foot. 'Should have brought the kites.'

'Should have worn trousers,' said Nadine, clinging on to the fly-away hem of her black chiffon skirt and directing a withering look at a passing pervert admiring her thighs. 'Can we find somewhere to sit? This skirt's pissing me off.'

They sat beneath an oak tree, hands in pockets, legs crossed at the ankles, and stared across the park for a while, in silence.

Nadine turned to Dig and smiled. He looked so sweet. His thick black hair was being furrowed by the wind, flattened into random partings all over his head and sticking up here and there in bizarre little horns. There were tiny rivulets of salt water running downwards from his wind-whipped eyes, and the end of his nose had turned a rather appealing shade of pink. He wasn't so bad looking, she supposed, smiling to herself. Quite cute, really. He was also wearing a somewhat serious, un-Dig-like expression on his face, and a couple of small creases had appeared in the area that should have been the gap between his eyebrows but was in fact just a bridge between the two. Nadine reached out to touch the little furrows with one long-nailed fingertip.

'Oooh, yes,' she said, 'I can see the signs of ageing already.'

'What?' laughed Dig, touching the offending wrinkles.

'Worry lines,' said Nadine, threading her arm through Dig's and resting her head on his shoulder, 'the carefree days of your youth are over, my friend.'

'You jest,' he said, leaning his head against hers and contemplating the brilliant blue and white sky above, 'but I think it might be true.'

'What's up?'

'Oh God. I don't know. It's that girl, last night . . .'

'What girl – Jailbait Girl?'

'Which other?'

'You're not still freaking out about that, are you?'

'Well – yes. I am actually. I just can't get it out of my head. I mean, *seventeen*! You were still a virgin when you were seventeen . . .'

'Well, they grow up faster these days, don't they?'

'I just feel really shitty.'

'I don't suppose *she* does.'

'That's not the point.'

'So what is the point?'

'The point is . . . the point is . . .' He turned to face her and then turned away again. 'I don't know what the point is. I just feel shitty, that's all.'

They stopped talking for a moment. Nadine didn't know what to say. 'Hey,' she changed the subject, 'what time were you born?'

'Eh?'

'What time of the day were you born?'

'Erm, I'm not sure,' replied Dig, 'but it must have been in the evening, because my folks were in the pub when my mum's waters broke.'

'Well. There you go then. You're not thirty yet. Not officially. You've got another four or five hours in your twenties. So . . .'

'What?'

Nadine leaped to her feet, leaned down and scooped up a large armful of russet, auburn and mustard leaves. 'So,' she said, 'you're not too old to have a jolly good leaf fight,' and with that she threw the leaves all over Dig's head like oversized confetti, turned on her heel and ran away laughing.

She ran away, as she would recollect, in an anticlockwise direction, and she would later wonder what uncontrollable forces had led her to that decision. If she'd analysed her thoughts in depth she might have found an answer. But more likely she would have found it to be no more than a random action, plucked from nothing more substantial than pure fancy.

Because what Nadine didn't know when she made that seemingly trivial choice was just *how important* it actually was. Fate had snuck up on her unawares that day on Primrose Hill and as she ran screaming with laughter across the springy grass, Dig in pursuit and closing in on her rapidly with an enormous pile of leaves in his hands and a look of vengeance about him, little did she know that fate was about leap into her path and change the course of her life for ever.

Because, had Nadine *not* taken the anticlockwise route that day, had she set off in the other direction, then they would have exited the park, walked the twenty minutes to Dig's flat, flopped on to his sofa, opened a couple of beers and watched some football, and they would never have bumped into Delilah.

He wasn't sure it was her at first. The hair threw him off a bit. It was a warm golden-brown instead of the five-alarm peroxide white he remembered. And the clothes were different: classic, well cut and definitely expensive. But the moment he saw her face he knew.

It was Delilah. Delilah Lillie! He ignored the scratchiness of the leaves trapped inside his clothing and made his way to the iron railings that separated the park from the pavement. She was walking towards him on Regent's Park Road, her hands full of carrier bags, a pair of sunglasses perched on top of her head. She was staring straight ahead and looked a bit stressed out. His pace quickened as she got closer.

'Where are you going?' Nadine's voice sounded like a whisper in the distance.

She was still very slim, small-waisted, elegant, she still walked with that sway in her hips and she was still quite jaw-droppingly beautiful.

'Di–ig. Where are you going?'

Dig ignored Nadine and carried on walking as if being irresistibly drawn towards a beam of light from an alien spaceship.

'Delilah?' he called. She didn't hear, carried on walking.

'Delilah?' She looked around her, confused.

'Delilah!' He'd reached the iron railings now. Leaves were dropping from his clothing as he walked, falling from beneath his jacket. He didn't notice, didn't care.

He grasped the railings with both hands as Delilah approached, a quizzical, slightly unsure expression on her face. 'It is, isn't it?' he began. 'Delilah. It is you, isn't it?'

Close up, she looked fantastically pretty, fresh-faced, glossy. She'd worn a lot of make-up at school and looked much younger now, bare-faced. She was looking at Dig with a combination of confusion, anticipation, concern and embarrassment. She nodded.

'Dig,' he said, placing a hand on his chest, 'Dig Ryan.'

Her face softened with recognition. 'Oh my God!' she exclaimed. 'Dig Ryan! I don't believe it!'

'God, how are you? How've you been? It's so good to see you.'

'Yeah . . . yeah. I'm great, just great. How're you?' She was smiling widely, looking genuinely pleased to see him.

'Great. I'm great, too. Shit – this is amazing! God, I mean, what've you been up to, what're you doing now, where are you living?'

Delilah indicated the iron railings that divided them.

'Wait,' said Dig, 'wait right there. I'm coming round.'

He skipped back across the grass to where Nadine was waiting for him. 'Quick,' he gestured at her, grinning like an idiot, 'quick! It's Delilah. Come on!'

'Delilah?' muttered Nadine, a shadow falling across her face. 'Delilah Lillie?'

She let the handful of leaves she'd gathered ready for a counter-offensive fall dolefully to the ground and grudgingly followed the bounding figure of Dig across the park and towards the gates.

# delilah lillie

Every school had a Delilah Lillie. They were usually blonde, they were always pretty and they were invariably the coolest girl in the school. Delilah Lillie was Debbie Harry, Leslie Ash and Kim Wilde all rolled into one. She had breasts before anyone else and a mop of thick bleached-blonde hair which hung over her eyes like flaxen curtains. She was moody and chewed gum and made her school uniform look sexy. She wore too much black eyeliner, and scuffed stilettos. All the boys wanted to go out with her and all the girls wanted to be her because she was so cool.

She was a woman.

Nadine could remember Delilah's first day at school as if it were yesterday. The corridors and classrooms of the Holy Trinity Convent School for Boys and Girls had been rumbling with the rumours all day. There was a new girl in 4H and she was *really cool.* Her name was Delilah. She'd been expelled from her last school for, among many suggested misdemeanours, getting pregnant, sniffing glue, beating up the headmistress, having sex in the showers, setting fire to the stationery cupboard and stealing the caretaker's car. She lived on the Gospel Oak Estate, the roughest estate in Kentish Town, and her dad was a burglar. She used to go out with Suggs from Madness and she'd slept with everyone in the sixth form of her last school. She sold drugs for a living and if you looked very closely you could see the track marks on her arms. She was a junky, a criminal, a slag and a hard-nut. And she was sexy as hell.

Dig and Nadine sat on the grass outside the science block on their first afternoon back at school. They were fourteen years old. At Dig's feet was his constant companion, a folded and battered copy of the *NME*, and pinned to the lapel of his red blazer was a new badge. It was shaped like a pork-pie hat and it said *Ska For Ever.* He had a big spot on his chin.

Nadine was wearing a baggy red school jumper, her thumbs emerging from tatty holes in the sleeves, and her tie was slung slovenly around her neck. Her frizzy copper hair was held back from her face with a green chiffon scarf and there were traces of mascara clinging to her pale eyelashes, mascara, Dig noticed, which hadn't been there last term.

Nadine had grown nearly four inches in the previous year and she was taller than Dig. Her limbs had stretched into her puppy fat and her knuckles were now the right way round. Dig had filled out a little and grown another inch or two but his eyebrows still joined forces in the middle and his hair still emerged from his scalp like dense black velour.

Dig 'n' Deen, that's what everyone at school called them, because they were inseparable. You never saw one without the other. They occupied a quiet and comfortable position within the school hierarchy – too studious to be cool but too cool to be drips. No one gave them any hassle, but then no one particularly made an effort to befriend them either. Which was fine with them. They lived in a cosy world of study, John Peel, back-combed hair and kite-flying.

Nadine hadn't forgotten the pledge she'd made to herself at eleven years old, and if you were to feel around under her mattress you would find her most secret diary, the one she fills with her deepest and darkest thoughts and desires. It is an old school exercise book and it is decorated on the front and the back with doodles – practice signatures, in fact, all loops and hearts and twirls. All of them say the same thing: *Nadine Ryan.* Because even though they're not boyfriend and girlfriend, even though they've never even kissed each other, she *is* going to marry him.

Dig 'n' Deen are going to live on Gloucester Crescent in Camden Town in a big house with shutters and marble floors. Their bed will be a huge pine one with a fluffy white duvet and the sun will shine on to it every morning. They will have parties in their big house every Saturday night, and on Sundays they'll pick up Dig's dad in their powder-blue E-type Jag and take him kite-flying on Primrose Hill. They will have four children – Sam, Ben, Emily and Alicia – and they will be incredibly happy.

It's not that Nadine has a crush on Dig or anything, it's just that she can't imagine anyone else marrying him and not being allowed to see him any more. One day they will be man and wife, but for now she is happy just to be his best friend.

'What have you got on Thursday mornings?' Nadine asked Dig, running her finger horizontally across her brand-new timetable.

'Erm . . . erm . . . erm . . .' He trailed off.

'Di–ig.' Nadine tutted and glanced up at Dig from her timetable, following his strange, glassy gaze with her eyes. He was staring across the grass to the netball courts, where a huddle of boys from the fifth form were jostling each other and play-fighting, vying for the attention of a tall girl with white-blonde hair, an awful lot of earrings and a very tight skirt.

'Aaaah,' said Nadine, sucking the end of a pencil, '*that* must be Delilah Lillie.'

Dig remained rigid and speechless, staring at the glamorous figure across the grass, his jaw hanging ever so slightly open.

'She doesn't look like a junky to me,' said Nadine casually, surveying her through her eyelashes, 'she's incredibly pretty.'

Dig gulped and nodded. He opened his mouth to say something but his still-breaking voice cracked and he cleared his throat. 'She . . . she . . . she looks like Leslie Ash in *Quadrophenia*,' he finally managed to squeak.

*Quadrophenia* was Dig's favourite film of all time and enough people had told Dig that he looked a bit like Phil Daniels for him to have developed a deep affinity with his character in the film. And now there was a girl in the playground, a girl just over there, in fact, a few metres away, who looked just like Leslie Ash, Phil Daniel's, and therefore *Dig's*, dream woman.

Nadine glanced across at her friend and saw the passion glimmering in his eyes, the longing oozing from his pores and the pain already piercing his soul as he looked at something he wanted so much but had already decided he could never have.

'She's beautiful,' he whispered, a blush rising from his frayed shirt-collar to his hairline and his ears. 'She is absolutely beautiful.'

And that was when Nadine knew. That was the moment that Nadine knew that things were never going to be the same again.

*

All the legends that had accompanied Delilah to the Holy Trinity were proven unfounded within those first six weeks of term. She wasn't a drug addict, she wasn't a dealer, her father wasn't a burglar and she hadn't been expelled from her last school. She had simply moved from south to north London and been put into a new school. She *did*, though, live on the Gospel Oak Estate, and she *had* apparently been out with Suggs's little brother, although only for two weeks. She also proved herself to be a fairly conscientious student who turned up for lessons on time, managed to hand in her homework nine times out of ten and wore her uniform very nearly within the guidelines set down by the school. This lack of sociopathic behaviour did nothing to dent her reputation as the coolest girl in school, however, and she still found herself surrounded wherever she went by swarms of buzzing boys and fussed over by shorter, plainer girls hoping that a little of her magnetism might rub off on them.

Nadine had been right. Things weren't the same between her and Dig after that first day of term. All Dig's priorities changed. Now everything was a constant reference to Delilah. He and Nadine would walk around the school grounds together, apparently aimlessly, but Nadine knew that they were Delilah-hunting, she knew that the moment Dig heard the sound of Delilah's gravelly voice echoing around a corner they would suddenly slow down and Dig would start walking differently and talking to Nadine in a really loud voice about something they hadn't been discussing before, usually something to do with music. He would walk past Delilah and stare resolutely ahead, avoiding her gaze.

Dig and Nadine's friendship ended one rainy Tuesday afternoon, just before the end of the first term.

They were sitting together in the canteen, munching on soggy chips and pasty pasta and speed-reading their set pieces from *Animal Farm* for English Lit that afternoon when they became aware of a sallow boy from 3G called Desmond hovering over their table. They looked up questioningly.

'Here,' he said, dragging a grubby finger across his nostrils, 'are you Dig Ryan?'

'Yeah,' he answered. 'Why?'

'Just thought you might want to know that there's a rumour going around' – he looked around shiftily – 'about you.'

'Oh yeah,' said Dig, folding the corner of the page and putting his book down.

'Yeah,' said Desmond, 'about you and Delilah Lillie.'

Dig's eyebrow shot off his forehead and nearly landed on the back of his neck. 'Oh yeah,' he managed, coolly, 'and what's that then?'

'Apparently, she's been going around saying that she thinks you're really cool. She says she wants to talk to you. She says she likes your attitude. She says you've got cha . . . cha . . . char . . . charisma?'

Nadine nodded at Desmond to indicate that he'd found the right word, and he continued. 'Anyway,' he said, 'I just thought you ought to know, you know, what she's been saying and' – he stuck one grimy hand out awkwardly and offered it to Dig to shake – 'I just wanted to say congratulations, like. You must be made up.'

And then he went shuffling back to his table and his mates, who were all eyeing Dig with a new-found respect.

Dig remained quite calm, considering, mindlessly prodding at his flaccid chips with his fork and muttering under his breath, 'Fucking-hell-Deen-fucking-hell-Deen-fucking-hell.' His face was flushed almost purple and his feet were banging together under the table. Suddenly he looked up and straight into Nadine's eyes. 'Fucking hell, Deen,' he almost shouted, 'what am I going to do?'

In the event, he hadn't had to do anything. During the last few days of that term Delilah Lillie became omnipresent. Dig's strategic patrols of the school were no longer necessary, as, wherever he went, Delilah was already there. For a couple of days nothing was said between them, but looks of intense significance were exchanged and the atmosphere between them was so charged that Dig became literally static, every object he touched perforating his skin with little bullets of electricity.

Nadine began to feel more and more superfluous and uncomfortable during these peculiar encounters, but whenever she suggested to Dig that she make herself scarce, find something else to do, he would grab on to her sleeve for dear life and beg her to stay.

Finally, on the last day of term, it happened. Nadine and Dig were sitting together on the stairs outside the language lab when Delilah appeared from nowhere, clutching a pile of books to her chest and apparently in a hurry. But she stopped dead when she rounded the corner and saw Dig on the steps, stopped and stood squarely in front of him. For a second the air tingled with electricity, and silence reverberated around the three of them. Nadine stopped breathing and waited for one of them to say something. Finally, Delilah opened her plump crimson lips, slowly enough, Nadine noticed, for two tiny peaks of skin to form between them and stick together briefly before pinging apart like little rubber bands.

'Hi,' she said.

'Hi,' said Dig, his voice not letting him down by cracking, but emanating resoundingly from beneath his ribcage.

Nadine sat with her hands on her lap and stared at the floor.

'You're Dig, aren't you?' said Delilah.

'Yeah,' he said, still in that deep, clear voice, 'that's right. And *you* are . . .?'

Nadine whistled silently under her breath. You had to hand it to him, she thought to herself, that was pretty fucking cool.

'I'm Delilah,' she said, 'Delilah Lillie. I'm in 4H. You know, Mr Harwood's class.'

'Oh,' said Dig, 'yeah. Right. You're the new girl, aren't you?'

'Yeah,' she said, 'pretty new.' There was a second's silence then, and Delilah bit her lip and threw Nadine a sideways glance, a look which told Nadine everything she needed to know. I'm taking over now, that's what that look said, it's my shift, off you go, you weird-looking, fat-arsed, ginger-haired nobody.

It was time to go, it was time to let Dig get on with this, without her. She pushed her papers together into a pile, swung her bag over her shoulder and got to her feet.

'Right,' she said unnecessarily, as neither of them was paying any attention to her, 'I'm off. See ya.' And then she walked, as fast as she'd ever walked, along corridor after corridor, pushing swing doors open with her shoulder as she went, walked and walked and walked until there was nowhere left to walk. And then she stopped, stopped in her tracks and turned to face the wall as the tears she'd been trying so hard to control spilled over her eyes and cascaded in sheets down her cheeks.

## the pub of perpetual darkness

It was a Saturday lunch-time, the week before Nadine was due to start her mock O Levels and four months since her friendship with Dig had ended.

Kentish Town Road was bright with the reflection of a dazzling sun on a slick wet pavement following a thirty-second deluge of rain. People emerged from shops where they'd taken temporary refuge and others shook out umbrellas and folded them up. Nadine was with her mother, looking for a book she needed for her history revision, sulking at the injustice of being in a place she didn't want to be, with a person she didn't want to be with, looking for something she wished she didn't need in the middle of a torrential downpour that had pissed on her quiff and left her drowning in a sea of melting Elnett.

'Take these, will you, Nadine?' her mother asked, handing her a soggy umbrella and a shopping bag full of cabbages. 'I've got to find a lavatory. It's this weather – all this rain,' she said, before disappearing into a nearby pub.

Nadine had never been inside a pub before. She wasn't allowed, which was hardly surprising as she wasn't allowed to do anything. She'd been in 'family' pubs on holiday, consigned to 'family' rooms full of fruit machines and bored children, but never inside an actual pub, a proper London sort of a pub. Curiosity inspired her to hover inside the entrance while she waited for her mother, a little closer to the innards of the pub than her mother would have liked.

The smell got to her first, stale, smoky and stagnant. Slivers of sunlight sneaked in through scratches in the black paint on the tall windows, picking out glittering mites of dust and ribbons of cigarette smoke curling across the top of the room, as if caught in the light of a cinema projector. A juke-box blared out the 'Ace of Spades', an artillery of fruit machines whizzed, crashed and banged and above all of this, from a table in the farthest corner, rose a loud and somewhat frightening cacophony of obscenities and profanities.

Nadine edged a bit further into the cavernous, unlit pub to view the source of this noise. Cloaked in shadow sat a small woman, with dyed black stringy hair, wearing a heavy gold crucifix. She was at least eight months pregnant, her bump accentuated by a too-small white T-shirt emblazoned with the faded legend 'I DON'T GIVE A **** WHAT FRANKIE SAYS.' She was smoking a roll-up and drinking a pint and screaming at the huge man sitting next to her in between drags and sips. He was staring straight ahead with a tightness in his face that threatened to turn from tolerance to violence at any moment.

In front of the table sat a buggy, into which were strapped two rather sullen-looking but attractive children, and to her right sat a beautiful blond-haired boy of about four years old, wearing an Arsenal football strip. He was talking to himself and scribbling in a colouring book with a red crayon. He looked like an angel.

'Mum,' he said, turning to look at the pregnant woman, 'Mum. I need the toilet, Mum.'

'Shut up, Kane,' she spat, stubbing out the spit-softened end of her roll-up and readying herself for the next stage of her verbal assault on the fat man. 'Can't you see I'm talking?'

'But, Mum, I need to go.' One hand had disappeared under the table to hold the end of his willy.

'Will you shut up! You'll just have to hold on! I'm talking!'

'But, Mum . . .'

The woman turned around and fixed the child with a terrifying expression, squeezed the tops of his arms with her bony hands and brought him upwards towards her face. 'If you don't shut up, Kane, I'm going to fucking belt you,' she said, and then, just to make sure he knew she was serious, she slapped him hard across his bare legs, a sharp crack resonating around the pub.

Nadine winced as the child dissolved into tears and watched in horror as a small trickle of pale yellow liquid began to dribble slowly from under the table, across the grubby linoleum. The woman rose up in her seat to view it better and then turned to the boy.

'You fucking little bastard!' She yanked him up by one puny arm. 'You disgusting little fucker!' A large damp patch adorned the front of his football shorts. She carried him by his arm to the men's toilets, pushed open the door with her shoulder and flung him through the door on to the grimy toilet floor. 'Clean yourself up, you filthy bastard.' The boy crouched on the tiled floor on all fours, tears coursing down his cheeks. Nadine gulped as the door came to a close between them, leaving just the muted sound of the boy's distress.

The girl sitting on the other side of the table, with her back to Nadine, stood up then and put out a cigarette.

She was wearing skin-tight drainpipe jeans with a pink-and-white-striped vest top. She fixed the woman with a look, blew out her last lungful of smoke and then marched towards the toilet door. She walked in and began to gather the boy into her arms, whispering soothing words into his ear and smoothing down his hair. The door closed, and the two of them emerged a few seconds later, the boy now shortless, his shirt hanging down to his thighs, and clinging on to the girl's leg with both arms. It was only at that moment that Nadine realized who the girl was.

It was Delilah.

Nadine turned then, turned away very quickly and walked out of the pub and into the sunny safety of the street outside. Her heart was beating frighteningly fast and she took in large mouthfuls of air. That was Delilah! And that was Delilah's mum. Oh my God. Poor Delilah. Poor, poor Delilah. Nadine had never witnessed anything quite so hellish before in her life.

That . . . woman, that horrible woman, drinking and smoking with a baby inside her and hitting that beautiful little boy. And how many children did she have? Nadine knew that Delilah had older brothers, too. She must have had millions. Making all her beautiful children sit indoors on a day like today, in that dark, dank, dismal place with all that noise and smoke, while she screamed foul language at some hideous fat man with stained clothes and greasy hair.

All of a sudden, what previously would have seemed to Nadine like the epitome of cool – a mother who actually let her fourteen-year-old daughter smoke in front of her, *with her* – now seemed to her to be a travesty. It was sick. Delilah's mum was sick.

Nadine suddenly realized why Delilah was allowed to do so much, why the rules and regulations which she felt strangled her own development didn't seem to apply to Delilah. It wasn't because Delilah was the lucky winner of the Parent Lottery, proud recipient of a wondrous mother who understood that girls *needed* to stay out later than eleven o'clock and *needed* to go out with boys, and *needed* more than one earring in each lobe and *needed* to do whatever they wanted with their hair. Delilah, she realized, wasn't lucky. She was unlucky. Because her mother didn't care, really didn't care about her or, it seemed, any of her other, numerous children. She didn't care about Delilah's hair or her ear lobes or the state of her health. It was unlikely that she cared about her education or her future or the status of her hymen. It no longer seemed cool to Nadine that Mrs Lillie (if that was her name) didn't turn up to parent-teacher meetings or check Delilah's homework.

Nadine's mother finally emerged from the pub, wiping the palms of her hands distractedly against the sides of her cotton dirndl skirt.

'Those,' she began, a distasteful expression hanging around her mouth, 'are the most terrible lavatories I have ever visited. Except for that hole-in-the-ground affair in Calais. No soap, no towels, no *seats*! I had to sort of squat over the bowl.' She shuddered and began to unburden Nadine of her bags. 'And there are *children* in that place. Can you believe it? Children! I mean who – *who* – would take children into a place like that? It's shocking, it really is . . .'

As they continued on their way that afternoon, stopping for a cup of tea and a Swiss Finger in the baker's shop, browsing through the Education section in

W. H. Smiths, searching through the bargain bin in the wool shop for a length of peacock blue angora to finish off a sweater her mother was knitting for her, Nadine began to regain a sense of normality, of humanity, of *cleanliness*. And, for the first time since she'd begun her journey through adolescence towards adulthood, she felt lucky.

Her mother was traditional and overbearing and her father was distant and predictable. Her little brother was a precocious pain in the arse who could do no wrong and she was treated like a wayward child who could do no right. Their flat was small and old-fashioned, furnished with her dead grandparents' dark and sombre pre-war furniture, and everyone in her family took this whole Catholicism thing just a bit too seriously.

But, she concluded, after the shock of seeing a fragment of Delilah's existence outside school, at least I have love. At least I have affection. At least my family cares about me, even if they care too much, sometimes. At least, she thought, I am not forced to be a grown-up when I am not ready. She would rather *want* to be an adult and not be allowed than be made to be one.

Delilah might have been the most beautiful girl at the Holy T but her life away from school was ugly and sordid; she might have been the queen of cool but she had a witch for a mother and a pig for a stepfather and she might have taken Nadine's best friend away from her, but she had to spend sunny afternoons in places like that.

Poor Delilah. Poor old Delilah.

Nadine vowed then that despite Delilah's sneering indifference to her initial attempts at friendship she would make one final attempt to befriend her.

*

The first thing she saw when she walked towards the doors of Holy T on Monday morning was Delilah, one leg bent up behind her against a wall, a fag in one hand and a crappy photo-strip magazine in the other, giving Nadine the evil eye. Nadine swallowed her feelings and walked towards her.

'Hi,' she said, forcing a smile, 'nice weekend?'

Delilah looked momentarily surprised by this unexpected encounter but quickly regained her composure and self-consciously flicked the long ash off the end of her cigarette. 'Yeah,' she said, 'it was all right.' She was unable to meet Nadine's gaze and began looking over her shoulder and then distractedly around the street, almost like she was panicking, hoping to be rescued. She spotted Dig walking up the road and beckoned to him with a trace of desperation. He came bounding towards them, and Delilah's face softened as she drew him to her and sunk into his embrace. She took a deep drag on her cigarette and smiled at Nadine. She had Dig. She was strong again.

Nadine didn't bother making an effort with Delilah after that day. She felt sorry for Delilah's unfortunate circumstances, but trying to be friends really wasn't worth it.

She had never liked Delilah, and Delilah had never liked her, and on that morning Nadine finally decided that it would be easier all round just to leave the two of them alone and get on with her life.

# the king and queen of the holy t

At around 4.15 p.m. on 17 July 1985 a loud bell from within the school walls pierced the silence, and the playground erupted.

It was the last day of school.

Folders and textbooks and feint-ruled pads with margins flew into the air, red-and-grey-striped nylon ties were unknotted from worn shirt-collars and spun like lassos around heads, previously muted transistors were turned up full blast and 120 red-blazered sixteen-year-olds moved as one out of the school gates for the last time, a mass of pent-up energy and hormones released from the confines of five years of study and discipline, erupting like a stream of red-hot molten larva on to the oven-baked summer streets of Kentish Town.

Nadine found her friends and they joined the crowds rushing towards Caledonian Park for an afternoon of fighting and drinking and pelting kids from other schools with flour and eggs. They drank flat cider from big plastic litre bottles that went floppy in their hands as the sun warmed the liquid inside. They watched the boys showing off. They talked about their plans for the summer and their plans for the rest of their lives. It was all ahead of them, but Nadine couldn't shake the feeling that the most important part was already behind her.

It was all over. Not just school, not just five years of

rules and regulations, homework and assembly, mass on Fridays and cross-country runs in the rain, wearing a tie and eating school dinners, but what remained of her friendship with Dig. It wasn't going to survive this, she knew that. He was going to do his A Levels at a college in Holloway; she was doing hers at a grammar school in Archway.

He was still firmly ensconced in his partnership with Delilah. They were the king and queen of the Holy T, together to the exclusion of everyone else, particularly Nadine. It looked horribly and sadly to Nadine as if it was all over between her and Dig, what had been and what could have been.

There were going to be no sunny mornings together on a big pine bed, no hosting of raucous Saturday-night parties and cosy shopping trips together. There would never again be any such thing as 'Dig 'n' Deen', only 'Dig and Delilah'. Delilah had him wrapped up like a fly in a web and he was happy to be there. There was nothing left over for Nadine, no bit of the Dig that Nadine had loved so much for so long, and the thought left her with a lump in her throat and an awful sense of incompleteness in her heart.

As if to add poignancy to her thoughts, a cloud moved across the sun, a small chill breeze wafted over her, and Nadine looked up just in time to see Dig and Delilah a few feet away exchanging a kiss. The sun was just starting to set across the tops of the council blocks that lined the horizon, they'd run out of cider and two of her friends had fallen asleep on the grass. It was nearly ten and Nadine decided it was time to go home. She gathered her belongings together, her transistor, her cardigan, the bits and pieces of stationery and equipment that symbolized the last five years of her life, got up and began walking.

Dig caught up with her at the park gates. He was breathless from running. 'Deen,' he squeaked incredulously, 'where are you going?'

Nadine could see Delilah across the park, sitting up stiffly, her back poker-straight, her eyes slanted closed against the low light, watching the exchange closely.

'Home,' said Nadine, pulling the sleeves of her cardigan tighter around her waist. 'It's getting late.'

Dig's face wrinkled in confusion. 'Oh,' he said, scratching his head, 'right.'

'So,' she said, 'goodbye and good luck, yeah?'

'What? I mean . . . yeah. But we'll still be meeting up, won't we? You know – the kites and everything?' He looked anxious.

Nadine shrugged. 'Oh,' she said, 'I don't know. I think we'll probably be too busy, what with schoolwork and being at different colleges, you know?'

Dig's eyes clouded over with sadness. 'Right. Yeah. I suppose you're right.'

Nadine squeezed a small smile through tight lips. 'So have a nice life . . .'

'Oh. Right. I see. You too. Yeah,' he said, looking like he had now given the matter some thought and was beginning to get used to the idea. 'Yeah. You have a good life, too, Nadine.'

And then they ran out of things to say, a few moments before they lost the desire to talk, standing together awkwardly, shuffling a little, smiling, making and losing eye contact. The screaming, shouting and swearing of the other kids faded into the background and slivers of light from the ebbing sun perforated through the branches of a large elm and painted the two of them with salmon-pink stripes. Nadine leaned down to pull up her socks. Dig picked up a folder that had slid from the top of her pile and handed it back to her. The furthest tips of their fingers touched and then retracted instantly.

In the background Delilah still sat and watched, a piece of grass between her lips, her long legs folded up beneath her, an expression of disquiet hewn into her features. Dig turned to look at her and then turned back to Nadine. He opened his mouth to say something but then realized that he didn't need to. He shrugged instead and began to back away. Nadine shot him one last smile and then turned to leave the park.

Outside the park, a Ford Cortina parked sideways across North Road billowed flames from an overheated engine while three firemen attacked the fire with wild hoses of water, watched by a small audience of people. A river of blackened water snaked along the pavement and Nadine skipped over it before walking blindly towards York Way, her feet leading her homewards while her heart urged her to turn around, tear through the park towards Dig, her best friend, her soulmate, to make amends and reseal their bond, before it was too late.

But she didn't – her pride wouldn't let her – and she carried on walking through the darkening streets of Kentish Town, walking and walking and feeling it all slowly slip away from her grasp. She let herself into her parents' tiny flat on Bartholomew Road, sat with them while they watched *Dynasty* and answered their questions about her last day at school. At eleven o'clock she yawned and padded upstairs to her bedroom. She stared around her dreary room for a while and let her mind fill up with memories and images of her and Dig. Her kite was pinned to one wall, little lines of dust forming in the creases, the bright colours starting to fade to shadows. The tail drooped sadly, looking like it had lost the will to live, ever to fly again.

It was to be two years before Nadine would unpin her kite from the wall, blow off the dust and watch it skitting once more across the London skyline.

# CHAPTER FIVE

Anticlockwise! Anticlockwise! Why had she gone anticlockwise? It was a fifty-fifty thing. She could have gone clockwise. She could have been back at Dig's by now, safe and cosy, watching the football, instead of sitting in some hoity-toity tea-shop in Primrose Hill drinking overpriced cappuccino and watching her best friend regress within seconds to the fourteen-year-old schoolboy he'd always been.

And oh my God, look at her. Just look at her, will you? It's sickening. How can she look younger now than she did then? How can she be more beautiful, more poised, more *everything*? She has acquired polish and gloss. Her accent is now neutral. She has a dazzling smile and even a certain amount of charm. That's definitely something with a designer label in it that she's wearing so *effortlessly*. And look at the size of that rock on her ring finger – Gibraltar has nothing on it.

She has expensive hair – what is it that hairdressers in expensive salons actually *do* to hair to make it look expensive like that? She's wearing the sort of make-up that looks like you're wearing none at all, and she has that smell about her, not quite perfume, but something more intrinsic, like cleanliness, like dew. She smells like she bathes in the morning dew. It probably costs about eighty quid a bottle.

Nadine looks at Dig. She hasn't seen him this excited

for years. Every angle of his body is directed towards Delilah, his elbows, his knees, his head. Nadine may as well not be here, may as well not exist. She's a big ginger gooseberry again.

They're talking about Delilah's marriage, about the life she's been living for the past twelve years. She's not called Delilah Lillie any more, she's called, somewhat unfortunately and much to Nadine's delight, Delilah *Biggins*. Her husband is called Alex. He owns a small chain of brasserie-style restaurants in the north-west and they live together in neo-Georgian splendour in Chester. When he's not overseeing his empire, he's to be found on the golf course, squash court and cricket pitch. They have three horses and a swimming pool. Every couple of months Alex pays for Delilah to fly to New York first class and slips her his platinum credit card. She shops till she drops and is the envy of every other woman in Chester.

It all sounds pretty dull to Nadine, but Dig's riveted by every word, like it was ten years' worth of *Brookside* storylines. But then, just as Nadine is about to nod off, the conversation suddenly changes direction in a most dramatic manner. All is not as it seems. Delilah admits, falteringly and nervously, her eyes glazing over with tears, that she's left Alex. She's taken off and left him in bed, with just a note to wake up to, which Nadine thinks is pretty cruel. But then, any man stupid enough to marry a heart-hazard like Delilah gets what he deserves, quite frankly. I mean, you can tell just by *looking* at her that she's going to leave you one day.

She doesn't expand on the subject and Dig doesn't ask her any of the *right* questions, about why she's left her husband and come back to London, but then he's a boy.

She'd ask them herself but she's in too much of a mood to give her voice that inquisitive, interested edge it needs to form questions.

And that's another thing. You'd have thought, wouldn't you, that Dig would be demanding some sort of explanation right now, demanding to know why exactly Delilah disappeared and left him all those years ago, why she broke his heart into so many pieces that he'd never found them all to glue back together again? You'd have thought he'd be a bit *frosty* with her about the way she behaved back then, but he's not. He's acting like none of that ever happened, like everything is all right.

Nadine makes little peaks in the froth on her coffee with a fingertip and looks around her. The place is packed full with people wearing expensive clothes, pink-cheeked after a bracing walk on Primrose Hill with their labs and retrievers, mud caked on to the soles of their Russell & Bromley walking boots, people who have so much money that they don't so much as *blanch* at the outrageous £4.50 they're charging for a rather slim slice of chocolate truffle cake in this place. Nadine decides that she doesn't like anyone in this tea-shop, that she doesn't, in fact, like Primrose Hill with its faux-village atmosphere, and its pretend pubs and its overpriced everything. Primrose Hill, concludes Nadine, does not belong in Inner London – it is too small and too twee and too genteel, and it should be disassembled piece by piece and taken to Esher, where it would make a charming side-street.

'So,' Dig is asking Delilah, 'how long have you been back?'

'I just arrived this morning, believe it or not. Got the first train down.'

‘Really?’ smiles Dig, the look of a man blessed with fantastic serendipity spreading across his face. ‘And where are you staying? At your mum’s?’

Delilah takes a slurp of her filter coffee – black, no sugar – and puts the cup down, shaking her head. ‘Oh God no,’ she says. ‘I haven’t spoken to her since I was eighteen. I moved out and went to stay with my cousin. Remember? Marina. That’s where I’m staying now. Just around the corner, up there.’ She indicates the road opposite. ‘Elsworthy Road,’ she says.

Why? Nadine wants to scream. Why did you move out when you were eighteen? Why did you move in with your cousin? Why didn’t you tell Dig you were going? And why the fuck isn’t Dig asking you these questions?

‘Very nice,’ says Dig, nodding respectfully in appreciation of the fact that Delilah’s cousin is obviously rolling in it and probably itching to ask her how another member of her Gospel Oak estate family found their way into the bourgeoisie. ‘Very nice.’ He controls himself. ‘And what are your plans? What are you going to do with yourself here?’

Delilah shrugs and looks anxious. This is obviously a tricky question for her to answer. Please, thinks Nadine, please say you’re just here for a couple of days, you’re very busy, people to see, places to go. Please say that you probably won’t be seeing us again because you’re *going to New York tomorrow.*

But Nadine already has this very strange, uncomfortable feeling that this isn’t to be the last time they see Delilah, that Delilah is, in fact, going to be around one hell of a lot, a portent that is borne out seconds later when Delilah smiles, tucks her Pantene-girl-eat-your-heart-out hair behind her ears with two beautifully manicured sets of fingertips and says, 'Well, I was just going to hang out, really, you know, catch up with old friends, that sort of thing.'

Dig's face performs a theatre of ecstatic emotions. 'Excellent,' he smiles, 'that's fantastic.' The two of them stop for a second then and beam, positively *beam*, at each other. Nadine wants to be sick.

Dig offers Delilah a cigarette. She waves it away. 'Not smoking any more?' he asks, surprised. In both of their minds, Delilah Lillie *invented* smoking.

She grimaces. 'Given up,' she says. 'Only twelve days. Don't want to talk about it.' Dig sucks in his breath in appreciation of the enormity of her sacrifice and withdraws the offered packet. 'It's just *so* great to see you,' he grins.

'I'm so glad I bumped into you, too,' smiles Delilah. 'I felt a bit lost and lonely when I arrived and then I ran into you two and now I feel much better.'

Nadine grits her teeth, hates Delilah for a moment, hates her and wants her dead, which makes her feel like a total bitch, the biggest bitch that ever lived. Which makes her feel ugly, makes her feel like a wicked, wart-faced witch, which in turn makes her feel like Delilah is some flaxen-haired, *flawless*, fucking fairy-princess type, which makes her hate her even more. Nadine smiles grimly and traces a happy face into the froth on top of her coffee, the coffee she hasn't actually drunk yet, the coffee she is feeling far too discomfited even to contemplate drinking.

'You two,' Delilah is saying, 'you two have changed so much. I would never have recognized you. Especially you, Deen. You're a . . . you're a babe, you really are. You're absolutely gorgeous. I love all these little clips in your hair. And I love your fingernails' – she takes Nadine's turquoise talons in her hands and examines them – 'how do you get them to grow so long? Mine always split down here.' She indicates the pink of her perfect nails.

'Jelly cubes,' says Nadine, 'I eat jelly cubes every day. Rowntrees, lemon and lime flavour.' And she's thinking, Oh no, don't do this, Delilah. Don't do this whole trying-to-make-me-like-you thing. I don't want to like you. I can't like you. I've never liked you. However many conversations we have about nails and cellulite and facial hair and cabbage-soup diets, I am not going to like you. I am never going to like you because no matter how much you might have changed, I will never be able to forget the way you treated me at school, the way you disregarded me and belittled me and broke my heart.

I know what women like you can do to normal, sane men. Women like you have ultimate power. Women like you just have to walk into a room for all hell to let loose and for all men to become retarded. Women like you can take the heart of a warm, trusting and gentle man like Dig and make mincemeat out of it. And I am always going to resent you, Delilah, because you're beautiful, and because the beauty you possess is something that no woman can ever buy, from a beauty counter, from a plastic surgeon or from South Molton Street. I can't compete with you on any level. I am deeply threatened by you and I don't want you in my life. I don't want you in my nice, safe, happy world, where I am secure and where I know my place. It has taken me a decade and a half to emerge from your shadow, to become desirable in my own right. Call me selfish, thinks Nadine, call me an egocentric bitch, call me insecure and call me paranoid,

I don't care. I just want you out of London, out of my life and out of Dig's life.

'So, you're a photographer, are you?'

'Uh-huh,' replies Nadine, 'that's me. I take pictures.' She tells Delilah briefly about the exotic locations and the financial rewards.

'Wow,' says Delilah, genuinely impressed, 'that must be amazing. I remember talking once about what we all wanted to be when we grew up and you said that you wanted to be married and writing cookbooks, or something, wasn't it? And look at you now. So glamorous and gorgeous and successful, with an exciting job and your own place. God, Deen' – she reaches out and squeezes Nadine's hand – 'I'm so jealous of you, I really am.'

Oh stop it, thinks Nadine. Just stop it. You're not jealous at all, you're just trying to make me feel better about not being as beautiful as you. You've got tons of money and satin hair and flawless skin – how could you possibly be jealous of me?

Nadine forces a saccharine smile and pats Delilah's hand back. 'Oh, don't be silly,' she says, wishing she could rise above all the small-minded, mean-spirited jealousy she's feeling. She looks across the table at Dig, trying to remind herself how to be nice – he always brings out the best in her – but he's lost in Delilahland. The Dig Ryan she knows and loves is nowhere to be seen.

'Well' – Delilah is knocking back the dregs of her coffee and making moves towards her handbag – 'I'd better get back. I've left my dog alone with a hundred starving cats. They've probably eaten *him* by now.' She smiles and drops a pile of coins on to the bill. She fixes them both with a deeply sincere gaze, brimming with warmth and good feeling, and says, 'I hope I'll see you both again soon. It would *so nice* if we could get together some time.'

'Yeah – definitely,' oozes Dig, 'definitely,' and Nadine can tell he's mentally reorganizing his entire diary to make sure there's no question that they'll be able to 'get together some time'.

'Actually,' he says, reaching into the pocket of his black leather coat and pulling out a scrappy piece of paper and a Biro, 'let me take your number at your cousin's. I'm not up to much this week. Maybe we could go out one night. You know. Catch up on old times.'

No, thinks Nadine. No. Please. Not again. This can't be happening again.

'That would be great, Dig. Thanks.'

Nadine's heart sinks.

They all exchange phone numbers, they schmooze all over each other and act delighted (which Nadine is, because Delilah's finally leaving) and then go their separate ways.

Nadine watches Delilah struggling across the road with her excess of carrier bags, trying to keep the curtain of hair out of her eyes with the back of one hand, and feels a brief flickering second of sympathy for her. The hairs on her arms stand up on end and a painful little lump forms in the back of her throat. Poor Delilah, she thinks, poor old Delilah.

Delilah gets to the other side of the road, whereupon a very handsome man who's just climbed out of a shiny red Lotus Elise approaches her and begins charmingly to unburden her of her shopping. 'Oh thank you, thank you so much,' she can just make out Delilah cooing to the gorgeous stranger. 'Really, you shouldn't have, you're too kind.'

The hairs on Nadine's arms fall flat, the lump in her throat deflates and her hands ball themselves up into tight little knots of hatred.

# CHAPTER SIX

On Monday morning, Dig gets to work at half past ten.

Late, by anybody else's standards, but perfectly acceptable by his, especially considering that he had to pick his car up from those thieving shysters in Tufnell Park on his way in.

Johnny-Boy Records is housed in a dinky little pink, stucco-fronted cottage in a Camden Town mews; it used to be Toby's home, when he started the label back in 1989, but now Toby lives in a five-bedroom house in Primrose Hill with his ex-model wife, their three strangely named children and a South African nanny, and the cottage is used as an office.

The inside hasn't changed much since Toby lived here; it's very cosy and homely. The floors are all distressed reclaim boards and threadbare kilims. There are table lamps and pictures and plants and flowers all over the place. In reception there is a widescreen Nicam TV and a big squidgy jacquard sofa where they all sit and watch *Neighbours* every day with their feet up on the Balinese coffee table. A wrought-iron spiral staircase leads to a galleried area overhead and from there another leads on to a tiny roof terrace where everyone eats their lunch in summer.

Dig loves the fact that his workplace is nicer than his flat. It's just one of many reasons why he's stayed here so long. Seven years, in fact. He's been here since he was twenty-three. He started off as an A&R assistant and was promoted to A&R manager the following year when his boss left to form a band of his own. Not that he actually manages anyone. He has the odd work-experience student in for a few weeks here and there, but on the whole, he's a one-man department and he likes it that way.

The other reasons why he's stayed here so long are:

1) It's a five-minute drive from home and he has a dedicated parking space

2) Nobody bats an eyelid when he gets in late

3) He gets on extraordinarily well with Toby, who is less like a boss and more like a second dad – well, one he can get stoned with, anyway

4) He's allowed to smoke at his desk, whenever and whatever he likes

5) He can spend an entire day making personal phone calls and no one even notices

6) He hardly has to do any work.

Dig didn't use to be this slack. He used to be a workaholic. He'd be in at nine, work through lunch, stay till seven and then hit the trail, going to two or three gigs every night, because in those days Dig was on a mission – a mission to find the 'next big thing'. A label the size of Johnny-Boy Records could easily support itself with a few reasonably successful acts, the occasional Top Fifty album. But Dig wanted more. And in 1995 he found more: Fruit. The biggest sensation of the year. He found them playing in a pub in Cheltenham, of all places, back in the days when he could be bothered to go outside the M25 to see bands playing in pubs. They were eighteen years old, good-looking and brilliant. Their first single went to number one and became the summer anthem, booming out of Oxford Street jeans shops and fairground rides all over the country for weeks on end. The first album went straight in at number one and stayed in the Top Fifty for nearly a year. They were on the front cover of all the music papers and appeared on every pop show on the telly.

It had been a mad year for Dig. He was headhunted by every A&R department in London and consequently given a payrise by a somewhat scared Toby, big enough for him to finally leave home and buy a flat at the ripe old age of twenty-seven. His reputation was made. Everyone knew who he was and what he'd achieved. So he sat back and relaxed for a while, safe in the knowledge that no one could touch him because he was the guy who discovered Fruit.

Dig can't ever imagine leaving Johnny-Boy Records. It's easy. It's cosy. It's *family.* He knows everyone, from the tiny elderly cleaner who turns up every evening in a vast Rolls-Royce Silver Shadow which was left to her by her ex-employer and which she refuses to sell even though she's paid only £6 an hour, to the guy who turns up once every three months sporting a ridiculously smart suit and over-gelled hair to service the photocopier. Dig knows where everything goes, where everything comes from and where everything belongs. Johnny-Boy Records is his second home.

'You're looking a bit pleased with yourself this morning,' says Charlie, their pneumatically blonde but strangely droll receptionist, shoving bits of paper into internal envelopes, which always makes Dig laugh because there's only seven of them. Charlie used to work for EMI and still does all her admin on a grand scale.

Dig considers his expression and realizes that he does

indeed have a smug smile hovering around his lips. He decides this is highly inappropriate for a Monday morning and removes it.

'You recovered from Friday night yet?' inquires Charlie, in a tone of voice laden with the suggestion that he'd been drunker than he thought.

'Just about,' he says, picking his mail out of the pile on her desk.

'You know that girl was only seventeen, don't you?'

Dig blushes and rips open an envelope.

'You shagged her, didn't you?'

Dig blushes even more and pretends to be very interested in the contents of a Viking Direct catalogue.

'You dirty old bastard,' she says, eyeing Dig with evident delight and tying the string on an internal envelope into a little bow, before handing it to him.

Dig climbs the spiral staircase and ignores Charlie's calls of 'Lock up your daughters – paed on the loose!'

'What are you looking so happy about?' says Toby, loitering around the coffee machine.

Dig again realizes he has that inappropriate smile on his face and quickly disassembles it.

'*Cradle-snatcher!*' Charlie bellows up the stairs.

'Aaah,' smiles Toby. 'Yes. That girl. Friday night. I take it you . . . er . . .'

Dig nods stiffly. 'She was totally up for it, you know.'

Toby nods, too. 'Of course,' he says, 'of course she was. You'd better get used to this now.'

'What?'

'Well, you're thirty now. You've got the *allure* of an older man. You'll have them throwing themselves at you. You want to get yourself one of these, too.' He points at his wedding band and winks. 'Fanny magnet,' he says and then turns away, laughing hoarsely.

Dig laughs, too, because he knows that as much as he moans about them and makes jokes about his supposed pulling power, Toby is tied completely to his wife and family and wouldn't have the energy even if he *did* have the opportunities. He's worked too hard and too long for everything he's got and he's far too clever to risk it all on a shag.

Dig pulls off his leather coat and hangs it up. He reaches into the inside pocket and feels around a bit until he locates what he's looking for. A small, manky shred of paper. He gently smooths it out, running his finger lingeringly across the creases, and places it on his desk, next to his phone. He looks at it for a while and feels that smile forming on his lips again.

He won't call her now. He'll call her later. He'll have a cup of coffee first, open his mail, check his e-mails.

And then he'll phone Delilah Lillie.

Nadine always feels a little shiver of excitement going to work. First of all there's the unadulterated *thrill* of driving around in her gleaming white Alfa Spider, which is beautiful beyond words and which she paid for herself. Even in the depths of winter she takes the roof down and cranks up the heating and drives around with the wind in her hair. Nadine can't see any point in owning a convertible if you only go topless for six weeks of the year.

And then there's the sign outside her studio, nailed

to the wall: NADINE KITE PHOTOGRAPHY. It gets her every time.

Her very own studio. She worked long and hard for it. Five years of underpaid and overworked assisting, first of all for a temperamental interiors photographer who called her *Nay*-deen even after three years, no matter how many times she told him it was *Nadd*-een and then for a wonderful, old page-three photographer called Sandy, who'd been her inspiration.

Nadine never expected to make a living from photographing half-naked women. She aspired, as most photography graduates do, to a much higher plane. Fashion, maybe, or portraiture. But she started doing freelance photography at around the same time that 'lads' magazines became big business and an ex-boyfriend who was a journalist on *Him* magazine at the time had recommended her for some still-life work. She'd built on that initial contact over the years and was now the magazine's most popular photographer, doing their main features and their cover shots. She'd found a niche for herself, a place where the rewards were high and the work enjoyable, a place she loved being. She got to meet Australian soap stars and TV presenters and DJs, and even the occasional Hollywood film star. She'd photographed everyone from Jeri Ryan to Danii Minogue to Denise van Outen, and she'd yet to work with a girl she hadn't liked.

Her subjects were always completely disarmed to meet Nadine. 'God,' they'd say, 'you don't look like a photographer.' And she doesn't suppose she does.

Nadine is in a particularly good mood for a Monday morning. She's already been to the gym for one of her thrice-weekly work-outs and it's left her feeling uncharacteristically energized and chirpy. The sun is shining and she's wearing a beautiful pink sequinned cardigan she picked up from a car-boot sale yesterday for a mere pound. One quid to make her feel like a million dollars. There's little in life as exhilarating and satisfying as a true bargain.

The scales at the gym this morning informed her that she'd finally got down to nine and a half stone, having hovered annoyingly around the ten stone mark since a gluttonous holiday in Disneyland six months earlier.

The bank statement that arrived in the morning's post informed her that her business has finally started to pay out after what had been a slow start.

And she's single again! She loves being single, she really does. And this time she's going to stay single for as long as it takes to find a decent bloke, not just give in at the first moment of insecurity or urge for a shag. This time she's going to do it properly, and this time she has a rather attractive financial carrot to make sure she does.

In the car park behind her studio Nadine clips up her soft top and attaches her Krooklok. She whistles under her breath as she approaches the front door and the big pink plastic sign with her name on it.

Nadine flicks on the kettle in the tiny kitchen and stretches out on her pink leather sofa to read her mail. It's going to be a quiet day today. For once. A meeting at the *Him* office in Shaftesbury Avenue to pick the shot for the February cover and lunch afterwards with the commissioning editor. She'll use the rest of the day to catch up on paperwork and have a bit of a tidy-up. And maybe start phoning around her girlfriends to see if anyone has a male friend she could borrow to win this bet with Dig.

She smiles to herself. She *is* going to win, there's no doubt about that. Nadine has a fierce competitive streak, especially when it comes to Dig. Maybe it has something to do with working in a man's world. Maybe it's the way her parents always compared her unfavourably to her little brother. Maybe it was spending two years at an all-boys school to do her A Levels. Who knows? But it's there, and it's got her where she is today. It's got her her flat and her car and a healthy bank balance. It's got her respect and status and a constant stream of high-quality commissions from some of the top magazines in the country.

And although she doesn't know it yet, it's just about to get her the prestigious Ruckham's Motor Oil calendar, a commission that will send her earning potential on a quite unbelievable trajectory, straight to the stars.

Mitchell Tuft, Ruckham's Brand Manager, asked her to bike over her portfolio last week. It was returned the same day with a blank compliment slip, and Nadine had assumed that was that.

But the phone has just rung and Mitchell Tuft is talking to her now, gushing forth about how much he loves her work, how fresh her style is and how he would like to offer her a month in the Polynesian Islands with some of the most beautiful women in the world and a pay-cheque big enough to mean that she could comfortably take the rest of the year off.

No nipples, states Nadine – that's her only rule, no nipples, says Mitchell Tuft.

It's time for an injection of new blood into the glamour-calendar scene. The same old photographers, he complains, year after year. It's a new millennium. It's time for a change. We'll give you a free hand, he says, we want

2001 to be as different and exciting as you can make it.

If she was interested, of course.

'Well, yes, Mitchell. Yes. I'd be honoured. Of course. Yes. I look forward to it very much. Thank you.' Nadine puts down the phone and takes a deep breath to calm her racing heart. '£40,000,' she whispers to herself, '£40,000. For four weeks' work. Jesus Christ.'

She silently congratulates herself, not for the first time, on deciding to work without an agent. And then she gets to her feet and starts screaming. 'Oh my God! Oh my God – I'm going to be *rich*!' She runs around her studio in circles. 'Rich! Rich! Rich! Totally bloody rolling in it!'

This is it. Her professional destiny. She's worked for so long without any real sense of where she's heading, just taking jobs as and when they're offered to her, but this is different – this feels right, somehow. Editorial work pays quite well, but calendars, that's where the real money is, and Ruckham's isn't any old calendar. It isn't like the tacky ones covered in tea-stains in mechanics' workshops. It's artistic and innovative. Some of the models even wear clothes.

Ruckham's. Jesus.

She has to tell Dig. Dig is always so impressed by Nadine's professional achievements and Nadine loves to impress him. She picks up the phone.

'Dig! Dig! Guess what?'

'Urm, Jenny McCarthy's breast implants have just exploded all over your Leica?'

'No no no.'

'You saw Gail Porter naked and she's got a knob?'

'Oh, don't be silly. Listen. I've got the Ruckham's calendar commission.'

'*Ruckham's!* Jesus! You're joking!'

'No. I'm serious. I'm going to be rich!'

'Sod rich,' says Dig, 'who cares about money? You're going to be sent off to some exotic paradise with twelve fantastic, incredible, stunning women. Oh man – can I come? I'll be the bikini valet. I'll be the baby-oil applicator. I'll do anything. Please, please, *please*, can I come?'

'Sounds like you already have.'

'When are you going?'

'Middle of January. Isn't that perfect? Could there be a better time to get out of England and go to Bora-Bora?'

'You're going to Bora-Bora! That's Polynesia, isn't it?'

'Uh-huh.'

'Shit, Deen. You're going to paradise. Do you realize that? And they're bound to put you up somewhere really swank, somewhere five star. I am so jealous.'

'I'll bring you back a stick of rock.'

'Thanks. A lot. Anyway. Look. We'll celebrate at the weekend, yeah? I'm just on my way out so I can't chat. I need your advice.'

'Fire ahead.'

'Restaurants. I need you to recommend me a restaurant.'

'What for?' Nadine wrinkles her nose in confusion. Dig doesn't go to restaurants.

Dig's voice is almost trembling with excitement. 'I asked her out.'

'Who?'

'Delilah, of course. I just phoned her and I asked her out.'

'What do you mean, asked her out?' Nadine's mouth has gone dry.

'I mean, I said, would you like to come out for dinner with me? And she said yes.'

'You're joking, right?' Nadine can feel bile rising unpleasantly at the back of her throat.

Dig appears not to have picked up on the sudden change of tone in Nadine's voice.

' . . . It's all just coming together, Deen, y'know? That girl on my birthday night, Katie, she was like my wake-up call. If I hadn't woken up in bed with her, I wouldn't have felt so shit. If I hadn't felt so shit, I wouldn't have suggested going for a walk in the park with you. And if I hadn't gone for a walk in the park with you, I'd never have bumped into Delilah and I wouldn't have asked her out and I wouldn't be feeling as fucking . . . *good* as I'm feeling right now. I mean, God – she's just *gorgeous*. Isn't she? Don't you think that she's actually *more* beautiful than she was when we were at school? . . . And nicer, too?'

Nadine feels her stomach constrict and her heart shrivel and is glad they're talking on the phone, otherwise Dig would be able to see the look in her eyes.

Delilah? How can he possibly fancy Delilah? She's stunningly beautiful, of course, but she's just not his type. She weighs more than five pounds for a start. She has breasts. She wears a bra. She's *taller* than him. She's nine months older than him. She has creases in the corners of her eyes. And she's *married*, for fuck's sake. What in God's name does he think he's playing at?

'Dig,' she hisses, petulantly, 'what are you expecting to actually *happen* with Delilah? She *is* still married, y'know.'

'Yes. I do realize that,' sniffs Dig, having finally picked up on Nadine's attitude. 'And I'm not expecting anything to *happen*. Well, not immediately. I just want to see her, that's all. You know, just be with her.'

'Well, in that case, might I suggest taking some *conversation cards* with you?'

'Eh?'

'You know. Delilah. She's not exactly the brightest girl in the world, is she? You might need some help.' She can almost feel her throat blistering with the acidity of the venom that is spewing forth from it, but she just can't help herself.

'That's a bit uncalled for, Deen.'

'I'm just saying, *Digby*, that Delilah was all well and good when you were teenagers, but she's not particularly your kind of girl nowadays, is she? I mean, she was fine for a first romance, you know, first love. But ultimately there's not much more to her than a pretty face, is there?' Oh dear God. She really hadn't meant to be like this – men found this sort of behaviour so *unbecoming* – but she's started now and she already knows there's no way she's going to be able to stop. ' . . . And if you think that this *date* qualifies for our bet you've got another think coming. This is not what I would call an attempt at a mature relationship. This is what I would call chasing around after an unattainable, unstable married woman who will never, ever make you happy in a million years, who is pre-programmed to fuck men over, who will break your heart into a thousand pieces and hand-feed them to her sodding dog!'

'Jesus, Deen. What the fuck's the matter with you? Getting your period, or something?'

'No, Digby. I'm not getting my period, I'm just . . . I just don't want to see you get hurt . . . I know how you feel about Delilah, how you *felt* about her, and I think you've probably lost any sense of objectivity – I'm just trying to give you a *little objectivity*. That's all.'

'Well, thanks all the same, Nadine, but I don't need your *objectivity*. OK? Delilah's back in town. She's just left her husband and she doesn't know anyone . . .'

'Oh yes! And have you actually asked her yet, what she's doing here, why she's in London, why she's *abandoned* her husband? Have you? Don't you think there might be a bit more to it than just wanting to "catch up with old friends"? Has it occurred to you that she might just want some space right now, she might want some room, to sort her head out? The woman's just left her husband, for Christ's sake. She's been here for five minutes and you're already plaguing her with phone calls and asking her out on dates!'

'Jesus, Nadine! I just want to spend the evening with her. That's all. And she wants to spend the evening with me, too.'

'OK. Fine. But I think you'll find that it's a disappointment. Being with Delilah. After all these years. You won't have anything in common, you know. She's been living in the sticks for ten years, living a completely different life to us.'

'*That* might not be such a bad thing . . .'

' . . . She's not the same girl you knew at school, she's not the same cool chick. I'll bet she listens to Phil Collins, these days. And did you notice, the other day, she was wearing *pearl* earrings. I mean . . . that's positively middle-aged . . . she's probably got a *Barbour* hidden away somewhere, as well.'

'My God! What's the matter with you? You're basing your entire opinion of her on a pair of *earrings*? How shallow is that, Deen? Delilah's got class. She dresses beautifully – that classic look really suits her. And by the way – I did not ask her out just to win this bet, but I have to say that I think it counts.'

'Forget it,' snaps Nadine. 'No way. Married women don't count.'

'Who said? Who said married women don't count? That wasn't in the rules.'

'Oh Jesus, Dig. Whatever. I really don't care any more. You go out on your stupid date with stupid Delilah and you have fun.'

'OK,' Dig says tersely, 'but what about restaurants? Where shall I take her?'

'What's wrong with the Bengal Lancer?'

'I can't take her there.'

'Why not?'

'Because – because she's Delilah, that's why. I want to take her somewhere special.'

'I'm sorry, Dig, I can't think of anywhere.'

'Fine,' Dig says angrily, 'just fine. I'll sort it out myself.' And then he hangs up, suddenly, leaving Nadine standing there in her studio, the barren receiver hanging limply from her hand and a film of tears forming rapidly over her eyes.

# CHAPTER SEVEN

People come to London from all over the world to dip into its enormous wealth of diverse cuisines. There are Korean, Vietnamese, Turkish, Brazilian, Burmese and Havanese restaurants everywhere you look. There are restaurants with Michelin stars and infamous chefs, restaurants with views over the Thames and the whole of London, restaurants with live music and conveyor-belted sushi. You can sip minted Algerian tea from tiny coloured glasses or chew on the ribs of a large cow with a bib around your neck. You can eat ostrich in Chiswick and octopus in Shepherds Bush. You can, in fact, eat anything you want, wherever you want, whenever you want.

So why was the only restaurant that Dig could think of in the whole extraordinary culinary melting-pot of London the Bengal Lancer on Kentish Town Road?

The Bengal Lancer was his favourite restaurant, without a doubt. The proprietor, Archad, was friendly and welcoming, the naan bread was the fluffiest in all of London and, most importantly, they served until midnight. But come on – he couldn't take *Delilah Lillie* there for dinner, could he?

He'd finally called her at midday. Her phone number had sat next to his phone, burning a hole into his consciousness all morning, and he had hardly been able to contain himself. They'd had a nice little chat and he'd suggested Tuesday night, for dinner, and she'd said yes, just like that. She'd actually said, 'Yes, that would be lovely,' and then commented at least three more times during the conversation, how much she was looking forward to it.

And then something vaguely surreal had happened. He'd been half-way through a sentence when Delilah had suddenly interjected with, 'Oh my God, I have to go – the cats are holding Digby hostage in the corner – I think one of them's got a gun.'

Eh? 'Digby?'

'Yeah, my dog, Digby. I named him after you. Ha. Look. Phone me tomorrow. Let me know where to meet you, or whatever. OK?'

'Er, yeah,' Dig had said, losing his composure, 'OK.'

And then she'd gone. Hung up. Left him feeling . . . all . . . all . . . Digby? *Digby?* She'd named her dog *Digby*? Jesus. I mean, in one way, he supposed, it was flattering. She'd obviously remembered him, thought about him over the years. But . . . a dog? He felt emasculated. God, he hoped it was a big dog, a Rotty or a Ridgeback. He'd die, just die, if it was something small and yappy. He was discomfited by the image of this dog, *Digby*, being held hostage by a few cats. He was obviously some kind of a wimp, a poofter dog.

It had taken Dig a while to get over the fact that Delilah had named her dog after him, before he started feeling his usual chirpy self again. It's a compliment, he'd persuaded himself, I'll bet she loves her dog more than anything, take it as a compliment.

And then he'd started feeling excited, incredibly excited. This was all just amazing, the timing, the coincidence. Within minutes of his conversation with Nadine in the café on Saturday, within minutes of making that bet with her, a bet which, in reality, neither of them had any intention of or capacity for honouring, who should stumble so fortuitously into his path but the only thirty-year-old woman on the face of the earth who he could ever seriously contemplate being with. Delilah Lillie. The Love of His Life. The One Who Got Away. It was like a . . . sign, like a message from God. Not only did he get to spend an evening with a woman who wouldn't look out of place on the cover of *Marie-Claire*, but he also got a hundred quid. Result.

Delilah could have let him down, been a disappointment after all these years. She could have been fat, or old-looking, or happily married with loads of children. She could've been rude or stand offish. But she wasn't – she was even better looking than he remembered, she was obviously unhappily married, had no children and was actually much nicer than she'd ever been when they were together – brighter, breezier, friendlier and easier to get on with.

'You choose,' she'd said, when Dig asked her where she fancied eating, 'you know London better than me. I haven't got a clue where's good these days.' Which was funny really, because neither had Dig.

And then Nadine had phoned with her incredible news about the Ruckham's calendar – jammy cow, she *always* landed on her feet – and he'd tried asking her for a recommendation for a good restaurant: she was a walking *Time Out Food Guide*. And now he really wished he hadn't. She'd been *awful*. Really bitchy and unpleasant, not like her usual self, at all. God knows what was the matter with her. She'd just been given the best news of her career – *£40,000*! What Dig could do with £40,000 – and she seemed just miserable. It seemed like she had something against Delilah, for some strange reason. It made no sense to Dig, no sense at all.

So he was now desperately scanning the food pages of the *Evening Standard* hoping that good old Fay Maschler would provide him with some little gem of inspiration, some wonderful Moroccan place just up the road from him that he'd never realized existed, twinkling with stained glass and brass filigree, scented with cumin and rose-water and only about fifteen pounds a head.

But no. Not today. Today she was reviewing some stark Modern European place, in *Victoria* of all places, that looked cold and echoey and was, anyway, horribly expensive, and a new restaurant in Mayfair that was the latest offering from one of those infamous Michelin-starred very *loud* chef-types. So that was out of the question – outrageously overpriced and you'd probably have had to have booked it back in January or something to secure a table.

Just as he was losing hope of ever finding somewhere to take Delilah, Nick Jeffries, PR Superstar and general wanker, wandered into Dig's office. Not that you could really call it 'his office', as such – Johnny-Boy Records was very lateral and non-hierarchical and flat-structured and all those other things that it was so fashionable for offices to be these days – it was more of an alcove, really.

Nick knew Meg Mathews. He knew everyone. He was always hanging out in hotel bars in the centre of town where models drank things with cranberry juice and where Madonna had been seen. (Was there anywhere left in London, apart from Dig's flat, where Madonna *hadn't* been seen?) He knew other people, too, like trendy novelists and conceptual artists and DJs and stylists. He would know about things like restaurants. He was bound to know a cool place that Dig could take Delilah.

'Where can I take a girl, tomorrow night, dinner, not too expensive, not too spicy, not too far away?'

'What sort of girl?'

'Sort of girl I've been in love with since I was fourteen who looks like a goddess.' Nick had a low boredom threshold so any attempts at conversation had to be succinct and to the point.

'Hmmmm' – Nick scratched at his bumfluff and perched his skinny, combats-clad butt on the edge of Dig's table – 'she in love with you?'

'She was. Not any more. Least, I don't think she is.'

'You still in love with her?'

'Don't know. Might be.'

'Hmmmm.'

'I was thinking Moroccan.'

'Yeah . . . Momo. Heddon Street. Not what it was, but you could probably get a table.'

'Expensive?'

'Yeah. Right. Got ya. What about sushi?'

'Nah. She's been living in the country. She won't want raw fish.'

'Got it.' Nick clicked his fingers, reached across Dig, grabbed his phone and began punching in numbers.

PR people always did this, Dig had noticed, brought third parties into conversations via the phone. They always had someone else's phone number on the tips of their fingers and they always used it.

'Freddie,' Nick was saying to him, 'mate of mine. Just opened a place in . . . oh, yeah, hi, Freddie. Nick. Listen. You got a table free tomorrow night? Two people? Great.

Dig. Thanks, mate. Take care. You too. Tomorrow. All sorted.' Dig started as he realized that Nick had put the phone down and was now talking to him again. 'Eight o'clock. Exmouth Market. It's called *ex*. He'll give you a good table. He'll give you a good night. Don't worry. She'll *love* it,' he said with a wink and a minimal grin.

'Yeah, but what sort of food is it?' asked Dig nervously. Nick didn't like too many questions.

'God, I dunno. Meat. Or something. It's a meat place.'

And then he was gone. Leaving Dig with a hundred unanswered questions, like, where in Exmouth Market? What sort of meat? How much? What sort of atmosphere? *ex* sounded a bit poncey, not much like his kind of place. But . . . oh well . . . it was more than he'd been able to come up with, wasn't it? And it was bound to be trendy, and at least Delilah would be able to tell people that she'd been to some new place in Clerkenwell, before anyone else, while it was still hot. Yeah. He'd go. He'd take Delilah to *ex*.

It couldn't be that bad, could it?

## CHAPTER EIGHT

It is.

That bad.

Jesus. Look at this place. Dig isn't actually sure whether they've even finished building it yet. Or is it supposed to look like this?

A pale Spanish girl with red lipstick has just led them to their table. It's an incredibly big table, stretching almost the entire length and width of the small concrete room. It's fashioned from one seamless piece of oak, limewashed and varnished to a glassy finish and must have cost a small fortune. It is laid with immense white china plates and chunky tumblers. It is also the only table in the room. There is a large chandelier overhanging the table constructed from what look like – sun-bleached bones? Extremely *long* sun-bleached bones. The shades covering the unpleasantly high-voltage bulbs appear to be pterodactyl eggshells, fissured all over with small cracks. Very *Jurassic Park*. Very bright. Very weird.

They are seated next to each other (thankfully – Dig had imagined for one worrying moment that they were going to be seated at opposite ends of this huge table, smiling regretfully at each other all night) somewhere near the middle of the table.

'So,' says Dig to the translucent Spanish girl as she helps him slide his pony-skin-clad chair towards the table, 'expecting a busy night tonight?'

'This is only our first week, you know?' she replies somewhat defensively, having obviously read sarcasm into Dig's innocent question. 'First week is always quiet.'

'Yeah. Of course.' Dig smiles nervously. 'Of course it is.'

She disappears then and Dig turns towards Delilah who is examining her cutlery with fascination. The fork is designed to look like a bird's leg, all gnarled and knobbly with talons for tines. The knife looks like some kind of feather thing, with vicious serrations, and the spoon is an egg, on the end of a twig. Delilah grimaces at Dig and puts them back down on the table. 'Weird,' she mouths, silently. Dig couldn't agree more.

There is no atmosphere in the place. Not one drop of it. Nothing even vaguely resembling an atmosphere is present here, in any form. Dig is suddenly blinded by the extent of his own stupidity to ever have taken a recommendation from Nick. I mean, *honestly.* He should have known Nick wouldn't have been thinking about what was best for him, for Dig, he'd just have been thinking how cool it was that he had one mate who needed customers for his new restaurant and another mate who needed somewhere to eat and how cool it was that he'd managed to put the two of them together. It would have given him a great sense of satisfaction. What the hell would Nick heart-of-an-anaconda Jeffries know about romance, about an atmosphere conducive to *conversation*, for God's sake? Nick didn't have conversations; he had public relations . . .

Still, thinks Dig, may as well make the most of it, the most of being alone in a room with Delilah Lillie. He turns to her and grins. 'So,' he says, looking around at their strangely unsettling surroundings, 'here's a bit of hip and happening London for you.'

'Looks more like Jeffrey Dahmer's basement to me,' whispers Delilah, and Dig sniggers, thinking that he's never heard Delilah crack a joke before.

He would love to launch into a conversation now – there's so much to talk about, so many questions to ask – but he can't because this place has an echo, and that Spanish girl is just standing there staring into space, and how the hell can you start having a deeply personal and intimate conversation when there's a bunch of old bones looming over your head and thirty empty places at your table and no music, anyway?

Dig has already explained to Delilah that he has no idea what the food is like at this place but that he has been told it has a meat 'bias'. Luckily for him, Delilah hasn't turned vegetarian in the years since school and sounded very pleased at the prospect. 'Great,' she said, 'I love meat.'

The way she said the word 'meat' raised a sweat on Dig's neck. 'Good,' he'd managed to squeak, 'that's good.'

Dig wishes they had a menu or a wine list or something that he could look at, something to do. He smiles hopefully at the waitress, who immediately snaps out of her reverie and almost runs towards them. 'Yes?' she demands, defensively again, obviously preparing for a complaint of some kind.

'Er – I wondered if we could maybe have a look at a wine list, maybe? And a menu? If possible. Thank you.' He grins, apprehensively, hoping she won't take his request the wrong way.

She positively *beams* at them then. Her mouth splits open from ear to ear, revealing a large set of intensely white teeth adorned with a small smudge of her lipstick. And then she shakes her head. Still smiling, she says, 'No.'

Dig decides he must have misheard her. 'Sorry,' he says, returning her wide smile.

'No menus. You are *at home* tonight. You understand?'

Dig and Delilah shake their heads slowly.

'*ex* is *our home.* You,' she points at them, 'are *our guests.* Chef is *your host.* This . . .' – she indicates the table – 'is *our dinner table.* This is like dinner party. You see?'

Dig and Delilah nod slowly.

'So. Chef has prepared one meal, four courses, for *his guests* and our *sommelier* will give you wine which will complement the food of the chef. And you will eat and you will drink and then, you will pay!' She has brightened considerably by this point. 'It is *brilliant* new concept!' she trills. 'So. You are comfortable?'

They nod again, and she smiles again. '*Sommelier* will be with you soon,' she says, before walking to the counter and going back into a trance.

Dig and Delilah exchange looks and shrug. Dig is imagining how pissed off she must be about him bringing her here and is just about to embark upon a nervous apology, try and explain about Nick and how this wasn't really his idea, and how they could leave if she wanted and how dreadful he is to have dragged her all the way out here to this awful *communist*-style place where their basic right to freedom of choice is being withheld, when he suddenly realizes that she's smiling.

'Damn,' she says, theatrically, 'I feel so rude. I should have brought our *host* a box of Black Magic.' Delilah begins giggling like a naughty kid.

Dig is confused for a second and then realizes with wonder that Delilah has cracked another joke. He sniggers and joins in. 'Wonder where they've taken our coats? D'you reckon they've put them on a *bed* upstairs?'

Delilah giggles even more and then pulls a serious face and pretends to get up from her seat. 'Just going to see if he needs a hand in the kitchen,' she says, before laughing uncontrollably and collapsing back into her chair.

'Here,' says Dig, leaning in to Delilah's ear, 'I hope we're getting Viennetta for pudding.'

They both dissolve into helpless laughter then, and the ice, it seems, is well and truly broken. Delilah Lillie, *circa* 1999, has a sense of humour! The Spanish girl finally has the sense to put some music on, lifting the atmosphere an iota above 'morgue', and Dig turns to Delilah, breathes in a lungful of her beauty and holds it inside, next to his heart, which is close to bursting with joy.

# CHAPTER NINE

Nadine slouches on her cracked-brown-leather Deco sofa in her marabou-trimmed fifties-starlet negligé and her Bart Simpson slippers, sipping Cadbury's Highlights from one of her *South Park* mugs and trying desperately *not* to think about what might be happening with Dig and Delilah tonight. She's failing miserably.

She looks at the time display on her video: 12.20. Which means that it's actually 9.45 p.m. Because that display's been wrong since 1994.

9.45 p.m. They're probably eating pudding by now. Nadine's mind fills up with images of Dig spoon-feeding strawberries into Delilah's soft, red welcoming mouth and laughing as a pink trickle of juice dribbles seductively down her chin. She imagines him in his new Jigsaw Menswear jumper, the camel cashmere one with the V-neck which she helped him choose and which he looks so cuddly in, and his big leather coat which makes him look chunkier than he is. It's his best outfit of the moment, his special-occasion outfit, and he's bound to be wearing it tonight. He'd have made an extra-special effort tonight, polished his teeth, perfumed his neck, deodorized his trainers, combed his eyebrow, shined his hair. She knows what he's like.

Nadine feels awful. She still can't get over the way she behaved yesterday on the phone to Dig. She still can't believe that she's fallen out with him, that he hung up on her, that they argued. It's all so out of character. What must Dig be thinking? she wonders. What must he be thinking of me? Nadine has always been his equal, someone he credits with a good, orderly, *male* rationale, someone he holds in high esteem in terms of her lack of what he sees as overtly female traits such as bitchiness, gossip-mongering, excessive vanity and general cloying girliness. He's always told her that she has just the right balance of oestrogen and testosterone, but for a few awful, poisonous moments she'd let her oestrogen wear the trousers and she'd been bitchy and catty and out of control.

Nadine wishes that life was like a word processor, complete with Undo and Delete buttons. She wishes that the entire phone call could be erased from both their memories.

As it is, the whole scenario is now festering away in her sub-and-not-so-subconscious like a sweaty sardine. Dig, she hopes, has by now put the episode down to some momentary hormonal aberration and forgotten all about it in his excitement about seeing Delilah – men don't tend to dwell too much on things of this nature. But the more she thinks about it, the more her general sense of gloom and despair deepens and the more she hates herself.

She is also hurt by what she, neurotically maybe, sees as the implicit assertion in Dig's comments that he doesn't like the way she dresses. 'Delilah's got class,' he'd said. 'She dresses beautifully.' What is that supposed to mean? Is that what Dig really wants? A classy woman? Someone who buys tailored suits from Escada? Who wears navy pumps and gold jewellery? Who has expensive highlights and pearl earrings? Nadine has always seen him with someone more interesting than that, someone with a bit more character, a bit more *style*. Someone a bit more like herself, quite frankly.

Nadine realizes that her own sense of style is maybe a bit . . . challenging, for some people's tastes. She's used to comments from cabbies and bus drivers and even from boyfriends, some of whom have been embarrassed by her appearance.

As far as men are concerned, women's clothes are a form of language, and they fall into two categories: clothes that they *can* understand and clothes they *can't*. These categories have nothing to do with fashionability. Women's clothes are meant either tantalizingly to camouflage their sexuality or brashly celebrate it. Anything else may as well be a foreign language.

Nadine knows that most men find her wardrobe as easy to understand as an ancient Flemish dialect. For a start, they don't understand why anyone who earns as much as she does would want to wear second-hand clothes or sew things herself.

Women, on the other hand, tend to appreciate the innate sense of style with which she puts the disparate elements of her wardrobe together so that they form one definitive and pleasing look. They appreciate the charm and craftsmanship of some of her unusual pieces of vintage clothing and they love the old-fashioned femininity of the fact that Nadine gets dressed up every day of her life, providing the glamour that's missing from their own lives. They like the fact that she does things with her hair when they can't find the time or the inclination to bother with their own. 'You're so brave,' they say. 'I'd love to have the nerve to wear things like that.'

Nadine has always assumed that Dig approves of her

dress sense, maybe even *admires* it. She's always assumed that he isn't like other men – that he *understands* the language of her dress. But now it seems that he finds it as alien as every other man.

And then there's her flat. It's the flat of a mad woman. Look at it. Miffy the Rabbit wallpaper and princess telephone. Flashing-neon Elvis mirror and flamenco-dancing lampstand. Leopardskin and zebra-print fake-fur cushions. Cocktail cabinet. Clarice Cliffe tea-set. Cactus fairy lights. Stuffed toys. Tack, memorabilia and other people's junk. It's mayhem in here, but somehow it works. They did a feature on her flat once in the *Observer* magazine. It's a great flat – everyone who sees it loves it – but if she lives alone for much longer it will go *too far* and she will probably start collecting newspapers and dead pigeons and carrier bags full of old men's shoes. They will have to break down her door when someone finally notices that she hasn't been seen for a few months, and they'll find her buried beneath an avalanche of back issues of *OK* magazine and weird second-hand clothes and empty fag packets. 'Poor old thing,' they'll say, 'she had a lonely life. But at least she had her junk to keep her company.'

Oh God. Nadine is about to have a crisis.

She puts on her negligé tonight with a sense of self-loathing. She is a hateful, gruesome, badly dressed, batty old bitch and she wants to look the part. She is tempted to rub some black eyeliner under her eyes and smudge her lipstick, drink a whole bottle of gin and start shouting at herself. She wants to be Bette Davis in *Whatever Happened to Baby Jane?* Faye Dunaway in *Mommie Dearest* and Elizabeth Taylor in *Who's Afraid of Virginia Woolf?* all rolled into one.

She wishes she had some curly-haired little lap-dog with a ribbon in its hair, and a Southern drawl to complete the picture. She wants to sit here all night, wallowing in her own misery and hatefulness and imagining Delilah in her 'classy' clothes and her expensive earrings and her huge solitaire diamond engagement ring, looking elegant and refined in some posh restaurant with lovely Dig, *her Dig*, wearing all his best clothes and being on his best behaviour, and making him fall in love with her all over again.

He can't. He *can't* fall in love with someone else. He just can't.

Where would that leave her?

Hot tears begin cascading down Nadine's cheeks. She's spiralling into a frenzied hysteria. A few days ago she was sane and normal. A few days ago she had a handsome boyfriend and a great life. A few days ago she was a free-living, happy girl with a brilliant job and a wonderful flat and a best mate who meant the world to her. Now she is a miserable, bitter and twisted old spinster with poison in her bloodstream and bad taste in clothes. She has fallen out with her best friend and fallen out with herself and she is once again the awkward, shy and frizzy-haired girl of her dim and distant youth.

And all because of Delilah-fucking-bloody-Lillie.

Nadine tips a cigarette from the pack on the coffee-table with the baby-blue-painted toenails of one foot and transfers it to her mouth. The cigarette falls to one side of her lips and hangs there, sluttishly.

She lets it.

# CHAPTER TEN

Half an hour after their arrival at the painful *ex* Dig and Delilah have relocated to an Indian restaurant a few doors down the road. The mausoleum atmosphere they could just about handle, the lack of choice they could have lived with, the empty table was not too much of a problem and the strange waitress was almost endearing.

But when she'd approached them bearing two steaming bowls of slightly grey soup, all afloat with what looked like bits of brain tissue, and told them that it was *menudo*, a very famous Spanish soup made with tripe, and then hastened to assure them after registering their apprehension that it was made using only the best tripe, the honeycomb tripe from the animal's second stomach chamber, and that chef was the most renowned offal chef currently working in London – didn't they know? Isn't that why they'd come? – they'd decided to cut their losses and run.

She'd tried to persuade them to stay and then the chef had emerged from the kitchen looking horribly anxious and tried to tempt them with descriptions of the high-quality baby-calf sweetbreads he employed in his famous Veal Soufflé, the glutinous succulence of his Twice-Cooked Smoked Pig-Foot Stew, and the wonderfully coarse texture of his signature Corned Tongue Hash. He knew, he pleaded with them, that most people were scared of offal, but that if they were only to try these things once in their lives, then it should be here, tonight, now. Please . . .

Dig liked to think of himself as an adventurous eater, but he was happy to be a coward on this occasion. So the two of them had collected their coats, apologized profusely to the waitress and the chef and spilled gratefully on to the pavement outside the restaurant, grimacing and laughing at each other as they contemplated their lucky escape.

In the Indian they chatted away over a pile of poppadams and a particularly good selection of chutneys. Dig was thoroughly enjoying himself. It was so long since he'd done this – taken a woman out to dinner, *conversed* with someone he didn't see every week of his life. He was so used to the young girls he met and slept with and went to parties and bars with, talking crap and messing about and playing the big man. This was different. This was serious. This was special.

'God . . . you know, Alex would have *loved* that place,' Delilah was saying, in her strange new voice, all Benson & Hedges and Bombay Sapphire, polo matches and shopping trips to New York. 'He loves offal – all those horrid bits – kidneys and livers and brains and things. Thank God he can get all that sort of stuff cooked for him at his restaurants, otherwise I'd be expected to do it.'

It was strange for Dig to hear Delilah talking like this, using words like 'horrid'. Delilah had customized her Kentish Town accent with new bits and pieces of pronunciation and intonation, accent and inflection picked up from her time mixing in another society, far removed from her own. Her voice had retained its gravelly hoarseness and some of its lost ends of words but had also acquired a polished sparkle and a soft northern lilt. She sounded unbelievably sexy.

'Thanks for tonight,' she said. 'I really appreciate it.'

'Oh – God – it's nothing. Sorry it's all been such a disaster.'

'Not at all – it's been great. And so good to see you. It's hard to know what to expect when you haven't seen people for so long – whether you'll still have anything in common or not. I've thought about you so often over the years, wondered what you were up to, where you were.'

'Oh yeah?' began Dig in trepidation. 'I thought about you, too. Wondered about you.'

'Really!' smiled Delilah. 'And what exactly did you wonder?'

'Well,' he said, seriously, 'I suppose, really, I worried, more than wondered. I was worried about you.'

The smile fell from Delilah's face. She fiddled awkwardly with her napkin and deftly changed the subject. 'You know,' she said, 'I think I could probably have guessed that this is what your life would be like now. Music biz. Still living in the area, not too far from your mum, eh?' She smiled wickedly. 'And I think I could have guessed that you wouldn't have settled down yet. You always used to say that you didn't want kids till you were forty, till you owned your own record label – d'you remember?'

Dig smiled wryly. 'Yeah, I did say that, didn't I? I was going to be a millionaire and we were going to go off and live on a tropical island somewhere. I was going to be the next Richard Branson.'

'Oh yes,' she laughed, 'you were, weren't you? I was going to sit on the beach all day drinking cocktails and waiting for you to return from your yachting trip. How hysterical!' Her laughter turned into a nostalgic smile and she looked into Dig's eyes, suddenly serious. 'God, we were great together, weren't we? Invincible. Dig and Delilah! We thought we could do anything. We thought we'd change the world one day. It's funny, when I first started at the Holy T, there were all these good-looking boys hanging around me all the time, Rob Dennis, Mark Barr, Tony whatsisname, all the fifth-formers, but I used to see you and Nadine wandering about together, always studying and looking so serious and so full of secrets. You had all that weird hair and knew so much about music, and Nadine had her big ginger quiff and holey jumpers and the two of you looked *so cool*. I was so jealous of you two. I wanted to be like you. I worshipped the ground you walked on . . .'

Dig choked on a fragment of poppadam. How had his life changed so dramatically? How come when he was a spotty fourteen-year-old geek he'd had women like Delilah 'worshipping the ground he walked on', and now he was reduced to chasing around after teenage girls like some pathetic middle-aged man?

'I remember our first date. I was so nervous, but you were so nice to me. You listened to me. I wasn't used to that in those days. You gave me so much confidence in myself . . . you shaped my life in a funny kind of way. I wouldn't be the person I am today if it wasn't for you. Isn't that weird?'

Dig nodded. It *was* weird. It was very weird. He'd never really thought about it before, but it was true. Parents expended so much energy worrying about the effect that their own actions and decisions would have on the development of their offspring when it seemed that your character was determined, on the whole, by your peers. It was friends who formed you: your first mate, your first girlfriend, your first party, your first day at school, your experiences away from home. Personalities, on the whole, were formed in the playground.

Delilah, Dig suddenly realized, was an enormous part of him.

Getting the most beautiful girl in the school, the girl everyone wanted, and feeling the jealousy and respect of every boy around him had filled him with an unshakeable confidence in his ability to attract women, despite not being conventionally attractive. If it hadn't been for Delilah, he would have probably left school with his virginity intact and ended up marrying the first girl who'd let him sleep with her just in case no one else ever let him again. He still had that confidence all these years later, and he owed it to Delilah.

'So,' he said, nervously, 'tell me about Alex.'

Delilah looked slightly surprised. 'What do you mean?'

'Well, I don't know. What's he like? How did you meet him? What went wrong? That kind of thing. Unless . . . you don't want to . . .'

Delilah shook her head affirmatively. 'No,' she said, 'it's OK. It's fine.' She took a deep breath, and a warm smile spread across her face. 'I met him on Primrose Hill. He was a business studies student. I was . . . I fell over. He picked me up and took me to Casualty.'

'Were you hurt?'

'No – well, not really – just a cut, some stitches. It was nothing.'

'When was this?'

'Not long after you and I split up. I was eighteen. He

was twenty-two. And so tall and so handsome. Here – look.' She grinned and began poking around in her handbag. She pulled out her purse and took a photo from it. 'This is Alex.'

Dig took the photo from her fingers and studied it. A black-haired man wearing a DJ and bow-tie. He looked like Pierce Brosnan. God. Dig gulped and handed it back.

Delilah slid it back into her purse and continued. 'Even though we were so different and came from such completely different backgrounds, we connected immediately. He was so strong and so together. Exactly what I needed.'

Dig felt the expression of interest freeze on to his features.

'Things were really tough for me around that time, and he became my best friend. There was no romance. But then he graduated and his father offered to set him up in business back in Cheshire, gave him the premises for his first restaurant.'

'So you went to live with him?'

'Not immediately. I had things to sort out down here. But we kept in touch and when his restaurant opened he offered me a job and a room above.'

'And what was that like?'

Delilah shrugged. 'Weird,' she said, 'I'd never been out of London before that, and I'd never really worked. I was incredibly lonely and it was really hard work. I nearly came home, but there was nothing to come back to and I couldn't let Alex down. So I stuck it out. And besides, I think I'd already fallen in love with him by then.'

'So, what er . . . what was the *arrangement* then, with you and Alex?'

'What? You mean sleeping-wise?'

Dig nodded. A rude question, he knew, but he just couldn't help it.

'Well, there wasn't one. We were just friends and colleagues. He was my boss. Until my twentieth birthday, that is.' She smiled warmly at what was obviously a treasured memory. 'It was so unexpected. I'd started to worry that I was just a pet project to Alex, a little urchin he'd picked up off the streets of London who'd scrubbed up nicely and kept him company. You know, some sort of *Pygmalion* scenario. There was never any indication that he had any sort of *amorous* feelings towards me. But on that night, my birthday, Alex had arranged a big dinner for me at the restaurant, all my favourite foods, candles, music, presents. He made a real fuss. And then he started saying things like how much he loved having me around, how I'd improved the quality of his life, how just knowing that I was there in my little room above the restaurant made him sleep easier. He said I was his "missing half", that he couldn't imagine his life without me.

'And then he got down on one knee and pulled out a little box with this' – she pointed at the rock on her finger – 'in it. And he asked me to marry him!'

'And you said yes?'

'On the spot. There and then. The minute he said it – "Will you marry me?" – I just knew that it was the right thing to do. It was perfect.'

'So. When did you, er . . . you know? You and Alex. When did you first . . .?'

'Sleep together? Oh, our wedding night. Not until our wedding night, believe it or not!'

Dig tried to look unfazed. 'And . . . how was that?'

'What – you mean – ?'

'No . . . no. I mean. Not in detail. Just generally. Waiting until your wedding night. Was it a mistake? Was it OK?'

Delilah smiled tightly and screwed up her napkin between her hands. 'Well, you know,' she said, 'the first time's never anything to write letters home about really, is it? And I, well, let's put it this way, sex isn't really a priority for me these days.' She laughed. Dig felt slightly shocked. 'You look shocked,' she smiled. 'Don't be. I'm just not a very sexual person any more. I am working on it, mind you, but right now – well . . . it's just something that has to be done.'

'Do you . . . well, do you still sleep together?' Dig was embarrassed asking Delilah about her personal life, but the picture she was painting of herself as an asexual loner just didn't fit in with his memories of her.

Delilah laughed, ironically. 'High days and holidays,' she said.

'Eh?'

'Special occasions. We sleep together on special occasions. Anniversaries, birthdays, that kind of thing.'

'And that's enough for you?!'

Delilah raised her eyebrows. '*More* than enough!'

'And Alex?'

'Oh. Alex doesn't mind. He'd much rather be working, or playing golf.'

They fell silent again. Dig didn't know what to say. What a waste. What an absolutely shocking waste of a beautiful woman in the prime of her sexuality. How could any man possibly share a bed with Delilah Lillie and not want to shag her senseless every night? This Alex character must be a raving shirt-lifter. It was the only explanation. Either that or he was shagging one of his waitresses on the sly.

'And you left him?'

'Hmm,' Delilah said, her face falling, 'I suppose I did.'

Dig composed himself to ask her the burning question. 'Why?'

For the first time in the conversation Delilah's body language closed in on itself and she became awkward. 'I'd rather not say,' she squirmed. 'It's er . . . it's rather personal.'

'OK. OK. No problem. But can I ask you just one more question?'

Delilah nodded cautiously.

'Are you back for good? This thing with Alex, is it over? Or what?' He looked straight into Delilah's eyes, hoping his gaze didn't betray the urgency inside, and then looked away again. 'I mean, are you staying?' Oh God, Delilah, he thought, please say you're staying, *please say you're staying.*

Delilah stiffened slightly and cleared her throat. 'Haven't quite decided about that yet,' she said, 'not quite sure.'

'Oh,' sighed Dig, 'right.'

'I've, er . . . I've got some stuff to deal with in London, stuff I need to do to sort my head out. It all depends, really, on how that all works out, you know.'

'Oh yeah,' said Dig, 'what sort of stuff?'

Delilah looked awkward again and was silent for a moment. Eventually she looked at him. 'Oh, you know. Emotional stuff.' Her eyes opened wide as she said the word 'emotional' and she smiled wryly.

She was being very cagey and Dig didn't know how to handle the conversation. It was obviously making her feel very uncomfortable and the last thing he wanted to do was make her uncomfortable. He would let it go – for now, anyway.

'So,' she said brightly, unselfconsciously changing the subject, 'what about you? How's *your* love life?'

'Well,' he smiled, 'existent. Active. But far from perfect.'

'Girlfriend?'

'Oh no,' he interjected briskly, 'I haven't got one of *those*,' as if she'd just said 'Mouldy toothbrush?' or 'Incontinent guinea-pig?' or something.

'Anyone special since . . . since . . . well, you know?'

'What – you mean since we split up?'

'Yeah.'

'No,' he answered. 'No. No one.' And then he laughed ironically as the sadness of this fact hit him.

'You're joking! No one special in ten years? How come?'

He shrugged, blew out a lungful of breath. 'I dunno,' he said, 'I just really haven't wanted anything like that from anyone, haven't needed it.'

'I find that surprising,' she said, 'I always thought you were the one-woman-man type.'

'Well, I guess I used to be' – he smiled, stubbed out his cigarette – 'when there was . . . just the one woman, if you see what I mean. But these days – I dunno – there just doesn't seem to be anyone else special out there and life's too short to mess around with people who aren't special. It's like, take Nadine. She drives me insane. Beautiful girl and everything – bright, funny, intelligent, talented and just all-round lovely person, but she keeps on getting involved with men who are – I don't know – just, unworthy of her. Underdogs. She always goes for the underdogs. She feels sorry for them and she gets involved with them, you know, gives them the key to her life – oh, do come in, make yourself at home, put your feet up, these are my parents, this is my social life, these are my closest friends, stay the night, stay for breakfast, here's a spare door key for you. And then two, three months later it's all over because she's finally realized that she doesn't want to spend any more time with a loser, she wants her life back, and then it all gets really messy and unpleasant. That's why I think it's safer just to stay uninvolved, so I go for the, er, younger woman, mainly, these days . . .'

Dig trailed off as he realized that Delilah probably wouldn't be too impressed by this admission, but she didn't seem to notice, as she leaned in towards him then and said, 'D'you mind if I ask you something, something personal?'

Dig bristled pleasantly and nodded. 'Please,' he said, 'be my guest.'

Delilah spooned a little yoghurt and mint on to her poppadam, popped it into her mouth and began crunching. She was flapping the spoon up and down in rhythm with her chewing, indicating her intention to start talking the moment she'd swallowed. Dig sat transfixed, watching her succulent lips in motion. Finally, she swallowed, took a slurp of water and looked Dig straight in the eye.

'What's the deal with you and Nadine?'

'Eh?'

'I mean, what's going on between you two? Are you sleeping together?'

Dig choked. 'I'm sorry,' he spluttered, 'me and Nadine? What on earth made you suggest that?'

'Oh,' she replied, picking bits of coriander-flecked tomato out of the relish and chewing on them, 'just a vibe I picked up on, that's all.'

'What do you mean?'

'Well. When I bumped into you. In the park. At first I just . . . assumed that you were together, you know, a couple. You looked like a couple. And then when we were in the coffee-shop and you and I were chatting. I'd worked out by then that you weren't together, that you were just mates, but Nadine seemed . . . she was very *prickly*, almost like she was sulking. And I got the feeling that I was treading on her toes – that she didn't want me around? And I couldn't work out why. I mean, we were never exactly great friends at school or anything, but that was so long ago, it couldn't be that, so all I could think of was that something had happened between you two, some other time, that she saw me as some kind of *threat*. For whatever reason. I mean, tell me if you think I'm being ridiculous or nosy or anything.'

'Well. No. Nothing. Nothing's ever happened between me and Deen. Well, not really.' Dig was rubbing his chin and beginning to feel very uncomfortable. 'It's always been just a friendship, pretty much.'

'Look. I'm sorry. I shouldn't have said anything. It's none of my business.'

'No. But you're right. Sort of. Nadine *has* been behaving very strangely lately.' He told Delilah how aggressive Nadine had been that morning on the phone.

'And she's never behaved like this before now?'

'Never. That's the great thing about Nadine. I've always known what makes her tick, I've always *understood* her.'

'Anything happened in her private life? Man troubles? Family troubles?'

'Well, she's just finished with *yet another* unsuitable underdog boyfriend. But I don't think it's that. I think she's happy about that. And she's just been offered the most fantastic job imaginable – loads of money and a month in paradise. She should be really happy.'

'Well,' said Delilah, moving out of the way to make room for their waiter to unload his trolley of steaming food, 'she doesn't seem happy. She doesn't seem *at all* happy. And she's got a real problem with me. That's why I left the coffee-shop in such a hurry – I was getting such bad vibes off Nadine. She was making me feel really uncomfortable.' She dipped her spoon into a dish of emerald-green spinach, flecked with creamy cubes of paneer cheese, and then flashed Dig an intense gaze. She took a deep breath.

'Have you ever considered the possibility that she might be in love with you?'

Dig's eyebrow shot off the top of his forehead. He snorted derisively. 'Nadine? Don't be daft! She wouldn't be in love with me if I was the last bloke on earth! She's my mate, that's all.'

'I wouldn't be quite so sure about that.'

'You don't know Nadine. There's no way, just no way, that she would *ever* feel that way about me. It's *unthinkable.* It's ridiculous! It's – it's – '

'True?' offered Delilah, raising an eyebrow at him.

'No! No! You've got it all wrong. You don't know Nadine the way I do. Nadine doesn't *do* love. All Nadine wants is a huge man with a small ego who she can boss around and then dump when she gets bored with him. She's the most independent person I've ever known. I don't think Nadine's *capable* of being in love, with anyone. Let alone with me.'

'Women know about these things, you know?'

'Yeah. I know. Female intuition. But I know Nadine and I know that what you're saying is laughable. I mean, I'm sorry, but it is.'

'Right. Well. Whatever, Dig. But I've been right about these things before. And *I* think that girl is in love with you. I can see it in her eyes.' She laughed wryly. 'And I can see in her eyes that she wishes I'd never come back on the scene.'

'No – that's not true.'

'Oh it is. She sees me as competition.'

Dig had to bite his lip to stop himself blurting out that in his opinion Nadine *did* see Delilah as competition but only in terms of losing this stupid bet. Nadine just couldn't bear to lose. At anything.

'And tell me this,' Delilah continued, leaning forward towards Dig with her elbows on the table, 'can you put your hand on your heart and swear to me that you've never, in all the years you've known Nadine, in all the years you've been friends, close friends, never felt more than just friendship? You've never been tempted to take things a step further? Never had a drunken night when things could have *happened*, you know? Never *fancied* her, even just a little bit?'

'No! God! No. Never. I mean, there might have been a time, you know, *years* ago, when we were younger, just before university, just after you and I . . . But then she met some photographer guy at college and I sort of grew up and – no. No. Nothing ever happened. And now – it's been so long and we're such good mates. It just wouldn't happen.'

'Really? I can't think why not, you know. She's very sexy, very attractive.'

'Oh I know. Of course she is. But she's . . . well, she's just Nadine, to me. Always has been. Always will be. And besides, she wouldn't want me even if I *did* fancy her.'

'So,' smiled Delilah, 'it's not true then. What they say. About how men can never be truly platonic friends, that there'll always be some sort of sexual tension, bubbling away, beneath the surface. You know, that *When Harry Met Sally* kind of thing.'

'Well. Obviously not.' Dig was hating every second of this conversation. He'd rather be discussing the fruits of Posh Spice's latest shopping spree, or the contents of Dale Winton's knicker drawer. This was all nonsense. Him? And Nadine? The concept was making his brain hurt. He didn't want to think about it. And he certainly didn't want to talk about it with Delilah.

' . . . Well, for what it's worth,' she was saying, 'I think you'd make a great couple. I think you'd be really good together. You've always had this bond. You've always been so similar.'

Similar? He and Nadine? Well, of course they were. That's why they were such good friends. That's why they spent so much time together. But that didn't mean to say that they should *fancy* each other, did it? That didn't mean they should be a couple? And anyway, why was Delilah saying all this? What did all this have to do with tonight – with *them*?

'But, anyway. It's none of my business so I'll shut up now.'

Thank God, thought Dig, thank God.

# CHAPTER ELEVEN

Nadine was feeling more and more insane by the second. More and more unhinged, churned up, inside out, upside-down and all over the place.

She hadn't known what else to do with herself, so she'd phoned Dig. She'd known he was going to be out, of course she had. But there was always a slight chance, wasn't there, that something might have gone wrong, he might have come home early? So she'd phoned him, listened to his answerphone message, the one with the James Bond theme playing in the background. And then she'd called him again. Five minutes later. Just in case, you know, he'd just that second walked into the flat. And then again, five minutes later. And again. And again. And again. Twenty-six times in all.

Pathetic. Absolutely pathetic. She didn't even have anything she particularly wanted to say to him. She just wanted to hear him say 'hello' so that she'd know he was home, that his night with Delilah was over, that *he wasn't with her any more*. That's all.

She could have called him on his mobile, but the bastard always had it switched off. Which was just as well, really. What would she have said? 'Are you having a good time with your dream-girl?' He'd have said, 'Yes, great, brilliant, you owe me a hundred quid.' The line would have been alive with the atmosphere of some groovy place, a place where she *wasn't*, and she'd have ended up feeling a hundred times worse. If that was possible.

It was now eleven thirty and possibly the sort of time they'd be leaving the restaurant. They could be back in about half an hour, depending on where they were coming from and how quickly they could get a cab. But it was also the sort of time when they would be deciding whether they wanted the evening to end or not, that standing-on-the-pavement, stamping-their-feet-to-keep-warm-and-discussing-the-options sort of time. If they decided to go on somewhere, then there was no knowing what time Dig would be home. Nadine didn't think she could stand it. She'd worked herself into such a frenzy by now that there was no way she'd be able to sleep. Her heart was pumping violently and adrenalin coursed dizzyingly through her body.

Suddenly she knew what to do. She stood up, marched towards the coat stand, pulled down her ankle-length fake fur, threw it on, picked up her car keys and headed for her Spider, the front door slamming heavily behind her and her Bart Simpson slippers making barely a sound as she ran along the cold pavement.

## CHAPTER TWELVE

After their meal Delilah seemed exhilarated, grinning widely and looping her arm through Dig's. Dig felt himself grow five inches taller. She asked him if he would take her to a gig – it had been so many years since she'd been to see a band. She didn't care who they saw – anyone, anyone at all, she said. Well, it was Dig's job to know exactly who was playing where, and he was on the guest list for at least a dozen different gigs around town every night of the week.

'Sure,' he said. 'What do you fancy? A bit of Britpop at a pub in Tufnell Park? Girl guitar band in Clapham South? Northern Soul revival band in Peckham?'

They decided to see a band called Paranoid who'd just been signed by Johnny-Boy Records' Camden Town rivals and were playing at a new venue in King's Cross, right on the canal. They'd been hyped up to a colossal extent and this was their first live outing since they'd signed their contract. It was going to be a big night, full of celebrities. He didn't know why he hadn't thought about this before. He'd been so overwhelmed by the prospect of spending an entire evening with Delilah that he'd had an imagination bypass. The only thing he could think of to do with a girl as beautiful as Delilah was to take her out for dinner. That's what you did with beautiful girls. Going to gigs was what he did with his colleagues every night of the week; it was work, it was standing at the bar with a load of cynical blokes coolly ignoring some poor kids playing their hearts out for them on the stage, and drinking freebie beers. It had been a long time since he'd been to a gig for pleasure. But judging by the expression of pure excitement on Delilah's face as she hailed a taxi on Rosebery Avenue and clambered into the back seat, it was going to be very pleasurable indeed.

Delilah switched on the cab heater, pulled down the window and began smiling into the cool autumn wind that blew into her face. 'You know,' she said, turning towards Dig suddenly, 'I've spent ten years in the countryside, ten years breathing in some of the cleanest air in the country, but nothing compares to the smell of London in winter. It smells so . . . so . . . full of possibility, doesn't it? Country air smells reassuring, safe, dependable. But this,' she said, taking in another deep breath of the chill air, 'this smells of life.'

Dig had certainly never thought about London's polluted oxygen in those terms before but, watching Delilah's exquisite face aglow with happiness, excitement exuding from her like an intoxicating perfume, he was prepared to believe anything.

'Oh my God! I just saw Robbie Williams!!' screamed Delilah, as they made their way down the steep basement steps leading to the main club area. 'Did you see? Robbie Williams!'

Dig smiled happily. This evening was going so well.

'I always liked him best, you know, when he was in Take That. I was *far* too old, of course, to be into Take That – it was a bit of a secret, really. Alex would have been horrified. But it's all right to like him now, isn't it?

It's quite cool to like Robbie these days. And I know loads of women my age who like him, too – he's the older woman's crumpet, isn't he? And I love all of his songs, I know the lyrics off by heart. Oh my God, Dig, being here with you, after all these years, being in London, going to gigs – it's like going back in time. I feel like a teenage girl again!'

Dig glanced quizzically at Delilah. Take That? Was this really the same girl who'd body-surfed through the crowds at a New Model Army gig at the Town & Country back in '84, wearing a shredded black T-shirt and stiletto-heeled pixie boots?

She grinned widely at him and he decided to forgive her – it was probably some kind of post-modern, ironic thing.

Downstairs was dark and dingy. The ceiling was low and the décor was all grubby red velveteen, scuffed mahogany, peeling gold and muted candle-light. It had obviously been styled to look like one of those night-clubs in old films where raunchy young women in spangles danced for penguin-suited gangsters and their glamorous lady friends to the crazy sounds of syncopated jazz.

They headed towards the bar at the back and Dig said 'All right' to a few people he recognized. He could see it in their eyes when they clocked Delilah following behind him: Fucking hell, they were thinking, Dig's done well for himself, didn't think he had it in him.

'Are you sure you don't want a proper drink?' he said, when Delilah asked if she could have an orange juice and lemonade.

'No. Really,' she said, 'I won't.'

'It's all right, you know. I'm not trying to get you

drunk. I'm not going to try and take advantage of you, or anything,' he said, smiling, feeling quite giddy at the thought.

'Don't be silly,' she said, disconcertingly quickly, 'I know you're not. It's not that.'

'Don't tell me you've given up drinking, too.' He laughed. 'I don't know – Delilah Lillie, given up the fags, given up the booze – what *have* they been doing to you up there in yokel-land?'

'Course I haven't given up,' she laughed, 'course I haven't. I'm just trying to cut back, that's all. You know, turning thirty and everything. Besides,' she said, patting his arm, 'who needs drink when you're having such a great time stone-cold sober, hmm?'

'I suppose so.' He smiled, ordering himself a double scotch on the rocks.

They took a table very close to the stage and spent half an hour celebrity-spotting.

'That's another great thing about London – you get to see famous people just sort of wandering about, don't you? Just shopping and eating and stuff. Not very common in Chester, although that fat girl from *Emmerdale* did come into Alex's Oldham branch for dinner once.'

Dig could listen to Delilah all night. He was so used to being with cynical people, people who'd lived and worked in London for so long, spent so many years struggling with the Tube every morning, trying to negotiate the tourists jamming up Oxford Street, dealing with truly dreadful, pretentious *arseholes* on a daily basis, that he'd forgotten how exciting and magical it could seem when seen through the eyes of someone less jaded.

Delilah's face was tinted pink from candle-light glowing through a red glass dome on the table, and her glossy hair swung backwards and forwards as she talked and laughed and looked around her. Her teeth were extraordinarily white and straight and she seemed to have an awful lot of them. As the support band left the stage, and the lights dimmed, the excitement mounted and Delilah turned towards him, smiled the most beautiful smile he'd ever seen and squeezed his hand on top of the table.

She turned back to watch the stage, but Dig's eyes remained glued to her, glued to her kneecap, where the sharp dome of bone pushed into the black twill of her tailored trousers, accentuating the length of thigh and calf, to the line of her nose in profile, the tiny fold in her stomach where she was bent at the waist and the indentations made by her breasts into the charcoal grey cashmere of her tight sweater.

She was perfect. In every way. Perfect.

Dig finally took his eyes from her and turned to watch the band.

# CHAPTER THIRTEEN

The heater in Nadine's Spider had packed up, and she was freezing, even in her furry coat and slippers. She'd been parked opposite Dig's flat for more than two hours now, and there was still no sign of him. She was listening to the Supernaturals on her Discman and smoking many, many cigarettes, her deep-violet fingernails tapping up and down on the synthetic wood of her steering-wheel. Where the hell was he? It was nearly two in the morning. She'd counted twelve cabs pull up in the vicinity since she'd arrived, twelve pairs of headlights, twelve sets of rumbling baritone diesel engines and twelve complete strangers disembarking. She'd crouched down in her seat every time she'd heard the familiar sound of a black cab applying its brakes and then sat up straight again when it wasn't Dig.

Her breath was leaving her lips in big icy clouds and she slipped her hands under her bottom to keep them warm. She knew she was being ridiculous. She knew that if anyone else had been doing what she was doing she would have felt terribly sorry for them, imagined them to be emotionally and psychologically deficient. But she wasn't someone else, she was herself, and it was *her* sitting in a freezing-cold car in a starlet negligé, fake-fur coat and Bart Simpson slippers at two in the morning, waiting for her best friend to get home from a date so that she could stand even the slightest chance of getting any sleep tonight at all. She knew she wasn't emotionally or psychologically deficient – she was just concerned for Dig's welfare. And besides, if she let herself admit that she was here because she was rancidly jealous, then she would never be able to look herself in the eye again.

Another rumble broke the silence of the traffic-free road. Nadine checked in her rear-view mirror: another cab. She slunk down in her seat as the cab passed her and took a deep breath when she heard the engine slowing down. It pulled up a few metres ahead and Nadine craned her neck to catch sight of the two silhouetted heads in the back seat.

'Are you sure you'll be all right?' Dig asked, as the cab pulled up outside his flat, 'I really don't mind walking back from yours.'

'Don't be silly, Dig. Of course I'll be all right.'

'Here,' he said, forcing a ten-pound note into her hand, 'I want to get this.'

'Why? Honestly, Dig. After everything you've done tonight, organized for me, I'm not going to let you pay for the cab, too.' She pushed his hand away from hers. 'Keep it. I don't want it.'

Dig finally gave up and tucked the note back into his pocket.

'So,' he said, pulling his leather coat around him and getting ready to get out of the cab, 'erm. Maybe see you at the weekend, or something?' He gulped.

'Yeah,' smiled Delilah, 'maybe.'

Dig nodded happily. 'Cool,' he said, 'that's great.' He leaned towards the door handle, took hold of it and then turned abruptly to Delilah. 'I've had a really, really good time tonight, you know. Really. Best night, in a long time. Thank you.'

'Me too,' she said warmly. 'Thank you for the restaurants! And for the gig and for reintroducing me to London. I haven't had so much fun in years. And you've been fantastic company. Isn't it funny – I thought I knew you so well when we were together, thought I knew everything about you, but in just one night, I feel like I know you a hundred times better than I ever did before. It's been a real pleasure getting to know you again, Digby Ryan!' She laughed then and leaned in towards him.

When Dig looked back on this moment afterwards, it took on a strange stretched-out quality, as if it had happened over a period of a few minutes rather than the second and a half it had actually lasted. He could remember every last detail, the rhythmic ticking of the cab's engine, the sound of a Heart FM DJ announcing the two o'clock news, the orange streetlight shining through Delilah's golden hair as she moved towards him, the little creases that formed in her lips as they puckered together, the shiver that ran down his spine as her hair whipped gently across his cheek and the spasm that rocked his body as he felt his lips being dampened by hers.

She pulled away slowly but left her arms where they were, loosely draped around his neck. She was staring deeply into his eyes and smiling. 'Mmm,' she drawled, touching her lips with the tip of her tongue, 'that was nice.'

Dig nodded and smiled and leaned in towards her again, his eyes slanting closed and his lips softening up for a repeat, but his descent towards her lips was impeded by her hands on his shoulders, gently pushing him away. 'That was nice,' she said, using a more measured intonation and raising her eyebrows, 'thank you.' She smiled. 'Thank you,' she said again.

Dig took his cue. He knew what she was saying. She was a married woman. She'd come to London to sort out her problems, not to get involved in any more. There'd be time. He lifted her hand and kissed the back of it. 'It's good to have you back,' he said as he stepped out of the cab and on to the freezing pavement, 'really good.'

Delilah slid across the seat and leaned through the open window. She grabbed his hand. 'Sleep tight, lovely Digby Ryan,' she said. And then the cab pulled off, executed a perfect turning circle and bore Delilah away towards Primrose Hill.

Dig stood where he'd been dropped, on the side of Camden Road, and watched the receding cab, his hands in his pockets, his heart in his mouth and a smile on his face.

As the cab pulled away from the traffic lights at the next junction and disappeared from view, Dig slowly pulled his hands from his pockets, bunched them up into triumphant fists and brought them down from the air above his head towards his chest. '*Yes!*' he said under his breath, '*YES!*'

Oh my God, thought Nadine, watching him from the shadows across the road, her face in her hands, her jaw slack, oh my God.

It's happening again.

Dig's in love.

## lime-green teeth

One morning, when Nadine was eighteen years old, an invitation dropped on to the doormat of her family home. Little did she know when she opened it that it was going to lead to one of the most unexpected nights of her life.

It was an invitation to a Holy T reunion. It had been organized by Anna O'Riordan, one of the perky, popular, button-nosed girls in their year, and was to be held at a wine bar in Camden Town. According to the invite it was meant as an 'opportunity to catch up with old friends and renew contact before we spread our wings to all four corners of the globe in the pursuit of a Higher Education'.

Anna O'Riordan always had been a pretentious cow.

The party was taking place on 12 September, Nadine's last weekend in London. She was all packed up, had passed her driving test, chucked in her summer job and cleared out her bedroom, which now stood empty and sad, nothing left of her eighteen years but her Enid Blyton books and her etiolated kite.

It had been a scorching-hot summer and Nadine's usually chalky-white complexion had been toasted to a shimmery golden-brown festooned with freckles, and her auburn hair had picked up strands of honey-coloured highlights. She didn't know it at the time – what eighteen-year-old girl does? – but she was at her peak. Her skin was as fresh as it would ever be, her hair as thick and shiny, her thighs as firm and her energy as boundless. Her life was free of worries, commitments and entanglements, her sights set firmly on the future. She was a vision to behold, a picture of youth, strength and vitality. When Nadine walked down the street men would stop and stare because she was more than just a good-looking girl – she was special, she was sexy, and energy oozed from her. She was the sort of girl who made middle-aged women want to weep for their lost youth and middle-aged men want to start afresh.

Nadine was, of course, blissfully unaware of her all-round gorgeousness and the power of her youth, and as she got ready for the party she felt incredibly nervous. Who was going to be there? What would they think of her? Would they even remember her? Would she have anything to say to anyone?

But, most importantly, would Dig and Delilah be there? The thought unleashed a mob of epileptic butterflies in her stomach. How was she going to handle that possibility? She envisaged herself walking into the wine bar and clapping eyes on them for the first time in two years. What should she be expecting? Delilah possibly full-term pregnant with three inches of black roots and a fag hanging out of her mouth? Dig looking like a man whose dreams have withered and died? That was a pleasing thought. Or maybe they just wouldn't turn up at all . . . Nadine began hoping nervously for this last option.

But as she walked from Bartholomew Road towards Camden that evening, the air still warm, the sun just starting to sink and a gentle breeze ruffling the crinkle cotton of her Indian skirt, she began to feel brave and strong. Why was she still bothered about Dig and Delilah after all this time? Who cared if they were there or not, happy or unhappy, together or apart? She'd just spent two of the best years of her life at St Julian's, one of only twelve girls in a sixth form of ninety boys. Her confidence had grown beyond belief while she was there. She was a different person now and she had more important things to worry about than Dig and bloody Delilah. She had a future, a degree, a career to think about. She didn't need anyone else's approval and she refused to be intimidated ever again by Delilah or her allegiance with her former best friend.

She was a kid then; she was an adult now.

She walked into the wine bar with her shoulders back and her head held high. She would show them, she would show everyone just how far mousy little Nadine Kite had come.

Dig was the first person she saw when she walked in.

He was standing on his own, wearing ripped jeans, moccasins and an old check flannel shirt. His thick hair had grown untidily long, flopping on to his forehead and covering his ears and he was sporting a sleeper in his right earlobe. He was holding a bottle of Sol and examining the slice of lime in the neck with some confusion, unsure what it was there for or what he was supposed to do with it. Nadine watched him with gentle amusement as he attempted to push the segment down the neck and into the bottle and, when this didn't work, pull it out again and try daintily to squeeze its juice into the beer. The slice released one drop of liquid and refused to yield any more, so Dig transferred it from his fingers to his mouth and began sucking on it.

And so it was that when Dig looked up and noticed Nadine staring at him, when their eyes locked for the first time in two years and their faces broke open into wide smiles of recognition, Dig Ryan was wearing a dazzling set of lime-green teeth.

'It's just meant to be for decoration, you daft bugger!'

'Deen!' he exclaimed, the lime segment falling from his lips and on to the floor. 'Didn't recognize you for a moment there. You look really . . . totally . . . shit. I didn't think you were going to come.'

'Of course I was going to come!' she laughed, hugging him to her. 'Why on earth wouldn't I?'

'I dunno,' he shrugged, smiling, 'I thought a St Julian's girl like you would be too posh for a do like this, it might be a bit beneath you.'

Nadine rolled her eyes at him. 'You shouldn't believe everything you hear.' Her gaze wandered up and down his face and she realized that Dig looked different. Not just older, but intrinsically *different*. Was it the hair? Or the increased facial shadow? No. Neither of those. Was it his manner – nervous, uncomfortable, slightly arrogant? No. So what was it? Her eyes traversed his face and then she saw it.

'Dig Ryan,' she laughed, staring at him intently and making him squirm, 'what the fuck happened to your eyebrow?!'

'What?' he demanded, affronted, putting a finger up to it.

'It's . . . it's *separated*!'

'What are you talking about?'

'Your eyebrow. It's two eyebrows. What have you done to the middle bit?!'

Dig blushed, looked away. 'Phphphphphph,' he mumbled.

'What?'

'*I shaved it off, all right! – I shaved it off.*' He brought his beer bottle to his lips and took a large mouthful, his eyes swivelling self-consciously around the room.

Nadine was doubled over with mirth. 'Oh Dig,' she cried, 'that's *hysterical*! You look so *weird* with two eyebrows. I just can't take it in! Oh come on,' she laughed, nudging him in the ribs, 'loosen up.'

A smile began to twitch at the corners of Dig's lips, and before long they were both laughing. 'It was Delilah's idea,' he wheezed through his laughter, 'she thought . . . she thought . . .' He fought to control himself. 'She thought it would make me look . . . *more intelligent*.' He dissolved again, and Nadine slapped her thighs and screamed with laughter. 'Oh don't,' she breathed, 'don't. I'm going to wet myself! You look so funny! Oh grow it back, Dig, please. For the love of God, grow it back! You just don't look like *you* any more!'

'Maybe,' laughed Dig, slowly regaining his composure, 'maybe. Anyway,' he said, indicating her empty hands, 'what about a drink? Do you want to go to the bar?'

Nadine shrugged, wiping a tear from under her eyes. 'Yeah,' she said, 'I guess so.'

They turned to survey the rest of the party then, and Nadine felt her spirits drop as she looked around her. 'Oh God,' she complained.

'Yeah, I know,' said Dig. 'Depressing, isn't it?'

'God. Just look at them all. They're all so *boring*.'

'I know. I know. I was going to leave after this drink. I tried to make an effort when I got here, but I got trapped in the corner with Anna O'Riordan for quarter of an hour, telling me all about her summer in the States and her American boyfriend in this pathetic pretend American accent. She must have told me how "neat" he was and how "cute" about a hundred times.' Dig put two fingers into his mouth and mock-gagged.

Nadine sneered in sympathy. 'So,' she said, looking around her, trying to appear unbothered, 'Delilah not here?'

Dig shook his head, took another slurp of beer. 'Nah.'

'Couldn't face it, eh?' she smiled. 'Don't really blame her.'

Dig shrugged. 'Don't even know if she was invited. I haven't seen her since March.'

Nadine quelled the wave of excitement in her belly and tried to look unfazed. 'Oh,' she said, 'why not?'

'You tell me,' he said bluntly. 'One minute everything was fine between us. Then she started behaving really oddly.'

'Oddly?'

'Yeah. After her eighteenth birthday. She just . . . Here' – he stopped suddenly – 'look. How d'you fancy making an escape. I'll tell you all about it over a decent pint. No one's noticed you're here yet. We could just go somewhere?'

Nadine nodded. There was nothing she would like more.

They wandered down Chalk Farm Road, past pine-furniture shops and window displays of black leather and studded belts, fluorescent wigs and enormous silver rings in the shapes of skulls. They stopped for a moment on the hump-backed bridge over the canal and watched the black water below shimmering with reflections of the purple streaks that the setting sun had left in the sky.

Someone was having a party on one of the roof terraces overhead and music blared out loudly as they passed by.

In a canalside pub, they bought pints at the bar and took them outside to a table overlooking the water. 'Pooh,' said Nadine, waving her hand in front of her nose, 'it *stinks* out here. It smells like rotten eggs.'

'We can go inside if you'd like.'

'No,' she said, 'don't worry. I'll get used to it.' She started ferreting around inside her duffel bag as she talked and brought out a packet of Silk Cut and a box of matches. Dig pretended to collapse. 'No!' he exclaimed, 'surely not. Not you! Not Nadine Kite! You can't *smoke*. It's not natural!'

She offered the packet to him, and lit them both up.

'Shit, Deen. You are the last person in the whole world I would ever have expected to smoke. How long . . . I mean . . . when did all this start?' He pointed at her mouth.

'About a week after I started at St Julian's,' she said, exhaling. 'You were treated like a freak there if you *didn't* smoke. It was actively encouraged, in fact.'

'But I thought that St Julian's was supposed to be really old-fashioned and tough?'

'Myth,' she said, 'complete myth. That's what they *want* people to think, otherwise they'd only get people applying who wanted to doss around for two years.'

'So it was good?'

'It was the best. I've just had the best two years of my life.' She told him all about the smoky common-room and the flexible timetables, the 'Call-me-Tony' teachers and the non-existent dress codes.

They discussed Holloway Tech, where Dig had taken his A Levels and which sounded like quite a laugh. He'd got fairly good grades but he'd already decided that he didn't want to go to university. He'd spent the summer doing unpaid work experience for a record company in Soho and now they'd offered him a permanent job as office assistant, starting on Monday.

They talked about their families – his parents were fine and so was his little sister, who'd just started at primary school; her parents were fine, too, and her little brother had just got ten 'A' grades in his O Levels and was currently held on a par with Jesus Christ in the Kite household.

'So,' said Nadine, finally, 'you were going to tell me about Delilah? About what happened with you and Delilah?'

'Yeah. Right.' Dig dropped the end of his cigarette on to the ground and crushed it with the heel of his moccasin. 'I dunno, it was really weird. Things probably *had* got a bit stuck in a rut towards the end – neither of us had any money so we just used to stay in at mine most of the time. It all got a bit routine after we left school. She started doing this secretarial course, but she dropped out after the first couple of weeks because she didn't like the teacher, or something, then she started on some YOP scheme, working in a florist's and she hated that, too. So in the end she just got some shitty weekend job in a chemist, cash in hand, and that created a bit of friction because I had all this college work to worry about and I was making all these new friends, and she was just stuck at home all day with her old hag of a mother.'

'Oh!' exclaimed Nadine, remembering her one unpleasant encounter with Delilah's mother years earlier. 'You met her mother?'

'Yeah,' Dig grimaced. 'Once or twice.'

'What was she like?'

'The devil's daughter.' He shuddered. 'I think she was a bit unbalanced, a bit schizo. Delilah never wanted me to go to her house – she hated it there, spent more time at mine. So yeah, things were a bit tense, but I thought once I'd finished my A Levels I'd get a job, work hard, get promoted and then I'd be able to afford a flat, somewhere for us to live together. You know, I wanted Delilah to be a lady of leisure, I wanted to look after her. I really thought we were going to be together for ever. I didn't think there was anything we couldn't work out.

'We even planned to get engaged on her eighteenth, we talked about where we'd live.

'But the night after her birthday I came home from college and Delilah didn't turn up. I phoned her at her mum's and one of her brothers answered the phone and said she wasn't there, he hadn't seen her since that morning, but that she'd left with a big bag and there'd been a lot of shouting and his mum was really angry with her.

'So all night, and the next and the next, I waited for her and I phoned her and nobody knew where she was and nobody seemed to give a shit . . . I mean, her family, they were just all so . . . *fucked.* I nearly went to the police. But then I thought of something. Wherever she was, she'd need money. And she was eighteen now, she could sign on, and I knew she would – she'd been talking about it for two years – so I bunked off college for a week and I hid behind a tree outside the DHSS, every day. She turned up on the Friday morning. She looked awful. Really awful. I almost didn't recognize her. I ran up to her and I grabbed her, and d'you know what? She couldn't even look me in the eye. It was like she was ashamed or something.

'Anyway. In the end, she came back to my house. She stayed for a couple of weeks but she was so miserable – she didn't want to go out, she didn't want to watch telly, she didn't want to have sex. I tried getting her to talk but she just kept saying that she was fine, nothing was wrong.

'Then one day I got back from college and she wasn't there. I asked my mum where she'd gone and she told me she'd popped out to get a paper. I knew instantly that something was wrong – Delilah would *never* pop out to get a paper. So I ran up to my room and all her stuff had gone. She'd left a note.'

'What did it say?' asked Nadine.

'Oh, exactly what I'd been expecting really. Sorry to hurt you but I can't be with you any more. It's not that I don't love you, I will always love you. But I have to go. It's over. Please don't try to contact me. Please forget about me.'

'I went round to her mum's place, demanded to know where Delilah was. But she just said, "I don't know no one called Delilah. I ain't got no daughter." And then she slammed the door in my face. Scary bitch.'

'Then what?'

Dig shrugged. 'Then just sort of trying to get over her, I suppose. Just getting on with things. Concentrating on my college work, revising, going to gigs.'

'You haven't seen her since?'

Dig shook his head glumly.

'Oh Dig,' said Nadine, putting on her best sympathetic voice, while thinking *'Good, I'm glad, I hated that girl.'* 'You poor, poor thing. How are you?'

'Oh,' he said, brightening, 'I'm fine, I'm cool. I really am. It was bad for a while – very bad. But this work experience, it's turned my life around. I know what I want now. I've got a direction in my life and that really helps.'

'So . . . have you started seeing anyone else, you know . . . since?'

Dig shook his head. 'Nah,' he said, 'I've been too busy, what with my A Levels and work experience and everything. Nah.' He breathed in, looked up at Nadine. 'What about you? You . . . seeing anyone?'

'Uh-uh.' She shook her head. 'No.'

A smile tickled Dig's lips.

'What?' smirked Nadine.

'Oh. Nothing,' he grinned.

'What!'

'Nothing!' he repeated, light-heartedly. 'Just wondering if you'd – you know – have you . . . lost it, yet?'

'It?'

'Yes. It. You know!'

Nadine blushed crimson. She'd never talked about sex with Dig before. 'Oh,' she muttered, 'right. That. No. Not yet.'

Dig nodded knowingly and took a swig of his beer, a smile still lingering on his face.

'What!'

'Nothing!'

'I'm only eighteen you know,' she smarted.

'Good,' smiled Dig infuriatingly, 'fine. That's just great.'

'I'm waiting,' she said, getting more indignant by the minute. 'It's just not something I want to rush into, that's all. I want to wait until *I'm* ready, and if I have to wait another ten years, then I will.'

'Deen. Calm down, will you! I think you're right. I think you're absolutely right.'

'Good,' said Nadine firmly, squirming slightly.

They fell silent for a second and sipped from their pints. Nadine looked up and found Dig staring at her intently. She looked away, embarrassed.

'That place suited you,' he commented, obscurely, scrutinizing her face as he spoke.

'What place?'

'That St Julian's.'

'What do you mean?' Nadine replied coyly.

'You just seem so . . . different. You look so . . . so . . .' A blush spread across Dig's face as he searched for a word. 'You look so . . .'

'Ye–es?' joked Nadine, tapping her fingernails up and down against the table-top.

'Jesus Christ, Deen, you look . . . *so fucking gorgeous*.' Dig's eyes seemed to bulge slightly as he said this and his blush went up a few gears from pale pink to throbbing purple.

Nadine snorted and burst into giggles, holding her cheeks in her hands. 'Oh,' she said finally, 'thank you!' Her blush matched his now, and the two of them sat side by side like a pair of matchsticks, giggling awkwardly. They stopped laughing every now and then and looked up at each other's crimson faces and started giggling afresh.

'Oh God – I am so embarrassed,' said Dig, putting his head in his hands. 'I can't believe I just said that to you! To you! Nadine. My old mate, Deen!'

'Neither can I!' laughed Nadine. 'In fact, I'm so embarrassed that I'm going to have to go to the toilet!'

Nadine was still smiling by the time she'd walked from

the beer garden, through the bar and to the toilets. She was still smiling as she peed and she was still smiling when she regarded herself in the mirror while she washed her hands. This was so weird. Seeing Dig again after so long, sitting in a pub with him like a grown-up, drinking and smoking and chatting like adults. And that, just now, that compliment. That was *bizarre.* Dig thought she was gorgeous. And the way he'd said it – it reminded her of something. It reminded her of a day years ago at the Holy T, a summer's day when Dig had first set eyes on Delilah Lillie and he'd said that she looked just like Leslie Ash in *Quadrophenia.* And then he'd said, 'Oh my God, she is absolutely beautiful,' and she'd known then that she'd lost him. He'd used exactly the same tone of voice just then, when he told her that *she* was gorgeous – definitely – exactly the same.

A shudder ran down her spine.

They stayed in the pub until closing time, until a chill breeze had started blowing across their table and Dig had put one arm around Nadine's shoulders to stop her shivering.

His arm stayed there, on her shoulder, as they walked home, and Nadine wondered whether or not she liked it being there. What did it mean? Was she supposed to collude by placing her arm around his waist? Was it just a casual gesture, an act of affection? Or was it a prelude to something altogether unthinkable? After all those years of indifference and disregard, was Dig Ryan suddenly and unexpectedly going to do what she'd wanted for so long? Was he going to *want* her?

Nadine tried to put these exciting but unsettling thoughts to the back of her mind as they wandered slowly through the Saturday-night mayhem of Camden Town. The streets were overrun with litter and people and pungent with the aroma of falafel and spicy sausages being fried up for the closing-time crowds. Dig and Nadine picked their way over old food containers and empty Coke cans and ignored the urgent whisperings of the dealers outside Camden Town Tube station as they passed.

But what if something were to happen? What then? It would be the worst timing imaginable. Tomorrow was her last day in London. On Monday she was going to Manchester, to start a new life, to become a new person. Did she really want to start something here that would tie her to the past, tie her to London? Instead of spending her weekends getting to know Manchester, making friends, concentrating on her photography, she would be on trains, constantly whizzing up and down between Manchester Piccadilly and Euston, living out of a holdall, missing someone, wanting to be somewhere else.

That wasn't what she wanted.

But then, wasn't *this* – Dig, her, together, no Delilah, just the two of them – wasn't *this* what she had always, always wanted?

She looked up towards Dig. He was animated, chatting away about his plans for world domination in the music business, how he was going to give himself a year to eighteen months, tops, as an office assistant at Electrogram Records before he would start pushing his way forwards into the A&R department. A year or two there and then he would move sideways to a smaller label where he could be a big fish in a small pond, make an impact. It would be another year or so before he would discover the greatest guitar band in the world, make his name, make a packet and then – his master plan: Dig-It Records, his own label, a millionaire by the time he was twenty-five. Sorted. In the bag. No problem.

He genuinely believed every word he was saying: it *was* going to happen, there was no doubt in his mind about that – his career progression, Dig-It Records, early retirement. All of it.

He was, Nadine realized, as full of ambition and plans for the future as she was. He had no room in his life for a long-distance love affair, that much was obvious.

They turned off Kentish Town Road and began the walk down Bartholomew Road towards her parents' flat. She'd already decided she wouldn't invite him in. Her parents would make a real fuss and say things like 'Well, howdy, stranger' and 'Long time no see' and 'Here's a blast from the past,' and he'd have to make small talk with them for ages about what he'd been up to for the past two years and how his parents were, and it was late, too late in the night, for all that, so when they arrived outside her house she stopped at the bottom of the steps to the front door and turned towards him.

'Well,' she said, shyly, 'thank you for rescuing me from the horrors of the Holy T reunion. I've had a really nice night. It's been . . . er . . .' She searched for the right words to bring the night to a close without spoiling it but Dig wasn't really listening. He was anxiously staring into her eyes, his lips open and poised to say something, his body stiff, his fists tightly furled.

'I have to see you again,' he stated firmly, his mouth hard, his eyes nervous.

Nadine shot him a look. 'Well,' she began, 'of course . . . I mean . . . of course we will . . . it's . . . er . . .'

'No,' he growled, 'I mean *I have to see you again*. Soon. Tomorrow. What are you doing tomorrow?' His voice was desperate, he was holding her hands in his, tightly, too tightly.

Nadine was confused. She didn't know what to say. She squeezed his hands back and decided. She wanted to see him tomorrow, romance or no romance. She *wanted* to spend her last day in London with Dig.

'Nothing,' she said, finally, shrugging and smiling goofily, 'I'm not doing anything tomorrow.'

Dig smiled. 'Let's do something. We'll do something tomorrow. You and me. Yeah?'

'Yeah,' smiled Nadine, relief at deferring the tearful farewells lighting up her face and widening her smile, 'we'll do something tomorrow.' Her heart was racing, and a light sweat had broken out on the palms of her hands.

And then, before she knew what was happening, before she had a chance to decide whether it was what she wanted or not, Dig had wrapped his arms tightly around her shoulders, brought his face down towards hers and kissed her squarely on the lips.

Nadine was unresponsive for a second or two, her lips firmly glued together, her body tensed. But then the smell of Dig's flesh under her nose joined forces with the quite spectacular effect his lips were having on her groin and suddenly she relaxed completely into the kiss. Dig's mouth was soft and gentle, his breath tasted like hers, of beer and cigarettes. His tongue, which was now snaking its way around her teeth and into the crevices of her mouth, was sensual and alive. It was happening – it was finally happening – Dig Ryan was kissing her! She was being kissed by Dig Ryan! She and Dig Ryan were kissing!

A Golf GTI with a loud engine and acid house music blaring from four open windows passed by and slowed down. 'Oi – give her one for me!' shouted a man in a baseball cap, laughing lecherously before screeching off again.

Dig and Nadine smiled and slowly pulled apart, staring with wonder into each other's eyes.

'Well,' said Nadine, eventually, 'I'd better get in.'

'Yeah,' said Dig, 'right. OK. Give us a ring when you wake up, yeah? If it's a nice day we could go for a picnic or something.'

'Yeah,' Nadine nodded enthusiastically. 'Yeah. That would be really lovely.'

They exchanged another kiss and another look of wonderment and then Dig turned to leave. Nadine watched him for a while as he sauntered down Bartholomew Road towards Kentish Town Road. He had his hands in his pockets and an awkward, slightly loping walk, as if he wasn't quite used to having legs yet. A warm feeling flooded Nadine's heart, a feeling of familiarity and cosiness seasoned with excitement and freshness. That's Dig Ryan, she thought to herself happily, that's Dig Ryan walking down my road, having just kissed me so firmly and passionately on the lips and turned all my insides to semolina, that's him, my soul mate, my dream man, the person I want to wake up with on Saturday mornings on a big pine bed. There he goes . . .

She smiled warmly to herself and was just about to turn and go indoors when she saw Dig, at the head of her road and thinking no one was watching him, suddenly break into a hop, skip and a jump, leap on to a garden wall, punch the air with his fist and whoop at the top of his voice before turning the corner and disappearing from view.

## see-through dress

The following morning Nadine knew exactly what she was going to do. She'd been thinking about it all night. What she was going to do was this: enjoy herself. She would go with the flow and let whatever unfolded unfold. She would act as if tomorrow was just any other Monday and not the end of her London life. And then, at the end of the day, when she and Dig came to say goodbye, she would walk away and say nothing about another meeting or discuss what happened next. She would walk away, go home, and forget that any of it had ever happened, forget that she had ever kissed Dig Ryan, forget that he had any feelings for her. And then the following day she and her mother would pack up her car and drive to Manchester and her new life would start, and her September Sunday with Dig Ryan would fade into a distant memory.

It was a golden late-summer morning when she awoke at ten o'clock. Her mother was at church – she'd long since stopped trying to drag Nadine along, faced with her daughter's protestations of atheism and paganism and, lately, just to prove her point, Satanism – and her father and brother had gone fishing together. She ran around the flat in her bra and knickers as she got ready, the windows open, the radio blaring, singing along at the top of her voice. At eleven o'clock she phoned Dig and arranged to meet him on Primrose Hill at half past twelve.

'Bring your kite,' he said. 'Apparently the wind's going to pick up later.'

Dig had two Cullens' carrier bags with him when they met on the brow of the hill. He was draped all over a bench and smoking a cigarette. He had on the same jeans as the night before and a Happy Mondays T-shirt. He sat up straight when he saw Nadine approaching and his face broke open into a lecherous grin.

'You know that dress is see-through, don't you?' he commented lasciviously when she sat down next to him.

Nadine pretended to be embarrassed, but she knew full well the diaphanous qualities of her ankle-length Indian voile dress. She was wearing black-leather monkey-boots with pink laces and her hair was tied on top of her head into a cascading pony-tail. It was what her mother disparagingly referred to as her 'hippy-dippy' look.

Dig peeled the Cullens' carrier bags apart to reveal warm baguettes and tubs of taramasalata, bags of Kettle Chips and twelve bottles of beer. Nadine had brought a blanket, and they wandered around together until they found a spot that would afford them a little privacy.

And then, for the rest of the day, from lunch-time, through the afternoon and as evening approached, they lay on Nadine's blanket and kissed. They kissed for five hours. They kissed so much and so hard that Nadine's lips felt like blisters, and a stubble rash broke out on her chin. Every now and then they would break apart to eat a little something or to take a swig of beer, quickly finding each other's mouths again seconds later. They barely talked all day; when they weren't kissing they would stare dreamily into the distance, smiling at the frisky dogs that scampered by every few minutes and at the overexcited children dashing around in circles. They watched the sun beginning to set in silence, silly smiles glued to their faces and their hands entwined.

And then, just as they were about to leave, their litter disposed of in a plastic bin, their blanket folded and their beer drunk, a breeze blew Dig's fringe off his forehead.

'Did you see that?' he said.

'What?'

Another breeze picked up the hem of Nadine's skirt and tossed it sideways.

'That,' he said, pointing at her skirt, '*that*,' he said, pointing at the furrows in the grass, '*THAT*,' he said, pointing at a candy-striped carrier bag filled with wind and bouncing across the footpath. 'Come on. *Quick*. Get your kite out!'

He grabbed her hand and they ran as fast as they could up towards the peak of Primrose Hill.

It didn't take long for Dig and Nadine's kites to become animated in the powerful wind that seemed to come from nowhere that evening. It was a warm wind, gentle but alive, tangling up their hair and clothes like the hands of an overenthusiastic lover. The sun sank down slowly in the sky as the last hour of daylight ebbed away, and their kites danced in front of a golden backdrop. Finally the sun dropped beneath the horizon and at the very moment that darkness descended upon Primrose Hill, the wind died away as suddenly as it had arrived and it was still and dark. Dig and Nadine looked around the hill. They were all alone, the last people there. They collected their kites from where they lay, spent, on the summer-dry grass, and arm-in-arm they began the walk back to Kentish Town.

'I've worked it out,' said Dig, as they walked down Prince of Wales Road. 'Even if I give my mum £20 a week rent *and* start payments on a car, say £20 a week, plus a Travelcard at £5 a week, I'll *still* be able to afford to come up and see you at least once a fortnight – I mean, it's not going to be much more than fifteen quid, is it, with a Young Person's Railcard?'

He turned to Nadine and smiled, squeezing her shoulders with his arm. She smiled tightly.

'And then, of course,' he continued, 'there'll be holidays as well, won't there? You'll come home for holidays, won't you? Do you have half-terms on degree courses?'

Nadine shrugged and smiled nervously.

'Yeah, anyway. So what with holidays and weekends we should get to see quite a bit of each other. The three years should go in a flash and you'll be back in London before you know it and . . .'

Oh God. Oh Jesus, thought Nadine, this is exactly what I *didn't* want to happen.

Hang on just a minute, buddy-boy, she wanted to shout out, hold your horses. If I was some girl you'd just met in a wine bar last night, you'd be taking it slowly right now, feeling your way. You wouldn't be making these enormous assumptions about what happens next, but because you knew me when I had scabs on my knees and buckle-up shoes, you think you know the score.

But you don't, actually, you don't know anything about what's going on in my head, about what I want or who I want. And I'm a strong woman, I have dreams and a direction and I have things I want to do, things that *don't involve you*, believe it or not. Just because Delilah-bitch-of-the-century-Lillie fell for your charms, it doesn't make you irresistible, it doesn't mean that I am going to drop my hopes and dreams for my future. *I* am the priority in my life, Digby Ryan, not you, not any more, never again. I am stronger than you. Yes! It's true! I *am* stronger than you and I don't need you.

Nadine felt a flush of excitement as these thoughts buzzed around her head. After all those miserable years at Holy T, watching Delilah Lillie slowly steal away her best friend and take apart her dreams, after so many years of wanting what she couldn't have and feeling like a third wheel, she was now firmly installed in the driver's seat and totally in control. She had Dig Ryan exactly where she'd always wanted him and now she was going to show him that she didn't need him.

'Dig,' she said, coming to a halt outside a record shop on Kentish Town Road and turning to face him, 'actually, I don't think this is a very good idea . . .'

'What?' Dig's face clouded over in confusion.

'This,' she said. 'You and me. I don't think it's going to work out.'

'What do you mean?'

Nadine sighed. 'Maybe we should just take things a bit slower, you know.' She explained her feelings to him, about her new life at Manchester, wanting a clean break from London, needing to be unfettered by the past. Dig blinked a lot and nodded stiffly.

'D'you understand, Dig?' she asked. 'It's just not the right time. It wouldn't be fair on either of us.'

Dig nodded again and attempted a smile.

'So you understand?'

Once again, Dig nodded, but the nod slowly became a shake.

'No!' he shouted, shrugging Nadine's hand from his arm and backing away from her. 'No, actually, I don't fucking understand. I don't fucking understand *at all*. I think it's all bollocks. Jesus, Deen. Since the minute I set eyes on you last night I have been . . . I have been . . . oh God, I don't even know *what* I've been, but it's been great. Feeling the way you've made me feel has been great and I want to carry on feeling like this. I want to look forward to the weekends. I want to queue up at Euston station on a Friday evening with a change of clothing in a bag and ask for a return ticket to Manchester Piccadilly. I want to sit on a train for three hours and imagine you waiting for me on the concourse wearing a see-through dress with your hair all over the place and dream about the weekend ahead. I want a chance to get to know you properly, not just as Nadine Kite, my old mate, but as this new wonderful person I only met last night, this amazing, *amazing* person who I've only known for forty-eight hours.'

'You've known me for years, Dig.'

'No! No I haven't! You were different before. You're a new person now and I can't just let you go without getting to know you properly, without giving us a chance. Jesus, Deen – I can't believe this is happening!'

Nadine stared at the ground. She couldn't believe this was happening either. She couldn't look into Dig's eyes. She was too scared of what she might find there. 'Sorry,' she mumbled, 'I'm sorry. But that's just the way things are. It's called bad timing and it's been the story of you and me, all through the years.'

'What do you mean?'

Nadine took a deep breath, opened her mouth and then closed it again. There was no point, no point whatsoever, in raking up the past. She shook her head. 'Nothing,' she sighed, 'nothing.'

'Look. Deen. Can't we even give it a try? Can't we at least see if things would work out, you know, instead of just writing it off from the outset? I know what you're saying, I really do, about new lives and fresh starts and all that, but, Deen, I have never felt like this before and I don't think I could cope if we didn't at least try.'

'Oh Dig! You don't understand, do you! Of course it will work! That's the whole fucking point. It will work. You and I would be perfect together and that's exactly why I don't want to get involved with you. Not now. Not the day before I leave London. It's not what I want!'

'But you want me?' asked Dig, his hand on his chest. 'You *do* want me?'

Nadine shrugged. Of course she wanted him. More than anything. But she'd made up her mind. If she said yes now, then she would lose control once again. 'No' – she shook her head firmly – 'no, Dig. I don't want you. I know you might find that hard to believe, but I don't want you. OK? I hate to dent your big macho ego, but that's just the way it is.' She spun around and began walking brusquely down Kentish Town Road. There were tears tickling at the back of her throat and she refused to let Dig see her crying.

Dig chased after her and grabbed her arm, forcing her to face him. 'So that's it, is it? Hmm? That's . . . it?'

Nadine nodded.

'And you're happy just to walk away tonight, are you? Just walk away and get on with your life without ever finding out what it could have been like?'

She nodded again. Dig sucked in his breath and eyed her with scepticism. 'I don't believe you, Nadine Kite' – he shook his head slowly from side to side – 'I really don't believe you.'

'That's your prerogative,' she replied sniffily, avoiding his gaze.

'Yeah,' he said, 'yeah. I suppose it is. And it's my prerogative to let you know that this isn't finished yet. I've never felt like this about anyone, ever. You are so beautiful and so special and so fucking *amazing*, Nadine, and this' – he indicated the two of them – '*us*, this isn't finished yet. Just remember I said that, OK? You're wrong, tonight, you're in the wrong. You're making a mistake, Nadine.'

'I'm sorry,' she said, as they turned to face each other outside her parents' house. 'I should have been more honest with you – I just didn't think things were going to work out like this. I had no idea – I'm really sorry.'

'Look – Deen.' Dig took her hands and looked deep into her eyes. 'I hear everything you're saying about not wanting to get involved but can't we at least be friends? I have to know that you'll still be in my life. Can I write to you? Maybe just see you to hang out with when you're home for the holidays? Please?'

Nadine nodded. 'Sure,' she said, desperate now to finish what she'd started, to get indoors and away from Dig. 'Sure. Why not?' And then she turned away abruptly as tears started rising again in her throat and her eyes began shimmering. 'See ya,' she managed to squeak before sliding her key in the lock and stumbling through the door, letting it slam loudly behind her.

'*Is that you, love?*' She heard her mother's concerned

voice drifting across the hallway from the living room, where her family were watching television.

'Yeah,' she said, brittlely, holding back a choke. 'I'll be in in a minute.' She ran then, two steps at a time, towards her bedroom and collapsed sobbing on to her bed. As she lay there she heard a strange scuffling noise coming from outside. She peered between her curtains and saw Dig slowly backing away from the front door with his hands in his pockets and then she watched him walking down Bartholomew Road, dragging his feet awkwardly and heavily along the pavement.

'*Nadine. Nadine, what is this on the carpet?*' Her mother was hollering up the stairs. '*I really do wish you'd learn to pick up after yourself – you won't have me to do it for you after tomorrow, you know.*'

Nadine waited until she heard her mother's slippers shuffling back into the living room before slipping down the stairs.

Sitting at the bottom of the stairs was something that looked like a very brightly coloured cat, with an extra long tail. As she approached it she saw that it wasn't a cat at all, but Dig's kite, the one with the red, white and yellow chequers, the one he'd brought with him to the park today.

She sat down heavily on the bottom stair and gently picked up the grubby old kite. She brought it to her nose and sniffed it. It smelled of fresh air and plastic. It smelled of today, her day with Dig. It smelled of their picnic and Dig's breath and the woollen blanket and the dried-out grass of Primrose Hill. It smelled of Kettle Chips and warm baguettes. It smelled of sunshine and hope and happiness. It smelled of her childhood, Dig's father. It smelled of the past.

She turned it over in her hands and noticed something written on the other side, in black Biro. Some of the letters hadn't come out properly, the Biro ink not taking to the plastic, so she held it up to the light and was eventually able to make out the words:

Dig 'n' Deen
13 September 1987
For ever ♥

She sadly folded the string around the kite, got to her feet and went back to her bedroom.

# CHAPTER FOURTEEN

Nadine had been expecting the inevitable gushing phone call from Dig all morning, the phone call that would crushingly confirm what she already knew: that he'd had a fantastic time with Delilah last night, that they'd had a laugh, stayed out late and kissed in the back of a black cab, that he'd never been happier, that Delilah was the most amazing woman he'd ever met, *that he was in love.*

She was working on an advertorial feature for *Him* magazine and had been casting models all day with the magazine's art director and some tedious little marketing person from the Korean car company whose brief it was. The client wanted an Emma Peel-type who'd look good in black PVC while brandishing a derringer on the bonnet of one of their nasty little cars. The normal procedure was to call in some girls who would arrive minimally made up and casually dressed, have a two-minute chat with them, look politely at their portfolios and tell them you'd be in touch.

However, the small and rather sweaty marketing person from Poowoo cars, or whatever they were called, had insisted that each girl in turn, all fifteen of them, squeeze themselves into the catsuit, pout, brandish a can of Spray-Mount in lieu of the derringer and pose for a Polaroid, which he deftly pocketed at the end of the casting, claiming that he had to take them to a 'top level' marketing meeting that afternoon.

Top-level bedside drawer, more like, Nadine had thought distastefully.

She hated advertorial work. Horrid businessmen. Had no idea about art, no idea about creativity. Thought that *Him* magazine was just a lower-shelf, more credible version of *Penthouse* or *Playboy.* Thought it was just a load of tits and arses. Which it was, to a certain extent. But there was more to it than that – articles on how to be a better boyfriend, how to be a better cook, dozens of pages of beautiful fashion photography, travel articles, sports, hobbies, health, music and film.

It was a quality magazine written by quality journalists and this was how Nadine justified her dependence on the magazine for her living.

So when nasty little businessmen turned up, all hot and sweaty under the collar at the prospect of leering over a parade of nubile women young enough to be their daughters, rustling the metaphorical rolls of banknotes in their trouser pockets and treating Nadine like she was some kind of pornmonger, it made her feel very angry.

They'd left her after lunch amid a sea of leftover Prêt sandwiches and empty sushi containers and she'd finally been able to give in to her feelings of total and utter abject misery by throwing herself on to her pink couch and having a tantrum.

'Men!' she shouted at Pia, her tiny, hyperactive assistant. 'Bloody fucking men. All they want is perfection, all they want is tits like this and arses like that and legs this long and thighs that firm and youth and sex and lots of it.'

Pia, twenty-two, with tits like this and an arse like that, nodded wholeheartedly in agreement.

'They don't want reality, they don't want longevity, they don't want character or personality or anything even vaguely three-dimensional. They want fantasy and unattainability and when will they all finally grow up and realize that they can't have it!

'Even Dig!' she continued. 'Even lovely, sane, together Dig. I thought he was different, but he's not. He's just the same. Show him a pair of long legs and a pair of 34Cs, show him perfect bone structure and long blonde hair and he's away – whoosh – just watch him go.'

Pia nodded sympathetically and handed Nadine half a satsuma she'd just unpeeled.

'So shallow' – Nadine shook her head slowly in disappointment – 'so very shallow. And he thinks he can win the bet – ha! Thinks that this counts! Well, it doesn't. When I said "over twenty-six" I meant a *nice* girl who was over twenty-six, not some blonde bimbo with a husband and a "To Let" sign where her personality should be. Delilah *does not count*.'

Pia shook her head sagely and plopped another segment of satsuma into her uncharacteristically silent mouth.

'That girl,' continued Nadine, 'that girl made me miserable at school, miserable. And I know I'm a grown woman and I should have got over it by now, but I haven't. From the second I set eyes on her on Saturday it all came flooding back. I hate her. I really, really hate her – aaargh!' She let out a frustrated cry and flopped about petulantly on the sofa for a while.

'Fuckin' hell, Deen,' said Pia, eyeing Nadine with concern, 'd'you fancy him, or something?'

'Eh?'

'Dig – have you got a thing about him?'

'Oh, don't be ridiculous.'

'Then why are you getting so worked up about him and this Delilah bird?'

'*I'm not getting worked up . . .*'

Pia shot her a hard, 'don't-give-me-that-bullshit' stare.

'I'm not getting worked up,' she said again, less aggressively, 'I just . . . it's just. Oh God – I dunno. I just don't want Dig to go out with Delilah, because I know what she's like, and Dig's my best mate and I don't want anything bad to happen to him. Because I love him. That's all.'

'But how come you've never been bothered in the past? About Dig's girlfriends?'

'Because . . .' Nadine paused and sat up straight. 'Because . . . they weren't real. Because they were pretend girlfriends.'

'Because they didn't threaten your friendship with Dig?'

'*Exactly!* That's exactly it!'

'You have really got to sort yourself out,' said Pia. 'You're a bloody disaster.'

'I know,' sniffed Nadine, 'I know. Oh God – d'you know what I did last night?' She groaned and told Pia about the humiliating stalking episode outside Dig's flat.

'Fucking hell, we have really got to sort this out. You are losing it – totally. There's only one thing for it, you've got to win the bet. Take your mind off this Delilah tart. What was your part of the deal?'

'Oh, I had to go out with someone I genuinely liked instead of someone I *wanted* to like.'

'OK. So, who do you like?'

'No one. That's the whole problem. I don't like anyone.'

'Oh, come on. You must like someone. Everyone likes someone. What about that stylist from *Him*. The blond guy? He's cute.'

'David? No way. Too trendy, too vain, too pretty.'

'OK – what about that guy you shot for *Cosmo*'s 50 Most Eligible last year, that merchant banker with the unpronounceable name. He really fancied you.'

Nadine shook her head firmly. 'Absolutely no way. He had a stupid accent and a horrible bottom.'

'All right. How about Danny, that courier bloke who's always flirting with you? He's quite sexy.'

'Uh-uh. No more couriers, thank you. And besides, he has that spit-build-up thing in the corners of his mouth – yuck.'

'Jesus, Deen. You're a fussy cow, aren't you?'

'Well, apparently not. Apparently that's the problem – not fussy enough. I can't just go on looks or the fact that they fancy me. It has to be someone I can honestly imagine having a proper relationship with.'

'And have you ever managed that before?'

'What do you mean?'

'Well – in the past. Have you ever been in love with someone who was right for you?'

Good question. Nadine squinted and thought back, through rows and rows of unsuitable men, wimps and weirdos and holes that needed filling. She thought back through Maxwell and Tony and John, through Simon and Raffy and Tom, and she didn't stop until she got to her first and only serious boyfriend, to the love of her life, the man who broke her heart.

'Phil,' she said, finally. 'Phil was right for me.'

Philip Rich had been everything that Dig wasn't. He was ten years older for a start, at twenty-eight, which had seemed enormously old to Nadine at the time and had been, without a doubt, the most handsome man at Manchester Polytechnic, with intense indigo eyes and a perfect Roman nose.

He drove a black MG Midget, he wore black-leather trousers and he had black shiny hair which was cut into a dramatic jaw-length bob. He was divorced. He arrived at college every morning carrying an aluminium brief-case and another metal-clad box full of state-of-the-art photography equipment. He was unfeasibly cool and completely unattainable and from the minute Nadine set eyes on him on her first day at poly, she knew she wanted him.

She'd lived with him for three years. He failed his degree and then broke off their relationship two weeks before the end of university, took the last £50 out of their supposed 'summer travel' piggy bank and just disappeared one Tuesday afternoon. She'd been devastated.

'So, what went wrong?' asked Pia.

Nadine shrugged. 'I've got absolutely no idea,' she said, 'it's a mystery. He just took off.'

'Why don't you ring him?'

'What!'

'Ring him. Arrange to see him.'

'Don't be ridiculous! I haven't seen him for ten years! He's probably married by now.'

'Yes, but he might not be. He might be single and

lonely.' Pia was an eternal optimist and a hopeless romantic.

'No,' said Nadine firmly, 'I can't phone him. He'll think I'm weird.'

'Of course he won't. He'll be made up. Have you still got his number?'

'Well, I've got his parents' number – somewhere – I think.'

'OK then – no excuses. Find it and phone them. Get his number. Meet up with him. You'll feel *so* much better about this Dig and Delilah thing.'

'D'you think?'

'I don't think,' said Pia sternly, '*I know.*'

# CHAPTER FIFTEEN

'You did *what*?!' Dig exclaimed loudly down the phone a few minutes later. 'You phoned *Phil*? What the fuck did you phone Phil for?'

'Well,' Nadine replied sniffily, 'why not?'

'Why not! How can you say "why not?" Because he was the most self-centred, arrogant, pretentious twat I have ever met, because he belittled you and controlled you and put you down, because he used you for money and sex and everything he could get out of you.'

'That is not true! He loved me! He did not use me!'

'So who paid the rent for the last two years you were there? Who went out to work in a bar every night to pay the rent while he sat around on his arse moaning about how nobody understood his "art"? Who paid for his clothes and his haircuts and his poncey fucking Australian shampoo? Eh?'

'He paid me back!'

'He gave you a hundred quid! That's about 5 per cent of what he owed you!'

'Look, it wasn't his fault his marriage didn't work out, it wasn't his fault he had to pay the woman all that alimony.'

'Students? Paying alimony? Didn't that strike you as wrong, Nadine? He was ripping you off and you were too blind and too gullible to see it! Jesus! I can't believe you! It took you months to get over what that bastard did to you. You were like a little mouse when you got back from Manchester.'

'I was not!'

'Yes you were! Don't you remember how you stopped wearing make-up, and the way you dressed, in all that baggy black stuff, and how you had no confidence whatsoever.'

'God, Dig! You're talking about nine years ago! People change, you know? Phil had a bad time at Manchester. He sounded completely different when I spoke to him on the phone, he sounded really relaxed and laid back.'

'Nadine. What are you doing? Why are you doing this? Why, after nine years of getting on with your life perfectly well, are you suddenly phoning up some fucked-up old wanker you used to go out with when you were nineteen?'

'*Exactly!* That's exactly it. I am *not* getting on with my life perfectly well. That's the whole problem. As you yourself have pointed out, I'm getting on with my life perfectly *unwell*.'

'I don't understand.'

Nadine sighed. 'Phil is the only bloke I've ever loved, ever cared about, and I want to see him. That's all there is to understand.'

'Oh! *I* get it! This is for the bet, isn't it?'

'Oh, don't be ridiculous!'

'Of course it is! Why else would you suddenly decide that you just have to see some bloke you went out with ten years ago?'

'Oh,' exclaimed Nadine, sarcastically, 'oh, I see! It's perfectly all right for you to go off on dates with disastrous women from your past, it's perfectly all right for you to go off with Delilah Lillie after what she did to you.

It's perfectly all right for you, but when *I* want to see someone who I used to be in love with, someone who hurt *me*, then there's something wrong with it! You fucking hypocrite!!'

'I haven't *gone off* with Delilah! What are you talking about? We had dinner, that's all. We had dinner and we went to see a band!'

'And that is all I intend to do when I see Phil tonight. We're going to have a drink together and see how it goes.'

'Well, that's fine. You go and you have a good time. But don't expect to come crying to me when he starts pulling you apart again and you're handing out cash left, right and centre and your self-esteem is in tatters.'

'I can assure you, I won't!'

'Good!'

'Fine!'

Oh dear. The conversation was unravelling at an alarming rate of knots. For the second time in less than a week, Dig and Nadine were having an argument that they couldn't joke their way out of.

'I'm going now,' said Dig, brusquely, after a short, tense silence, 'I'm really busy.'

'That's fine,' sniffed Nadine, '*I* happen to be rather busy, too.'

'See you?' he ventured, unenthusiastically.

'Yeah. See you,' she returned with a corresponding lack of enthusiasm. She took the receiver from her ear and was about to replace it when she decided she had one last thing to say. 'Oh,' she began, 'by the way. I'm not *stupid*, you know? You don't need to lie to me, about you and Delilah. I know *everything* about you and Delilah. So don't give me all that "just good friends" bullshit, OK, because it won't wash.'

And with that she forcefully and noisily dropped the receiver back on to its cradle, threw herself down on to her studio sofa and started crying again.

Dig forcefully and noisily dropped the receiver back on to its cradle, lit a cigarette and sighed deeply. Jesus, he thought to himself, what the fuck is going on here? I mean, will someone please tell me what the fuck is happening?

He'd phoned Nadine to make things up with her, to patch over their argument of Monday, and instead things had ended up a hundred times worse.

Phil?

Philip Rich?

How could it be possible that this awful character was re-entering his life after so many years?

Dig hadn't liked many of Nadine's boyfriends over the years but there'd been none he'd disliked as heartily as Philip Rich. Philip Rich with his ridiculous shiny bob and effeminate leather trousers. Philip Rich with his long words and condescending manner. Philip Rich with all his supposed good taste and maturity and sophistication. Philip Rich who'd morphed into Philip Poor so suspiciously quickly.

Philip Rich who'd picked up his tender, teenage heart with hairless, careless hands and snapped it clean in two.

# the worst weekend . . . ever

Nadine had been in Manchester nearly two months and Dig was in a bad way, still reeling from the emotional punch in the stomach she'd dealt him after their day in the park.

He wrote to her nearly every day. He sent her letters and comical postcards; he sent her promo copies of new singles, and posters and stickers and T-shirts, all freebies from his new job. He tried to keep things light-hearted, pretend that he was only interested in the so-called friendship he'd conjured up so desperately on Nadine's doorstep that night, pretend that he was too busy being successful and indispensable in his exciting job to have time to think about what had happened between the two of them on that September weekend.

Which was, of course, completely and utterly not true.

The truth was, that Dig Ryan had fallen madly, passionately and devotedly in love with Nadine Kite.

He dreamed of her at night. He wrote songs for her by day. He pinned up the Holy T class photo by his bed and kissed Nadine's fuzzy-haired image good-night before he went to sleep. He kept dried blades of grass from their day on Primrose Hill in a paper bag in his drawer.

Nadinc wrote back occasionally, not as often as he, and after seven weeks, three days and fourteen hours of this façade, Dig felt that strong enough foundations had been laid for him to suggest a weekend visit to Manchester, without scaring her away. She put him off at first, but eventually they organized a date, and it was all he could think about for the week before he went.

So, here he was, as he'd imagined himself so many times, clutching his weekend bag, striding purposefully up the concourse at Euston station towards the train that was to bear him Nadine-wards, to the land of see-through dresses and radiant skin, spring-water laughs and silken mouths. She'd moved out of digs and into a flat now, and he presumed that he'd be bunged on to some kind of sofa and treated like a kid brother, but he didn't care. Just to be there would be enough, actually to be in Nadine's flat.

*Nadine's flat.* It sounded like poetry to Dig. He had images of it in his mind, images of voiley, floaty things and joss sticks, coloured muslins, embroidered throws and dried flowers, Water Lilies posters on the walls and loads of green-packaged Body Shop stuff in the bathroom.

It seemed she had a flatmate of some sort, who she referred to in her letters as 'Phil' – he was probably gay – but hopefully he'd be out a lot and he and Nadine could hang out together in her jasmine-scented living room, listening to all the records he'd brought up with him from Electrogram and smoking the hash he'd gone to so much trouble acquiring from a bloke with gold teeth in Ealing Broadway.

Dig was prepared to accept that there was unlikely to be any kissing this weekend. Nadine was more than likely still going to be in her 'independent woman' phase and he didn't want to rush things. All he could do for now was develop the intimacy between them. The rest, despite everything his surging, raging hormones were trying so hard to tell him, could wait till later.

He resisted the urge to buy Nadine a bunch of flowers as he dismounted his train at Piccadilly and instead bought her a bag of Cola Bottles and a stupid lighter with 'Welcome to Manchester – Britain's Second City' on it and thought to himself how glad he was to have had the good fortune to have been born in Britain's *first* city. He'd made an arrangement to meet Nadine outside, by the taxi rank, and as he emerged from the train station he looked around him for a fountain of auburn hair flecked with gold and an elusive shimmer of translucent cotton.

He was therefore more than a little surprised when he turned around to see Nadine, her beautiful hair chopped off into a severe bob at her chin, dressed entirely in black and wearing a vicious slash of red lipstick across her mouth. She looked very pale and very thin and very trendy.

She was nervous with him as they sat in the back of the taxi on the way to her flat. She kept talking about this Phil character and how much she hoped Dig would like him and how he shouldn't be put off by his manner – he could be a bit abrupt with people sometimes – and how he was very interested to meet Dig as he hadn't met any of her London friends yet and Dig was thinking, all right, all right, what's the big deal, it's you I've come to see, not your bender flatmate. But instead he smiled reassuringly and said that he was looking forward to meeting him, too, and he was sure they'd get on fine, and Nadine had looked disproportionately relieved to hear him say so.

Dig should have twigged when she started saying

things like 'I don't know how much we'll be able to do this weekend, *we* haven't got much money at the moment' and 'there's a vegetarian café around the corner from *us* where *we* go for breakfast sometimes' but he didn't. He certainly should have twigged when she referred to '*our* bedroom', but he didn't. When he looked back on the whole episode the following day, he would wonder at his own stupidity and never again would he snort sceptically at those 'cross wires' comedy sketches on the telly when two people manage to discuss entirely different topics together without either of them realizing it.

Dig's first sense that something was afoot came as he crossed the threshold into Nadine's flat. It was horrible. Not that this fact aroused any suspicion in itself. But it was absolutely horrible. It was on the second floor of a discoloured thirties block, built above a parade of shops, with bucket-shaped concrete balconies attached to the front and paint peeling off the walls in enormous flaps. The flat itself had no central heating and was wretchedly furnished with the sort of furniture more usually associated with skips outside buildings and house-clearance sales. Many of the aluminium-framed windows were cracked or missing entirely and patched over with gungy layers of mud-coloured parcel tape.

Far from the feminine bouquet of jasmine and white musk and Body Shop peppermint foot lotion that Dig had expected to encounter, the flat smelled overpoweringly and depressingly of damp and mildew. No attempt had been made to personalize it or to camouflage its ugliness, other than the rows of rather pretentious and badly composed black and white photographs in Clip-frames which hung on nearly every wall in the flat.

'We're going to decorate it next term, when we've both got a bit more money,' said Nadine, hanging her black nylon bomber jacket from a hook in the hallway and leading Dig towards a door at the bottom of the corridor.

This time the 'we' reference resonated a little more unambiguously and Dig began to feel vaguely uncomfortable. He tucked his hair behind his ears self-consciously as Nadine pushed open the door, and attempted to flatten his fringe on to his forehead.

The door creaked open slowly and somewhat dramatically and there, sitting cross-legged on the floor, smoking a stinking Gauloise and reading the *Guardian* was the most enormous arsehole Dig had ever set eyes on. On a bleak November morning, in a dank and overcast flat, this man was wearing sunglasses.

Really and truly, without a word of a lie.

RayBans.

Tortoiseshell ones.

Unbelievable.

He was barefoot and wearing pristine white jeans with a big black linen shirt, the sleeves held up to his elbows by stretchy metal suspenders. His hair was ludicrous, a soigné wedge of over-polished black, tied back from his face into a stumpy pony-tail. He was in possession of a proud and well-constructed nose of which, Dig could tell, he was inordinately enamoured and when he looked up slowly, calcu*late*dly slowly, from his paper to acknowledge Dig's presence in the room, his expression arranged itself into a strange and unnatural contortion of his facial features which didn't suit him in the slightest. Dig suspected he was trying to smile.

'All right,' he said, lifting his glasses an inch or two from the bridge of his nose and leaving them resting on his forehead while he regarded Dig through squinted eyes. After a second or two, he tapped the glasses nonchalantly, letting them fall back on to his nose, before going back to his newspaper and his smouldering Gauloise.

It was antipathy at first sight. Dig had never before in his life felt so much dislike towards another person within such a short space of time. This bloke, whoever he was, was a complete wanker. He was a wanker of the highest order and of the greatest magnitude. He was the beginning and the end of the wanker universe, the original wanker, the top wanker, the wanker to end all other wankers. You had to hand it to him: this bloke was at the cutting edge of wankerdom.

Dig hated him.

As Dig stood awkwardly at the edge of the room, absorbing this unexpected surge of negative feelings and the fact that the lovely and ravishing Nadine was living in near-squalor with the Antichrist, the most terrible thing happened.

Nadine, who, he now noticed, was wearing a worryingly similar black linen shirt, the sleeves hoisted up with the same metal suspenders, suddenly dropped her bag on to the sofa, kicked off her DM shoes, walked up to Phil, crouched down behind him and wrapped her lovely arms around his shoulders, squeezed him gently and planted a great big kiss on the back of his neck.

Dig's jaw dropped and his eyelids sprung apart. All of a sudden, everything fell into place; all of a sudden, everything made blindingly obvious, disgusting, foul and rancid sense. This *person*, this ridiculous, affected and contrived assortment of mannerisms, pretensions and vanities was Nadine's lover. This person who represented in one full set of human organs and limbs everything that Dig could possibly find to hate in another person, was sharing his bed with Nadine Kite – the same Nadine Kite who had by her own admission been a lush and lovely virgin as little as eight short weeks ago, waiting sensibly for the right time with the right person, prepared to hold out till her thirtieth year if necessary. And now here she was giving it out, every night and with bountiful generosity, he presumed, to the foulest man he'd ever met.

Dig couldn't really remember much about the rest of the weekend. He didn't let his surprise show and he didn't ask Nadine about her relationship with Phil. He acted like he'd been expecting to find her in this cohabitation. He played it cool, he played the role of the scruffy, innocuous schoolfriend from years gone by, up to see his old pal for the weekend, exchanging nostalgic tales from the past around the breakfast table with Phil and Nadine, messing around, making adolescent jokes and talking with overblown enthusiasm about his new job and his new car. In fact, cars were the only thing that he and Phil found in common that weekend, and Phil even took him for a drive around the block in his little MG Midget – the high spot in an otherwise wretched weekend.

Dig had no time alone with Nadine and he didn't get to play her any of his records. Phil seemed to think that the hunk of hash Dig had brought with him was some sort of *gift*, hijacked it entirely and smoked the whole lot, constructing painstakingly complicated little spliffs as if performing origami, the Rizlas all folded on the diagonal and the tip folded into some kind of triangle, which took fifteen minutes each to make and smoked like shit.

By the time Dig had decided that the whole weekend had sunk as low as it possibly could, and that all he had to do now was get through the night and then he could go home, things got even worse.

After an excruciating evening in a miserable pub watching Phil become more and more morose and distant as the night and the conversation ground on, Dig was installed, as he'd predicted, on the sofa in the living room. The sofa was spectacularly uncomfortable, the room Arctically cold and the quilt they'd given him to sleep under was thin and smelled of old people.

And then, just as he was starting to drift off, to forget where he was, something woke him up. A squeak. Followed by another squeak. Followed by yet another. Rhythmic squeaks, one after the other. And then a soft banging, in time with the squeaks. Bangsqueak, bangsqueak, bangsqueak . . .

Dig's heart fell into his toes as it dawned on him what he was listening to – the sounds of Nadine, *his* Nadine, being soundly and roundly porked by Philip Rich. He felt instantly nauseous and pulled a cushion over his head. The cushion, however, proved insufficient in the face of what was to come. After about fifteen minutes of a progressively louder and more insistent bangsqueak, Nadine started to wail – a whimpery sort of moan to start with, developing into a blood-curdling howl later. This continued for another five minutes or so and was then augmented by the voice of Philip Rich, whose loins were quite obviously fit to explode, judging by the rawness of his groaning.

The banging reached pneumatic-drill proportions, the

shouting began to crescendo and Dig stuck fingers in both his ears and started humming gently to himself in an attempt to drown out the noise. By the time he pulled his fingers from his ears and emerged from under the quilt, all was quiet again, except for the sound of the tap running in the bathroom and the toilet being flushed.

He heard Phil and Nadine's bedroom door close and turned sadly on to his side.

He really, really, hadn't wanted to hear that. That was, in fact, the last thing in the entire world he had ever wanted to hear. He felt sick. He felt dirty. He felt disgusting. He felt contaminated.

He felt as jealous as fucking hell.

He left fairly early the following morning, politely turning down Phil's offer of a lift and claiming that he'd rather get a cab, not put him to any trouble. He refused Nadine's offer to accompany him to the station also, as he really couldn't think of one thing that he would have to say to her if she did. He would either break down uncontrollably and start sobbing, 'Why? Why? Why? For the love of God, tell me why?' or he'd be sarcastic and unpleasant and scathing and make Nadine hate him. So he shook hands with Phil and thanked him for his hospitality, and Nadine saw him off from outside the flat.

'God, Dig,' she said, looking inexplicably happy, 'thanks so much for coming – it's been really, really nice having you here. I wasn't sure how things were going to work out, you know, with Phil being around but – he really liked you!' She was bursting over with excitement about this. 'He told me last night, when we were in bed . . .'

Dig shuddered at the thought.

'. . . He says you can come and stay any time, he thinks you're a really sweet bloke . . .'

Oh God – she was so thrilled and he was quite obviously expected to be thrilled, too. He smiled grimly and said something inconsequential and filthily dishonest along the lines of 'Yeah, he's a nice bloke,' before a well-timed taxi appeared at the head of the road and he stuck his arm out for it. There was just enough time for a quick peck on the cheek and a couple of niceties before the cab took him away and deposited him, like a half-demented hostage being thrown from a moving car after twenty-four hours of interrogation, at Manchester Piccadilly.

Dig never returned to Manchester, despite Nadine's numerous and regular invitations.

He did, however, meet up with the dreaded Phil on a few more occasions, when the happy couple returned to London for holidays and the odd weekend. Phil did appear to have a genuine fondness for Dig, a patronizing, big-brotherly sort of fondness which consisted of poking fun at him whenever possible and using him to magnify his own rather small reserves of humour and intelligence. Dig took this in his stride for Nadine's sake but after a while began making excuses and turning down invitations.

Nadine became a different person during those three years with Philip Rich. She appeared to have no opinions or ideas of her own, and it broke Dig's heart to think of that strong, determined, stubborn girl who'd turned him down all those years ago because there was more she wanted from life than the constraints of a relationship would allow, so easily surrendering herself and her independence to a waste of space like Phil.

Very infrequently Nadine would be in London on her own and on these occasions, Dig would always try his hardest to make her see sense, to convince her that it was *him*, not Phil, who should be the object of her fragrant affections. But she was in love – completely. Nadine would shrug his arm from her shoulder, slap his fingers from her bottom, push his lips from her mouth, but always with a sense of humour. There was never again any *serious* reference to the weekend of 12 September 1987 – it got used in moments of piss-take and teasing, it was treated as a rather amusing incident from their past, as a joke. And even when Nadine returned to London for good, her heart in tatters and her relationship with Phil categorically over, there was no looking back. He still tried his luck with the occasional affectionate gesture but something had grown between them in the time she was in Manchester that left such gestures impotent.

Gradually Nadine found herself again. Her career was a success story from the start, her wardrobe and disposition accumulated layers of colour day by day, and as the years went by she developed into one of the most extraordinary, incredible people Dig knew. Dig loved Nadine more than anyone – he loved her as much as he loved his mum, and that was saying something. The love he'd felt for her that weekend in 1987 when she'd broken his heart and hurt him more than he'd ever thought possible was just the building block for a lifetime of love.

Occasionally, even now, he would look at Nadine and something deep inside him would stir, something beyond platonic love, something *carnal*. But that was only occasional and he was a horny bastard, so it was inevitable really. He held her in the highest esteem and had the greatest respect for her. He loved her, cherished her and cared for her.

He would go so far as to say that he *adored* her.

But right now, at this precise moment in time, Dig Ryan thought that Nadine Kite was the stupidest, most ridiculous, idiotic, irrational, absurd and preposterous *fool* of a woman he had ever had the misfortune to know and love.

Phil?

Philip Rich?

Jesus Christ.

# CHAPTER SIXTEEN

As the day drew to a close, and Dig's frustration had matured nicely into a full-blown bad mood, he became overcome by a desperate desire to get steaming drunk. Images of ice-cold lagers and chunky tumblers of iced whiskey danced in front of his eyes and the scent of a good old-fashioned boozer tickled his nostrils. Anything to take his mind off Nadine and her ridiculous 'date'.

Nobody in the office had been interested in the suggestion of a post-work drink so Dig had attempted to track down Delilah to suggest that maybe they do something together. He was intending to tempt her with the offer of another gig, or maybe even two. But there'd been no answer at the Primrose Hill number all day, and by the time he got home at eight o'clock he'd given up on the idea.

As ever, there were any number of gigs and general music-biz schmoozathons he could have attended but, glancing out of his window at a wet and chilly Wednesday evening, he decided on reflection that his fridgeful of big Buds, two packets of Marlboro Lights and something on video that he'd taped earlier on in the week would make for a mighty pleasant night in, so he plumped up his cushions, stretched out his legs and settled down for a night of vegetating.

At about nine o'clock his stomach started growling and he leafed through his ever-expanding library of takeaway menus, deciding on a meat vindaloo and a prawn dopiaza from the Indian down the road.

Half an hour later his doorbell rang and he padded down his hall towards the entry phone clutching a twenty-pound note. 'Top floor,' he said into the mouthpiece, without waiting to be addressed. He opened his front door and listened to the sound of footsteps against the cold linoleum, resentful footsteps that grew slower and slower as they neared the dizzying heights of the top floor. Restaurant-delivery drivers hated him for making them take the stairs and always arrived at his door in very poor spirits indeed. Consequently Dig had prearranged his features into his usual disarming toothy smile, ready to be charming and placatory.

The smile fell off his face like a badly hung painting from a wall, however, when a dishevelled, small and extremely ugly Yorkshire Terrier suddenly bounded up the top flight of stairs and came careering round the corner and straight into his flat, leaving a trail of tiny grubby footprints all over his oatmeal seagrass.

'Digby!' echoed a female voice around the stairwell. 'You bad boy! Come back here this instant!' The female voice was followed a couple of seconds later by the form of Delilah, equally as dishevelled as the deliriously damp Digby and shaking out a half-furled and very soggy umbrella. 'Hi,' she said, stopping in her tracks when she saw Dig's shocked expression.

'Hi,' replied Dig, mindlessly folding his twenty-pound note into a square and tucking it into his pocket.

They stood like that for a moment or two, Delilah slowly dripping all over the floor, Digby running around Dig's flat in frenetic circles, while he himself stared in wonderment at Delilah.

'I was . . . er . . . expecting a curry,' said Dig, eventually, in the absence of anything more relevant to say.

'Oh,' said Delilah, 'and you got me instead!'

'Yeah,' laughed Dig, wondering whether Delilah was ever going to offer an explanation for her presence.

'So,' said Delilah, running her fingers through her damp hair and peering around the doorway, 'are you going to invite me in?'

Dig started and moved out of the way. 'Oh God,' he said, 'of course. Yeah. Come in. Come in.'

He held open the door for Delilah and caught his breath as her sheepskin coat flapped open briefly to reveal a thoroughly waterlogged cotton blouse sticking like clingfilm to her breasts. The collar was slightly askew, revealing just a hint of damp cleavage and the smell emanating from Delilah's dripping personage was quite overpoweringly delicious.

He had no idea what she was doing here, but she was a lot more welcome than a dopiaza.

# CHAPTER SEVENTEEN

That same evening, a quarter of a mile away to the east, Nadine finds herself sitting in a low-level seventies red-brick monstrosity loudly advertising 'sizzlin' steaks for £2.99' and going under the name of the Brecknock Arms.

She's only been here a few minutes but she's already sensing, very strongly, that she's made a mistake. This is all Dig's fault, she thinks to herself. *He* drove me to it.

She is sitting on a torn red vinyl barstool, wearing – inappropriately, she now feels – an emerald-green angora cardigan over a fuchsia crocheted dress, a silk poppy in her hair, staring at a beer- and ash-stained *swirl* of tan and orange carpeting, drinking a watered-down pint of Theakstones and wondering what has happened to the mysterious and debonair Phil of her memories, the Phil with the shiny black bob and the slick leather trousers and the elegant Roman nose.

The man now sitting in front of her is *so old*. His face has the crumpled-newspaper look of an over-the-hill rock star. His cheekbones, once such a feature, now give his face a desolate geography, and his teeth are in the sort of condition that would give a Californian nightmares. The once glossy black hair now hangs limply and finely over his ears and forehead in a style better suited to a man half his age, and his beautiful nose has acquired sharp lines and large open pores, overpowering his hollow face.

He has dark circles around his eyes and an earring with a crucifix hanging off it and he is wearing an old lambswool jumper, black jeans and a pair of football boots. There's an indistinguishable black-ink tattoo on his very white forearm that wasn't there before, and he smells faintly of fags and booze.

Looking back, Nadine supposes that Phil always had the kind of face that would age cruelly, but it still shocks her to see someone she last remembered as a young man so drained of his youth.

This is what Keith Richards would have looked like if he'd left the Stones twenty years ago and become a bus driver, she thinks to herself.

All Nadine's foolish, pathetic little fantasies about some over-the-top romantic reunion with her first love, her idiotic visions of their eyes meeting and twelve years disappearing, her naïve dreams of a charming, atmospheric pub, dazzling conversation and reignited passion, all crumpled and died within seconds of walking into the Brecknock Arms. Phil was supposed to look the same as she remembered, with maybe just a touch of distinguished grey at the temples. He wasn't supposed to look like this. The pub wasn't supposed to be like this.

This is a huge mistake. She is a fool.

Phil, on the other hand, had been speechless with joy to see Nadine walk in.

'Nadine Kite,' he'd drawled, grasping her hands, 'Nadine Kite. You fucking came, man. You're here! Look at you. You look great. I love your outfit, it's wild!' And then he looked like he was about to hug her, so Nadine deftly extricated herself from his grip and balanced herself on her barstool. He introduced her to the man behind the bar, a large, white-haired Scotsman wearing a nylon shirt and slightly too tight trousers. 'Murdo, this is Nadine Kite,' he said, beaming, 'we used to live together, at university. Murdo served me my first legal pint when I was eighteen.'

Murdo smiled grimly, gave Nadine's hand a good hard shake and turned round to remove a rather half-hearted ploughman's from the dumb waiter behind him, obviously as unsure as Nadine as to why they'd been introduced.

Phil insisted on paying for the first round, despite Nadine's best efforts to swing the balance of the evening towards a *Dutch* sort of thing by paying for them herself, and he then, worse still, insisted on carrying her drink to their table, thereby potentially setting the tone for a night of false expectations and crossed wires.

'So,' she says, keeping her body language neutral and taking a measured sip from her Theakstones, 'Phil. How've you been?'

'Oh, you know. Not bad.' He takes a noisy slurp of his beer and wipes his mouth with the back of one hand. 'You?' He looks nervous, as if he's scared of her.

'Fine,' she smiles, 'great, in fact.'

'So,' he says, 'what *inspired* you to get in touch again, after all this time – do I owe you money?' He laughs, extra loud to ensure that Nadine knows he's only joking, but it occurs to her that this is what he's really thinking.

'Well,' she replies, 'there was that fifty quid you took out of the piggy-bank! But seriously – I just wanted to find out how you were. What you've been up to. I just felt . . . I dunno . . . you spend so many years with someone, you're so close to someone and then suddenly, overnight, they're not in your life any more. They just get on a train and disappear for ten years. I wanted to hear your story, I suppose, the "Story of Philip Rich"!'

Phil exhales through tight lips and eyes her sceptically. 'You got all night?' he asks.

Nadine nods, enthusiastically. She senses a story here, something behind that look, and suddenly decides that the only way she is going to be able to get through this evening is by pretending that Phil isn't really a part of her history, isn't a bloke she lived with and loved ten years ago, but is in fact someone she's interviewing for a magazine or researching for a novel, that sort of thing. 'Start at the beginning,' she says. 'Start at the end of us . . .'

Nadine was disappointed to learn that Phil had gone back to London when they split up, gone back home and not to the remote Yorkshire village she'd been fondly imagining for some strange reason. He had come back, moved in with his parents, sold all his camera equipment, extended his bank loan and, with a shocking lack of business judgement, at the height of an international recession bought back the photographic lighting company he'd sold to fund his degree. For a song, he said, laughing wryly at his own stupidity.

He was made bankrupt six months later and had a nervous breakdown.

His life then, it seemed, took a series of very unexpected and out-of-character turns, and Phil spent most of the nineties trying to 'find himself' through one alternative route after another – crystals, meditation, Chinese herbs, Buddhism and Taoism. He moved from town to town and from woman to woman in search of happiness and fulfilment until his failure to find either led him to a drink problem and yet another broken relationship on a travellers' site in Warwickshire.

On the day he left the site, he walked three miles to Nuneaton in the rain clutching a bottle of Taunton Dry, walked into a launderette, pissed in a tumble-drier, swore at an old man and nicked the money he'd left out for his next wash. He stole £1.50 and for that he got a three-month prison sentence.

'Best thing that ever happened to me,' he said, 'cut through all my bullshit.'

'What do you mean?' said Nadine, who was as gripped by his story as any *Cutting Edge* documentary.

'Being inside – I dunno, I'd spent so much of my life convinced that there was some big reason for me being here. First I thought it was to be rich, to be the consummate businessman with the mobile phone and the sharp suit and the keen mind. That didn't work out. Then I thought I was supposed to be creative and stylish, on the cutting edge, you know, some really cool photographer-type with dark glasses and a sexy girlfriend.' He glanced at Nadine and raised his eyebrows at her. She laughed. 'And that, as you know, didn't work out *at all*. So I got into all that alternative stuff, thought maybe I was meant to be a great healer or something. And when that didn't make me happy I moved towards the whole lifestyle thing, thought that if I could immerse myself in another world, then that would make me special.

'It was like . . . it was like I was trying on personas for fit, d'you know what I mean? Seeing what suited me. And then discarding them when I realized that they made me look like a twat.' He laughed hoarsely.

'It took a stretch inside to make me understand that some people aren't here for any big reason – they're just here. And I realized then that I'm one of those people and that there's nothing actually wrong with that – d'you know what I mean? It's all right just to be a normal bloke, do a normal job and have normal friends. It was like a huge weight off my shoulders working that one out. And the pressure just sort of disappeared – it had been like this great big ugly parrot sitting on my shoulder all my life, and while I was inside it flew away.' Phil shrugged and lit a Rothman.

Nadine breathed out deeply. 'Fuck, Phil,' she said, 'I mean – I always knew that you wouldn't have had a boring life, but I can't believe how much has happened to you, how many changes you've made. It makes me feel so boring and . . . predictable. God – I haven't done *anything* with my life.'

'What about the photography? Still taking pictures?'

She nodded.

'Making a living from it?'

'Yeah,' she said, 'a very good living, actually.'

'Oh yeah?' His body language suddenly became very focused on Nadine. 'Got a nice flat and all that?'

'Yes,' nodded Nadine, proudly.

'That's great. I'm really pleased for you. What sort of work have you been doing?'

'Oh' – she shrugged, suddenly remembering what Phil's attitude towards commercial photography had been at university, and expecting him to judge her – 'editorial, mainly. *Him* magazine. Do you know it?'

'Yeah. Tits and arses, isn't it?'

'Well, there's a lot more to it than that. But I have been known to take the odd picture of an arse, yes.' She smiled, nervously, waiting for Phil to chastise her for selling out. But he didn't. He smiled, too, and then he almost laughed. Nadine breathed a sigh of relief. 'I thought you'd be horrified,' she said. 'I thought I was about to get a lecture about the evils of commerce!'

'Nah,' said Phil, 'I think it's great. Really great. Christ, I was a right wanker at Manchester, wasn't I? So pretentious. Who the fuck did I think I was?' He laughed then, properly and, as the conversation progressed, it became more and more obvious that Phil wasn't the same person she'd known all those years ago, at all. He was ten years older, at least a stone thinner, and seemed to have a completely different set of priorities.

'So,' she said, 'when did you move back to London again?'

'Straight from the nick. March 1997.'

'Back to your parents?'

'Yeah.'

'And you're still there?'

Phil shook his head. 'Nah,' he said, 'nah. I've got a place in Finsbury Park now. A Peabody flat. My . . . er . . . grandparents sublet it to me.'

Nadine was confused. 'But you were at your parents' when I phoned their number?'

Phil shook his head, again. 'Nah. I was at mine, in Finsbury Park. I took the number with me when I went.'

'But . . . but . . . didn't your parents want to keep their number?'

Phil put down his pint and took a deep breath. He stared deep into Nadine's eyes, hardened his mouth and clenched his jaw.

'No. They don't need their number any more. They're dead.'

The bluntness of his response took Nadine somewhat by surprise. 'I see,' she said, having managed to train herself out of the knee-jerk response of apologizing for the bereaved's misfortune. 'How long? How long have they been dead?'

Phil shrugged and took a slug of his beer. 'A year,' he said, 'a year and a bit.'

'What? Both of them?'

'Uh-huh.'

'They died together?'

'Yeah.'

'Oh God – how awful. What happened?'

'You don't want to know.'

'Yes I do.'

'It's not nice.'

'Tell me,' said Nadine, her curiosity now stimulated beyond her control. 'I can take it.'

Phil sighed and fell into a thoughtful silence, staring into the depths of his pint. Nadine thought he wasn't going to tell her, but eventually he looked up and opened his mouth, gazing into the distance while he waited, like a sluggish standpipe, for the words to come.

'My mum had lung cancer,' he began, 'she'd fought it for three years. They thought she was dead at one time, performed last rites and everything. But my mum wasn't having any of that. You remember my mum? She was a right old battleaxe and she fought it. And the tumour just kind of *dissolved*. They X-rayed her lungs one day and the tumour had gone. Everyone said it was a miracle. She said it was the evil thoughts she'd sent it – she called it Beelzebub, that lump. She hated it.' He smiled wryly. 'She reckoned that's what killed it – none of this positive-thinking malarkey, none of all that alternative stuff that I was into. Anyway, she makes a full recovery, and then two months later my dad's diagnosed with breast cancer.

Nah,' he said, 'I didn't know men could get it either, but they can. Here.' He indicated his pectorals. 'So, he's in hospital, having tests, operations, treatments, just like my mum, and it's looking bad for a while – the lump's quite big and they have to remove most of the flesh from around his chest, they've taken away his nipple and everything – it was a fucking mess' – he winced – 'but a year later and he's got the all-clear from the hospital and he's told he can get on with his life.

'So, after, you know, everything the pair of them have been through, they decide that they deserve a bit of a break, a bit of time away in the sunshine. So they cash in some Premium Bonds and book themselves a two-week cruise around the Mediterranean – it was off-season, so it wasn't too pricey. And I wave them off at Portsmouth and away they go. I'll never forget their faces on that deck – they looked so happy and, you know, excited.

'Anyway. And this is all according to witnesses, you know, obviously I wasn't there, but this is what happened, apparently. Mum had had a bad sardine, or something – she wasn't used to that sort of food – and she had a dodgy gut, you know, puking up, the squits, the works. So she's hanging off the side of the boat one night, puking her guts up while my dad's stroking her back and all that. Suddenly the ship lurches to one side, quite violently, and Mum's thrown to the other side of the boat, puking up as she goes, and there's puke absolutely everywhere. She's landed by some steep steps down to the next deck, metal steps, you know, like you get on boats, and knocked her head off one of those pipe things, and when Dad sees the blood starting to drip down her face he comes legging it across the deck towards her, not noticing that the floor's all slick with vomit.

'So' – Phil took a deep breath and slurp of beer before continuing – 'he's legging it across all this vomit, and he slips, and as he slips the boat lurches again and he's gone, according to someone who saw it all, he's gone *gliding* like a fucking ice-skater over the floor and then sort of tipped over, head first, through the door-way leading to the staircase and straight down those metal steps, head over heel over head, over heel, bang bang bang bang bang bang . . .'

He stopped again for a second to compose himself. Nadine held her breath. 'He copped it immediately, according to the ship's doctor. The fall snapped his spine. He didn't suffer . . .'

'Oh God. That's awful,' gasped Nadine, 'and what about your mother? What happened to your mother?'

Phil exhaled loudly. 'Well, she was in a bit of a state, obviously, what with my dad being dead and everything, and she was still puking up. The doctor sticks a plaster on her head where it's cut and gives her a sedative and something for her stomach, and she's sent back to her cabin. When the doctor knocked on her door early the next morning there was no answer so he got the steward bloke to let him in, and there she was, lying in bed' – he took another swig of his drink and looked at Nadine – 'dead.'

'What! But how?!'

'It was the knock on the head. It was worse than they'd thought. A blood clot, apparently. She would've died in her sleep. She wouldn't have suffered, either. At least neither of them suffered.'

‘Oh, Phil. You poor thing. That’s one of the worst stories I’ve ever heard.’

‘I told you, didn’t I? Told you it was bad. My dad died from slipping over in my mum’s puke. Nice, isn’t it?’

‘Oh, Phil’ – Nadine instinctively grabbed his hand across the table – ‘you poor, poor thing.’

‘Yeah,’ he muttered, ‘well.’

‘So. You couldn’t bear to live in the house any more after they went?’

‘Eh?’

‘You know. Your parents’ house . . .?’

‘Oh. Right. No. It . . . er . . . I did live there for a while after they died. It was mine, legally. They left it to me.’

‘What. And you sold it?’

‘Erm . . . no. Not exactly. I . . . I . . . Oh God. This is another bad thing, you know. The house. Another bad thing.’

‘Go on,’ soothed Nadine.

‘You sure you want to hear this?’

Nadine nodded. ‘If you’re sure you want to tell me.’

‘I haven’t really talked about all this before, properly, you know.’

‘Well, maybe you should.’

Phil sighed and took a deep breath. ‘Yeah,’ he said, ‘you’re right. I might as well tell you everything then, eh? Since you’re listening.’ He stopped and stared at her then, intently. ‘You know something,’ he said, ‘you’re still as beautiful as you ever were. Even more beautiful, if anything.’

Nadine blushed and looked away, embarrassed by the unexpected compliment and Phil’s piercing gaze.

‘Sorry,’ he smiled, ‘sorry. I shouldn’t have said that. Anyway. The house. I met this girl, Mandy, when I was inside. She was a visitor. Came to see me every day. We were both in our late thirties, both single, both a bit lost and lonely. She was such a great girl, a real laugh, game for anything, you know what I mean? She kind of brought me out of myself, gave me self-confidence, that sort of thing. It was different this time – she was a real person and I wasn't looking for anything from her, I wasn't looking for this mystical life any more. I just wanted to settle down with her, maybe a kid or two, an ordinary life. Anyway, when I got out we got engaged. I wanted to do it properly – the traditional way. My parents were made up, her parents were made up, everyone was over the moon. She was working for a computer company, technical stuff, and I'd just started working for this company, erecting marquees, earning a fair bit, and we opened a joint bank account, started putting away a couple of hundred quid a month. Saving up for the wedding. She wanted a big wedding. That was her dream. Big white dress and flower arrangements and string quartets – she wanted the lot, not just what our parents could afford. I wasn't bothered, myself, but I went along with it. Anything Mandy wanted was fine by me. So we're both working all the hours, saving every month, staying in, watching this money growing slowly, day by day.

'After a year, we had five grand in that bank account. Then Mandy gets a promotion – becomes a programmer – and suddenly she's earning, three, four, five times as much as me, and she's putting that much more in the account. A few months later and there's twelve grand in it. We'd reached our goal, we can afford the silver-service dinner and the master of ceremonies and the real champagne and the honeymoon in Antigua. Mandy's really excited. We set a date, we send out the invites, we book the honeymoon, the reception. It's all systems go.

'Then Mandy phones me at work one day – she's going off to pick up her wedding dress after work. It was costing two grand, this thing, it's all she could talk about – the dress this, the dress that, the dress the other. This dress was the most important thing in the world to her. Anyway. I'm on my way home that night, and I happen to be driving past this dress shop, you know, where she's picking her dress up from, and I decide to pop in, give her a lift. So, I walk into this shop and the assistant tells me, "Oh no, Miss Taylor, she's already left. She left about ten minutes ago. Are you the groom?" "Yes, I say, I'm the groom." "Well," she says, "maybe you should make sure she's all right, she seemed a bit" – what was it she said? – she seemed a bit *agitated*, yeah, agitated when she left." "Agitated?" I say. "Yeah," she says, "a bit upset."

'So, I suddenly get this really bad feeling. You know how they say – someone walking over your grave? Well, that's what it was like. So I goes legging it from this shop, and it was summer so it was still light, and I'm running towards the river as fast as I can – I don't know why, I've just got this feeling. And then, as I get towards Putney Bridge, dodging the traffic, running between the cars, I see her, half-way up the bridge. And I'm shouting her name, over and over – "Mandy! Mandy!" She's got her dress on, this huge wedding dress, and a big veil and tiara and everything. And she's just standing there, staring into the river. I'm calling her name but she doesn't turn around, and I'm running towards her, towards the bridge. And as I'm running I'm watching her, like it's in slow motion, watching her lift up this big petticoat skirt of her dress and climbing on to the bridge, on to the actual stone-wall thing. She's standing there on the wall and staring into the water, just staring.' Phil stopped talking for a while and Nadine didn't try to fill the silence.

'I'm nearly on the bridge by now and I'm still calling out her name, and then, just as I set foot on the bridge, she turns towards me and I can see that she's smiling. She's smiling straight at me, a strange sort of smile. She slowly lifts up her veil and throws it back over her head, and then she turns back towards the water, and I'm running and running, and even though it feels like she's doing all this really slowly, she can't be because I don't get there in time, and as I'm running towards her I see her reach up on to her tiptoes, and then she puts her arms out, like this, out by her sides, and then . . . then she just lets herself fall, she doesn't jump, just lets herself fall, face first into the water, and all the fabric in her dress makes her sort of float down, like a parachute. And I stop, just for a second, I stop running and I turn to look in the water, because, and this sounds really bad, but because it looks so extraordinary, *she* looks so extraordinary, floating there, in the black water, in her big white dress. She looks like a swan or something, you know? It was *surreal* . . .

'So – obviously I'm straight in there, straight in the water, but I'm not a very good swimmer, as you might remember, I'm a doggy-paddler, and it's taking me ages to get to her, and the tide's quite strong, and I'm flailing around, calling her name, swallowing loads of this rancid disgusting water, and she just seems to be floating away from me – the closer I get, the further she gets – and I'm choking by now, I've got so much water in my pipes and I'm getting really tired. But I keep on swimming towards her, I can still see this white blob, and it's not moving, and I feel like I've been in the water for hours now. Then suddenly this boat appears, it's a speedboat and there's some posh people on it, sunning themselves and drinking champagne, and I can hear the engine being turned off and the boat slowing down, and then someone's dragging me out of the water and I'm saying "Mandy. Get Mandy." "There's no one there," they're saying. "She's wearing a white dress," I tell them. But we went round and round in circles looking for her, all round that part of the river, for about an hour, and she wasn't there. She was gone.' Phil fell silent again.

'Her body washed up in Rotherhithe, three days later.'

Nadine gasped.

'We still don't know why she did it. Nobody knows why she did it. Everyone who knew her said she was happy, everyone said she really loved me, that she was so excited about the wedding, about the future. It doesn't make any sense. You know, that was nearly a year ago, and every day that goes by I want to talk to her, even if it's only for a minute, just so I can ask her why. It's the worst thing in the world not to know why. I know how, I know where and I know when – I just need to know why. That's all.'

'Oh God. Phil. I couldn't imagine . . . how can you . . . it must have been just awful . . . I mean . . .'

'It's all right,' he smiled, 'you're not supposed to know what to say. Don't worry. No one knows what to say. There's nothing anyone can say . . . That was a year ago. Then, like I told you, a couple of months later, my parents died. I was a bit of a mess for a while, as you can probably imagine, didn't really have much faith in anything, nearly lost my job, messed up a lot of friendships, a lot of drinking, drugs, self-pitying, you know. I was wallowing in it, really.

'And then one morning, earlier this year, I woke up and the sun was shining and I could hear kids playing outside in the street, and I thought, Phil, you're nearly forty years old and what have you got? Nothing, I thought, nothing except this house and this body. That's all you've got. So I decided to take more care of them, and I started doing up my parents' house and looking after my body. No drugs, booze only at the weekends, a healthy diet. I bought myself a recipe book and I learned to cook – you know, Indian veg stuff, pasta, stir-fries – healthy stuff. I bet you can't believe that, eh! And I spent a fortune on my folks' house, every penny I earned went into that house. I put central heating in, a new bathroom, I knocked through from the front room to the back room and put these big adjoining doors in between. I chucked out all their old furniture and bought all new, stripped off all the wallpaper, painted the whole house, every room, every door. I replaced the door-handles with these really expensive brass ones, pulled up the carpets and polished the floorboards. It took me six months but it was the most rewarding thing I'd ever done. And it took my mind off the . . . bad stuff. When it was finished I put on my best clothes and I just sort of walked around it for ages, you know, imagining that it was somebody else's house, trying to imagine it through somebody else's eyes. And it looked fantastic! You should have seen it, Nadine. It was immaculate.

'So. I start feeling better about myself, you know, I'm getting back some self-respect, and there's this girl at work, a secretary at the office, called Fiona. I've always thought she was really nice but I'd never have done anything about it before, would have been too scared she'd turn me down, humiliate me. But one day I'm in the office, talking to Payroll about something that's gone wrong with my overtime, and on my way out I bump into Fiona, and I suddenly find myself asking her out and she's saying yes! Just like that. So we arrange to have a drink on the Friday night. It's the first time I've been out for six months, and I'm in a bit of a state getting ready, you know, not being able to decide what to wear, that sort of thing. So I'm running around, I'm scared I'm going to be late, and I just kind of run out the front door and slam it behind me.

'So anyway. Me and Fiona, we're drinking and chatting, and I'm not doing what I'm doing here with you, I'm not telling her about everything that's happened, I'm keeping it light-hearted, keeping it lively, making her laugh, asking her all about herself. You know, being the *other* Phil. And it's going really well. We go off and have dinner and I order some champagne, and she's really impressed, and for the first time in months I'm feeling like a human being again. This girl, this Fiona, she really likes me, and I start feeling like I like myself, too. Before we know it, it's one in the morning and we're both a bit pissed, so I suggest that she comes back to mine to order a cab. I really want her to see my house, I want her to be the first person to see how beautiful it looks, how hard I've worked. So she says, yeah, that would be lovely and then she says maybe she could stay the night, and I'm thinking, Christ, what a result, and I'm so excited I'm almost running home. We're laughing and we're chatting and we're holding hands, and as we get towards the house, there's this smell in the air, it's acrid, it catches in the back of the throat. And then' – he stopped and pointed at Nadine's empty glass – 'd'you want another drink, by the way?'

Nadine shook her head vigorously. 'No,' she said, 'no thanks. I'm fine. Carry on.'

He nodded. 'OK,' he said. 'Yeah. So. There's this smell in the air, and as we get closer to home there's smoke, too. Thick, thick clouds of black smoke. We turn the corner into my road and the street's wall-to-wall fire engines – dozens of them – and I start walking faster now, really fast, and Fiona's running behind me in these high heels, saying, "It's not your house, is it, Phil, it's not your house?" And you know what? It *was* my house. It was *my* fucking house, man. Gutted, from top to bottom. All the windows gone, all the furniture, fixtures, fittings, everything. Gone. It was a shell.'

'Oh my God,' cried Nadine. 'How? What happened?'

'Huh.' He shrugged. 'It was my fault. I left a fag burning, didn't I? Can you believe it? One fag, one measly little fag.' He took one out of the packet in front of him and held it under Nadine's gaze. 'Something that small, that *puny*, it's hard to believe. If you'd seen what it did to my house – to three storeys and four bedrooms, and the way it just ate up all those months of hard work. It's frightening,' he said.

'What did you do?'

'Well, that's the thing, right. I don't know what happened after that. Not really. Only what other people have told me. I think I must have gone into some sort of shock. Fiona took me to the hospital, and they treated the shock, and then she took me home with her and got in touch with my grandparents, who came and picked me up and took me back with them to Bournemouth. I don't really remember any of this. I was there for three weeks apparently – it was summer, I can remember vague things like the beach and the seagulls, the fat people with sunburn, the smell of frying onions, the sound of fruit machines, but I can't remember any *events*, I can't remember what I was actually doing there. I reckon I had some kind of breakdown because I became quite unmanageable apparently, talking to myself, disappearing for hours on end, not washing, not eating. I was a bit of a nutter by all accounts and eventually my grandparents couldn't take it any more, so they sent me to a hospital.

'I was there for three months and they gave me pills and they gave me psychotherapy and they gave me counselling, all that bollocks, and then they sent me home. My grandparents kicked another tenant out of their old Peabody flat and got it ready for me. I've been there for a couple of months, you know, trying to live a normal life, getting to know people.'

'What about Fiona?' asked Nadine. 'What happened to Fiona?'

Phil shrugged. 'Never heard from her again. I got my job back at the marquee company, but she wasn't working there any more. Got a job in the City or something.'

'So, you're all alone?'

'Well,' he said, 'I met this girl called Jo a couple of weeks ago, down the pub with all her mates, and we got talking. Turns out she was a student, and her and all her student mates ended up coming back to mine because most of that lot live with their parents or in tiny rented flats with no living rooms. They come round most nights now – all of them, just for a drink and a smoke and somewhere to hang out. It's nice for them to have somewhere to come and I like having them around. It makes me feel like I'm not all alone, even though none of them really talk to me or anything. I think they think I'm a bit boring, you know?' he smiled. 'A bit of a weird old fart. But I don't mind, really. The company's nice. I feel safe. I don't feel safe when I'm on my own. Not really. Not any more. When I'm on my own I feel like if I look out the window the streets could be deserted and everyone could have disappeared and I'd be the only person left in the whole world, d'you know what I mean? The only person left . . .

'Everything feels so – so – ephemeral sometimes. I don't know what's real and what's not. It's like, I wasn't expecting you to come tonight, not really. I thought maybe I'd imagined your phone call, imagined *you*. But you came! You're here, man. And it's so great. D'you know something?' he continued happily. 'I don't care what we do tonight. I don't care what we talk about, and I don't care where we talk about it. Just so long as you're actually here, in front of me, where I can see you. That's all. That's all I want.'

Phil fell into another silence then and Nadine fished her purse out of her bag. 'Let me get you a drink,' she said, resting her hand on his shoulder, her heart close to bursting with sympathy and pity. Poor, poor Phil.

'Great,' he said, 'thanks.'

At the bar, Murdo leaned towards Nadine. 'Everything all right?' he asked in his Highland growl.

'Yes,' said Nadine lightly, 'of course.'

'You better be careful with that lad,' he said, swivelling his eyes in the direction of Phil's slouched figure, 'he's had a hard life, you know?'

'Yes. I know. He's just been telling me.'

'He's trouble, that one, so you better look out for him. He dis'nae need any more trouble in his life than he's already had. Anyway, what'll it be?'

Nadine took the drinks back to their table and Phil looked up at her gratefully. 'Thanks,' he said, 'thank you, Nadine Kite.'

And Nadine smiled back at him nervously and thought to herself that she was not just walking but positively *sprinting* up a path in her life that she was never, ever supposed to take, and then she thought to herself how even if she tried to turn around now, this very minute, and get off the path, it was already too late, far too late to ever find her way back.

# CHAPTER EIGHTEEN

Delilah hadn't arrived at Dig's empty handed. As well as her tiny and unattractive dog, she had produced from somewhere, God knows where, a pair of enormous and ominously bulging suitcases.

'You going somewhere?' Dig asked, eyeing the cases with deep suspicion.

Delilah smiled and shrugged. 'Well,' she said, 'that's the thing. It's not really working out for us at Marina's. I've . . . er . . . I've just had a huge row with her.'

'With Marina? What about?'

'Oh God. Nothing. Nothing, really. She's just such a pious, sanctimonious old cow. I don't know why I ever thought it would be a good idea to stay with her. I'd have stayed in a hotel, you know, but I can't because of the dog. And *then* she threatened to tell my mum I was back in town, so I just told her to fuck off, packed a bag and walked.

'You should have seen her face. It was as if she'd never heard the word "fuck" before. I tell you, there's little in life worse than a frustrated nun, there really isn't . . .'

There was a brief silence as Dig absorbed this information, waiting tensely for the inevitable.

'So, anyway, I – er – was sort of hoping that me and Digby could maybe crash here for a while. We won't be any trouble, I promise you and we'll be gone as soon as we can find somewhere else to go. It's just that there's no one else for me to turn to right now, what with me not talking to my mum and my brothers all with houses full of children and everything, and it would only be for a few days. And Digby's fully house-trained and very quiet.'

The tiny creature suddenly threw himself on to Dig's corduroy sofa and began yapping incredibly loudly.

' . . . Well, usually he's quiet. He's just excited to be somewhere new. I'll cook for you and keep the place tidy. Not,' she said, peering around the door-way into Dig's spotless flat, 'that it actually needs it. So. What do you think?' She beamed at him.

Dig was speechless for a second, his head telling him that there wasn't enough room in his flat for a girl and a dog and two suitcases full of their belongings, while his heart told him that there was a devastatingly beautiful woman who he might well be in love with on his doorstep begging most appealingly for a place to stay and of course he should invite her in. As he grappled with his dilemma, the awkward silence was broken by the buzz of the doorbell.

'*Takeaway*,' said a muffled Indian voice.

'Top floor,' said Dig, suddenly flustered by the preponderance of issues bearing down on him all at once and the thought of so many people, animals and large objects jostling for space on his tiny landing. Something would have to give.

'Right,' he said, turning back to Delilah, 'I'd better give you a hand with these cases.'

'Oh,' squeaked Delilah, 'really? I can stay? Oh thank you! Thank you so much.' And then she threw her arms around Dig's neck and hugged him hard.

Dig's arms crept slowly around her waist and through

the dampness of her coat he could feel the shape of her backbone, the softness of the flesh that covered her hips, the squashiness of her breasts against his chest and the heat of her body emanating through her clothes and as her lips found his cheek and pressed themselves against his flushed skin, Dig decided that this arrangement could actually work out after all.

# CHAPTER NINETEEN

Nadine is on *at least* her fifth large tumbler of vodka.

And they've been *extremely* large. Equivalent to two or three pub measures. She started off drinking them with some lime cordial she found in the kitchen but gave up on the mixer after the first couple. Since then, she's been drinking them neat – without ice. She can't actually taste the vodka any more.

She'd said no, at first, when Phil had invited her back to his flat after the pub closed. Despite the fact that they'd ended up having a fairly pleasant evening together, helped along considerably by the four pints of Theakstones she'd consumed, the weight of the dreadful unfolding of events in Phil's life had started to make itself felt around her temples and she wanted to get away before things got any heavier.

But he'd looked so deflated by her refusal, almost like he was going to cry, and all of a sudden she'd thought, 'Oh my God, he's an orphan, he's got no one.' And before she knew what was happening she was agreeing to come back for a smoke, just to assuage her conscience.

Phil's flat was in the Peabody estate off the Holloway Road, up three flights of echoing concrete stairs, and very strangely decorated, like an old people's home. 'I haven't done anything with it since I moved in. You can probably guess why.' He smiled ironically.

There were about half a dozen people already in his

draughty living room when they walked in, listening to Gomez and sitting under a thick fleece of smoke. None of them looked up when Phil walked in, except for one tall, skinny girl with waist-length hair and enormous breasts straining beneath a child's T-shirt who unfolded herself from a cushion on the floor to greet him.

'Nadine, this is Jo. Jo, this is Nadine. Me and Nadine used to live together at university.'

'Oh yeah,' said Jo, handing Phil the bum end of a spliff and lowering herself back on to her cushion, 'didn't know you went to university.'

Nadine looked around her. Everyone in this room was so young and so distant, she felt almost as if she didn't exist in their eyes, as if she was of no consequence – which was ridiculous considering the fact that they were a bunch of students and she was a successful photographer with a sports car, a flat and a £40,000 commission. But if she was going to stand even the slightest chance of enjoying herself with these people, then she was going to have to get a lot more drunk than she was right now.

Phil led her to the kitchen and fixed her what would be the first of many vodkas.

An hour and five large vodkas later and Nadine is suddenly feeling very brave and self-confident, and all the incredibly strong spliff she's smoked has given her surroundings a slightly surreal edge. She feels like she's in some kind of lovely floaty dream, and now Phil feels like one of those strange characters who wander in and out of your dreams sometimes, pretend-people who you don't know in real life – made-up people.

She's been using Phil as a sounding-board for the last half an hour, chewing his ear off about Dig and Delilah and what a mistake Dig's making and how he won't pay any attention to what Nadine has been trying to tell him *for his own good*, and how he's going to end up getting his heart broken all over again, and Phil, despite having so many problems of his own, real problems, big problems, has turned out to be a great, great listener, agreeing wholeheartedly with everything Nadine says and endearing himself to her more than he could possibly imagine in the process. He met Dig a few times in London during holidays, so Nadine respects his opinion. He also has a large personal supply of grass and is being very generous with it, letting Nadine roll spliff after spliff while they chat.

And now he's smiling at her and ferreting around his jeans pockets looking for something. He reaches into his pocket and brings out a tiny Indian pillbox encrusted with multicoloured stones. 'You sound like you could do with a little something to *lift* your spirits,' he says, pulling the lid off the tiny box.

'What's that?' Nadine asks.

'Little miracles,' he smiles. 'One of these, and the whole world will seem like a better place.'

Nadine's eyes open wide. 'Eeeeeeeee?' she asks, thinking that even though that's what it looks like, it can't be, because Phil was always so anti-anything connected with rave culture.

Phil nods and hands her a pill. 'You might just want half,' he says, 'if it's your first.'

'Oh no,' she says 'let me have a whole one.' Despite having lived what she considers to be a fairly colourful life, Nadine's never done an E before and she swallows it, gleefully and quickly and waits for it to take effect.

Half an hour later and she doesn't really feel any

different. She's much more stoned, that's for certain, and much more pissed, and maybe that's why she's suddenly feeling so strangely drawn to Phil, suddenly feeling like she'd like to touch him, hug him, maybe even kiss him.

'So, you must be very muscly now, I suppose, under that baggy top, *erecting* all those big, heavy marquee things.' She pulls at the fabric of his lambswool sleeve. She's feeling very brazen, very forward, very *physical*.

He laughs. 'Nah,' he says, 'not really. Still as puny as ever.'

'Are you sure you're not really a *drug-dealer*?' she asks, jokingly, even though she's secretly started to think that maybe he is. It would explain all these students in his flat and the abundance of strong weed and the pill she's just swallowed.

'Nah,' he smiles. And then, suddenly and most unexpectedly, he turns and stares into her eyes and says, 'God, Nadine, you're so fucking beautiful.'

Nadine chokes on her vodka. 'Oh,' she says, 'don't be daft.'

Phil shakes his head very slowly and stares at her. 'I'm not being daft,' he says. 'You're fucking gorgeous.' He leans in towards her as he says this, so that his face is only a couple of millimetres from hers. He locks his eyes on to hers, and she starts to feel vaguely uncomfortable but strangely excited. He pulls his face away from hers unhurriedly, gently takes the spliff from between her stiff fingers, puts it to his lips, inhales deeply, inhales again and disposes of it in an empty beer can. 'And you've really kept your body in good nick.' His gaze slowly pans up and down her, eating her up.

Nadine feels a shudder run up and down her spine in

time with the rhythm of his eyes. She feels exposed and titillated at the same time. She blushes.

'You've still got those great tits,' he says, staring at them like they were a pair of juicy rare fillet steaks, 'those perfect, perfect tits. Just the right size, right shape. They haven't drooped at all. Some women's tits start *drooping*, you know.'

Any feminist leanings that Nadine may once have had desert her. She knows that she should, in all decency, slap him round the face and storm off with some rant or other about how she will not be spoken to like that by a sexist pig like him. But her ego is suffering from malnutrition and she laps up his graceless compliment like it was vintage wine. She is grateful to him for thinking that she has great tits and actually says *thank you*.

'Thank you,' she says, smiling coyly.

Nadine's head is spinning; a combination of booze, spliff and too many knee-trembling compliments. Not to mention the Class A chemical currently swishing around her brain cells.

Inside Nadine's drug-and-alcohol-addled head, Phil is now larger than life – he is a legend. Phil has lived a big life, full of change and adversity. He has battled with depression. He has been to prison. He has lost his parents and the love of his life killed herself. His house burned down. He's had two nervous breakdowns. He has been accepted into the homes and worlds of so many different people. He has taken risks and lived life according to his heart. He has reinvented himself and pulled himself out of the quagmire time after time. He is strong and resilient. He is brave and unpredictable.

He is everything that Nadine is not.

He is better than Nadine.

And all of a sudden, through the blur of her thoughts, Nadine realizes that this is what's been wrong with every man she's been out with since she and Phil split up. None of them have been better than her. They've all been inferior – at least in her mind – and she has been unable to respect them. Weak, weak men, they seemed to follow her around. It was like she was giving out some ultrasound, audible only to men with gaps in their lives and low self-esteem.

She's had enough of weak men. She wants a strong man, a man like Phil. Phil isn't perfect – he is far from perfect – he is as flawed as it is possible for a man to be. But he is strong. He is special. He's different. He's exciting.

If Nadine was sober and straight and happier, if Nadine hadn't just taken an E, she would be thinking exactly the opposite; she would probably call it a night now, start making her excuses, get her coat, order a cab, go home, because it is becoming increasingly obvious what sort of turn this evening is about to take, and there is a sensible, wise part of Nadine deep down somewhere beneath all the narcotics which knows that she shouldn't be following this path, knows that Phil has always managed to manipulate her and control her and that if she stays now she is more or less bound to let him do it again.

But she is not sober and she is not straight and she is not happy, so she smiles at Phil instead and thinks how much she's enjoying herself and how she still loves him in a funny kind of way, and how, if he was to try to kiss her, she probably wouldn't fight him off.

As if reading her thoughts, Phil puts one hand on her

shoulder and the other over her hand, and his fingers are moving over her flesh. Nadine would like to touch him, too, feel his flesh, his bones, his heartbeat through his jumper. She grabs hold of his hand and traces her fingertips over the smooth, hairless skin, skin she hasn't touched for twelve years, skin she used to love so much – and it's beautiful, so beautiful to be with this man, this man who she's missed so much, who's changed so much, who's *lived* so much and who's turned out to be so *beautiful* and full of kindness and warmth, and just to be able to touch him, touch him and feel the blood running through his veins, and he's been through so much these last years, and now she wants to hold him in her arms and look after him and protect him and be even closer to him and share herself with him and have *sensations* with him and just to *love him* like she used to . . .

'I think,' says Phil, stroking the side of Nadine's neck, 'we should – go somewhere else – a bit quieter, y'know? Let's go somewhere?' Phil reaches out to touch her hair again. He strokes it and then brings the back of his hand down softly against her cheek. It is such a tender gesture that Nadine immediately turns to blancmange inside and knows that she has to do this, that this is what life is all about, after all, people and being with people and loving people, and that it's not wrong, it's all right, it's all right, because Phil is good and Phil is beautiful and it will be beautiful and it's the right thing to do, the most perfect thing to do, just to love someone . . .

'I want to get to know you all over again, Nadine Kite. I want to be alone with you. Come with me.' He holds out his hand for her.

'Where are we going?'

'Just come with me.'

There is something so surreal about all this, about Phil, this flat, this evening, that Nadine is starting to feel like she's in a film or something, that none of this is really happening to her.

She takes his hand and follows him.

## CHAPTER TWENTY

Dig was trying to be chilled out but was finding it very hard. Delilah had just committed the greatest domestic crime known to man. There were many domestic crimes – not replacing the toilet roll when it was finished, not rinsing things before putting them in the dishwasher, not putting lids back on things, not rewinding videos and not plumping up cushions – but that one, just now – leaving CDs out of their boxes – was the worst, by far. He'd tried so hard not to say anything. It had been his suggestion, after all, that she choose some music to put on. But he'd just meant for her to select one CD and put it on. Instead, she'd been completely overwhelmed by his shelves and shelves of alphabetically organized CDs and was now playing DJ, excitedly pulling one plastic case after another off the shelves. Dig lost the battle to control his neurosis.

'Erm – you couldn't put those back in their boxes, could you?'

'Sure,' replied Delilah, distractedly, pulling some shit by Vengaboys off the shelf and sticking it in the machine. She slid the Shania Twain album she'd just listened to back into its case and seemed satisfied that this act constituted a reasonable response to Dig's request.

Dig sat back and sighed. His CD shelves were full of music that he didn't like. He got it all free. Every day he came home with a handful of new CDs that he was never going to listen to. He used to consider these free CDs to be a perk of the job, but over the last couple of years British pop music had slipped tragically and dramatically into a cesspool of bland Euro-bollocks music-by-numbers, and Dig was now starting to feel that these freebies were more of an encumbrance. Steps, for Christ's sake. B*witched. Billie. Britney Spears. How had this happened? What sort of children were we breeding?

He winced as he heard the opening bars to 'Boom Boom Boom Boom' and then stared in horror at Delilah, who was jauntily bouncing up and down and humming under her breath. She couldn't really like this sort of thing, could she?

'This is great,' she beamed at him.

Oh dear God, thought Dig.

'I've really lost touch with music over the years. I've only bought one CD this year: Robbie Williams, *I've Been Expecting You*. Which is brilliant, of course! But Alex likes jazz, on the whole. So that's what we listen to. But this new stuff is *great*, isn't it? So simple and such good tunes. Good old-fashioned pop music!' She grinned and turned away and began rifling through Dig's shelves to find something else dreadful to put on.

Dig dropped his head into his hands. Nadine had been right. Delilah *wasn't* the same girl he remembered from years ago. Phil Collins would have been a *relief* right now. The old Delilah had thrown empty beer cans at Bucks Fizz on the telly and used a selection of well-chosen swearwords to express her disgust at such blandness and unoriginality. The old Delilah had stalked around the Holy T raining disdain upon screaming Duranies, pulling posters off notice-boards and peeling stickers off desks. The old Delilah had sat on his shoulders waving a pint of snakebite in the air while they watched the Cure and Echo and the Bunnymen and the Smiths at lager-soaked venues all over London.

The new Delilah had the musical taste of a twelve-year-old girl.

The passage of time could do cruel things to people.

Anyway. He would give them to her. All of them. Tomorrow he would get a big cardboard box, pick every technicolored, vacuous and sterile CD off his shelves, put them in the box and give them to her. With pleasure.

Digby was sitting at his feet staring up at him with watery eyes. He vibrated briefly and then emitted a strange little high-pitched whimper.

God he was an ugly dog. Not cute-ugly. Not bred to be ugly, like a pug or a bulldog. Just ugly.

'What do you want?' he said quietly.

Digby whimpered again.

'Delilah. I think there's something wrong with your dog. He keeps shivering and moaning.'

'Oh no,' said Delilah, 'he just needs to go to the toilet, that's all. D'you mind taking him?'

'Taking him? Where?' Dig had an image in his mind of some plastic contraption in Delilah's luggage with a seat and a lid – a little doggy-toilet.

'The nearest tree would be good,' she replied, a little sarcastically, Dig thought.

'Oh. Right. OK.' He glanced from his window and noticed that it was still raining. Great. He pulled on his leather coat and picked up an umbrella, attached Digby to his Louis Vuitton lead – pausing for a second to register the fact that the dog had a Louis Vuitton lead: good grief – and then dragged him down the stairs to the chestnut tree outside his house.

Digby cocked his leg and then released the smallest squirt of urine that Dig had ever seen in his life.

'Is that it?' he barked at the dog. 'Is that it? Are you telling me that you dragged me out here in the pissing rain in the middle of the night just for that? That . . . that dribble? I've seen more liquid come out of a fucking teat! Jesus.' He sighed and began dragging the dog back towards the house, but the dog seemed to have decided that he quite liked it out there in the rain and wanted to go out walking, explore the neighbourhood.

'No,' shouted Dig, 'we're going in. You've had your lot.'

The dog ignored him and stood his ground, looking pleadingly into Dig's eyes.

'That's it,' sighed Dig, 'if you can't behave like a grown-up, then I'm going to have to treat you like a puppy. Come here.' He leaned down to pick Digby up and the dog scampered backwards. He bent down again and the dog moved back even further. This continued for a few seconds until they were nearly in the road, and just as Dig managed to get his hands on the animal and pick him up, a large lorry drove past and threw the entire contents of an enormous puddle all over him.

Dig stood for a second, in shock, water rolling down his face from his hair, and his trousers sticking heavily to his legs.

'Oh,' he muttered, 'for fuck's sake.'

When he returned to the flat Delilah had moved away from the CD player, having left every single CD out of its case and strewn around the place, and was now busily unpacking, chucking items of clothing and undergarments randomly around the room. She spun round when she heard the front door go.

‘Oh,’ she said, ‘you’re back. Did he go all right?’

‘Yes,’ murmured Dig, dripping on to the floor and waiting for some sort of sympathetic comment from her about his dramatic state of wetness.

Instead, Delilah turned her attention immediately to Digby and began petting him furiously. ‘Good boy,’ she squeaked in some kind of strange, other-worldly voice, ‘’oos a good boy then? Did ’oo do a wee-wee for your uncle Dig, did you? Good boy!’ And then she went back to her haphazard unpacking.

Dig watched her fiddling around in a small black-suede pouch. She emptied four glistening crystals into the palm of her hand and rubbed them gently with a thumb. They were attached to lengths of thread. She got to her feet and began placing them carefully in the four corners of the room.

Dig watched her with bemusement.

‘Crystals,’ she said, illuminatingly. ‘Room Pattern Crystals. They create an energy field which projects positive vibrations, removes all negativity and strengthens your energies every day.’

‘Aaaah,’ said Dig, nodding and feeling that sense of nervous anxiety he always experienced whenever anyone started talking about ‘alternative’ stuff. It was the same sense of tension that seized him when people started talking about God as if he was more than just a vague notion or a mild swearword.

‘White jade,’ she said, pointing out a stone. ‘Said to help direct energies to their most advantageous outlet, help filter out distraction and aid in solution-oriented thinking. Which is just what I need.

‘Peridot’ – she indicated another – ‘helps connect us to our destinies and attain spiritual truth. Emerald –

said to give wisdom so that the possessor is motivated to give love and wisdom to others. Aquamarine – a great healer. It helps you to understand difficult situations from a love-filled viewpoint.

'And this one,' she said, sombrely, reaching enticingly into her still-damp blouse and pulling out a shard of something prismatic and luminescent, 'this one I wear next to my heart. Mother-of-pearl. This stone is a great protector. It's meant to represent a mother's love.' She stared meaningfully at the stone and caressed it between her fingertips.

Dig didn't know what to say, and the room fell silent. He watched her tuck the stone sadly back inside her bra and gulped.

Delilah sighed and pulled her hair back from her face. 'I wouldn't mind turning in now, Dig, if that's all right with you? It's been kind of a long day.'

Dig looked at his watch. It was ten past ten. He didn't usually go to bed until at least midnight. He didn't have a television in his room. He hadn't even *begun* to digest his curry yet. He wasn't quite sure what he was going to do. 'Er – yeah – sure. I'll get the sofabed up for you.'

Shit, he thought as he made up the bed for her – without even a glimmer of an offer of help – I'm going to have to read a book. What a nightmare. He'd been reading *The Beach* for the last six months and was still only on page 85. He used it as a coaster for his morning cup of coffee, mainly. Dig wasn't one of life's great readers.

'Right,' he said, scratching his head, 'I'll see you in the morning. You know where everything is, don't you? Do you need me to wake you up tomorrow morning or anything?'

'No,' said Delilah, smiling, 'no. I'll just get up when you get up.' She walked towards him and placed her hands on his arms. 'Thank you, Dig. Thank you so much. This is so kind of you. I just . . . I . . . er – oh, just thank you! You're lovely, you really are.'

She grabbed him then, and squeezed him to her in a bear-hug, and Dig thought, *excellent*, and lifted himself on to his tiptoes to match her height. He squeezed her back and buried his face into her cool, silky hair and breathed in that smell, that morning-dew fragrance. Oh Jesus, he thought, oh Delilah. You have *no idea* what you do to me. You are so fucking beautiful and so fucking sexy and I just want to drag you into my bedroom right now and lick every inch of you and fuck you senseless.

Dig could feel Delilah caressing his back through his wet clothes and – *boing* – right on cue, there he was, Mr Happy, in his trousers.

'Oh Delilah,' he murmured into her hair, bringing his nose up towards her face, 'oh Delilah.' He closed his eyes and puckered up, almost exploding with the intensity of the desire he was experiencing, and then, suddenly, she was gone. Slithered from his embrace like a Vaselined cat.

She was half-way to the hallway. 'Sleep tight,' she said, and threw him a little wave before disappearing into the bathroom.

Dig shook his head in confusion.

Fuck.

What happened? One minute she was . . . and the next she was . . . And now he had a huge hard-on. And . . . and . . .

He sighed, turned off the central light, looked briefly around at the four crystals hanging ominously in the corners of his living room and went to bed.

## CHAPTER TWENTY-ONE

Nadine wasn't sure how she and Phil had got here.

They had walked in and out of a few of the rooms in his flat at first, all of which had been occupied by small groups of people in shadow who looked up guiltily from whatever they were doing as the door opened. Then they left by the front door of the flat and walked along a corridor, under an archway, through a door, through another door, and Nadine had lost track of where they were by the time they emerged in a small lock-up garage with a low ceiling.

The floor was concrete and the atmosphere was scorching hot and dry, heat emanating from three wall-mounted gas fires on full power. The air was rank with the smell of used cat litter and Whiskas Supermeat and a dozen or more cats of varying shapes and sizes were dozing, eating and playing in the room.

Before Nadine had a chance to ask about the garage or to wonder why all these cats were locked up in it, Phil had his tongue half-way down her throat and was running his hands up and down her back like he was playing a zither. Within seconds they were tearing at each other's clothing: they were unbuttoning, unzipping, unpopping, pulling off, pulling down and pulling over.

Her clothes were in a heap on the floor at her feet, Phil's jeans and lambswool jumper were draped over a trestle-table, their underwear was in varying stages of removal and a coffee-and-cream Persian with a face like Les Dawson had begun sharpening his claws on Phil's abandoned trainers.

He picked her up; she wrapped her legs around his back. He carried her and deposited her gently upon the edge of the trestle-table. A large marmalade with odd-coloured eyes mewed loudly and leaped out of their way. Phil deftly removed her knickers, even more deftly removed his own (yellow cotton briefs, Nadine observed for one fleeting, worrying second). He bent down and fiddled around inside the socks that he was still wearing, and bizarrely, and Nadine thought miraculously, came up bearing a condom.

'Gosh,' she said breathlessly, 'that was a bit of luck!'

Phil smiled and tore open the glossy purple packet with his teeth. He unfurled it expertly and then, effortlessly, without Nadine even really noticing, he was inside her.

For a few moments they stayed like that, barely moved, staring into each other's eyes, breathing in rhythm. Nadine surrendered all conscious thought to wave after wave of pure physical sensation. Nadine had never before felt so in tune with the rhythm of her own body, with the rhythm of someone else's body. It was like making music, like playing the most sublime duet on the piano, singing together in perfect harmony, two pairs of hands caressing the same harp. It was beautiful . . .

An elderly black cat with white whiskers snaked nervously around Phil's bare ankles, sniffed at them delicately, turned slowly, raised his tail elegantly and then silently released a squirt of bright yellow urine all over the backs of his legs.

'Shit,' hissed Phil, kicking backwards at the cat, who scampered off nimbly, avoiding the blow.

They were moving faster now, but still together, still as one, and Nadine found herself lost in mesmeric synchronicity. And then she started to think about the beautiful, *beautiful* differences between them, the way she was soft and he was hard, and how she was smooth and he was hairy, and he was strong and she was weak, but that when they were together like this it all made perfect sense, it was like a key in a lock, and how come she'd never noticed any of this before, how come she'd never realized before how beautiful sex really was and how this must be what God meant it to be like . . .

A skinny blue cross-eyed Burmese stared meaningfully at her from a tartan bed, looked away, abruptly cocked one back leg stiffly into the air and proceeded to lick his anus, meticulously and enthusiastically.

Nadine closed her eyes, dug her fingers into Phil's hair and was amazed by the feel of his scalp underneath her fingertips, by the fact that you could see it but you could never touch it because there was hair on it, and then she wondered what it would feel like if Phil was to shave it all off, but then there'd be stubble, so you'd have to wax it off, *wax it off*, to be able to really feel what that scalp skin felt like. She began to imagine spreading hot wax on to Phil's scalp, hot, red, wet wax, and peeling it off with big bits of white paper . . .

A fat-faced English Blue who'd been sniffing the end of her nose jumped through the air with a blood-curdling howl and landed on Phil's back.

Phil screamed.

Nadine opened her eyes to find Phil staring into them. 'Oh my God, are you all right?' she exclaimed.

Phil nodded and kept thrusting.

Nadine found herself lost again in the natural rhythm of their movements, in the way their bodies produced sweat where they touched, in the whiteness of the skin on Phil's shoulders, in the feel of him moving up and down inside her, so smooth, so slick, so in and out and in and out, and just perfect, perfectly designed pieces of machinery, working in perfect hydraulic harmony. In and out and in and out and in and out . . . like a well-oiled piston. Imagery flooded her head: huge shining, gleaming chrome apparatus and engines moving constantly and smoothly . . .

The machinery pumped away, and Nadine was oblivious to everything. She didn't notice the passage of time, she didn't notice that her arms had gone numb, she didn't notice the cats, didn't notice how sore she was getting or how fast Phil was now going. She didn't notice his eyes suddenly screw close, and she didn't hear him saying, 'oh thank Christ oh thank Christ I'm coming I'm coming I'm coming.'

They dropped to the floor, kissing, sweating, sighing. Phil wrapped his legs around Nadine and held her tight, very tight. He kissed the top of her sweaty head and stroked her face. The English Blue approached stealthily and began sniffing Phil's bottom.

They lay together silently for a while and Nadine let her eyes close. She was suddenly very, very tired and wanted to sleep. It was hot in here, like a jungle, and Nadine felt miles away from anywhere, detached from reality. Her head was full of lovely, meandering thoughts.

'That was very special, Nadine Kite,' Phil whispered in her ear, ignoring the cat now licking the soles of his feet, 'you'll never, ever know how much that meant to me.' He kissed her eyelids and brought her head back into his embrace.

Nadine smiled and let herself drift away.

'Saffron! Amber! Dill! Jethro! Here babies! Come to Mummy!'

Nadine awoke.

'Murphy! Mack! Topaz! Where are you, my angels?'

Nadine sat bolt upright, covering her naked breasts with her hands.

'Sienna! Mummy's here.'

Phil sat up, too. They looked at each other.

'Shit,' whispered Phil, looping his frighteningly yellow briefs around his ankles and working them up his legs. 'Shit. It's Freda. Hide!' He lifted the plastic cloth from the trestle-table next to them and indicated that she should scoot underneath. She grabbed her clothes and slid under. A pair of alabaster-white Siamese shot out from under the table.

'Who's Freda?' hissed Nadine.

'Shhhhh.'

'Philip?' She could hear the woman's voice, maybe a couple of feet away from her. She could see her feet. She was wearing enormous silver platform shoes, and her fat ankles were covered in broken blood vessels and flea-bites. Nadine scratched an imaginary itch.

'Philip? What*ever* are you doing in here with my babies?' The woman had a bizarre telephone-voice accent.

'Sorry, Freda,' said Phil, sheepishly, 'just . . . er . . . just wanted to come and say hello to the cats . . . make sure they were all right . . . hello, boy, hello.' He put on a rather silly voice and waggled his fingers at a passing Persian with an imperious face who sniffed haughtily at his fingers, regarded him with disdain and immediately began curling himself around the woman's legs.

'At two o'clock a.m. in the bally morning? With half of your apparels removed?' she said, sounding unconvinced.

'Oh – yeah – right. Well. It's pretty hot in here. You know.'

Nadine could see his feet nervously stepping from side to side.

'Hmmmm,' said the woman. 'Well. I must say that I think the hour for visiting my babies has passed. And by the by,' she began in rather a loud, deliberate voice, almost like she wasn't talking to Phil any more, was talking to somebody else, '*by the by*. There's been an almighty commotion in the vicinity of your so-called flat this evening, Philip. A rather elderly and distressed gentleman claiming to be your *father* and wailing about a portable television set. He was taken away by the caretaker but he voiced his intention to return *most* vociferously and to keep on returning until he and his portable television set are reunited. So I suggest that you return to your "flat" and to your so-called "flatmates", forthwith, Philip.'

Nadine saw her lean down to stroke a few of the cats, who were knitting themselves around her legs. She was about seventy, with an extraordinary meringue of yellow spun-sugar hair and a dazzling spectrum of apricot and baby-blue cosmetics trowelled all over her features without, it appeared, benefit of a mirror. Nadine watched her lavishly mascaraed eyes sweep along the floor of the room like searchlights, sweep under the cat hammocks and behind the scratching posts and then under the trestle-table. Nadine flinched and brought her feet closer into her body, made herself into a smaller ball.

'So, Philip,' continued Freda, straightening herself briskly, 'might I suggest that you *move upstairs*, *immediately*, and maybe you and your young friends could contemplate the prospect of *bed*. Tonight. Soon. You understand, of course, that no one appreciates the party *esprit* like Freda appreciates the party *esprit*. But it is no longer the hour for festivity and jolly-making and it is, in fact, the hour for sleeping. Please. Philip. Thank you.'

And then she went. Nadine watched her platformed feet clomping across the concrete floor. She heard the door at the other end of the garage slide open and closed and heard the footsteps recede to a distant echo.

She began to breathe again. She scrambled out from under the table and Phil pulled her into his open arms.

'Who the hell was that?' she said, gently extricating herself from his embrace, which suddenly felt constricting and overpowering.

'Freda,' he said, nuzzling her ear.

'Who's Freda?'

'Mad old coot. Lives next door. This is her garage. Used to be an erotic dancer or something in the fifties – thinks she's a famous film star.'

'These hers?' asked Nadine surveying their feline company.

'Yeah,' he said, 'she keeps them in here because she doesn't like all the hair and smell in her flat.'

'Bit cruel, isn't it?'

He shrugged and kissed her shoulders.

'And what was all that about old men and televisions?'

'Fuck knows,' he sighed, 'this building's full of deranged old pensioners who think their mother's still alive and the country's still at war. He probably thought I was someone else. Probably never even *owned* a TV. Anyway,' he drawled, 'anyway – who cares about senile old men, come over 'ere, you gorgeous sex-goddess.' He grinned and pulled her firmly towards him, leaving her little choice in the matter. 'You are incredible,' he whispered into her ear. 'I could fuck you for ever.'

Oooh, she thought to herself, I wish you hadn't said that. I feel all *weird* now. In fact, Nadine was starting to feel all weird about this whole situation. What the hell was she doing in here? What was she doing disappearing into some stinking, cat-pissy hole in the middle of the night to have sex with a deeply damaged man, on a cocktail of drugs and alcohol. It might have been rock 'n' roll but it certainly wasn't her style.

She knew that he'd tugged her heart-strings nearly to oblivion in the pub earlier on and then, in his living room he'd been a really good listener, he'd been sympathetic and attentive and kind, and then she knew that he'd hit her with some pretty powerful compliments and that she'd agreed quite willingly to come down here with him, and she particularly remembered how much she'd enjoyed the sex – it was *mind-blowing* – but now . . . well, what the hell was she doing down here?

Despite her lingering feelings of love and affection for him, Phil *really* wasn't her type, at all. Too thin, too pale and all that *very black* body hair that stood out in such stark contrast to his lime-washed flesh that you could see each individual follicle. And those long, shapely legs that looked like women's legs. She'd forgotten about those. His hair, which she had been so enthusiastically grabbing hold of a couple of hours ago, looked like it could do with a good wash, and his hands didn't have any hair on them, were all smooth and fleshy like he didn't have any bones, like he was wearing surgeon's gloves. But worst of all were those *underpants* – Nadine had never slept with a man who wore *underpants* before, particularly not bright-lemon underpants.

She was just starting to notice his eyes, too. Those denim-blue eyes she'd loved so much at poly. There was something strange about them now. They stared too much, ate through what they observed like blowtorches through a metal door. He was like a manta ray. Nadine shuddered a little.

'We could just stay here – no one will find us in here,' he was saying, 'no one knows about this room except me.'

And he had bad teeth! Really bad teeth.

'Just another half an hour. Give me another half an hour and I'll see if I can make it *even better* this time.'

Oh what! Oh no. No no no no no. Nadine dragged her knickers up her legs and over her hips as quickly as she could, using them as some kind of symbolic chastity belt.

She stood up and pulled on her crocheted dress. 'Sorry, Phil,' she said, 'but I've got to go home now. Really.' She looked at her watch. 'Shit! It's nearly two! We've been in here for ages.'

'Yeah,' smiled Phil proudly, 'I know.'

'Better get back then, eh?' she said brightly, starting to pull her cardigan sleeves up her arms.

She looked at Phil. He was sitting in his lemon briefs, cross-legged, strangling a strand of his grubby-looking hair into a knot. His stomach had folded itself into a small pale flap of skin over the waistband of his briefs and an aged Siamese cat with only one eye was gingerly settling himself into his lap.

Nadine shuddered.

She wanted to go home.

The girl called Jo was waiting anxiously in the hallway when they finally walked back into the flat, picking at the skin around her nails and holding a smouldering cigarette.

'Where the fuck have you been?' she demanded rudely of Phil. 'It's been a fucking nightmare here.' She threw Nadine a contemptuous look and blew a cloud of cigarette smoke into the air around her head. 'Your old man turned up and had a screaming fucking fit about some fucking TV, and then that old hag from next door started snooping around and moaning about the noise, and then . . .'

'Chill, girl,' said Phil, putting a hand firmly on her shoulder and turning to smile at Nadine. 'Just chill. I've been showing Nadine Freda's cats, that's all. I'm here now.'

'Yeah, but what about your old man? He said he's going to come back every night until . . .'

'*Just. Chill.* He's just a senile old man. OK?' he said firmly, putting a finger to Jo's lips and turning her around. And then he turned and winked at Nadine before placing his hand firmly on Jo's back and disappearing with her into one of the many rooms leading off his hallway.

Nadine stood blinking for a moment or two, feeling slightly foolish. Was he coming back? Was she supposed to be waiting for him? Was she supposed to have followed him? And what the hell was all that about his 'old man'? He didn't have an 'old man'. His father was dead.

After a couple of minutes she decided that he wasn't coming back and that she was presently making a giant fool of herself, so she located a mini-cab card on the telephone table and started to dial.

She didn't want to be here any more.

She arranged to meet the cab on the street outside the flats and paced up and down agitatedly while she waited. A few minutes later a dark-blue Granada Ghia pulled up and she gratefully fell into the back seat and explained to the Turkish driver where she wanted to be taken.

The entire area between her legs felt raw and used and her thigh muscles had begun to ache tenderly. The skin around her mouth was taut and sore and her head felt thick and woolly and dense with confusing images and blurred thoughts. The streetlights and window displays danced in front of her eyes and made pinhead patterns of light on her retinas.

Nadine didn't know what had happened tonight. She didn't know who she was or where she'd been or where she was going.

She was all alone.

She wanted a bath.

She wanted to go home.

# CHAPTER TWENTY-TWO

Dig woke with a start at seven o'clock, emerging from a very peculiar but pleasant dream involving ice-cream cones and Kylie Minogue to find a greasy-snouted, curry-breathed Digby frantically snuffling at his ear.

Imagining that this urgent awakening might have something to do with the fullness of Digby's bladder and the severity of his need to empty it, not to mention any unexpected effect that his snaffling of last night's vindaloo might have had on his doubtless delicate stomach, Dig hopped briskly out of bed, jumped into a pair of boxers and encouraged the creature into the living room with a slap to the back of his bare thighs, hoping that he would then leap up on to the recumbent figure of Delilah nestled into Dig's sofabed, and begin snuffling into *her* ear the news of his full bladder.

This plan didn't work. Instead of waking his mistress, Digby sat stiffly on the floor at the foot of her bed, staring imploringly at Dig and whimpering very quietly, a grain of yellow rice hanging resolutely from his oily whiskers. Dig patted gently at the duvet covering the apparently dead Delilah in an attempt to lure Digby towards her ear but the dog just looked at him as if he was slightly retarded and whimpered again, and Dig realized that he had only three choices:

a) wake up the angelically, beautifully slumbering Delilah and insist that she take the dog outside

b) take responsibility himself for the emptying of Digby's bladder, or

c) let him piss on the carpet.

Option a) seemed a bit cruel, and option c) was a complete no-no, which left him only one feasible alternative. However, it was seven o'clock in the morning, it was still raining and Dig would have to get properly dressed and take the dog outside, as he had no access to a garden. These were all truly horrible considerations and it was the prospect of these that led to Dig gingerly gripping the beast around his bony undercarriage, picking his way over the scavenged foil curry containers strewn around the kitchen floor, and holding him firmly aloft out of the kitchen window, over the early rush-hour noises of Camden Road, while making 'whooshing' noises under his breath in an attempt to charm open Digby's urethra.

The dog reacted badly to the situation he found himself in, flailing around wildly in Dig's hands and staring at him with madly bulging eyes as if to ask, 'Why are you trying to kill me? What have I ever done to you?'

Dig realigned his fingers beneath Digby's belly and began to push his fingertips into the point where he imagined his bladder sat, attempting to *squeeze* the business out of him as if emptying a hot-water bottle. Digby liked this even less and started kicking his tiny legs around ever more frantically, but finally Dig felt the animal begin to relax in his hands and breathed a sigh of relief as a jet of dog pee streamed elegantly from between the creature's legs like the squirt of water from a cherubic statue in a water fountain, arcing gently and cascading down towards the lower branches of the chestnut tree outside Dig's window. 'Good boy,' said Dig, 'that's a good boy . . .'

'Oh my God!! Oh Jesus!! What are you *doing*?'

Dig jumped in his skin as a shrill female voice reverberated around the kitchen, and he felt a pair of hands dragging him away from the window.

'Put him down – let go of him, for God's sake!!'

He spun around without thinking and certainly without first verifying with the dog that his bladder was fully empty and watched in horror as Digby's still-active spray sprinkled in a generous crescent all over the kitchen surfaces, across the hob, into the sink and, finally, all down the front of Delilah's bra and knickers and into a foil container at her feet.

Dig barely had time to register the disaster before he was overcome by the breathtakingly erotic realization that Delilah was standing in front of him in her bra and knickers looking like some kind of Greek goddess, despite the rivulets of lemon-coloured dog-pee trickling down her fantastically flat stomach and into the waistband of her knickers. He gulped. The stream of pee stopped as suddenly as it had started, and the shell-shocked trio found themselves rooted silently to the spot in horror, the only sound that of the last few droplets of Digby's pee hitting the tiled floor . . . *splish* . . . *splish* . . . *splish*.

Delilah opened her mouth and looked down with disgust at her dampened body, her face contorting as the full horror of her situation hit her. 'Eeeeeegh!!' she squeaked, ineffectually flapping her arms up and down. 'Eeeegh!!'

Dig dropped the dog to the floor, where he began slipping and sliding around in the puddles he'd made there. 'Oh Jesus! Oh Delilah! I'm so sorry . . . oh God . . . here' – he grabbed a brand-new J-cloth from the side of the sink – 'here – let me help you.' He started sponging at Delilah's rigid body, desperately trying to avoid the rude bits, which was tricky as that's where most of the pee was.

'Eeeeegh!' said Delilah.

'Here,' said Dig, handing her the damp cloth, 'you do the other . . . bits. I'll . . . er . . . put the shower on for you.'

'Eeeeegh!' said Delilah again, picking the cloth gingerly from his hands and rubbing it stiffly along her inside legs. Dig tried not to stare at the soft golden down poking from her knickers as he made his way past her towards the bathroom.

He had to negotiate piles of Delilah's belongings in the overcast gloom of what had been his living room and was now effectively Delilah's bedroom. Her two suitcases had been left on the floor and opened wide, their entrails spilt all over the floor and piled up in small heaps here and there. There were *three* glasses of water balanced on the table by the bed and stacks of paperwork spread out all over the place. Dig had to resist the urge to start tidying things as he made his way across the room, and he clenched his fists into balls as he walked, repeating silently to himself, 'Don't be anal, don't be anal, don't be anal.'

The bathroom, too, was unrecognizable, sporting a sophisticated array of white-packaged bottles and jars containing all manner of fluids for the removal, cleansing and general facilitation of the contact lenses that Dig hadn't realized Delilah wore, plus a variety of beauty products housed in mint-green packaging that promised to perform what sounded to Dig like the stuff of miracles, and a simply *enormous* bag of cotton-wool balls on top of the cistern. She had also used one of *his* towels, which threw his weekly towel rota into complete disarray, and had left the bathmat *on the floor*, instead of leaving it on the side of the bath, so that it was still damp this morning even though she'd used it the night before and – oh God – she'd finished a toilet roll at some point and had left the new one just sitting balanced on top of the empty one – just sitting there – balanced – when all she had to do – it was *so simple* – was to take the old roll off, throw it in the bin and slip the new one on. I mean – for God's sake – how could anyone be so *lazy*.

Don't be anal. Don't be anal. Don't be anal.

He flicked the switch for the shower and tested the temperature, straightened the towels, replaced the toilet roll and put all of Delilah's bottles into nice straight, satisfying lines before heading back towards the kitchen, where Digby was still where Dig had left him, curled up on the floor in a puddle of his own pee, wondering where he was and why strange men were trying to throw him out of windows, and where Delilah was still scrubbing at herself with the new-five-minutes-ago-but-soon-to-be-thrown-in-the-bin J-cloth.

Dig stopped at the threshold of the kitchen, stopped and just stared for a moment at the sight before him – not the mess, not the dog pee all over everything and the bits of turmeric-tinted sauce staining his porous white floor tiles and the grains of oily rice slowly solidifying and sticking to the floor – but the glorious sight of Delilah, standing with her back to him, her long legs splayed out at strange angles to allow for cleaning, her golden hair swinging back and forth in the slowly pervading sunlight from the window, her stretch-jersey underwear dazzlingly white. She looked like the models in the photographs on the underwear packets he'd seen in M&S. She was magnificent. How could he have ever let her get away, all those years ago? He should have followed her to the ends of the earth and back, he should have been there at the church ten years ago to stop her marrying this Alex person, he should have fought for her. Girls like Delilah only came along once in a lifetime . . . or did they?

His fantastic reverie was disturbed at that moment when Delilah suddenly spun around violently on the spot, regarded him with bulging, tearful eyes, brought one hand up to her mouth and charged past him, pushing him out of the way with her other hand and running noisily towards the bathroom.

'Are you OK?' he called after her, following.

He caught up with her just in time to see her grip the wash-basin firmly with one hand, pull her hair back from her face with the other and throw up rambunctiously into the sink.

'Oh God,' he thought to himself, 'not the sink! Please – not the sink! That's what toilets are for.' But instead he said, 'Oh Delilah! You poor thing. Are you OK?', and patted her back and brought her a glass of water. She assured him that she was fine while she sat shivering and shaking on the edge of the bath, her creamy skin looking clammy and damp, gripping the glass to death between her hands.

He shuffled out when she said she wanted to take a shower and wandered blindly through his messy living room, deliberately ignored the rancid mayhem and disoriented dog in his kitchen and made his way towards the blessed sanctuary of his bedroom. He flopped wearily on to his bed and turned his head to view the time.

7.15 a.m. Had so many disgusting things really occurred in such a short amount of time? Could so much have gone so disastrously wrong in the space of just fifteen minutes? He turned the other way, brought his knees into chest and closed his eyes. His mind soon filled with images of Delilah in her underwear, but this time without the dog and the pee and the curry and the mess and the vomit – this time, just Delilah, her underwear and him . . .

By the time Dig's alarm went off at 8.15, he'd had a couple of gorgeous day-dreams and a long and, he thought, extremely well-deserved wank and he was feeling ready to start the day again, putting his previous attempt at day-starting well behind him.

The rain had stopped and the sun was positively bursting through his curtains. Delilah was wearing a pair of faded jeans, black crocodile-skin boots with high heels and a black polo neck when he walked into the now-uncurtained brightness of the living room. She was one of the few women who Dig considered suited to wearing jeans. She was crouching on the floor and leafing frantically through her paperwork, spreading the piles ever further and slurping on a mug of coffee as she went. She turned around when she sensed Dig behind her.

'Hi!' she beamed happily, rocking on her heels, 'you recovered from earlier on yet?'

'I think so,' he said, scratching his head and balancing himself on the arm of the sofabed, which had not, he noted, been put away.

'Sorry about all that. And sorry about shouting at you about the dog – I should have known that you weren't trying to harm him – I'm probably a bit over-protective sometimes.'

'Oh,' said Dig, dismissively, 'don't worry about that. How are *you*, anyway? You know . . .' He rubbed his tummy.

'Oh God. Sorry about that, too! I've had a bit of a dodgy gut lately. I'll try to do it in the toilet next time!' She laughed, getting to her feet and rubbing at the knees of her jeans.

'Oh don't be silly! It's fine. I mean – when you've gotta puke, you've gotta puke really, haven't you?' He giggled foolishly and then cleared his throat.

'So, Dig,' she asked, 'heard anything from Nadine yet?'

Dig jumped a little – for such a closed book, Delilah had a disarming ability to ask awkward questions at very unexpected junctures. 'Yeah,' he said, tersely, 'I spoke to her yesterday afternoon, actually. We had another row.'

'About me?'

Dig shook his head. 'Nah. About her. She's an idiot. She's getting back in touch with this wanker she went out with at university. She saw him last night. I don't understand her.'

'Well,' said Delilah, decisively, 'I do. She's trying to get back at you.'

'What are you talking about?'

'It's obvious. She's pissed off with you for spending time with me, so she's phoned up her ex to try and make you jealous.'

'Oh, don't be ridiculous.'

'I'm not. I'm right. I know I am. She wants you to know what she feels like. Why else would she choose now, of all times, to get back in touch with this bloke?'

Dig shrugged petulantly.

'You gonna call her?'

'No.' Dig was aware that he sounded like a child but he didn't care. If Nadine could play it like a brat, then he could play it like an even bigger brat.

'Jesus,' sighed Delilah, 'you two are behaving like a pair of kids. It's just like when we were at school, remember? When you and me first started going out together and Nadine wouldn't talk to you any more? Twelve years later and nothing's changed – it's pathetic.' She scooped together a pile of papers and beat them off the floor to straighten the edges.

'She started it,' said Dig, continuing his brat theme.

'So. Why can't you finish it? Just pick up the phone and say, "All right, Deen, fancy a drink?" You'll go out, you'll chat, within an hour everything will be back to normal – I guarantee you. Honestly. You two should be married to each other and instead you're not even *talking* to each other – it's infuriating!'

Dig winced at this new reference to him and Nadine.

'D'you want another coffee?' he asked, gesturing at her mug with his eyes.

'Er . . . no thanks,' she said, 'I'm actually really late for something.'

'Oh yeah? What's that then?'

'Oh – nothing really. I've just got be somewhere in twenty minutes, somewhere in Surrey.'

She suddenly became deeply distracted, flapping the papers about ever more wantonly, and Dig thought better of probing her with more questions and made his way to the kitchen to get himself a coffee. He was alarmed to note that Delilah had apparently managed to manoeuvre herself around the kitchen to make herself a cup of coffee *and* a bowl of porridge, with hot milk (the slimy-looking pan had been left unwashed and *unrinsed* in the sink), without feeling the need to clean up any of Digby's piss or at the very least pick the curry containers off the fucking floor. Dig was rendered speechless for a moment, well aware that even though he was cleaner and had higher standards than most, there could be very few people in this world who would feel happy about preparing food in amongst congealed curry and dog pee.

Delilah wandered into the kitchen, busily rearranging things in her handbag and clutching the spare set of door keys he'd given her the night before, a black sheepskin jacket slung crookedly over her shoulders. 'Erm,' she began, biting at her lower lip, 'Dig. I . . . er . . . need to ask you a favour.'

'Oh God,' thought Dig, 'what now?'

'Sure!' he smiled. 'No problem!'

'I was sort of hoping, if it wasn't too much trouble, that you could maybe have Digby today?' She smiled at him apprehensively.

'Eh?' said Dig.

'Well, I wouldn't normally ask, but I'll be on trains and God knows what today, and I don't know when I'll be home, and it would just make everything so much easier if he wasn't with me . . .'

'But I've . . . um . . . I've got to go to work, Delilah. I can't look after him. Can't you just leave him here?'

Delilah shook her head sadly. 'He's awful when he's left alone – he makes this terrible noise, like goats being tortured or something – painful. And he deliberately pees on beds. And he eats things. Toilet paper and stuff. It's a spite thing. Can't you take him with you? He's ever so small and incredibly well-behaved – just stick him under your desk, I'm sure no one will mind.' She opened up her face pleadingly.

'Well . . . it's not really up to me, you see – it's my boss – we get all sorts of important people coming to the office, and he might not like it very much if Digby here was around.'

'Oh I'm sure he won't mind little Digby – he'll probably love him! Please Dig – please. I'm begging of you. I'll make it up to you tonight – I'll cook you my famous lamb casserole – it's Alex's favourite! Please!'

Dig stared into Delilah's huge blue eyes and felt his minuscule reserves of resolve diminish rapidly to nothing. Toby wouldn't mind about the dog – he would probably think it was quite cool having a dog around the place – and he was sure that Digby could behave himself for at least a day, and poor old Delilah really, *really* needed him to help her – she would be so grateful, and grateful women were, generally speaking, a *very good thing.*

So he nodded and he smiled and he said, 'Yeah, sure, why not?', and Delilah hugged him yet again, and Dig thought to himself that he really was building up a good, big stock of brownie-points here and that at some stage all this Good Samaritan stuff was going to start paying dividends, surely, and he hugged her back and imagined the lovely luminous *white* stuff she had on underneath all those clothes.

Delilah didn't get back to Dig's flat until half past ten that night. She didn't tell him where she'd been all day and Dig didn't ask, and there was certainly no mention whatsoever of the promised lamb casserole.

# CHAPTER TWENTY-THREE

Nadine was experiencing what could fairly be described as the worst hangover of her life. Without a doubt. Her head was throbbing, her heart was racing, her blood was fizzing, her stomach was churning and she was feeling as miserable as sin. She was having rather severe difficulty piecing together the fragmented bits of last night's events. She could just about remember having sex with Phil (bleugh), but she had absolutely no idea how such a terrible thing could have happened.

She'd managed to crawl out of bed forty-five minutes ago and had been dragging her pained body around the flat ever since, trying to make it do the things it normally did in the mornings, like wash its hair and make its toast and brush its teeth. It had been extremely difficult and extremely unpleasant, but she'd managed it somehow, and had been about to leave for work when she'd heard the phone ringing.

'Hello,' she sighed, painfully, perching on the arm of the sofa, expecting to hear her mother's voice on the end of the line, telling her something bizarre, like that she'd been clearing out the loft and found Nadine's old retainer brace and would she like her to bring it over that weekend or should she throw it away?

'Is that the sexiest woman in Kentish Town?' said a strange male voice.

'I'm sorry?'

'Hello, darlin'. It's me, Phil.'

Nadine experienced a sudden knot of tension in her stomach.

'Hello . . . hello . . . are you there?'

'Oh . . . yeah . . . sorry.' Nadine let her weary body flop sideways on to the sofa. 'So . . . how are you?'

'Yeah. Great. Great. You?'

'Not so great, actually.'

'Feeling bad?'

'Yeah – you could say that.'

'Can't say I'm surprised, really. All that vodka you were drinking and then – you know – what I gave you, later?'

'What?'

'That pill.'

'What pill?'

'You know – I gave you a pill – when you were getting upset about things.'

Oh yes. That E! Oh my God – she had, hadn't she? She'd taken an E. Jesus – she was thirty years old and she'd just taken her first E. That would explain *a lot* of things about last night.

'You might feel a bit low, today, a bit blue. Just drink a lot of coffee. Keep yourself busy.'

God – she was so stupid. She could have killed herself. She could imagine the headlines: PHOTOGRAPHER FOUND DEAD AFTER LETHAL COCKTAIL OF ALCOHOL AND DRUGS – *Police Say 'She Was Very Stupid.'*

'Yeah. Right. I will . . . Thanks.' She buried her face into the cushions on the sofa and closed her eyes. She was aware that the line had gone silent but was feeling too dreadful to be able to think of anything to say.

'Hey, Nadine' – Phil's voice broke the silence – 'you

know something? I haven't slept since you left. I've been up all night. Just thinking about you, about *us* . . . about how great we still are together.'

Oh no, thought Nadine, oh God.

'I've been wanting to phone you since you left. And I just wanted to say thanks, for getting in touch, for last night, for listening, for being you.'

Nadine wanted to reciprocate his enthusiasm, to say something nice – she felt *so sorry* for him – but all she could manage was a weak laugh.

'I meant everything I said last night, you know. I meant it.'

What did he say? What had he said? Nadine couldn't remember.

' . . . You are . . . special. Totally.'

Ooooh, thought Nadine, stop it.

'So I . . . er . . . just wondered. What are you up to later? Thought we could, like, meet up. Or something. Yeah?'

Nadine sat up straight. This was all a bit much, all a bit full-on for 8.30 on a Thursday morning with a raging hangover. 'Oh well,' she stalled, 'later? Erm, well – the thing is, I'm off to Barcelona at the weekend so . . .'

'Oh right, yeah. Fair enough. You'll want an early night, I suppose.'

'Yeah. That sort of thing.'

'Well, when are you back? Maybe we could get together then?'

'Back on Tuesday evening, actually.'

'So – maybe late next week?'

'Yeah. Maybe.'

'Great. Cool,' he said, and the line went quiet again. 'Erm, Nadine?' he said, eventually.

'Yeah.'

'I just wanted to say to you, I'm so glad you're back in my life. It feels like a miracle, you know, a fucking miracle.'

Nadine managed another weak laugh.

'. . . And next week, when I see you, I'm going to prove it to you, prove how much I care.'

Nadine felt a sickly little butterfly start fluttering its wings inside her tummy.

'I should never, ever have let you go, before. I should never have let my ego come between us the way it did. I'm older now and I've learned so much in life, and one thing I realize now, the most important thing I've learned, is that true love is what life is all about and nothing should ever, *ever* get in its way. And you were my true love, Nadine. I knew it then and I sure as hell know it now.'

Nadine's cheeks pinkened with horror.

'I can't believe I'm lucky enough to be given a second chance with you. I wanna make it work this time, I wanna make it perfect. Yeah? So I'll give you a ring on Tuesday, OK? And we'll meet up?'

'Yeah,' said Nadine, not knowing what else to say and wondering, not for the first time in her life, why it was so hard to use the word 'no'. 'Yes, sure.' It wasn't until she put the phone down that she realized her voice had gone up by about twelve octaves during the course of the conversation so that by the time she'd made her parting comments she'd sounded like Sandra Dickinson on helium.

She wondered for a moment why this should be and then decided that it really didn't matter.

## CHAPTER TWENTY-FOUR

The next morning Dig waited until he heard the door slam behind Delilah and her footsteps bouncing down the front steps before crawling out of bed and into the living room.

Bloody hell – it was a nightmare in here. She hadn't even opened the curtains this time. There was half a bowl of porridge encrusting on the coffee-table, half her wardrobe strewn across her bed, and Digby was shivering furiously under the radiator.

'Great,' Dig muttered under his breath.

He strode towards the television and switched it off. Quarter to eight in the morning was no time for Johnny Vaughan, as far as he was concerned. He dragged the curtains apart and peered through the window. Delilah was standing on the other side of the road pacing back and forth and looking at her watch. Christ, she looked gorgeous. She was wearing leggings, which accentuated the shape of her fantastic legs, pristine white trainers and a huge knee-length puffa jacket. She'd put her hair up into a sort of fluffy, tufty thing on the back of her head, which bounced up and down as she walked around, giving her the look of a dressage pony. A very beautiful dressage pony.

A cab screeched to a halt next to her, and a couple of seconds later she was gone.

Dig scratched his chin, yawned and turned towards

the kitchen, the smell of Delilah's freshly brewed coffee luring him away from the window. He took one step forward and then recoiled in agony, clasping his knee to him and rubbing furiously at the sole of his foot.

'Aaargh! Fucking shitting bollocking FUCK!' he yelled, hopping around. He looked down and saw one of Delilah's high-heeled shoes lying on its side. He'd trodden on the heel and it fucking hurt.

What the *fuck* was Delilah's shoe doing over here anyway? Where was the other one? Why couldn't she keep them together? In a pair? Like a normal human being?

Dig felt anger percolating in his chest. He picked the shoe up and hurled it across the room with a roar, and then he sat down heavily on the arm of the sofa and took a lot of deep breaths, to calm his inner rage.

He couldn't stand this, he really, really couldn't bear it. He knew he was being anal, he knew other people would be able to ignore all this . . . this *shit*, all this stuff everywhere, clothes and mess and paper and dogs and fucking *crystals*. Other people would just think, Well, it's not perfect, but it's only temporary, and she's a friend and it's only a bit of mess. But Dig just couldn't. It fucked his head up. He couldn't concentrate. He couldn't relax. He couldn't *breathe*, for God's sake.

He hobbled towards his stereo and traced his finger across the 'B' section of his CD collection. There was only one thing for it, only one person who could help him now.

He reverently laid the disc in its tray, slid shut the door and pressed play. There was different music for different moments. Music to work to (Radiohead, Travis, the Manics), music to bathe to (Paul Westerberg, Paul Weller), music to cook and wash up to (Blondie, Abba, 70s compilations), music to have sex to (Portishead, Chris Isaaks, Dean Martin), music to dance to (*Saturday Night Fever* soundtrack and any Northern soul) and then there was music to tidy up to, and when it came to a mess of this magnitude, there was only one man for the job.

The One and Only.

The Godfather.

James.

Brown.

Get down.

Dig swivelled the volume as loud as it would go without bouncing ornaments off his shelves and set to it.

Dig loved to tidy, he really did. It was one of his favourite occupations. But this was a bit trickier than usual because it wasn't his stuff. It was weird, alien bits and pieces from somebody else's life, stuff that belonged on the shelves and in the cupboards of a house he'd never visited, in a part of the country he'd never been to. And a lot of it was underwear.

Digby still sat quaking under the radiator and watched Dig as he picked up tailored trousers, sweatshirts, jeans and cashmere jumpers and folded them painstakingly into perfect little cubes. Episode. Phase Eight. Donna Karan. Marks and Spencer. Tommy Hilfiger. He feigned disinterest in her bits of white-jersey underwear, lumping them together nonchalantly, like old rugby socks, almost as if someone might be watching him for signs of sad-old-gitness. He collected her mugs and bowls and glasses of water and put them in the kitchen sink. He rolled up the duvet and shoved it in the hall cupboard, along with the pillows. He heaved the sofabed back into its cavity, retrieved his cushions from where they lay scattered around the room, plumped them up voraciously and arranged them into a nice overlapping pattern across the sofa back.

He stepped back to appraise his cushions, screwing up his face as he joined James to hit a high note. Now – where to put all these beautifully folded bits of designer clothing? He spotted one of her vast suitcases in the corner, dragged it into the middle of the room and threw it open. And then he stopped in his tracks. Paper. Loads of it. Loose-leaf papers in clear plastic folders. Notebooks. Folders. Letters.

Clues.

Again, acting as if there might be a CCTV in operation in his flat, he pretended not to notice. Oh no, he thought to himself, I most certainly am *not* the sort of fellow who would snoop in other people's possessions, thank you very much. Not me. Oh no.

He hoped that the imaginary people watching him on their imaginary monitor were impressed by his restraint.

He shuffled the papers around a bit to make room in the case for her clothes, and let his eyes wander across the letter that lay on the top as he put her clothing, piece by piece, into the case. It was an official-looking letter on crisp white laid.

Dig scanned it quickly.

Rosemary Bentall
Clinical Psychologist
The Old School Buildings
Liverpool Road
Chester
CH2 1UL

**Phone: 01244 555000**
**Fax: 01244 555129**

10th November 1999

Mrs Delilah Biggins
Dorrington Lodge
Chester
CH8 7LN

Dear Delilah,

I have been trying to phone you since you walked out of our session yesterday afternoon but your housekeeper was unable to tell me where you were.

I am very concerned about you, Delilah, and can only hope that you haven't carried out your threat to return to London. I understand your need to uncover the past, especially in the light of what you told me yesterday, but I really feel that this trip will not be in your best interests and could in fact be detrimental to your progress at this stage in our work together. We have both worked so hard to get to this point and leaving now will put your recovery in jeopardy.

However, if you do insist on going ahead with your plans, then I beseech you to talk to Alex about it. He has supported you in everything over the years and shutting him out now would be unfair on both of you.

I don't think there is anything else I can say, except to urge you once more to heed my advice and postpone this visit until you're stronger.

Warm wishes,

Rosie

**Dr Rosemary Bentall**

Dig closed his mouth, cleared his throat and quickly piled the rest of the clothes on top of the paperwork.

His heart raced in rhythm to the music as he tried to go about his business, but he found it impossible to feel normal. 'Uncover the past'? What did that mean? And what the hell was Delilah doing seeing a shrink? Delilah wasn't mad. OK – so she was into crystals and feng shui and stuff. She was messy and disorganized and talked too much. But she wasn't *mad*.

This threw a new complexion on everything. When Delilah had told Dig that she was in London to 'sort her head out', he'd interpreted it as meaning that she wanted to get away from Alex. He'd thought she was here to contemplate her marriage, which was why he'd kept out of her face. But it was nothing to do with her marriage.

It was to do with the past. Of which he was a part. It was his business, now. He had a right to know.

He was about to zip up Delilah's suitcase when he had a sudden thought. He grabbed a pen and scribbled down Dr Rosemary Bentall's phone number. Just in case. He probably wouldn't need it.

But if a woman in Chester with letters after her name was worried about Delilah, then so was he.

# CHAPTER TWENTY-FIVE

Nadine had received a most unexpected phone call the previous day.

From Delilah.

It had thrown her completely, suffering, as she was, so terribly with a hangover, not to mention the guilt and anxiety and spine-chilling remorse her reckless actions of Wednesday evening were punishing her with.

'Hi,' she'd said, jauntily, 'it's me. Delilah' – as if they were old mates.

'Oh,' Nadine had said, 'hi.'

'Look – I was talking to Dig last night,' she'd continued.

Oh yes, thought Nadine, I bet you were.

'And he mentioned that you go to the gym regularly.'

'Ye–es.'

Delilah wondered whether Nadine would mind if she came to the gym with her, because, in her own highly amusing words, she was starting to feel really fat. Apparently she used to go running every day in the countryside and she was missing the exercise – oh, and the reason she didn't want to go jogging in London was because she felt self-conscious about her 'wobbly bottom'.

If there was one thing more annoying than a naturally thin girl, it was a naturally thin girl who went on about being fat all the time.

So Nadine had had approximately one and a half

seconds to form a reply and because she was incapable of using the word 'no', the only alternative had been to say, 'Of course, great, no problem – that would be lovely.'

She had no one to blame but herself.

Delilah arrived at Nadine's flat on Friday morning on the dot of eight o'clock. Nadine had managed to forget about this arrangement until half past seven and had consequently spent the last half an hour frantically running around her flat trying to clear up, defumigate and make herself look beautiful all at the same time.

When the doorbell rang at eight o'clock she'd achieved none of the above. She had been unable to find any of her sexy, expensive, *shiny* Lycra gym things, those tight purple, black and red things that skimmed gleamingly over her body, sucking her in and making her look like a Gladiator, and instead had had to throw on her baggy old *grey* things with the holes in them that made her look like a dumpy housewife with low self-esteem who doesn't know that her husband is shagging his secretary.

She'd attempted to put her hair up in some sort of jaunty, sporty-looking pony-tail thing and had ended up with this strange *cottage-loaf*-type structure on her head that looked like it might be housing a pair of chaffinches. And, in an attempt to rid her flat of the stench of three weeks' worth of Marlboro Light emissions (the last time she'd opened a window), she'd actually managed to *smash* the kitchen window. Actually broken the fucking thing. No idea how. And there was now a force-ten icy gale wailing through the angry-looking hole. She'd taped a carrier bag over it, to no great effect, and given that she didn't have time to phone a glazier, was just hoping and praying that the burglars in her area weren't quick-witted enough to break in in the hour or so she'd be out of the house.

She opened the door breathlessly and was greeted, unsurprisingly, by a vision of female perfection. There she was, her golden hair scraped back immaculately into a sleek pony-tail, her body encased in a simple pair of black cotton leggings, black vest top and an enormous, all-enveloping black puffa jacket which made her look like a fragile little doll. Pah! Her skin was glowing like she'd already been for a two-mile jog, and she was grinning from ear to ear.

'Hi! I'm not late, am I?' she oozed.

'No . . . no' – Nadine suddenly realized she had left her fag hanging out of her mouth and quickly transferred it to her fingers – 'no . . . not at all. Come in.'

Nadine wasn't a flake. Not usually. She wasn't one of those girls who couldn't get out of the front door without laddering her tights or who couldn't cook a lasagne without setting the house on fire. She was usually pretty cool and poised. So why was she now falling apart at the seams just because of the mere presence, the sheer *existence* of a girl called Delilah Lillie? It was pathetic. If this was any other girl, literally any other girl, she would have just said, 'Come in, excuse the mess, sorry about the fag smell, and don't I look dreadful.' So why did she feel this overwhelming need to be perfect for Delilah?

'Wow,' said Delilah, as she moved through Nadine's cluttered hallway, 'what an incredible place. I love what you've done to the walls.' She was running her fingers across the rose-pink foil. 'Where did you get this stuff from?'

'It's sweet wrapping. I found a big box of it in one of

the studios upstairs from mine when they moved out. It was a fucking nightmare to put up.'

'Amazing,' sighed Delilah, 'you've got such an imagination. I would *never* have thought of something like that. So original.'

Oh God. She was doing that thing again, that self-effacing, you're-so-much-better-than-crappy-little-old-me bollocks.

'Oh my God! That's so cute!' said Delilah, eyeing up the tiny motifs on Nadine's wallpaper in the living room. 'It's Miffy the Rabbit, isn't it?' She put her index fingers to her upper lip and crossed them over each other, into an X, and then giggled. 'I used to love Miffy the Rabbit. Where did you get it?'

'Oh' – Nadine gritted her teeth at Delilah's cloying attempt at cuteness – 'it was from a children's shop in Crouch End that was closing down. It wasn't a top-selling line, apparently – couldn't compete with Thomas the Tank Engine and Postman Pat.'

'Incredible. Absolutely incredible . . . So clever the way it looks like little flowers from a distance and you can't see it till you get close up. Magnolia's about my limit on the home-décor front.'

Delilah loved her car, too – of course. 'Wow. Sex on wheels. What is it?'

'It's an Alpha. Spider.'

'It's beautiful. God, you're so lucky. Only car I've ever driven is my Renault Clio. It's nice but not exactly sexy, though.'

Yeah right, thought Nadine, yawn yawn. If you got much more self-deprecating you'd cease to exist, you'd end up vanishing vaporously into the ether. Either this girl was suffering from a severe case of low self-esteem or this really was the only way she could communicate with women who weren't as beautiful as her. Either way, it was beginning to grate on her nerves. She'd almost preferred the old-style cocky, arrogant Delilah.

Nadine was aware that she was being rather unfair on Delilah. She knew that Delilah was just trying to be friendly, trying to be a girl's girl. But that was the problem. She just *wasn't* a girl's girl and she sounded insincere and fake. She wasn't the cool Delilah that Nadine had known and hated at school. She was just plain irritating.

Unpeeled and bobbing up and down on the step machine, Delilah looked extraordinary – she made it look so effortless. Not a drop of sweat on her, not a hair out of place.

'Ever used one of these before?' puffed Nadine.

'Nah,' replied Delilah, sounding frighteningly *un*breathless.

'What setting are you on?' Nadine asked her.

Delilah moved her towel away from the dot-matrix screen. 'Erm . . . thirteen, I think. No – fourteen.'

Fourteen! *Fourteen!* Nadine had almost thrown a party when, after weeks and weeks, she'd finally gone up to level *ten* on the step machine. 'Uh-huh,' she squeaked, breathlessly, 'really.'

Nadine was desperately trying to control her urge to ask after Dig. The question was sitting, quivering, on the tip of her tongue, like a diver's toes gripping the edge of the diving-board.

She could hear herself asking the question in her head, it echoed over and over, varying in intonation and construction, but try as she might, she just couldn't launch the words from her mouth. She was scared her voice would suddenly crack and that tears would appear from nowhere and that right here, in the middle of this gym, in front of *Delilah Lillie*, of all people, she would lose control.

She couldn't bear to ask Delilah the question because she didn't think she'd be able to handle even the smallest hint of intimacy in her reply. It made her feel bad enough as it was to imagine that Delilah had been talking to Dig last night, having normal conversations with him, being a part of his life, while she herself – *his best friend* – was not even on talking terms with him. Nadine couldn't believe how much things had changed over the last few days.

On the treadmill, Delilah ran as if being swept along by the wind through an endless, sunlit field of cornflowers and poppies, her feet not making a sound against the rubber tread, her pony-tail flying out behind her as if on a gust of summer breeze. Nadine had tried the treadmill only once and had felt so paranoid that she was going to lose her footing and go shooting off the back end and into the lap of someone doing sit-ups behind her that she'd not tried it again since.

They stood side by side on the machines that Nadine had never found a name for and so referred to as the 'swish' machines. Nadine always felt a little insecure on this contraption, too, gripping on to the handlebars for dear life while her legs 'swished' away beneath her. Delilah, she noticed, was fearlessly unattached to the machine, positively *marching* back and forth, her arms swinging freely at her sides. And she was on the highest ramp setting.

Delilah turned and hit Nadine with a wide, adrenalin-fuelled grin that seemed to suggest that she was actually enjoying herself, and then turned away again.

It had taken Nadine a long time to feel comfortable at the gym. She'd first joined after realizing with an overpowering sense of desolation that only a few years after finally shedding her puppy-fat she was about to experience the ill-effects of a rapidly slowing metabolism. The carefree life of one who could eat Mars Bars and burgers and cream cakes with impunity was not to be hers.

It had been anathema to her at first, lining up at these soulless machines to walk up and down or cycle on the spot for forty-five minutes or so feeling utterly ridiculous and thinking, Is this what God intended? Is this what two hundred million years of evolution have boiled down to? Me – paying a hundred quid a month to run on the spot in a stupid outfit?

But she'd got used to it eventually, it had become just another part of her routine, and she no longer thought about it. Felt almost at home in this peculiar place, in fact. She knew the form, could programme any of these machines in two or three deft button configurations, no longer felt embarrassed doing her stretches in front of other people, looked positively *cool* at the water fountains, had it all down pat.

But now, accompanied by Delilah, she was feeling like a graceless, lumpen novice again.

'God – I enjoyed that,' said Delilah, joyfully, after effortlessly executing 150 sit-ups in the manner of a US marine in training, and leaping down the stairs towards the changing rooms. Nadine followed behind, her legs wobbling slightly as a result of her efforts to keep pace with Delilah's work-out.

‘Yeah. Me too,’ said Nadine, her leaden, exhausted voice suggesting anything *but*.

In the changing room Delilah began to remove her barely damp clothes with the confidence of one who has nothing to hide: no bumps, no lumps, no ripples, no hairs.

Yup, thought Nadine, as she glanced at a startlingly naked Delilah, she was that sort of clotted-cream colour all over, and she was definitely a natural blonde, and she did have the body of a finely tuned race horse and her bottom did stand up all by itself.

She hoped sincerely that Delilah got down on her hands and knees every morning when she woke up and thanked God for what he’d chosen to give her.

Over a cup of coffee in the gym’s café, Delilah seemed less nervous and eager to please than she’d been earlier, and Nadine was surprised by how easy-going and pleasant she was – she’d always been so sullen and moody at school. Nadine couldn’t recall ever seeing her smiling in those days. But now she was almost enjoying the conversation. They’d been talking generally about keeping fit, healthy eating, giving up smoking – which Delilah was having trouble with and which Nadine had been meaning to get around to for the last ten years – and the shock of turning thirty.

‘And of course,’ said Nadine, ‘the scariest thing about turning thirty is that you’re running out of time to defer the *baby* issue, aren’t you? You know, for years and years you’ve said that you’ll have kids before you’re thirty – that seems reasonable enough – and then you turn twenty-eight, twenty-nine, and suddenly you’re thinking, hold on a sec, not sure if I’m ready quite yet, maybe when I’m thirty-two. Then you turn thirty and realize that you're no more ready for it than you were ten years ago – *less* ready, if anything, and you start wondering if you'll ever actually be ready.' She stopped stirring her sugar lump into her coffee and looked up at Delilah. 'Do you know what I mean?'

Delilah smiled and shrugged. 'Haven't really given it that much thought,' she said, which struck Nadine as very odd. Thirty-year-old women who hadn't given the baby issue much thought simply didn't exist as far as she was concerned.

'Oh, come on, Delilah,' she snorted, 'you've been married for ten years. You must have at least *talked* about it?'

'Well,' she said, 'Alex – his business is his life. I don't think there's any room for a child.'

'Yeah, but what about you? Don't you want kids?'

Delilah was turning Nadine's lighter over and over between her fingers and staring at the top of the table. 'Oh God,' she said, 'I don't know. I suppose so. One day. I just feel too . . . *selfish* right now. I feel I've got too much to sacrifice. Do you know what I mean?'

Nadine nodded enthusiastically. She knew *exactly* what she meant. 'I sometimes wish that I'd done it when I was younger. Got it out of the way when I was eighteen. My kid would have been in school by the time I was twenty-four and I could have caught up with my life then, without being deafened by the sound of my biological clock nagging at me.' She laughed. 'Don't you ever wish you'd done it when you were younger?'

Delilah laughed, too. 'Not really,' she shrugged. And then she glanced at her watch. 'Oh God,' she said, 'it's nearly ten! Look, Deen. I'm sorry, but I've really got to dash.' She was collecting her belongings to her, her puffa, her bag, her scarf.

'Here,' said Nadine, picking up her car keys and getting to her feet, 'let me give you a lift home – your cousin's place isn't far from the studio.'

'Oh. No. Really, thanks. I'll be fine walking. I'd like to walk,' she smiled tightly and threw her bag over her shoulder. 'Really.'

'If you're sure?'

She nodded effusively. 'Yeah – there's some things I need to do, you know, on the way home. But thanks. And thanks for this' – she indicated the gym – 'maybe we could do this again?'

Nadine nodded and smiled and thought, 'Yeah – *maybe*.'

'Actually, Nadine,' said Delilah, sliding her hold-all off her shoulder and putting her hands on the table, 'I haven't been entirely honest with you. I'm not . . . um . . . I'm not here just for the sake of my bottom, actually.' Nadine saw her take a deep breath. She was nervous.

'Oh yeah,' said Nadine, apprehensively.

'No,' she said, 'I wanted to talk to you, really. There was something I wanted to say to you.'

Nadine sat down and put her car keys back on the table.

'I know you don't really like me, Nadine and I know that you see me as some sort of threat to your friendship with Dig. But that's not why I'm here – honestly. There's nothing going on between Dig and me and there never will be. I've always liked you, Nadine. I was a bit in awe of you at school and maybe that sometimes came across as rudeness, but I suppose I was just jealous of you. You were so clever and so cool and you had everything going for you. I used to want to *be* you, you know, and if I was ever mean to you it was only because I was scared of you. I never meant to come between you and Dig then, and I really, *really* don't want to come between you again now. I hate it that you're not speaking.

'Dig's so stubborn,' continued Delilah, 'and he's not going to call you even though I can tell he's desperate to. And I know you're just as stubborn as him. But please. Call him,' she pleaded. 'Don't waste any more time, Nadine. Life's too short. Make up. Be friends. You two need each other, you two were made for each other. You two,' she said pointedly, 'should be *together*.'

And with that highly overdramatic and perfectly ludicrous closing comment, she disappeared, leaving behind her a cloud of her unidentifiable morning-dew perfume and an atmosphere of sadness and confusion.

# CHAPTER TWENTY-SIX

The arsehole driver of the Porsche 911 in front of him finally ran out of water. Dig felt like he'd been here for ever, parked behind him, watching him circle round and round his precious extra inch of manhood, squirting at it mincily with the water jet-spray like he was the only man in the history of the world who'd ever owned a Porsche.

Dig watched him drying his hands distastefully on a piece of paper towel pulled from a barrel attached to the wall, and just when Dig thought he was finally going to get into his car and drive away, he began circling it again, eagle-eyed, with a soft cloth in his hand, rubbing meticulously at various points on the paintwork.

He was taking his time. He could see Dig waiting behind him, but he wasn't going to let that unsettle him. Because he was a Porsche driver and in the evolutionary scale of car ownership he was the boss, Dig, in his silver G-reg Honda Civic was just Monkey-Boy to him, a lower form of life.

Finally, the man in the Porsche lowered himself into his car, fiddled around with his stereo a bit, adjusted his wing mirrors electronically and drove away, apparently quite pleased with himself. Dig sighed and moved his car forward towards the jet-spray.

Dig had been driving home from work tonight, Digby vibrating nervously in the passenger seat next to him, when he'd stopped to fill up at the petrol station on Oval Road and had had a sudden and unprecedented urge to wash his car. This had never happened to him before – especially not at one of those manual jet-spray jobs where you actually had to *get out* of your car.

Despite his domestic fastidiousness, Dig operated a complete set of double standards when it came to his car. The inside of his car resembled Notting Hill the morning after the carnival, strewn with fast-food packaging and empty cans, the outside festooned with monochromatic bird-shits and tear-drops of sticky red sap.

The reason he kept his flat so clean and his car so dirty was simple. He loved his flat and he hated his car. Hated it. He'd had to fork out another £150 on Monday morning to get it fixed – the fifth time in six years he'd had major problems with it. He'd already paid for the car twice over in maintenance alone. And it wasn't even a car he'd ever actually wanted. It was a car he'd somehow ended up with. But tonight, strangely, he felt warmly disposed towards his car. Tonight he decided that maybe if he treated his car a little more nicely then his car might treat him a little more fairly.

He aimed the spray at the side panels and watched with satisfaction as layers of grime and goo began to fall away and a fresh new skin of shiny silver revealed itself. It symbolized, he realized in an uncharacteristic moment of philosophical reflection, the way he himself was feeling today.

He'd had a revelation today, at work – in fact, he'd had a series of revelations, and washing his car was just the start. A new Dig was going to be born tonight.

After the disastrous start to his unplanned cohabitation with Delilah, after the dreadful scene with Digby the other morning, and the puking up and the mess everywhere and disorganized towel rotas, Dig wanted to bring some *class* to the situation.

Delilah, in her Chester palace, was probably accustomed to eating her evening meal at a dining table. She was used to large rooms and open spaces, fresh air and privacy. She probably had her own en-suite bathroom. She *wasn't* accustomed to living in cramped quarters, eating off her lap and tidying up after herself. She had a *housekeeper*, for God's sake.

Despite Delilah's ignominious start in life, she had always exuded a kind of star quality and it was easier for Dig to imagine her living in neo-Georgian splendour than living as she had done on the Gospel Oak estate, among dirty nappies, empty beer cans, bawling, snot-nosed infants and overflowing ashtrays. Delilah *belonged* in her huge six-bedroomed, feng-shui-ed house with its ruffles and valances, its conservatory and water feature in the garden, she was born to be pampered and spoiled. She didn't belong on his sofabed. It was all wrong.

So tonight he was going to do everything he could to make his lifestyle compare favourably with Delilah's life in Chester. Why? Because, as inconvenient and uncomfortable as it was sharing his tiny flat with Delilah, as much as he hated her mess and her mood swings, her crystals and her dog, he wanted her to stay.

Not necessarily in his flat, but in London.

He didn't want her to turn around to him and say, 'This sucks, London sucks, your flat sucks, I'm going home.' Because it felt very suspiciously to Dig like he was falling in love with Delilah.

Yes, he knew: he knew exactly what Nadine would

think of that, he knew that he shouldn't, he knew it was probably a huge mistake, but he couldn't help it. She was just so . . . so unutterably delicious. The smell of her, like fresh laundry and damp grass, the feel of her, like marshmallows and satin, and the sight of her, that extraordinary hair which you could almost see your reflection in, those lips, those legs, those duck-egg-blue eyes . . .

But it was more than all that. It was her *vulnerability* more than anything that made Dig love her – or want to love her. She was like a lost little girl, all alone in the world, full of secrets and pain. He wanted to help her, protect her, look after her. Reading that letter from her shrink had unleashed a whole new set of emotions within him. He'd looked up 'clinical psychologist' on the Internet at work this morning, trying to find out more about what they did, and it sounded like they were pretty serious shit. It was more than just 'my father never hugged me' kind of stuff. Clinical psychologists, it seemed, tried to mend broken people.

Dig's water allocation ran out and he replaced the jet-spray in its holder. He got back into his car, gave the increasingly quivering Digby a reassuring chuck under the chin and drove towards the vacuum machine.

Far from putting Dig off Delilah, finding out that she was a fruitloop had intensified his feelings for her. It made her more real, more attainable in a way, like finding out that she was more than just the coolest girl in school, finding the soft spots that she'd let only him see, was what had made him fall in love with her all those years ago. People with weaknesses made Dig feel strong in the same way that small women made him feel big.

Since reading that letter, Dig had been consumed by

an overwhelming desire for intimacy. He missed the way he'd been in his youth, he missed the time in his life when he'd been carefree and careless with his heart, when he'd been capable of falling helplessly and hopelessly in love. He'd been such a soft-hearted romantic when he was young, his heart on his sleeve and his emotions on a plate. And since he'd first set eyes on Delilah, last Saturday, he had begun to experience similar sensations again. It was incredibly exciting to discover that he was still capable of feeling this way.

For the first time since he was a teenager, since that hideous weekend in Manchester, Dig could imagine, without a hint of queasiness or panic, a future life which involved somebody else. He could imagine seeing the same face on the pillow next to him every single morning, and he could imagine saying 'we' a lot instead of 'I'. He could imagine being a provider and taking care of someone. He could envisage the golden world that Nadine had conjured up in the café the other day, the world full of teenage children and mess and noise and joyful rites of passage.

Dig was ready to open up again. He was ready for anything, including getting hurt.

He slid into the back seat of his car, thinking briefly what an alien place the back seat of one's own car was to be, and began stuffing handfuls of rubbish into a carrier bag.

Him and Delilah.

Delilah and him.

It was a distinct possibility.

He just had to persuade her to stay. He had to convince her that whatever it was she had going on with Alex in Chester was not that special. And let's face it, this Alex couldn't be all that, could he, if he didn't even manage it more than once or twice a year? Not to mention the fact that Delilah had left him in Chester without warning and without involving him in her plans, whatever they were. She couldn't love him that much, could she, to have left him with a note and an empty bed?

Alex did, however, have a six-bedroom house in his favour, plus acres of land, horses, cars and enough cash to send Delilah off shopping first-class all over the world whenever she felt like it.

But Dig took this as a sign – this was another facet of his major revelation – it was time to step his career plans up a gear. He was thirty years old – he was supposed to be the millionaire owner of his own record label by now. He was supposed to be driving a big fuck-off Mercedes and spending half the year abroad in his tax haven in Monaco. He should be up there with Alan McGee in the *Times* 1000 Richest supplement. He wasn't ever supposed to have ended up in a poky flat on Camden Road driving a clapped-out old Honda Civic and feeling pleased to be earning £27,000 a year.

Somewhere between his A levels and his thirtieth birthday, Dig realized, he'd lost his fire. Somewhere along the line he'd become complacent and *laissez-faire*, happy to get by with the bare minimum. When he'd first started work at Electrogram Records music had been his life. He used to pinch himself in disbelief that he was *being paid* to go to gigs. He felt *privileged* to be working in the music industry. What had happened to his ambition, his overpowering need to be a success, leave his mark, make something of himself? Contentment was a dangerous thing.

There were guys out there, guys still in their twenties,

making twice, three times, *ten* times what he was making. There were guys out there who'd done it, made it, got there, achieved – *and they were younger than him.*

He thought about Nick Jeffries – twenty-four, hyperactive, restless and always on the move, always sniffing around, asking questions, pushing, pushing, pushing. He was a pain in the arse but you could bet your bottom dollar that in a year or two he'd be gone from Johnny-Boy Records, gone and on to the next salary increment, the next rung of the ladder. He'd be running his own company by the time he was twenty-eight and rolling in it two years later.

Nick Jeffries would *not* be driving a G reg Honda Civic when he was thirty years old.

*This* was what Dig had missed most about being in love. This was the effect that being in love had on Dig. It lit a fire in his belly. And now he could feel it returning, like the blood rushing back to an anaemic complexion.

£27,000 a year *wasn't enough.*

A Honda Civic *wasn't enough.*

Seventeen-year-old students *weren't enough.*

Signing up only one big band in his career *wasn't enough.*

Delilah expected more, and he wanted more.

He pulled the vacuum nozzle out of its holder and began ferreting around the fluff-laden nooks and crannies of his car, sucking out years' worth of dust and fag-ash and tiny ribbons of Cellophane unfurled from cigarette packets.

Pretty phallic places, petrol stations, Dig thought, looking around him. Nozzles, pumps, cars, dipsticks and all those things that were designed to fit into holes and spew forth petrol, air, water and oil. Even this innocent-looking vacuum was behaving like a lascivious old pervert, groping around frantically inside his car's underwear.

The first weapon in Dig's anti-Alex arsenal was his 'groovy' London lifestyle. Alex might have cash and assets and a business but he couldn't excite Delilah the way Dig could, with nights out schmoozing with celebrities, first viewings of hot new bands and cab rides all around London Town with that air that 'smells of life' rushing up her nostrils.

The second weapon was his libido. He had one. Alex didn't. Full stop.

And the third weapon was his culinary skills. Dig was very proud of his attention to detail and his eye for aesthetics. Nothing pleased him more than the simplest of high-quality ingredients, plainly cooked and beautifully presented, and it had always saddened him slightly that he had no one special to regale with his lovingly prepared plates of food. It wasn't the sort of food you would cook for just anyone, for your mates, or your mum, or some girl who you weren't all that serious about.

Delilah was giving him the perfect opportunity to show off.

So – it was all sorted.

Dig and Delilah's Big Night Out.

A gig at the Forum – an all-girl band called Pesky Kids who Dig, personally, couldn't stand but who Delilah would love, because they were fresh and trendy and poppy and all those things that seemed to appeal to her so much.

Then on to the after-show party – lots of celebs for Delilah to get her rocks off over. A couple of drinks, a bit of a mingle and then back home, where Dig was going to surprise her with a slap-up midnight feast.

He'd been to the fishmonger in his lunch hour and bought a pound of absolutely enormous prawns – complete bruisers – plus a great thick wedge of Loch Fyne smoked salmon and a small pot of caviar. He'd bought a packet of blinis and a large pot of smetana from the organic supermarket on Parkway, and he was going to boil up some dinky miniature new potatoes and serve them crushed with melted butter and rock salt. Nice and simple. The sort of stuff he could just whisk out of the fridge at the last minute and have ready with the minimum of preparation and fuss. And very, very classy.

And during dinner, over the candle-light, he would talk to her, *really* talk to her, about her plans, her trip to London, about that letter from her shrink, and her mission to 'uncover the past'. After all, he couldn't help her if he didn't know what her secret was.

Dig sneered a bit as he unpeeled half a Harvest Crunch bar from the floor of his car. This was somewhat confusing, as he'd never in his entire life eaten a Harvest Crunch bar and could only imagine that someone else, someone he'd been kind enough to offer a lift to, had left it there. It was one thing chucking litter about in your own car, but in somebody else's? Fucking cheek . . .

Dig gave his dashboard a last going over with a cloth and clambered from his car to appraise his handiwork. Not bad, not bad at all.

'What d'you think of that then, you little gremlin?' he said, bending to address Digby, who was now shivering on the forecourt, looking like an abandoned orphan. 'Pretty good, huh?' It looked almost like it belonged to someone who actually *liked* their car.

He opened the passenger door for Digby and patted the seat. 'In you get, titch. We're going home now.'

Digby sat motionless.

'Come on, mate. Get in.'

The dog eyed Dig fearfully, and then the passenger seat, and began to quake even more.

'Oh Jesus, what kind of a dog are you? You're descended from the *wolf*, for God's sake. Do you realize that? Come on – show some balls.'

Digby emitted a small whimper and looked at Dig imploringly.

'You can look at me all you like, and you can make your pathetic little noises, but I'm not going to put you in the car. We're going to stay here until you get in on your own.'

Digby whimpered a bit louder.

'Listen, you raggedy little excuse for a dog, I am not going to help you, OK? You might be used to the life of Riley where you come from – you've probably got your very own personal valet, or something, but you're in Dig country now and you're going to have to learn to fend for yourself. So get in.'

He patted the seat once more, and this time Digby seemed to have a change of attitude. He girded his loins and readied himself, an expression of determination on his face, and suddenly launched himself, with a tremendous effort, towards the passenger seat. He looked like he was just about to make it – his little legs gripped for dear life on to the edge of the seat, his eyes bulged with strenuous effort, his claws dug into the beige upholstery, his back legs scrabbled to keep him aloft – and then he fell off, rolling on to his back on the forecourt.

Dig couldn't help it. He burst out laughing. The dog threw him an injured look.

'If at first, mate, if at first. Try again.'

Digby did try again, and again he fell. He tried twice more in fact before finding enough impetus to finally land on the chair.

'Yeah!' cheered Dig, patting the distinctly triumphant-looking dog on the head. 'What a geezer! What a dude!' He picked up Digby's paw and shook his hand. 'See – wasn't so bad, was it?'

Dig gently closed the door, walked around the car and got into the driver's seat. He turned to look at the dog, and the dog turned to look at him, and Dig could have sworn he smiled at him.

'OK, boy. Let's go home and show your mum how much we've both changed, eh?'

He switched on his ignition and pulled out of the garage.

# CHAPTER TWENTY-SEVEN

Nadine stopped off at her local corner shop on the way home that Friday evening and bought a fresh loaf of bread and a packet of bacon. She was going to eat lots of bacon sandwiches. She couldn't remember the last time she'd let herself eat a bacon sandwich, and then a courier had walked into her studio eating one a couple of hours ago and she hadn't been able to get the smell out of her nostrils or the thought out of her mind since. And besides, she deserved a big fat bacon sandwich after her hugely strenuous work-out with Delilah at the gym this morning – she must have burned off at least twice as many calories as she usually did, when she was on her own.

She'd spent most of that day and the last thinking about what Delilah had said to her that morning at the gym. It had been a revelation. Delilah had been jealous of *her* at school. It all made sense now and threw a different complexion on two of the worst years of her life. She felt stupid for all the angst she'd put herself through and she respected Delilah hugely for her honesty. Of course Delilah wasn't interested in Dig. Why would she want Dig, with his skinny legs and his poky flat when she had a mansion and a handsome husband waiting for her at home? For the first time since she was fourteen years old, Nadine could feel her resentment towards Delilah fading away.

She'd also been thinking a lot about what had happened between her and Phil on Wednesday night, and shuddering a lot – how could she? how could she? *how could she?* – but it had been nearly forty-eight hours now and there'd been no word from him, so maybe, just maybe, *please God*, he was just going to disappear down whatever dark, dank hole he'd emerged from, and she'd never have to see him again.

She dropped a thick stack of paperwork on the table in her hallway, hung up her coat and kicked off her shoes. She dropped the plug into the bath-tub, flicked on the hot tap, bunged in a huge dollop of marshmallow and rosehip bubbles and padded into her living room.

As she passed the telephone she noticed the answerphone flashing and did a double take. It was telling her that she had eighteen new messages!

The display must have malfunctioned. Either that or something bad had happened. Oh God. Maybe her mother. Or . . . or . . . maybe it was Dig, trying to make things up with her, maybe he wanted to see her that night. Nadine's heart began racing as she pressed the Play button.

'Er – hi,' began the first message, 'Nadine. It's me. Phil.' Nadine's burgeoning excitement deflated like a punctured tyre. 'It's . . . erm . . . it's eight fifteen. On Friday morning. I must have just missed you. Just phoning to say hi and that I hope you have a great time in Barcelona, and I can't wait till you get back.'

So much for her theory that he'd forgotten about her, thought Nadine. She tapped her fingers impatiently against the plastic covering of the machine while she waited for the next message, hoping for the sound of Dig's voice.

'Hi. It's me again. It's . . . eight thirty now. I know you're not there, but I was just thinking about you. So . . . I'll call back. Bye.'

Oh for God's sake. Nadine didn't have time to listen to this crap. She had bacon sandwiches to eat, packing to do, Channel Four comedy shows to watch. A beep heralded the next message.

'Me again. It's nine thirty now. I was thinking – maybe I could see you off at the airport tomorrow. Maybe. If you like. I just really, really need to see you, Deen. Soon. So give me a call. OK?'

Oh God. Oh God. Nadine fast-forwarded to the next message.

'Nadine Kite. It's me again. At . . . er . . . ten o'clock. Thinking about you still, about Wednesday night. I'm still just . . . blown away, by you, by what happened between us.'

She fast-forwarded again.

'It's ten thirty. I've been thinking about Wednesday night again. I can't wait to see you, Nadine Kite. I don't think I can wait till next week, y'know? I think we should meet sooner . . . I'd really like to see you before you go . . . Anyway – give me a call.

'Hi. Me again. Ten forty-five. Yeah. Definitely meet up before you go to Barcelona, I think. Let's talk later.

'Hi. It's ten fifty. I've got to go out now. I'll . . . er . . . I'll call you later.

'Nadine Kite. I'm back. It's amazing, everything feels so different. You've changed everything. Everything felt so black and so fragile and now I feel like I'm alive again.'

Oh Jesus. Oh no. Oh no. Nadine began fast-forwarding through the messages faster and faster.

'Hi – it's me again . . .

'Nadine – it's me . . .

'It's three fifteen, still thinking about you . . .

'It's me. What time do you get home? Shit – I wish I had your work number. I need to talk to you . . .

'Hi – it's Phil again . . .

'It's five twenty . . .

'It's me. It's five forty-five . . .

Nadine heavy-heartedly wound the tape on to the last message.

'You'll be home any minute. How many messages have I left? Yeah. Too many, probably. Look, I have to see you. Tonight. OK? I'll call you again. Please, Nadine Kite. I have to see you. Bye.'

*Beep*, said the machine, *you have no more messages.*

A chill went up and down Nadine's spine. Oh God.

She felt herself beginning to panic. The flat felt suddenly oppressive and horribly, horribly empty. The phone sat ominously in its cradle, frighteningly silent but pregnant with the prospect of the next ringing tone and the inevitable sound of Phil's voice invading her home and her freedom.

She sat like that for a few minutes, listening to the sound of her own heartbeat in her ears, trying to assimilate the fact that what she'd done on Wednesday night wasn't over, and was in fact just beginning, until she heard the bath water change its pitch as it reached the top. She got up slowly and shuffled towards the bathroom. As she approached the door the phone finally rang, making her jump in spite of her expectation.

She turned and watched as the answerphone clicked on.

'Oh. Hi. Thought you'd be back by now. It's . . . er . . .

six forty-five. Where are you? Maybe you got stuck at work? I'll phone you later. Bye.'

Nadine sighed and turned off the bath taps.

Oh God, she thought, I can't handle this.

I've got to get out of here.

*I have got to get out of here.*

She picked up her handbag, threw on her coat and left her flat, the door slamming loudly behind her.

She was going to the place in the world where she felt safest. She was going to Dig's and she was going to apologize for her hideous behaviour, and by the time she left, everything was going to be back to normal.

## CHAPTER TWENTY-EIGHT

Dig's prawns tasted like unwashed towelling socks.

His smoked salmon tasted like damp kitchen roll, and the blinis had all the flavour and consistency of old cardboard.

'Mmmmmm,' he murmured, through a mouthful of mush, 'these prawns are excellent, aren't they?'

Delilah nodded sadly, and sighed.

She had slipped into a pair of pyjamas, and her hair was hanging limply around her face. Dig had seen her looking better. She hadn't said a word since they'd sat down to eat a quarter of an hour ago, just nodded and sighed and made the odd grunting noise in response to his questions.

This evening was not turning out how he'd planned.

Delilah had claimed to be feeling unwell when she'd finally returned from wherever it was she'd been all day at eight thirty that evening. The Pesky Kids were due on stage at eight so they'd blown that one, and she didn't want to go out anyway, so she said, fancied a 'quiet night in'.

Funny, Dig had thought, how people in bad moods always take precedence over people in good moods.

Dig had been trying so hard to get her to open up, but it seemed he'd chosen the wrong night. All his questions hit a dead end and were ricocheted back at him. Delilah was quite patently *not* in the mood for talking. Dig's heartfelt concern from earlier in the day had dissipated, and now he was just plain irritated.

He didn't know what to do. He knew what he *wanted* to do. He wanted to slam his cutlery down on the table and shout at the top of voice, *'Delilah Lillie, what the fucking hell is the matter with you?!'* But he couldn't, because this was Delilah, and Delilah didn't give answers; you weren't allowed to ask her questions – that was against the rules. So he just had to swallow it and pretend that her deathly silence wasn't happening, compensating for her cerebral absence from the table by being ludicrously jolly and gratingly convivial.

But he'd run out of mindless prattle now, spent the last dollar in his jolly-bank. He wanted to walk over to the stereo, turn it off and switch on the telly instead. That would take the pressure off. But he couldn't, because that would be an acknowledgement of the fact that something was wrong, that they weren't talking. It would make a mockery of the candles and the lollo rosso fronds and the shiny cutlery.

Delilah was pushing a tiny, ant-like ball of caviar around her plate with the tine of her fork, and Dig could feel her long bare feet tap-tap-tapping against the table leg. This latest silence had lasted about two minutes, so far. The longest yet. What was it, thought Dig, what was it that was so painfully unbearable about silences between people? It was like a failure. A silence in the midst of a lively conversation could negate in a second everything that had come before, as if the rest of the evening's seamless chatter had been just a fluke and it had always been only a matter of time before the truth emerged – that nobody *really* had anything to say to each other. Why couldn't people just sit together in silence without feeling inadequate, boring and distanced from their companions? Silence also seemed to act as a laxative for bullshit, desperation to fill the hole in the conversation leading to ever more frantic and tedious commentary.

'So,' began Dig, admitting defeat, breaking the silence, splitting open a prawn, belly-up, 'what are you up to tomorrow?' He felt like an emotionally withdrawn father trying to make conversation with a recalcitrant teenage daughter.

Delilah gently rested her fork on the side of her plate and sighed again.

'I've . . . er . . . I've got a lot to do tomorrow . . .' She trailed off.

Dig sensed an opening. Finally. He took a deep breath. 'Anything I can help with?'

Delilah shrugged and picked up her fork again. 'No,' she said, eventually, 'no – I'll be fine. But thanks.' She looked up briefly through heavy eyes and then down again.

Dig sighed with frustration.

'What are *you* doing?'

'What?' replied Dig, slightly shocked by Delilah's first opening gambit of the evening.

'Tomorrow. What are you doing tomorrow?'

'Oh. Right. I don't know.' That was a point, thought Dig. It was Saturday tomorrow, and for as long as he could remember, Saturday had been Nadine day. A fry-up either round the corner from her, or round the corner from him, and then, depending on the weather, a walk in the park, flying the kites, or just sitting in and watching some sport on the telly before getting ready to go out. That was what he did on Saturdays. Well, that was what he *used* to do on Saturdays, before he and Nadine had fallen out with each other. He wasn't quite sure what he would do now that they weren't talking to each other.

The thought made him feel single. Which struck him as odd, because he'd been single, pretty much, for the last ten years. But, with Nadine in his life, he'd never actually *felt* single. He'd never had to contemplate huge, empty weekends with no one to share the minutiae. Even when Nadine was going out with someone, she usually spent her Saturdays with him, grateful to have whichever hugely unsuitable man she currently had in her life out of her hair for a few hours.

Dig felt his stomach swill with unexpected anxiety. What would life be like, without Nadine? It was impossible to imagine. Horrible, probably, absolutely horrible. That settled it. He would definitely, definitely make things up with her, tomorrow. He would phone her first thing and they would go out for breakfast and everything would be back to normal.

He smiled and looked up. Delilah was still pushing the bead of caviar around her plate and appeared to be having trouble controlling her breathing. Her chest was rising and falling like billows and her mouth was slightly puckered.

'Are you all right?'

As he watched her, he saw a slick of sweat appear on her upper lip and the colour drain entirely from her face.

'Are you OK? Delilah?'

She dropped her fork noisily on to her plate, scraped back her chair, cupped her hands to her mouth and ran towards the bathroom, her napkin falling from her lap as she went.

A moment later Dig heard his prawns, his caviar, his

blinis and his smoked salmon hitting the toilet bowl in a dramatic stampede from Delilah's stomach.

He sighed and began clearing away the food. He heard the shower being operated and the lock going on the bathroom door. Well, that was that, then. It looked as if Delilah's problems and her secret mission to uncover the past were to remain a mystery for at least another night.

Dig was just about to blow out the candles, when he heard the doorbell ring.

Dig's disembodied voice on the entry phone sounded surprised to hear her – 'Oh, Nadine. Hi' – almost like he'd been expecting someone else.

She took the linoleum-clad steps two at a time, oblivious to her already tender, post-gym leg muscles screaming at her to stop. She hadn't yet thought about how she was going to tell Dig that she'd had E'd-up sex with Philip Rich within hours of meeting up with him again and how he was now turning out to be a bit of a psycho, plaguing her with phone calls and scaring her half to death. She hadn't thought about any of that. None of that mattered any more. All she wanted to do was make up and be friends again.

She rounded the corner at the top of the last flight of stairs and stood nervously outside Dig's front door. He was standing in his hallway, looking tired and uncomfortable, wearing his best shirt, his new jeans and a pair of oatmeal socks.

'Hi,' she said, squeezing out a smile. She felt suddenly and inexplicably tearful.

'Er – hi.' Dig scratched his head and looked distinctly unthrilled to see her.

'Sorry to – er – turn up like this.'

'That's OK.'

'Are you going to invite me in then, or what?' She grinned, attempting to bring a little levity to the tense atmosphere.

Dig didn't smile, didn't say anything, just scratched his head again and moved out of her way.

'So – how've you been?' she asked.

'Oh – fine. Fine. You?'

'Yeah. Fine.'

There was a silence. It was awkward.

She dropped her bag and coat where she always left them and made her way into the living room – which was when she became slowly aware of the seductive surroundings, of the veritable *come-on* spread out all over the table, and candles, and the music – it sounded like – sounded like – *Robbie Williams*? Couldn't be, couldn't possibly be. Dig wouldn't be listening to Robbie Williams. And the lights were very low, and what was that *thing*, that furry little thing on the sofa? It looked like one of those Russian hats, except smaller and hairier. Nadine jumped in her skin when the Russian hat thing wriggled and then she screamed when it jumped off the sofa and started walking towards her.

'Oh God!' she exclaimed, clutching at her heart. 'What the fuck is that?'

As it approached it revealed itself to be a very, very small dog.

'It's a dog,' said Dig, helpfully.

'Yes. I can see it's a dog. But what's it doing here?' She crouched down to pet the trembling little creature, who immediately flopped on to his back and offered up his stomach.

'It's – er – he's Digby.'

It took a second for Nadine to twig. She thought it was a feeble joke at first, and then it dawned on her. Digby. Delilah's dog. This was Delilah's dog. What the hell was Delilah's dog doing in Dig's flat? Nadine was starting to think that she'd stumbled into some parallel universe; empty prawn shells, jars of caviar, Robbie Williams, small dogs – she fully expected a wife and kids to appear from nowhere at any second.

And then her thought processes began to clarify.

Sexy food – low lighting – Delilah's dog.

Oh God.

Oh God.

Oh no.

At the very second that Nadine worked out what was going on she heard a click and there was a sudden blast of light and steam from the bathroom door. And there she stood, emerging from the steam like a rock star coming on stage through a cloud of dry ice, her hair tied up in a towelling turban and her body wrapped in a minute towel that barely covered the tops of her thighs. She smiled widely when she saw Nadine standing there.

'Deen,' she said, 'what are you doing here? We weren't expecting you.'

Oh God. Oh God. Nadine's chest constricted and her breath came fast and furious.

She looked at Delilah, towelled and scrubbed and steaming.

She looked at Dig, shirted and combed and blushing.

Shc looked at the table, laden and clothed and sparkling.

Nadine had never felt less like she belonged somewhere before, in her life. The flat stank of Delilah. She'd scented it, like a cat. She saw Dig and Delilah exchange a look. There was single moment of dreadful silence.

'You two-faced, conniving, lying *BITCH*!'

The words came from nowhere. Nadine's anger was uncontrollable.

She stood rooted to the spot for a while, staring at Delilah through teary eyes. Delilah was staring back at her in horror.

'No . . . no,' she began, 'you don't understand, honestly, it's fine, Nadine.' She put a hand out towards Nadine.

Nadine shook it off, picked up her coat and bag and pushed Dig out of the way. At the door she turned around. 'You haven't changed, have you, Delilah, you haven't changed at all.' She slammed the door closed behind her and ran down the stairs. Behind her she heard Dig's door opening and his voice echoing down the stairs: 'Deen, where the fuck are you going?' She heard his footsteps, faster than hers, catching up with her, and she increased her pace.

She spun herself around the twists and turns of the narrow stairwell, her hand gripping the rail, her feet moving faster than Michael Flatley's. She snagged her tights on the pedal of a bicycle crammed into the entrance hall and threw open the front door, clattering down the stone steps leading to the pavement.

Dig caught up with her on the street.

'Nadine! What the fuck is going on?'

'Nothing – I'm going home.'

'But what's the matter with you? What was all that about?'

'I don't want to talk about it. Just go back inside. Go

and look after your precious, *beautiful* Delilah! Poor helpless innocent little Delilah. Go and wrap yourself back around her little finger. Go on!'

'Nadine!' Dig grabbed her arm. She shook his hand off her.

'*Leave me alone!*'

Dig stood back and eyed Nadine with surprise. 'All right then,' he sniffed, 'all right. Fuck off then, go on – fuck off.'

For a moment they stood and stared at one another, both breathing heavily and both wearing expressions of disbelief that something this horrible could be happening to their perfect friendship.

Nadine opened her mouth to say something, then turned and ran away. A gap in the four lanes of traffic on Camden Road prevented her from killing herself as she sped across the road towards her car, flinging open the door and grinding her gears before screeching away.

The last thing she saw before she took off was Dig, standing in his socked feet in the middle of Camden Road, rain pouring down his face, staring after her with his jaw hanging open and his hands outstretched in front of him in a gesture of pure bewilderment.

## CHAPTER TWENTY-NINE

Nadine started talking to herself as she threw her little white car around corners, across roundabouts and over traffic lights, muttering, under her breath, like a mad woman.

What had she done? What was happening to her? What had happened to all those years she'd spent being cool and together and happy and well adjusted? Had she actually been but a whisker's width away from this insanity all along, without ever realizing?

In the space of less than a week Nadine had dumped a perfectly lovely man because she didn't like his choice of mugs, had spent an entire evening phoning Dig when she knew he was going to be out, had actually driven round to his bloody flat in the middle of the night in her Bart Simpson slippers, for Christ's sake, to spy on him, had impulsively telephoned her horribly beautiful ex-boyfriend of ten years ago only to find that he was just horribly horrible now, had ignored this, and the fact that he was completely fucked up, and slept with him anyway, in someone's garage, on a cocktail of drugs and alcohol, she had broken her kitchen window while in the throes of a ridiculous Delilah-induced panic and now she'd done that. That thing just now, in Dig's flat. That hideously embarrassing, Scarlett O'Hara-style exit, all flouncing and tripping and hands-held-to-throat drama-queen.

'Oh my God,' she muttered, 'oh my God, I'm a fucking psycho. Maybe I deserve Phil. Maybe we were made for each other. We could *stalk* each other and send each other sick letters and video tapes.' Tears sprang to her eyes. 'I'm mad,' she sniffed, 'I'm barking mad. I used to be sane but that part of my life is over now . . . oh God!' The tears were now splashing down her cheeks as she contemplated a life of unwashed hair, episodes of uncontrolled eccentricity and stretches of residential care wearing paper clothes.

Dig had told her to fuck off. Her stomach lurched and wriggled and rucked. She felt nauseous. She scratched at her tears distractedly and tried to ignore the little voice inside her head telling her something that she'd known all along, really, ever since Delilah had first reappeared six days ago, the little voice that was telling her that the reason she was so jealous was that she wanted Dig for herself, that she loved Dig – that she was *still in love with Dig.*

'*Ridiculous!*' she exclaimed, slamming the heels of her hands against the steering-wheel, '*completely, totally and utterly ridiculous!*'

A woman in a Fiat Uno and a bobble hat shot her an alarmed glance and Nadine cleared her throat and collected herself. 'Ridiculous,' she muttered again, this time barely moving her lips, and caressing her steering-wheel apologetically.

How could she possibly still be in love with Dig? She'd always loved him, of course she had, but this was a completely different story. She'd never felt jealous of him before. She'd sat next to him at parties and night-clubs while he was chewing young, flat-stomached girls' faces off. She'd listened with relish to every last detail of every last encounter he'd ever had with nubile, perky-breasted little imps. They'd even shared a bedroom together once, at some cottage in the country, him with a girlfriend, her with a boyfriend, and they'd giggled at each other's half-hearted attempts to keep their respective noises down. All without even the smallest sign of the green-eyed monster.

'"*You two need each other*"' – she mimicked Delilah's husky voice – '"*you two were made for each other. You two should be together.*"' Pah!' she exclaimed, under her breath. 'Pah! Two-faced, sneaky, conniving, secretive, lying BITCH!

'He's *my* Dig, Delilah Lillie,' she moaned, as she drove past her house for the fourth time, frantically looking out for a parking space, '*he's my Dig, not your Dig. Go and get your own Dig, you bitch. Leave mine alone. He's my Dig, my Dig, my Dig, my Dig . . .*'

But it was too late, she knew that now, too late for her and Dig. She was never going to see Dig again, ever. It was over . . .

At this thought, yet more tears sprung from her churning stomach and erupted like a geyser all over her face. Rain cascaded down her windscreen and tears ran down her cheeks, and she couldn't see a bloody thing. The world was a blur of orange and white saucers, splintered discs of light that grew and danced and converged together.

She indicated left to make one final attempt at parking somewhere within walking distance of her home and swung her car violently around the corner. 'Why do I live in this *fucking* city?' she muttered. 'Can't even park outside your own *fucking* home, bloody palaver, every single *fucking* time . . .' Her eyes swivelled this way and that, looking desperately through tear-soaked lashes for a space, or a gap, or a person getting into a car, or anything, anything a-fucking-t'all . . .

And then she saw it – there it was, definitely – a car, about to pull out of a space, literally twenty feet from her own front door. She felt a moment of elation, slammed her indicator to the right and brought her car to a screeching halt parallel to the car behind it, so full of determination and defensive territorialism, so paranoid that another car would appear from nowhere and claim the space before her, her eyes so clouded with tears and her vision so obstructed by the sheets of rain bouncing frantically off her windscreen that she didn't see the thin, bowed-over figure in front of her, she didn't notice that he'd stepped out into the street, without warning, from between two parked cars, and the first she knew of his existence was the sound of his knees crunching against her bumper.

'Oh Jesus!' screamed Nadine, her hands jumping off the steering-wheel to cover her mouth. 'Oh no, oh *Jesus*!' She pulled on her handbrake till it almost came off in her hand and started desperately trying to get out of her car, her hands shaking, the old handle clunking and creaking but refusing to budge. 'Jesus Jesus Jesus, oh Jesus, let me out of *this car*!' She suddenly remembered that she'd locked it from the inside, force of habit, to stop car-jackers, and finally threw the car door open. A passing car swerved out of the way and let loose a loud and frightening blast of its horn. Nadine's handbag fell from her lap and everything in it fell on to the wet, black Tarmac. She skipped over the pile of her belongings and ran to the front of her car. 'Oh God, oh God, oh God!'

There was a small, raggedy bunch of bones lying at

the foot of her bonnet, not moving, its limbs arranged at strange angles.

'Oh no oh no oh no,' she thought to herself, whimpering slightly, 'I've killed someone, I've only gone and killed someone.'

She crouched down next to the crumpled figure and leaned in towards his face.

'Hello,' she ventured tentatively, gently prodding his shoulder, 'hello. Can you hear me? Are you all right? Oh Jesus oh Jesus . . . hello . . . hello . . . hello.' The figure remained still. Nadine started thinking *ER*, thinking recovery position, thinking mouth-to-mouth resuscitation, thinking 'mustn't move him, mustn't move him,' thinking '*Defib! Clear!*', thinking 'oh my God will someone please call an ambulance?' The rain cascaded down her damp curls and all over her face. She was paralysed with fear and indecision.

She turned feebly to face the empty street and shouted at the top of her voice, '*Will someone help me – please!*'

And then the man moved, moved just a few inches, and groaned. Nadine spun round and stared at him. He groaned again.

'Oh God – you're alive! Oh thank God!' Tears of relief began to flow down Nadine's face.

The thin, wet figure turned slightly from where he lay on his stomach, on to his side, and began moaning under his breath, 'Oh my leg, my fucking leg.'

Nadine stopped in her tracks – she recognized that voice.

'You dopey cow, you dopey fucking cow – what 'ave you done to me?'

He was beginning to sit up now, his back to her, clutching his knee and rocking back and forth. Nadine definitely recognized that voice. And, now she came to think of it, that hair was pretty familiar, too. And those jeans. And that raggedy old jumper.

'What the fuck were you playing at?' The man turned to face Nadine with this last question, and his jaw dropped when he looked at her.

'Nadine!'

Oh God, thought Nadine, her eyebrows dancing in disbelief, this can't be happening, this just *can't be happening.*

'Phil!' she reciprocated painfully, staring in horror at her worst nightmare. 'Christ – are you OK?'

# CHAPTER THIRTY

Nadine peeled down Phil's sodden and grimy jeans while he perched on the edge of her bath, wincing and clenching his teeth. He was, she noticed, wearing lemon underpants. She hoped they weren't the same pair he'd had on on Wednesday night.

As his jeans unfurled she sucked in her breath.

'Oh Jesus,' she said. His lower thigh was blooming into huge, misshapen roses of black and purple and grey. There was a small trickle of blood seeping from a deep graze where the corner of her number plate had embedded itself into his skin. His knee was swollen up to twice its normal size. 'Oh Jesus,' she said again. 'I'm taking you to the hospital.'

'No,' stated Phil, too firmly.

'Yes,' retaliated Nadine, disbelievingly, 'come on.' She got to her feet and held her hand out to him.

'No. No hospitals. It's only a bruise. I just need to rest it.'

'Phil – you're bleeding. And look at the size of your knee, for fuck's sake. Now will you please let me take you to the hospital – you should have this X-rayed.'

'No,' he stated again, 'I'm not going to the hospital. If it hasn't gone down by tomorrow, then I'll go.'

Nadine took a deep breath. 'OK. Fine,' she said, 'so let me take you home.'

Phil winced again and doubled over in agony. 'Aaaah,'

he moaned under his breath, 'aaah. Have you got any painkillers?'

Nadine passed him a couple of Advils from her bathroom cabinet and headed towards the kitchen to get him a glass of water. As she stood over the sink, staring through the broken and taped-over window into the wet blackness outside, she started feeling a little uncomfortable. She still hadn't asked Phil what exactly he'd been doing hanging around in the rain outside her house at half past nine on a Friday evening and she wasn't sure that she wanted to.

She turned off the tap and headed back to the bathroom. Phil wasn't there. Her heart missed a beat. Maybe he'd gone. Gone away. Stumbled back out into the darkness. A selfish and worried voice deep inside her said, 'I hope so.'

She stuck her head around the living-room door – no sign of him. Neither was he in the toilet nor in the entrance hall. She pulled back the 1950s *Homemaker* print curtains in her living room and surveyed the street outside. It was empty.

And then she wandered into her bedroom, not expecting at all to find him sprawled all over the Bollywood duvet cover on her bed in nothing but his lemon briefs and a pair of black ribbed socks, smoking a cigarette and with the remote control for her TV in his hand.

'Oh,' she said, when what she'd really wanted to say was 'Get the fuck off my bed and take your horrid lemon pants with you!'

'Had to lie down,' he said, sucking on his Rothman and wincing a bit theatrically. 'Don't suppose you've got a TV guide, have you?' He blew out a stream of smoke and regarded Nadine defiantly through faded-denim-blue eyes. He was challenging her, daring her to make him leave, to get off her bed and out of her flat.

Nadine flinched a little in the face of his audacity. She didn't want him on her bed. She didn't want him in her flat. She didn't, in fact, want him anywhere within a five-mile radius of her. But what could she do? She'd nearly run him over out there. That was her fault. Bad driving, lack of concentration. And just look at the state of his leg – there was no way he'd be able to walk on that unaided, and she couldn't *force* him into her car, she couldn't force him to do anything.

She approached her bedside table stealthily and placed the glass of water on a mother-of-pearl coaster embedded with tiny little mirrors.

'There you go,' she said, in her best jolly voice. 'I'll – er – just get you a TV guide, then. Won't be a sec.'

'Cheers.' He was staring ahead at the TV, not even looking at her.

She glanced at him as she left the room, at the rock-star pallor, the twelve-year-old-girl legs, the white skin sprouting incongruous black hairs in places, the thin arms and the yellow briefs. An involuntary shudder worked its way up her body.

But the minute she walked into her living room she started feeling bad. Oh God, she thought. Poor Phil. Poor poor Phil. He's got no one. He's all alone in this world. His parents are dead. His fiancée's dead. His house is burned down. And now I've run him over. None of this is *his* fault. None of it.

And it was me – *me* – who invited him back into my life. It was me who phoned him out of the blue and me who sat in a pub with him, ghoulishly pushing him for more and more details about the tragedy that was his life. He didn't ask to get involved with me again. He didn't force me to take an E. He didn't force me to have sex with him.

She remembered what Murdo, the Scots landlord, had said to her in the pub on Wednesday night, about looking out for Phil. He was right. Phil was her responsibility now – she'd taken on that responsibility when she'd agreed to go back to his flat. Murdo had warned her and she hadn't listened and now she was paying the price. She sighed and began pulling animal-print cushions from her sofa as she searched for last week's Culture section from the *Sunday Times*. It was only one night, she told herself. Just one night. She would let him stay in her bed – she would sleep on the sofa – and then she'd drop him home tomorrow on her way to the airport.

It was the least she could do.

# CHAPTER THIRTY-ONE

The front door slammed, staccato heels clattered down the front steps and Digby bounced joyfully on to Dig's bed.

'OK,' thought Dig, chucking him under the chin, 'I'm awake now.' It was eight forty-five. Dig couldn't remember the last time he'd been awake before eleven on a Saturday morning. And not just awake, but unhungover and somewhat refreshed. He'd been in bed by ten thirty the previous night – because Delilah had wanted to turn in early – and pretty much stone-cold sober.

He stepped out of bed into a little rectangle of sunshine that was warming up his seagrass and strolled towards the window. As he pulled his curtains apart he saw Delilah on the street below. She was standing on the corner of Hilldrop Crescent and Camden Road looking around distractedly for a cab. She was wearing her sheepskin over a very smart suit and high heels, and her hair was held back from her face with sunglasses. In one hand she held her incredibly expensive-looking little Hermès doeskin attaché case and in the other a huge Hamleys carrier bag, poking from one corner of which was the tip of what looked like a large rabbit's ear. Dig scratched his head and wondered where the Hamleys bag had come from, what the rabbit was doing in it and how come he hadn't noticed it when he'd cleared the living room for dinner last night. Delilah must have hidden it somewhere. Why?

He watched as Delilah impatiently paced the corner, back and forth, back and forth, swivelling her head constantly as she listened for the rumble of a cab. She glanced at her watch a couple of times. Dig untwisted the security lock on his sash window and lifted it up a couple of inches, letting in a blast of fresh autumn air and the roar of early morning traffic.

A cab appeared on the horizon and Delilah lifted the attaché-attached hand to hail it. Dig pushed his head further through the gap in the window, stretching his legs backwards into the seagrass to flatten himself out and straining to hear Delilah's voice above four lanes of traffic.

He was sick of this. Sick of tiptoeing around Delilah and avoiding the truth. Sick of not being able to discuss anything of any importance with her, sick of doing everything in his power to make her life comfortable and easy while she rewarded his efforts with nothing more than evasion, avoidance, bad moods and the dubious honour of looking after her dog and putting her bed away every fucking morning.

Yesterday night had been the last straw. He had, officially, run out of patience.

It was clear to Dig that the only way he stood a chance of getting close to Delilah now was to know all her secrets, to know everything that Dr Rosemary Bentall knew. And if she thought that he was too immature and unprepared to deal with them, then he was going to uncover them for himself.

He poked his head a little further through the window

and, as if by magic, just as Delilah grabbed hold of the cab door-handle and twisted her head towards the driver to tell him where she wanted to go, a hush fell across Camden Road. The traffic stopped and the wind died and Delilah's words were carried from her lips on a puff of fresh air and deposited on Dig's window-sill.

'Waterloo Station, please.'

Dig cracked his head off the window, withdrawing too quickly in his panic to reach his jeans and top and get out of the flat.

'Ow fuck . . .' He rubbed his head.

Within two minutes he had dressed, knocked back half a mug of cold coffee left by Delilah in the kitchen, thrown on his leather coat, scooped Digby up in his arms and was pacing up and down Camden Road looking for a cab.

He briefly wondered at this strange, alien world, this early-morning-Saturday world peopled by the kind of men and women who didn't spend every Friday night down the pub, who didn't go to bed at two in the morning and who didn't have to spend their entire Saturdays stumbling from one attempt at curing their hangovers to another. There was something appealing about that, something refreshing. A whole new array of possibilities. His thoughts returned once more to the golden world of Nadine's imagination – the one with the kids and everything. It was becoming more alluring by the minute.

Dig flapped his free hand up and down like an over-excited schoolboy who knows the right answer when he saw a little amber lozenge glowing mutely in the distance.

The cab pulled up next to him.

'Do you mind taking a dog?' Dig asked pleasantly,

as the bleary-eyed driver looked disapprovingly at the quivering furball in his arms.

'Trained, is 'e?'

Dig nodded frantically. 'Better trained than me,' he joked feebly.

'OK – get in. Any mess though, an' you'll 'ave to clear it up.'

Dig nodded again and placed Digby on the ribbed plastic floor.

'Where you going?' asked the driver brusquely.

'Waterloo station, please – and I'm in a real hurry.'

'No problem,' said the driver, his face relaxing at the prospect of a breakneck drive around the near-empty streets of London. 'No problem at all.'

# CHAPTER THIRTY-TWO

It was five thirty a.m. and Nadine was doing one of her five-minute, condensed, early-morning preparations. It was possible, if in a big enough rush, to do everything one normally squeezed into forty-five minutes in only five. She'd packed the night before, laid out her travelling outfit, put coffee, milk and sugar in a mug, and had a good long soak in the bath just before she had gone to bed so she wouldn't have to shower.

The only thing she had to do this morning that she didn't normally have to fit into her five-minute regime was to make sure that Phil was up and ready to go. She'd spent the night on her sofa, and when her alarm went off, the first thing she'd done was throw open the bedroom door and switch on the overhead light. It was cruel, but she didn't care – this was a military-style operation.

'How's your leg?' she'd said, when she popped her head around the door thirty seconds later, her toothbrush protruding from between frothy lips.

'Uuuuuppphhhh,' Phil had said, throwing his arm over his face.

'Come on,' she'd said, all brisk efficiency, 'all you have to do is put your clothes on – here.' She lobbed them on the bed. 'I left them on the radiator overnight so they'll be nice and dry and snug. You've got' – she looked at her watch – 'two and a half minutes. Chop-chop.'

Thirty seconds later and Phil did not appear to have moved a muscle, let alone a limb.

'Phil! Will you please move it!'

'Fucking hell, Deen,' he mumbled, squinting at her from beneath his own elbow, 'you've turned into a right little sergeant-major.'

'Yes – well – lots of things about me have changed,' she said. 'Let me have a look at your leg.' She strode around to his side of the bed and flung the duvet back mercilessly.

Phil watched her carnivorously, a smug smile twitching the corners of his mouth. 'Ooh yes,' he drawled, 'I like you much more like this. All stern and Miss Whiplashy. Are you going to spank me?' He said this last in a flesh-crawlingly horrible little-boy voice.

Nadine blanched and her face dropped in horror. Jesus. Who was this repulsive person?

'Hey,' he said, attempting to sit up a little, 'this is like *Misery*, isn't it? You could just leave me tied up on your bed all weekend and then come back next week, tie my ankles together and hobble me!' He laughed, too loud, and searched Nadine's face for a trace of amusement. He raised his eyebrows in a 'suit yourself' sort of way when he failed to find one and lay back against the pillows.

She tutted and turned her attention to his leg, which resembled an overcooked chipolata sausage, all gnarled and blackened and knobbly. 'Jesus,' she said, 'you really are going to have to do something about that leg, you know. Do you want me to drop you at the hospital now, or can you make your own way there from home?'

Phil looked at Nadine with bemusement. 'I don't think I'm going anywhere, to be honest.'

Nadine let the duvet drop back over Phil's legs and regarded him with growing horror. 'What do you mean?'

'I mean – this leg ain't going to get me anywhere beyond the bedroom door, not for a while, anyway.'

'What? But it was fine yesterday – you walked all the way from the road to here and then you made it on your own from the bathroom to the bedroom and . . .'

Phil nodded sagely. 'Yeah – that was *yesterday*. It's sort of seized up overnight.' He wiggled his chipolata leg and winced. 'You know, it's gone all stiff. I can hardly move it. I reckon I'm gonna need a wheelchair to get me out of here.'

Nadine gulped. Her five-minute plan was unravelling – this was a nightmare. Wheelchairs, cripples, lascivious comments, men in her bed – at five thirty in the morning. Part of her thought Phil was lying about his leg – the swelling, as far as she could see, appeared to have gone down, and Phil was in mighty high spirits for someone who was supposed to be a cripple. But what could she do? She could hardly accuse him of lying, could she? She couldn't say, 'Oh yeah, pull the other one, it's got bruises on,' and yank him out of bed and into her car. The only thing she could do was believe him. And if she was going to believe him, then she was going to have to get the situation sorted. She couldn't leave him in her flat – alone – without her. It was unthinkable. She looked at her watch again. She had a bit more time now that she didn't have to drop Phil off at Finsbury Park, time to organize things.

Think – think – think . . . But the only thing that Nadine could think was that it was five thirty in the morning and there was no one – not even her father – who she would feel comfortable phoning at this time of day to help her remove an immobile ex-boyfriend from her flat.

She reached for the phone book.

'What are you doing?' asked Phil, suddenly alarmed.

'I'm going to call the hospital, see if they'll send someone round for you with a wheelchair.'

'No!' snarled Phil, grabbing her wrist, 'I told you – no hospitals.'

Nadine loosened his grip on her arm and eyed him uncomfortably. 'OK.' She placed the phonebook carefully on the floor. 'Why not?'

'Because,' he said, 'because it's . . . er . . . I've got some stuff in my bloodstream that shouldn't be there – *comprende*? And the last thing I need right now is a bunch of fucking hassle off a load of junior doctors – all right?'

'OK – OK. I won't call the hospital. But I've got to call someone. Is there anyone I can call?' she asked hopefully. 'A friend or something – maybe that Jo girl – who could come and collect you, or sort out a wheelchair for you?' She bit her lip, hoping that her sense of selfish desperation hadn't come through too loudly in her words.

Phil winced again and shook his head. 'Not at this time of the morning,' he breathed, 'no way. Jo's probably still out clubbing and, as you know' – he eyed her poignantly – 'there's no one else . . .' He lowered his eyes and let his shoulders slump forwards.

Nadine was harpooned, once again, by guilt. Oh God. She kept forgetting. Every time she started feeling antipathetic towards Phil, he would say something or do something to remind her how mean-hearted and self-centred she was, she who had everything, a family, friends, a future, a beautiful home – legs that worked.

She sighed and gave in to the guilt. It couldn't hurt, could it? To leave Phil here in her flat. I mean – what could he *actually* do, when you thought about it?

Make a mess? Big deal.

Snoop through her things? He wouldn't find anything very interesting.

Eat all her food? He was welcome to it, it was only going to go off otherwise.

Invite his young student friends over? Where was the harm in that?

Still be here when she got back? She shuddered. No – that wasn't going to happen. No way.

Oh God, she wailed silently, why is this happening? *Why is this happening?*

'OK,' she said, firmly, 'you can stay. But promise you'll get some help. Promise you'll call Jo a bit later. Yes?'

Phil did that awful little-boy thing again, pouting ever so slightly and nodding chastely. 'I pwomise,' he said, and Nadine had to fight back a burst of nausea.

'Right,' she said, backing uncertainly out of the room, 'I'm just going to load up the car. I'll be back in a second.'

She felt vaguely sick as she lugged boxes and boxes of aluminium-clad photographic equipment down her front steps and out to her Spider. It was still dark outside, and invisible birds chattered happily from shrouded tree tops. Jesus, she thought, am I mad? I'm leaving my flat, my beautiful flat, my refuge from the world, in the hands of Philip Rich, a man I was hoping just yesterday that I would never, ever see again as long as I lived. He's lying in my bed, in his foul underpants, on my lovely Indian-cotton sheets, under my Bollywood duvet cover *that I made with my own hands*, and I don't want him to be there, but there's nothing I can do about it because my flight to Barcelona leaves in two and a half hours and there's a whole team of models, hairdressers and stylists expecting to meet me in an hour, and if I'm not there I'll get sacked, and it's five thirty in the morning and I don't want him to be there, I just really, really don't want him to be there.

She threw her coat over the boxes in the boot to stop them being bounced about, slammed down the door and locked it, taking a deep breath to try to calm her nerves.

Back indoors, she performed a last-minute check of the flat, making sure she hadn't forgotten anything. In the kitchen she stopped for a second, noticing the yellow plastic bucket sitting by the back door, and picked it up. Well – it wouldn't hurt, would it – you never know – he might be telling the truth. And then she opened the door to her bedroom, warily and heavily.

'Right,' she said, over-brightly, a spare set of keys clutched in one hand, the plastic bucket in the other and her bag slung over her shoulder, 'I'm off.' She walked briskly towards the bedside table and dropped the keys. 'Spare set of keys for you,' she said, twirling a strand of hair behind her ear. 'Just drop them back through the letter box when you go. I've . . . er . . . left tea and coffee stuff out for you but I don't suppose you'll be able to get to it, will you?'

He looked at her and shrugged sadly, as if he was growing used to the idea of life as a helpless cripple.

'Make any phone calls you need and – um' – she glanced down at the bucket and put it down next to the bed – 'I thought you'd probably need this. You know, seeing as you can't get to the toilet.'

He smiled at her warmly.

'So, good luck. Hope everything works out with the leg. And, Phil . . . I'm so sorry. So, so sorry for what happened last night. I hope you can forgive me.' She forced a smile and Phil picked her hand up from where it hung at her side. She looked at him awkwardly and he smiled at her gratefully. Very slowly and very measuredly he brought her hand to his mouth and kissed the back of it, deeply, passionately and intensely, breathing the scent of her skin into the depths of his lungs and letting his lips moisten her skin. She looked down at him, willing him to stop, resisting the urge to pull her hand away from his mouth. She attempted a smile and failed.

'Nadine Kite,' he drawled, letting her hand drop from his lips but not letting go of it, 'you're the best. The best girl ever. Look at you – bringing me buckets, worrying about me, looking after me. I could so easily fall in love with you all over again, you know. In fact' – he smiled and squeezed her hand – 'I think I might already have done.'

Nadine managed to extricate her hand from his without seeming rude and began backing away from him. Her face was flaming red, which was annoying, because Phil was arrogant enough to presume that she was blushing with desire and pleasure rather than the all-consuming revulsion and horror she was feeling.

'I really have got to go now, Phil,' she said, looking at her watch, 'I'll try calling later, from the airport, or something. Good luck.'

Phil stuck one hand in the air and smiled again. 'Farewell, lovely lady,' he said, in a pretend Shakespearean tone, and then performed a ridiculous little twiddle of his hand and the mock-bow of a courtesan.

Nadine smiled stiffly, found the door handle and left the room.

She felt horribly sad as she closed the door on her lovely little flat, like a mother forced to leave her beautiful daughter alone with a lecherous baby-sitter.

'Sorry,' she mouthed to her front door as she made her way towards the car. 'I'm sorry.'

She flopped down into the driving seat and locked the door. Her heart was heavy and full of dread as she switched on the ignition and began the drive out west to Heathrow.

# CHAPTER THIRTY-THREE

Who was that? Up ahead?

Dig slunk down in the back seat as he recognized the shape of Delilah's head in the cab in front, leaving just his eyebrow visible above the partition. His driver had certainly made up time, flying through the streets of north London, and now Dig's cab was sitting directly behind Delilah's at the traffic lights on the Strand, about to turn left on to Waterloo Bridge.

Dig glanced at his watch. It was twenty past nine. The lights changed and Dig grabbed the armrest as the cab took the corner a little too fast. He wanted to tell the driver that he could slow down now, but realized how silly that would sound. He just hoped that they wouldn't overtake Delilah's cab.

Dig stared in disbelief at the top deck of a tourist bus, which had pulled over in the bus lane on the bridge and was packed full of cagouled tourists listening raptly to a man in a blue-nylon blazer with a microphone. It was nearly December, for Christ's sake, and it wasn't even ten o'clock yet. If Dig was a tourist in London, he would be making his second visit to the breakfast buffet bar right now, buttering his croissant, slicing the top off his hard-boiled egg and hatching gentle plans for a trip to the Royal Academy or Fortnum and Mason's later in the day, maybe. He would *not* be sitting on an open-topped bus, on the windiest bridge in London, in a day-glo cagoule with some bloke from Kidderminster shouting in his ear.

'*Which entrance do you want*?' came the tinny, disembodied voice of the driver as they approached the Imax cinema on Waterloo roundabout.

Dig sat up straight and tried to look like he knew where he was going. 'Oh,' he said, 'the main one, please.' He realized instantly that this was the wrong answer when he heard the driver sighing wearily through the intercom.

'*Eurostar? Mainline? The Underground? Which one, mate?*'

Oh God. He was going to have to say it, wasn't he? Ten years ago he'd have been excited at the prospect, but now – well, it was a bit embarrassing, really.

'Can you just, um' – he cleared his throat – 'would you mind just following that cab?' He cringed a little as he heard the words leave his lips and saw the driver's eyebrows arch sceptically.

'*Bet you've wanted to say that all your life*,' he chuckled happily.

Delilah's cab pulled up in front of the creamy stone steps leading towards the main concourse of the station and Dig watched her extricating herself from the vehicle – one long, trousered, heeled leg followed by another, and then the Hamley's bag with the rabbit in it.

His cab squeaked to a halt behind hers and the driver eyed Dig as he attempted to pay the fare from an almost entirely prone position in the back seat, sliding a ten-pound note through the crack in the window and crouching down to open the door only once he was sure that Delilah had fully disembarked and was half-way up the steps.

As Dig picked his way carefully up the magnificent stairway, Digby started quivering with excitement in his arms, his little suede nose exploring the air. He could smell her – Delilah. He let out an excited, high-pitched groan and tried to wriggle his way out of Dig's arms, towards his mistress. 'Shhhh,' said Dig, clamping his hand over the dog's tiny, damp snout. 'Shhhh.'

On the concourse Dig hid behind a row of phone booths to watch Delilah's movements. She was striding towards the ticket office, her heels clicking against the marble flooring, the rabbit ear flopping up and down as she walked.

Dig waited until Delilah was firmly ensconced in a queue and then dashed furtively to a leaflet stand offering colourful information about day trips to Hampton Court and Loseley Park. He dropped his head and pretended to study the leaflets, scooting quickly to the other side of the stand as Delilah picked up her change and turned to leave the ticket office.

He had no idea where she was going. According to the clattering arrival boards set high above the platform entrances, she could be going anywhere from Basingstoke to Bagshot, from Exeter to Epsom. She could be going to Hook, Fleet, Liss or Wool, not to mention Surbiton, Staines or Sunningdale.

Dig's heart was starting to race now. This really was primeval, bringing out deeply buried instincts and emotions, stalking his prey, hiding in the undergrowth, using the pillars and phone booths of Waterloo station as trees and bushes.

Delilah was walking slowly now, heading back towards the far end of the station, past platform nine, eight, seven, six – stopping at the Accessorize shop, feeling up some fur wraps, leather gloves, fake pashminas, beaded handbags, before wandering past platform five, four, three, popping into Knickerbox, fingering bits of silk and satin, lime-green G-strings, gingham bras and tiny jersey vest tops printed with rosebuds. Did women have any idea how absolutely devastating they looked browsing in lingerie shops?

As she emerged she glanced up at the arrival board above platform one. Dig followed her gaze from where he stood in the doorway of a closed pub, on the other side of the concourse. He squinted to make out the words.

9.52 to GUILDFORD via CLAPHAM JUNCTION

OK, he thought, Guildford here I come.

Dig moved stealthily down the platform, following Delilah's swaying hips and floppy bunny ear. Digby was still frantically trying to liberate himself from Dig's arms, squeaking every time he saw Delilah's form in the distance, and Dig was starting to wish he'd brought a lead or a harness to restrain the creature. The mutt was jeopardizing the whole operation.

When Delilah stopped midway down the platform and mounted the train, Dig increased his pace. He got into the carriage one down from her, so that he could keep an eye on her through the adjoining windows. There she was, sitting with her back to his carriage, thankfully, and flipping through a sheaf of paper. Yet another blessed sheaf of paper. What was it with all that paper? Maybe she was practising to be a newsreader . . .

Between stations, Dig cupped his chin in his hand and stared through the window, watching the grey, grimy backside of inner London morph into the shampoo and set of suburbia.

He watched as the tiny, rust-filled, overgrown gardens of Battersea, Clapham and Streatham gave way to the conservatories and aluminium-framed windows of Wimbledon, Kingston and New Malden, where the gardens sprouted bright plastic swings and slides, shiny barbecues and pristine sheds, and where Dig felt entirely alien. Suburbia, he considered, might well be a hotbed of creativity and inspiration, its very blandness acting as an inducement to escape and achieve, but he hated it. It made him feel trapped and suffocated, as if he were entering a big, green plastic bag that someone was about to tie a knot in.

As the train slunk through Surbiton – the fatherland, Dig had always thought, of suburbia – Dig threw a furtive glance towards the next carriage. Delilah had stopped flicking through papers now and was staring out of the window, nervously nibbling at the skin around her fingernails. God, thought Dig, as inappropriately as ever, she really is so shockingly beautiful.

Nondescript office building followed nondescript shopping parade followed nondescript garden; anonymous station after anonymous station zipped by in little flashes of red, white and blue Network Southeast insignia, and within twenty minutes Dig found himself being deposited somewhere called Walton-on-Thames.

Delilah dismounted and turned left, leaving Dig in a perfect position to follow her unseen. His heart, which had slowed down while sitting on the train, resumed its frenetic tattoo as he pulled his sunglasses from his coat pocket and slipped them on. Not, he hastened to reassure himself, in a sad attempt at subterfuge but because the sun was quite blindingly bright.

He held back as he made his way down the platform – only a handful of people had dismounted the train and he was highly visible – and then had hurriedly to throw himself behind a pillar when an increasingly anxious Digby spotted Delilah in the distance and emitted a high-pitched yap. Dig saw Delilah slow down like a suspicious cat when she heard the yap, and his breathing stopped momentarily as he held his hand over Digby's muzzle and waited for her to continue on her way.

This rat was a fucking liability. Dig should have left him at home and, besides, he thought with a growing sense of horror, he probably looked like a sad homosexual walking around with this ugly thing under his arm like an Alexander McQueen clutch-bag. Why, he wondered, not for the first time, had Delilah chosen this dog from among the packs of puppies she would have had access to, the spaniels and the collies, the sheepdogs and the retrievers? What was it about this greasy, quivering little bag of bones that had appealed to her? It was a mystery to him, a complete mystery.

Delilah disappeared into the ticket hall up ahead, and Dig quickened his pace, narrowing the gap between them. He rounded the corner into the ticket hall and leaped ahead when he saw Delilah crossing the road outside the station, striding purposefully away from him.

He headed briskly through the chilly hall and nearly jumped out of his skin when a man with a big scar on his cheek, a broken nose and a cauliflower ear suddenly bellowed into his face, '*Can I see your ticket please, sir?*'

Oh fuck. Dig glanced at the man and then at the road opposite, where he could see Delilah shrinking to doll-sized proportions. Oh bloody hell. He stepped from foot to foot as he desperately tried to think of what to do next. He could stay here and waste five minutes trying to sweet-talk this unfortunate-looking fellow into letting him off with a fine or a telling-off or he could just make a run for it.

'*Sir, I need to see your ticket.*'

Oh sod it. He clutched Digby tightly to him, threw the man a deeply apologetic look which he hoped conveyed within it every nuance of the story that had brought him to Walton-on-Thames without a ticket, and legged it. It was a risk – the guy looked like an ex-bare-knuckle fighter, but he might be a bit slow now in his middle age. The risk paid off. The mashed-up ticket collector sighed deeply and returned to his newspaper, tired beyond words, apparently, of breathless homosexuals with greasy terriers arriving at his barrier without the required piece of cardboard.

Dig stood impatiently at the edge of the road, waiting for a bus to complete its U-turn before dashing across the road towards the now empty street he'd last seen Delilah disappearing up. He looked around very quickly and was startled to notice that he was in the middle of nowhere – literally – but not in the good sense of the phrase, not in the way of endless meadows and wide horizons and featureless panoramas, not in the way that suggested solitude and space and mind-expansion, just . . . nowhere . . . nowhere at all. Apart from the station, all that existed in this silent and eerily uninhabited junction of two slumbering roads was an estate agents' office and a bus stop.

The heaving, creaking bus disappeared up the road in a miasma of grey smoke, leaving the area feeling even more abandoned, Dig's T-shirt was sticking to his back with the layer of viscous sweat that had broken out all over his body. He was operating on more than just conscious thought, his body was producing all sorts of reactions, effluents and chemicals as he hunted his prey. He was feeling curiously stimulated.

Dig breathed in sharply and slowed down when he heard Delilah's heels echoing around the next corner – thank God, he'd been worried that she might have disappeared into one of the overgrown Wendy houses that lined this meandering avenue and that he would be left stranded in Walton-on-Thames for the rest of his life.

Finally, the interminable road gave way to a fork, and signs of civilization and human life began to appear: a school, a church, a low-level office block, people. Within a few seconds a busy high street emerged, and Dig found himself jostling for space on the pavement with large, meaty-armed families, with nervously shuffling pensioners and pushchairs, prams and double buggies. Delilah kept striding.

Robert Dyas, Dorothy Perkins, Boots, Fads, Smiths and Marks.

Dig mopped his brow.

He ducked into a doorway when Delilah stopped in her tracks ahead of him. What must he look like, he wondered to himself, all sweaty and unkempt, with uncombed hair and a weird dog, dashing around furtively and hiding in doorways? If he could see himself in the street today, he would be able to reach only one conclusion: Care in the Community.

Delilah was consulting one of her bits of paper, turning it round and viewing it from all angles in a manner that suggested she was looking at a map. Dig looked at his watch: 10.51 a.m. They'd been walking for bloody ages. He hoped they were nearly there – wherever the hell 'there' was. He didn't think he could stand the suspense for much longer.

Delilah slid the piece of paper back into her doeskin attaché and continued on her way, her heels beginning to echo again as the pedestrian population thinned out once more.

Outside a pink pub, she turned right, and Dig followed her down a steep footpath, his heartbeat increasing with every loose pebble his trainered feet dislodged. At the bottom of the footpath Dig stopped and caught his breath and had his first reality check of the day. What the *fuck* was he doing? I mean – what the *fuck*? Where was he? Where was he going? Why was he here? He didn't do things like this, people in films did things like this, not him.

He looked down with disgust when he noticed that Digby was greedily licking the salty sweat off the palm of his hand with a hot little pink tongue, sneered and wiped his hand down the leg of his jeans. And then he felt guilty again when he realized that the poor creature was probably parched, not to mention starving, and possibly, probably, almost definitely, in need of voiding some part or parts of his body. Dig looked at Digby. Digby looked back at him, blinked and gulped. There were tears in his eyes, and he looked desperately unhappy. Dig felt mean beyond belief.

The river lay beyond the fringe of trees in which Dig was hiding. Despite the name of the town, Dig was slightly surprised to find it there, wide and curved and sparkling, small flotillas of rented boats peopled by families in overcoats skimming the surface, a large lock to the left, a small reservoir to the right. Behind him sat a fantastic clapboard pub covered in flaking white paint and lichen, a large balustraded balcony on the first floor and several tables outside. What a gem of a place, thought Dig, as he mentally added it to the 'summer' section of his infinite list of nice-looking pubs he'd like to drink in one day.

A panting pack of varied dogs scampered by on the sand-covered towpath, followed by strolling, Barboured owners clutching limp, unclipped leads. Digby twitched in his arms and Dig soothed him by purring into his ear.

Finally, Delilah came off the path and disappeared up a small turning, and Dig breathed a sigh of relief as he realized that they were probably there. They had to be. The sun was beating down on him even harder now and he was boiling. There were big damp patches under his arms and he could feel sweat trickling down his back and collecting in his sternum. He pulled at the collar of his T-shirt with a crooked index finger and blew down his top on to his chest. He just wanted to sit down now. He didn't want to walk any further.

At the top of the turning were three houses, set well back from the road and all backing directly on to the river. These weren't the mini-mansions that Dig had seen on the way from the station, these were the real McCoy. Gravel drives that hadn't just been tipped off the back of a delivery van, tangles of ancient laburnum climbing to the top floors, uncurtained sash windows, old estate cars in the driveways, hexagonal turrets and warped old boot-scrapers embedded into doorsteps. Delilah was walking towards the middle of the three houses, her pace diminishing, the Hamley's bag no longer swinging.

Even from fifty feet away, Dig could hear her nervously clearing her throat.

He stationed himself behind a small skiff that was being decorated and had been left upturned and unfinished, painted half white and half green. It was called 'Sun King' and had been pulled on to the verge next to a mulberry bush, where it provided Dig with more than sufficient cover.

Delilah slowed down even more as she approached the large, handsome house. And then she did something really annoying. After all this, after a ten quid cab ride at the crack of dawn, after nearly being done for fare evasion, after walking through some godforsaken bit of Surrey for nearly half an hour, after everything that Dig had been through this peculiar and surreal morning to discover what Delilah was up to, she rewarded him by placing both of her bags side by side on a bench and sitting on it.

Dig grimaced and ground his teeth. What was she doing? For God's sake. What the *hell* was she doing? Sitting down. In Walton-on-Thames. Sitting down – on a bench – for no discernible reason – apropos of nothing at all – just sitting there. In Walton-on-Thames. *Why?*

The bench was situated between the middle and right-hand houses and faced away from the road, directly towards the river. It afforded, it had to be said, a very attractive view of the river and a small eyot accessed by a charming wooden bridge. It was very pretty indeed. Extremely pretty. But, *why*?

Dig took the weight off his toes and sat back on his bottom. The ground underneath was cold and damp, but he didn't care – he was knackered and hot, and now he was also deeply frustrated. He searched his coat pockets for a piece of chewing gum or a packet of mints – his breath tasted like curdled milk – and sighed with ever-increasing frustration when he failed to find either.

Delilah had crossed her legs on the bench and draped one elbow across the back of it. Dig watched her knock her sunglasses from the top of her head to her nose and then do something vaguely peculiar with her hair, arranging it over her face, almost as if she were drawing curtains, and then she turned up the collar of her sheep-skin jacket. She was, Dig realized with a sense of mounting excitement, attempting to disguise herself. This was more like it, he thought gleefully, this was more like it. He was about to witness some kind of illicit rendezvous, some kind of espionage, something a bit . . . *exciting*.

As he sat behind the boat and the bush, clasping a very-keen-to-escape Digby to his chest and keeping an eye on Delilah, Dig's imagination began to run away with itself. His mind filled with images of wartime escapades, of James Bond shenanigans, of the trench-coated woman in *Allo Allo* who says, 'Listen very carefully', of excellent bits of electronic surveillance equipment, of false moustaches and video cameras in briefcases. This was starting to look more interesting than he'd imagined. He rubbed his hands gleefully and waited for the excitement to begin.

Nearly an hour later Dig was starting to run out of enthusiasm.

His body had lost every degree of the heat it had built up on the walk here. His hands and nose were freezing and his arse had gone numb. He was starving hungry and bored stiff.

Nothing had happened in Eyot Reach for nearly an hour – not a single thing. Someone's dog had strayed from the towpath at one point and come haring towards Dig when it spied the tasty morsel sitting shivering on his lap, but had been quickly recovered by its owner. The weather-vane on top of one of the houses had turned a few times. A car had used the road for a three-point-turn a few minutes ago. And that was it.

Delilah was still sitting on the bench, still wearing her sunglasses and still hiding behind her hair.

Five more minutes, Dig told himself, five more minutes and then I'm going home.

And then he heard something – a click, followed by another click, followed by laughter. Someone was finally coming out of one of the houses. He tucked Digby into his coat and rearranged himself to give himself a better view of the proceedings.

The front door of the middle house was wide open now and Dig could see the silhouetted form of a family as they jostled to leave the house, bickering and squawking and shouting. Delilah, he noticed, had swivelled slightly on the bench and was regarding the open door with interest, her fingertips touching the arm of her sunglasses.

'Maddie, stop it!' he heard a woman's voice shouting, in perfect Surrey tones. 'Leave the dog alone!'

A large Newfoundland bounded through the door and across the gravel, bearing a small child on his back, who was gently whipping the dog's bottom with a plastic ruler. 'Gee up, Monty! Gee up!' squeaked the pretty, dark-haired little girl.

'Get off the dog, Maddie!' A tall woman emerged from the house, carrying a large duvet and a pressure cooker.

She was too thin and had obviously been extremely beautiful in her youth. Her hair was jet black and cut into a big tousled wedge which suited her. She was wearing an enormous ex-army greatcoat with a fur collar and green wellingtons.

She was followed by a young boy of about ten, who had his nose stuck in a Harry Potter book while simultaneously dribbling a football across the crackling gravel.

The mother pulled a clunking set of keys from her battered old handbag, selected one with her teeth and thrust it into the keyhole at the back of her silver Mercedes estate. The door sprung open, and the dog, the duvet and the pressure cooker landed in the boot.

Maddie was now pretending to ride a horse, trotting round and round in circles, kicking up the gravel and making neighing and clip-clopping noises.

'Maddie, stop it! Get into the car!'

The dark-haired boy kicked his football towards the garage and slid into the back seat, his eyes still glued to his Harry Potter book, and Maddie continued to ignore her mother, who was getting into the driver's seat, tucking her acres of coat around her.

*'Maddie! Get into the car right now or I shall leave you here and you won't get a McDonald's.'*

Maddie immediately dropped her ruler and skidded across the gravel towards the car, hopping into the back seat next to her brother and strapping herself into some kind of harness. The Newfoundland in the back snuffled at the top of Maddie's head and she turned towards him and beamed.

Well, thought Dig, this is all very sweet – cute dog,

cute girl, wonderful domestic vignette and all that – but what the hell has this got to do with anything? Where's the swarthy stranger in the raincoat, where's the mysterious package, where's the excitement?

The woman sounded her car horn and Dig jumped a mile. *Jesus*, he muttered, clutching his heart, *Jesus*. She wound down her car window and stuck her head through it.

'*Sophie!*' she roared, banging the car horn with the heel of her hand again in exasperation. '*Will you get down here immediately!*'

Dig had the feeling that she was one of those women who made everything in life far more complicated and dramatic than it needed to be.

The front door squeaked open a few seconds later and Dig saw Delilah stiffening on the bench, cupping the side of her face with one hand in a further attempt, he presumed, to disguise herself, as a very tall and slim young girl emerged into the sunshine.

'*Honestly, mother*,' the young girl shouted, turning to look at her while she locked the front door behind her, '*the neighbours must think you're a bloody child-abuser*.' She tutted and tucked her door keys into the pocket of her rucksack. She looked about twelve years old, and was wearing black pedal-pushers, chunky fluorescent trainers and an outsized grey fleece. Her hair was long and parted in the centre and was a warm, shining golden-brown, in stark contrast to that of the other members of her dark-haired family. She was the sort of fresh-faced, lanky and even-featured young girl who Dig could imagine being approached in shopping centres by scouts from modelling agencies. She might have been only twelve, thirteen years old, but she was gorgeous, completely drop-dead, slaveringly, put-a-spring-in-an-old-man's-step gorgeous.

Stop it, you pathetic pervert, he chastised himself, stop it.

As she walked around the car and approached the passenger door, Dig got a better look at her. Full, plump lips, like silken cushions, wide blue eyes with dark lashes, creamy skin and a sulky, resentful attitude. Her mother said something to her as she slid into the passenger seat, and she smiled – a reluctant smile, he noticed, her mouth trying to persuade the rest of her face to join in – and as she smiled she turned towards Dig and, like a brick lobbed through a window, a thought splintered his mind.

Oh my God, he thought, she looks just like Leslie Ash in *Quadrophenia*.

He turned to look at Delilah, who hadn't moved a muscle since the young girl emerged from the house, and then he turned back to the girl, who was strapping herself into her seatbelt. Uncanny, he thought, uncanny the resemblance between the two, the same height, attitude, lips and smile, the same rangy figure, swaying hips and peaches-and-cream complexion. The same . . . exactly the same. Realization coursed through him and he began to experience difficulty breathing. He was back in the playground at the Holy T, cross-legged on the grass, perusing his new timetable and experiencing the character-forming shock of seeing Delilah for the very first time. Jesus, he thought, this is eerie. That girl, he thought, that girl is the spitting bloody image of Delilah.

He turned to look at Delilah again, who was clutching the back of the bench with two white-knuckled hands and staring helplessly at the Mercedes as it reversed out of the driveway and away from her. Her hair had fallen away from her face and her jaw was slack with shock and dismay. As the car straightened itself out on the street, Delilah mindlessly pushed her sunglasses from her nose to her hair, and Dig could see tears shimmering on her cheeks. He felt bad. He felt elated. He felt cheated. He felt horrified. He felt scared. He felt excited.

He looked back at the car and at the girl in the passenger seat, who was now arguing with her brother in the back. Is it possible, he thought to himself, that that girl, that that beautiful, sullen, wonderful girl, is my daughter?

# CHAPTER THIRTY-FOUR

Nadine hadn't had time today to think about Dig and Delilah, about Phil in her flat, about anything very much apart from exposure levels, light readings and F-stops. Which was a good thing. But then, after four hours of lugging all her equipment around the streets of Barcelona, sweet-talking policemen and bribing shopkeepers into letting her use locations, not to mention holding back the drooling crowds of men trying to get a look at Fabienne, the eighteen-year-old star of the new Renault advertising campaign, in a gold-sequinned bikini, it had started raining. Absolutely bucketing down. And Nadine had had to abandon the shoot for the day.

She was sitting in her hotel room now, listening to the rain ricocheting off the tiled roof overhead, sorting narrow yellow canisters of film into piles and trying desperately to resist the temptation to phone home. It would do her no good at all to hear the sound of Phil's voice echoing down the line from hundreds of miles away. It would only upset her. Better not to know. But the second she managed to tear her thoughts away from Philip Rich, lying in all his underpanted splendour on her bed, in her flat, her mind filled instead with the equally alarming image of Delilah in Dig's flat, all scrubbed and shining and ready to have sex with Dig. Urgh. She shuddered at the thought.

Jesus, thought Nadine, last night was just *horrible*.

She looked at her watch. It was only three o'clock, but the dark, low cloud that hung over Barcelona, inches, it seemed, from the roof-tops, made it feel more like early evening. She yawned, stretched out on her lovely, firm, quilty hotel bed and closed her eyes. A little snooze would be nice – just a few moments of luxurious, foreign hotel-room shut-eye. After all, she had been up since five thirty.

The sounds from outside her window soothed her. Angry cabs, impatient trucks, the doorman at the front entrance whistling for taxis, rain beating in treble off the roof and in bass off the canvas awning stretched over the front door, like long fingernails tapping a drum. Every few seconds muffled foreign voices would drift past her door, reminding her that it was the middle of the day and other people were busy doing things, didn't have time to lie around.

She pulled up the bedcover and wrapped it over her cold bare feet and naked arms. Her thoughts drifted as she warmed up and snuggled down. Ideas for tomorrow's shoot, plans for dinner tonight, a reminder to herself to get some more Polaroid from the camera shop downstairs because she hadn't packed enough . . . just . . . stuff . . . nice, normal, boring . . . stuff.

And then – *wallop* – there it was. Bang – right there, in the midst of all that lovely driftiness. Delilah. In her fucking towel. In Dig's fucking flat. About to have fucking sex with fucking Dig. And *bang* – there she is again, silhouetted in the back of a black cab at two in the morning, with her arms around Dig's neck and her lips against his mouth. *Crack* – Delilah in the playground at the Holy T, sitting on Dig's lap, throwing Nadine ice-blue daggers, making Nadine feel small and fat and ugly, insufficient, inconsequential and inadequate.

Nadine threw the quilted cover off her and leaped to her feet. Delilah was even robbing her of her sleep. She wanted to scream at the injustice of it all.

Delilah, Delilah, Delilah.

She threw open the door of the mini-bar and eyed it furiously, challenging it to offer her *a real drink*, something that could even *begin* to take the edge off her wretchedness and misery, and sheer, belly-rotting jealousy. Come on you pathetic excuse for a fridge, what have you got, eh? What have you got?

She eyed a quarter-bottle of Louis Roederer and a dinky little bottle of José Cuervo. There was something horribly sad about the idea of doing tequila slammers alone, in the middle of the afternoon but, in her current frame of mind, it appealed to her. To fuck with it. The rain outside was even heavier, the sky was growing darker, she was in a foreign country and she was in a foul mood. If there had ever been a moment to pay a visit to Alcy-land, this was it.

She pulled a tooth mug off her bedside table, poured in the little bottle of tequila, filled it to the top with lovely, cold, frothing champagne, covered it with her hand, slammed it down hard on the table-top and necked it in one.

The bubbles and the taste made her shudder. Disgusting. She burped loudly and licked the champagne off the palm of her hand.

The alcohol reacted immediately, lending a lovely soft focus to the room, the view from her window and her mood. Now she wanted a cigarette. Not just wanted but *craved* a cigarette. Her room was non-smoking. Her window was fixed closed.

She poured the remainder of the champagne into the mug, gulped it down, put on her shoes and a cardigan, picked up her door key and made her way downstairs to the hotel bar.

Hotels, especially extremely *posh* hotels like this one, were like another world, for Nadine. She could quite happily spend the rest of her life in a hotel, absolve herself of all responsibility for the minutiae of life like housework and cooking and plumbers and paying bills and calling mini-cabs and remembering to buy Cornflakes and ironing things and polishing your own shoes and deciding where to eat and buying stamps and ordering newspapers.

But the best thing about smart hotels was that they were the same the world over. From continent to continent, from First World to Third World you could always depend upon the availability of a boiled egg or a decent bottle of champagne, a safety-deposit box or a mini-bar. Wherever you were, the moment you stepped into a smart hotel you were in another country, entirely unconnected to the land in which it happened to have been constructed. You were in *Hotel-land*, one of the nicest countries in the world as far as Nadine was concerned.

And look at all these lovely twiddly bits you get with everything. Look at this little paper coaster she's been given with her champagne cocktail, with the pretty scalloped edges, and look at all those newspapers over there, hanging off polished mahogany poles. This carpet's great – it's got the hotel insignia all over it. Nadine wants some personalized carpet in *her* flat, with 'NK' woven into it and swirls and curlicues all over the place.

Nadine was hidden in a cosy little corner of the bar, nestled on to a tiny, squishy sofa but within easy eye-contactable distance of the barman. Her head swam pleasantly and the lines of Spanish current affairs she was attempting to translate, using her school Spanish, in the newspaper in front of her were starting to lose their clarity. It was five thirty and it was still raining outside. Nadine was drunk.

'God – there you are! Thank God!' A small pixie-faced girl with cropped black hair and a bindi on her forehead collapsed next to Nadine on the sofa. 'We've been looking everywhere for you.' It was Pia. 'Fabienne's doing all the shops in the lobby and Sarah's doing a corridor-by-corridor trawl for your butchered body. We've been phoning your room all afternoon. I was about to call the fucking police.' Her tiny little nose wrinkled up and down with the drama of it all and she slapped Nadine on the arm with annoyance at so much expended worry.

'God, I'm sorry,' said Nadine, suddenly very conscious of her lips not working in harmony with her tongue, of the fact that if she didn't watch out she could very easily start slurring. 'I didn't think. I'm sorry. Hit me again.'

Pia grimaced and slapped her arm again. 'Bad photographer,' she scolded, teasingly. 'What are you?'

'I'm a bad photographer,' said Nadine, dropping her head into her chest.

'You're also a *pissed* photographer, aren't you? Breathe on me,' Pia ordered, pointing her minute nostrils towards Nadine's mouth. Nadine let out a small puff of air. 'You are! You're drunk! Blimey, Deen. It's not even six o'clock yet, and you're off your trolley! Well,' she said, getting to her platformed feet, 'there's only one thing for it. I'm going to find Sarah and Fab and get them down here. I expect a full round of whatever that is you're drinking, on the table by the time I get back. OK?'

'OK.'

Nadine watched Pia striding across the insignia-ed carpeting towards the twinkling lobby outside, her tiny little hips twitching from side to side in skintight black pedal-pushers, her ankles looking like they might snap with the weight of the platform shoes that were strapped onto them. Every man in the room turned to watch her as she went.

She was back within minutes with Sarah, the Sloaney, blonde, pencil-thin make-up artist with the dirty laugh, and Fabienne, the voluptuous and ripe-fleshed Renault-ad girl with the vertiginous cleavage. Nadine supposed that in company like this she was probably the dumpy red-head with the stupid clothes on. Nadine smiled to herself. She didn't care. She *loved* drinking with beautiful women. It was so much fun, the night-time equivalent of going to the park with a cute dog. You got loads of attention and everyone talked to you.

'You dirty old lush,' said Sarah, peeling off a cashmere cardigan and revealing elegant arms and shoulders in a tiny pink vest-top, 'how much have you had to drink?'

Nadine giggled, shrugged and hiccuped. The three girls laughed. 'Say no more,' said Sarah.

The bartender arrived at their table and off-loaded four more champagne cocktails, each with its own little scalloped coaster, and a tiny bowl of pistachios. Brave now, in the company of other women, Nadine threw him her best smile and said *gracias* with all the Spanishness she could muster. He smiled back at her and she blushed, and the girls all nudged each other and teased her and Nadine settled down to enjoy what was obviously going to be a top girly night.

By eight o'clock the previously sedate bar had exploded into Saturday-night mayhem, and the quartet of lary English girls drinking champagne cocktails in the corner were no longer drawing quite so much attention to themselves. Pia had been entertaining them, as ever, with hilarious accounts of the men in her life, peppering her stories with well-chosen swear-words and physical demonstrations of various events using her tiny little stick-drawing body to great comic effect. Nadine was so drunk by now that she was hugely appreciative of Pia's diverting behaviour, meaning as it did that she could just sit there grinning like a fool and not have to make any kind of intelligent conversation.

Her bladder was telling her that a trip to the *Señoritas* was imminent, but her head was telling her that she was too pissed and too red in the face and her heels were too high and she didn't know where they were and she'd have to wander around for ages, gormlessly trying to locate them, and that when she did there'd probably be some poor anaemic Spanish woman in there whose job it was to sit in a toilet all day, and there'd be three pesetas in her little saucer and Nadine would feel really guilty about not leaving her anything and it was all far, far too much trouble, so she should just cross her legs and not drink anything for a while because that would just make her need to go even more, and she was half-way through this desperate mental monologue when she suddenly realized that Sarah was asking her a question.

'Sorry,' she muttered, pulling herself back into the proceedings.

'I said, are you still going out with that really cute-looking bloke I met last time I saw you?' said Sarah.

Nadine racked her mind. The last time she'd seen Sarah socially was about six months ago when she was going out with? . . . with? . . . Jimmy, of course, the thirty-nine-year-old chiropodist whose hair, spookily enough, was exactly the same shade of red as hers. Everyone had taken them for brother and sister in the couple of months they'd been together, which Nadine had found deeply insulting given the age difference and the fact that he was – well, not *bad*-looking as such, but certainly not what you would describe as a 'really cute-looking bloke'. Sarah couldn't possibly mean Jimmy.

'You know,' said Sarah, noticing Nadine's confusion, 'the guy with all the hair and the big eyebrows – he had some kind of weird name. The A&R guy.'

Nadine choked on her cocktail. 'What!' she exclaimed, wiping her chin with the back of her hand and laughing, unnaturally loudly. 'You mean Dig?'

'That's it,' cried Sarah, 'Dig! I knew he had a silly name. Yeah, Dig. What happened to him – are you still seeing him?'

Nadine laughed over-loudly again and shook her head. 'Dig and I are just friends,' she said, 'we're not going out together.'

'God, you're joking,' said Sarah, 'could have sworn the two of you were as together as Posh and Becks.'

Nadine laughed again.

'No, really,' continued Sarah, her eyes glittering with the excitement of intimate revelation, 'what is it with the two of you? There was a real chemistry there. I remember it really well – he had his arm around your shoulders.'

'Yeah, well,' said Nadine, 'we've known each other for a long time. We're very affectionate with each other.'

Sarah was shaking her head. 'No,' she said, 'no. There's more to it than that. I told Neil about you two when I got home that night. I said to him that I'd never been able to understand why you never went out with decent men, but that it looked like you'd finally found one. I was full of it, how happy I was for you and how lovely he seemed and how well matched and all that. Have you ever met him?' She turned towards Pia.

Pia nodded, effusively. 'He's *gorgeous*,' she drawled and Nadine wondered, not for the first time, at Pia's ability to tailor her opinions to fit the moment. She'd always agreed with Nadine, before, that he was too skinny and too short and had too much hair.

'Honestly,' said Sarah, addressing Fabienne, 'he's really cute-looking and sweet and polite, and you should see the way he looks at Nadine – Neil never bloody looks at me like that and he's asked me to marry him!'

Nadine laughed again. This wasn't the first time someone had told her what a lovely couple she and Dig made – many other people had made that mistake over the years – but tonight, with her heart broken and her head full of Delilah and all the stuff that had happened over the last week, it was hugely reassuring to hear. Her stomach did a strange floppy thing that made her feel all weak.

'What do you mean,' she asked, 'the way he looks at me?'

'I dunno,' said Sarah, 'he just seemed – so *proud* of you. It was like he was showing you off. The way he had his arm around your shoulder and the way he laughed at your jokes. I honestly thought that he was some new boyfriend who was completely besotted with you.'

'Hm,' smiled Nadine, 'well. He's not. He's my mate.' Nadine was feigning nonchalance. She wanted to hear more – more about how Dig looked at her and more about how good they looked together and more about what a great couple they made. She needed to hear it.

'So why haven't you two ever got it together?' asked Sarah. 'Is he gay?'

Nadine snorted and slapped her thighs. 'Dig? God, you're joking. He's deeply heterosexual. *Too* heterosexual, if anything.'

'So why not? Oh – don't tell me. He's trapped in some long-term relationship with the wrong woman?'

'No! He's a serial monogamist, like me – except his relationships are even shorter than mine.'

'So, the two of you are unattached, you're affectionate with each other, you're best friends and you've known each other half your lives?'

Nadine nodded.

'Why the hell aren't you going out together? That's more than most supposed couples have going for them, y'know?'

Nadine nodded again and felt a little hysteria building in her stomach.

'Don't you fancy him, even a little bit?' asked Pia, nudging her playfully in the ribs.

Nadine was about to give her usual knee-jerk response to this question, asked of her in the past, many times. 'Oh no,' she was about to sneer, 'he's too small for me.' That's what she always said – he's too short. And then she'd make some joke at his expense about his lack of stature and his skinny legs and his big eyebrow and his sticky-uppy hair, and everyone would laugh and the subject would get dropped immediately. But tonight – tonight she was going to be honest. She needed to get it off her chest, off-load on to someone else the frightening realization that she was in love with her best friend. And Dig was gorgeous. Of course he was. Anyone could see that. His eyes twinkled and his lips curled when he smiled. He was small, but he was taller than her. He had great eyelashes and wonderful buttocks. He was sexy as hell. As sexy as he'd always been.

Nadine looked at Pia and grinned mischievously. 'We–ell,' she grinned, and all three girls began screeching with pleasure, 'he is kind of cute.' Blood rushed to Nadine's head as the words left her lips. She felt strangely excited and unburdened. She joined in the excited laughter of her companions and then had to stop herself sharply when she realized that she'd almost peed herself – almost, but not quite – a very close thing. 'Ooh,' she said, covering her mouth with a hand, 'excuse me, girls. Nature is shouting very loudly.'

'Oh no!' sighed Pia, in dismay. 'Not now. You can't go now. You've just admitted to fancying your best friend, for God's sake!'

She stood up stiffly, every muscle in the lower half of her body clenched tightly. 'Gotta go, girls, really, really gotta go.' She shuffled from foot to foot while she waited for Pia to get out of her way and then made as inconspicuous a dash for it as she possibly could, across the insignias and towards the large marble lobby.

Nadine felt a bit wobbly on her feet as she negotiated the small gaps between tables and chairs in the crowded bar. She was much more drunk than she'd thought. She felt heavy and ungainly. Her shoes felt like breezeblocks and the cool, high-ceilinged lobby felt as vast as a skating rink as she tapped her way across it towards the toilets. She was sure everyone – all these business types with their smart little suitcases and their unsmiling, not-on-holiday faces – was staring at her, staring at the red-faced, slightly panic-stricken girl with the ginger hair and the strange dress walking uncertainly across the marble floor. It was like another world out here – Nadine had that odd walking-out-of-a-cinema-into-bright-sunshine feeling.

She pushed open the toilet door with her shoulder and was pleased to find the large, plush, mirrored and wallpapered room empty. Not an anaemic Spanish woman clutching a paper napkin in sight. She threw open the door of the first cubicle, lifted the hem of her dress and then began fumbling with the tops of her knickers, which just didn't seem to be where they usually were. She started panicking as she felt her bladder weakening and threatening to explode before she'd sat down. She finally located the tops of her knickers, yanked them down and then landed somewhat heavily on the seat, sighing with unspeakable pleasure as she released her tensed muscles and let it all out. 'Aaaaah,' she smiled to herself. 'Aaaah.'

Afterwards, she confronted her reflection in the mirror and started giggling. She wasn't quite sure why: it was a combination of how awful she looked (flushed and wild-eyed) and how pissed she was feeling (it was always a sure-fire sign that you were really drunk, when you started laughing at your reflection in the toilets).

But it was also a slightly nervous reaction to what had happened just now, in the bar. That comment about

Dig. That sudden rush of feelings. Admitting to a bunch of girls she hardly knew that she thought Dig was 'cute', when she hadn't even admitted it to herself since she was eighteen years old.

'So – do you? Do you fancy Dig?' she asked her reflection, trying to pull a serious face and dissolving into laughter yet again. 'Do you? Do you want him? Do you want to see him naked? Do you want to see his *willy*?' She slapped her hands down on the marble surface and laughed out loud. 'How do you feel about Dig's willy, Nadine? Do you want to hold it in your hand? Do you want to kiss it, kiss its little shiny head?' She nearly overbalanced as her laughter increased and had to grip on to the marble to keep herself upright.

'Do you *want* him? . . . Do you want him to kiss you? Would you like it if Dig held your face in his hands and kissed you on the lips?'

Nadine eyed her blurred reflection, her blotchy, disproportional features, her messy hair, her diametrically opposed eyes – the woman in the mirror who looked like an older, fatter and sartorially less refined sister.

'I *vont* you, Dig' – she experimented with a Garbo approach – 'I *vont* you.' She laughed at her reflection again and then let her head fall into her chest. She sighed heavily. 'Oh God,' she moaned to herself, 'oh God. Dig. I do. I want you. Oh, bollocks.' Her head felt too small, far too small, to accommodate all the stuff that was going on in there.

Her mind started sending her picture postcards from the past. There was one postmarked 12 September 1987, a shot of Dig wandering down Bartholomew Road in the dark, jumping up on that wall when he didn't know she was looking and punching the air. There were the doodles she'd drawn all over her old diary when she was a teenager. *Nadine Ryan Nadine Ryan Nadine Ryan.* And there was Dig's old kite, the one he'd given her the day they went to Primrose Hill. *Dig 'n' Deen, 13 September 1987, for ever* ♥.

More pictures flashed through her mind. Flying kites on Southend beach with Dig and his dad. Waiting for buses in the rain on Saturday mornings with Dig to go down to the Notting Hill Record and Tape Exchange. Queuing up outside the Electric Ballroom on Saturday nights, hair thick with backcombing and Elnett. Saying goodbye in the setting sun on the last day of school, the burning car outside Caledonian Park that was now inextricably linked with her memories of that night – broken hearts and burnt-out cars.

She pictured Dig's flat, his anally arranged knick-knacks and ornaments, his spotless little kitchen, his plumped-up cushions and fluffed-out duvet. She saw him launching himself from the sofa, suddenly, in the middle of a film, as he often did, to pick a bit of lint off his floor. She remembered his endearing excitement at finally leaving home at the age of twenty-seven and buying his flat, all those nightmarish weekend trips to Ikea in Brent Park and hours spent discussing the relative merits of seagrass carpeting versus wooden floors, and then trawling around Allied Carpets for two, three hours at a time to find exactly the right shade of beige.

She imagined the two of them, sitting side by side on his blue-cord sofa drinking big bottles of Bud, watching the telly, smoking and snuggling up to each other, the warmth where their thighs pressed together, the weight of his head on her shoulder, the smell of his sweet, beery breath when he turned to share a joke with her. All that stuff she'd taken for granted for ten years, all that lovely, warm, easy, intimate Diggy stuff.

All that lovely stuff that Delilah was currently getting her perfectly manicured mitts all over.

As these thoughts surged through her mind, Nadine became filled with a sense of resolve and strength. She couldn't let Delilah win, not again, not this time.

Nadine squinted to focus and glanced at her watch. Quarter past eight. Quarter past seven in London. She felt her pocket for her door key, pushed open the toilet door and strode purposefully towards the lifts. She didn't feel self-conscious now as her heels clattered against the hard marble. A smile twitched at the corners of her mouth while she waited for the smoothly humming lift to slink its way down to the foyer and collect her.

She wove a bit as she made her way down corridor after corridor on the fourth floor, her heels sinking into the soft carpeting, one stiff flower arrangement blurring into another, brass-plated light fittings with pleated shades guiding her on her way. Nadine liked being drunk and alone in a hotel. She wanted to break into a run and start careering around the place like a kid. She wanted to shout and scream and play hide-and-seek.

She wanted to speak to Dig. Right now. This instant.

She was going to tell Dig that she was in love with him. Why should she let Delilah win again?

In her room, Nadine threw off her shoes and landed with a bounce on her freshly made bed. She found the bit of laminated plastic that gave instructions on how to make an international call and began dialling.

Her heart raced as she waited for the call to connect. 'Come on,' she muttered to herself, 'come on, Diggy-boy, pick it up.' The phone rang, five times, six times, seven times, and Nadine was about to hang up when there was a click, a second's silence and the muffled sound of someone's skin rubbing against the mouthpiece. Nadine caught her breath.

'*Hello?*' came a woman's breathless voice.

Nadine dropped the receiver and it landed with a crash on to the cradle. Delilah. Delilah Lillie. Answering Dig's phone. In Dig's flat on a Saturday night. The slightly insane smile that had been etched on to Nadine's face for the last quarter of an hour disappeared. Stinging, salty tears sprung to her eyes, taking its place.

Nadine pulled a handful of Kleenex from the box on her bedside table and rubbed her damp face into them. Her hysterical happiness turned to hysterical misery, and the more she wiped away her tears, the more she produced. She didn't have a place on Dig's corduroy sofa any more, she didn't belong in his flat. She'd lost again – lost to Delilah Lillie. She'd had ten years to love Dig, to have Dig, to be Dig's – *ten years*. And she'd left it a week too late.

She didn't laugh now as she looked at herself in the mirror opposite her bed. There was nothing funny about the blotchy-faced girl staring back at her; there was nothing funny about being in love with her best mate; there was nothing funny about Dig being in love with Delilah. None of it was even vaguely amusing.

She slowly lifted two fingers to her head, made them horizontal, pressed them into her temple and pulled the trigger with her thumb.

'Bang,' she said, sadly, letting her hand drop to her side.

## CHAPTER THIRTY-FIVE

Dig had sat numbly for a moment after the family disappeared in their Mercedes estate, unable to absorb what had just taken place. He looked over at Delilah, who had turned to face the water and was staring pensively across the river, her hands clasped together tightly in her lap and, for a moment, he desperately, desperately wanted to rush over to her and take her in his arms and share her trauma. He had to bite his tongue and hold himself down.

Instead he waited for a while and watched her. After a few minutes she stood up and shuffled down the grass towards the towpath. She stopped a man with a red setter and he nodded and pulled something out of his inside pocket. As she walked back up the hill, Dig saw what he'd given her. She was smoking a cigarette. She took a couple of puffs, looked down at it between her fingers, scowled and threw it out towards the river.

She stood at the top of the grassy hill, nibbling at her fingernails. And then, finally, she picked up her two bags and strode towards the middle house. She stopped at the front door, pulled the gigantic bunny from inside the Hamley's bag and perched it on the doorstep.

It was a grey and white rabbit, with a large bow round its neck, and was carrying in its paws a red-felt heart with the words 'Birthday Girl' printed on it.

Jesus Christ, Dig thought, this is so fucking heavy.

And then he started doing some pretty basic maths. Today was 21 November. He counted nine months backwards on his fingers: 21 February. Delilah's eighteenth birthday. The last time they'd had sex. The last time they'd been happy together. Just before everything had gone sour and Delilah had disappeared. There was still the possibility that the girl was younger than twelve, had been born long beyond the end of his relationship with Delilah, but it was looking increasingly unlikely. She couldn't have been younger than twelve – she looked sixteen as it was.

And then another thought occurred to him. Maybe she *was* older than twelve. Maybe Delilah had had her and given her away before she'd moved to north London, before he'd ever even met her. But then . . . but then . . . no – he would have known. She would have told him. She used to say that young girls who got themselves pregnant were pathetic. She said that she would never let that happen to her. She said that she never wanted children. She said . . . oh God. Dig dropped his forehead on to his fist with frustration and confusion. This was so heavy, so unbelievably heavy.

Delilah was crouched down on the front doorstep of the middle house. She was fussing with the rabbit, arranging it, trying to balance it. She leaned in towards it, and Dig was rooted to the spot with sadness and tenderness when he saw her suddenly grab it in her arms and squeeze it tightly, her face buried against its cheek and tears rolling down her face.

Enough, he thought to himself, I've seen enough.

He got to his feet and very quickly, before she turned around, scampered down towards the towpath and ran, through the crowds, along the river, down the high street and back to the station.

He was home a couple of hours later.

His thought processes were dizzying as he went from train to Tube, from Tube to bus and from bus to front door. Absolutely breathtaking. His head felt like it was strapped into a terrifying fairground ride. He was frightened, exhilarated and nauseated, all at the same time.

Most days the most important thing Dig had to think about was his car breaking down or having a row with Nadine or forgetting to send his mum a Mother's Day card. Today he was being forced to reconsider his entire existence, his history, his identity.

He felt bigger, physically larger, as he paced his flat back and forth that afternoon, waiting for Delilah to get back. His feet felt wider, his arms felt thicker, his legs felt chunkier. He felt older, too, like all those grown-up people he'd seen out and about at quarter to nine this morning.

His initial instinct was to say nothing to Delilah when she returned. He might have been reeling from the shock of it all, but Delilah would be feeling worse. He'd spied on one of the most intensely private moments of her life. He'd seen her crying into the rabbit's fur when she'd thought nobody was looking. He'd been somewhere he had no place to be. He felt guilty. The last thing Delilah would need on her return from such a traumatic event was Dig sticking his nose in, asking questions, turning the whole shocking situation into his own drama.

But as afternoon turned to evening and the sky darkened and his head became so inflated with questions it felt like it would explode, his mood changed. He became angry. Delilah was in the wrong. No matter whether that beautiful girl was her daughter or not and whether he was the father or not, no matter what the truth of the situation, Delilah should have involved him. She should have told him why she was in London. She'd treated him like a child with no capacity for dealing with adult realities. Which was, he supposed, true on many levels. But still, she'd found other uses for him, hadn't she? He was grown-up enough to own the flat she was staying in, to have paid cash for the sofabed she was sleeping on, and he was responsible enough, apparently, to look after her precious dog every day.

As his frustration and impatience had grown during the course of the afternoon he'd tried phoning Nadine. Over and over. He'd never before needed to speak to Nadine so badly, never needed to hear her voice, the voice of normality and routine, of light-heartedness and easiness, the voice of his best friend in the world. He didn't care about all that awfulness the previous evening. He just wanted to see her. But where was Nadine when he needed her? Not at home, that was for sure. Nadine's absence in his hour of need had served only to compound his sheer, throbbing panic, and by the time he heard the key in the lock and lifted himself from the sofa to confront Delilah at the front door, he'd lost all sense of reason. He no longer cared whether or not Delilah was emotionally ready to discuss the blonde girl in Surrey, and he was no longer ashamed of his act of deception and craftiness in following her there this morning. All Dig cared about now was getting answers to questions.

And, it had to be said, that of all the possible opening gambits to such a monumental conversation, he'd probably chosen the most bizarre and unsuitable.

'So,' began Dig, 'what happened to the rabbit?'

Delilah jumped and clutched her heart. 'Oh God, Dig,' she said, 'you nearly gave me a heart attack.' She hooked her sheepskin on to the coatstand and clicked the front door shut behind her. Digby bounced off the sofa and went hurtling towards her. Dig leaned against the living-room doorpost and folded his arms.

'What did you do with the rabbit?'

Delilah glanced at him curiously and then with concern. 'What rabbit?' she asked, slipping her sunglasses off her head and dropping them on to a table.

'Oh, you know, the big one' – he extended his arms to describe the height – 'the big one, with the floppy ears.'

She looked at him quizzically. 'Sorry, Dig. You've lost me.' She moved towards the kitchen and Dig followed her.

'You had him when you left the house this morning.'

Delilah stopped in her tracks for a moment and then spun round towards Dig. 'Ah!' she said, brightly, '*that* rabbit.'

'Yes,' said Dig, '*that* rabbit.'

'Oh he was a – er – gift. For a little girl I know. In Surrey. It was her – um – birthday.' She pulled open the fridge and removed a large jar of pickled onions, twisted off the lid nervously and forced an onion the size of a satsuma into her mouth. 'Mmmm,' she mumbled through the sphere, 'yummy.'

Dig looked at her with disbelief.

'Anyway,' she frowned, 'why do you ask?' A dribble of vinegar ran down her chin and she wiped it away with the back of her hand. Dig was surprised to notice that this failed to ignite in him even the slightest flicker of desire. In fact, it almost disgusted him.

'Did she like it?'

'Hmm?'

'The little girl. In Surrey. Did she like the rabbit?'

Delilah shrugged and crunched. 'Yes. I think so.'

'It was a nice rabbit.'

'Yes,' said Delilah, looking at Dig worriedly, 'it was.'

She popped another onion in her mouth, picked up the jar and walked out of the kitchen.

Dig leaned back against the work surface and put his face in his hands. Great, he thought, bloody great. I really am a *smooth* operator, aren't I? I really handled that so well. 'It was a nice rabbit.' Jesus. What an arse.

But then what, exactly, was the right way to handle a situation like this? Dig was fairly sure that no rules applied to how to conduct yourself on discovering that you have unknowingly fathered a child in your youth and that the mother of that child has kept you in blissful ignorance of the situation while taking full advantage of your flat, your facilities and your good nature.

He'd thought that by mentioning the rabbit he would immediately confer upon Delilah a full realization of the day's events, that she would instantly understand that he'd followed her to Surrey and watched her crying into the rabbit's fur and that a luminously enlightening conversation would immediately follow. Instead, she probably thought he was mad.

It was time to start this all over again.

'Delilah,' he said sternly, striding into the living room, 'I know about Sophie.'

His heart bounced into his throat as the words left his mouth, and his voice caught on the last syllable. It was the most dramatic thing he'd ever said in his life. He suddenly felt like an actor playing a part in a silly soap opera. He didn't know quite what to do with his arms while he waited for her to respond.

Delilah looked up at him. She'd been unzipping her black-suede boots. She kicked one off mindlessly and continued to stare at Dig.

'What?'

'Sophie. I know about Sophie.' His arms felt like strange, long things over which he had no control. He folded them across his chest to get them out of the way.

'Sophie who?'

Oh God, this was starting to sound like the rabbit conversation. Dig walked over to the sofa and sat down next to Delilah. He turned towards her, looked into her red eyes and felt himself relax. He stopped feeling like a soap actor.

'I followed you today, Delilah. I followed you to Surrey and to the river. I watched you. I saw everything.'

Delilah froze momentarily, one boot suspended from her hand.

'I saw the girl. I saw Sophie. She's beautiful . . .'

Delilah placed the boot carefully on the floor and rested her hands on her kneecaps. She stared into space for a moment and then turned towards Dig. 'Why did you do that, Dig?' she sighed, and Dig suddenly felt ten years old again.

'I don't know,' he shrugged. 'I didn't give it too much thought really. Just saw you outside, waiting for a cab this morning, and something snapped. I didn't plan it, or anything . . .' He tailed off.

There was a moment's silence. Dig contemplated the dirt under his thumbnail while he waited for Delilah to say something. The silence continued, leaving Dig more than enough time to ponder again his lack of emotional finesse. He wanted, as ever, someone else to take responsibility for the situation. He wanted Delilah to take over now – he'd done his bit. But he realized that that wasn't going to happen. He'd started this, therefore it was his responsibility. There were a million questions he could ask her right now, but only one truly definitive one. He took a deep breath and opened his mouth.

'Is she – Sophie – is she mine?'

Delilah spun round and stared at him. Dig held his breath. This was it. This was, potentially, the biggest moment of his life.

Delilah's eyebrows knitted together and she frowned. And then she grimaced. 'No,' she stated, 'of course not.'

Dig exhaled, felt his heart start beating again, a little too fast. He licked his dry lips and nodded distractedly. 'Ah,' he murmured, feeling curiously deflated, 'of course not.'

Dig had never known his flat so quiet before, as if the entire building had been wrapped in cotton wool. He heard the pilot light flick on in the kitchen, signalling the arrival of central heating. It was the only sound.

This wasn't what he'd expected. He'd expected floodgates to open at the mere mention of the girl in Surrey, he'd expected Delilah to abandon her reticence of the last few days and open up to him. Instead she was still keeping it all locked away inside, even now she didn't have to. Dig took a deep breath and forced himself to keep pushing. He hadn't come this far to let it all slip away again.

'But she is yours – right?'

Delilah was silent again. She let out a huge sigh and turned towards Dig. 'I can't believe you followed me,

Dig. I really can't.' There was a trace of disappointment in the tone of her voice which cut right through him like a switchblade.

He looked at her then and felt suddenly and icily detached from her. Who was she? Who the hell was this girl, Delilah 'Biggins', who he thought had left him twelve years ago because she was scared of commitment but who'd actually gone off and had someone else's baby, who lived some fairy-princess existence in the countryside that he couldn't even come close to relating to, who had a horrible dog and terrible taste in music, who veered constantly between onerous silence and bubblegum chatter, who was incapable of hanging up a wet towel or cleaning a cup?

He had absolutely no idea.

The Delilah of his dreams and memories was a girl; this person eyeing him with disappointment and disdain was a woman, a real woman, a woman who'd given birth and had to give her child away, a woman who had moved on in her life and had left her past behind her. Including him.

He'd been a fool to imagine that there was a future for him and Delilah. He felt faintly ridiculous to have ever considered such a notion.

Dig suddenly felt a burst of intense anger.

'Jesus, Delilah,' he shouted, 'what the hell was I supposed to do? You turn up here at my flat without warning, you – you kiss me in the back of a cab, you dump your dog on me, you make – you make – you make a . . . a . . . fucking *mess*, you tell me *nothing* about what you're doing here. You treat me like a mug. You haven't made me a casserole. I clean up after you all the time. And then I ask you a perfectly *normal* question and you don't even give me the decency of a straight answer. I'm sorry, Delilah, if I stuck a toe into your private areas, but I didn't know what else to do.'

Dig gulped when he realized he'd just said 'stuck a toe into your private areas'. What a ludicrous thing to say . . .

'I just want some answers, Delilah,' he sighed, before getting up off the sofa and walking meaningfully towards the kitchen.

He pulled open the fridge door and enjoyed the blast of cold air against his flushed skin. He picked up the last of his big Buds and made a pig's ear of trying to get the lid off on the corner of the work surface before giving up and taking it off with a bottle-opener. Had he ever, he wondered, been less cool?

He stomped back into the living room and sat next to Delilah again.

She turned towards him and placed a cool hand over his hot one. Her face had softened. 'Dig. I'm sorry. You're right. I've been unfair. I hadn't really thought about any of this from your point of view. I've been so preoccupied, trying to track the family down, trying to avoid . . . trying not to see other people, and you've been so patient and so sweet. You've kept out of my way and I don't know what I'd have done without you.'

Dig pulled his hand away. 'There you go again,' he said, 'you're doing it again, treating me like a pet, or something, treating me like Digby here.' He pointed at the dog. 'Well, you might have named him after me but I am *not* a Yorkshire Terrier, Delilah, I am not your pet,' he finished indignantly, his features set with pride, his thoughts in shock at the sheer idiocy of some of the things he was coming out with this evening.

Quote of the Night: 'I am not a Yorkshire Terrier', closely followed by 'you haven't made me a casserole' and 'it was a nice rabbit'. It wasn't like this on the television.

'Look, Delilah. I'm not very good at this sort of thing, as you've probably noticed. But I'm confused. I appreciate what you must have gone through for the last week – well, the last twelve years, I imagine. I appreciate how hard this must all have been for you, how emotional and tough. And I understand why you kept it all from me, I really do. But I haven't had a moment's peace since you kissed me in the back of the cab on Tuesday. You sent me down the wrong turning when you did that. Made me think you were here because of me. Made me think that what we had when we were kids still existed. You being here has made me re-evaluate my entire life, you know. I was *happy* before you turned up. And then you kissed me. And then you moved into my flat. And then I thought we'd had a bloody kid. I've fallen out with my best mate over you. And now – and now, I'm just in a right old two and eight.'

Nice finish, he thought, really stylish closing line.

'Please include me in your life, Delilah,' he said, 'please tell me everything. What happened twelve years ago?'

Delilah pinched the bridge of her nose between two fingers. 'God, I've made a real mess of this, haven't I?' she sighed. 'It wasn't supposed to be like this. I was just supposed to come to London, find Isab– find Sophie, have a look at her, make sure she was all right and then decide what to do about . . .' She cast her gaze downwards, cryptically, towards her crotch. Dig eyed her with confusion but she ignored him and carried on. 'I had no idea

I was going to bump into you and Nadine and how that was going to make me feel.'

'How d'you mean?'

'Look – I saw you first, on Saturday, in the park. I saw you before you saw me and I actually sped up, you know, to avoid you.'

'Why?'

'It just wasn't part of the plan. The plan was all so clean and simple. But then you saw me and you caught up with me and I found myself feeling nostalgic. And I thought, why not? Why not have a bit of fun while I'm in London. You know, I'm the same age as you and Nadine, but the life I live and the life I've *lived*, I feel like a middle-aged woman most of the time. Which is fine. But when I sat there in that coffee-shop with you and Nadine I suddenly felt so old and you seemed so young, with your wacky clothes and your free-and-easy lifestyles, and I was so envious of you both.

'So I went back to Marina's and started thinking about the old days, about going to gigs with you and wearing outrageous clothes and behaving like a rebel, drinking and smoking, sneering and pouting and being obnoxious, and I suddenly really missed that person. I missed that person who didn't give a toss what anyone thought, who was streetwise and rude and true to herself. So I met up with you. I wanted a holiday from being Delilah Biggins, Chester Wife, I wanted a night out as Delilah Lillie, Kentish Town Rebel, and there was no one I enjoyed being Delilah Lillie with more than you, Dig.

'It was only going to be the one night. That's why I kissed you, I suppose. I didn't think I'd ever see you again, and I was so full of adrenalin and so excited to be out with you, away from Alex, away from the country and back, very briefly, in my youth, that I just got carried away. And I kissed you. I shouldn't have. I know you, Dig. I know how sensitive you are. I should have realized how seriously you would have taken that kiss. It was stupid and self-indulgent of me. Please forgive me . . . I didn't mean to lead you on.'

Dig nodded sagely, wondering at the irony of a beautiful woman asking his forgiveness for kissing him on the lips.

'I didn't think twice about turning up here and asking you for a bed. You've always been one of the kindest-hearted men I knew, Dig. It didn't occur to me that you still had any feelings towards me – I felt like a charity case, not a woman, when I turned up on your doorstep. I was so desperate, I didn't think about your feelings. I'm sorry. And I'm sorry about the mess. I'm terrible, I know that. I always mean to be tidier – I always intend to put things away – but then I get distracted and I completely forget. And as for the casserole,' she smiled, 'let me take you out for one. Tonight. Please! I'll take you anywhere you like, for any kind of casserole you like.'

'How about a curry-flavoured one?' teased Dig.

'Absolutely,' smiled Delilah, 'a curry-flavoured casserole it is.'

'God, Delilah. I'm sorry to have lost my temper with you like that. It was out of order and it was selfish. It's just been so frustrating, and then I've spent all day thinking I was a dad.' He laughed wryly. 'I shouldn't have got on your case – not after the day you've had. You must be feeling shitty.'

Delilah shook her head and smiled again. 'D'you know

what?' she said. 'I'm really not. I thought I would be, but I'm not. Because she's fine, isn't she? Sophie's just fine. The woman who adopted her – her mother – seems a bit of a panicker, but then, maybe if my mother had been a bit more like her . . . She's just fine. Lovely house, brother and sister, she's got everything. The thing I was most scared of was that she'd look like her father – that I'd see him in her. But he's not there – not at all. She's all me. She's fine.'

'Delilah,' said Dig, seriously, 'promise me, over dinner, promise me you'll tell me everything. About Alex and Sophie and who her father is and what happened? Yes?'

'Yes,' nodded Delilah, 'I promise.'

'Bengal Lancer?'

'Bengal Lancer sounds great.'

Dig slugged back the end of his beer and got to his feet. 'I'm sorry I followed you – it was sneaky and low.'

Delilah shook her head. 'No,' she said, 'don't be sorry. I'm glad you followed me. It's good to be able to talk to someone about things. And' – she paused for a moment – 'I'm going to need your advice, too. There's something else I haven't told you – haven't told *anyone*. We can talk about that, too. OK?'

'OK.'

Dig held his hand out to Delilah. As she stood up she leaned into Dig's chest and wrapped her arms around him. 'You really are the loveliest bloke in the world, Dig Ryan,' she said, and Dig squeezed her back, and was delighted to note that there was no sexual response anywhere in his body to the proximity of her warm, fragrant body.

Well – only a tiny bit.

He grabbed his coat and passed Delilah her sheepskin,

and just as they were about to leave the house, the phone rang.

'Leave it,' he shouted out to Delilah, 'let the answerphone pick it up.'

'No,' she said, 'I'll get it.'

She was frowning when she wandered back into the hall a few seconds later.

'Who was it?' asked Dig.

She shrugged. 'God knows,' she said, 'they hung up when I answered. I did 1471 but it was "*from a network which doesn't transmit numbers.*"'

Dig shrugged, too, and held the front door open for Delilah.

He felt curiously light-hearted as he pushed his front door closed behind them and locked it. He was going out for a curry on a Saturday night with a beautiful woman, who, he suddenly and overwhelmingly realized, he wasn't in love with.

For the first time in over a week, a sense of normality began to return to him, a sense that things might just be getting better.

## CHAPTER THIRTY-SIX

Delilah was in one of her effervescent moods as they walked down Camden Road towards Kentish Town Road, bubbling enthusiastically about a deli she'd found in Great Portland Street earlier in the week that had made her the best salt-beef sandwich she'd ever had in her entire life, even better than the ones she'd had in New York on her shopping trips there, and really, really good coffee – but then London was finally getting to grips with the whole coffee thing, wasn't it, what with Seattles and Aromas and Coffee Republics all over the place, and it was about time, too, because how could London ever hope to be taken seriously as a sophisticated city if you couldn't even get a decent cup of coffee, for God's sake?

Crossing over Torriano Avenue she babbled on, about how awful the suburbs were and how she'd never realized because she'd gone straight from inner London to the deepest depths of the countryside, and it really was very depressing to see how the vast majority of the population actually lived, in terracotta-coloured houses with funny little porches and their two allocated parking spaces among the garden-centre rockeries, with their characterless high streets full of Nexts and Robert Dyases and lacklustre branches of Marks and Spencer which didn't sell any of the top-of-the-range lines they sold in town, and how she'd actually rather live in an unheated squat in Mile End than live her life in suburban mediocrity with borders on her walls and all over her garden.

As they trotted briskly down Caversham Road, Delilah regaled him with her thoughts on Gwyneth Paltrow's love life, and how it looked like she was turning into another Julia Roberts, constantly falling in and out of love with the wrong men, trying to find something real inside all that Hollywood bullshit while labouring under the weight of self-doubt and feelings of insecurity, and how if she wasn't careful she could end up single and lonely.

Unsurprisingly, Dig found himself zoning out, and his eye was caught by a couple walking the other way down the road.

The man was average-looking with a bad haircut and a damp raincoat and the woman was small and more than a little overweight. There was a sense of completeness to them and when the woman reached up on to her tiptoes and put her lips to the back of his neck, softly, slowly and unselfconsciously, Dig felt an overwhelming sense of sadness. The gesture suddenly struck him as the most intimate thing one person could do to another, more intimate than sex. The back of the neck, he thought, is where it's at, where all of human intimacy can be found.

Dig couldn't remember the last time he'd been intimate enough with someone to want to kiss the back of their neck.

In fact, the last person he'd felt that way about was Nadine, and that had been twelve years ago. Twelve years! The hairs on Dig's arms stood on end as the enormity of this realization hit home. He was thirty years old, and he had no intimacy in his life whatsoever.

He remembered the conversation he'd had with Nadine in the café, what felt like months ago now, about their disastrous love lives, and how they'd made a joke out of it and made that stupid bet. It had seemed funny then, the fact that none of his relationships lasted longer than a couple of weeks, the fact that his taste in women was veering towards the jailable-offence end of things, the fact that ever since he'd had his heart broken twice in his eighteenth year, he'd been able to relate to women only on either a purely sexual or platonic basis. It had seemed funny then, but now, walking down Caversham Road with Delilah and watching love's slightly overweight dream walking the other way, oblivious to anyone else on the street, Dig felt suddenly and desperately overcome with disappointment.

He looked at Delilah and analysed his responses to her now that he knew for a fact that he wasn't in love with her. Well, there was the obvious and most immediate response, that of the unblemished desire to undo all her buttons and clips and zips and watch her clothes fall effortlessly to the floor leaving her luminously white-underweared and ready to party, but then, that was Dig's obvious and most immediate response to looking at any beautiful woman. There was nothing that Dig could do about this constituent of his character – he was *always* going to want to undress beautiful woman. It was just the way he was made.

But did he feel intimacy for Delilah? Did he feel close to her, part of her, *connected* to her? Did he want to kiss the back of her neck on the street? It was an interesting question.

As he followed Delilah's still talking figure through the streets of Kentish Town, he looked at her narrow back and swaying hips and shiny golden hair, and he realized that they were strangers, complete and utter strangers, and that he most certainly did not want to kiss the back of her neck.

Delilah was still going on, about some film that he'd never heard of that had just come out in London and had been number one in the States for the last eight weeks, which was amazing apparently because it had been directed by a twenty-two-year-old woman, and Dig felt that no intelligent response to this conversation was required on his part and he could therefore safely drift back into his thoughts without fear of being asked to comment.

As they walked, Dig found himself staring at other couples, watching the ways they interacted together, deciphering their body language, judging the attractiveness differential between the two parts of each couple and then wondering what other people might make of the Dig and Delilah pairing. Well, they'd probably think that she was very tall and he was very . . . not so tall. But would other people assume that they were an established couple, nothing out of the ordinary, been together for a couple of years – or maybe they looked like they were on a first date? Would anyone be able to guess just by looking at them that they were ex-teenage-sweethearts reunited coincidentally after twelve years and currently sharing a tiny one-bedroom flat together with a ratty dog that she'd named after him? Would anyone guess that he looked at Delilah now and wondered who the hell she was, that he'd once been completely bonded to this person who was now so thick with secrets that talking to her about anything of any importance was like wading through molasses?

Dig had had a strange week, a week of change and metamorphosis. For the first time since he was twenty years old Dig was thinking seriously about the future. His ill-judged and unsuccessful attempt at romance last night had been just the tip of the iceberg, because, as he looked at the top of Delilah's golden head, he realized with a mind-cleansing start that even if he wasn't *in love* with Delilah, he wanted to be *in love* with somebody. Anybody. He was on for it. Totally.

## CHAPTER THIRTY-SEVEN

At the Bengal Lancer, Archad greeted Dig warmly and with surprise.

'You are very early this evening,' he joked, looking at his watch, and Dig thought, Yes, I am – I have never, in fact been here before eleven o'clock, I have never been here sober and I've never said a word to you that wasn't pliant with alcohol.

Dig was surprised to find the restaurant heaving. It alarmed him to see his favourite restaurant full of so many smart, sober and quiet people – like finding out that your best mate sings folk songs in his spare time.

Archad seated them in a booth at the back of the restaurant and handed them a pair of menus, smiling with excitement at Delilah as he backed away. As Dig looked at Delilah across the table he had a sudden *déjà vu* – the two of them, in Exmouth Market, on Tuesday night – God, had it really been only five days ago? – when he'd been so entranced by her, so thrilled to be sitting in a restaurant with *Delilah Lillie*, the Love of his Life, praying that she'd stay in London, hoping that . . . hoping that – What had he been hoping? Hoping that something would happen, he supposed, that someone would let him fall in love with them, *hoping that something would change.*

And there was no denying that things had changed, although not in any of the ways he might have imagined.

It had been a week of firsts. He'd cleaned his car, he'd woken up before nine on a Saturday and arrived at the Lancer before eleven. He'd taken a woman out to dinner, he'd been seen in public with a Yorkshire Terrier, he'd been to Walton-on-Thames and his towel rota was now so royally fucked that he no longer cared whether he was using Tuesday's towel or Thursday's, let alone whether it was black, green, red, dry, damp or dirty.

But most importantly, he felt unblocked. He felt free and alive. Delilah had changed everything. He was ready for love.

He looked up from his menu and scanned the busy restaurant, looking for potential lovees. There were plenty of attractive women in there, that was for sure. *Women* being the operative word. But they were all sitting at little tables for two, smiling at the large, smug men sitting opposite them, men who'd worked it out before Dig, worked out the whole love thing and got there first. The world, he reminded himself, was full to the brim with couples. Everyone knew that. That was what he and Nadine always joked about together. The 'ands', they called all their friends these days. Tim *and* Cat. Si *and* Angela. Robbie *and* Rachel.

Alex *and* Delilah.

Couples. Everywhere. No wonder Dig went out with young girls – they might not be on his wavelength, they might have different interests and priorities, but at least they were available. You know – at least after you'd gone to all the trouble of approaching them and talking to them and getting to know them, they didn't turn round and say, 'Sorry, you're a lovely bloke and everything, but I'm in a long-term committed relationship with that large, smug guy over there.' Or, 'Sorry, but I'm married to a handsome restaurateur who buys me horses and sends me on shopping trips to New York and I only kissed you for a laugh and I'm really only here to track down my long-lost daughter and . . .'

'Dig?'

Dig shook the thoughts from his head and looked up at Delilah. 'Sorry,' he smiled, 'miles away.'

'Are you ready to order?'

'Yeah,' he said, closing his menu, 'yeah.' He didn't have to look at the menu to know what he was going to order. 'So, what are you going to do now?'

'What do you mean?'

'Well – now that you've found Sophie. What are your plans?'

He tensed his body as he waited for her to answer. Please say you're going home, he thought to himself, please say you'll be tidying all your shit away and packing those enormous suitcases and going back to Chester with your weird dog and your pickled onions and your crystals. Please.

'Are you trying to get rid of me?' teased Delilah, grinning at Dig.

'No!' he almost shouted. 'No! Of course not. I just wondered . . .'

'Well. I guess I'll be going back home. To Alex.'

'Is that what you want?'

She nodded. 'More than anything. I've missed him so much.'

'I don't get it,' said Dig, 'if Alex means so much to you, why didn't you tell him you were coming to London? Why did you leave him? You must have really hurt him.'

Delilah nodded again, stiffly, and Dig was alarmed to notice her eyes glaze over with tears. Oh shit – now he'd made her cry. Dig couldn't bear it when girls cried, especially when it was his fault.

'I'm sorry,' he said, grasping her hand across the table, 'I didn't mean to . . .'

She shook her head. 'It's all right,' she said, 'it's fine. It's just that – you're right. I should have told him what I was doing but I was in such a state, it was all so unexpected, I couldn't think about anything else for two weeks and then I just took off. I just never thought it would happen to us, it didn't seem possible, and I never wanted it, I really never wanted it and . . .'

'Delilah!' barked Dig. 'Slow down, for God's sake. I've got no idea what you're talking about.'

'Oh God – I'm pregnant, Dig! I'm pregnant for fuck's sake. Can you believe it? We had sex three times last year *and* we used a diaphragm and I still managed to get pregnant!'

Dig clicked his hanging jaw closed. 'A-ha,' he said. That explains all that puking, he thought.

'And I never wanted a baby. Never. What would I know about being a mother? Look at the example I had.' She raised her eyebrows indignantly. 'I've already given one away and I don't want to do that again. But I can't have a baby, Dig, I just can't! I don't want one and Alex would be so angry. He complained enough when I got the dog.'

Dig was panicking. More heavy stuff. Oh God. 'Can't you – you know,' he stammered, 'can't you?'

'Get rid of it? Oh God – I've thought about it. That was one of the reasons why I came down to London. I couldn't have an – an – a termination at home. It would have been round Chester in seconds, and it's no one's business, is it?' She eyed him angrily. 'And ever since I found out I was pregnant I haven't been able to stop thinking about Isab– about Sophie. She's been haunting me. I suddenly felt like I couldn't make any decisions about this' – she looked at her groin again and Dig realized what she'd been trying to say earlier on when she'd eyed her crotch so cryptically – 'until I'd put a full-stop on the Sophie chapter. The agency told me she'd gone to a good family, a nice family, but at the time I didn't care. I just wanted her away from me – gone. I couldn't bear to look at her or touch her. I didn't care whether she went to live with the Queen or the fucking Yorkshire Ripper, just so long as I never had to see her again. Because, you see, she looks like me now, but when she was born she looked just like him – she really did.'

'The father?'

She nodded, and her face hardened, and Dig sensed that they were approaching the crux of the matter.

He leaned back into the red velvet of the banquette and waited for Delilah to start talking.

## silver toenails

The sun was shining the day after Delilah's eighteenth birthday. She'd spent the previous night at Dig's, as she did nearly every night. He'd taken her out for a birthday treat to a wine bar off Oxford Street and they'd shared a bottle of Mateus Rosé and felt like grown-ups. Her mother's house was empty when Delilah let herself in at nine thirty. She'd left a birthday card outside her bedroom door. It was the first time her mother had remembered her birthday in ten years, and Delilah felt a curious surge of warmth rising in her chest.

In her bedroom, Delilah ripped open the envelope and pulled out an embossed and gilded card with a picture of a young girl riding a pony on the front.

*Daughter Dearest,* said the printed message inside the card,

*Once you were a tiny thing, with toes and thumbs so small*
*And now you are a woman, strong and proud and tall*
*I've fed you and I've loved you, I've nurtured you through strife*
*But now it's time to let you go and learn to live your life*
*I'm so proud of you, daughter dearest*
*Happy 18th Birthday*

She'd signed it 'All love, Mum' and she'd even scribbled a couple of kisses underneath her name. Delilah felt choked with strange emotions. Despite the fact that a stranger had worded the message inside the card, it was her mother who had chosen it, who'd picked it up in a shop and paid for it, put a Biro to it, licked the envelope and left it outside Delilah's room. It was the kindest, least selfish thing her mother had ever done. Delilah felt a wondrous sense of her life opening up: she and Dig were going to get engaged, he was going to get them a place to live, she could sign on at last and stop working at that shitty chemist, and now this – an unprecedented gesture of maternal love. The future looked brighter than it had ever done before.

She had a bath, washed her hair, slipped into her dressing-gown and enjoyed the rare peace and quiet in her usually chaotic home. On her bed, she stretched out a long, white leg, picked up a bottle of silver nail polish and began to paint her toenails.

Downstairs, the front door slammed shut, loudly enough to make Delilah jump. The brush slipped in her hand and left a smear of polish down the side of her toe.

'Fuck.'

She got to her feet and peered down the stairwell, towards the front door ahead.

It was Michael, her stepfather.

He was leaning heavily against the door, his clothing awry, his face caked in dirt and bloody scabs.

'What the fuck happened to you?' she said, climbing down the stairs. Michael looked at her sheepishly. 'Jesus Christ, look at your face.'

Delilah had known Michael since she was five years old. He was a quiet, repressed, almost terminally shy man who rarely spoke. Delilah suspected he had learning difficulties. He'd been teetotal when he'd met Delilah's mother, just after her father died of cirrhosis, but thirteen years and five children later was a consummate drinker, his life punctuated by pub opening times and visits to the off-licence. He lived on beef-and-onion crisps, which he ate six packs at a time, and he had about him a permanent aroma of stale smoke and Monster Munch.

Michael let Delilah manoeuvre him into the front room and on to the threadbare sofa. He stank. She peeled his leather jacket from his obese frame and threw it over the arm of the sofa.

'Where've you been, Michael? What's happened?' Delilah often found herself talking to Michael as though he were a child.

Michael shook his head distractedly.

'Did someone hit you?'

He opened his mouth to speak and Delilah was almost knocked sideways by his vaporous breath. 'Oh Jesus, Michael, you're pissed. It's bloody ten o'clock in the morning and you're pissed.'

'Your mother,' he said, shaking his head slowly, 'your mother.'

'What did she do?'

'She kicked me out, didn't she? Kicked me out last night. Your mother. Hadn't even finished eating my tea. And it was sausages and all.'

'Why did she kick you out, Michael?'

He shrugged. 'Hadn't even finished my tea. Your fucking mother . . .'

Delilah raised her eyebrows. She wasn't going to get any sense out of him, that much was obvious. 'Here,' she said, 'I'll go and put the kettle on, make us both a coffee, eh?'

'Yes please, D'lilah – that would be nice.'

Delilah had always felt sorry for Michael. He'd gone straight from the home of his overbearing and abusive mother into the home of another overbearing and abusive woman, taken on her four children and given her another five. Despite the indubitable quality of his sperm, there was no respect in this household for Michael, and now that Delilah was escaping, could see a future beyond these four oppressive walls, she almost wanted to help him. He was more a victim of the Lillie curse than her, in a lot of ways. He was never going to escape. He dug himself further into this open grave with every pint he drank.

She walked back into the front room holding the two mugs of coffee. Michael looked pathetic – fat, unkempt, drunk and pointless.

'There you go,' she said, guiding the mug into his dirty fingers, making sure he'd got a firm grip on it, 'that should make you feel a bit better.'

She stood over him while he took a first tentative sip. He looked up at her, over the rim of the mug, his eyes brown and nicotine-stained, full of disappointment. As he pulled the mug away from his lips, Delilah could see he was smiling.

'Thank you, D'lilah,' he said, 'thank you.'

And for a moment Delilah felt warm and good.

'Delightful . . . de-lovely . . . delicious . . . Delilah,' said Michael. He laughed to himself under his breath. 'Delightful . . . de-lovely . . . delicious . . . Delilah . . . delightful . . . de-lovely . . . delicious . . . Delilah.' He was laughing loudly now and rocking back and forth as he repeated his strange mantra. Delilah began to back away – he was weirding her out – but suddenly the smile fell from his face and he began to cry. He stretched his vast arms upwards and grasped Delilah by the waist. He buried his face into her stomach and began muttering into the cotton of her dressing-gown. 'Thank you, D'lilah, thank you, D'lilah.'

Delilah didn't know what to do. His hair was greasy and smelled bad. His breath was hot against her flesh, his arms suffocating around her waist. She tried to peel his fingers apart and extricate herself from the foul embrace, but the more she tried to get away from him, the harder he held her. Beautiful Delilah, he kept saying, such a beautiful girl, such a nice girl . . . such a nice girl.

She could feel a damp patch on her stomach where his snot and tears were seeping through the cotton. Her heart began to race as a feeling of being trapped overcame her. And then suddenly she was on her back. Suddenly Michael had her by the wrists and was pinning her to the sofa. But you're not a girl, he was saying, his face inches from hers, you're not a girl, not any more, you're a woman now, aren't you, you're eighteen, and you're a woman, and you can do whatever you like, and I can do whatever I like because we're both adults, isn't that right, isn't it, and his breath, his breath smelt like raw meat, and his tongue, when it forced its way through her clenched lips, tasted of stale vomit.

Delilah heard a song in her head while it was happening. It was a song she'd heard on the radio at Dig's that morning. It played over and over in her head in rhythm with Michael's laboured thrusting. As she listened to the song in her head, she stared at her feet, her eyes focusing on the smudge of silver nail polish left on her toe, a reminder of the last thing she'd done before this had happened, the last thing she'd done while she was still happy. Because, even as it was happening, Delilah knew for sure that she was never going to be happy again.

He lay on top of her afterwards, breathing heavily and sweating on to her skin. Delilah felt her breath escaping her as his bulk crushed her diaphragm. And then the front door went. Delilah heard her brothers shouting and careering around, and her mother's harsh Golden Virginia voice telling them to shut up. Thank God, she thought, thank God, Mum's home, she'll look after me.

'*Mum*,' she wheezed, trying to lever Michael's frame off hers, '*Mum. In here.*'

She should have known better. All those years of disinterest and she'd let herself be sucked in by one flimsy birthday card, let herself believe that her mother cared.

'You filthy little fucking slapper!' Delilah felt herself being dragged from the sofa by her elbow and thrown to the floor. 'You *whore*!' She felt the toe of her mother's shoe connecting with her stomach. 'You disgusting *whore*!

'Can't you get your own man, is that it?' she said. 'What's wrong with that eyebrow-on-legs you're always hanging around with? Isn't he giving you enough?'

And then she slapped Delilah around the face, there, in the living room, her husband with his stinking knob still hanging out of his trousers, her daughter with her husband's cum running down the insides of her legs, and her children clinging to her legs, watching everything.

She didn't give Delilah a chance to wash herself, or pack more than a few essentials. 'Get out of my house and never come back! As far as I am concerned, I don't have a daughter any more.'

She'd slammed the door behind her, opening it again two seconds later to throw Delilah's jacket out after her, on to the pathway.

Delilah picked it up, dusted it off and began to walk. As she walked, she turned briefly to look behind her at a house where she'd known no joy, and she knew for a fact that she would never see it again.

# CHAPTER THIRTY-EIGHT

Dig gulped. 'Why didn't you come to me, Delilah? That day. Why didn't you come to me?'

Delilah had been looking at the ceiling, but now she dropped her head, and the tears that had been suspended in her eyes tumbled down her cheeks. She rubbed her face with her pink napkin and looked into Dig's eyes for the first time since she'd started talking. She looked so vulnerable and so young and Dig wanted to absorb her slight frame into his own.

'I didn't want to be with *anyone*, Dig. I was ruined. Michael ruined me that day. You have to understand that. You were good and pure and kind. You were love to me, Dig, and after that day, for a long, long time, I was a tiny shrivelled-up lump of dog-shit. I couldn't even think about being anywhere near you and your lovely mum and your neat little house and your clean, clean lives. And when you found me that day, at the DSS, I just wanted to disappear. I was standing there with you in the rain and you were so concerned about where I'd been, there was so much love in your eyes – and all I wanted was for the rain to turn to acid and dissolve me, there and then, dissolve me into a pile of mush and wash me away down a drain.

'I tried to make it work with you, for your sake, not for mine. But every time I touched something in your house, every time I got into bed with you I felt like I was contaminating things, dirtying your bedsheets. Every time you touched me I wanted to tell you not to, almost like you'd tell a child not to put their finger in an electric socket. Your mum would bring me a cup of tea in every morning and I used to wash the mug in the bathroom sink before I gave it back to her. I was totally fucked up, Dig, the most fucked up I've ever been, and when my period was late I just lost it. Packed up my stuff and went back to Marina's.

'Of course, it was the last place I should have gone. Once it was confirmed that I was pregnant there was never any question of an abortion, it didn't even come into the equation. Marina's such a devout Catholic. It was unthinkable. And I was too much of a vegetable to do anything about it. I just sat in my room, staring at the walls, feeling this thing growing inside me, day by day totally resigned to my fate, totally resigned to bringing this thing into the world, to giving it life. I felt like a vessel, not a human being. I wasn't Delilah Lillie any more. I didn't wear make-up any more, stopped dying my hair, didn't watch telly, listen to music, anything.

'But that was when I met Alex – he was studying on Primrose Hill. I was nine months pregnant and I tripped and fell. He took me to the hospital and they had to induce the baby because I was bleeding internally and there was a chance that it might have gone into trauma from the fall. So Alex was there when Sophie was born. I told him everything, about Michael. He was so acceptant – he didn't even flinch. He made me feel so calm. Clean, almost. I don't suppose there are many twenty-two-year-old men who would have had the maturity to deal with a situation like that, are there? I knew he was special.

'He kept in touch after that day, took me out every now and then. And then – well – you already know the rest, don't you? Alex always understood, about the sex thing, about me not wanting it. He didn't have a problem with it. I've been seeing someone about it – a shrink – trying to get better, trying to be a sexual person again. It's a very slow process. Every now and then I burst over with love for Alex and I want to give him something. He never asks me for it. I offer it, when I feel strong, when I feel clean. And, if I'm really honest, when I get scared that he's going to find it somewhere else. And I offered it to him six weeks ago and now I'm pregnant, and I thought that coming back to London, finding Sophie, would help me decide what to do. And it just hasn't, Dig. It hasn't at all.'

She started crying then, not loud sobbing, but silent tears. 'What do you think, Dig? Do you think I should have it? Do you think I'd make a good mother? I wouldn't be like my mother, would I? Do you think?' Her expression changed abruptly. 'Sorry. Sorry. That's not fair. I shouldn't have asked you that. You haven't asked for any of this. Oh God. Oh God. Just when you're starting to think that maybe life's quite simple really, it turns around and asks you to divide a hundred and twenty-eight by nineteen.' She smiled, unexpectedly. 'That's something Alex always says,' she said. She put her elbows on the table and ran her fingers through her hair.

Jesus, thought Dig. We might be the same age, but Delilah Lillie is centuries older than I'll ever be. Thirty, to me, just means being a slightly-older-than-I'd-like-to-be teenager. Thirty to Delilah means a lifetime of growing and surviving and really living. I'm just a child, he thought, compared to Delilah, an overgrown child.

I've done nothing. I'm still living in Kentish Town, still in the same job, hanging out with the same people in the same places – I'm even wearing the same jeans. My parents adore me and everything I do. They adore each other. Nothing bad's ever happened to me. I've never known what it's like to be broke. I've never had to make sacrifices or life-and-death decisions. I've never had to keep secrets or face the truth. I've never even been mugged. I've had it *so easy*, he thought, so fucking easy.

'So,' Delilah was saying, 'that's the story. That's Sophie's heritage. She'd be *so* proud, I'm sure, to know where she came from.'

'Fuck, Delilah,' sighed Dig, eloquently, 'what a fucking nightmare.' He shook his head slowly and exhaled loudly and hated himself for being so ill-equipped to deal with this sort of situation, especially as it was him who'd been so desperate for Delilah to open up and talk about things in the first place. He exhaled again and felt his brain scrambling with the effort of finding something, *anything* substantial or helpful to say.

And then, through the fug of thoughts, it came to him, the one thing he could say that he knew was true, that he meant wholeheartedly and that might actually help Delilah.

He took hold of her hands and looked her in the eye. 'You'll be a wonderful mother,' he said, 'I know you will. You shouldn't worry about that.'

Her face softened and she sniffed loudly. 'Do you think so?' she said, and Dig thought to himself that tonight was the first time in a week that he'd seen the old Delilah, the tender, vulnerable, scared girl he'd fallen in love with all those years ago, the Delilah who'd leaned on him so heavily and needed him so much, and made him feel like a man even though he'd been only eighteen years old.

He felt strong suddenly and gripped Delilah's hands even harder. 'You want this baby, don't you?' he said. 'You really want it?'

She nodded, snottily.

'And you're scared, aren't you, scared that you won't be able to love it, like you couldn't love Sophie?'

She nodded again.

'And like your mother couldn't love you?'

'Mmm.' She blew her nose into her napkin.

'Delilah – you're not your mother. I sometimes find it hard to believe that you're from the same gene pool as your mother. You are so full of love. You loved me, I know you did, and look how much you love Alex. You love your horses. You love your dog. You love your little brothers. And I think that deep down somewhere, you did love Sophie. I saw your tears today on her doorstep, I saw the way you looked at her. You love, Delilah, and you will be a great, great mother. Really.'

Delilah looked at Dig with watery eyes and he was moved to see the warmth inside them. 'Thank you, Dig,' she sniffed, 'thank you. That means a lot. It really does. It means – it means – you know – Alex – he'd be such a wonderful dad.' She started to brighten. 'He doesn't think he would. But he would be, I know it. And his parents have got this big treasure chest full of fancy-dress things and there's china dolls and old teddy bears and so much land. We've got ponies and dogs and ducks and trees to climb and secret gardens to explore. Any child would be happy there, don't you think? Even with an old bag like me for a mother!' And then she laughed and Dig laughed, and he noticed that she'd picked up her cutlery and was spooning cubes of chicken tikka on to her plate, and he supposed that must mean that the crisis was over. But there was still something he wanted to ask her.

'Don't you ever want, you know – revenge? Don't you ever want to kill him?'

Delilah stopped, her spoon suspended over her plate. 'Who? Michael?'

Dig nodded.

'No,' she said, thoughtfully, 'no. He's going to spend the rest of his life with my mother. In that house. That's punishment enough. That's a life sentence.' She cleared her throat and deposited some rice on to her plate.

'I would have,' said Dig, decisively, 'I would have killed him. If you'd come to see me that night and told me what he'd done I would have gone straight round there and killed him. With my bare hands. Honestly.' Dig stopped when he realized that Delilah was smiling at him. 'What?'

'Oh, Dig. You're so lovely, aren't you? So good.' She patted his hand, which he'd unconsciously furled into a fist, and Dig blushed. 'Why the hell haven't you got a girlfriend? What are you doing wasting your time with all these young things when you could be making someone so happy? Someone real?'

Dig averted his gaze from hers and busied himself piling curry on to his plate, barely aware of what he was doing. His face was burning crimson. He wasn't used to people telling him how lovely he was.

'I mean,' continued Delilah, 'you're hardly the archetypal playboy, are you? It's not you. It doesn't suit you. Don't you ever want – more?'

Dig laid down his cutlery and rested his head in his hands, as much an attempt to cover his blazing face as to compose himself. Still feeling rather pleased with himself for the way he'd handled the whole drama-in-the-Lancer scenario just then, for having been able to dispense useful, helpful advice to a friend in distress, he now felt capable of doing the mature thing and opening up to Delilah.

'Never even thought about it till you turned up,' he said, frankly. He told her about the girl he'd slept with on his thirtieth birthday and the conversation he and Nadine had had over breakfast, which neither of them had taken at all seriously. He told her about his reaction to bumping into her in the park, how excited he'd been about their dinner date, how spellbound he'd been by her that night and blown away by their unexpected kiss in the back of the cab. He described the feelings of growth and change that her presence instilled in him, his sudden need to extend himself and expect more from life – more money, more success, more respect, more ambition and, most importantly, more love.

'This morning, when I left the flat to follow you, I was looking at all those people out and about, doing their thing, with their kids and their jobs and their responsibilities, and for the first time ever I found myself thinking, Yeah, I could do that, I could be like those people. You know, a nice woman, a kid, a dog – a nice, *big* dog – a proper flat instead of a shoebox, holidays twice a year, in-laws, anniversaries, early nights, all that. But then I realized something. It's too late, isn't it? I've left it too late. Basically, the foundation for all that stuff is the right woman – yeah? None of that is going to happen without the woman, that's where it all starts.

But all the women I know are in couples. Everywhere I look – couples. There aren't any decent single women around. I thought you were single and look how wrong I was. All the good ones are taken.'

Delilah smiled and nodded. 'You're just saying what women of my age have been saying for years. But I don't think it's true, actually. This is about the age when a lot of relationships that started at school or college or whatever start showing the strain, start breaking down. There's a whole seam of newly single men and women looking for someone, but the *right* person this time, someone they can spend the rest of their lives with, have children with.'

'Desperate women, you mean. I'm not interested in desperate, last-chance-saloon women who are looking for sperm and – and – ' he puffed a bit as he ran out of steam and held his hands up in defeat.

'What are you looking for, Dig? Who's your ideal woman? Describe her to me.'

'Well – she'd be you, I suppose, but without the husband and the baby and the dog.'

Delilah raised her eyebrows. 'Seriously.'

'Hmm. Well, seriously, she'd be beautiful, of course, and slim, definitely. Blonde would be good and nice perky tits. Sorry' – he shrugged – 'I'm shallow about that sort of thing – I live in London, I can't help it. And – well – she'd be the same sort of age as me – or she could be a very mature twenty-two, I suppose.

'She'd have to be intelligent, but not intellectual. Intellectual people scare the life out of me and you could never go to the cinema to see crap films or watch *EastEnders*. She'd have to have a healthy appetite, you know, really enjoy her food. Especially curry. And it would be great if she could cook.

'She'd like pubs, have similar taste in music to me, be sociable, but sensible, too, if we're going to have babies. She couldn't be too much of a party animal. I'd want her to be someone who I could rely on, who'd be where she said she was going to be, not too flighty.

'And . . . and' – he tapped his fingernails off his teeth as he considered – 'money would be good.' He nodded. 'I wouldn't object to a woman with a nice healthy bank balance. A family girl would suit me, too – someone who's as close to her parents as I am, who understands the little apron-strings I can't quite cut off. And' – he clicked his fingers at the arrival of a new thought – '*tidy*. She would absolutely have to be reasonably tidy. I mean, I wouldn't expect her to be quite as over-the-top as me, obviously. But reasonably tidy would be good.'

'So, you're not too fussy, then?' smiled Delilah, teasingly.

Dig smiled and leaned back in the banquette. 'I guess,' he said, 'the most important thing is a girl who I can look at in bed when I wake up on a Saturday morning and just think – great, it's the weekend and I'm with my girl, and whatever we do today it's going to be great because she's my best friend and I love being with her.'

Delilah was nodding and smiling. 'Well, congratulations,' she said, offering him her hand to shake, 'that was the correct answer. You are, officially, mature enough to handle a grown-up relationship. But hmm . . . let me think . . . there's only one problem, isn't there?' She was camping it up, rubbing her chin with her fingertips and feigning confusion. Dig wondered what the hell she was doing.

'What's that?' he said.

'Well, where *on earth* are you going to find a woman to fit those criteria. I mean, they don't exist, do they?'

'Exactly!' said Dig. 'Exactly.'

'There's just no such thing as a beautiful, intelligent, single woman who likes curry and pubs, who's tidy and sensible and family-minded and who you could consider to be your best friend, is there?' She slapped her forehead with the palm of her hand in mock-exasperation. Dig was thoroughly confused by her strange carrying-on.

'Not in my experience, no,' he said, conclusively.

'Oh, but wait! Silly me! I know just the girl. I can't believe I didn't think of her before. She's perfect for you. You'll love her.' She leaned down to pick up her handbag and started ferreting around in it. 'I'll give you her number.'

Dig was suddenly all ears. 'Oh yeah,' he said, 'who is she? What's she like?'

'She's like your perfect woman, Dig. She's thirty, she's beautiful, she's successful, she's sweet and she's kind, and you'll absolutely love her.'

'Yeah but – will she like me? If she's that great won't she just think I'm a bit of a wanker?'

'No,' said Delilah, scribbling on a piece of Filofax paper, 'no. She'll think you're perfect. You're just her type, I promise you.' She clicked the lid back on to her pen and slid the piece of paper across the table towards Dig. 'Ring her,' she said, sternly, 'ring her right now.'

Dig picked up the sliver of paper and held it in front of his nose:

020 7485 2121

His face creased in confusion. 'But – but – I don't get it. This is *Nadine's* number.'

Delilah smiled at him.

'Why have you given me Nadine's number?'

Delilah frowned. 'Blimey, Dig,' she said, 'no wonder intellectuals scare you. You're not exactly bright spark of the month, are you?'

'Oh,' said Dig, smiling grimly, 'oh, *I see.* You're back on one of these matchmaking crusades. *I* get it.' He shook his head and handed the piece of paper back to Delilah. 'You just don't get it, do you? This isn't going to happen. Nadine and I are never going to be like that. If it was going to happen, it would have happened by now.'

'*Why?*' exclaimed Delilah. 'I don't understand. What the hell is the matter with you two? Why hasn't it happened?'

Dig sighed and rubbed his face with the palms of his hands. 'I dunno,' he sighed, 'it just wasn't meant to be, I guess. I tried and she wasn't interested and she's never shown even the slightest sign of . . . you know?'

Delilah slapped her hand down on the table-top and made Dig jump. 'So you have! I knew it! I knew that there must be something more than just this supposed platonic friendship bullshit. Tell me what happened. Tell me everything.'

Dig was starting to regret his candour – it was taking him places he had no interest in being. He took a breath and composed himself to tell Delilah the story of September 1987.

'So,' he said, afterwards, 'Nadine didn't want me, OK? She told me: "I don't want you." You don't get the truth much plainer than that. She wanted more than me.

She wanted a Man. She wanted sports cars and trendy clothes and life experience and brooding good looks. Not spotty little Dig Ryan with his Honda Civic and his crappy job and his skinny legs. And it took me a while to get used to the idea, you know. For months I found it hard to be around her without wanting to – you know – but it's good now. She's my mate. She's a huge part of my life and I'm grateful for that. Life without Nadine would be empty and meaningless. But, Delilah – I know you mean well and everything, but forget it, OK. Because it just isn't going to happen.'

Delilah was shaking her head. 'God, Dig. I wish you could sit where I'm sitting just for a few moments, see what I see, what *anyone* can see when they look at you and Nadine. I wish you could see it, get over some stupid, childish shit that happened ten years ago and see it objectively.' She sighed deeply and passed the piece of paper back to Dig. 'Keep this,' she said, folding it into his palm, 'keep this bit of paper. Maybe one day you'll find it in your wallet and you'll remember this conversation and you'll do the right thing. Yes?' she said, beetling her eyebrows and squeezing his clamped hand.

'Yeah,' sighed Dig, 'whatever.'

He slid the piece of paper into his coat pocket and set about trying to consume some of the food that was congealing on his plate.

What a day, he thought to himself as he masticated on a flavourless piece of lamb – why did food always taste so awful when he was with Delilah? – what a fucking unbelievable day. He suddenly felt exhausted beyond words. He wasn't hungry, he wasn't thirsty, and there was no way he could revert to smalltalk with Delilah now.

But the funniest thing of all was that in spite of the painful conversation they'd just had and everything that had happened in the past week, as he sat there contemplating his cold curry and absorbing the strange atmosphere, Dig suddenly realized that all he wanted in the whole world was to see Nadine.

# CHAPTER THIRTY-NINE

*Bang Bang Bang*

'Uuurgghh.'

*Bang Bang Bang*

'Neuuughhh.'

'*Nadine!*'

'Oh. Jesus.' Nadine peeled open one eye and then the other. The blurred images of textiles, bits of furniture and the watercolours on the wall that were forming on her retinas meant nothing to her.

She attempted to stand up. 'Oh, Jesus!' She started to panic. She couldn't move her legs. She didn't *have* any legs. She was crippled. She was paralysed. She was . . . oh . . . she was all twisted up in the bedcovers.

'*Nadine! Are you in there? Are you all right? Let me in.*' *Bang Bang Bang.*

It was Pia. It was . . . she was . . . oh, God. Nadine's head was like a . . . like a . . . a horrible thing, just a horrible, horrible, *horrible* thing. Where was she? Where the hell was she? What was this place?

She opened her mouth to try to shout something through the door, but nothing left her lips but foul, sticky breath. Uuugghh. She was going to have to get to the door somehow. It was dark, the only light coming from a tangerine streetlight just outside her open curtains. Barcelona, she suddenly remembered – she was in Barcelona. But what day was it?

She finally managed to extricate herself from the bed-clothes and crawled across the carpet towards the door. 'Coming,' she managed to croak, as she dragged herself along on hands and knees, 'I'm coming.'

She hauled the door open and blinked into the bright light. Looming above her was Pia and, on either side of her, two enormous Spanish men wearing black jackets and concerned expressions.

'Christ, Deen,' squeaked Pia, crouching down and putting her skinny little arm around her shoulders, 'are you OK?'

'Mmmm,' grunted Nadine, shielding her eyes from the light and the gaze of the two huge men above her, 'my head. My head. What day is it? How long have I been asleep?'

'It's still Saturday night, Deen,' said Pia, stroking some hair out of Nadine's face. 'It's nearly half ten. You've been gone two hours.' She turned to smile at the two men behind her, one of whom, Nadine could now see, was carrying a large bunch of keys.

'Looks like it's OK,' she grinned at them, 'sorry to have dragged you all the way up here. *Muchos gracias* and everything.'

'The señorita is well?' asked the man with the keys.

'The señorita's going to be just fine,' she soothed.

'We get room service maybe, to bring up some coffee?'

'That,' grinned Pia, 'would be absolutely smashing. Make it two. *Multo gracias*!'

Pia clicked the door closed behind them and lay down on the floor next to Nadine's prone figure. They lay and contemplated the ceiling for a moment.

'You know your phone's off the hook, don't you?' said

Pia, turning towards Nadine, who had covered her face with her elbow and was groaning under her breath.

'Shit,' she moaned, 'fuck.'

'When you didn't come back from the toilet, we tried to phone you, and when it was engaged we just assumed you must have run up here to phone Dig. After two hours we started thinking that even *you* couldn't spend that long on the phone. So, did you? Did you call Dig? Were we right? Were we right?!' She rolled over on to her stomach and faced Nadine, holding her chin on her hand.

Nadine nodded. 'Mmmm,' she mumbled.

'Yes!' exclaimed Pia triumphantly. 'I knew it. Jesus – that Sarah really opened a can of worms, didn't she, coming out with all that stuff about you and Dig? You should have seen your face, Deen – it was priceless! So – what did you say to him? What happened? Did you declare undying love, or what?!'

Nadine rolled on to her side. 'Got to hang the phone up, Pia, it might still be – you know – what's the word? Attached. No . . . no . . . that other word – you know? Urrgghh.'

Pia leaped to her feet and strode towards the telephone. She put the misplaced receiver to her ear and listened. 'No,' she said, replacing it, 'it's all right. You're not connected.' She perched on the edge of the bed. 'So. Tell me. What happened?'

Nadine pulled herself to a sitting position. It was all coming back to her now. Oh yes – it most certainly was. Oh bloody hell. Oh bloody bloody hell. Blood rushed to her head with the shame of it and her face creased up with mortification. 'Oh no,' she muttered, 'oh Pia. I can't believe what I did. It's too awful. I can't tell you.'

Pia's face blossomed with excitement. 'What?' she screeched. 'What have you done?'

'Oh no. Oh no. I'm never going to be able to face him again. Oh fucking hell.' She cradled her head on her knees and began rocking back and forth as she remembered every last detail.

'What happened – will you just tell me – please. I can't bear it!'

'I left a message on his answerphone.'

'Oh no!' Pia clasped her hands over her mouth. 'You mean like Rachel did in that episode of *Friends*.'

Nadine threw her a bemused look.

'You know! When she went on a date with that bloke and got really drunk and phoned Ross and said "this is closure" to his answerphone and then' – she picked up on Nadine's lack of comprehension and trailed off – 'no? Never mind. Anyway' – she brightened – 'what did you say?'

Nadine shuddered and caught the cigarette that Pia had just thrown her. 'Well – first time I phoned him, *Delilah* answered.'

'Delilah? Who the fuck is Delilah?' Pia lit her cigarette and threw the lighter to Nadine.

Nadine sighed. 'Delilah,' she said, 'remember? I told you about her last week. The Love of Dig's Life. They were teenage sweethearts.'

'Oh, yes,' nodded Pia, although Nadine knew full well she had no recollection whatsoever of the conversation.

'She and Dig split up when they were eighteen and they lost touch. And now she's back, for some unknown reason. And ever since she's been here she's been attached to Dig like a fucking leech. I don't *exist* any more as far as Dig's concerned. We haven't even been talking to each other for the past week.' She hauled herself off the floor and joined Pia on the bed, to share the empty champagne bottle she was using as an ashtray. 'And then last night I went round there because of Phil . . .'

Pia rolled her eyes dramatically. 'Who is Phil?'

'Don't ask. No one. Nothing. Anyway, I turned up there and there was this flash meal laid out on the table – candles, music, the works. And this disgusting little dog who turns out to be – guess who? – *Delilah's* dog. And then *she* appears, just got out of the shower, all skinny, wearing a towel this big.' She indicated half a centimetre between finger and thumb. 'I just lost it, you know? I suppose it was pretty immature of me but I couldn't help it. It just really, really upset me. I ran off, got into the car, went home – all very drama-queen. But it was just – it was just – *Delilah*, you know? Delilah-fucking-Lillie. All over again. She gets to me, she's under my skin, even after all these years, she's there and I've tried so hard to put it all in the past, start afresh with her, but I just can't do it. She has this effect on me. And she has this other effect on Dig. He can't see sense while she's around. He turns into a total spaz.'

Pia nodded empathetically.

'So when I heard her voice just now on the phone, in Dig's flat, like she fucking *owned* the place, I went a bit mad. I burst into tears first – snot and everything – and then afterwards I calmed down a bit. And then . . . and then – oh God' – she ran her fingers through her mussed-up hair – 'I managed to convince myself that I needed to be a grown-up about all of this. I decided that the best thing to do would be to confront Delilah, talk to her, find out what her intentions were, kind of thing.

So I called back – but this time there was no answer. I hung up. I was *furious*, convinced that they were both there, deliberately not picking up the phone. I got myself really wound up, imagining them there, looking at the phone, laughing at poor, mad Nadine.'

'*Room service*.'

Pia stubbed out her cigarette and grinned widely at the embarrassed young waiter who'd arrived with their coffee. 'Gracias,' she beamed at him as he backed nervously out of the oestrogen-rich room.

As she lowered herself back on to the bed, her smiling, flirting face automatically rearranged itself back into its former picture of sympathetic attentiveness. 'Go on,' she said.

'Yeah. So. I got myself more and more wound up, and before I knew it I'd picked up the phone again and – and – when the answerphone clicked on I just let rip.'

'Oh God – what? What did you say?' Pia passed her a cup of coffee.

Nadine slurped on it gratefully. 'I said something along the lines of' – she cleared her throat – '"I give up. He's yours. Have him."'

Pia winced.

'Oh but it gets worse,' warned Nadine, ruefully, reddening as her words echoed in her ears, 'it gets much worse.'

She'd thought she was being so calm, so mature, so *wise*.

'Have him,' she'd said, trembling, a hastily lit and illicit cigarette shaking between her fingers. 'He's yours. I've had ten years to do something about it and I didn't, so I guess it's fair enough. I'm not going to let you get to me any more – oh no – I'm moving on, Delilah and you're welcome to him. Have him, wind him round your finger for a while and then dump him again. See if I care. Break his little heart again. It's not my problem any more. I'm done. I'm through. Goodbye.'

She'd put the phone down then, her heart thumping loudly under her viscose dress and before she'd even had a chance to think about what she'd just done, she'd had another thought and was picking up the phone again and dialling.

She'd stubbed her cigarette out viciously as she waited for Dig's bloody stupid James Bond message to finish. She was on a roll now and couldn't stomach delays and time-wasting.

'And,' she'd said, hysterically, after the beep, 'another thing. This is a message for you, Dig. *I lied*!' she'd cried, adrenalin almost leaking from her ears, 'I lied when I said I didn't want you. OK? L-I-E-D. Because I did. I did want you, actually. And I always have and I still do. And – and – I'm drunk. I'm very, very, *very* drunk. I'm plastered. And I've been thinking about things and thinking about *your* things, you know, your willy, mainly, and your flat and your sofa and Ikea and bits of lint on the carpet and I miss them all and I miss you and I lied. Just so long as you know that I lied. Have a good life. Bye. I'll always love you. Bye.'

And then she'd hung up – and then again and then again as the blessed phone refused to sit in its cradle. She remembered feeling quite pleased at the time, quite pleased with the way it had gone. 'That's that sorted, then,' she'd thought to herself, her mouth set hard and her hands still shaking. She'd lit another cigarette, opened her mini-bar, made some kind of hellish cocktail from brandy, gin and San Miguel, knocked it back, been to the bathroom, thrown it up and then collapsed on the bed into a stuporous and immediate sleep.

'Oh shitting hell, Deen,' tutted Pia, shaking her head from side to side, her eyes like saucers. 'Shitting bloody hell. You've really done it now, haven't you?'

Nadine nodded heavily and collapsed backwards on to the bed. 'This is – awful. This is the most awful, awful thing. Just awful . . .'

'Did you mean all that, then? All that stuff about wanting him?'

Nadine nodded. And then shook her head. And then nodded again. 'Oh God. I don't know. This is all too much. I can't deal with it. My head hurts.'

'You know something, Deen. If all that was true, then it's good, you know? It's good that you said it. Life's too short and you're not getting any younger and at least this way you'll know. You'll know one way or the other. And I wouldn't get too worked up about this Delilah chick. It's like . . . it's like – ' her face lit up suddenly – 'it's like *Dawson's Creek*! You know – Joey not realizing how she really felt about Dawson until glam Jen came along with all her New York sophistication. But Dawson wasn't really into Jen, not really. She was just a fantasy. But she was also the catalyst for both of them to wake up and see that they really wanted each other. Except they split up – but then, they are only sixteen, I suppose. Even though you wouldn't think it, the way they talk to each other . . .'

Nadine eyed Pia with disbelief. 'You watch *way* too much television,' she sighed disparagingly, 'and besides. This isn't television. This is real life. *My* life. And I've just fucked it up.'

Pia shook her head sagely. 'Television *is* life. And life *is* television.'

'Well, your life is, obviously,' snorted Nadine, wondering at the shallowness of the youth of today.

'No. Everyone's lives. And I'll bet you that by the time we get back to London, Delilah will be gone and you'll see Dig and you'll kiss, and it'll be Ross and Rachel and Joey and Dawson and Harry and Sally all rolled into one. I mean – *Delilah* – honestly. There is *no way* Dig could end up with someone called Delilah. It just wouldn't happen. It's not real life.'

Nadine wanted Pia to go now. The conversation was getting unbelievably silly, and her head hurt, and she just wanted to lie there for a while on her own, torturing herself with word-perfect recollections of the messages she'd left on Dig's answerphone. She clutched her face as she remembered what she'd said about his willy.

Oh God.

How could she have said that? How could she have mentioned Dig's willy? Nadine had never even *seen* Dig's willy. It threw the entire dynamic of their friendship, their relationship, inside out. It changed everything. She could have covered up everything else she'd said, made out she was just being drunkenly overemotional. She could have got away with all the other stuff – but not that. Not the willy thing.

It was all over now. Things were never going to be the same again.

# CHAPTER FORTY

A sense of madness descended upon Dig as he drove towards Nadine's.

That message. It can't have been real. It just can't have. Must have been some kind of joke. There was just no way – no way.

'Did you put her up to this?' he'd asked Delilah after the stunned silence that had followed the end of the second message. Delilah had just shaken her head, numbly.

'Do you promise?' he'd asked desperately.

'Of course I didn't,' she'd snapped. 'Don't be so ridiculous. I've had slightly more important things to worry about the last few days than constructing some kind of elaborate practical joke. I told you. It's what I've been telling you all along. That's all. It's the truth and now you're actually going to have to do something about it. I'll put the kettle on,' she'd sighed, stroking his arm, 'you'd better give her a ring.' She'd looked horribly tired and Dig had felt guilty, inadvertently dragging her through yet another emotional quagmire after the day she'd had.

He'd phoned Nadine after he'd recovered from the initial shock and had been more than a little surprised to find that she was having a party. He couldn't believe that she hadn't invited him. Some girl whose voice he didn't recognize had answered the phone, and there'd been loud music in the background. He'd said, 'Is Nadine there?', and she'd said, 'I dunno, I dunno. Hold on.' She'd sounded very drunk, and when he was still holding on nearly three minutes later he'd hung up and attempted to watch the telly, instead, intending to deal with it in the morning. No point discussing it with her now, he'd thought, she'll be too pissed. Better to wait until tomorrow, until we've both had a chance to think about this, much better to wait. But waiting had, of course, been impossible. This had to be talked about now. It was too weird and too scary. It was *madness.*

She couldn't really have said that thing, could she? That thing about his willy. He must have misheard it.

It was a clear night for once as Dig drove in a daze towards Gordon House Road. A Saturday night, he reminded himself, the night when he and Nadine would usually be in a pub somewhere, either locally or in town, either with friends or just the two of them, either single or with current partners. They would be getting their last round in about now, a curry would be imminent. The world would be a simple place, full of warm friendship and deep affection and unspoken feelings of love and togetherness all wrapped up in a lovely, lagery blur. Nadine would be wearing some outrageous dress or other that she'd picked up earlier in the week from a second-hand shop, and wherever they were, her loud laughter and loud clothes, her vociferousness and her humour would light the place up, even the dingiest corner of the dingiest pub. There'd usually be some bloke sitting next to her, some sad idiot, shell-shocked by his extraordinary companion, amazed that someone like her had ever agreed to go out with someone like him, his face inert with nervous delight.

Could that incredible, bright, flamboyant and utterly unattainable woman, that self-contained, self-assured, and infuriatingly independent woman really be the same one who'd left that hysterical message on his answerphone, the same one who claimed to have been thinking about his willy? Nadine? Thinking about his willy? Maybe she was on drugs. Maybe someone at this party of hers had slipped her a little something. Yes, he decided, turning left into her road, that was the only explanation. Nadine was on drugs.

He could hear the music pounding from her flat even before he'd got out of his car – which was another worrying thing. Nadine had never had a party at her flat before. She'd had parties, but she'd always hired rooms and studios and restaurants because she couldn't bear the thought of her lovely, mad, overstuffed, piled-up, spilling-over, bright and colourful flat being trashed by a load of drunken friends who she'd feel too guilty to shout at. Dig felt a little uneasy concern rising in his chest.

It took a few minutes for someone to come to the door. Dig watched the smudged blur of a human form making its way to the internal front door through the thick opaque glass. Looked like a bloke. Dig cleared his throat and breathed in deeply, trying to quieten his thumping heart. He felt suddenly and overwhelmingly awkward. What was he going to say once he was face to face with Nadine? What the hell was he going to say? He'd been in such a rush to get round here that he'd hardly given a thought to what would happen once he *was* here.

'*Yeah – who is it?*' rumbled a hoarse male voice on the entry phone.

'It's Dig,' he shouted back, 'who's that?'

'*Eh?*'

'It's Dig,' he yelled, this time through the letter-box.

'*Dig! Little Dig! Cool. Fucking excellent!*' He could hear various locks and chains being undone and then the door slowly opened. A very thin, gaunt man with a mop of dirty hair and a threadbare lambswool sweater on shuffled out into the hallway. He was barefoot against the mosaic terracotta tiling in the communal hall and was holding in one hand a can of Kestrel and half a mangy-looking spliff. He was grinning so much that Dig could see his gums. He had terrible teeth. And he was limping.

As he opened the front door he placed his hands on Dig's shoulders and grinned at him even more. 'Looking good, Dig, looking really good. Fuck, man, it's great to see you.'

He enveloped Dig in a minor hug then, and Dig was almost knocked out by the smell of fags and booze and unwashed hair. Jesus Christ, who *was* this person? It was only as the man released him from the hug and pulled back to appraise him that Dig realized who it was. He hadn't recognized him because he'd been smiling, and he'd never seen him smiling so genuinely before.

'Phil?' he said, uncertainly.

'Come in, man, come in. I tell you – it's fucking blinding in there.' He began limping across the tiled flooring again, towards the door.

Dig followed him, suspiciously. Phil? What was Phil doing here? And what the hell had happened to him in the last ten years? He looked terrible – ravaged, ill and half destroyed. There was nothing left to remind Dig of that shiny, pretentious, leather-trousered tosser he'd first encountered all those years ago, except maybe the shape of his jaw and the line of his nose. But these once-defining features were lost now in a network of sharp angles and deep crevasses that looked like they'd been carved into his face by a psychopath.

As they entered Nadine's pink-foil-wrapped hallway Dig stopped in his tracks. This wasn't right. Something wasn't right. These weren't Nadine's friends. They were all far too young. There was a girl sitting on Nadine's art deco cabinet, the one she'd picked up off a skip in Highgate one night after a party and had made Dig help her carry all the way home. It had taken them two and a half hours and they'd had to keep stopping every minute or so to put it down because it weighed a ton and was cutting into their hands. Dig had resented every minute of it and complained the whole way, but he'd had a soft spot for it since, feeling that although it was Nadine's cabinet it was for ever a part of him. And now there was a girl he didn't know sitting on it, sitting on a pile of Nadine's precious magazines, swinging her fat-trainered feet back and forth and hitting the shiny walnut of the cabinet clunk clunk clunk. She had several facial piercings and was drinking Ernest & Julio Chardonnay from the bottle. She threw Dig a disinterested look as he walked past her and knocked back another mouthful. There was a bloke sitting at her feet on the floor, also multi-pierced and flicking through a copy of *Red* magazine. He was tapping his feet manically, to the beat of some kind of unidentifiable dance music emanating very loudly from Nadine's living room.

Dig followed Phil's skinny, limping figure towards the living room, stepping over the man on the floor, and began scanning the flat for any sign of Nadine. He saw a nugget of ash drop from the end of Phil's spliff, and rubbed it into the dark-green carpet with the sole of his foot as he passed over it, tutting under his breath at Phil's lack of respect for other people's carpets. He was starting to make a little sense of the situation now. These were obviously *Phil's* friends. Nadine had thrown a party and invited Phil and he'd invited some of his mates, and it explained entirely why Nadine hadn't invited him – quite apart from the fact that they weren't on speaking terms: because she knew he didn't like Phil.

Poor Nadine he thought to himself. She must be hating this. I bet she's wishing she'd never even suggested the idea now. And I bet she's wishing she'd never got in touch with Phil again, out of the blue – he's not exactly heart-throb material any more. And all this weirdness here might go some way to explaining her bizarre telephone messages.

Dig tapped Phil on the shoulder and shouted into his ear. 'Just going to get myself a drink,' he said, indicating the kitchen at the top of the hallway. He suddenly realized that there was no way he'd be able to face Nadine without at least a glass of wine.

'Yeah,' said Phil, effusively, 'yeah. Of course, man. Get yourself a drink and I'll see you in there. We can have a chat – I want to find out what you've been up to. Yeah?'

'Yeah,' said Dig, straining to hear him over the thump of the music.

As he approached the kitchen, Dig noticed that someone had spilt a bottle of red wine on to the green carpet, leaving a large brown stain roughly the same shape as South America seeping into the pile. The bottle was still on its side, next to the stain. Dig leaned down to pick it up and tutted again. He couldn't *believe* that Nadine was letting her flat get trashed like this. There were about ten people in the kitchen. Most of them were sitting around her table, making spliffs and flicking mindlessly through yet more of her beloved magazines. Some of the glossy publications were being used as table mats and had buckled with spilt liquid. A copy of *Wallpaper* lay on the floor and had been walked all over a few times by the look of it. It was smeared with muddy brown footprints, and pages from it had been dislodged and dragged across what Dig could now see was a sodden, booze-soaked linoleum.

There was a page at his feet. '*Pouffes*,' ran the now-grubby headline, '*the last bastion of bad taste*.'

A girl with scarlet hair was in the middle of telling the rest of the room what was, she seemed to think, a very interesting story about her mother's new boyfriend. 'He's a fuck-in' wanker,' she said in a soft Cardiff accent. 'He calls me Tania – I keep tellin' him it's pronounced Tar-nia, but 'e's so thick. It's always Tan-ia. And I wouldn't be at all surprised if he was a fuck-in' *paedo*phile, you know? The way he looks at my little sister . . .' She shuddered and a few people mumbled in response. It was quite obvious from the reaction that nobody was very interested in what Tarn-ia thought of anything.

A couple of people looked up as Dig walked in and then looked down again. He walked towards the fridge and nearly gasped out loud when he saw the state of the kitchen work surfaces. There was a veritable *Withnail and I*-style arrangement of festering washing-up piled up in the sink, which made no sense, as Nadine had a dishwasher. There were empty soup cans just left, their lids only semi-removed and sticking up like snapping jaws, and there was some kind of multicoloured, unidentifiable goo slavered all down the white plastic sides of the swing bin. The pools of liquid all over the oak surfaces had attracted particulated detritus – ash, sugar, crumbs and tobacco clung to the work surfaces, hardened and dried. Packets of cereal sat around, open-mouthed, and a crumb-embedded tub of Olivio had developed a rancid yellow coating.

Jesus, thought Dig, this is disgusting. And look – how the hell had that happened? – one of the panes in the window that looked out over Nadine's neighbour's garden had been smashed, and there was a Dorothy Perkins carrier bag taped over it.

This was all wrong. The image confronting him was at complete odds with everything he knew about Nadine's kitchen, with every memory of it. Nadine's kitchen was one of the best places in the world. He lost count of the hours he'd spent sitting at her faux-gingham, Formica-topped table (donated by the Italian owner of their previously favourite greasy spoon when it had closed down three years ago) watching her knocking together a quick pasta or a moussaka or – it made him drool just thinking about it – one of her home-made pizzas with chorizo and chilli. She always had some kind of music playing, it had been Belle and Sebastian last time, he recalled.

Her smart little CD-player was festooned now with destitute CDs, the neat pile that usually rested against it up-ended, disordered and pilfered.

On summer evenings, the sun set directly into Nadine's kitchen, it sometimes seemed. She'd have the windows wide open, and as the sun sank the walls of the room would turn a warm, toasty peach, and the birds outside would turn up the volume and Nadine would twitch her floral-clad bottom from side to side in time to the music, and the smell of garlic would hit the air, and at moments like that Dig would feel a happiness that emanated almost entirely from his belly, a happiness that had a short shelf-life but was unspeakably wonderful nonetheless.

How was he supposed to reconcile that with this, with this dark, stinking, dirty, soulless room full of strangers and their mess? Finding no wine, he plucked a beer from the fridge and strode towards the living room. He was now thoroughly unsettled. He had to see Nadine. This couldn't be right, it just couldn't. The vibe was all wrong, totally negative. Nadine's flat felt like it was being squatted. There was no one, he decided, in this room, who he could even vaguely imagine liking, even if they all tried their hardest.

He pulled his cigarettes from his coat pocket and lit one from a dripping red candle before picking his way back over the shredded magazine pages stuck to the floor. He was now so unsure of his place in this once-familiar environment that he wouldn't have been at all surprised to find Nadine stripped naked and cross-legged in the middle of the floor having rashers of raw bacon stapled to her body by a team of gimps in head-to-toe leather.

The living room was almost pitch black and, at first, appeared to be empty, but as Dig's eyes grew accustomed to the dark he could see that it was, in fact, heaving. The beat pulsated gently through the floorboards, fizzing into the soles of his feet and making him want to dance, despite himself. The Homemaker curtains at the other side of the room had been left open and the window on to the road let in wafts of cool, fresh air which did nothing to alleviate the intense, syrupy body heat that suffused the room.

There was, he could now see, a proper DJ set up at the far side of the room, and as he walked towards the centre of the room the bpm. tripled and the room exploded into dazzling strobe lighting. At least thirty people seemed to jump in the air at the same time, their eyes wide and staring.

Jesus, thought Dig, Nadine's having a bloody rave in her flat.

He scanned the room nervously for Nadine, his brain throbbing in time with the flashing lights. All her furniture had been cleared out of the room – her leather deco sofa, her mirrored cocktail cabinet, her bookshelves and bucket chairs, her fluffy leopardskin cushions and purple suede pouffe. Every picture and mirror on the wall had been knocked to a dishevelled angle and – oh no – her favourite mirror of all, the oval bevelled one with the chrome frame, had been smashed cleanly in half.

There were fag-ends on the carpet.

Unable to spy Nadine anywhere, Dig began walking towards Phil, who was sitting on the window-ledge with his bad leg resting on an upturned plastic crate in front of him. The tip of his tongue was just protruding from his lips as he licked the corner of a Rizla, and his face broke open into another gummy smile when he saw Dig approach.

'Dig. Mate. Sit down.' He slid along the window-seat and patted the space.

Dig didn't want to sit next to Phil. 'Erm – actually – I wouldn't mind just going to say hello to Nadine first. I haven't seen her yet. D'you know where she is? Is she in here?'

Phil burst into uproarious laughter. 'Come on,' he

said, 'sit down. *Sit down.*' He patted the seat next to him again. He stuck a roach into the end of the spliff he was constructing, adjusted it, lit it and passed it to Dig. 'Yeah,' he said, immediately starting to make another one, 'Nadine told me you two had fallen out. Over a girl, yeah?' He was pinching pale-green grass from the most enormous bag of grass that Dig had ever seen.

'Yeah,' Dig said, inhaling, 'sort of. It's all really complicated.'

'Isn't it always, mate, isn't it always?'

'Look – I really need to speak to her. Where is she?'

Phil exploded into another peal of blood-curdling laughter. 'I couldn't say, precisely, Digby. No – not precisely. You'd have a long search on your hands, let's put it that way.' He guffawed happily to himself and then looked up at a young man with a mop of peroxide hair who'd just whispered something in his ear. He whispered something back to him and patted his arm. ''Scuse me a minute, Dig. I'll be back in a tick.' He heaved his bad leg off the crate and hobbled towards the corner of the room with the young man.

Dig frowned. What was that supposed to mean, 'I couldn't say, precisely'? That sounded . . . ominous. Deeply, deeply ominous. Dig began to feel the slightly nauseous sensation of butterflies in his stomach.

What had Phil done to her? He stood up abruptly and strode from the room. He checked the kitchen again. Tarn-ia was still talking. He stepped over the *Red*-reading bloke in the hallway and threw open Nadine's bedroom door. He backed out immediately when he saw the haphazard piles of Nadine's furniture, *thrown*, seemingly, from a distance into the room. The sofa was sitting on her bed, on top of her Bollywood duvet cover, and everything else was just lying where it had landed. There was certainly no one in the room.

The bathroom door was locked. He banged on it hard with his fists.

'*Busy*,' came a gruff, male voice.

'Is Nadine in there?' Dig shouted.

'*Who*?'

'Nadine. I'm looking for Nadine.'

'*Come back later. We're busy*.'

Oh Jesus. Oh Jesus. Dig ran his fingers through his hair despairingly. He was half-tempted to kick the bathroom door down. Oh Jesus. Nadine. What the hell had happened to Nadine?

He strode back to the living room and towards Phil, who was just tucking a banknote of some description into his jeans pocket.

'What the fuck have you done with her?' he demanded, his face inches from Phil's.

'Whoa,' grinned Phil, 'calm down, man. Calm down.' He rested one hand gently on Dig's arm. Dig shrugged it off.

'Where is she? Where the fuck is Nadine?'

'What are you trying to say, Digby?' Phil was frowning, confused.

'I'm saying, what's happened to Nadine? Where is Nadine?'

'I told you, man. I don't know for sure . . .'

'What do you mean, you don't know? This is her flat, for fuck's sake. Now where is she?' A fleck of spit flew off the end of Dig's tongue and landed on Phil's cheek. He didn't notice.

'Shit. I dunno,' he shrugged, 'Spain, somewhere. Take it easy, for fuck's sake.'

'Eh?' Dig grimaced. Spain? That was the last thing he'd been expecting Phil to say.

'Yeah. Spain. She's on a business trip, taking pictures of tits and arses.' He laughed again and lowered himself back on to the window-seat.

Dig's head began to swim. Spain? Actually, that did sound kind of familiar now he came to think about it. She might have mentioned something about a Spanish trip a while back. But that explained nothing. It didn't explain her desperate visit to his flat last night. It didn't explain the messages on his answerphone and it certainly didn't even *begin* to explain this nightmare of a party currently taking place in her lovely flat. Dig rubbed his face with the palms of his hands and sat down heavily next to Phil on the window-seat.

'When did she go?' he sighed.

'This morning. Really fucking early this morning. Woke me up and all,' he laughed, 'expected me to get up, cheeky bint!'

'You were here this morning?'

Phil nodded.

Dig digested this unsavoury little fact with a dry gulp. Phil was here, this morning. Which meant, of course, that Phil had been here last night. Dig shuddered.

'So,' he managed to squeak, 'what's the story, then?' He attempted to imbue his voice with a blokish camaraderie but couldn't quite veil the creeping nausea rising in his gut. Surely not. *Surely not.*

'The story, man? What story?'

'You. And Nadine. What's happening?'

He could hardly bear to hear Phil's answer.

'Not too sure myself, mate,' he grinned. 'Nadine just phoned me, out of the blue. We went out for a drink, went back to mine, and suddenly she was all over me, like nothing had ever changed, you know. That girl is something else, isn't she? That girl is – *hot*.' He nudged Dig and Dig had to stop himself punching him in the face.

'So, it's all on again. Me and Nadine. I've got the front-door key, mate.' He winked and Dig felt sick.

'So,' he said, taking a deep breath, 'where are you living now, Phil?'

Phil shrugged and indicated the room with his eyes. 'Wherever I lay my hat, Digby, wherever I lay my hat.'

'And have you – have you laid your hat here?'

'It certainly looks that way. I could do much worse than Nadine, couldn't I? She's an angel, that girl, a true angel. She's got a lovely little place here and a nice bit of money coming in. You seen her motor?' He made on 'O' of his mouth.

'So Nadine's asked you to move in?' Dig's eyes were starting to bulge with the improbability of it all.

'That's right, mate. That's right. Bit of a result, *non*?'

'But – but – but – '

'That's taken you a bit by surprise, hasn't it?'

Dig nodded.

'Look,' said Phil, draping one arm around Dig's shoulders, 'you've got to understand a woman like Nadine. She's got everything, right. She's got the looks and the job and the flat and the car. But she hasn't got a man. Not a real man. So she's flailing around for ten years, making do, compromising, and then she turns thirty – the old biological clock clicks in and it gets her thinking – about the old days – about what we had together. She phones me – her lost love. Who can blame her? I was a bit surprised, to be honest, by how fast everything happened, especially the sex – you know – on the first night. But it was blinding, Digby, blinding. Some of the best sex I've ever had.'

Dig felt bile rising in the back of his throat. He swallowed it.

'So I give her a load of what I know she wants – sweet talk, messages on the answerphone, declarations of undying love – and the next night, I'm in. Foot in the door, hat on the old metaphorical bed. In – like – Flynn.' He nodded smugly and inhaled deeply on a spliff. 'It's a shame she had to go away, really. She would have loved this.' He indicated the party.

'Does she know?' muttered Dig. 'Does she know about this party? Does she know you're having a party?'

'Nah. Nah. But she won't mind. You know what she's like. Sweet. Laid back. Make yourself at home, she said, help yourself to anything, this is your flat now, treat it like your own.'

Two small girls with spiky pony-tails wandered towards Phil. 'Yes, sweethearts,' he smiled. One of them leaned down to his ear. He nodded and leaned into hers and then the three of them disappeared into the corner of the room, Phil turning to wink at Dig before he went.

Dig's eyes were wide open and his mouth was shut tight. This was all surreal. He must be dreaming all of this. Nadine was in Spain. Phil was in Nadine's flat. Nadine had had sex with this mop-haired skeleton. She'd invited him to live with her. All this at the same time as phoning *him* and leaving bizarre messages on *his* answerphone about *his* willy. No no no. The entire universe had gone stark staring raving mad.

He felt suddenly and horribly claustrophobic. There were too many people in here, not enough air, too much noise, and this terrible strobing light was sending him just about over the edge. He had to get out of here, absolutely had to get out, fresh air, clear his head . . .

As he left the room he saw the two girls walking away from Phil and examining something in their hands. Phil tucked yet another banknote into his jeans pocket and started chatting to a bald bloke who was dancing.

Right, thought Dig, OK. Phil's a dealer. Phil's a dealer.

He put the realization into a mental To-Do list for digesting later, when he was out of here, away from here, gone.

As he passed the bathroom, the door opened and in the brief second before it snapped closed again, Dig had a fleeting vignette. Toilet bowl: broken. Bath: full of people. Sink: full of sick. Cistern: busy heads bowed down over it. Floor: covered in wet toilet paper. He backed away. He couldn't bear it. Not for another second. He found the front door handle and forced it open, stumbling into the relative tranquillity of the tiled hallway. He stood statue-still for a split second. His head was spinning. He pushed open the main door and felt a sense of release when he heard it slam loudly behind him.

His feet sounded like giant's feet as he clambered clumsily down the front steps. A fat tabby cat perched on the bottom step eyed him up. Where had he parked his car? Where? Shit. Yes. Over there. That's right. He ran down the pavement, unlocked the front door, slipped into the driver's seat, locked the door, leaned into the beige upholstery, breathed out – big, long, deep, out. Jesus – Jesus. Pulled on his seatbelt, switched on his ignition, reverse, forward, reverse, out of here, gone.

The world seemed to get brighter as Dig left Gordon

House Road. Brighter and lighter. His racing heart slowed down, his strobe-blinded eyes regained clarity, the tape playing in his car stereo was melodic and clean. A group of fresh-faced, friendly-looking people were gathered on the corner of Chetwynd Road, waiting for a cab. They looked like nice people. It was only eleven thirty.

Slowly, yard by yard, Dig's head cleared. He turned left into Highgate Road and tried to focus his thoughts. He should be doing something, that was what he was aware of above all – he should definitely be doing something. What? What should he be doing? Nadine had invited that man into her flat. She'd slept with him. She'd given him a front-door key. She had no one to blame but herself. But parties – drugs, students, broken toilets and trashed carpets – she hadn't asked for any of that.

Dig pulled up at the traffic lights at the top of Highgate Road and rested his head on his steering-wheel. This had been the weirdest fucking twenty-four hours of his life.

As he lifted his head to check the lights, another light caught his eye. A light on Kentish Town Road to his right. A deep-blue, trapezium-shaped light. It said 'Police'. Of course, he thought, of course. Absolve himself. Let someone else deal with it. Clean it up. Sort it out. That's what they were there for, after all. That's what we paid them for. Let them take the strain.

The car behind him hooted as he dithered in front of the now-green light. He slipped into first, flicked his indicator to the right and pulled up in front of the police station.

## CHAPTER FORTY-ONE

Dig returned to Nadine's flat, with DCs Farley, Stringer, Short and McFaddyen. He rang on the doorbell, asked for Phil, waited until both doors were opened and then stood back and allowed the officers to go about their business.

He'd never seen anything like it. Within seconds, hordes of people began spilling from the house like insects, hurriedly pulling on jackets and shoes and hats as they went. A second later the music died, leaving the entire street with a strange, dead, ringing sound. And then a couple of minutes later Dig watched with a morbid fascination from his hiding-place across the street as Phil himself was marched firmly towards the waiting police car and lowered into it.

He was still smiling.

Dig remembered what Phil had said at the party: 'Wherever I lay my hat, Digby, wherever I lay my hat.' Of course. It made perfect sense to Dig. He probably thought of prison as just another place to lay his hat and, no doubt, when he got out, he'd find somewhere new to 'lay his hat', some other poor woman's lovely flat.

He didn't believe a word Phil had said earlier on. There was no way, *just no way*, that a wrinkly old git like Philip Rich with his dead eyes and his dirty hair and his bad teeth could possibly have got Nadine to drop her drawers, to invite him to move into her flat. It made him feel sick just thinking about it.

There must have been some other explanation for it. There must be more to Philip Rich than met the eye. Dig had always had his suspicions about him, never trusted him. He would get to the bottom of this peculiar state of affairs. But first he needed to speak to Nadine.

For the first time ever Dig felt protective and tender towards Nadine, Nadine who needed no one, least of all Dig Ryan. He'd protected her property. He'd looked after her. The thought left him feeling curiously warm inside.

He watched the blue-and-white car pull away from Gordon House Road and then walked sadly towards Nadine's house. The front door was open. He moved into the hallway and towards Nadine's flat.

Inside he wandered around desolately. The mass stampede from the flat had created even more damage. Nadine's weird pink-foil wallpaper had been shredded by the hordes of people all rushing to the front door at the same time. The pile of magazines on the deco cabinet had been thrown to the floor and mashed underfoot. Wine bottles and lager cans littered the carpet.

Dig's head filled up with images of happier times, thoughts of all the evenings he'd spent here with Nadine in her eccentric little castle, listening to music, getting stoned, getting ready to go out, discussing their disastrous love lives. He'd been with her when she'd first been to see the flat. She'd fallen madly in love with it and he'd tried to persuade her it wasn't right for her. It's characterless, he'd told her, it's got no soul and it's overpriced. But she hadn't listened to him. She'd bought it for the asking price and he'd shaken his head and said, 'You're making a huge mistake – you're going to be desperate to move in six months' time, and then you'll be imprisoned in here by negative equity and you'll start hating it. Take my word.'

Nadine had, of course, proved him entirely wrong, compensating for the beige Anaglypta, dark-stained-oak and magnolia walls of her childhood with flights of fancy and bright colours, turning the dull, echoing flat she'd bought into a mad, welcoming, warm and cosy refuge from the world. Dig loved it in Nadine's flat.

Imagine, he thought with a sudden sense of dread, if something happened and I was never allowed to come back here again. Imagine if something happened to Nadine and I never saw *her* again. What would be the point, he wondered, of going on? Would he have any desire to get up in the mornings or to go out at the weekends if there was no Nadine?

Imagine if she died. Imagine if she got run over by a bus and someone phoned him and said, 'It's Nadine, something's happened.' He couldn't, he just couldn't countenance it – he'd never smile again . . .

Dig was surprised and just a little horrified to find that his eyes were filling up with tears as he explored this morbid train of thought. He gulped to force them back and wiped away an escapee as it slid down the side of his nose. How ridiculous. He must be over-tired. That was the only explanation. Over-tired and over-emotional and – and – Jesus, what a day.

. . . and imagine, his mind forced him to keep thinking, imagine if something happened to Nadine and you never got a chance to apologise for not phoning her last night when she was so upset, never got the chance to explain to her about Delilah, to assure her that nothing had happened between you, to ask her about that message on the answerphone, to find out why she lied to you all those years ago about how she felt about you.

There was so much that needed talking about, and where was Nadine? In Spain, that's where, in bloody Spain, while his head pounded and his heart ached and his life twisted itself in and out and all around like a fucking Möbius strip.

Dig sighed heavily and lowered himself on to his haunches. He picked up one of Nadine's poor, destroyed magazines and held it to his chest.

Please come home, Nadine, he breathed to himself, please come home.

# CHAPTER FORTY-TWO

Nadine piled all her cases and aluminium-clad boxes on to the pavement and eyed her front door with suspicion.

London was still soggy and unhappy, and the crisply sunny days of her weekend in Barcelona suddenly seemed like a distant memory. Her neighbour's cat leapt up onto the wall to greet her and Nadine gently scooped the bedraggled creature into her arms, let herself into the house and deposited him in the terracotta-tiled hallway, where he could dry out while he waited for his owners to get home from work.

She felt for her key in her pocket and breathed in deeply as she brought it towards the keyhole. She'd managed to work herself up into a complete paranoid frenzy over the course of the weekend about what might have happened to her flat while she was gone. She had images in her mind of spilt wine, broken glass, wild parties and police raids. Ridiculous, of course, she knew she was being ridiculous. Pia and Sarah had spent most of the last three days persuading her how silly she was being. 'Don't be daft,' they kept saying, 'don't be so over-dramatic. The flat's going to be just fine. Phil will be home by now, back in Finsbury Park,' they soothed. 'The worst thing that could happen is that you might be minus a few cornflakes or he might have finished the bog roll. Take it easy.'

Instead they encouraged her to discuss the whole

'Phoning Dig' fiasco. That was *much* more interesting as far as they were concerned – a real-life soap opera for Pia, unfolding in front of her very eyes. They were all convinced she'd done the right thing, especially Sarah, of course, who'd started the whole bloody thing in the first place and was already planning what she going to wear to the wedding. They'd been on her case all weekend to phone him again.

'No way,' she'd insisted, 'don't even waste your time thinking about it. I am never phoning Dig again. Ever, OK?' She had a plan anyway. A plan to work her way out of the awful nightmare she'd landed herself in. If Dig *did* ever phone her again, for whatever bizarre reason, then she'd just tell him that she'd been playing Truth or Dare with the girls and that phoning him and telling him she'd been thinking about his willy was the punishment they'd concocted for her.

OK. So it was a crap excuse. But at least it was an excuse. And actually, she supposed, men were generally so bemused by the carryings-on of drunken women *en masse* that he'd probably just shrug and accept it as gospel. Of course, he'd think, 'Women – they're weird, we all know that.'

But that was just on the very slim off chance that he did ever phone her again. There was no reason why he should. She'd dissed his new girlfriend, she'd been pissed and belligerent and slightly insane – she'd been deeply unattractive.

'Ah yes,' she could hear Dig sighing in years to come, 'Nadine. She was a great girl. We were so close. But I had to let her go when she became unstable. Poor Nadine. It's all rather tragic.' And then he'd squeeze Delilah's hand and throw her a slightly sad but very relieved look and they'd both silently thank God for the day that they excised Mad Nadine from their perfect, pure, *impeccable* fucking lives.

Hmph. She clenched her jaw and stabbed the front-door key into its hole.

It was going to be fine, she told herself. Everything was going to be just fine. Her flat would be fine. Her life would be fine. It was all going to be perfectly – fine. She took a few deep breaths to psych herself into believing that everything really was going to be fine before slowly twisting the key in the lock and pushing the door open.

She flicked the hall light on and clamped her hand over her mouth.

A strange, strangulated little yelp slipped through her fingers.

A million thoughts landed in her mind at once as she absorbed the physical reality of her trashed hall, the most insistent of which was that this wasn't, *couldn't possibly be*, physical reality at all, was, in fact, some kind of dream or psychological trick precipitated by the preceding three days of irrational concern. Like a mirage. Yes – that's right – a mirage.

This comforting thought lasted less than a micro-second before reality hit with a vengeance. Her flat was destroyed. She'd been burgled. Her hand still clamped to her mouth, she slumped her shoulders and fell to her knees, bags and cases slipping from her shoulders and hands, her keys clanging to the ground. Oh God. Look at this place. Look at it. Look at her walnut cabinet. Look at all her magazines everywhere. Look at the pink-foil wallpaper, all scuffed and ripped.

She hobbled on her knees down the hallway. Spilt wine, fag-ends, ripped pages from magazines, huge, dirty footprints – everywhere. There was a lump the size of an egg in her throat. She breathed deeply to prevent useless tears escaping and got to her feet using the bathroom doorframe to pull herself up. She pushed open the bathroom door and waited helplessly while it creaked open.

'Oh God,' she moaned, when she saw what was within, 'oh no. Oh no.' Tears began spilling, despite her attempts to control them. 'Oh no,' she sniffed.

She began moving more quickly then, from room to room, from kitchen to living room, and everything she saw increased the knot in her stomach and the sadness in her heart. Her flat. Her lovely, lovely flat. The flat she'd created with her bare hands, from skips and second-hand shops, from clearance sales and her parents' generosity, month by month, year after year, piece by piece. All ruined. All dirty. All broken and shitty and fucking fucking *horrible*.

Anger started to erupt inside her as she stepped over empty wine bottles, and she felt a primal scream building in her chest. Her fists clenched themselves tightly and then she let it go. She opened her mouth, closed her eyes and screamed, not a scream of fear but a deep, sonorous scream of pure rage.

'*FUCKING BASTARDS!*'

She began half-heartedly to collect bits and pieces together – empty beer cans, half-full beer cans afloat with stinking, swollen fag-butts and spliff-ends. There were articles of discarded clothing lying around the place – *other people's* discarded clothing. She picked up a rancid-looking flannel shirt gingerly, between two fingernails. A soft-top packet of Camels fell from the pocket. She let the shirt drop to the floor. She hadn't been burgled – that was obvious now. There was nothing actually missing. Just lots of grim stuff added, things moved around and other things broken. She hadn't been burgled – she'd been partied.

Phil.

Fucking Phil.

She'd known this was going to happen, from the minute she'd closed her front door behind her on Saturday morning to the minute she'd opened it again just now. Her instincts had been spot on. She felt sick. She found it impossible now to rustle up even the smallest shred of sympathy for Philip Rich. She was *glad* in fact, glad his parents had died, glad his girlfriend had topped herself, glad his house had burned down. He deserved it. All of it. He deserved worse. He deserved more. Much more.

Her head filled with thoughts of retribution, most of which revolved around the general theme of cutting off various bits of his horrible pasty body and making him eat them.

'*You fucking bastard*,' she shouted out loud, '*you fucking bastard*.' She kicked the doorframe, collapsed to her knees and began to howl. She wailed and thrashed and sobbed and shouted. And then had rapidly to pull herself together when she heard the doorbell ring.

'Oh Jesus,' she muttered to herself, pushing tear-sodden tendrils of hair from her cheeks and wiping her eyes. She got heavily to her feet and stumbled towards the front door. As she crossed the hallway towards the main door she saw a sight she knew would stay with her for ever, a vision that brought goosebumps to her flesh and a lump to her throat, that turned her stomach to liquid and her knees to jelly, the sweetest, most beautiful thing she'd ever seen in her life. Everything that had occurred in the past week and a half, from sleeping with Phil to running him over, from having her flat trashed to leaving appalling messages on answerphones, every bad moment of every bad day, every feeling of insanity and misery and unhappiness just dissolved when she pulled open her front door and saw Dig standing there.

He was wearing a frilly apron, a cap and a daft smile.

In one hand was his precious purple Dyson, in the other a dustpan and brush and at his feet sat a tiny, quivering Yorkshire Terrier.

'I've come about the cleaning position,' he grinned. 'I've got excellent credentials and references. I've been voted the cleanest person in NW5.'

Nadine melted then and dissolved into fresh tears. 'Oh Dig,' she snuffled into his shoulder, 'oh Dig. Thank God you're here. Thank God.'

Dig squeezed her back, hard as anything, tighter than he'd ever hugged her before.

'God, I've missed you,' he said, smiling at her.

Nadine smiled back at him and looked into his soft, dark eyes, pain just falling away from her as she did so. 'It feels like ages,' she sniffed. She looked down at the trembling dog. 'Is that the feather duster?'

Dig laughed and leaned down to pick him up. 'No,' he said, 'this is the world's smallest and most unappealing dog and this small and unappealing dog is getting the early train back to Chester tomorrow morning. Aren't you, mate?' The dog looked at him fearfully, as if he'd just suggested thc knacker's yard.

'What?' said Nadine. 'On his own?'

Dig threw her a pitying look.

'Oh,' she said, breathlessly, 'you mean Delilah's going home?'

'Yes,' smiled Dig, 'Delilah's going home. Back to her husband. Back to have a baby.' He smiled.

'But – but – but . . .'

'Nothing ever happened between me and Delilah, you know. Nothing. We had one kiss. I've done a lot of thinking since you went away and there's a lot of stuff you need to know, Nadine. About Delilah. You need to hear about Delilah. You've got her so wrong. She's a good person. She's a very good person who's had a very hard time. And we need to talk about Phil. About why he let this happen to your flat. He *isn't* a good person. But,' he said, seriously, 'most importantly, we really, *really* need to talk about us.'

'What do you mean – about us?' Her stomach fizzed at the very concept, at the fact that Dig had even mentioned it.

'Look,' he said, ushering her into the hallway, 'get your rubber gloves on and get into the kitchen. We'll talk as we clean.'

## CHAPTER FORTY-THREE

There was a lot of talking that rainy Tuesday afternoon and a lot of explaining. Dig had spent twenty minutes on the phone the previous day to a DI Wittering, who had been more than expansive on the subject of Philip Rich, a character who the Metropolitan Police had been familiar with since his ex-wife had first reported him twelve years earlier for the theft of her black MG and the contents of her savings account.

They'd come into contact with him again seven years later when his suicide was reported to them by a distraught woman called Mandy Taylor, claiming to be his fiancée. She'd watched in horror as he threw himself off Putney Bridge two weeks before they were due to be married. He had, apparently, taken the precaution of emptying their joint bank account before taking his life and when Mandy Taylor bumped into him coming out of a pub off Tottenham Court Road six months later she'd been too shocked to press charges.

His parents – who were alive and well and had attended his funeral – refused to have anything to do with him after their first reunion and these days he was a squatter dabbling in a bit of small-time drug-dealing.

'You . . . you mean, he made all that up – all that stuff about his parents and his girlfriend and everything?'

Dig nodded. 'He's a con artist, Nadine. He's been a con artist from the day you met him.'

After a tip-off from Phil's elderly father, Haringey council had evicted him and eight students from a flat in Finsbury Park on Friday morning, and it seemed he'd decided that Nadine and her flat would make a much better alternative to finding a new building to squat.

'Of course,' sighed Nadine, 'of course. That flat. It didn't seem right. All those students and that strange furniture. And . . . and' – she was growing quite animated as so many of the events of the last few days began to make sense – 'and – of course! The old man. And the portable telly. That was his father! And that's why he left me all those messages. That's why he was hanging around outside my flat. That's why he wouldn't leave. He had nowhere else to go. I thought he was desperate to see me, but he was just desperate for a roof over his head. Oh my God. To think . . . I just . . . oh God, Dig, I'm such an *idiot*. I can't believe I fell for all that . . .'

Her face fell even further after Dig had related the story of Delilah's visit to London, of Sophie and Michael and her unplanned pregnancy.

'Oh Jesus,' she said, 'I feel so bad. All that time I spent bitching about her and hating her and she was going through so much. And I had no idea. None at all. I just thought she was here to make trouble, to take you away from me. Oh God, Dig, I feel like such a fucking bitch . . .'

It was getting dark by the time they'd finished cleaning the kitchen and discussing the events of the past week and they still hadn't even brushed on the subject of the answerphone messages.

Both of them were aware that it was next on the agenda but both of them industriously spun out the other subjects until finally, at five o'clock, they ran out of things to say. The atmosphere in the kitchen was plump with the prospect of their next conversation.

'Well,' said Dig, getting off his knees and looking around the kitchen, 'I think we've done in here. Pretty much spotless, I'd say.'

'Mmm,' murmured Nadine, looking around her and feeling awkward with Dig for the first time in years. 'Do you want to get started on the other rooms now? Or we could have a cup of tea? Or you can go if you like? You don't have to stay. I'll be all right. I'll make you dinner, though, obviously, if you do stay. So . . .' She trailed off and turned abruptly towards the sink, stowing a jumbo-sized bottle of Domestos into a cupboard and feeling her cheeks flush to a warm pink.

Dig smiled at her back. Of course he was going to stay. This was the only place in the world he could think of that he wanted to be right now. It was where he'd wanted to be since Saturday night. Here, in Nadine's kitchen, with Nadine looking fantastically cute in threadbare old grey jogging bottoms, a crappy old Paul Weller T-shirt that he'd given her years ago and a lime-green pinny with Miffy the Rabbit patch pockets. Her thick copper hair was all over the place, her toenails were bubblegum pink and she had a smudge of something grey across her upper lip that made her look like she had a tache. She looked like a madwoman. She *was* a madwoman. A gorgeous, lovable, sexy, red-haired, successful, together, strong-minded and about-to-be fabulously wealthy madwoman. He smiled again. What a combination.

Dig opened his mouth to say something. He wasn't sure what. A compliment, maybe, or a joke. Nothing came out. He closed his mouth again.

Nadine spun around. 'I just thought of something,' she said, 'we should do it now – in case we don't get round to it later – all that furniture on my bed – I'm going to need a hand getting it off. Do you mind?'

Digby had made a little nest for himself on the corner of Nadine's duvet that was still showing, and Dig gently scooped the sleepy creature off the bed with the palm of one hand and laid him on his jacket in the hallway.

'Aw,' smiled Nadine, watching him tenderly, 'cute. You're quite fond of him, aren't you?'

Dig started. 'No,' he said. Then more softly, 'Well, he's all right, I suppose. He's sort of grown on me the last few days. But he's just not my kind of dog. Well, he's not *any* kind of dog, really, is he? I mean, look at him.'

They both cast their eyes downwards at the slumbering little ball of greasy whiskers and bulging eyes. He sighed deeply in his sleep and emitted a little whistle.

'He's knackered,' said Nadine.

'Well,' said Dig, 'it's not surprising, really. He's had a tough few days.'

'Yeah,' said Nadine, moving back towards the bedroom, 'haven't we all.'

'It's been a very strange week,' agreed Dig.

'Mmm,' murmured Nadine, turning pink again, 'to put it mildly.'

'But good, I think – a good week.'

'Do you?'

'What?'

'Think it's been a good week?'

'Yes. In a funny way.'

'In spite of everything?'

They were on either side of Nadine's bed now, each holding an arm of her leather sofa.

Dig nodded.

'Why?'

Not just yet, thought Dig. In a minute.

'Here,' he said, 'let's get this sofa into the living room.'

Nadine nodded stiffly, and on the count of three they heaved the ancient sofa off the bed and lumbered around with it for a while until they'd manoeuvred it through the bedroom door and into the living room. Exhausted, they both collapsed on to the sofa and gasped in unison.

'D'you remember getting this thing in here, when you moved in?' asked Dig, turning to smile at Nadine.

'Yeah. Of course I do. This was the first thing I bought for the flat. From that old house-clearance place that used to be up on Agar Grove. £38.50. I always wondered what the 50p was for.'

'I thought you were mad. Why would anyone want to buy some rancid, stinky sofa with horsehair falling out of the bottom and cracks all over the place? I kept trying to get you to go to Habitat but you just weren't interested in anything new – or clean – or' – he cast Nadine a cheeky look – '*nice.* "Oh no, I don't want something that hasn't been used by at least twelve people before me – oh no, that's *far too clean* – you mean, it came in a box? How common."'

Dig flinched and laughed as Nadine picked up a cushion and hit him over the head with it. 'You bastard! You're just jealous because you've got no imagination. "Ooh, I *just* don't know – shall I go for the mid-beige or the light beige? Or maybe I'll be *really* daring and go for the deep beige. Or do you think that'll clash with the navy blue . . .?"'

Dig picked up a cushion now and boffed Nadine with

it, harder than he'd intended, accidentally clipping her on the temple with his knuckle.

'Ow!' she yelled, rubbing the side of her face. 'That really hurt!'

'Oh God,' said Dig, immediately dropping the cushion and sliding along the cracked leather towards Nadine, 'oh God. I'm sorry.' He cupped the side of Nadine's face with his hand and stroked his thumb across her temple. 'I'm really sorry, Deen.' Her skin was smooth and flushed under his and her eyes were still slightly red around the rims. She looked so young and vulnerable. He brought his thumb down to her upper lip and wiped away the grey smudge.

As he touched her and looked into her green eyes Dig could feel something stirring deep down inside him, something almost magnetic forcing his body and his face closer and closer to hers. She eyed him with a mixture of fear and excitement.

Dig could tell she'd stopped breathing.

So had he.

'Oh, Deen,' he said finally, pushing a messy copper curl away from her face, tucking it behind her ear, 'we're such a pair of idiots, aren't we?'

Nadine nodded, and Dig knew then that they were on the same wavelength, knew that he wouldn't have to do too much explaining.

And for once Dig wasn't stuck for words. For once he was going to open his mouth and all the right words were going to come out of it. Because, for once, Dig had it all planned.

He took a deep breath and started talking.

'We've been a couple for the last ten years, do you realize that? We go shopping together. We go on holiday together. We spend our weekends together. We even spend alternate Christmases with our parents. We bicker. We hug. We help move each other's furniture around. You know all my colleagues, I know all yours. The only thing we *don't* do is sleep together and wake up together. And I used to think that that was because you'd rather die than even contemplate the idea of being – *intimate* with me.'

Nadine opened her mouth to say something and Dig put a finger up to hush her. 'Shhh,' he said, 'listen to me.

'Remember that weekend – in Manchester, when I came to stay?'

Nadine nodded again.

'I didn't show it at the time because I didn't want to make you feel bad, but I didn't know that you were living with Phil until I got there – I still thought I was in with a chance. And that weekend – it was the worst weekend of my life, Deen. Pretending I didn't care was the hardest bit of acting I've ever done. I had to listen to you and him – having sex – and I thought my heart was going to break, I really did.

'It wasn't Delilah who broke my heart, Nadine, it was you. And I never got over it. I really didn't. And now I know what I've been doing for the last ten years. With all these young girls. Now I know why I haven't had a decent, proper girlfriend in all this time. It's because I didn't *need* one. *You've* been my girlfriend, Nadine, and I've subconsciously chosen women who were no threat whatsoever to what I have with you. And all this time I've thought that I could be happy living this compromise for the rest of my life, happy loving you and having sex with other women because I thought that friendship was all I'd ever get from you. But then you left that message on my answerphone and now everything's changed. Did you mean it? Did you mean what you said? About lying – about wanting me?' He stared into her unblinking eyes.

Nadine stared back into his in wonder. She felt almost faint with excitement. 'Yes,' she said, 'I meant it.'

'So why?' said Dig. 'Why did you tell me you didn't want me? Why did you reject me? Why did you go off to Manchester and fall in love with someone else?'

Nadine sighed. 'Because of Delilah,' she said.

'Delilah? What did Delilah have to do with it?'

'You were my best friend – my world. Delilah broke my heart when she took you away from me. It wasn't just *you* that she wanted at the Holy T, it was what you and I had – that intimacy, that exclusivity, that complicity. She wanted to take my place. Dig 'n' Deen. Dig and Delilah. I knew it, and I hated her. I didn't know who I was without you. My last two years at school were miserable and lonely.

'And then I went to St Julian's and I felt strong again. I became someone in my own right, and when we met up and spent that weekend together and you started making all these plans for the future, I just got scared. I couldn't bear to lose you all over again, not when I'd only just found myself. So I rejected you. It made me feel strong. I wasn't expecting to meet Phil, to fall in love so quickly, and I really thought, that weekend when you came up, that you'd got to grips with the idea that we were never going to be together. And, you know, I've done it too, what you've done. The reason I've been out with so many unsuitable people is because I had the most suitable person right here, all along. I haven't been looking for love because I haven't needed to. Because I love you and

I don't want to love anyone else and I really don't think I *can* love anyone else . . .'

'No! That's exactly it. Neither can I. I thought I could love Delilah, because I'd loved her before. I thought it would be different. But it wasn't. I tried to love her, but I couldn't . . .'

'And I thought I could love Phil again! But . . . bleughhh.' She grimaced and she laughed, and Dig laughed, and for the first time in ten years Nadine could feel herself getting a grip on one of those happiness seeds. She could feel her hand tightening over the little seed, she could feel it nestling against the palm of her hand, and this time she was not going to let go of it.

'It's always been you, Nadine. You and me. Dig 'n' Deen. Nobody else stood a chance, did they?'

Nadine shook her head and smiled widely. 'I used to think that you and I would get married when we left school. I used to think . . . here – wait.' She ran from the room, into her bedroom, ferreted around inside her wardrobe for a minute and then came back clutching something in her hands. 'Look,' she said, handing it to Dig, 'look at this.'

It was a diary. It was old and musty. On the front was a sticker of Steve Strange wearing a silver hat and black Cupid's-bow lipstick. Funny the way that schoolgirls couldn't resist a blatantly gay man, thought Dig. He turned it over. And there it was, written over and over again in selfconscious adolescent handwriting.

*Nadine Ryan. Nadine Ryan. Nadine Ryan.*

'And look,' said Nadine, turning the pages, 'look at this.' She pointed at a section at the back entitled 'Mrs Nadine Ryan'. 'Read that bit,' she said.

Dig threw her an amused look and started reading.

He chuckled as he read. 'Oh yes, I like this bit – powder-blue E-type,' he smirked.

'*Four children!*' he cried at one point.

'Gloucester Crescent. Yes. I could live in Gloucester Crescent. So,' he said, closing the book and turning to face Nadine, 'when shall we start?'

'Start what?'

'House-hunting, of course.'

Nadine searched for the hint of sarcasm in his voice, but it wasn't there.

'Jesus, Nadine. We've wasted so much time, haven't we? Ten years. Let's not waste any more. Eh?'

And then he put the book down, took Nadine's hands in his, and he kissed her. On the lips. And even though he'd thought it might feel strange, kissing Nadine, it didn't. It felt the opposite of strange. It felt so unbelievably right.

And Nadine gripped Dig's hands in hers and felt his lips moving against hers, and she couldn't believe they'd waited so long to do this because this was what her lips were designed for. For kissing Dig Ryan.

They fell backwards together into the leather of Nadine's deco sofa and smiled at each other, and then they kissed again.

It grew dark while they kissed and soon the only light in the room came from the cactus fairy lights over the fireplace, and in that cool, green glow, in the debris of her flat, on a rainy November evening, Dig and Nadine finally got it together.

# EPILOGUE

Dig looked out through the tangles of ice-blue clematis and snowflake jasmine that framed his study window. The sky outside was turquoise and smudged with white. The air was warm and full of pollen. It had taken its time but, finally, in the second week of July, summer had come to London.

Dig's study was a minimal refuge in the chaos of their new home. He'd acceded to Nadine's taste in interior décor and let her run amok with her strange wallpapers and bits of bohemian junk in the rest of the flat. It was funny how easy he found it to live with Nadine's mess – it was so much a part of her that he almost loved it. He could *breathe* amongst her clutter. But in here was all white walls and modern furniture, angle-poise lamps and linen filing boxes from Muji. His old corduroy sofa sat against the wall.

This tiny, neat, well-organized room was now home to Dig-It Records, the smallest independent label in the world. Only two weeks old and only one band to its name but – they were *the* greatest guitar band since Oasis. Absolutely. Dig could feel it in his gut, his heart and his soul. He just had to persuade the rest of the world now.

This new life still felt a little like playing at grown-ups. He and Nadine kept expecting someone to come to the front door in a uniform and ask them what the hell they thought they were doing living in this adult's house in this adult's road, to march them out, throw them into the back of a van and deposit them in a bedsit in Tufnell Park.

Dig gulped back the dregs of his tea and looked at the clock. Six thirty. Nadine should be back any minute. He smiled at the thought. It was her turn to cook tonight. His stomach growled appreciatively in anticipation.

The doorbell rang and Dig made his way wearily down the hallway but he snapped out of his long-day-in-the-office reverie when he opened the door and saw a stunningly beautiful woman with golden hair and skin standing on the doorstep.

'Delilah!'

Delilah's face burst open into an enormous smile and she threw her arms around Dig and squeezed him hard.

'Oh Dig,' she said, 'it's so great to see you!'

'What are you doing here?'

'God. I'm *so sorry*. I was determined not to turn up unannounced again, not after last time. I kept trying to call you and there was no answer so I wrote to you. Two weeks ago. We've been shopping all day and then we turned up at your flat this afternoon and there was no one there, so we drove round to your mum's and she told me you'd moved . . .'

Stunning, thought Dig, eyeing Delilah with amazement, you are absolutely stunning.

'She told me you'd moved up in the world and she wasn't wrong – I mean, *look at this place*!'

She poked her head into the hallway and began looking around. She was wearing a pure white crêpe viscose dress, short and flirty with shoestring straps. On her feet were pale-blue strappy sandals. Her hair was twisted up and clipped back with some kind of plastic claw affair. Dig could see her knickers through the semi-opaque viscose. She was wearing a G-string. He gulped. Jesus bloody Christ.

The sound of a car door slamming drew Dig's attention away from Delilah's underwear and towards the road. There was a large four-wheel-drive jeep parked opposite, and a tall man was unloading stuff from it – funny bags made from quilted fabric, and plastic boxes. He was about six foot four with coal-black hair and an imposing physique. He was wearing jeans in the same effortless way that Delilah wore hers, with a grey V-neck T-shirt. He was very brown and, when he turned around, quite guttingly handsome. He threw Dig a smile and Dig worked it out.

Alex.

Alex reached further into the jeep and brought out something very carefully with both arms – a Ming vase, maybe, thought Dig, or a particularly large Fabergé egg. No – it was another plastic contraption with a large handle, and nestled within it was a small pink thing wearing a stripy all-in-one.

Alex picked up all his quilted things and plastic things and headed towards them. Delilah beamed. 'Dig,' she said, 'let me introduce you to the two most gorgeous men in the world. Dig – this is Alex – Alex, *this is Dig*.' Dig was touched to notice a trace of pride in Delilah's voice when she said his name. He went to shake Alex's hand and laughed because his hands were all being used up for other things. Alex laughed, too, and Dig was nearly blinded by the fabulous whiteness of his teeth and shaken again by the uncanny resemblance to Pierce Brosnan.

'And,' continued Delilah, taking the contraption with

the pink thing in it from Alex and thrusting it towards Dig, 'this is the fantastic Oliver – isn't he *beautiful*?'

Dig looked down into the contraption, at the funny little sausage of pinky-white flesh and into the cloudy blue of the sausage's eyes and tried to think of something to say. 'Lovely,' he managed, eventually, 'he's lovely.'

They went indoors then, and Dig felt inordinately proud as he showed this perfect family his elegant and classy new home, with its high ceilings and original features, this airy two-bedroom flat that spoke of hitherto alien concepts such as *being settled* and having *made it*.

He made tea and sat his guests down in the garden, on dark-green wrought-iron furniture. The garden looked spectacular – tiny but mature, all brambly rose bowers and ivy-clad walls. The air was heavy with heat and fragrant with jasmine. The sound of a violin being played somewhere further down the street wafted into the garden.

Delilah fiddled with a plastic bottle and slipped it into the sausage's mouth. 'Dig,' she said, looking around her, 'this is incredible. Gloucester Crescent. Did you win the lottery or something?'

Dig laughed. 'No,' he said, 'I wish. No. This is a childhood dream of Nadine's. A *very expensive* childhood dream. I have never been poorer in my entire life. I had more money was I was eighteen, earning £6,000 a year. But we sat down together and worked out that we could afford it, even with me giving up my job. Just. We both made quite a lot on our old flats and Deen's doing so fucking well and – oops.' He covered his mouth and glanced apologetically at the sausage.

Delilah laughed. 'His language skills aren't quite up

to picking up swearwords just yet. He's only four weeks old. Don't worry.'

'Anyway, Nadine's career has really taken off, since the Ruckham's calendar – she's earning a mint. The mortgage repayments are crippling, we can't afford to go out or buy clothes or go on holiday or anything but' – he looked around him – 'it's worth it, you know. I could die here, do you know what I mean?'

They both murmured affirmatively and for a second or two it was silent. Delilah fed her baby. Alex appraised the back of the house. Dig stared at Alex and imagined him wearing a tux, leaping from a moving BMW Z3 and shooting at Chinese men with a ballpoint pen. The small patch of baby vomit on the sleeve of his T-shirt somewhat spoiled the image.

Delilah and Alex glanced at each other and exchanged a look.

'Shall I tell him?' said Delilah.

Alex nodded happily.

Delilah turned to face Dig, anticipation pulling at her face. 'Dig,' she said, 'we've got something we'd like to ask you. Well – two things, actually.'

Dig felt his face muscles tense up. Delilah asking him favours was, in his experience, a very worrying thing.

'Ye–es,' he said, smiling stiffly, trying to sound excited.

'The first thing is – and I know, you're not religious or anything, but neither are we so it doesn't matter – but I'd – *we'd* – be so honoured if you would be Oliver's godfather.' She beamed at him and Dig was surprised to notice a little flush of pleasure in his stomach area. He looked down at the suckling sausage and felt a burst of warmth. He looked at Alex and Delilah, who were both staring desperately at him as if they'd just proposed marriage, and he smiled. 'Shit,' he said, 'yeah. Definitely. I mean – yeah!' And everyone just sat there and beamed for a while.

'That's fantastic,' said Delilah grabbing the back of Dig's neck and kissing him on the cheek. Alex gave him a large hand to shake, and Dig couldn't believe how happy he was to be asked to stand in a church and tell lies with a stupid suit on, all for the sake of a dimply sausage who couldn't have cared less either way.

'So,' he said, happily, 'what was the other favour?' He was on a favour roll now – he could handle favours like this.

'Well,' said Delilah, her face becoming serious, 'it's – er – actually, hold on, just a sec. Alex – can I have the car keys?'

She plopped the sausage down into Dig's arms, took the keys from Alex and disappeared back into the house.

Dig sat for a while, holding the sausage as if it were an unpinned hand-grenade.

'Here,' said Alex, smiling, 'let me take him. You don't look very comfortable there. It takes a bit of getting used to, this baby lark.' He grinned warmly at Dig and gently scooped the pink thing from his arms.

Dig felt awkward for a second, now that Delilah was gone, not sure what he and Alex were going to have to talk about, but Alex saved him from himself.

'Dig,' he said, and Dig nearly jumped out of his skin because his voice was so deep – he sounded like he should be doing trailers for Hollywood movies. 'Dig. I wanted to thank you.'

Dig threw him a not-sure look.

'For what you did for Delilah last year.' He was *very* posh.

'What do you mean?' said Dig, thinking about his complete lack of doing anything for Delilah last year, except for following her around and sprinkling her with dog pee and ogling her in her underwear.

Alex put the sausage back in its contraption and tucked a blanket round its legs. 'For looking out for her. For having her to stay. For talking her out of not having this little chap. She told me what you said to her, about being a great mother, about her ability to love. You were very wise and you were right. I dread to think what would have happened if you hadn't talked her round.'

They both turned to survey the pink thing and Dig felt himself blushing. 'Well,' he said, 'God. You know. It was nothing. It was . . .' And then, just in the nick of time, just before Alex would have reached the conclusion that he was an illiterate buffoon, the proper grown-up bit of Dig came to the rescue and he realized there was something important he wanted to say. 'It was the least I could do,' he said, breathing easy, 'after all, Delilah did the same for me.'

'Oh yes?' said Alex, crossing his legs and looking at Dig with interest.

'Yes. She set me on the path to true happiness.'

'Really. How?'

Dig looked at Alex and tried to gauge how honest he could be. His eyes were brown and gentle. He looked like he could take a bit of romance. 'She stopped me being blind. I'd been in love with someone for ten years and was too much of a coward to risk rejection so I just made do with being her friend. Delilah showed me that I could have more. That this girl loved me, too. I thought she was interfering at the time. But she was right. And now I've got the girl of my dreams.'

Alex smiled. 'And you're happy?'

Dig lit a fag, inhaled and nodded. 'I have never been happier in my life. This is it' – he indicated their surroundings – 'this is my castle and Nadine's my queen.'

And Alex and he exchanged a long, deep look, and Dig knew that Alex knew exactly how he felt and that they were both lucky, lucky men. Dig decided he liked Alex.

'What are you boys talking about?' said Delilah, striding back into the garden. Dig was about to make a joke of some description when he noticed what Delilah was holding in her arms.

'No way,' said Dig immediately, crossing his hands in front of his chest.

'You don't know what I'm going to ask you yet.'

'I don't need to. I don't care. There's just no way . . .'

In Delilah's arms, shivering even in this balmy heat, was Digby. He wagged his tail when he saw Dig and tried to escape from Delilah's arms.

'See,' whined Delilah, 'see how much he loves you. He's never forgotten you, you know. He's had this empty look about him since I took him home last year.'

'What do you want? Do you want me to look after him? OK. One night only, though. One night and that's it.'

Delilah shook her head slowly from side to side and deposited the dog on Dig's lap. 'It's a bit more than that,' she said, nervously, 'you see, you wouldn't think it to look at him but he can be quite aggressive, and the thing is, is that – and there's no way we could have known this in advance – but he hates babies. Hates them. And he hates Oliver. Snarls at him. It's awful. And I couldn't bear to give him away to a stranger. And I just keep remembering how well the two of you got on together. And . . .'

'He hates babies?' asked Dig.

'Mmm,' Delilah nodded, sadly.

'All babies?'

'Well. Yes. At first we thought it was just Oliver, but now we've noticed it's all babies.'

A large, smug smile spread across Dig's face, and he shook his head. 'Sorry,' he said.

'Can't you just give it a go? You could have a trial run?'

Dig shook his head and looked up when he saw someone walk into the garden. A stunning redhead in a blue crushed-silk dress wearing red 1950s plastic sunglasses and butterflies in her hair.

She stopped in her tracks when she saw the group in the garden and looked quizzically at Dig. And then she smiled widely when she recognized Delilah and stooped to hug her. Delilah introduced her to Alex and Oliver.

'Nadine,' said Dig, tucking his arm around her waist and drawing her hips towards his shoulders, 'Delilah's just asked us a favour. She needs a new home for little Digby and she thought maybe we'd like to have him.'

Nadine smiled at little Digby. 'Oh,' she said, 'well . . . we *could*, I suppose.'

'There's only one thing, though. He hates babies.'

'Hates babies?'

'Uh-huh.'

'Oh dear.'

'Oh dear indeed.'

Delilah looked at them questioningly and they smiled

at each other and then at her, and Dig spun Nadine round so that she was sideways on. Nadine pulled at her dress so that it clung tightly to her body and there, silhouetted by the white-gold sun and barely perceptible, was a tiny, hard, perfect little bump.

Delilah screamed, leaped to her feet and cupped the bump with the palm of her hand, asking a million questions all at once about due dates and scans.

Alex smiled warmly and shook their hands.

Digby ran around barking in an attempt to draw attention to himself.

And Dig and Nadine just beamed at each other because although it was scary as hell, although it was entirely unplanned, although they felt far too young and far too immature to bring another life into the world, and although they had no idea how they were going to afford it, none of that mattered because that little bump was the best thing that had ever happened to them.